PENGUIN BOOKS

A PLACE OF GREATER SAFETY

'Concentrating on the tortuously interwoven relationship between its three most important protagonists, Robespierre, Danton and Desmoulins, Hilary Mantel has pulled off the apparently impossible ... an ambitious, gripping epic ... The host of minor characters and the swirling mob who form the necessary background to the story are never lost from sight, but are expertly marshalled on and off the bloodstained stage ... a *tour de force* of the historical imagination' – *Vogue*

'Intriguing ... She has grasped what made these young revolutionaries – and with them the French Revolution – tick ... This is the perfect complement to Simon Schama's history of the French Revolution, *Citizens*' – *Independent*

'A formidably talented novelist ... She has seen deeply into her characters and their involvements with one another, and makes them live for us, with vivid invented detail, day by day, as they are battered or seduced by public events'– *London Review of Books*

'Mantel's grasp both of detail and the complex sweep of events is quite remarkable ... "her people" are firmly rooted in physical and historical reality ... Little is known of the personal lives of most revolutionary leaders before 1789, and after they became famous, they lived constantly in the public eye. Yet Mantel has managed to get inside them by feeling her way through their writings, families and, quite brilliantly, their women' – *The Times Literary Supplement*

'Much, much more than an historical novel, this is an addictive study of power, and the price that must be paid for it ... a triumph' – *Cosmopolitan*

ABOUT THE AUTHOR

Hilary Mantel was born in Derbyshire in 1952, and has lived and worked in Africa and the Middle East. In 1987 she was awarded the Shiva Naipaul Memorial Prize for travel writing. Her previous novels, all published by Penguin, are *Every Day is Mother's Day*, *Vacant Possession*, *Eight Months on Ghazzah Street* and *Fludd*. Hilary Mantel is married and lives in Berkshire.

A Place of Greater Safety was the winner of the 1992 *Sunday Express* Book of the Year Award.

HILARY MANTEL

A PLACE OF GREATER SAFETY

PENGUIN BOOKS

PENGUIN BOOKS

Published by the Penguin Group
Penguin Books Ltd, 27 Wrights Lane, London W8 5TZ, England
Penguin Books USA Inc., 375 Hudson Street, New York, New York 10014, USA
Penguin Books Australia Ltd, Ringwood, Victoria, Australia
Penguin Books Canada Ltd, 10 Alcorn Avenue, Toronto, Ontario, Canada M4V 3B2
Penguin Books (NZ) Ltd, 182–190 Wairau Road, Auckland 10, New Zealand

Penguin Books Ltd, Registered Offices: Harmondsworth, Middlesex, England

First published by Viking 1992
Published in Penguin Books 1993
1 3 5 7 9 10 8 6 4 2

Copyright © Hilary Mantel, 1992
All rights reserved

To Clare Boylan

Contents

Author's Note

THIS IS A NOVEL about the French Revolution. Almost all the characters in it are real people and it is closely tied to historical facts – as far as those facts are agreed, which isn't really very far. It is not an overview or a complete account of the Revolution. The story centres on Paris; what happens in the provinces is outside its scope, and so for the most part are military events.

My main characters were not famous until the Revolution made them so, and not much is known about their early lives. I have used what there is, and made educated guesses about the rest.

This is not, either, an impartial account. I have tried to see the world as my people saw it, and they had their own prejudices and opinions. Where I can, I have used their real words – from recorded speeches or preserved writings – and woven them into my own dialogue. I have been guided by a belief that what goes on to the record is often tried out earlier, off the record.

There is one character who may puzzle the reader, because he has a tangential, peculiar role in this book. Everyone knows this about Jean-Paul Marat: he was stabbed to death in his bath by a pretty girl. His death we can be sure of, but almost everything in his life is open to interpretation. Dr Marat was twenty years older than my main characters, and had a long and interesting pre-revolutionary career. I did not feel that I could deal with it without unbalancing the book, so I have made him the guest star, his appearances few but piquant. I hope to write about Dr Marat at some future date. Any such novel would subvert the view of history which I offer here. In the course of writing this book I have had many arguments with myself, about what history really is. But you must state a case, I think, before you can plead against it.

The events of the book are complicated, so the need to dramatize and the need to explain must be set against each other. Anyone who writes a novel of this type is vulnerable to the complaints of pedants. Three small points will illustrate how, without falsifying, I have tried to make life easier.

When I am describing pre-revolutionary Paris, I talk about 'the police'. This is a simplification. There were several bodies charged with law enforcement. It would be tedious, though, to hold up the story every time there is a riot, to tell the reader which one is on the scene.

Again, why do I call the Hôtel de Ville 'City Hall'? In Britain, the term 'Town Hall' conjures up a picture of comfortable aldermen patting their paunches and talking about Christmas decorations or litter bins. I wanted to convey a more vital, American idea; *power* resides at City Hall.

A smaller point still: my characters have their dinner and their supper at variable times. The fashionable Parisian dined between three and five in the afternoon, and took supper at ten or eleven o'clock. But if the latter meal is attended with a degree of formality, I've called it 'dinner'. On the whole, the people in this book keep late hours. If they're doing something at three o'clock, it's usually three in the morning.

I am very conscious that a novel is a cooperative effort, a joint venture between writer and reader. I purvey my own version of events, but facts change according to your viewpoint. Of course, my characters did not have the blessing of hindsight; they lived from day to day, as best they could. I am not trying to persuade my reader to view events in a particular way, or to draw any particular lessons from them. I have tried to write a novel that gives the reader scope to change opinions, change sympathies: a book that one can think and live inside. The reader may ask how to tell fact from fiction. A rough guide: anything that seems particularly unlikely is probably true.

Cast of Characters

PART I

In Guise:
Jean-Nicolas Desmoulins, a lawyer
Madeleine, his wife
Camille, his eldest son (b. 1760)
Elisabeth, his daughter
Henriette, his daughter (died aged nine)
Armand, his son
Anne-Clothilde, his daughter
Clément, his youngest son

Adrien de Viefville   }   their snobbish relations
Jean-Louis de Viefville

The Prince de Condé, premier nobleman of the district
   and a client of Jean-Nicolas Desmoulins

In Arcis-sur-Aube:
Marie-Madeleine Danton, a widow, who marries
Jean Recordain, an inventor
Georges-Jacques, her son (b. 1759)
Anne Madeleine, her daughter
Pierrette, her daughter
Marie-Cécile, her daughter, who becomes a nun

In Arras:
François de Robespierre, a lawyer
Maximilien, his son (b. 1758)

Charlotte, his daughter
Henriette, his daughter (died aged nineteen)
Augustin, his younger son
Jacqueline, his wife, née Carraut, who dies after giving birth to a fifth child
Grandfather Carraut, a brewer
Aunt Eulalie ⎫
Aunt Henriette ⎭ François de Robespierre's sisters

In Paris, at Louis-le-Grand:
Father Poignard, the principal – a liberal minded man
Father Proyart, the deputy principal – not at all a liberal-minded man
Father Herivaux, a teacher of classical languages
Louis Suleau, a student
Stanislas Fréron, a very well-connected student, known as 'Rabbit'

In Troyes:
Fabre d'Églantine, an unemployed genius

PART II

In Paris:
Maître Vinot, a lawyer in whose chambers Georges-Jacques Danton is a pupil
Maître Perrin, a lawyer in whose chambers Camille Desmoulins is a pupil
Jean-Marie Hérault de Séchelles, a young nobleman and legal dignitary

François-Jérôme Charpentier, a café owner and Inspector of Taxes

Angélique (Angelica) his Italian wife
Gabrielle, his daughter

Françoise-Julie Duhauttoir, Georges-Jacques Danton's
mistress

At the rue Condé:
Claude Duplessis, a senior civil servant
Annette, his wife
Adèle ⎱
Lucile ⎰ his daughters
Abbé Laudréville, Annette's confessor, a go-between

In Guise:
Rose-Fleur Godard, Camille Desmoulins's fiancée

In Arras:
Joseph Fouché, a teacher, Charlotte de Robespierre's beau
Lazare Carnot, a military engineer, a friend of Maximilien
de Robespierre

Anaïs Deshorties, a *nice* girl whose relatives want her to
marry Maximilien de Robespierre

Louise de Kéralio, a novelist: who goes to Paris, marries
François Robert and edits a newspaper

Hermann, a lawyer, a friend of Maximilien de Robespierre

The Orléanists:
Philippe, Duke of Orléans, cousin of King Louis XVI
Félicité de Genlis, an author – his ex-mistress, now Gover-
nor of his children
Charles-Alexis Brulard de Sillery, Comte de Genlis –
Félicité's husband, a former naval officer, a gambler
Pierre Choderlos de Laclos, a novelist, the Duke's secretary

Agnès de Buffon, the Duke's mistress
Grace Elliot, the Duke's ex-mistress, a spy for the British
    Foreign Office

Axel von Fersen, the Queen's lover

At Danton's chambers:
Jules Paré, his clerk
François Deforgues, his clerk
Billaud-Varennes, his part-time clerk, a man of sour tem-
    perament

At the Cour du Commerce:
Mme Gély, who lives upstairs from Georges-Jacques and
    Gabrielle Danton
Antoine, her husband
Louise, her daughter

Catherine ⎫
            ⎬   the Dantons' servants
Marie   ⎭

Legendre, a master butcher, a neighbour of the Dantons
François Robert, a lecturer in law: marries Louise de
    Kéralio, opens a delicatessen, and later becomes a radi-
    cal journalist
René Hébert, a theatre box-office clerk
Anne Théroigne, a singer

In the National Assembly:
Antoine Barnave, a deputy: at first a radical, later a royal-
    ist
Jérôme Pétion, a radical deputy, later called a 'Brissotin'
Dr Guillotin, an expert on public health
Jean-Sylvain Bailly, an astronomer, later Mayor of Paris.
Honoré-Gabriel Riquetti, Comte de Mirabeau, a renegade
    aristocrat sitting for the Commons, or Third Estate

Teutch, Mirabeau's valet

Clavière ⎫
Dumont ⎬ His 'slaves', Genevan politicans in exile
Duroveray ⎭

Jean-Pierre Brissot, a journalist

Momoro, a printer

Réveillon, owner of a wallpaper factory
Hanriot, owner of a saltpetre works
De Launay, Governor of the Bastille

PART III

M. Soulès, temporary Governor of the Bastille

The Marquis de Lafayette, Commander of the National Guard

Jean-Paul Marat, a journalist, editor of the *People's Friend*

Arthur Dillon, Governor of Tobago and a general in the French army; a friend of Camille Desmoulins

Louis-Sébastien Mercier, a well-known author

Collot d'Herbois, a playwright

Father Pancemont, a truculent priest
Father Bérardier, a gullible priest

Caroline Rémy, an actress

Père Duchesne, a furnace-maker: fictitious *alter ego* of René Hébert, box-office clerk turned journalist

Antoine Saint-Just, a disaffected poet, acquainted with or related to Camille Desmoulins

Jean-Marie Roland, an elderly ex-civil servant
Manon Roland, his young wife, a writer

François-Léonard Buzot, a deputy, member of the Jacobin Club and friend of the Rolands
Jean-Baptiste Louvet, a novelist, Jacobin, friend of the Rolands

PART IV

At the rue Saint-Honoré:
Maurice Duplay, a master carpenter
Françoise Duplay, his wife
Eléonore, an art student, his eldest daughter
Victoire, his daughter
Elisabeth (Babette), his youngest daughter

Charles Dumouriez, a general, sometime Foreign Minister

Antoine Fouquier-Tinville, a lawyer; Camille Desmoulins's cousin

Jeanette, the Desmoulins's servant

PART V

Politicians described as 'Brissotins' or 'Girondins':
Jean-Pierre Brissot, a journalist
Jean-Marie and Manon Roland
Pierre Vergniaud, member of the National Convention, famous as an orator
Jérôme Pétion
François-Léonard Buzot

Jean-Baptiste Louvet

Charles Barbaroux, a lawyer from Marseille and many others

Albertine Marat, Marat's sister

Simone Evrard, Marat's common-law wife

Defermon, a deputy, sometime President of the National Convention

Jean-François Lacroix, a moderate deputy: goes 'on mission' to Belgium with Danton in 1792 and 1793

David, a painter

Charlotte Corday, an assassin

Claude Dupin, a young bureaucrat who proposes marriage to Louise Gély, Danton's neighbour

Souberbielle, Robespierre's doctor

Renaudin, a violin-maker, prone to violence

Father Kéravenen, an outlaw priest

Chauveau-Lagarde, a lawyer: defence council for Marie-Antoinette

Philippe Lebas, a left-wing deputy: later a member of the Committee of General Security, or Police Committee; marries Babette Duplay

Vadier, known as 'the Inquisitor', a member of the Police Committee

Implicated in the East India Company fraud:

Chabot, a deputy, ex-Capuchin friar

Julien, a deputy, former Protestant pastor

Proli, secretary to Hérault de Séchelles, and said to be an Austrian spy

Emmanuel Dobruska and Siegmund Gotleb, known as

Emmanuel and Junius Frei: speculators

Guzman, a minor politician, Spanish-born

Diedrichsen, a Danish 'businessman'

Abbé d'Espanac, a crooked army contractor

Basire
Delaunay } deputies

Citizen de Sade, a writer, formerly a marquis

Pierre Philippeaux, a deputy: writes a pamphlet against the government during the Terror

Some members of the Committee of Public Safety:
Saint-André

Barère

Couthon, a paraplegic, a friend of Robespierre

Robert Lindet, a lawyer from Normandy, a friend of Danton

Etienne Panis, a left-wing deputy, a friend of Danton

At the trial of the Dantonists:
Hermann (once of Arras), President of the Revolutionary Tribunal

Dumas, his deputy

Fouquier-Tinville, now Public Prosecutor

Fleuriot
Liendon } prosecution lawyers

Fabricius Pâris, Clerk of the Court

Laflotte, a prison informer

Henri Sanson, public executioner

Map of Revolutionary Paris

FAUBOURG ST-HONOR[É]

AVENUE DES CHAMPS ÉLYSÉES

FAUBOURG ST - HONORÉ

Madeleine

Robespierre's lodging

Place Vendôm[e]

Riding School

Place Louis-XV
(Place de la Révolution)

Seine

Tuileries gardens

Pont Louis-XVI
(Under construction)

Pont-Royal

Champs-de-Mars

Invalides

FAUBOURG
ST- GERMAIN

RUE DE SÈVRES

Revolutionary
Paris

FAUBOURG
ST-MICHEL

FAUBOURG
ST-DENIS

(lace des Piques)

cobins
ub

Palais-Royal

FAUBOURG
ST-MARTIN

FAUBOURG
DU TEMPLE

T—HONORÉ

Les Halles

RUE ST–DENIS

RUE ST–MARTIN

RUE DU TEMPLE

ouvre

Conciergerie   Châtelet

Pont-Neuf

City
Hall

La Force
prison

Place
de Grève

RUE ST–ANTOINE

Palais de Justice

Abbaye prison

ÎLE DE
LA CITÉ

Notre-Dame

Bastille

Pont-Marie

Cordeliers
Club

ÎLE
ST-LOUIS

t Sulpice

R. CONDÉ

RUE DES CORDELIERS

Pont de la
Tournelle

RUE D'ENFER

RUE ST–JACQUES

RUE

Luxembourg

FAUBOURG
ST-VICTOR

Panthéon

MOUFETARD

Seine

FAUBOURG
ST-JACQUES

PART ONE

Louis xv is named the Well-Beloved. Ten years pass.
The same people believe the Well-Beloved takes baths
of human blood ... Avoiding Paris, ever shut up at
Versailles, he finds even there too many people, too
much daylight. He wants a shadowy retreat ...

In a year of scarcity (they were not uncommon then)
he was hunting as usual in the Forest of Sénart. He met
a peasant carrying a bier and inquired, 'Whither he was
conveying it?' 'To such a place.' 'For a man or a woman?'
'A man.' 'What did he die of?' 'Hunger.'

Jules Michelet

I. *Life as a Battlefield*

(1763–1774)

NOW THAT THE DUST has settled, we can begin to look at our situation. Now that the last red tile has been laid on the roof of the New House, now that the marriage contract is four years old. The town smells of summer; not very pleasant, that is, but the same as last year, the same as the years to follow. The New House smells of resin and wax polish; it has the sulphurous odour of family quarrels brewing.

Maître Desmoulins's study is across the courtyard, in the Old House that fronts the street. If you stand in the Place des Armes and look up at the narrow white façade, you can often see him lurking behind the shutters on the first floor. He seems to stare down into the street; but he is miles away, observers say. This is true, and his location is very precise. Mentally, he is back in Paris.

Physically, at this moment, he is on his way upstairs. His three-year-old son is following him. As he expects the child to be under his feet for the next twenty years, it does not profit him to complain about this. Afternoon heat lies over the streets. The babies, Henriette and Elisabeth, are asleep in their cribs. Madeleine is insulting the laundry girl with a fluency and venom that belie her gravid state, her genteel education. He closes the door on them.

As soon as he sits down at his desk, a stray Paris thought slides around his mind. This happens often. He indulges himself a little: places himself on the steps of the Châtelet court with a hard-wrung acquittal and a knot of congratulatory colleagues. He gives his colleagues names and faces. Where is Perrin this afternoon? And Vinot? Now he goes up twice a year, and Vinot – who used to discuss his Life Plan with him when they were students – had walked right past him in the Place Dauphine, not knowing him at all.

That was last year, and now it is August, in the year of Grace 1763. It is Guise, Picardy; he is thirty-three years old, husband, father, advocate, town councillor, official of the bailiwick, a man with a large bill for a new roof.

He takes out his account books. It is only two months ago that Madeleine's family came up with the final instalment of the dowry. They pretended – knowing that he could hardly disabuse them – that it was a kind of flattering oversight; that a man in his position, with steady work coming in, would hardly notice the last few hundred.

This was a typical de Viefville trick, and he could do nothing about it. They hammered him to the family mast while, quivering with embarrassment, he handed them the nails. He'd come home from Paris at their behest, to set things up for Madeleine. He hadn't known that she'd be turned thirty before her family considered his situation even half-way satisfactory.

What de Viefvilles do, they run things: small towns, large legal practices. There are cousins all over the Laon district, all over Picardy: a bunch of nerveless crooks, always talking. One de Viefville is Mayor of Guise, another is a member of that august judicial body, the Parlement of Paris. De Viefvilles generally marry Godards; Madeleine is a Godard, on her father's side. The Godards' name lacks the coveted particle of nobility; for all that, they tend to get on in life, and when you attend in Guise and environs a musical evening or a funeral or a Bar Association dinner, there is always one present to whom you can genuflect.

The ladies of the family believe in annual production, and Madeleine's late start hardly deters her. Hence the New House.

This child was his eldest, who now crossed the room and scrambled into the window-seat. His first reaction, when the new-born was presented: this is not mine. The explanation came at the christening, from the grinning uncles and cradle-witch aunts: aren't you a little Godard then, isn't he a little Godard to his fingertips? Three wishes, Jean-Nicolas thought sourly: become an alderman, marry your cousin, prosper like a pig in clover.

The child had a whole string of names, because the godparents could not agree. Jean-Nicolas spoke up with his own preference, whereupon the family united: you can call him Lucien if you like, but We shall call him Camille.

It seemed to Desmoulins that with the birth of this first child he had become like a man floundering around in a sucking swamp, with no glimmering of rescue. It was not that he was unwilling to assume responsibilities; he was simply overwhelmed by the perplexities of life, paralysed by the certainty that there was nothing constructive to be done in any given situation. The child particularly presented an insoluble problem. It seemed inaccessible to the processes of legal reasoning. He smiled at it, and it learned to smile back: not with the amicable toothless grin of most infants, but with what he took to be a flicker of amusement. Then again, he had always understood that the eyes of small babies did not focus properly, but this one – and no doubt it was entirely his imagination – seemed to look him over rather coolly. This made him uneasy. He feared, in his secret heart, that one day in company the baby would sit up and speak; that it would engage his eyes, appraise him, and say, 'You prick.'

Standing on the window-seat now, his son leans out over the square, and gives him a commentary on who comes and goes. There is the curé, there is M. Saulce. Now comes a rat. Now comes M. Saulce's dog; oh, poor rat.

'Camille,' he says, 'get down from there, if you drop out on to the cobbles and damage your brain you will never make an alderman. Though you might, at that; who would notice?'

Now, while he adds up the tradesmen's bills, his son leans out of the window as far as he can, looking for further carnage. The curé recrosses the square, the dog falls asleep in the sun. A boy comes with a collar and chain, subdues the dog and leads it home. At last Jean-Nicolas looks up. 'When I have paid for the roof,' he says, 'I shall be flat broke. Are you listening to me? While your uncles continue to withhold from me all but the dregs of the district's legal work, I cannot get by from month to month without making inroads into your mother's dowry, which is supposed to pay for your education. The girls will be all right, they can do needlework, perhaps people will marry them for their personal charms. We can hardly expect you to get on in the same way.'

'Now comes the dog again,' his son says.

'Do as I tell you and come in from the window. And do not be childish.'

'Why not?' Camille says. 'I'm a child, aren't I?'

His father crosses the room and scoops him up, prising his fingers away from the window frame to which he clings. His eyes widen in astonishment at being carried off by this superior strength. Everything astonishes him: his father's diatribes, the speckles on an eggshell, women's hats, ducks on the pond.

Jean-Nicolas carries him across the room. When you are thirty, he thinks, you will sit at this desk and, turning from your account books to the piffling local business on which you are employed, you will draft, for perhaps the tenth time in your career, a deed of mortgage on the manor house at Wiège; and that will wipe the look of surprise off your face. When you are forty, and greying, and worried sick about your eldest son, I shall be seventy. I shall sit in the sunshine and watch the pears ripen on the wall, and M. Saulce and the curé will go by and touch their hats to me.

WHAT DO WE THINK about fathers? Important, or not? Here is what Rousseau says:

The oldest of all societies, and the only natural one, is that of the family, yet children remain tied to their father by nature only as long as they need him for their preservation . . . The family may perhaps be seen as the first model of political society. The head of the state bears the image of the father, the people the image of his children.

So here are some more family stories.

M. DANTON had four daughters: younger than these, one son. He had no attitude to this child, except perhaps relief at its gender. Aged forty, M. Danton died. His widow was pregnant, but lost the child.

In later life, the child Georges-Jacques thought he remembered his father. In his family the dead were much discussed. He absorbed the content of these conversations and transmuted them into what passed for memory. This serves the purpose. The dead don't come back, to quibble or correct.

M. Danton had been clerk to one of the local courts. There was a little money, some houses, some land. Madame found herself coping. She was a bossy little woman who approached life with her elbows out. Her sisters' husbands came by every Sunday, and gave her advice.

Subsequently, the children ran wild. They broke people's fences and chased sheep and committed various other rural nuisances. When accosted, they talked back. Children of other families they threw in the river.

'That girls should be like that!' said M. Camus, Madame's brother.

'It isn't the girls,' Madame said. 'It's Georges-Jacques. But look, they have to survive.'

'But this is not some jungle,' M. Camus said. 'It is not Patagonia. It is Arcis-sur-Aube.'

Arcis is green; the land around is flat and yellow. Life goes on at a steady pace. M. Camus eyes the child, where outside the window he throws stones at the barn.

'The boy is savage and quite unnecessarily large,' he says. 'Why has he got a bandage round his head?'

'Why should I tell you? You'll only bad-mouth him.'

Two days ago, one of the girls had brought him home in the early warm dusk. They had been in the bull's field, she said, playing at Early Christians. This was perhaps the pious gloss Anne Madeleine put on the matter; it was possible of course that not all the Church's martyrs agreed to be gored, and that some, like Georges-Jacques, went armed with pointed sticks. Half his face was ripped up from the bull's horn. Panic-stricken, his mother had taken his head in her hands and shoved the flesh together and hoped against hope it would stick. She bandaged it tightly and put another bandage around his head to cover the bumps and cuts on his forehead. For two days, with a helmeted, aggressive air, he stayed in the house and moped. He complained that he had a headache. This was the third day.

Twenty-four hours after M. Camus had taken his leave, Mme Danton stood at the same window and watched – as if in a dazed, dreadful repeating dream – while her son's remains were manhandled across the fields. A farm labourer carried the heavy body in his arms; she could see how his knees bent under the dead-weight. There were two dogs running after him with their tails between their legs; trailing behind came Anne Madeleine, bawling with rage and despair.

When she reached them she saw that the man had tears in his eyes. 'That bloody bull will have to be slaughtered,' he said. They went into the kitchen. There was blood everywhere. It was all over the man's shirt, the dogs' fur, Anne Madeleine's apron and even her hair. It went all over the floor. She cast around for something – a blanket, a clean cloth – on which to lay the corpse of her only son. The labourer, exhausted, swayed against the wall, marking the plaster with a long rust-coloured streak.

'Put him on the floor,' she said.

When his cheek touched the cold tiles of the floor, the child moaned softly; only then did she realize he wasn't dead. Anne Madeleine was repeating the *De profundis* in a monotone: 'From the morning watch even until night: let Israel hope in the Lord.' Her mother hit her across the ear to shut her up. Then a chicken flew in at the door and got on her foot.

'Don't strike the girl,' the labourer said. 'She pulled him out from under its feet.'

Georges-Jacques opened his eyes and vomited. They made him lie still, and felt his limbs for fractures. His nose was broken. He breathed bubbles of blood. 'Don't blow your nose,' the man said, 'or your brains will drop out.'

'Lie still, Georges-Jacques,' Anne Madeleine said. 'You gave that bull something to think about. He'll run and hide when he sees you again.'

His mother said, 'I wish I had a husband.'

NO ONE HAD LOOKED at his nose much before the incident, so no one could say whether a noble feature had been impaired. But the place scarred badly where the bull's horn had ripped up his face. The line of damage ran down the side of his cheek, and intruded a purple-brown spur into his upper lip.

The next year he caught smallpox. So did the girls; as it happened, none of them died. His mother did not think that the marks detracted from him. If you are going to be ugly it is as well to be whole-hearted about it, put some effort in. Georges turned heads.

When he was ten years old his mother married again. He was Jean Recordain, a merchant from the town; he was a widower, with one (quiet) boy to bring up. He had a few little eccentricities, but she thought they would do very well together. Georges went to school, a small local affair. He soon found that he could learn anything without the least trouble, so he did not allow school to impinge on his life. One day he was walked on by a herd of pigs. Cuts and bruises resulted, another scar or two hidden by his thick wiry hair.

'That's positively the last time I'll be trampled on by any animal,' he said. 'Four-legged or two-legged.'

'Please God it may be,' his stepfather said piously.

A YEAR PASSED. One day he collapsed suddenly, with a burning fever, chattering teeth. He coughed sputum stained with blood, and a scraping, crackling noise came from his chest, quite audible to anyone in the room. 'Lungs possibly not too good,' the leech said. 'All those ribs driven into them at frequent intervals. Sorry, my dear. Better fetch the priest.'

The priest came. He gave him the last rites. But the boy failed to die that night. Three days later he still clung to a comatose half-life. His sister Marie-Cécile organized a cycle of prayers; she took the hardest shift, two o'clock in the morning till dawn. The parlour filled up with relations, sitting around trying to say the right thing. There were yawning silences, broken by the desperate sound of everyone speaking at once. News of each breath was relayed from room to room.

On the fourth day he sat up, recognized his family. On the fifth day he cracked jokes, and demanded food in quantity.

He was pronounced out of danger.

They had planned to open the grave, and bury him beside his

father. The coffin, which they had put in an outhouse, had to be sent back. Luckily, they had only put a deposit on it.

When Georges-Jacques was convalescent, his stepfather made an expedition to Troyes. Upon his return, he announced that he had found the boy a place in the minor seminary.

'You dolt,' his wife said. 'Confess it, you just want him out of the house.'

'How can I give my time to my inventions?' Recordain asked reasonably. 'I'm living on a battlefield. If it's not stamping pigs it's crackling lungs. Who else goes in the river in November? Who else goes in it at all? People in Arcis have no need to know how to swim. The boy's above himself.'

'Perhaps he could be a priest, after all,' Madame said, conciliatory.

'Oh yes,' Uncle Camus said. 'I can just see him ministering to his flock. Perhaps they'll send him on a Crusade.'

'I don't know where he gets his brains from,' Madame said. 'There's no brains in the family.'

'Thanks,' her brother said.

'Of course, just because he goes to the seminary it doesn't mean he has to be a priest. There's the law. We've got law in the family.'

'And if he disliked the verdict? The mind recoils.'

'Anyway,' Madame said, 'let me keep him at home for a year or two, Jean. He's my only son. He's a comfort to me.'

'Whatever makes you happy,' Jean Recordain said. He was a mild, easy-going man who pleased his wife by doing exactly as she told him; much of his time nowadays he spent in an outlying farm building where he was inventing a machine for spinning cotton. He said it would change the world.

His stepson was fourteen years old when he removed his noisy and overgrown presence to the ancient cathedral city of Troyes. Troyes was an orderly town. The livestock had a sense of its lowly place in the universe, and the Fathers did not allow swimming. There seemed an outside chance that he would survive.

Later, when he looked back on his childhood, he always described it as extraordinarily happy.

IN A THINNER, greyer, more northerly light, a wedding is celebrated. It is 2 January, and the sparse, cold congregation are able to wish each other the compliments of the season.

Jacqueline Carraut's love affair occupied the spring and summer of 1757, and by Michaelmas she knew she was pregnant. She never made mistakes. Or only big ones, she thought.

Because her lover had now cooled towards her, because her father was a choleric man, she let out the bodices of her dresses, and kept herself very quietly. When she sat at her father's table and could not eat, she shovelled the food down to the terrier who sat by her skirts. Advent came.

'If you had told me earlier,' her lover said, 'we would have only had the row about a brewer's daughter marrying into the de Robespierre family. But now, the way you're swelling up, we have a scandal as well.'

'A love child,' Jacqueline said. She was not romantic by nature, but she felt the posture forced upon her. She held up her chin as she stood at the altar, and looked the family in the eye all day. Her own family, that is; the de Robespierre family stayed at home.

François was twenty-six years old. He was the rising star of the local barrister's association and one of the district's most coveted bachelors. The de Robespierre family had been in the Arras district for three hundred years. They had no money, and they were very proud. Jacqueline was amazed by the household into which she was received. In her father's house, where the brewer ranted all day and bawled his workers out, great joints of meat were put upon the table. The de Robespierres were polite to each other, and ate thin soup.

Thinking of her, as they did, as a robust, common sort of girl, they ladled huge watery platefuls in her direction. They even offered her father's beer. But Jacqueline was not robust. She was sick and frail. A good thing she had married into gentility, people said spitefully. There was no *work* to be got out of her. She was just a little china ornament, a piece of porcelain, her narrow shape distorted by the coming child.

François had stood before the priest and done his duty; but once he met her body between the sheets, he felt again the original, visceral passion. He was drawn to the new heart that beat in her side, to the primitive curve of her ribs. He was awed by her translucent skin, by the skin inside her wrists which showed green-ish marble veins. He was drawn by her myopic green eyes, wide-open eyes that could soften or sharpen like the eyes of a cat. When she spoke, her phrases were like little claws, sinking in.

'They have that salty soup in their veins,' she said. 'If you cut them, they would bleed good manners. Tomorrow, thank God, we shall be in our own house.'

It was an embarrassed, embattled winter. François's two sisters hovered about, taking messages and being afraid of saying too much. Jacqueline's child, a boy, was born on 6 May, at two in the morning. Later that day, the family met at the font. François's father stood godparent, so the baby was named after him, Maximilien. It was a good, old, family name, he told Jacqueline's mother; it was a good, old family to which her daughter now belonged.

There were three more children of this marriage within the next five years. The time came to Jacqueline when sickness, then fear, then pain, was her natural condition. She did not remember any other kind of life.

THAT DAY AUNT EULALIE read them a story. It was called 'The Fox and the Cat'. She read very quickly, snapping the pages over. It is called not giving your full attention, he thought. If you were a child they would smack you for it. And this book was his favourite.

She was quite like the fox herself, jutting her chin up to listen, her sandy eyebrows drawing together. Disregarded, he slid down on to the floor, and played with the bit of lace at her cuff. His mother could make lace.

He was full of foreboding; never was he allowed to sit on the floor (wearing out your good clothes).

His aunt broke off in the middle of sentences, to listen. Upstairs, Jacqueline was dying. Her children did not know this yet.

They had evicted the midwife, for she had done no good. She was in the kitchen now eating cheese, scraping the rind with relish, frightening the servant-girl with precedents. They had sent for the surgeon; at the top of the stairs, François argued with him. Aunt Eulalie sprang up and closed the door, but you could still hear them. She read on with a peculiar note in her voice, stretching out her thin, white, lady's hand to Augustin's cradle, rocking, rocking.

'I see no way to deliver her,' the man said, 'except by cutting.' He did not like the word, you could see; but he had to use it. 'I might save the child.'

'Save her,' François said.

'If I do nothing, they'll both die.'

'You can kill it, but save her.'

Eulalie clenched her fist on the cradle, and Augustin cried at the jolt. Lucky Augustin, already born.

They were arguing now – the surgeon impatient at the layman's slow comprehension. 'Then I might as well fetch the butcher,' François shouted.

Aunt Eulalie stood up, and the book slipped out of her fingers, slithered down her skirt, fell and opened itself on the floor. She ran up the stairs: 'For Jesus' sake. Your voices. The children.'

The pages fanned over – the fox and the cat, the tortoise and the hare, wise crow with his glinting eye, the honey bear under the tree. Maximilien picked it up and straightened the bent corners of the pages. He put his sister's fat hands on the cradle. 'Like this,' he said, rocking.

She raised her face, with its slack infant mouth. 'Why?'

Aunt Eulalie passed him without seeing him, perspiration broken out along her upper lip. His feet pattered on the stairs. His father was folded into a chair, crying, his arm thrown over his eyes. The surgeon was looking in his bag. 'My forceps,' he said. 'I shall make the attempt, at least. The technique is sometimes efficacious.'

The child pushed the door just a little, making a gap to slip in. The windows were closed against the early summer, against the buzzing fragrance from gardens and fields. There was a good fire, and logs lay ready in a basket. The heat was close and visible. His mother's body was shrouded in white, her back propped against cushions, her hair scraped from her forehead into a band. She turned to him just her eyes, not her head, and the threadbare remnants of a smile. The skin around her mouth was grey.

Soon, it seemed to say, you and I shall part.

When he had seen this he turned away. At the door he raised a hand to her, a feeble adult gesture of solidarity. Outside the door the surgeon had taken off his topcoat and stood with it over his arm, waiting for someone to take it away from him and hang it up. 'If you had called me a few hours ago . . .' the surgeon remarked, to no one in particular. François's chair was empty. It seemed he had left the house.

The priest arrived. 'If the head would emerge,' he said, 'I should baptise it.'

'If the head would emerge our troubles would be over,' the surgeon said.

'Or any limb,' the priest said hopefully. 'The church countenances it.'

Eulalie passed back into the room. The heat billowed out as she opened the door. 'Can it be good for her? There is no air.'

'Chills are disastrous,' the surgeon said. 'Though anyway – '

'Extreme Unction, then,' the priest suggested. 'I hope there is a convenient table.'

He took out of his bag a white altar cloth, and delved in again for his candles. The grace of God, portable, brought to your hearth and home.

The surgeon's eyes roamed around the stairhead. 'Get that child away,' he said.

Eulalie gathered him into her arms: the love child. As she carried him downstairs the fabric of her dress chafed his cheek, made a tiny sound of rasping.

Eulalie lined them up by the front door. 'Your gloves,' she said. 'Your hats.'

'It's warm,' he said. 'We don't really need our gloves.'

'Nevertheless,' she insisted. Her face seemed to quiver.

The wet-nurse pushed past them, the baby Augustin tossed against her shoulder, held with one hand as if he were a sack. 'Five in six years,' she said to Eulalie, 'what can you expect? Her luck's run out, that's all.'

They went to Grandfather Carraut's. Later that day Aunt Eulalie came, and said that they must pray for their baby brother. Grandmother Carraut mouthed, 'Christened?' Aunt Eulalie shook her head. She cast an eye down at the children, a can't-say-too-much look. She mouthed back at Grandmother: 'Born dead.'

He shuddered. Aunt Eulalie bent down to kiss him. 'When can I go home?' he said.

Eulalie said, 'You'll be all right with Grandmother for a few days, till your mother's feeling better.'

But he remembered the grey flesh around her mouth. He understood what her mouth had said to him: soon I shall be in my coffin and soon I shall be buried.

He wondered why they told lies in this way.

He counted the days. Aunt Eulalie and Aunt Henriette went to and fro. They said, aren't you going to ask us how your mother is today? Aunt Henriette said to Grandmother, 'Maximilien doesn't ask how his mother is.'

Grandmother replied, 'He's a chilly little article.'

He counted the days until they decided to tell the truth. Nine days passed. It was breakfast time. When they were having their bread and milk, Grandmother came in.

'You must be very brave,' she said. 'Your mother has gone to live with Jesus.'

Baby Jesus, he thought. He said, 'I know.'

When this happened, he was six. A white curtain fluttered in the breeze from the open window, sparrows fussed on the sill; God the Father, trailing clouds of glory, looked down from a picture on the wall.

THEN IN A DAY OR TWO, sister Charlotte pointing to the coffin; his smaller sister Henriette grumbling in a corner, fractious and disregarded.

'I will read to you,' he told Charlotte. 'But not that animal book. It is too childish for me.'

Later the grown-up Henriette, who was his aunt, lifted him up to look in the coffin before it was closed. She was shaking, and said over his head, 'I didn't want to show him, it was Grandfather Carraut who said it must be done.' He understood very well that it was his mother, the hatchet-nosed corpse with its terrifying paper hands.

Aunt Eulalie ran out into the street. She said, 'François, I beg of you.' Maximilien ran after her, grabbing at her skirts; he saw how his father did not once turn back. François strode down the street, off into the town. Aunt Eulalie towed the child with her, back into the house. 'He has to sign the death certificate,' she said. 'He says he won't put his name to it. What are we going to do?'

Next day, François came back. He smelled of brandy and Grand-father Carraut said it was obvious he had been with a woman.

During the next few months François began to drink heavily. He neglected his clients, and they went elsewhere. He would disappear for days at a time; one day he packed a bag, and said he was going for good.

They said – Grandmother and Grandfather Carraut – that they had never liked him. They said, we have no quarrel with the de Robespierres, they are decent people, but him, he is not a decent person. At first they kept up the fiction that he was engaged in a lengthy and prestigious case in another city. He did return from time to time, drifting in, usually to borrow money. The elder de Robespierres – 'at our time of life' – did not feel they could give his children a home. Grandfather Carraut took the two boys, Maximilien and Augustin. Aunt Eulalie and Aunt Henriette, who were unmarried, said they would take the little girls.

At some point during his childhood, Maximilien found out, or was told, that he had been conceived out of wedlock. Possibly he put the worst construction on his family circumstances, because during the rest of his life he never mentioned his parents at all.

IN 1768 FRANÇOIS de Robespierre turned up in Arras after an absence of two years. He said he had been abroad, but he did not say where, or how he had lived. He went over to Grandfather Carraut's house, and asked to see his son. Maximilien stood in a passageway and heard them shouting from behind a closed door.

'You say you have never got over it,' Grandfather Carraut said. 'But have you stopped to ask your son whether he has got over it? The child is her image, he's not strong; she was not strong; you knew that when you forced yourself on her after each childbirth. It's only thanks to me that they have any clothes to their backs and are growing up Christians.'

His father came out and found him and said, he's thin, he's small for his age. He spent a few minutes talking to him in a strained and embarrassed way. Leaving, he bent down to kiss him on the forehead. His breath was sour. The love child jerked his head back, with an adult expression of distaste. François seemed disappointed. Perhaps he wanted a hug, a kiss, to swing his son around in the air?

Afterwards the child, who had learned to measure out sparingly his stronger emotions, wondered if he ought to be sorry. He asked his grandfather, 'Did my father come to see me?'

The old man grumbled as he moved away. 'He came to borrow money again. Grow up.'

Maximilien gave his grandparents no trouble at all. You would hardly know he was in the house, they said. He was interested in reading and in keeping doves in a cote in the garden. The little girls were brought over on Sundays, and they played together. He let them stroke – very gently, with one finger – the doves' quivering backs.

They begged for one of the doves, to take home and keep for themselves. I know you, he said, you'll be tired of it within a day or two, you have to take care of them, they're not dolls you know. They wouldn't give up: Sunday after Sunday, bleating and whining. In the end he was persuaded. Aunt Eulalie bought a pretty gilt cage.

Within a few weeks the dove was dead. They had left the cage outside, there had been a storm. He imagined the little bird dashing itself in panic against the bars, its wings broken, the thunder rolling overhead. When Charlotte told him she hiccupped and sobbed with remorse; but in five minutes, he knew, she would run out into the sunshine and forget it. 'We put the cage outside so he would feel free,' she sniffed.

'He was not a free bird. He was a bird that needed looking after. I told you. I was right.'

But his rightness gave him no pleasure. It left a bitter taste in his mouth.

His grandfather said that when he was old enough he would take him into the business. He escorted the child around the brewery, to look at the various operations and speak with the men. The boy took only a polite interest. His grandfather said that, as he was more bookish than practical, he might like to be a priest. 'Augustin can go into the business,' he said. 'Or it can be sold. I'm not sentimental. There are other trades than brewing.'

When Maximilien was ten years old, the Abbot of Saint-Waast was induced to interest himself in the family. He interviewed Maximilien in person, and did not quite take to him. Despite his self-effacing manner, he seemed basically contemptuous of the Abbot's opinions, as if he had his mind on higher things and plenty of tasks to engage him elsewhere. However, it seemed clear that he had a good brain going to waste. The Abbot went so far as to think that his misfortunes were not his fault. He was a child for whom one might do something; he had been three years at school in Arras, and his teachers were full of praise for his progress and industry.

The Abbot arranged a scholarship. When he said, 'I will do something for you,' he did not mean a mere trifle. It was to be Louis-le-Grand, the best school in the country, where the sons of the aristocracy were educated – a school that looked out for talent, too, and where a boy with no fortune might get on. So the Abbot said: moreover, he enjoined furious hard work, abject obedience, unfailing gratitude.

Maximilien said to his Aunt Henriette, 'When I go away, you will have to write me letters.'

'Of course.'

'And Charlotte and Henriette are to write me letters, please.'

'I'll see they do.'

'In Paris I shall have a lot of new friends, as well.'

'I expect so.'

'And when I am grown up I will be able to provide for my sisters and my brother. No one else will have to do it.'

'What about your old aunts?'

'You too. We'll get a big house together. We won't have any quarrels at all.'

Fat chance, she thought. She wondered: ought he to go? At twelve he was still such a small boy, so softly spoken and unobtrusive; she was afraid he would be overlooked altogether once he left his grandfather's house.

But no – of course he had to go. These chances are few and far between; we have to get on in this world, no good to be done by clinging to women's apron strings. He made her think of his mother, sometimes; he had those sea-coloured eyes, that seemed to trap and hold the light. I never disliked the girl, she thought. She had a feeling heart, Jacqueline.

During the summer of 1769 he studied to advance his Latin and Greek. He arranged about the care of the doves with a neighbour's daughter, a little girl slightly older than himself. In October, he went away.

IN GUISE, under the de Viefville eye, Maître Desmoulins's career had advanced. He became a magistrate. In the evenings after supper he and Madeleine sat looking at each other. Money was always short.

In 1767 – when Armand was able to walk, and Anne-Clothilde was the baby of the household – Jean-Nicolas said to his wife:

'Camille ought to go away to school, you know.'

Camille was now seven years old. He continued to follow his father about the house, talking incessantly in a de Viefville fashion and rubbishing his opinions.

'He had better go to Cateau-Cambrésis,' Jean-Nicolas said, 'and be with his little cousins. It's not far away.'

Madeleine had a great deal to do. The eldest girl was persistently sick, servants took advantage and the household budget required time-consuming economies. Jean-Nicolas exacted all this from her; on top of it, he wanted her to pay attention to his feelings.

'Isn't he a bit young to be taking the weight of your unfulfilled ambitions?' she inquired.

For the souring of Jean-Nicolas had begun. He had disciplined himself out of his daydreams. In a few years' time, young hopefuls at the Guise Bar would ask him, why have you been content with such a confined stage for your undoubted talents, Monsieur? And he would snap at them that his own province was good enough for him, and ought to be good enough for them too.

THEY SENT CAMILLE to Cateau-Cambrésis in October. Just before Christmas they received an effusive letter from the principal describing the astonishing progress that Camille had made. Jean-Nicolas waved it at his wife. 'Didn't I tell you?' he said. 'I knew it was the right thing to do.'

But Madeleine was disturbed by the letter. 'It is as if,' she said, 'they are saying, "How attractive and intelligent your child is, even though he has only one leg."'

Jean-Nicolas took this to be a witticism. Only the day before Madeleine had told him that he had no imagination and no sense of humour.

A little later the child arrived home. He had developed an appalling speech impediment, and could hardly be persuaded to say anything at all. Madeleine locked herself in her room and had her meals sent up. Camille said that the Fathers had been very kind to him and opined that it was his own fault. His father said, to cheer him, that it was not a fault but an inconvenience. Camille insisted that he was obscurely blameworthy, and asked coldly on what date it would be possible to return to school, since at school they did not worry about it and did not discuss it all the time. Jean-Nicolas contacted Cateau-Cambrésis in a belligerent mood to ask why his son had developed a stutter. The priests said he came with it, and Jean-Nicolas said he assuredly did not leave home with it; and it was concluded that Camille's fluency of speech lay discarded along the coach-route, like a valise or a pair of gloves that has gone astray. No one was to blame; it was one of those things that happen.

In the year 1770, when Camille was ten years old, the priests advised his father to remove him from the school, since they were unable to give him the attention his progress merited. Madeleine said, 'Perhaps we could get him a private tutor. Someone really first-class.'

'Are you mad?' her husband shouted at her. 'Do you think I'm a duke? Do you think I'm an English cotton baron? Do you think I have a coal mine? Do you think I have serfs?'

'No,' his wife said. 'I know what you are. I've no illusions left.'

It was a de Viefville who provided the solution. 'To be sure,' he said, 'it would be a pity to let your clever little boy come to nothing for the want of a little cash. After all,' he said rudely, 'you yourself are never going to set the world ablaze.' He ruminated. 'He's a charming child. We suppose he'll grow out of the stutter. We must think of scholarships. If we could get him into Louis-le-Grand the expense to the family would be trifling.'

'They'd take him, would they?'

'From what I hear, he's extraordinarily bright. When he is called to the Bar, he will be quite an ornament to the family. Look, next time my brother's in Paris, I'll get him to exert himself on your behalf. Can I say more?'

LIFE EXPECTANCY in France has now increased to almost twenty-nine years.

THE COLLÈGE Louis-le-Grand was an old foundation. It had once been run by Jesuits, but when they were expelled from France it was taken over by the Oratorians, a more enlightened order. Its alumni were celebrated if diverse; Voltaire, now in honoured exile, had studied there and Monsieur the Marquis de Sade, now holed up in one of his châteaux while his wife worked for the commutation of a sentence passed on him recently for poisoning and buggery.

The Collège stood on the rue Saint-Jacques, cut off from the city by high solid walls and iron gates. It was not the custom to heat the place, unless ice formed on the holy water in the chapel font; so in winter it was usual to go out early to harvest some icicles and drop them in, and hope that the principal would stretch a point. The rooms were swept by piercing draughts, and by gusts of subdued chatter in dead languages.

Maximilien de Robespierre had been there for a year now.

When he had first arrived he had been told that he would want to work hard, for the Abbot's sake, since it was to the Abbot he owed this great opportunity. He had been told that if he were homesick, it would pass. Upon his arrival he sat down to make a note of everything he had seen on the journey, because then he would have done his duty to it, and need not carry it around in his head. Verbs conjugated in Paris just as they did in Artois. If you kept your mind on the verbs, everything would fall into place around them. He followed every lesson with close attention. His teachers were quite kind to him. He made no friends.

One day a senior pupil approached him, propelling in front of him a small child. 'Here, Thing,' the boy said. (They had this affectation of forgetting his name.)

Maximilien stopped dead. He didn't immediately turn around. 'You want me?' he said. Quite pleasant-offensive; he knew how to do that.

'I want you to keep your eye on this infant they have unaccountably sent. He is from your part of the country – Guise, I believe.'

Maximilien thought: these ignorant Parisians think it is all the same. Quietly, he said, 'Guise is in PICARDY. I come from ARRAS. ARRAS is in ARTOIS.'

'Well, it's of no consequence, is it? I hope you can take time from your reputedly very advanced studies to help him find his way about.'

'All right,' Maximilien said. He swung around to look at the so-called infant. He was a very pretty child, very dark.

'Where is it you want to find your way to?' he asked.

Just then Father Herivaux came shivering along the corridor. He stopped. 'Ah, you have arrived, Camille Desmoulins,' he said.

Father Herivaux was a distinguished classicist. He made a point of knowing everything. Scholarship didn't keep the autumn chills out; and there was so much worse to come.

'And I believe that you are only ten years old,' Father said.

The child looked up at him and nodded.

'And that altogether you are very advanced for your years?'

'Yes,' said the child. 'That's right.'

Father Herivaux bit his lip. He scurried on. Maximilien removed the spectacles he was obliged to wear, and rubbed the corners of his eyes. 'Try "Yes, Father,"' he suggested. 'They expect it. Don't nod at them, they tend to resent it. Also, when he asked you if you were clever, you should have been more modest about it. You know – "I try my best, Father." That sort of thing.'

'Groveller, are you, Thing?' the little boy said.

'Look, it's just an idea. I'm only giving you the benefit of my experience.' He put his glasses back on. The child's large dark eyes swam into his. For a moment he thought of the dove, trapped in its cage. He had the feel of the feathers on his hands, soft and dead: the little bones without pulse. He brushed his hand down his coat.

The child had a stutter. It made him uneasy. In fact there was something about the whole situation that upset him. He felt that the *modus vivendi* he had achieved was under threat; that life would become more complicated, and that his affairs had taken a turn for the worse.

WHEN HE RETURNED to Arras for the summer holiday, Charlotte said, 'You don't grow much, do you?'

Same thing she said, year after year.

His teachers held him in esteem. No *flair*, they said; but he always tells the truth.

He was not quite sure what his fellow pupils thought of him. If you asked him what sort of a person he thought he was, he would tell you he was able, sensitive, patient and deficient in charm. But as for how this estimate might have differed from that of the people around him – well, how can you be sure that the thoughts in your head have ever been thought by anyone else?

He did not have many letters from home. Charlotte sent quite often a neat childish record of small concerns. He kept her letters for a day or two, read them twice; then, not knowing what to do with them, threw them away.

Camille Desmoulins had letters twice a week, huge letters; they became a public entertainment. He explained that he had first been sent away to school when he was seven years old, and as a consequence knew his family better on paper than he did in real life. The episodes were like chapters of a novel, and as he read them aloud for the general recreation, his friends began to think of his family as 'characters'. Sometimes the whole group would be seized by pointless hilarity at some phrase such as 'Your mother hopes you have been to confession', and would repeat it to each other for days with tears of merriment in their eyes. Camille explained that his father was writing an *Encyclopaedia of Law*. He thought that the only purpose of the project was to excuse his father from conversing with his mother in the evenings. He ventured the suggestion that his father shut himself away with the *Encyclopaedia*, and then read what Father Proyart, the deputy principal, called 'bad books'.

Camille replied to these letters in page after page of his formless handwriting. He was keeping the correspondence so that it could be published later.

'Try to learn this truth, Maximilien,' Father Herivaux said: 'most people are lazy, and will take you at your own valuation. Make sure the valuation you put on yourself is high.'

For Camille this had never been a problem. He had the knack of getting himself into the company of the older, well-connected pupils, of making himself in some way fashionable. He was taken up by Stanislas Fréron, who was five years older, who was named after his godfather, the King of Poland. Fréron's family was rich and learned, his uncle a noted foe of Voltaire. At six years old he had been taken to Versailles, where he had recited a poem for Mesdames Adelaide, Sophie and Victoire, the old King's daughters; they had made a fuss of him and given him sweets. Fréron said to Camille, 'When you are older I will take you about in society, and make your career.'

Was Camille grateful? Hardly at all. He poured scorn on Fréron's ideas. He started to call him 'Rabbit'. Fréron was incubating sensitivity. He would stand in front of a mirror to scrutinize his face, to see if his teeth stuck out or if he looked timid.

Then there was Louis Suleau, an ironical sort of boy, who smiled when the young aristocrats denigrated the status quo. It is an education, he said, to watch people mine the ground under their own feet. There will be a war in our lifetime, he told Camille, and you and I will be on different sides. So let us be fond of each other, while we may.

Camille said to Father Herivaux, 'I will not go to confession any more. If you force me to go, I will pretend to be someone else. I will make up someone else's sins and confess them.'

'Be reasonable,' Father Herivaux said. 'When you're sixteen, then you can throw over your faith. That's the right age for doing it.'

But by the time he was sixteen Camille had a new set of derelictions. Maximilien de Robespierre endured small daily agonies of apprehension. 'How do you get out?' he asked.

'It isn't the Bastille, you know. Sometimes you can talk your way out. Or climb over the wall. Shall I show you where? No, you would rather not know.'

Inside the walls there is a reasoning intellectual community. Outside, beasts file past the iron gates. It is as if human beings have been caged, while outside wild animals range about and perform human occupations. The city stinks of wealth and corruption; beggars sit in roadside filth, the executioner carries out public tortures, there are beatings and robberies in broad daylight. What Camille finds outside the walls excites and appals him. It is a benighted city, he said, forgotten by God; a place of insidious spiritual depravity, with an Old Testament future. The society to which Fréron proposed to introduce him is some huge poisonous organism limping to its death; people like you, he said to Maximilien, are the only fit people to run a country.

Camille also said, 'Wait until Father Proyart is appointed principal. Then we shall all be stamped into the ground.' His eyes were alight at the prospect.

This was an idea peculiar to Camille, Maximilien thought: that the worse things get, the better they get. No one else seems to think this way.

BUT, AS IT HAPPENED, Father Proyart was passed over. The new principal was Father Poignard d'Enthienloye, a relaxed, liberal, talented man. He was alarmed at the spirit that had got about among his charges.

'Father Proyart says you have a "set",' he told Maximilien. 'He says you are all anarchists and puritans.'

'Father Proyart doesn't like me,' Maximilien said. 'And I think he overstates the case.'

'Of course he overstates it. Must we plod? I have to read my office in half an hour.'

'Are we puritans? He ought to be glad.'

'If you talked about women all the time he would know what to do, but he says that all you talk about is politics.'

'Yes,' Maximilien said. He was willing to give reasonable consideration to the problems of his elders. 'He is afraid that the high walls don't keep American ideas out. He's right, of course.'

'Each generation has its passions. A schoolmaster sees them. At times I think our system is wholly ill-advised. We take away your childhoods, we force your ideas in this hothouse air; then we winter you in a climate of despotism.' Delivered of this, the priest sighed; his metaphors depressed him.

Maximilien thought for a moment about running the brewery; very little classical education would be required. 'You think it is better if people's hopes are not raised?' he said.

'I think it is a pity that we bring on your talents, then say to you – ' the priest held his palm up – 'this far, but no further. We cannot provide a boy like you with the privileges of birth and wealth.'

'Yes, well.' The boy smiled, a small but genuine smile. 'This point had not escaped me.'

The principal could not understand Father Proyart's prejudices against this boy. He was not aggressive, did not seem to want to get the better of you. 'So what will you do, Maximilien? I mean, what do you intend?' He knew that under the terms of his scholarship the boy must take his degree in medicine, theology or jurisprudence. 'I gather it was thought you might go into the Church.'

'Other people thought so.' Maximilien's tone was very respectful, the principal thought; he offers a due deference to the opinions of others, then takes no notice of them at all. 'My father had a legal practice, once. I hope to pick it up. I have to go home. I am the eldest, you see.'

The priest knew this, of course; knew that unwilling relatives doled out a pittance for what the scholarship did not provide, so that the boy must always be acutely conscious of his social standing. Last year the bursar had to arrange for him to be bought a new topcoat. 'A career in your own province,' he said. 'Will this be enough for you?'

'Oh, I'll move within my sphere.' Sardonic? Perhaps. 'But Father, you were worrying about the moral tone of the place. Don't you want to have this conversation with Camille? He's much more entertaining on the topic of moral tone.'

'I deplore this convention of the single name,' the priest said. 'As if he were famous. Does he mean to go through life with only one name? I have no good opinion of your friend. And do not tell me you are not his keeper.'

'I'm afraid I am, you see.' He thought. 'But come, Father, surely you do have a good opinion of him?'

The priest laughed. 'Father Proyart says that you are not just puritans and anarchists, but strikers of poses too. Precious, self-conscious . . . this is the Suleau boy as well. But I see that you are not like that.'

'You think I should just be myself?'

'Why not?'

'I usually feel some greater effort is called for.' Later, putting down his breviary, the priest brooded over the interview. He thought, this child will just be unhappy. He will go back to his province, and he will never amount to anything.

THE YEAR NOW is 1774. Poseurs or not, it is time to grow up. It is time to enter the public realm, the world of public acts and public attitudes. Everything that happens now will happen in the light of history. It is not a midday luminary, but a corpse-candle to the intellect; at best, it is a secondhand lunar light, error-breeding, sand-blind and parched.

Camille Desmoulins, 1793: 'They think that gaining freedom is like growing up: you have to suffer.'

Maximilien Robespierre, 1793: 'History is fiction.'

II. *Corpse-Candle*

(1774-1780)

Just after Easter, King Louis XV caught smallpox. From the cradle his life had been thronged by courtiers; his rising in the morning was a ceremony governed by complex and rigid etiquette, and when he dined he dined in public, hundreds filing past to gape at every mouthful. Each bowel movement, each sex act, each breath a matter for public comment: and then his death.

He had to break off the hunt, and was brought to the palace weak and feverish. He was sixty-four, and from the outset they rather thought he would die. When the rash appeared he lay shaking with fear, because he himself knew he would die and go to Hell.

The Dauphin and his wife stayed in their own rooms, afraid of contagion. When the blisters suppurated the windows and doors were flung wide open, but the stench was unbearable. The rotting body was turned over to the doctors and priests for the last hours. The carriage of Mme du Barry, the last of the Mistresses, rolled out of Versailles for ever, and only then, when she had gone and he felt quite alone, would the priests give him absolution. He sent for her, was told she had already left. 'Already,' he said.

The Court had assembled, to wait events, in the huge antechamber known as the Œil de Boeuf. On 10 May, at a quarter past three in the afternoon, a lighted taper in the window of the sickroom was snuffed out.

Then suddenly a noise exploded like thunder from a clear sky – the rush, the shuffle, the tramp of hundreds of feet. Of blank and single mind, the Court charged out of the Œil de Boeuf and through the Grand Galerie to find the new King.

The new King is nineteen years old; his consort, the Austrian princess Marie-Antoinette, is a year younger. The King is a large, pious, conscientious boy, phlegmatic, devoted to hunting and the pleasures of the table; he is said to be incapable, by reason of a painfully tight foreskin, of indulging the pleasures of the flesh. The Queen is a selfish little girl, strong-willed and ill-educated. She is fair, fresh-complexioned, pretty because at eighteen almost all girls are pretty; but her large-chinned Hapsburg hauteur is already beginning to battle with the advantages conferred by silk, diamonds and ignorance.

Hopes for the new reign run high. On the statue of the great Henri IV, the hand of an unknown optimist writes '*Resurrexit*'.

WHEN THE LIEUTENANT of Police goes to his desk – today, last year, every year – the first piece of information he requires concerns the price of a loaf in the bakers' shops of Paris. If Les Halles is well supplied with flour, then the bakers of the city and the faubourgs will satisfy their customers, and the thousand itinerant bakers will bring their bread in to the markets in the Marais, in Saint-Paul, in the Palais-Royal and in Les Halles itself.

In easy times, a loaf of brown bread costs eight or nine sous. A general labourer, who is paid by the day, can expect to earn twenty sous; a mason might get forty sous, a skilled locksmith or a joiner might get fifty. Items for the budget: rent money, candles, cooking fat, vegetables, wine. Meat is for special occasions. Bread is the main concern.

The supply lines are tight, precise, monitored. What the bakers have left over at the end of the day must be sold off cheap; the destitute do not eat till night falls on the markets.

All goes well; but then when the harvest fails – in 1770, say, or in 1772 or 1774 – an inexorable price rise begins; in the autumn of 1774, a four-pound loaf in Paris costs eleven sous, but by the following spring the price is up to fourteen. Wages do not rise. The building workers are always turbulent, so are the weavers, so are the bookbinders and (poor souls) the hatters, but strikes are seldom to procure a wage rise, usually to resist a cut. Not the strike but the bread riot is the most familiar resort of the urban working man, and thus the temperature and rainfall over some distant cornfield connects directly with the tension headaches of the Lieutenant of Police.

Whenever there is a shortage of grain, the people cry, 'A famine pact!' They blame speculators and stockpilers. The millers, they say, are conspiring to starve the locksmiths, the hatters, the bookbinders and their children. Now, in the seventies, the advocates of economic reform will introduce free trade in grain, so that the most deprived regions of the country will have to compete in the open market. But a little riot or two, and on go the controls again. In 1770, the Abbé Terray, the Comptroller-General of Finance, acted very quickly to reimpose price controls, levies, restrictions on the movement of grain. He sought no opinions, just acted by royal decree. 'Despotism!' cried those who had eaten that day.

Bread is the main thing to understand: the staple of speculation, the food for all theories about what happens next. Fifteen years from now, on the day the Bastille falls, the price of bread in Paris will be at its highest in sixty years. Twenty years from now (when it is all over), a woman of the capital will say: 'Under Robespierre, blood flowed, but the people had bread. Perhaps in order to have bread, it is necessary to spill a little blood.'

THE KING CALLED to the ministry a man named Turgot, to be Comptroller-General of Finance. Turgot was forty-eight years old, a new man, a rationalist, a disciple of *laissez-faire*. He was energetic, bursting with ideas, full of the reforms he said must be made if the country was to survive. In his own opinion, he was the man of the hour. One of his first actions was to ask for cuts in expenditure at Versailles. The Court was shocked. Malesherbes, a member of the King's Household, advised the minister to move with greater caution; he was making too many enemies. 'The needs of the people are enormous,' Turgot replied brusquely, 'and in my family we die at fifty.'

In the spring of 1775 there was widespread rioting in market towns, especially in Picardy. At Versailles, eight thousand townspeople gathered at the palace and stood hopefully gazing up at the royal windows. As always, they thought that the personal intervention of the King could solve all their problems. The Governor of Versailles promised that the price of wheat in the town would be pegged. The new King was brought out to address the people from a balcony. They then dispersed without violence.

In Paris, mobs looted the bakers on the Left Bank. The police made a few arrests, playing the situation softly, avoiding clashes. There were 162 prosecutions. Two looters, one a boy of sixteen, were hanged in the Place de Grève. May 11, 3 p.m.; it served as an example.

IN JULY 1775, it was arranged that the young King and his lovely Queen would pay a visit to the Collège Louis-le-Grand. Such a visit was traditional after coronations; but they would not stay or linger, for they had more entertaining things to do. It was planned that they should be met, with their retinue, at the main gate, that they should descend from their carriage, and that the school's most industrious and meritorious pupil would read them a loyal address. When the day came, the weather was not fine.

An hour and a half before the guests could reasonably be expected, the students and staff assembled at the rue Saint-Jacques gate. A posse of officials turned up on horseback, and pushed them back and rearranged them, none too gently. The scanty spots of rain became a steady drizzle. Then came the attendants and bodyguards and persons-in-waiting; by the time they had disposed themselves everyone was cold and wet, and had stopped jockeying for position. No one remembered the last coronation, so nobody had any idea that it was all going to take so long. The students huddled in miserable groups, and shifted their feet, and waited. If anyone stepped out of line for a moment the officials jumped forward and shoved him back, flourishing weapons.

Finally the royal carriage drew up. People now stood on their toes and craned their necks, and the younger ones complained that it wasn't fair that they couldn't see a thing after waiting all this time. Father Poignard, the principal, approached and bowed. He began to say a few words he had prepared, in the direction of the royal conveyance.

The scholarship boy's mouth felt dry. His hand shook a little. But because of the Latin, no one would detect his provincial accent.

The Queen bobbed out her lovely head and bobbed it in again. The King waved, and muttered something to a man in livery, who conveyed it by a sneer down a line of officials, who conveyed it by dumb show to the waiting world. All became clear; they would not descend. The address must be read to Their Majesties as they sit snug in the coach.

Father Poignard's head was whirling. He should have had carpets, he should have had canopies, he should have had some kind of temporary pavilion erected, perhaps bedecked with green boughs in the fashionable rustic style, perhaps with the royal arms on display, or the monarchs' entwined monograms made out of flowers. His expression grew wild, repentant, remote. Luckily, Father Herivaux remembered to give the nod to the scholarship boy.

The boy began, his voice gathering strength after the first few nervous phrases. Father Herivaux relaxed; he had written it, coached the boy. And he was satisfied, it sounded well.

The Queen was seen to shiver. 'Ah!' went the world. 'She shivered!' A half-second later, she stifled a yawn. The King turned, attentive. And what was this? The coachman was gathering the reins! The whole ponderous entourage stirred and creaked forward. They were going – the welcome not acknowledged, the address not half-read.

The scholarship boy did not seem to notice what was happening. He just went on orating. His face was set and pale, he was looking straight ahead. Surely he must know that by now they are driving down the street?

The air was loud with unvoiced sentiment. All term we've been planning this . . . The crush moved, aimlessly, on the spot. The rain was coming down harder now. It seemed rude to break ranks and dash for cover, yet no ruder than what the King and Queen had done, driving off like that, leaving Thing talking in the middle of the street . . .

Father Poignard said, 'It's nothing personal. It's nothing we did, surely? Her Majesty was tired . . . '

'Might as well talk to her in Japanese, I suppose,' said the student at his elbow.

Father Poignard said, 'Camille, for once you are right.'

The scholarship boy was now concluding his speech. Without a smile, he bid a fond and loyal goodbye to the monarchs who were no longer in sight, and hoped that the school would have the honour, at some future time . . .

A consoling hand dropped on his shoulder. 'Never mind, de Robespierre, it could have happened to anybody.'

Then, at last, the scholarship boy smiled.

THAT WAS PARIS, July 1775. In Troyes, Georges-Jacques Danton was about half-way through his life. His relatives did not know this, of course. He was doing well at school, though you could not describe him as settled. His future was the subject of family discussion.

SO: IN TROYES one day, near the cathedral, a man was drawing portraits. He was trying to sketch the passers-by, throwing occasional glances at the sky and humming to himself. It was a catchy, popular air.

No one wanted to be sketched; they pushed past and bustled on. He did not seem put out – it seemed to be his proper occupation, on a fine and pleasant afternoon. He was a stranger – rather dandified, with a Parisian air. Georges-Jacques Danton stood in front of him. In fact, he hovered conspicuously. He wanted to look at the man's work and to get into conversation. He talked to everyone, especially to strangers. He liked to know all about people's lives.

'Are you at leisure to be portrayed?' The man did not look up; he was putting a fresh sheet of paper on his board.

The boy hesitated.

The artist said, 'You're a student, you've no money, I know. But you do have that face – sweet Jesus, haven't you had a busy time? Never seen a set of scars quite like it. Just stay still while I do you in charcoal a couple of times, then you can have one of them.'

Georges-Jacques stood still to be drawn. He watched the man

out of the corner of his eye. 'Don't talk,' the artist said. 'Just do me that terrifying frown – yes, just so – and I'll talk to you. My name is Fabre, Fabre d'Églantine. Funny name, you say. Why d'Églantine? you ask. Well, since you ask – in the literary competition of 1771, I was awarded a wreath of eglantine by the Academy of Toulouse. A signal, coveted, memorable honour – don't you think? Yes, quite right, I'd rather have had a small gold bar, but what can you do? My friends pressed me to add the suffix 'd'Églantine' to my own homely appellation, in commemoration of the event. Turn your head a little. No, the other way. So – you say – if this fellow is fêted for his literary efforts, what is he doing making sketches in the street?'

'I suppose you must be versatile,' Georges-Jacques said.

'Some of your local dignitaries invited me to read my work,' Fabre said. 'Didn't work out, did it? I quarrelled with my patrons. No doubt you've heard of artists doing something of that sort.'

Georges-Jacques observed him, as best he could without turning his head. Fabre was a man in his mid-twenties, not tall, with unpowdered dark hair cut short. His coat was well-brushed but shiny at the cuffs; his linen was worn. Everything he said was both serious and not serious. Various experimental expressions chased themselves across his face.

Fabre chose another pencil. 'Little to the left,' he said. 'Now, you say versatile – I am in fact a playwright, director, portraitist – as you see – and landscape painter; a composer and musician, poet and choreographer. I am an essayist on all subjects of public interest, and speak several languages. I should like to try my hand at landscape gardening, but no one will commission me. I have to say it – the world doesn't seem to be ready for me. Until last week I was a travelling actor, but I have mislaid my troupe.'

He had finished. He threw his pencil down, screwed up his eyes and looked at his drawings, holding them both out at arms' length. 'There you are,' he said, deciding. 'That's the better one, you keep it.'

Danton's unlovely face stared back at him: the long scar, the bashed-in nose, the thick hair springing back from his forehead.

'When you're famous,' he said, 'this could be worth money.' He looked up. 'What happened to the other actors? Were you going to put on a play?'

He would have looked forward to it. Life was quiet; life was dull.

Quite abruptly, Fabre rose from his stool and made an obscene gesture in the direction of Bar-sur-Seine. 'Two of our most applauded thespians mouldering in some village dungeon on a drunk-and-disorderly charge. Our leading lady impregnated months ago by some dismal rural wight, and now fit only for the most vulgar of low comedy roles. We have disbanded. Temporarily.' He sat down again. 'Now you –' his eyes lit up with interest – 'I don't suppose you'd like to run away from home and become an actor?'

'I don't think so. My relatives are expecting me to become a priest.'

'Oh, you want to leave that alone,' Fabre said. 'Do you know how they pick bishops? On their pedigree. Have you a pedigree? Look at you. You're a farm boy.. What's the point of entering a profession unless you can get to the top?'

'Could I get to the top if I became a travelling actor?'

He asked civilly, as if he were prepared to consider anything.

Fabre laughed. 'You could play the villains. You'd be well received. You've got a good voice there, potentially.' He patted his chest. 'Let it come from here.' He pounded his fist below his diaphragm. 'Breathe from here. Think of your breath as a river. Let it just flow, flow. The whole trick's in the breathing. Just relax, you see, drop those shoulders back. You breathe from *here* –' he stabbed at himself – 'you can go on for hours.'

'I can't think why I'd need to,' Danton said.

'Oh, I know what you think. You think actors are the bottom of the heap, don't you? You think actors are ambulant shit. Like Protestants. Like Jews. So tell me, boy, what makes your position so brilliant? We're all worms, we're all shit. Do you realize that you could be locked up tomorrow, for the rest of your natural life, if the King put his name to a piece of paper that he's *never even read*?'

'I don't see why he should do that,' Danton said. 'I've hardly given him cause. All I do is go to school.'

'Yeah,' Fabre said. 'Exactly. Just make sure to live the next forty years without drawing attention to yourself. He doesn't have to know you, that's the *point*, don't you see, Jesus, what do they teach you at school these days? Anybody, anybody who *is* anybody, who doesn't like you and wants you out of the way, can go to the King with their document – "Sign here, Your Moronship" – and that's you in the Bastille, chained up fifty feet below the rue Saint-Antoine with a bunch of bones for company. No, you don't get a cell to yourself, because they never bother to shift the old skeletons. You know, of course, they have a special breed of rat in there that eats the prisoners alive?'

'What, bit by bit?'

'Absolutely,' Fabre said. 'First a little finger. Then a tiny toe.'

He caught Danton's eye, burst into laughter, balled up a spoiled piece of paper and tossed it over his shoulder. 'Bugger me,' he said, 'it's a body's work educating you provincials. I don't know why I don't just go to Paris and make my fortune.'

Georges-Jacques said, 'I hope to go to Paris myself, before too long.' The good voice died in his throat; he had not known what he hoped, till he spoke. 'Perhaps when I'm there I'll meet you again.'

'No perhaps about it,' Fabre said. He held up his own sketch, the slightly flawed one. 'I've got your face on file. I'll be looking out for you.'

The boy held out his vast hand. 'My name is Georges-Jacques Danton.'

Fabre looked up, his mobile face composed. 'Goodbye,' he said. 'Georges-Jacques – study law. Law is a weapon.'

ALL THAT WEEK he thought about Paris. The prizewinner gnawed at his thoughts. Maybe he was just ambulant shit – but at least he'd been somewhere, might go somewhere else. Breathe from *here*, he kept saying to himself. He tried it. Yes, it was all true. He felt he could keep talking for days.

WHEN M. DE VIEFVILLE des Essarts went to Paris, he would call on his nephew at the Collège Louis-le-Grand, to see how he did. By now, he had reservations – grave ones – about the boy's future. The speech impediment was no better, perhaps worse. When he talked to the boy, an anxious smile hovered about his lips. When the boy got stuck part-way through a sentence, it was embarrassing – sometimes desolating. You could dive in, help him out with what he was going to say. Except with Camille, you never knew quite where he was heading. His sentences might begin in the ordinary way, and end up anywhere at all.

He seemed, in some more important way, disabled for the life they had planned for him. He was so nervous you could almost hear his heart beating. Small-boned, slight and pallid, with a mass of dark hair, he looked at his relative from under his long eyelashes and flitted about the room as if his mind were only on getting out of it. His relative's reaction was, poor little thing.

But when he got outside into the street, this sympathy evaporated. He would feel he had been verbally carved up. It was not fair. It was like being tripped in the gutter by a cripple. You wanted to complain, but when you saw the circumstances you felt you couldn't.

Monsieur's primary purpose in visiting the capital was to attend the Parlement of Paris. The Parlements of the realm were not elected bodies. The de Viefvilles had bought their membership, and would pass it to their heirs: to Camille, perhaps, if he behaves better. The Parlements heard cases; they sanctioned the edicts of the King. That is, they confirmed that they were the law.

Occasionally, the Parlements grew awkward. They drafted protests about the state of the nation – but only when they felt their interests threatened, or when they saw that their interests could be served. M. de Viefville belonged to that section of the middle classes that did not want to destroy the nobility, but rather hoped to merge with it. Offices, positions, monopolies – all have their price, and many carry a title with them.

The Parlementarians worried a great deal when the Crown began to assert itself, to issue decrees where it had never issued them before, to produce bright new ideas about how the country should be run. Occasionally they got on the wrong side of the monarch;

since any resistance to authority was novel and risky, the Parlementarians managed the difficult feat of being both arch-conservatives and popular heroes.

In January 1776, the minister Turgot proposed the abolition of the feudal right called corvée – a system of forced labour on roads and bridges. He thought that the roads would be better if they were built and maintained by private contractors, rather than by peasants dragged from their fields. But that would cost, wouldn't it? So perhaps there could be a property tax? And every man of means would pay it – not just commoners, but the nobility too?

Parlement turned this scheme down flat. After another bitter argument, the King forced them to register the abolition of the corvée. Turgot was making enemies everywhere. The Queen and her circle stepped up their campaign against him. The King disliked asserting himself, and was vulnerable to the pressures of the moment. In May, he dismissed Turgot; forced labour was reinstated.

In this way, one minister was brought down; the trick bore repetition. Said the Comte d'Artois, to the back of the retreating economist: 'Now at last we shall have some money to spend.'

When the King was not hunting, he liked to shut himself up in his workshop, doing metalwork and tinkering with locks. He hoped that by refusing to make decisions he could avoid making mistakes; he thought that, if he did not interfere, things would go on as they always had done.

After Turgot was sacked, Malesherbes offered his own resignation. 'You're lucky,' Louis said mournfully. 'I wish I could resign.'

1776: A DECLARATION of the Parlement of Paris:

The first rule of justice is to conserve for each individual that which belongs to him. This is a fundamental rule of natural law, human rights and civil government; a rule which consists not only in maintaining the rights of property, but also those rights vested in the individual and derived from prerogatives of birth and social position.

WHEN M. DE VIEFVILLE arrived home, he would make his way

through the narrow huddle of small-town streets, and through the narrow huddle of provincial hearts; and he would bring himself to call on Jean-Nicolas, in his tall white book-filled house on the Place des Armes. Maître Desmoulins had an obsession nowadays, and de Viefville dreaded meeting him, meeting his baffled eyes and being asked once again the question that no one could answer: what had happened to the good and beautiful child he had sent to Cateau-Cambrésis nine years earlier?

On Camille's sixteenth birthday, his father was stamping about the house. 'I sometimes think,' he said, 'that I have got on my hands a depraved little monster with no feelings and no sense.' He has written to the priests in Paris, to ask what they teach his son; to ask why he looks so untidy, and why during his last visit home he has seduced the daughter of a town councillor, 'a man,' he says, 'whom I see every day of my working life'.

Jean-Nicolas did not really expect answers to these questions. His real objections to his son were rather different. Why, he really wanted to know, was his son so emotional? Where did he get this capacity to infect others with emotion: to agitate them, discomfit them, shake them out of their ease? Ordinary conversations, in Camille's presence, went off at peculiar tangents, or turned into blazing rows. Safe social conventions took on an air of danger. You couldn't, Desmoulins thought, leave him alone with anybody.

It was no longer said that his son was a little Godard. Neither did the de Viefvilles rush to claim him. His brothers were thriving, his sisters blooming, but when Camille slipped in at the front door of the Old House, he looked as if he had come on a message from the Foundling Hospital.

Perhaps, when he is grown up, he will be one of those boys who you pay to stay away from home.

THERE ARE SOME noblemen in France who have discovered that their best friends are their lawyers. Now that revenue from land is falling steadily, and prices are rising, the poor are getting poorer and the rich are getting poorer too. It has become necessary to assert certain privileges that have been allowed to lapse over the years. Often, dues to which one is entitled have not been paid for a generation; that lax and charitable lordship must now cease. Again, one's ancestors have allowed part of their estates to become known as 'common land' – an expression for which there is usually no legal foundation.

These were the golden days of Jean-Nicolas; if, privately, he had worries, at least professionally he was prospering. Maître Desmoulins was no bootlicker – he had a lively sense of his own dignity, and was moreover a liberal-minded man, an advocate of reform in most spheres of national life. He read Diderot after dinner, and subscribed to the Geneva reprint of the *Encyclopédie*, which he took in instalments. Nevertheless, he found himself much occupied with registers of rights and tracing of titles. A couple of old strongboxes were brought around and trundled up to his study, and when they were opened a faint musty smell crept out. Camille said, 'So that is what tyranny smells like.' His father swept his own work aside and delved into the boxes; very tenderly he held the old yellow papers up to the light. Clément, the youngest, thought he was looking for buried treasure.

The Prince de Condé, the district's premier nobleman, called personally on Maître Desmoulins in the tall, white, book-filled, very very humble house on the Place des Armes. Normally he would have sent his land agent, but he was piqued by curiosity to know the man who was doing such good work for him. Besides, if honoured by a visit, the fellow would never dare to send in a bill.

It was late afternoon, autumn. Warming in his hand a glass of deep red wine, and mellow, aware of his condescension, the Prince lounged in a wash of candlelight; evening crept up around them, and painted shadows in the corners of the room.

'What do you people *want*?' he asked.

'Well ... ' Maître Desmoulins considered this large question. 'People like me, men of the professional classes, we would like a little more say, I suppose – or let me put it this way, we would welcome the opportunity to serve.' It is a fair point, he thinks; under the old King, noblemen were never ministers, but, increasingly, all the ministers are noblemen. 'Civil equality,' he said. 'Fiscal equality.'

Condé raised his eyebrows. 'You want the nobility to pay your taxes for you?'

'No, Monseigneur, we want you to pay your own.'

'I do pay tax,' Condé said. 'I pay my poll tax, don't I? All this property-tax business is nonsense. And so, what else?'

Desmoulins made a gesture, which he hoped was eloquent. 'An equal chance. That's all. An equal chance at promotion in the army or the church . . .' I'm explaining it as simply as I can, he thought: an ABC of aspiration.

'An equal chance? It seems against nature.'

'Other nations conduct themselves differently. Look at England. You can't say it's a human trait, to be oppressed.'

'Oppressed? Is that what you think you are?'

'I feel it; and if I feel it, how much more do the poor feel it?'

'The poor feel nothing,' the Prince said. 'Do not be sentimental. They are not interested in the art of government. They only regard their stomachs.'

'Even regarding just their stomachs – '

'And you,' Condé said, 'are not interested in the poor – oh, except as they furnish you with arguments. You lawyers only want concessions for yourselves.'

'It isn't a question of concessions. It's a question of human beings' natural rights.'

'Fine phrases. You use them very freely to me.'

'Free thought, free speech – is that too much to ask?'

'It's a bloody great deal to ask, and you know it,' Condé said glumly. 'The pity of it is, I hear such stuff from my peers. Elegant ideas for a social re-ordering. Pleasing plans for a "community of reason". And Louis is weak. Let him give an inch, and some Cromwell will appear. It'll end in revolution. And that'll be no tea-party.'

'But surely not?' Jean-Nicolas said. A slight movement from the shadows caught his attention. 'Good heavens,' he said, 'what are you doing there?'

'Eavesdropping,' Camille said. 'Well, you could have looked and seen that I was here.'

Maître Desmoulins turned red. 'My son,' he said. The Prince nodded. Camille edged into the candlelight. 'Well,' said the Prince, 'have you learned something?' It was clear from his tone that he took Camille for younger than he was. 'How did you manage to keep still for so long?'

'Perhaps you froze my blood,' Camille said. He looked the Prince up and down, like a hangman taking his measurements. 'Of course there will be a revolution,' he said. 'You are making a nation of Cromwells. But we can go beyond Cromwell, I hope. In fifteen years you tyrants and parasites will be gone. We shall have set up a republic, on the purest Roman model.'

'He goes to school in Paris,' Jean-Nicolas said wretchedly. 'He has these ideas.'

'And I suppose he thinks he is too young to be made to regret them,' Condé said. He turned on the child. 'Whatever is this?'

'The climax of your visit, Monseigneur. You want to take a trip to see how your educated serfs live, and amuse yourself by trading platitudes with them.' He began to shake – visibly, distressingly. 'I detest you,' he said.

'I cannot stay to be abused,' Condé muttered. 'Desmoulins, keep this son of yours out of my way.' He looked for somewhere to put his glass, and ended by thrusting it into his host's hand. Maître Desmoulins followed him on to the stairs.

'Monseigneur – '

'I was wrong to condescend. I should have sent my agent.'

'I am so sorry.'

'No need to speak of it. I could not possibly be offended. It is not in me.'

'May I continue your work?'

'You may continue my work.'

'You are really not offended?'

'It would be ungracious of me to be offended at what cannot possibly be of any account.'

By the front door, his small entourage had quickly assembled. He looked back at Jean-Nicolas. 'I say out of my way and I mean well out of my way.'

When the Prince had driven away, Jean-Nicolas mounted the stairs and re-entered his office. 'Well, Camille?' he said. A perverse calm had entered his voice, and he breathed deeply. The silence prolonged itself. The last of the light had faded now; a crescent moon hung in pale inquiry over the square. Camille had retired into the shadows again, as if he felt safer there.

'That was a very stupid, fatuous conversation you were having,' he said in the end. 'Everybody knows those things. He isn't mentally defective. They're not: not all of them.'

'Do you tell me? I live so out of society.'

'I liked his phrase, "this son of yours". As if it were eccentric of you, to have me.'

'Perhaps it is,' Jean-Nicolas said. 'Were I a citizen of the ancient world, I should have taken one look at you and popped you out on some hillside, to prosper as best you might.'

'Perhaps some passing she-wolf might have liked me,' Camille said.

'Camille – when you were talking to the Prince, you somehow lost your stutter.'

'Mm. Don't worry. It's back.'

'I thought he was going to hit you.'

'Yes, so did I.'

'I wish he had. If you go on like this,' said Jean-Nicolas, 'my heart will stop,' he snapped his fingers, 'like that.'

'Oh, no,' Camille smiled. 'You're quite strong really. Your only affliction is kidney-stones, the doctor said so.'

Jean-Nicolas had an urge to throw his arms around his child. It was an unreasonable impulse, quickly stifled.

'You have caused offence,' he said. 'You have prejudiced our future. The worst thing about it was how you looked him up and down. The way you didn't speak.'

'Yes,' Camille said remotely. 'I'm good at dumb insolence. I practise: for obvious reasons.' He sat down now in his father's chair, composing himself for further dialogue, slowly pushing his hair out of his eyes.

Jean-Nicolas is conscious of himself as a man of icy dignity, an almost unapproachable stiffness and rectitude. He would like to scream and smash the windows: to jump out of them and die quickly in the street.

THE PRINCE WILL SOON forget all this in his hurry to get back to Versailles.

Just now, faro is the craze. The King forbids it because the losses are so high. But the King is a man of regular habits, who retires early, and when he goes the stakes are raised at the Queen's table.

'The poor man,' she calls him.

The Queen is the leader of fashion. Her dresses – about 150 each year – are made by Rose Bertin, an expensive but necessary modiste with premises on the rue Saint-Honoré. Court dress is a sort of portable prison, with its bones, its vast hoops, its trains, its stiff brocades and armoured trimmings. Hairdressing and millinery are curiously fused, and vulnerable to the *caprice du moment*; George Washington's troops, in battle order, sway in pomaded towers, and English-style informal gardens are set into matted locks. True, the Queen would like to break away from all this, institute an age of liberty: of the finest gauzes, the softest muslins, of simple ribbons and floating shifts. It is astonishing to find that simplicity, when conceived in exquisite taste, costs just as much as the velvets and satins ever did. The Queen adores, she says, all that is *natural* – in dress, in etiquette. What she adores even more are diamonds; her dealings with the Paris firm of Böhmer and Bassenge are the cause of widespread and damaging scandal. In her apartments she throws out furniture, tears down hangings, orders new – then moves elsewhere.

'I am terrified of being bored,' she says.

She has no child. Pamphlets distributed all over Paris accuse her of promiscuous relations with her male courtiers, of lesbian acts with her female favourites. In 1776, when she appears in her box at the Opéra, she is met by hostile silences. She does not understand this. It is said that she cries behind her bedroom doors: 'What have I done to them? What have I done?' Is it fair, she asks herself, if so much is really wrong, to harp on one woman's trivial pleasures?

Her brother the Emperor writes from Vienna: 'In the long run, things cannot go on as they are ... The revolution will be a cruel one, and may be of your own making.'

In 1778 Voltaire returned to Paris, eighty-four years old, cadaverous and spitting blood. He traversed the city in a blue carriage covered with gold stars. The streets were lined with hysterical crowds chanting 'Vive Voltaire.' The old man remarked, 'There would be just as many to see me executed.' The Academy turned out to greet him: Franklin came, Diderot came. During the performance of his tragedy *Irène* the actors crowned his statue with laurel wreaths and the packed galleries rose to their feet and howled their delight and adoration.

In May, he died. Paris refused him a Christian burial, and it was feared that his enemies might desecrate his remains. So the corpse was taken from the city by night, propped upright in a coach: under a full moon, and looking alive.

A man called Necker, a Protestant, Swiss millionaire banker, was called to be Minister of Finance and Master of Miracles to the court. Necker alone could keep the ship of state afloat. The secret, he said, was to borrow. Higher taxation and cuts in expenditure showed Europe that you were on your knees. But if you borrowed you showed that you were forward-looking, go-getting, energetic; by demonstrating confidence, you created it. The more you borrowed, the more the effect was achieved. M. Necker was an optimist.

It even seemed to work. When, in May 1781, the usual reactionary, anti-Protestant cabal brought the minister down, the country felt nostalgia for a lost, prosperous age. But the King was relieved, and bought Antoinette some diamonds to celebrate.

Georges-Jacques Danton had already decided to go to Paris.

It had been so difficult to get away, initially; as if, Anne-Madeleine said, you were going to America, or the moon. First there had been the family councils, all the uncles calling with some ceremony to put their points of view. They had dropped the priest business. For a year or two he had been around the little law offices of his uncles and their friends. It was a modest family tradition. Nevertheless. If he was sure it was what he wanted . . .

His mother would miss him; but they had grown apart. She was a woman of no education, with an outlook that she had deliberately narrowed. The only industry of Arcis-sur-Aube was the manufacture of nightcaps; how could he explain to her that the fact had come to seem a personal affront?

In Paris he would receive a modest clerk's allowance from the barrister in whose chambers he would study; later, he would need money to establish himself in practice. His stepfather's inventions had eaten into the family money; his new weaving loom was especially disaster prone. Bemused by the clatter and the creak of the dancing shuttles, they stood in the barn and stared at his little machine, waiting for the thread to break again. There was a bit of money from M. Danton, dead these eighteen years, which had been set aside for when his son grew up. 'You'll need it for the inventions,' Georges-Jacques said. 'I'll feel happier, really, to think I'm making a fresh start.'

That summer he visited the family. A pushy and energetic boy who went to Paris would never come back – except for visits, perhaps, as a distant and sucessful man. So it was proper to make these calls, to leave out no one, no distant cousin or great-uncle's widow. In their cool, very similar farmhouses he had to stretch out his legs and outline to them what he wanted in life, to submit his plans to their good understanding. He spent long afternoons in the parlours of these widows and maiden aunts, with old ladies nodding in the attenuated sunlight, while the dust swirled purplish and haloed their bent heads. He was never at a loss for something to say to them; he was not that sort of person. But with each visit he felt that he was travelling, further and further away.

Then there was just one visit left: Marie-Cécile in her convent. He followed the straight back of the Mistress of Novices down a corridor of deathly quiet; he felt absurdly large, too much a man, doomed to apologise for himself. Nuns passed in a swish of dark garments, their eyes on the ground, their hands hidden in their sleeves. He had not wanted his sister to come here. I'd rather be dead, he thought, than be a woman.

The nun halted, gestured him through a door. 'It is an inconvenience,' she said, 'that our parlour is so far within the building. We will have one built near the gate, when we get the funds.'

'I thought your house was rich, Sister.'

'Then you are misinformed.' She sniffed. 'Some of our postulants bring dowries that are barely sufficient to buy the cloth for their habits.'

Marie-Cécile was seated behind a grille. He could not touch or kiss her. She looked pale; either that, or the harsh white of the novice's veil did not suit her. Her blue eyes were small and steady, very like his own.

They talked, found themselves shy and constrained. He told her the family news, explained his plans. 'Will you come back,' she asked, 'for my clothing ceremony, for when I take my final vows?'

'Yes,' he said, lying. 'If I can.'

'Paris is a very big place. Won't you be lonely?'

'I doubt it.'

She looked at him earnestly. 'What do you want out of life?'

'To get on in it.'

'What does that mean?'

'I suppose it means I want to get a position, to have money, to make people respect me. I'm sorry, I see no point in being mealy-mouthed about it. I just want to be somebody.'

'Everybody's somebody. In God's sight.'

'This life has turned you pious.'

They laughed. Then: 'Have you any thought for the salvation of your soul, in the plans you've made?'

'Why should I have to think about my soul, when I've a great lazy sister a nun, with nothing to do but pray for me all day?' He looked up. 'What about you, are you – you know – happy?'

She sighed. 'Think of the economics of it, Georges-Jacques. It costs money to marry. There are too many girls in our family. I think the others volunteered me, in a way. But now that I'm here – yes, I'm settled. It really does have its consolations, though I wouldn't expect you to acknowledge them. I don't think you, Georges-Jacques, were born for the calmer walks of life.'

He knew that there were farmers in the district who would have taken her for the meagre dowry she had brought to the convent, and who would have been glad of a wife of robust health and cheerful character. It would not have been impossible to find a man who would work hard and treat her decently, and give her some children. He thought all women ought to have children.

'Could you still get out?' he asked. 'If I made money I could look after you, we could find you a husband or you could do without, I'd take care of you.'

She held up a hand. 'I said, didn't I – I'm happy. I'm content.'

'It saddens me,' he said gently, 'to see that the colour has gone from your cheeks.'

She looked away. 'Better go, before you make me sad. I often think, you know, of all the days we had in the fields. Well, that is over now. God keep you.'

'And God keep you.'

You rely on it, he thought; I shan't.

III. At Maître Vinot's

(1780)

SIR FRANCIS BURDETT, British Ambassador, on Paris: 'It is the most ill-contrived, ill-built, dirty stinking town that can possibly be imagined; as for the inhabitants, they are ten times more nasty than the inhabitants of Edinburgh.'

GEORGES-JACQUES came off the coach at the Cour des Messageries. The journey had been unexpectedly lively. There was a girl on board, Françoise-Julie; Françoise-Julie Duhauttoir, from Troyes. They hadn't met before – he'd have recalled it – but he knew something of her; she was the kind of girl who made his sisters purse their lips. Naturally: she was good-looking, she was lively, she had money, no parents and spent six months of the year in Paris. On the road she amused him with imitations of her aunts: 'Youth-doesn't-last-for-ever, a-good-reputation-is-money-in-the-bank, don't-you-think-it's-time-you-settled-down-in-Troyes-where-all-your-relatives-are-and-found-yourself-a-husband-before-you-fall-apart?' As if, Françoise-Julie said, there were going to be some sudden shortage of men.

He couldn't see there ever would be, for a girl like her. She flirted with him as if he were just anybody; she didn't seem to mind about the scar. She was like someone who has been gagged for months, let out of a gaol. Words tumbled out of her, as she tried to explain the city, tell him about her life, tell him about her friends. When the coach came to a halt she did not wait for him to help her down; she jumped.

The noise hit him at once. Two of the men who had come to see to the horses began to quarrel. That was the first thing he heard, a vicious stream of obscenity in the hard accent of the capital.

Her bags around her feet, Françoise-Julie stood and clung to his arm. She laughed, with sheer delight at being back. 'What I like,' she said, 'is that it's always changing. They're always tearing something down and building something else.'

She had scrawled her address on a sheet of paper, tucked it into his pocket. 'Can't I help you?' he said. 'See you get to your apartment all right?'

'Look, you take care of yourself,' she said. 'I *live* here, I'll be fine.' She spun away, gave some directions about her luggage, disbursed some coins. 'Now, you know where you're going, don't you? I'll expect to see you within a week. If you don't turn up I'll come hunting for you.' She picked up her smallest bag; quite suddenly, she lunged at him, stretched up, planted a kiss on his cheek. Then she whirled away into the crowd.

He had brought only one valise, heavy with books. He hoisted it up, then put it down again while he fished in his pocket for the piece of paper in his stepfather's handwriting:

> The Black Horse
> rue Geoffroy l'Asnier,
> parish of Saint-Gervais.

All about him, church bells had begun to ring. He swore to himself. How many bells were there in this city, and how in the name of God was he to distinguish the bell of Saint-Gervais and its parish? He screwed the paper up and dropped it.

Half the passers-by were lost. You could tramp for ever in the alleyways and back courts; there were streets with no name, there were building sites strewn with rubble, there were people's fireplaces standing in the streets. Old men coughed and spat, women hitched up skirts trailing yellow mud, children ran naked in it as if they were country children. It was like Troyes, and very unlike it. In his pocket he had a letter of introduction to an Île Saint-Louis attorney, Vinot by name. He would find somewhere to spend the night. Tomorrow, he would present himself.

A hawker, selling cures for toothache, collected a crowd that talked back to him. 'Liar!' a woman screamed. 'Get them pulled out, that's the only way.' Before he walked away, he saw her wild, mad, urban eyes.

*

MAÎTRE VINOT was a rotund man, plump-pawed and pugnacious. He affected to be boisterous, like an elderly schoolboy.

'Well,' he said, 'we can but give you a try. We . . . can . . . but . . . give . . . you . . . a try.'

I can give it a try, Georges-Jacques thought.

'One thing's for sure, your handwriting is atrocious. What do they teach you nowadays? I hope your Latin's up to scratch.'

'Maître Vinot,' Danton said, 'I've clerked for two years, do you think I've come here to copy letters?'

Maître Vinot stared at him.

'My Latin's fine,' he said. 'My Greek's fine, too. I also speak English fluently, and enough Italian to get by. If that interests you.'

'Where did you learn?'

'I taught myself.'

'How extremely enterprising. Mind you, if we have any trouble with foreigners we get an interpreter in.' He looked Danton over. 'Like to travel, would you?'

'Yes, I would, if I got the chance. I'd like to go to England.'

'Admire the English, do you? Admire their institutions?'

'A parliament's what we need, don't you think? I mean a properly representative one, not ruined by corruption like theirs. Oh, and a separation of the legislative and executive arms. They fall down there.'

'Now listen to me,' Maître Vinot said. 'I shall say to you one word about all this, and I hope I shall not need to repeat it. I won't interfere with your opinions – though I suppose you think they're unique? Why,' he said, spluttering slightly, 'they're the commonest thing, my coachman has those opinions. I don't run around after my clerks inquiring after their morals and shepherding them off to Mass; but this city is no safe place. There are all kinds of books circulating without the censor's stamp, and in some of the coffee houses – the smart ones, too – the gossip is near to treasonable. I don't ask you to do the impossible, I don't ask you to keep your mind off all that – but I do ask you to take care who you mix with. I won't have sedition – not on my premises. Don't ever consider that you speak in private, or in confidence, because for all you know somebody may be drawing you on, ready to report you to the authorities. Oh yes,' he said, nodding to show that he had the measure of a doughty opponent: 'oh yes, you learn a thing or two in our trade. Young men will have to learn to watch their tongues.'

'Very well, Maître Vinot,' Georges-Jacques said meekly.

A man put his head around the door. 'Maître Perrin was asking,' he said, 'are you taking on Jean-Nicolas's son, or what?'

'Oh God,' Maître Vinot groaned, 'have you *seen* Jean-Nicolas's son? I mean, have you had the pleasure of conversation with him?'

'No,' the man said, 'I just thought, old friend's boy, you know. They say he's very bright, too.'

'Do they? That's not all they say. No, I'm taking on this cool customer here, this young fellow from Troyes. He reveals himself to be a loud-mouthed seditionary already, but what is that compared to the perils of a working day with the young Desmoulins?'

'Not to worry. Perrin wants him anyway.'

'That I can readily imagine. Didn't Jean-Nicolas ever hear the gossip? No, he was always obtuse. That's not my problem, let Perrin get on with it. Live and let live, I always say,' Maître Vinot told Danton. 'Maître Perrin's an old colleague of mine, very sound on revenue law – they say he's a sodomite, but is that my business?'

'A private vice,' Danton said.

'Just so.' He looked up at Danton. 'Made my points, have I?'

'Yes, Maître Vinot, I should say you've driven them well into my skull.'

'Good. Now look, there's no point in having you in the office if no one can read your handwriting, so you'd better start from the other end of the business – "cover the courts", as we say. You'll do a daily check on each case in which the office has an interest – you'll get around that way, King's Bench, Chancery division, Châtelet. Interested in ecclesiastical work? We don't handle it, but we'll farm you out to someone who does. My advice to you,' he paused, 'don't be in too much of a hurry. Build slowly; anybody who works steadily can have a modest success, steadiness is all it takes. You need the right contacts, of course, and that's what my office will give you. Try to work out for yourself a Life Plan. There's plenty of work in your part of the country. Five years from now, you'll be nicely on your way.'

'I'd like to make a career in Paris.'

Maître Vinot smiled. 'That's what all the young men say. Oh well, get yourself out tomorrow, and have a look at it.'

They shook hands, rather formally, like Englishmen after all. Georges-Jacques clattered downstairs and out into the street. He kept thinking about Françoise-Julie. Every few minutes she flitted into his head. He had her address, the rue de la Tixanderie, wherever that was. Third floor, she'd said, it's not grand but it's mine. He wondered if she'd go to bed with him. It seemed quite likely. Presumably things that were impossible in Troyes were perfectly possible here.

ALL DAY, and far into the night, traffic rumbled through narrow and insufficient streets. Carriages flattened him against walls. The escutcheons and achievements of their owners glowed in coarse heraldic tints; velvet-nosed horses set their feet daintily into the city filth. Inside, their owners leaned back with distant eyes. On the bridges and at the intersections coaches and drays and vegetable carts jostled and locked their wheels. Footmen in livery hung from the backs of carriages to exchange insults with coalmen and out-of-town bakers. The problems raised by accidents were solved rapidly, in cash, according to the accepted tariff for arms, legs and fatalities, and under the indifferent eyes of the police.

On the Pont-Neuf the public letter-writers had their booths, and traders set out their goods on the ground and on ramshackle stalls. He sorted through some baskets of books, secondhand: a sentimental romance, some Ariosto, a crisp and unread book published in Edinburgh, *The Chains of Slavery* by Jean-Paul Marat. He bought half a dozen for two sous each. Dogs ran in packs, scavenging around the market.

Every second person he met, it seemed, was a builder's labourer, covered in plaster dust. The city was tearing itself up by the roots. In some districts they were levelling whole streets and starting again. Small crowds gathered to watch the more tricky and spectacular operations. The labourers were seasonal workers, and poor. There was a bonus if they finished ahead of schedule, and so they worked at a dangerous pace, the air heavy with their curses and the sweat rolling down their scrawny backs. What would Maître Vinot say? 'Build slowly.'

There was a busker, a man with a strained, once-powerful baritone. He had a hideously destroyed face, one empty eye-socket overgrown with livid scar tissue. He had a placard that read HERO OF THE AMERICAN LIBERATION. He sang songs about the court; they described the Queen indulging in vices which no one had discovered in Arcis-sur-Aube. In the Luxembourg Gardens a beautiful blonde woman looked him up and down and dismissed him from her mind.

He went to Saint-Antoine. He stood below the Bastille, looked up at its eight towers. He had expected walls like sea-cliffs. The highest must be – what? Seventy-five, eighty feet?

'The walls are eight feet thick, you know,' a passer-by said to him.

'I expected it to be bigger.'

'Big enough,' the man said sourly. 'You wouldn't like to be in there, would you? Men have gone in there and never come out.'

'You a local?'

'Oh yes,' the man said. 'We know all about it. There are cells under the ground, running with water, alive with rats.'

'Yes, I've heard about the rats.'

'And then the cells up under the roof – that's no joke either. Boil in summer, freeze in winter. Still, that's only the unlucky ones. Some get treated quite decent, depends who you are. They have beds with proper bed-curtains and they can take their own cat in to keep the vermin down.'

'What do they get to eat?'

'Varies, I suppose. Again, it's according to who you are. You do see the odd side of beef going in. Neighbour of mine a few years back, he swears he saw them taking in a billiard table. It's like anything else in life, I suppose,' the man said. 'Winners and losers, that's all about it.'

Georges-Jacques looks up, and his eye is offended; it is impregnable, there is no doubt. These people go about their lives and work – brewing by the look of it, and upholstery – and they live under its walls, and they see it every day, and finally they stop seeing it, it's there and not there. What really matters isn't the height of the towers, it's the pictures in your head: the victims gone mad with solitude, the flagstones slippery with blood, the children birthed on straw. You can't have your whole inner world rearranged by a man you meet in the street. Is nothing sacred? Stained from the dye-works, the river ran yellow, ran blue.

And when evening came the civil servants hurried home; the jewellers of the Place Dauphine came clank, clank with their keys to lock away their diamonds for the night. No homeward cattle, no dusk over the fields; shrug away the sentimentality. In the rue Saint-Jacques a confraternity of shoemakers settled in for a night's hard drinking. In a third-floor apartment in the rue de la Tixanderie, a young woman let in her new lover and removed her clothes. On the Île Saint-Louis, in an empty office, Maître Desmoulins's son faced, dry-mouthed, the heavy charm of his new employer. Milliners who worked fifteen hours in a bad light rubbed their red-rimmed eyes and prayed for their families in the country. Bolts were drawn; lamps were lit. Actors painted their faces for the performance.

PART TWO

WE make great progress only at those times when we become melancholy – at those times when, discontented with the real world, we are forced to make for ourselves one more bearable.

'The Theory of Ambition', an essay:
Jean-Marie Hérault de Séchelles

I. *The Theory of Ambition*

(1784-1787)

THE CAFÉ DU PARNASSE was known to its clients as the Café de l'École, because it overlooked the Quai of that name. From its windows you could see the river and the Pont-Neuf, and further in the distance the towers of the Law Courts. The café was owned by M. Charpentier, an inspector of taxes; it was his hobby, his second string. When the courts had adjourned for the day, and business was brisk, he would arrange a napkin over his arm and wait at table himself; when business slackened, he would pour a glass of wine and sit down with his regular customers, exchanging legal gossip. Much of the small-talk at the Café de l'École was of a dry and legalistic nature, yet the ambience was not wholly masculine. A lady might be seen there; compliments leavened with a discreet wit skimmed the marble-topped tables.

Monsieur's wife Angélique had been, before her marriage, Angelica Soldini. It would be pleasant to say that the Italian bride still enjoyed a secret life under the matron's cool Parisienne exterior. In fact, however, Angélique had kept her rapid and flamboyant speech, her dark dresses which were indefinably foreign, her seasonal outbursts of piety and carnality; under cover of these prepossessing traits flourished her real self, a prudent, economic woman as durable as granite. She was in the café every day – perfectly married, plump, velvet-eyed; occasionally someone would write her a sonnet, and present it to her with a courtly bow. 'I will read it later,' she would say, and fold it carefully, and allow her eyes to flash.

Her daughter, Antoinette Gabrielle, was seventeen years old when she first appeared in the café. Taller than her mother, she had a fine forehead and brown eyes of great gravity. Her smiles were sudden decisions, a flash of white teeth before she turned her head or twisted her whole body away, as if her merriment had secret objects. Her brown hair, shiny from long brushing, tumbled down her back like a fur cape, exotic and half-alive: on cold days, a private warmth.

Gabrielle was not neat, like her mother. When she pinned her hair up, the weight dragged the pins out. Inside a room, she walked as if she were out in the street. She took great breaths, blushed easily; her conversation was inconsequential, and her learning was patchy, Catholic and picturesque. She had the brute energies of a washerwoman, and a skin – everybody said – like silk.

Mme Charpentier had brought Gabrielle into the café so that she could be seen by the men who would offer her marriage. Of her two sons, Antoine was studying law; Victor was married and doing well, employed as a notary public; there was only the girl to settle. It seemed clear that Gabrielle would marry a lawyer customer. She bowed gracefully to her fate, regretting only a little the years of trespass, probate and mortgage that lay ahead. Her husband would perhaps be several years older than herself. She hoped he would be a handsome man, with an established position; that he would be generous, attentive; that he would be, in a word, distinguished. So when the door opened one day on Maître d'Anton, another obscure attorney from the provinces, she did not recognize her future husband – not at all.

SOON AFTER Georges-Jacques came to the capital, France had been rejoicing in a new Comptroller-General, M. Joly de Fleury, celebrated for having increased taxation on foodstuffs by 10 per cent. Georges-Jacques's own circumstances were not easy, but if there had not been some financial struggle he would have been disappointed; he would have had nothing to look back on in his days of intended prosperity.

Maître Vinot had worked him hard but kept his promises. 'Call yourself d'Anton,' he advised. 'It makes a better impression.' On whom? Well, not on the real nobility; but so much civil litigation is pressed by the massed ranks of the socially insecure. 'So what if they all know it's spurious?' Maître Vinot said. 'It shows the right kind of urges. Have comprehensible ambitions, dear boy. Keep us comfortable.'

When it was time to take his degree, Maître Vinot recommended the University of Rheims. Seven days' residence and a swift reading list; the examiners were known to be accommodating. Maître Vinot searched his memory for an example of someone whom Rheims had failed, and couldn't come up with one. 'Of course,' he said, 'with your abilities, you could take your exams here in Paris, but . . . ' His sentence trailed off. He waved a paw. He made it sound like some effete intellectual pursuit, the kind of thing they went in for in Perrin's chambers. D'Anton went to Rheims, qualified, was received as an advocate of the Parlement of Paris. He joined the lowest rank of barristers; this is where one begins. Elevation from here is not so much a matter of merit, as of money.

After that he left the Île Saint-Louis, for lodgings and offices of varying degrees of comfort, for briefs of varying number and quality. He pursued a certain type of case – involving the minor nobility, proof of title, property rights. One social climber, getting his patents in order, would recommend him to his friends. The mass of detail, intricate but not demanding, did not wholly absorb him. After he had found the winning formula, the greater part of his brain lay fallow. Did he take these cases to give himself time to think about other things? He was not, at this date, introspective. He was mildly surprised, then irritated, to find that the people around him were much less intelligent than himself. Bumblers like Vinot climbed to high office and prosperity. 'Goodbye,' they said. 'Not a bad week. See you Tuesday.' He watched them depart to spend their weekends in what with Parisians passed for the country. One day he'd buy himself a place – just a cottage would do, a couple of acres. It might take the edge off his restless moods.

He knew what he needed. He needed money, and a good marriage, and to put his life in order. He needed capital, to build himself a better practice. Twenty-eight years old, he had the build of the successful coal-heaver. It was hard to imagine him without the scars, but without them he might have had the coarsest kind of good looks. His Italian was fluent now; he practised it on Angelica, calling at the café each day when the courts rose. God had given him a voice, powerful, cultured, resonant, in compensation for his battered face; it made a *frisson* at the backs of women's necks. He remembered the prizewinner, took his advice; rolled the voice out from somewhere behind his ribs. It awaited perfection – a little extra vibrancy, a little more colour in the tone. But there it was – a professional asset.

Gabrielle thought, looks aren't everything. She also thought, money isn't everything. She had to do quite a lot of thinking of this kind. But compared to him, all the other men who came into the café seemed small, tame, weak. In the winter of '86, she gave him long, private glances; in spring, a chaste fleeting kiss on closed lips. And M. Charpentier thought, he has a future.

The trouble is, that to make a career in the junior ranks of the Bar requires a servility that wears him down. Sometimes the signs of strain are visible on his tough florid face.

MAÎTRE DESMOULINS had been in practice now for six months. His court appearances were rare, and like many rare things attracted a body of connoisseurs, more exacting and wonder-weary as the weeks passed. A gaggle of students followed him, as if he were some great jurist; they watched the progress of his stutter, and his efforts to lose it by losing his temper. They noted too his cavalier way with the facts of a case, and his ability to twist the most mundane judicial dictum into the pronouncement of some engirt tyrant, whose fortress he and he alone must storm. It was a special way of looking at the world, the necessary viewpoint of the worm when it's turning.

Today's case had been a question of grazing rights, of arcane little precedents not set to make legal history. Maître Desmoulins swept his papers together, smiled radiantly at the judge and left the courtroom with the alacrity of a prisoner released from gaol, his long hair flying behind him.

'Come back!' d'Anton shouted. He stopped, and turned. D'Anton drew level. 'I can see you're not used to winning. You're supposed to commiserate with your opponent.'

'Why do you want commiseration? You have your fee. Come, let's walk – I don't like to be around here.'

D'Anton did not like to let a point go. 'It's a piece of decent hypocrisy. It's the rules.'

Camille Desmoulins turned his head as they walked, and eyed him doubtfully. 'You mean, I may gloat?'

'If you will.'

'I may say, "So that's what they learn in Maître Vinot's chambers?"'

'If you must. My first case,' d'Anton said, 'was similar to this. I appeared for a herdsman, against the seigneur.'

'But you've come on a bit since then.'

'Not morally, you may think. Have you waived your fee? Yes, I thought so. I hate you for that.'

Desmoulins stopped dead. 'Do you really, Maître d'Anton?'

'Oh Christ, come on, man, I just thought you enjoyed strong sentiments. There were enough of them flying around in court. You were very easy on the judge, I thought – stopped just this side of foul personal abuse.'

'Yes, but I don't always. I've not had much practice at winning, as you say. What would you think, d'Anton, that I am a very bad lawyer, or that I have very hopeless cases?'

'What do you mean, what would I think?'

'If you were an impartial observer.'

'How can I be that?' Everybody *knows* you, he thought. 'In my opinion,' he said, 'you'd do better if you took on more work, and always turned up when you were expected, and took fees for what you do, like a normal lawyer.'

'Well, how gratifying,' Camille said. 'A neat, complete lecture. Maître Vinot couldn't have delivered it better. Soon you'll be patting your incipient paunch and recommending to me a Life Plan. We always had a notion of what went on in your chambers. We had spies.'

'I'm right, though.'

'There are a lot of people who need lawyers and who can't afford to pay for them.'

'Yes, but that's a social problem, you're not responsible for that state of affairs.'

'You ought to help people.'

'Ought you?'

'Yes – at least, I can see the contrary argument, perhaps as a philosophical position you ought to leave them to rot, but when things are going wrong for them under your nose – yes.'

'At your own expense?'

'You're not allowed to do it at anyone else's.'

D'Anton looked at him closely. No one, he thought, could want to be like this. 'You must think me very blameworthy for trying to make a living.'

'A living? It's not a living, it's pillage, it's loot, and you know it. Really, Maître d'Anton, you make yourself ridiculous by this venal posturing. You must know that there is going to be a revolution, and you will have to make up your mind which side you are going to be on.'

'This revolution – will it be a living?'

'We must hope so. Look, I have to go, I'm visiting a client. He's going to be hanged tomorrow.'

'Is that usual?'

'Oh, they always hang my clients. Even in property and matrimonial cases.'

'To visit, I mean? Will he be pleased to see you? He may think you have in some way failed him.'

'He may. But then, it is a Corporal Work of Mercy, visiting the imprisoned. Surely you know that, d'Anton? You were brought up within the church? I am collecting indulgences and things,' he said, 'because I think I may die at any time.'

'Where is your client?'

'At the Châtelet.'

'You do know you're going the wrong way?'

Maître Desmoulins looked at him as if he had said something foolish. 'I hadn't thought, you see, to get there by any particular route.' He hesitated. 'D'Anton, why are you wasting time in this footling dialogue? Why aren't you out and about, making a name for yourself?'

'Perhaps I need a holiday from the system,' d'Anton said. His colleague's eyes, which were black and luminous, held the timidity of natural victims, the fatal exhaustion of easy prey. He leaned forward. 'Camille, what has put you into this terrible state?'

Camille Desmoulins's eyes were set further apart than is usual, and what d'Anton had taken for a revelation of character was in fact a quirk of anatomy. But it was many years before he noticed this.

AND THIS CONTINUED: one of those late-night conversations, with long pauses.

'After all,' d'Anton said, 'what is it?' After dark, and drink, he is often more disaffected. 'Spending your life dancing attendance on the whims and caprices of some bloody fool like Vinot.'

'Your Life Plan goes further, then?'

'You have to get beyond all that, whatever you're doing you have to get to the top.'

'I do have some ambitions of my own,' Camille said. 'You know I went to this school where we were always freezing cold and the food was disgusting? It's sort of become part of me, if I'm cold I just accept it, cold's natural, and from day to day I hardly think of eating. But of course, if I do ever get warm, or someone feeds me well, I'm pathetically grateful, and I think, well, you know, this would be nice – to do it on a grand scale, to have great roaring fires and to go out to dinner every night. Of course, it's only in my weaker moods I think this. Oh, and you know – to wake up every morning beside someone you like. Not clutching your head all the time and crying, my God, what happened last night, how did I get into this?'

'It hardly seems much to want,' Georges-Jacques said.

'But when you finally achieve something, a disgust for it begins. At least, that's the received wisdom. I've never achieved anything, so I can't say.'

'You ought to sort yourself out, Camille.'

'My father wanted me home as soon as I qualified, he wanted me to go into his practice. Then again, he didn't . . . They've arranged for me to marry my cousin, it's been fixed up for years. We all marry our cousins, so the family money interbreeds.'

'And you don't want to?'

'Oh, I don't mind. It doesn't really matter who you marry.'

'Doesn't it?' His thinking had been quite other.

'But Rose-Fleur will have to come to Paris, I can't go back there.'

'What's she like?'

'I don't know really, our paths so seldom cross. Oh, to look at, you mean? She's quite pretty.'

'When you say it doesn't matter who you marry – don't you expect to love someone?'

'Yes, of course. But it would be a vast coincidence to be married to them as well.'

'What about your parents? What are they like?'

'Never seem to speak to each other these days. There's a family tradition of marrying someone you find you can't stand. My cousin Antoine, one of my Fouquier-Tinville cousins, is supposed to have murdered his first wife.'

'What, you mean he was actually prosecuted for it?'

'Only by the gossips at their various assizes. There wasn't enough evidence to bring it to court. But then Antoine, he's a lawyer too, so there wouldn't be. I expect he's good at fixing evidence. The business rather shook the family, and so I've always regarded him as, you know,' he paused wistfully, 'a sort of hero. Anyone who can give serious offence to the de Viefvilles is a hero of mine. Another case of that is Antoine Saint-Just, I know we are related but I can't think how, they live in Noyon. He has recently run off with the family silver, and his mother, who's a widow, actually got a *lettre de cachet* and had him shut up. When he gets out – they'll have to let him out one of these days, I suppose – he'll be so angry, he'll never forgive them. He's one of these boys, sort of big and solid and conceited, incredibly full of himself, he's probably steaming about at this very minute working out how to get revenge. He's only nineteen, so perhaps he'll have a career of crime, and that will take the attention off me.'

'I can't think why you don't write and encourage him.'

'Yes, perhaps I shall. You see, I do agree that I can't go on like this. I have had a little verse published – oh, nothing really, just a modest start. I'd rather write than anything – well, as you can imagine, with my disabilities it's a relief not having to talk. I just want to live very quietly – preferably somewhere warm – and be left alone till I can write something worthwhile.'

Already, d'Anton did not believe this. He recognized it as a disclaimer that Camille would issue from time to time in the hope of disguising the fact that he was an inveterate hell-raiser. 'Don't you care for anyone respectable?' he asked.

'Oh yes – I care for my friend de Robespierre, but he lives in Arras, I never see him. And Maître Perrin has been kind.'

D'Anton stared at him. He did not see how he could sit there, saying 'Maître Perrin has been kind.'

'Don't you mind?' he demanded.

'What people say? Well,' Camille said softly, 'I should prefer not to be an object of general odium, but I wouldn't go so far as to let my preference alter my conduct.'

'I'd just like to know,' d'Anton said. 'I mean, from my point of view. Whether there's any truth in it.'

'Oh, you mean, because the sun will be up in an hour, and you think I'll run down to the Law Courts and tell everybody I spent the night with you?'

'Somebody told me . . . that is, amongst other things they told me . . . that you were involved with a married woman.'

'Yes: in a way.'

'You do have an interesting variety of problems.'

Already, by the time the clock struck four, he felt he knew too much about Camille, and more than he was comfortable with. He looked at him through a mist of alcohol and fatigue, the climate of the years ahead.

'I would tell you about Annette Duplessis,' Camille said, 'but life's too short.'

'Is it?' D'Anton has never thought about it before. Creeping towards his future it sometimes seems long, long enough.

In July 1786 a daughter was born to the King and Queen. 'All well and good,' said Angélique Charpentier, 'but I expect she'll be needing some more diamonds to console her for losing her figure.'

Her husband said, 'How would we know if she's losing her

figure? We never see her. She never comes. She has something against Paris.' It was a matter of regret to him. 'She doesn't trust us, I think. But of course she is not French. She is far from home.'

'I am far from home,' Angélique said heartlessly. 'But I don't run the nation into debt because of it.'

The Debt, the Deficit – these were the words on the lips of the café's customers as they occupied themselves in trying to name a figure. Only a few people had the ability to imagine money on this scale, the café believed; they thought it was a special ability, and that M. Calonne, now the Comptroller-General, had not got it. M. Calonne was a perfect courtier, with his lace cuffs and lavender-water, his gold-topped cane and his well-attested greed for Périgord truffles. Like M. Necker, he was borrowing; the café thought that M. Necker's borrowing had been considered, but that M. Calonne's borrowing stemmed from a failure of imagination and a desire to keep up appearances.

In August 1786 the Comptroller-General presented to the King a package of proposed reforms. There was one weighty and pressing reason for action: one half of the next year's revenues had already been spent. France was a rich country, M. Calonne told its sovereign; it could produce many times more revenue than at present. And could this fail to add to the glory and prestige of the monarchy? Louis seemed dubious. The glory and prestige were all very well, most agreeable, but he was anxious to do only what was right; and to produce this revenue would require substantial changes, would it not?

Indeed, his minister told him, from now on everybody – nobles, clergy, commons – must pay a land tax. The pernicious system of tax exemptions must be ended. There must be free trade, the internal customs dues must be abolished. And there must be some concessions to liberal opinion – the corvée must be done away with completely. The King frowned. He seemed to have been through all this before. It reminded him of M. Necker, he said. If he had thought, it would have reminded him of M. Turgot, but by now he was getting muddled.

The point is, he told his minister, that though he personally might favour such measures, the Parlements would never agree.

That, said M. Calonne, was a most cogent piece of reasoning. With his usual unerring accuracy, His Majesty had pinpointed the problem.

But if His Majesty felt these measures were necessary, should he allow himself to be baulked by the Parlements? Why not seize the initiative?

Mm, the King said. He moved restlessly in his chair, and looked out of the window to see what the weather was doing.

What he should do, Calonne said, was to call an Assembly of Notables. A what? said the King. Calonne pressed on. The Notables would at once be seized by a realization of the country's economic plight, and throw their weight behind any measures the King deemed necessary. It would be a bold stroke, he assured the King, to create a body that was inherently superior to the Parlements, a body whose lead they would have to follow. It was the sort of thing, he said, that Henri IV would have done.

The King pondered. Henri IV was the most wise and popular of monarchs, and the very one that he, Louis, most desired to emulate.

The King put his head in his hands. It sounded a good idea, the way Calonne put it, but all his ministers were smooth talkers, and it was never quite as simple as they made out. Besides, the Queen and her set . . . He looked up. The Queen believed, he said, that the next time the Parlements got in his way they should simply be disbanded. The Parlements of Paris, all the provincial Parlements – chop, chop, went the King. All gone.

M. Calonne quaked when he heard this reasoning. What did it offer but a vista of acrimonious dealings, a decade of wrangling, of vendettas, of riots? We have to break out of this cycle, Your Majesty, he said. Believe me – please, you must believe me – things have never been this bad before.

GEORGES-JACQUES came to M. Charpentier, and he put his cards on the table. 'I have a bastard,' he said. 'A son, four years old. I suppose I should have told you before.'

'Why so?' M. Charpentier gathered his wits. 'Pleasant surprises should be saved up.'

'I feel a hypocrite,' d'Anton said. 'I was just lecturing that little Camille.'

'Do go on, Georges-Jacques. You have me riveted.'

They'd met on the coach, he said, on his first journey to Paris. She'd given him her address, he'd called on her a few days later. Things had gone on from there – well, M. Charpentier could imagine, perhaps. No, he was no longer involved with her, it was over. The boy was in the country with a nurse.

'You offered her marriage, of course?'

D'Anton nodded.

'And why wouldn't she marry you?'

'I expect she took a dislike to my face.'

In his mind's eye he could see Françoise raging round her bedroom, aghast that she was subject to the same laws as other women: when I marry I want it to be worth my while, I don't want some clerk, some nobody, and you with your passions and your self-conceit running after other women before the month's out. Even when the baby was kicking inside her, it had seemed to him a remote contingency, might happen, might not. Babies were stillborn, they died in the first few days; he did not hope for this to happen, but he knew that it might.

But the baby grew, and was born. 'Father unknown', she put on the birth certificate. Now Françoise had found the man she wanted to marry – one Maître Huet de Paisy, a King's Councillor. Maître Huet was thinking of selling his position – he had something else in mind, d'Anton did not inquire what. He was offering to sell it to d'Anton.

'What's the asking price?'

D'Anton told him. Having received his second big shock of the afternoon, Charpentier said, 'That's simply not possible.'

'Yes, I know it's vastly inflated, but it represents my settlement for the child. Maître Huet will acknowledge paternity, it will all be done in the correct legal form and the matter will be behind me.'

'Her family should have made her marry you. What kind of people can they be?' He paused. 'In one sense the matter will be behind you, but what about your debts? I'm not sure how you can raise that amount in the first place.' He pulled a piece of paper towards him. 'This is what I can let you have – let's call it a loan for now, but when the marriage contract is signed I waive the debt.' D'Anton inclined his head. 'I must have Gabrielle well set up, she's my only daughter, I mean to do right by her. Now, your family can come up with – what? All right, but that's little enough.' He jotted down the figures. 'How can we cover the shortfall?'

'Borrow it. Well, that's what Calonne would say.'

'I see no other solution.'

'I'm afraid there is another part to this deal. You won't like it. The thing is, Françoise has offered to lend me the money herself. She's well-off. We haven't gone into the details, but I don't suppose the interest rate will be in my favour.'

'That's iniquitous. Good God, what a bitch! Wouldn't you like to strangle her?'

D'Anton smiled. 'Oh, yes.'

'I suppose you are quite sure the boy's yours?'

'She wouldn't have lied to me. She wouldn't dare.'

'Men like to think that ... ' He looked at d'Anton's face. No, that was not the way out. So be it – the child was his. 'It is a very serious sum of money,' he said. 'For one night's work five years ago it seems disproportionate. It could dog you for years.'

'She wants to wring what she can out of me. You can understand it, I suppose.' After all, she had the pain, he thought, she had the disgrace. 'I want to get it settled up within the next couple of months. I want to start off with Gabrielle with a clean slate.'

'I wouldn't call it a clean slate, exactly,' Charpentier said gently. 'That's just what it isn't. You're mortgaging your whole future. Can't you –'

'No, I can't fight her over it. I was fond of her, at one time. And I think of the boy. Well, ask yourself – if I took the other attitude, would I be the kind of person you'd want for a son-in-law?'

'Yes, I see that, don't mistake me, it's just that I'm old and hardboiled and I worry about you. When does this woman want the final payment?'

'She said '91, the first quarter day. Do you think I should tell Gabrielle about this?'

'That's for you to decide. Between now and your wedding, can you contrive to be careful?'

'Look, I've got four years to pay this off. I'll make a go of things.'

'Certainly, you can make money as a King's Councillor. I don't deny that.' M. Charpentier thought, he's young, he's raw, he has everything to do, and inside he cannot possibly be as sure as he sounds. He wanted to comfort him. 'You know what Maître Vinot says, he says there are times of trouble ahead, and in times of trouble litigation always expands.' He rolled his pieces of paper together, ready for filing away. 'I daresay something will happen, between now and '91, to make your fortunes look up.'

MARCH 2 1787. It was Camille's twenty-seventh birthday, and nobody had seen him for a week. He appeared to have changed his address again.

The Assembly of Notables had reached deadlock. The café was full, noisy and opinionated.

'What is it that the Marquis de Lafayette has said?'

'He has said that the Estates-General should be called.'

'But the Estates is a relic. It hasn't met since – '

'1614.'

'Thank you, d'Anton,' Maître Perrin said. 'How can it answer to our needs? We shall see the clergy debating in one chamber, the nobles in another and the commons in a third, and whatever the commons propose will be voted down two to one by the other Orders. So what progress – '

'Listen,' d'Anton broke in, 'even an old institution can take on a new form. There's no need to do what was done last time.'

The group gazed at him, solemn. 'Lafayette is a *young* man,' Maître Perrin said.

'About your age, Georges.'

Yes, d'Anton thought, and while I was poring over the tomes in Vinot's office, he was leading armies. Now I am a poor attorney, and he is the hero of France and America. Lafayette can aspire to be a leader of the nation, and I can aspire to scratch a living. And now this *young* man, of undistinguished appearance, spare, with pale sandy hair, had captured his audience, propounded an idea; and d'Anton, feeling an unreasoning antipathy for the fellow, was compelled to stand here and defend him. 'The Estates is our only hope,' he said. 'It would have to give fair representation to us, the commons, the Third Estate. It's quite clear that the nobility don't have the King's welfare at heart, so it's stupid for him to continue to defend their interests. He must call the Estates and give real power to the Third – not just talk, not just consultation, the real power to do something.'

'I'll believe it when I see it,' Charpentier said.

'It will never happen,' Perrin said. 'What interests me more is Lafayette's proposal for an investigation into tax frauds.'

'And shady underhand speculation,' d'Anton said. 'The dirty workings of the market as a whole.'

'Always this vehemence,' Perrin said, 'among people who don't hold bonds and wish they did.'

Something distracted M. Charpentier. He looked over d'Anton's shoulder and smiled. 'Here is a man who could clarify matters for us.' He moved forward and held out his hands. 'M. Duplessis, you're a stranger, we never see you. You haven't met my daughter's fiancé. M. Duplessis is a very old friend of mine, he's at the Treasury.'

'For my sins,' M. Duplessis said, with a sepulchral smile. He acknowledged d'Anton with a nod, as if perhaps he had heard his name. He was a tall man, fifty-ish, with vestigial good looks; he was carefully and plainly dressed. His gaze seemed to rest a little behind and beyond its object, as if his vision were unobstructed by the marble-topped tables and gilt chairs and the black limbs of city barristers.

'So Gabrielle is to be married. When is the happy day?'

'We've not named it. May or June.'

'How time flies.'

He patted out his platitudes as children shape mud-pies; he smiled again, and you thought of the muscular effort involved.

M. Charpentier handed him a cup of coffee. 'I was sorry to hear about your daughter's husband.'

'Yes, a bad business, most upsetting and unfortunate. My daughter Adèle,' he said. 'Married and widowed, and only a child.' He addressed Charpentier, directing his gaze over his host's left shoulder. 'We shall keep Lucile at home for a while longer. Although she's fifteen, sixteen. Quite a little lady. Daughters are a worry. Sons, too, though I haven't any. Sons-in-law are a worry, dying as they do. Although not you, Maître d'Anton. I don't intend it personally. You're not a worry, I'm sure. You look quite healthy. In fact, excessively so.'

How can he be so dignified, d'Anton wondered, when his talk is so random and wild? Was he always like this, or had the situation made him so, and was it the Deficit that had unhinged him, or was it his domestic affairs?

'And your dear wife?' M. Charpentier inquired. 'How is she?'

M. Duplessis brooded on this question; he looked as if he could not quite recall her face. At last he said, 'Much the same.'

'Won't you come and have supper one evening? The girls too, of course, if they'd like to come?'

'I would, you know . . . but the pressure of work . . . I'm a good deal at Versailles during the week now, it was only that today I had some business to attend to . . . sometimes I work through the weekend too.' He turned to d'Anton. 'I've been at the Treasury all my life. It's been a rewarding career, but every day gets a little harder. If only the Abbé Terray . . . '

Charpentier stifled a yawn. He had heard it before; everyone had heard it. The Abbé Terray was Duplessis's all-time Top Comptroller, his fiscal hero. 'If Terray had stayed, he could have saved us; every scheme put forward in recent years, every solution, Terray had worked it out years ago.' That had been when he was a younger man, and the girls were babies, and his work was something he looked forward to with a sense of the separate venture and progress of each day. But the Parlements had opposed the abbé; they had accused him of speculating in grain, and induced the silly people to burn him in effigy. 'That was before the situation was so bad; the problems were manageable then. Since then I've seen them come along with the same old bright ideas —' He made a gesture of despair. M. Duplessis cared most deeply about the state of the royal Treasury; and since the departure of the Abbé Terray his work had become a kind of daily official heartbreak.

M. Charpentier leaned forward to refill his cup. 'No, I must be off,' Duplessis said. 'I've brought papers home. We'll take you up on that invitation. Just as soon as the present crisis is over.'

M. Duplessis picked up his hat, bowed and nodded his way to the door. 'When will it ever be over?' Charpentier asked. 'One can't imagine.'

Angélique rustled up. 'I saw you,' she said. 'You were distinctly grinning, when you asked him about his wife. And you,' she slapped d'Anton lightly on the shoulder, 'were turning quite blue trying not to laugh. What am I missing?'

'Only gossip, my dear.'

'*Only* gossip? What else is there in life?'

'It concerns Georges's gypsy friend, M. How-to-get-on-in-Society.'

'What? Camille? You're teasing me. You're just saying this to test out my gullibility.' She looked around at her smirking customers. 'Annette Duplessis?' she said. 'Annette Duplessis?'

'Listen carefully then,' her husband said. 'It's complicated, it's circumstantial, there's no saying where it's going to end. Some take season tickets to the Opéra; others enjoy the novels of Mr Fielding. Myself I enjoy a bit of home-grown entertainment, and I tell you, there's nothing more entertaining than life at the rue Condé these days. For the connoisseur of human folly . . . '

'Jesus-Maria! Get on with it,' Angélique said.

II. *Rue Condé: Thursday Afternoon*

(1787)

ANNETTE DUPLESSIS was a woman of resource. The problem which now beset her she had handled elegantly for four years. This afternoon she was going to solve it. Since midday a chilly wind had blown up, draughts whistled through the apartment, finding out the keyholes and the cracks under the doors: fanning the nebulous banners of approaching crisis. Annette, thinking of her figure, took a glass of cider vinegar.

When she had married Claude Duplessis, a long time ago, he had been several years her senior; by now he was old enough to be her father. Why had she married him anyway? She often asked herself that. She could only conclude that she had been serious-minded as a girl, and had grown steadily more inclined to frivolity as the years passed.

At the time they met, Claude was working and worrying his way to the top of the civil service: through the different degrees and shades and variants of clerkdom, from clerk menial to clerk-of-some-parts, from intermediary clerk to clerk of a higher type, to clerk most senior, clerk confidential, clerk extraordinary, clerk *in excelsis*, clerk-to-end-all-clerks. His intelligence was the quality she noticed chiefly, and his steady, concerned application to the nation's business. His father had been a blacksmith, and – although he was prosperous, and since before his son's birth had not personally been anywhere near a forge – Claude's professional success was a matter for admiration.

When his early struggles were over, and Claude was ready for marriage, he found himself awash in a dismaying sea of light-mindedness. She was the moneyed, sought-after girl on whom, for no reason one could see, he fixed his good opinion: on whom, at last, he settled his affection. The very disjunction between them seemed to say, here is some deep process at work; friends forecast a marriage that was out of the common run.

Claude did not say much, when he proposed. Figures were his medium. Anyway, she believed in emotions that ran too deep for words. His face and his hopes he kept very tightly strung, on stretched steel wires of self-control; she imagined his insecurities rattling about inside his head like the beads of an abacus.

Six months later her good intentions had perished of suffocation. One night she had run into the garden in her shift, crying out to the apple trees and the stars, 'Claude, you are dull.' She remembered the damp grass underfoot, and how she had shivered as she looked back at the lights of the house. She had sought marriage to be free from her parents' constraints, but now she had given Claude her parole. You must never break gaol again, she told herself; it ends badly, dead bodies in muddy fields. She crept back inside, washed her feet; drank a warm tisane, to cure any lingering hopes.

Afterwards Claude had treated her with reserve and suspicion for some months. Even now, if she was unwell or whimsical, he would allude to the incident – explaining that he had learned to live with her unstable nature but that, when he was a young man, it had taken him quite by surprise.

After the girls were born there had been a small affair. He was a friend of her husband, a barrister, a square, blond man: last heard of in Toulouse, supporting a red-faced dropsical wife and five daughters at a convent school. She had not repeated the experiment. Claude had not found out about it. If he had, perhaps something would have had to change, but as he hadn't – as he staunchly, wilfully, manfully hadn't – there was no point in doing it again.

So then to hurry the years past – and to contemplate something that should not be thought of in the category of 'an affair' – Camille arrived in her life when he was twenty-two years old. Stanislas Fréron – her family knew his family – had brought him to the house. Camille looked perhaps seventeen. It was four years before he would be old enough to practise at the Bar. It was not a thing one could readily imagine. His conversation was a series of little

sighs and hesitations, defections and demurs. Sometimes his hands
shook. He had trouble looking anyone in the face.

He's brilliant, Stanislas Fréron said. He's going to be famous.
Her presence, her household, seemed to terrify him. But he didn't
stay away.

RIGHT AT THE BEGINNING, Claude had invited him to supper. It
was a well-chosen guest list, and for her husband a fine opportunity
to expound his economic forecast for the next five years – grim –
and to tell stories about the Abbé Terray. Camille sat in tense near-
silence, occasionally asking in his soft voice for M. Duplessis to be
more precise, to explain to him and to show him how he arrived at
that figure. Claude called for pen, paper and ink. He pushed some
plates aside and put his head down; at his end of the table, the meal
came to a halt. The other guests looked down at them, nonplussed,
and turned to each other with polite conversation. While Claude
muttered and scribbled, Camille looked over his shoulder, disputing
his simplifications, and asking questions that were longer and more
cogent. Claude shut his eyes momentarily. Figures swooped and
scattered from the end of his pen like starlings in the snow.

She had leaned across the table: 'Darling, couldn't you . . . '

'One minute – '

'If it's so complicated – '

'Here, you see, and here – '

' – talk about it afterwards?'

Claude flapped a balance sheet in the air. 'Vaguely,' he said. 'No
more than vaguely. But then the comptrollers are vague, and it
gives you an idea.'

Camille took it from him and ran a glance over it; then he looked
up, meeting her eyes. She was startled, shocked by the – emotion,
she could only call it. She took her eyes away and rested them on
other guests, solicitous for their comfort. What he basically didn't
understand, Camille said – and probably he was being very stupid –
was the relationship of one ministry to another and how they all got
their funds. No, Claude said, not stupid at all: might he demonstrate?

Claude now thrust back his chair and rose from his place at the head of the table. Her guests looked up. 'We might all learn much, I am sure,' said an under-secretary. But he looked dubious, very dubious, as Claude crossed the room. As he passed her, Annette put out a hand, as if to restrain a child. 'I only want the fruit bowl,' Claude said: as if it were reasonable.

When he had secured it he returned to his place and set it in the middle of the table. An orange jumped down and circumambulated slowly, as if sentient and tropically bound. All the guests watched it. His eyes on Claude's face, Camille put out a hand and detained it. He gave it a gentle push, and slowly it rolled towards her across the table: entranced, she reached for it. All the guests watched her; she blushed faintly, as if she were fifteen. Her husband retrieved from a side-table the soup tureen. He snatched a dish of vegetables from a servant who was taking it away. 'Let the fruit bowl represent revenue,' he said.

Claude was the cynosure now; chit-chat ceased. If . . . Camille said; and but. 'And let the soup tureen represent the Minister of Justice, who is also, of course, Keeper of the Seals.'

'Claude – ' she said.

He shushed her. Fascinated, paralysed, the guests followed the movement of the food about the table; deftly, from the under-secretary's finger ends, Claude removed his wine glass. This functionary now appeared, hand extended, as one who mimes a harpist at charades; his expression darkened, but Claude failed to see it.

'Let us say, this salt cellar is the minister's secretary.'

'So much smaller,' Camille marvelled. 'I never knew they were so low.'

'And these spoons, Treasury warrants. Now . . . '

Yes, Camille said, but would he clarify, would he explain, and could he just go back to where he said – yes indeed, Claude allowed, you need to get it straight in your mind. He reached for a water jug, to rectify the proportions; his face shone.

'It's better than the puppet show with Mr Punch,' someone whispered.

'Perhaps the tureen will talk in a squeaky voice soon.'

Let him have mercy, Annette prayed, please let him stop asking questions; with a little flourish here and one there she saw him orchestrating Claude, while her guests sat open-mouthed at the disarrayed board, their glasses empty or snatched away, deprived of their cutlery, gone without dessert, exchanging glances, bottling their mirth; all over town it will be told, ministry to ministry and at the Law Courts too, and people will dine out on the story of my dinner party. Please let him stop, she said, please something make it stop; but what could stop it? Perhaps, she thought, a small fire.

All the while, as she grew flurried, cast about her, as she swallowed a glass of wine and dabbed at her mouth with a handkerchief, Camille's incendiary eyes scorched her over the flower arrangement. Finally with a nod of apology, and a placating smile that took in the voyeurs, she swept from the table and left the room. She sat for ten minutes at her dressing-table, shaken by the trend of her own thoughts. She meant to retouch her face, but not to see the hollow and lost expression in her eyes. It was some years since she and Claude had slept together; what relevance has it, why is she stopping to calculate it, should she also call for paper and ink and tot up the Deficit of her own life? Claude says that if this goes on till '89 the country will have gone to the dogs and so will we all. In the mirror she sees herself, large blue eyes now swimming with unaccountable tears, which she instantly dabs away as earlier she dabbed red wine from her lips; perhaps I have drunk too much, perhaps we have all drunk too much, except that viperous boy, and whatever else the years give me cause to forgive him for I shall never forgive him for wrecking my party and making a fool of Claude. Why am I clutching this orange, she wondered. She stared down at her hand, like Lady Macbeth. What, in our house?

When she returned to her guests – the perfumed blood under her nails – the performance was over. The guests toyed with *petits fours*. Claude glanced up at her as if to ask where she had been. He looked cheerful. Camille had ceased to contribute to the conversation. He sat with his eyes cast down to the table. His expression, in one of her daughters, she would have called demure. All other faces wore an expression of dislocation and strain. Coffee was served: bitter and black, like chances missed.

*

NEXT DAY CLAUDE referred to these events. He said what a stimu-
lating occasion it had been, so much better than the usual supper-
party trivia. If all their social life were like that, he wouldn't mind
it so much, and so would she ask again that young man whose name
for the present escaped him? He was so charming, so interested, and
a shame about his stutter, but was he perhaps a little slow on the
uptake? He hoped he had not carried away any wrong impressions
about the workings of the Treasury.

How torturing, she thought, is the situation of fools who know
they are fools; and how pleasant is Claude's state, by comparison.

THE NEXT TIME Camille called, he was more discreet in the way he
looked at her. It was as if they had reached an agreement that
nothing should be precipitated. Interesting, she thought. Interesting.

He told her he did not want a legal career: but what else? He was
trapped by the terms of his scholarship. Like Voltaire, he said, he
wanted no profession but that of man of letters. 'Oh, Voltaire,' she
said. 'I'm sick of the name. Men of letters will be a luxury, let me
tell you, in the years to come. We shall all have to work hard, with
no diversions. We shall all have to emulate Claude.' Camille pushed
his hair back a fraction. That was a gesture she liked: rather
representative, useless but winning. 'You're only saying that. You
don't believe it, in your heart. In your heart you think that things
will go on as they are.'

'Allow me,' she said, 'to be the expert on my heart.'

As the afternoons passed, the general unsuitability of their friendship was borne in on her. It was not simply a matter of his age, but
of his general direction. His friends were out-of-work actors, or
they slid inkily from the offices of back-street printers. They had
illegitimate children and subversive opinions; they went abroad
when the police got on their trail. There was the drawing-room life;
then there was this other life. She thought it was best not to ask
questions about it.

HE CONTINUED to come to supper. There were no further incidents.
Sometimes Claude asked him to spend the weekend with a party at

Bourg-la-Reine, where they had some land and a comfortable farmhouse. The girls, she thought, had really taken to him.

FROM QUITE TWO YEARS ago, they had begun to see a great deal of each other. One of her friends, who was supposed to know about these things, had told her that he was a homosexual. She did not believe this, but kept it to hand as a defence, in case her husband complained. But why should he complain? He was just a young man who called at the house. There was nothing between them.

ONE DAY SHE ASKED HIM, 'Do you know much about wild flowers?'

'Not especially.'

'It's just that Lucile picked up a flower at Bourg-la-Reine and asked me what it was, I hadn't the least idea, and I told her confidently that you knew everything, and I pressed it – ' she reached out – 'inside my book, and I said I'd ask you.'

She moved to sit beside him, holding the large dictionary into which she would cram letters and shopping lists and anything she needed to keep safe. She opened the book – carefully, or its contents would have cascaded out. He examined the flower. Delicately with a fingernail he turned up the underside of its papery leaf. He frowned at it. 'Probably some extremely common noxious weed,' he said.

He put an arm around her and tried to kiss her. More out of astonishment than intention, she jumped away. She dropped the dictionary and everything fell out. It would have been quite in order to slap his face, but what a cliché, she thought, and besides she was off balance. She had always wanted to do it to someone, but would have preferred someone more robust; so, between one thing and another, the moment passed. She clutched the sofa and stood up, unsteadily.

'I'm sorry,' he said. 'That lacked finesse.'

He was trembling a little.

'How could you?'

He raised a hand, palm upwards. 'Oh, because, Annette, I want you.'

'It's out of the question,' she said. She picked her feet out of the scattered papers. Some verses he had written lay on the carpet folded with a milliner's bill she had found it necessary to conceal from Claude. Camille, she thought, would never in a thousand years ask questions about the price of a woman's hats. It would be beyond him; beyond, and beneath. She found it necessary to stare out of the window (even though it was a bleak winter's day as unpromising as this one) and to bite her lips to stop them from quivering.

This had been going on for a year now.

THEY TALKED about the theatre, about books and about people they knew; really though, they were only ever talking about one thing, and that was whether she would go to bed with him. She said the usual things. He said that her arguments were stale and that these were the things people always said, because they were afraid of themselves and afraid of trying to be happy in case God smote them and because they were choked up with puritanism and guilt.

She thought (privately) that he was more afraid of himself than anyone she had ever known: and that he had reason to be.

She said that she was not going to change her mind, but that the argument could be prolonged indefinitely. Not indefinitely, Camille said, not strictly speaking: but until they were both so old that they were no longer interested. The English do it, he said, in the House of Commons. She raised a shocked face. No, not what she had so clearly on her mind: but if someone proposes a measure you don't like, you can just stand up and start spinning out the pros and cons until everybody goes home, or the session ends and there's no more time. It's called talking a measure out. It can go on for years. 'Considered in one way,' he said, 'since I like talking to you, it might be a pleasant way to spend my life. But in fact I want you now.'

AFTER THAT FIRST OCCASION she had alway been cool, fended him off rather expertly. Not that he had ever touched her again. He had seldom allowed her to touch him. If he had brushed against her, even accidentally, he had apologized. It was better like this, he said. Human nature being what it is, and the afternoons so long; the girls visiting friends, the streets deserted, no sound in the room except the ticking of clocks, the beating of hearts.

It had been her intention to end this non-affair smoothly, in her own good time; considered as a non-affair, it had had its moments. But then, obviously, Camille had started talking to somebody, or one of her husband's friends had been observant: and everybody knew. Claude had a host of interested acquaintances. The question was contended for in robing rooms (scouted at the Châtelet but proposed in the civil courts as the scandal of the year, in the middle-class scandals division); it was circulated around the more select cafés, and mulled over at the ministry. In the gossips' minds there were no debates, no delicately balanced temptations and counter-temptations, no moral anguish, no scruples. She was attractive, bored, not a girl any more. He was young and persistent. Of course they were – well, what would you think? Since when, is the question? And when will Duplessis decide to know?

Now Claude may be deaf, he may be blind, he may be dumb, but he is not a saint, he is not a martyr. Adultery is an ugly word. Time to end it, Annette thought; time to end what has never begun.

She remembered, for some reason, a couple of occasions when she'd thought she might be pregnant again, in the years before she and Claude had separate rooms. You thought you might be, you had those strange feelings, but then you bled and you knew you weren't. A week, a fortnight out of your life had gone by, a certain life had been considered, a certain steady flow of love had begun, from the mind to the body and into the world and the years to come. Then it was over, or had never been: a miscarriage of love. The child went on in your mind. Would it have had blue eyes? What would its character have been?

AND NOW THE DAY HAD COME. Annette sat at her dressing-table. Her maid fussed about, tweaking and pulling at her hair. 'Not like that,' Annette said. 'I don't like it like that. Makes me look older.'

'No!' said the maid, with a pretence at horror. 'Not a day over thirty-eight.'

'I don't like thirty-eight,' Annette said. 'I like a nice round number. Say, thirty-five.'

'Forty's a nice round number.'

Annette took a sip of her cider vinegar. She grimaced. 'Your visitor's here,' the maid said.

The rain blew in gusts against the window.

IN ANOTHER ROOM, Annette's daughter Lucile opened her new journal. Now for a fresh start. Red binding. White paper with a satin sheen. A ribbon to mark her place.

'Anne Lucile Philippa Duplessis,' she wrote. She was in the process of changing her handwriting again. 'The Journal of Lucile Duplessis, born 1770, died ? Volume III. The year 1786.'

'At this time in my life,' she wrote, 'I think a lot about what it would be like to be a Queen. Not our Queen; some more tragic one. I think about Mary Tudor: "When I am dead and opened they will find 'Calais' written on my heart." If I, Lucile, were dead and opened, what they would find written is *"Ennui."*'

'Actually, I prefer Maria Stuart. She is my favourite Queen by a long way. I think of her dazzling beauty among the barbarian Scots. I think of the walls of Fotheringay, closing in like the sides of a grave. It's a pity really that she didn't die young. It's always better when people die young, they stay radiant, you don't have to think of them getting rheumatics or growing stout.'

Lucile left a line. She took a breath, then began again.

'She spent her last night writing letters. She sent a diamond to Mendoza, and one to the King of Spain. When all was under seal, she sat with open eyes while her women prayed.

'At eight o'clock the Provost Marshal came for her. At her prie-dieu, she read in a calm voice the prayers for the dying. Members of her household knelt as she swept into the Great Hall, dressed all in black, an ivory crucifix in her ivory hand.

'Three hundred people had assembled to watch her die. She entered through a small side door, surprising them; her face was composed. The scaffold was draped in black. There was a black cushion for her to kneel upon. But when her attendants stepped forward, and they slipped the black robe from her shoulders, it was seen that she was clothed entirely in scarlet. She had dressed in the colour of blood.'

Here Lucile put down her pen. She began to think of synonyms. Vermilion. Flame. Cardinal. Sanguine. Phrases occurred to her: caught red-handed. In the red. Red-letter day.

She picked up her pen again.

'What did she think, as she rested her head on the block? As she waited: as the executioner took his stance? Seconds passed; and those seconds went by like years.

'The first blow of the axe gashed the back of the Queen's head. The second failed to sever her neck, but carpeted the stage with royal blood. The third blow rolled her head across the scaffold. The executioner retrieved it and held it up to the onlookers. It could be seen that the lips were moving; and they continued to move for a quarter of an hour.

'Though who stood over the sodden relic with a fob-watch, I really could not say.'

ADÈLE, HER SISTER, came in. 'Doing your diary? Can I read it?'

'Yes; but you may not.'

'Oh, Lucile,' her sister said; and laughed.

Adèle dumped herself into a chair. With some difficulty, Lucile dragged her mind back into the present day, and brought her eyes around to focus on her sister's face. She is regressing, Lucile thought. If I had been a married woman, however briefly, I would not be spending the afternoons in my parents' house.

'I'm lonely,' Adèle said. 'I'm bored. I can't go out anywhere because it's too soon and I have to wear this disgusting mourning.'

'Here's boring,' Lucile said.

'Here's just as usual. Isn't it?'

'Except that Claude is at home less than ever. And this gives Annette more opportunity to be with her Friend.'

It was their impertinent habit, when they were alone, to call their parents by their Christian names.

'And how is that Friend?' Adèle inquired. 'Does he still do your Latin for you?'

'I don't have to do Latin any more.'

'What a shame. No more pretext to put your heads together, then.'

'I hate you, Adèle.'

'Of course you do,' her sister said good-naturedly. 'Think how grown-up I am. Think of all the lovely money my poor husband left me. Think of all the things I *know*, that you don't. Think of all the fun I'm going to have, when I'm out of mourning. Think of all the men there are in the world! But no. You only think of one.'

'I do not think of him,' Lucile said.

'Does Claude even suspect what's germinating here, what with him and Annette, and him and you?'

'There's nothing germinating. Can't you see? The whole point is that nothing's going on.'

'Well, maybe not in the crude technical sense,' Adèle said. 'But I can't see Annette holding out for much longer, I mean, even through sheer fatigue. And you – you were twelve when you first saw him. I remember the occasion. Your piggy eyes lit up.'

'I have not got piggy eyes. They did not light up.'

'But he's exactly what you want,' Adèle said. 'Admittedly, he's not much like anything in the life of Maria Stuart. But he's just what you need for casting in people's teeth.'

'He never looks at me anyway,' Lucile said. 'He thinks I'm a child. He doesn't know I'm there.'

'He knows,' Adèle said. 'Go through, why don't you?' She gestured in the direction of the drawing room, towards its closed doors. 'Bring me a report. I dare you.'

'I can't just walk in.'

'Why can't you? If they're only sitting around talking, they can't object, can they? And if they're not – well, that's what we want to know, isn't it?'

'Why don't you go then?'

Adèle looked at her as if she were simple-minded. 'Because the more innocent assumption is the one that you could be expected to make.'

Lucile saw this; and she could never resist a dare. Adèle watched her go, her satin slippers noiseless on the carpets. Camille's odd little face floated into her mind. If he's not the death of us, she thought, I'll smash my crystal ball and take up knitting.

CAMILLE WAS PUNCTUAL; come at two, she had said. On the offensive, she asked him if he had nothing better to do with his afternoons. He did not think this worth a reply; but he sensed the drift of things.

Annette had decided to employ that aspect of herself her friends called a Splendid Woman. It involved sweeping about the room and smiling archly.

'So,' she said. 'There are rules, and you won't play by them. You've been talking about us to someone.'

'Oh,' Camille said, fiddling with his hair, 'if only there were anything to say.'

'Claude is going to find out.'

'Oh, if only there were something for him to find out.' He stared absently at the ceiling. 'How *is* Claude?' he said at last.

'Cross,' Annette said, distracted. 'Terribly cross. He put a lot of money into the Périer brothers' waterworks schemes, and now the Comte de Mirabeau has written a pamphlet against it and collapsed the stocks.'

'But he must mean it for the public good. I admire Mirabeau.'

'You would. Let a man be a bankrupt, let him be notoriously immoral – oh, don't distract me, Camille, don't.'

'I thought you wanted distraction,' he said sombrely.

She was keeping a careful distance between them, buttressing her resolve with occasional tables. 'It has to stop,' she said. 'You have to stop coming here. People are talking, they're making assumptions. And God knows, I'm sick of it. Whatever made you think in the first place that I would give up the security of my happy marriage for a hole-and-corner affair with you?'

'I just think you would, that's all.'

'You think I'm in love with you, don't you? Your self-conceit is so monstrous – '

'Annette, let's run away. Shall we? Tonight?'

She almost said, yes, all right then.

Camille stood up, as if he were going to suggest they start her packing. She stopped pacing, came to a halt before him. She rested her eyes on his face, one hand pointlessly smoothing her skirts. She raised the other hand, touched his shoulder.

He moved towards her, set his hands at either side of her waist. The length of their bodies touched. His heart was beating wildly. He'll die, she thought, of a heart like that. She spent a moment looking into his eyes. Tentatively, their lips met. A few seconds passed. Annette drew her fingernails along the back of her lover's neck and knotted them into his hair, pulling his head down towards her.

There was a sharp squeal from behind them. 'Well,' a breathy voice said, 'so it is true after all. And, as Adèle puts it, "in the crude technical sense".'

Annette plunged away from him and whirled around, the blood draining from her face. Camille regarded her daughter more with interest than surprise, but he blushed, very faintly indeed. And Lucile was shocked, no doubt about that; that was why her voice came out so high and frightened, and why she now appeared rooted to the spot.

'There wasn't anything crude about it,' Camille said. 'Do you think that, Lucile? That's sad.'

Lucile turned and fled. Annette let out her breath. Another few minutes, she thought, and God knows. What a ridiculous, wild, stupid woman I am. 'Well now,' she said. 'Camille, get out of my house. If you ever come within a mile of me again, I'll arrange to have you arrested.'

Camille looked slightly overawed. He backed off slowly, as if he were leaving a royal audience. She wanted to shout at him 'What are you thinking of now?' But she was cowed, like him, by intimations of disaster.

'Is THIS YOUR ULTIMATE INSANITY?' d'Anton asked Camille. 'Or is there more to come?'

Somehow – he does not know how – he has become Camille's

confidant. What he is being told now is unreal and dangerous and perhaps slightly – he relishes the word – depraved.

'You said,' Camille protested, 'that when you wanted to get on terms with Gabrielle you cultivated her mother. It's true, everybody saw you doing it, boasting in Italian and rolling your eyes and doing your tempestuous southerner impersonation.'

'Yes, all right, but that's what people do. It's a harmless, necessary, socially accepted convention. It is not like, it is a million miles from, what you are suggesting. Which is, as I understand it, that you start something up with the daughter as a way of getting to the mother.'

'I don't know about "start something up",' Camille said. 'I think it would be better if I married her. More permanent, no? Make myself one of the family? Annette can't have me arrested, not if I'm her son-in-law.'

'But you ought to be arrested,' d'Anton said humbly. 'You ought to be locked up.' He shook his head . . .

THE FOLLOWING DAY Lucile received a letter. She never knew how; it was brought up from the kitchen. It must have been given to one of the servants. Normally it would have been handed straight to Madame, but there was a new skivvy, a little girl, she didn't know any better.

When she had read the letter she turned it over in her hand and smoothed out the pages. She worked through it again, methodically. Then she folded it and tucked it inside a volume of light pastoral verse. Immediately, she thought that she might have slighted it; she took it out again and placed it inside Montesquieu's *Persian Letters*. So strange was it, that it might have come from Persia.

And then, as soon as the book was back on the shelf, she wanted the letter in her hand again. She wanted the feel of the paper, the sight of the looped black hand, to run her eye across the phrases – Camille writes *beautifully*, she thought, *beautifully*. There were phrases that made her hold her breath. Sentences that seemed to fly from the page. Whole paragraphs that held and then scattered the light: each word strung on a thread, each word a diamond.

Good Lord, she thought. She remembered her journals, with a sense of shame. *And I thought I practised prose* . . .

All this time, she was trying to avoid thinking about the content of the letter. She did not really believe it could apply to her, though logic told her that such a thing would not be misdirected.

No, it was she – her soul, her face, her body – that occasioned the prose. You could not examine your soul to see what the fuss was about; even the body and face were not easy. The mirrors in the apartment were all too high; her father, she supposed, had directed where to hang them. She could only see her head, which gave a curious disjointed effect. She had to stand on tiptoe to see some of her neck. She had been a pretty little girl, yes, she knew that. She and Adèle had both been pretty little girls, the kind that fathers dote on. Last year there had been this change.

She knew that for many women beauty was a matter of effort, a great exercise of patience and ingenuity. It required cunning and dedication, a curious honesty and absence of vanity. So, if not precisely a virtue, it might be called a merit.

But she could not claim this merit.

Sometimes she was irritated by the new dispensation – just as some people are irritated by their own laziness, or by the fact that they bite their nails. She would like to work at her looks – but there it is, they don't require it. She felt herself drifting away from other people, into the realms of being judged by what she cannot help. A friend of her mother said (she was eavesdropping, as it happened): 'Girls who look like that at her age are *nothing* by the time they're twenty-five.' The truth is, she can't imagine twenty-five. She is sixteen now; beauty is as final as a birthmark.

Because her skin had a delicate pallor, like that of a woman in an ivory tower, Annette had persuaded her to powder her dark hair, and knot it up with ribbons and flowers to show the flawless bones of her face. It was as well her dark eyes could not be taken out and put back china blue. Or Annette would have done it, perhaps; she wanted to see her own doll's face looking back. More than once, Lucile had imagined herself a china doll, left over from her mother's childhood, wrapped up in silk on a high shelf: a doll too fragile and too valuable to be given to the rough, wild children of today.

Life for the most part was dull. She could remember a time when her greatest joy had been a picnic, an excursion to the country, a boat on the river on a hot afternoon. A day with no studies, when the regular hours were broken, and it was possible to forget which day of the week it was. She had looked forward to these days with an excitement very like dread, rising early to scan the sky and predict the weather. There were a few hours when you felt 'Life is really like this'; you supposed this was happiness, and it was. You thought about it at the time, self-consciously. Then you came back, tired, in the evening, and things went on as before. You said, 'Last week, when I went to the country, I was happy.'

Now she had outgrown Sunday treats; the river looked always the same, and if it rained, and you stayed indoors, that was no great disaster. After her childhood (after she said to herself, 'my childhood is over') events in her imagination became more interesting than anything that happened in the Duplessis household. When her imagination failed her, she wandered the rooms, listless and miserable, destructive thoughts going around in her head. She was glad when it was time for bed and reluctant to get up in the mornings. Life was like that. She would put aside her diaries, consumed with horror at her shapeless days, at the waste of time that stretched before her.

Or pick up her pen: Anne Lucile Philippa, Anne Lucile. How distressed I am to find myself writing like this, how distressed that a girl of your education and refinement can find nothing better to do, no music practice, no embroidery, no healthy afternoon walk, just these death-wishes, these fantasies of the morbid and the grandiose, these blood-wishes, these *images*, sweet Jesus, ropes, blades and her mother's lover with his half-dead-already air and his sensual, bruised-looking mouth. Anne Lucile. Anne Lucile Duplessis. Change the name and not the letter, change for worse and worse for it's much less dull than better. She looked herself in the eye; she smiled; she threw back her head, displaying to her advantage the long white throat that her mother deems will break her admirers' hearts.

Yesterday Adèle had begun on that extraordinary conversation. Then she had walked into the drawing room and seen her mother slide her tongue between her lover's teeth, knot her fingers into his hair, flush and tremble and decline into his thin and elegant hands. She remembered those hands, his forefinger touching paper, touching her handwriting: saying Lucile, my sweet, this should be in the ablative case, and I am afraid that Julius Caesar never *imagined* such things as your translation suggests.

Today, her mother's lover offered her marriage. When something – blessed event, however strange – comes to shake us out of our monotony – then, she cried, things should happen in ones.

CLAUDE: 'Of course I have said my last word on the matter. I hope he has the sense to accept it. I don't know what can have led him to make the proposal in the first place. Do you, Annette? Once it might have been a different story. When I met him at first I took to him, I admit. Very intelligent . . . but what is intelligence, when someone has a bad moral character? Is basically unsound? He has the most extraordinary *reputation* . . . no, no, no. Can't hear of it.'

'No, I suppose you can't,' Annette said.

'Frankly, that he has the nerve – I'm surprised.'

'So am I.'

He had considered sending Lucile away to stay with relations. But then people might put the worst construction on it – might believe she had done something she shouldn't have.

'What if . . . ?'

'If?' Annette said impatiently.

'If I were to introduce her to one or two eligible young men?'

'Sixteen is too young to marry. And her vanity is already great enough. Still, Claude, you must do as you feel. You are the head of the household. You are the girl's father.'

ANNETTE sent for her daughter, having fortified herself with a large glass of brandy.

'The letter.' She clicked her fingers for it.

'I don't carry it on my person.'

'Where then?'

'Inside *Persian Letters*.'

An ill-advised merriment seized Annette. 'Perhaps you would like to file it inside my copy of *Les Liaisons Dangereuses*.'

'Didn't know you had one. Can I read it?'

'No indeed. I may follow the advice in the foreword, and give you a copy on your wedding night. When, in the course of time, your father and I find you someone to marry.'

Lucile made no comment. How well she hides, she thought – with the help of only a little brandy – a most mortifying blow to her pride. She would almost like to congratulate her.

'He came to see your father,' Annette said. 'He said he had written to you. You won't see him again. If there are any more letters, bring them straight to me.'

'Does he accept the situation?'

'That hardly matters.'

'Did it not seem proper to my father that I be consulted?'

'Why should you be consulted? You are a child.'

'I might have to have a chat with my father. About certain things I saw.'

Annette smiled wanly. 'Ruthless, aren't you, my dear?'

'It seems a fair exchange.' Lucile's throat was constricted. On the precipice of these new dealings, she was almost too frightened to speak. 'You give me time to think. That's all I'm asking for.'

'And in return you promise me your infant discretion? What is it, Lucile, that you think you know?'

'Well, after all, I've never seen my father kiss you like that. I've never seen anybody kiss anybody like that. It must have done something to brighten your week.'

'It seems to have brightened yours.' Annette rose from her chair. She trailed across the room, to where some hothouse flowers stood in a bowl. She swept them out, and began to replace them one by one. 'You should have gone to a convent,' she said. 'It's not too late to finish your education.'

'You would have to let me out eventually.'

'Oh yes, but while you were busy with your plain chant you

wouldn't be spying on people and practising the art of manipulation.' She laughed – without merriment now. 'I suppose you thought, until you came into the drawing room, how worldly-wise and sophisticated I was? That I never put a foot wrong?'

'Oh no. Until then, I thought what a boring life you had.'

'I'd like to ask you to forget what has happened in the last few days.' Annette paused, a rose in her hand. 'But you won't, will you, because you're stubborn and vain, and bent on seizing what you – quite wrongly – feel to be your advantage.'

'I didn't spy on you, you know.' She wanted, very badly, to put this right. 'Adèle dared me to walk in. What would happen if I said yes, I want to marry him?'

'That's unthinkable,' her mother said. One flower, icy-white, escaped to the carpet.

'Not really. The human brain's a wonderful thing.'

Lucile retrieved the long-stemmed rose, handed it back to her mother. She sucked from her finger a bead of blood. I may do it, she thought, or I may not. In any event, there will be more letters. She will not use Montesquieu again, but will file them inside Mably's disquisition of 1768: *Doubts on the Natural Order of Societies*. Those, she feels, have suddenly become considerable.

III. *Maximilien: Life and Times*

(1787)

MERCURE DE FRANCE, June 1783: 'M. de Robespierre, a young barrister of great merit, deployed in this matter – which is in the cause of the arts and the sciences – an eloquence and wisdom that give the highest indications of his talents.'

> 'I see the thorn that's in the rose
> In these bouquets you offer me . . . '
>   Maximilien de Robespierre, *Poems*

THE CUTTING was growing yellow now, worn from much handling. He had been trying to think how to preserve it and keep it clean, but the whole sheet was curling at the edges. He was certain that he knew it by heart, but if he simply repeated it to himself, it might have been something he had made up. But when you read it, held the paper in your hand, you could be sure that it was another person's opinion, written by a Paris journalist, set up by the printers. You could not say that it had not happened.

There was quite a long report of the case. It was, of course, a matter of public interest. It had all begun when a M. de Vissery of Saint-Omer got himself a lightning conductor and put it up on his house, watched by a dour crowd of simpletons; when the work was finished they had clumped off to the Municipality and claimed that the thing actually attracted lightning, and must be taken down. Why would M. de Vissery want to attract lightning? Well, he was in league with the devil, wasn't he?

So, to law over the subject's right to have a lightning conductor. The aggrieved householder consulted Maître de Buissart, a leading figure at the Arras Bar, a man with a strong scientific bent. Maximilien was well in with de Buissart, at the time. His colleague got quite excited: 'You see, there's a principle at stake; there are people trying to block progress, to oppose the dissemination of the benefits of science – and we can't, if we count ourselves enlightened men, stand idly by – so would you like to come in on this, write some letters for me? Do you think we should write to Benjamin Franklin?'

Suggestions, advice, scientific commentary poured in. Papers were spread all over the house. 'This man Marat,' de Buissart said, 'it's good of him to take so much trouble, but we won't push his hypotheses too strongly. I hear he's in bad odour with the scientists of the Academy.' When, finally, the case went to the Council of Arras, de Buissart stood aside, let de Robespierre make the speeches. De Buissart hadn't realized, when the case began, what a strain on his memory and organizational powers it would be. His colleague didn't seem to feel the strain; de Buissart put it down to youth.

Afterwards, the winners gave a party. Letters of congratulation came – well, *pouring* in would be an exaggeration, but there was no doubt that the case had attracted attention. He still had all the papers, Dr Marat's voluminous evidence, his own concluding speech with the last-minute emendations down the side. And for months when people came calling the Aunts would take out the newspaper and say, 'Did you see about the lightning conductor, where it said Maximilien did so well?'

Max is quiet, calm and easy to live with; he has a neat build and wide, light eyes of a changeable blue-green. His mouth is not without humour, his complexion is pale; he takes care of his clothes and they fit him very well. His brown hair is always dressed and powdered; once he could not afford to keep up appearances, so now appearances are his only luxury.

This is a well-conducted household. He gets up at six, works on his papers till eight. At eight the barber comes. Then a light breakfast – fresh bread, a cup of milk. By ten o'clock he is usually in court. After the sitting he tries to avoid his colleagues and get home as soon as he can. His stomach still churning from the morning's conflicts, he eats some fruit, takes a cup of coffee and a little red wine well diluted. How can they do it, tumble out of court roaring and backslapping, after a morning shouting each other down? Then back to their houses to drink and dine, to address themselves to slabs of red meat? He has never learned the trick.

After his meal he takes a walk, whether it is fine or not, because dog Brount does not care about the weather and makes trouble with his loping about if he is kept indoors. He lets Brount tow him through the streets, the woods, the fields; they come home looking not nearly so respectable as when they went out. Sister Charlotte says, '*Don't* bring that muddy dog in here.'

Brount flops down outside the door of his room. He closes the door and works till seven or eight o'clock; longer, of course, if there is a big case next day. When finally he puts his papers away, he might chew his pen and try some verse for the next meeting of the literary society. It's not poetry, he admits; it's proficient, unserious stuff. Sometimes more unserious than others; consider, for example, his 'Ode to Jam Tarts'.

He reads a good deal; then once a week there is the meeting of the Academy of Arras. Their ostensible purpose is to discuss history, literature, scientific topics, current affairs. They do all this, and also purvey gossip, arrange marriages, and start up small-town feuds.

On other evenings he writes letters. Frequently Charlotte insists on going over the household accounts. And the Aunts take offence if they are not visited once a week. They have separate houses now, so that takes up two evenings.

There had been many changes when he returned to Arras from Paris, with his new law degree and his carefully modulated hopes. In 1776, the year of the American war, Aunt Eulalie to the general amazement announced that she was getting married. There is hope for us all, said the spinsters of the parish. Aunt Henriette said Eulalie had taken leave of her senses: Robert Deshorties was a widower with several children, including a daughter, Anaïs, who was almost of marriageable age. But within six months, Aunt Henriette's sour grapes had turned to secretive pink blushes and an amount of unbecoming fluttering and hint-dropping. The following year she married Gabriel du Rut, a noisy man, aged fifty-three. Maximilien was glad he was in Paris and could not get away.

For Aunt Henriette's godchild, there was no marriage, no cele-bration. His sister Henriette had never been strong. She couldn't get her breath, she didn't eat; one of these impossible girls, destined to be shouted at, always with her nose in a book. One morning – this news came to him a week old, in a letter – they found her dead, her pillow soaked in blood. She had haemorrhaged, while downstairs the Aunts were playing cards with Charlotte; while they were enjoy-ing a light supper, her heart had stopped. She was nineteen. He had loved her. He had hoped they might be friends.

Two years after the amazing marriages, Grandfather Carraut died. He left the brewery to Uncle Augustin Carraut, and a legacy to each of his surviving grandchildren – to Maximilien, to Charlotte and to Augustin.

By courtesy of the abbot, young Augustin had taken over his brother's scholarship at Louis-le-Grand. He'd turned into a nice, unremarkable boy, reasonably conscientious but not particularly clever. Maximilien worried about him when he went to Paris – whether he would find the standard too exacting. He had always felt that someone from their background had little to recommend him unless he had brains. He assumed that Augustin was making the same discovery.

When he arrived back in Arras he had gone to lodge with Aunt Henriette and the noisy husband – who reminded him, before the week was out, that he owed them money. To be exact, it was his father François who owed the money – to Aunt Henriette, to Aunt Eulalie, to Grandfather Carraut's estate – he dared not inquire further. The legacy from his grandfather went to pay his father's debts. Why did they do this to him? It was tactless, it was grasping. They could have given him a year's grace, until he had earned some money. He made no fuss, paid up; then moved out, to save embar-rassment to Aunt Henriette.

If it had been the other way around, he'd not have asked for the money – not in a year, not anytime. And now they were always talking about François – your father was like this, he was like that, your father always did such-and-such at your age. For God's sake, he thought, I am not my father. Then Augustin came back from

Louis-le-Grand, suddenly and decisively grown-up. He had an in-
cautious mouth, he wasted his time and he was an avid though
inept chaser of women. The Aunts said — not without admiration —
'He really is his father's son.'

Now Charlotte came home from her convent school. They set up
house together in the rue des Rapporteurs. Maximilien earned the
money, Augustin lounged about, Charlotte did the housekeeping
and thought up cutting remarks about them both.

During his vacations from Louis-le-Grand, he had never neglected
his round of duty calls. A visit to the bishop, a visit to the abbot, a
visit to the masters at his first school to tell them how he was
getting on. It was not that he was enchanted with their company; it
was that he knew how later he would need their good will. So
when he returned home, his carefulness paid off. The family had
one opinion, but the town had another. He was called to the Bar of
the Council of Arras, and he was made as welcome as anyone could
be. Because of course he was not his father and the world had
moved on; he was sober, neat and punctilious; he was a credit to
the town, a credit to the abbot, and a credit to the respected
relatives who had brought him up.

If only that unspeakable du Rut would quit his reminiscing . . . If
only you could order your own mind, so that certain conversations,
certain allusions, certain thoughts even, did not make you nauseated.
As if you were guilty of a crime. After all, you are not a criminal,
but a judge.

IN HIS FIRST YEAR he had fifteen cases, which was considered
better than average. Usually his papers would be prepared a clear
week in advance, but on the eve of the first hearing he would work
till midnight, till dawn if necessary. He would forget everything he
had done so far, lay his papers aside; he would survey the facts
again; he would build the case once more, painstakingly, from its
foundations. He had a mind like a miser's strongbox; once a fact
went in, it stayed there. He knew he frightened his colleagues, but
what could he do? Did they imagine that he was going to be less
than a very very good lawyer indeed?

He began to advise his clients to settle out of court where they could. This brought little profit to himself or his opponent, but it saved clients a lot of time and expense. 'Other people aren't so scrupulous,' Augustin said.

After four months of practice he was appointed to a part-time judicial position. It was an honour, coming so soon, but immediately he wondered if it were double-edged. In his first weeks he had seen things that were wrong, and said so, naturally; and M. Liborel, who had sponsored him in his introduction to the Bar, seemed to think he had made a series of gaffes. Liborel had said (they had all said), 'Of course, we agree on the need for a certain degree of reform, but we in Artois would prefer things not to be rushed.' In this way, misunderstandings began. God knows, he had not set out to ruffle anyone's feelings, but he seemed to have managed it. And so whether this judicial position was because they thought he merited it, or whether it was a sop, a bribe, a device to blunt his judgement, or whether it was a prize, a favour, or even a piece of compensation . . . compensation for an injury not yet inflicted?

THAT DAY CAME: that day appointed, for him to give a judgement. He sat up, the shutters open, watching the progress of the night across the sky. Someone had put down a supper tray among his papers for the case. He got up and locked the door. He left the food untouched. He expected to see it rot before his eyes; he looked, as if it were putrescent, at the thin green skin of an apple on a plate.

If you died it might be, like his mother, in a way never discussed; but he remembered her face, when she sat propped against the bolsters waiting to be butchered, and he remembered how one of the servants had said afterwards that they were going to burn the sheets. You might die like Henriette: alone, your blood pumping out on to white linen, unable to call, unable to move, shocked to death, paralysed – while downstairs, people were making small talk and passing cakes around. You might die like Grandfather Carraut – palsied and decrepit and disgusting, memory gone, fretting about the will, chattering to his under-manager about the age of the wood for the barrels; breaking off, from time to time, to chide the family for faults committed thirty years before, and to curse his pretty dead daughter for her shameful swollen womb. That was not Grandfather's fault. That was old age. But he couldn't imagine old age. He couldn't imagine approaching it.

And if you were hanged? He did not want to think about it. The workaday criminal death could take half an hour.

He tried praying: some beads to keep his mind ordered. But then slipping through his fingers they reminded him of a rope, and he dropped them gently on to the floor. He kept count: '*Pater noster, qui es in coeli, Ave Maria, Ave Maria*', and that pious addendum, '*Gloria Patri, et Filio, et Spiritui Sancto, Amen*'. The blessed syllables ran together. They made nonsense words, everted themselves, darted in and out of sense. Anyway, what is the sense? God is not going to tell him what to do. God is not going to help him. He does not believe in a God of that sort. He's not an atheist, he tells himself: just an adult.

Dawn: he heard the clatter of wheels below the window, the leathery creak of the harness and the snort and whinny of the horse drawing a cart bringing vegetables for those who would still be alive at dinner-time. Priests were wiping their vessels for early Mass, and the household below was rising, washing, boiling water and lighting fires. At Louis-le-Grand, he would have been at his first class by now. Where were they, the children he had known? Where was Louis Suleau? Pursuing his sarcastic path. Where was Fréron? Cutting a swathe through society. And Camille would be sleeping still, this morning, gathered to the city's dark heart: sleeping unconscious of his perhaps damned soul draped about in muscle and bone.

Brount whined at the door. Charlotte came, called him sharply to come away. Brount's reluctant paws scrabbled down the stairs.

He unlocked the door to let the barber in. The man looked into the face of his regular, amiable client; he knew better than to try his morning chatter. The clock ticked without compunction towards ten.

It occurred to him at the last moment that he need not go; he could simply sit here and say, I'm not going into court today. They would wait for him for ten minutes, post a clerk to look along the road, and then they would send a message; and he would reply that he was not going into court today.

They could not drag him out, or carry him, could they? They could not force the sentence out of his throat?

But it was the law, he thought wearily, and if he could not carry it out he should have resigned: should have resigned yesterday.

THREE P.M.: the aftermath. He is going to be sick. Here, by the side of the road. He doubles up. Sweat breaks out along his back. He goes down on his knees and retches. His eyes mist over, his throat hurts. But there's nothing in his stomach; he hasn't eaten for twenty-four hours.

He puts out a hand, gets to his feet and steadies himself. He wishes for someone to take his hand, to stop him from shivering; but when you are ill, no one comes to help.

If there were anyone to watch his progress along the road they would see that he is staggering, lurching from foot to foot. He tries consciously to stand up straight and put some order in his steps, but his legs feel too far away. The whole despicable body is teaching him a lesson again: be true to yourself.

This is Maximilien de Robespierre, barrister-at-law: unmarried, personable, a young man with all his life before him. Today against his most deeply held convictions he has followed the course of the law and sentenced a criminal to death. And now he is going to pay for it.

A MAN SURVIVES: he comes through. Even here in Arras it was possible to find allies, if not friends. Joseph Fouché taught at the Oratorian College. He had thought of the priesthood but had grown away from the idea. He taught physics, and was interested in anything new. Fouché came to dinner quite often, invited by Charlotte. He seemed to have proposed to her — or at any rate, they had come to some understanding. Max was surprised that any girl would be attracted by Fouché, with his frail, stick-like limbs and almost lashless eyes. Still, who's to know? He did not like

Fouché at all, in point of fact, but Charlotte had her own life to lead.

Then there was Lazare Carnot, a captain of engineers at the garrison; a man older than himself, reserved, rather bitter about the lack of opportunities open to him, as a commoner in His Majesty's forces. Carnot went for company to the Academy's meetings, formulae revolving in his head while they discussed the sonnet form. Sometimes he treated them to a tirade about the deplorable state of the army. Members would exchange amused glances.

Only Maximilien listened earnestly – quite ignorant of military matters, and a little overawed.

When Mlle de Kéralio was voted in by the Academy – its first lady member – he made a speech in her honour about the genius of women, their role in literature and the arts. After this she'd said, 'Why don't you call me Louise?' She wrote novels – thousands of words a week. He envied her facility. 'Listen to this,' she'd say, 'and tell me what you think.'

He made sure not to – authors are touchy. Louise was pretty, and she never quite got the ink scrubbed off her little fingers. 'I'm off to Paris,' she said, 'one can't go on stagnating in this backwater, saving your presences.' Her hand tapped a rolled sheaf of manuscript against a chair-back. 'O solemn and wondrous Maximilien de Robespierre, why don't you come to Paris too? No? Well, at least let's take off for the afternoon with a picnic. Let's start a rumour, shall we?'

Louise belonged to the real nobility. 'Nothing to be thought of *there*,' said the Aunts: 'poor Maximilien.'

'Noble or not,' Charlotte said, 'the girl's a trollop. She wanted my brother to up and go to Paris with her, imagine.' Yes, just imagine. Louise packed her bags and hurtled off into the future. He was dimly aware of a turning missed; one of those forks in the road, that you remember later when you are good and lost.

Still, there was Aunt Eulalie's stepdaughter, Anaïs. Both the Aunts favoured her above all other candidates. They said she had nice manners.

ONE DAY BEFORE LONG the mother of a poor rope-maker turned

up at his door with a story about her son who was in prison because the Benedictines at Anchin had accused him of theft. She said the accusation was false and malicious; the Abbey treasurer, Dom Brognard, was notoriously light-fingered, and had in addition tried to get the rope-maker's sister into bed, and she wouldn't by any means be the first girl . . .

Yes, he said. Calm down. Have a seat. Let's start at the beginning.

This was the kind of client he was beginning to get. An ordinary man – or frequently a woman – who'd fallen foul of vested interests. Naturally, there was no hope of a fee.

The rope-maker's tale sounded too bad to be true. Nevertheless, he said, we'll let it see the light. Within a month, Dom Brognard was under investigation, and the rope-maker was sueing the abbey for damages. When the Benedictines wanted to retain a lawyer, who did they get? M. Liborel, his one-time sponsor. He said, gratitude does not bind me here, the truth is at stake.

Little hollow words, echoing through the town. Everyone takes sides, and most of the legal establishment takes Liborel's. It turns into a dirty fight; and of course in the end they do what he imagined they would do – they offer the rope-maker more money than he earns in years to settle out of court and go away and keep quiet.

Obviously, things are not going to be the same after this. He'll not forget how they got together, conspired against him, condemned him in the local press as an anti-clerical troublemaker. *Him?* The abbot's protégé? The bishop's golden boy? Very well. If that's how they want to see him, he will not trouble from now on to make things easy for his colleagues, to be so very helpful and polite. It is a fault, that persistent itch to have people think well of him.

The Academy of Arras elected him president, but he bored them with his harangues about the rights of illegitimate childen. You'd think there was no other issue in the universe, one of the members complained.

'*If your mother and your father had conducted themselves properly,*' Grandfather Carraut had said, '*you would never have been born.*'

*

CHARLOTTE would take out her account books and observe that the cost of his conscience grew higher by the month. 'Of course it does,' he said. 'What did you expect?'

Every few weeks she would round on him and deliver these wounding blows, proving to him that he was not understood even in his own house.

'This house,' she said. 'I can't call it a *home*. We have never had a home. Some days you are so preoccupied that you hardly speak. I may as well not be here. I am a good housekeeper, what interest do you display in my arrangements? I am a fine cook, but you have no interest in food. I invite company, and when we take out the cards or prepare to make conversation you withdraw to the other side of the room and mark passages in books.'

He waited for her anger to subside. It was understandable; anger these days was her usual condition. Fouché had offered her marriage – or something – and then left her high and dry, looking a bit of a fool. He wondered vaguely if something ought to be done about it, but he was convinced she'd be better off without the man in the long run.

'Sorry,' he said. 'I'll try to be more sociable. It's just that I've a lot of work on.'

'Yes, but is it work you'll be paid for?' Charlotte said that in Arras he had got himself the reputation of being uninterested in money and soft-hearted, which surprised him, because he thought of himself as a man of principle and nobody's fool. She would accuse him of alienating people who could have promoted his career, and he would begin again to explain why it was necessary to reject their help, where his duties lay, what he felt bound to do. She made too much of it, he thought. They could pay the bills, after all. There was food on the table.

Charlotte would go round and round the point, though. Sooner or later, she would work herself into a crying fit. Then out it would come, the thing that was really bothering her. 'You're going to marry Anaïs. You're going to marry Anaïs, and leave me on my own.'

IN COURT he was now making what people called 'political speeches'. How not? Everything's politics. The system is corrupt. Justice is for sale.

JUNE 30 1787:

It is ordered that the language attacking the authority of justice and the law, and injurious to judges, published in the printed memoir signed 'De Robespierre, Barrister-at-Law', shall be suppressed; and this decree shall be posted in the town of ARRAS.

BY ORDER OF THE MAGISTRATES OF BÉTHUNE

EVERY SO OFTEN, a pinpoint of light in the general gloom: one day as he was coming out of court a young advocate called Hermann sidled up to him and said, 'You know, de Robespierre, I'm beginning to think you're right.'

'About what?'

The young man looked surprised, 'Oh, about everything.'

HE WROTE AN ESSAY for the Academy of Metz:

The mainspring of energy in a republic is *vertu*, the love of one's laws and one's country; and it follows from the very nature of these that all private interests and all personal relationships must give way to the general good ... Every citizen has a share in the sovereign power ... and therefore cannot acquit his dearest friend, if the safety of the state requires his punishment.

When he had written that, he put his pen down and stared at the passage and thought, this is all very well, it is easy for me to say that, I have no dearest friend. Then he thought, of course I have, I have Camille.

He searched for his last letter. It was rather muddled, written in Greek, some business about a married woman. By applying himself to the dead language, Camille was concealing from himself his misery, confusion and pain; by forcing the recipient to translate, he was saying, believe that my life to me is an élitist entertainment, something that only exists when it is written down and sent by the posts. Max let his palm rest on the letter. If only your life would come right, Camille. If only your head were cooler, your skin thicker, and if only I could see you again … If only all things would work together for good.

Now it is his daily work to particularize, item by item, the iniquities of the system, and the petty manifestations of tyranny here in Arras. God knows, he has tried to placate, to fit in. He has been sober and conformist, deferential to colleagues of experience. When he has spoken violently it has only been because he hoped to shame them into good actions; in no way is he a violent man. But he is asking the impossible – he is asking them to admit that the system they've laboured in all their lives is false, ill-founded and wicked.

Sometimes when he is faced with a mendacious opponent or a pompous magistrate, he fights the impulse to drive a fist into the man's face; fights it so hard that his neck and shoulders ache. Every morning he opens his eyes and says, 'Dear God, help me to bear this day.' And he prays for something, anything, to happen, to deliver him from these endless polite long drawn-out recriminations, to save him from the dissipation of his youth and wit and courage. Max, you can't afford to return that man's fee. He's poor, I must do it. Max, what would you like for dinner? I haven't an idea. Max, have you named the happy day? He dreams of drowning, far far under the glassy sea.

He tries not to give offence. He likes to think of himself by nature as reasonable and conciliatory. He can duck out, prevaricate, evade the issue. He can smile enigmatically and refuse to come down on either side. He can quibble, and stand on semantics. It's a living, he thinks; but it isn't. For there comes the bald question, the one choice out of two: do you want a revolution, M. de Robespierre? Yes, damn you, damn all of you, I want it, we need it, that's what we're going to have.

IV. *A Wedding, a Riot, a Prince of the Blood*

(1787–1788)

LUCILE has not said yes. She's not said no. She's only said, she'll think about it.

ANNETTE: her first reaction had been panic and her second rage; when the immediate crisis was over and she had not seen Camille for a month, she began to curtail her social engagements and to spend the evenings by herself, worrying the situation like a dog with a bone.

Bad enough to be deemed seduced. Worse to be deemed abandoned. And to be abandoned for one's adolescent daughter? Dignity was at its nadir.

Since the King had dismissed his minister Calonne, Claude was at the office every evening, drafting memoranda.

On the first night, Annette had not slept. She had tossed and sweated into the small hours, plotting herself a revenge. She had thought that she would somehow force him to leave Paris. By four o'clock she could no longer bear to remain in her bed. She got up, pulled a wrap about her shoulders, walked through the apartment in the dark; walked barefoot, like a penitent, for the last thing she wanted was to make any noise at all, to wake her maid, to wake her daughter – who was sleeping, no doubt, the chaste and peaceful sleep of emotional despots. When dawn came she was shivering by an open window. Her resolution seemed a fantasy or nightmare, a monstrous baroque conceit dreamed by someone other than herself. Come now, it's an incident, she said to herself: that's all. She was left, then as now, with her grievance and her sense of loss.

Lucile looked at her warily these days, not knowing what was going on in her head. They had ceased to speak to each other, in any sense that mattered. When others were present they managed some vapid exchanges; alone together, they were mutually embarrassed.

LUCILE: she spent all the time she could alone. She re-read *La Nouvelle Heloïse*. A year ago, when she had first picked up the book, Camille had told her he had a friend, some odd name, began with an R, who thought it the masterpiece of the age. His friend was an arch-sentimentalist; they would get on well, were they to meet. She understood that he himself did not think much of the book and wished a little to sway her judgement. She remembered him talking to her mother of Rousseau's *Confessions*, which was another of those books her father would not allow her to read. Camille said the author lacked all sense of delicacy and that some things were better not committed to paper; since then she had been careful what she wrote in her red diary. She recalled her mother laughing, saying you can do what you like I suppose as long as you retain a sense of delicacy? Camille had made some remark she barely heard, about the aesthetics of sin, and her mother had laughed again, and leaned towards him and touched his hair. She should have known then.

These days she was remembering incidents like that, turning them over, pulling them apart. Her mother seemed to be denying – as far as one could make out what she was saying at all – that she had ever been to bed with Camille. She thought her mother was probably lying.

Annette had been quite kind to her, she thought, considering the circumstances. She had once told her that time resolves most situations, without the particular need for action. It seemed a spineless way to approach life. Someone will be hurt, she thought, but every way I win. I am now a person of consequence; results trail after my actions.

She rehearsed that crucial scene. After the storm, a struggling beam of late sun had burnished a stray unpowdered hair on her mother's neck. His hands had rested confidingly in the hollow of her waist. When Annette whirled around, her whole face had seemed to collapse, as if someone had hit her very hard. Camille had half-smiled; that was *strange*, she thought. For just a moment he had held on to her mother's wrist, as if reserving her for another day.

And the shock, the terrible, heart-stopping shock: yet why should it have been a shock, when it was – give or take the details – just what she and Adèle had been hoping to see?

Her mother went out infrequently, and always in the carriage. Perhaps she was afraid she might run into Camille by accident. There was a tautness in her face, as if she had become older.

MAY CAME, the long light evenings and the short nights; more than once Claude worked right through them, trying to lay a veneer of novelty on the proposals of the new Comptroller-General. Parlement was not to be bamboozled; it was that land tax again. When the Parlement of Paris proved obdurate, the usual royal remedy was to exile it to the provinces. This year the King sent it to Troyes, each member ordered there by an individual *lettre de cachet*. Exciting for Troyes, Georges-Jacques d'Anton said.

On 14 June he married Gabrielle at the church of Saint-Germain l'Auxerrois. She was twenty-four years old; waiting patiently for her father and her fiancé to settle things up, she had spent her afternoons experimenting in the kitchen, and had eaten her creations; she had taken to chocolate and cream, and absently spooning sugar into her father's good strong coffee. She giggled as her mother tugged her into her wedding dress, thinking of when her new husband would peel her out of it. She was moving on a stage in life. As she came out into the sunshine, hanging on to Georges's arm harder than convention dictated, she thought, I am perfectly safe now, my life is before me and I know what it will be, and I would not change it, not even to be the Queen. She turned a little pink at the warm sentimentality of her own thoughts; those sweets have jellified my brain, she thought, smiling into the sun at her wedding guests, feeling the warmth of her body inside her tight dress. Especially, she would not like to be the Queen; she had seen her in procession in the streets, her face set with stupidity and helpless contempt, her hard-edged diamonds flashing around her like naked blades.

The apartment they had rented proved to be too near to Les Halles. 'Oh, but I like it,' she said. 'The only thing that bothers me are those wild-looking pigs that run up and down the street.' She grinned at him. 'They're nothing to you, I suppose.'

'Very small pigs. Inconsiderable. But no, you're right, we should have seen the disadvantages.'

'But it's lovely. It makes me happy; except for the pigs, and the mud, and the language that the market ladies use. We can always move when we've got more money – and with your new position as King's Councillor, that won't be very long.'

Of course, she had no idea about the debts. He'd thought he would tell her, once life settled down. But it didn't settle, because she was pregnant – from the wedding night, it seemed – and she was quite silly, mindless, euphoric, dashing between the café and their own house, full of plans and prospects. Now he knew her better he knew that she was just as he'd thought, just as he'd wished: innocent, conventional, with a pious streak. It would have seemed hideous, criminal to allow anything to overshadow her happiness. The time when he might have told her came, passed, receded. The pregnancy suited her; her hair thickened, her skin glowed, she was lush, opulent, almost exotic, and frequently out of breath. A great sea of optimism buoyed them up, carried them along into midsummer.

'MAÎTRE D'ANTON, may I detain you for a moment?' They were just outside the Law Courts. D'Anton turned. Hérault de Séchelles, a judge, a man of his own age: a man seriously aristocratic, seriously rich. Well, Georges-Jacques thought: we are going up in the world.

'I wanted to offer you my congratulations, on your reception into the King's Bench. Very good speech you made.' D'Anton inclined his head. 'You've been in court this morning?'

D'Anton proffered a portfolio. 'The case of the Marquis de Chayla. Proof of the Marquis's right to bear that title.'

'You seem to have proved it already, in your own mind,' Camille muttered.

'Oh, hallo,' Hérault said. 'I didn't see you there, Maître Desmoulins.'

'Of course you saw me. You just wish you hadn't.'

'Come, come,' Hérault said. He laughed. He had perfectly even white teeth. What the hell do you want? d'Anton thought. But Hérault seemed quite composed and civil, just ready for some topical chat. 'What do you think will happen,' he asked, 'now that the Parlement has been exiled?'

Why ask me? d'Anton thought. He considered his response, then said: 'The King must have money. The Parlement has now said that only the Estates can grant him a subsidy, and I take it that having said this they mean to stick to it. So when he recalls them in the autumn, they will say the same thing again – and then at last, with his back to the wall, he will call the Estates.'

'You applaud the Parlement's victory?'

'I don't applaud at all,' d'Anton said sharply. 'I merely comment. Personally I believe that calling the Estates is the right thing for the King to do, but I am afraid that some of the nobles who are campaigning for it simply want to use the Estates to cut down the King's power and increase their own.'

'I believe you're right,' Hérault said.

'You should know.'

'Why should I know?'

'You are said to be an *habitué* of the Queen's circle.'

Hérault laughed again. 'No need to play the surly democrat with me, d'Anton. I suspect we're more in sympathy than you know. It's true Her Majesty allows me the privilege of taking her money at her gracious card table. But the truth is, the Court is full of men of good will. There are more of them there than you will find in the Parlement.'

Makes speeches, d'Anton thought, at the drop of a hat. Well, who doesn't? But so professionally charming. So professionally smooth.

'They have good will towards their families,' Camille cut in. 'They like to see them awarded comfortable pensions. Is it 700,000 livres a year to the Polignac family? And aren't you a Polignac? Tell me, why do you content yourself with one judicial position? Why don't you just buy the entire legal system, and have done with it?'

Hérault de Séchelles was a connoisseur, a collector. He would travel the breadth of Europe for a carving, a clock, a first edition. He looked at Camille as if he had come a long way to see him, and found him a low-grade fake. He turned back to d'Anton. 'What amazes me is this curious notion that is abroad among simple souls – that because the Parlement is opposing the King it somehow stands for the interests of the people. In fact, it is the King who is trying to impose an equitable taxation system – '

'That doesn't matter to me,' Camille said. 'I just like to see these people falling out amongst themselves, because the more they do that the quicker everything will collapse and the quicker we shall have the republic. If I take sides meanwhile, it's only to help the conflict along.'

'How eccentric your views are,' Hérault said. 'Not to mention dangerous.' For a moment he looked bemused, tired, vague. 'Well, things won't go on as they are,' he said. 'And I shall be glad, really.'

'Are you bored?' d'Anton asked. A very direct question, but as soon as it popped into his head it had popped out of his mouth – which was not like him.

'I suppose that might be it,' Hérault said ruefully. 'Though one would like to be – you know, more lofty. I mean, one likes to think there should be changes in the interest of France, not just because one's at a loose end.'

Odd, really – within a few minutes, the whole tenor of the conversation had changed. Hérault had become confiding, dropped his voice, shed his oratorical airs; he was talking to them as if he knew them well. Even Camille was looking at him with the appearance of sympathy.

'Ah, the burden of your wealth and titles,' Camille said. 'Maître d'Anton and I find it brings tears to our eyes.'

'I always knew you for men of sensibility.' Hérault gathered himself. 'Must get off to Versailles, expected for supper. Goodbye for now, d'Anton. You've married, haven't you? My compliments to your wife.'

D'Anton stood and looked after him. A speculative expression crossed his face.

*

THEY HAD STARTED to spend time at the Café du Foy, in the Palais-Royal. It had a different, less decorous atmosphere from M. Charpentier's place; there was a different set of people. And – one thing about it – there was no chance of bumping into Claude.

When they arrived, a man was standing on a chair declaiming verses. He made some sweeping gestures with a paper, then clutched his chest in an agony of stage-sincerity. D'Anton glanced at him without interest, and turned away.

'They're checking you out,' Camille whispered. 'The Court. To see if you could be any use to them. They'll offer you a little post, Georges-Jacques. They'll turn you into a functionary. If you take their money you'll end up like Claude.'

'Claude has done all right,' d'Anton said. 'Until you came into his life.'

'Doing all right isn't enough though, is it?'

'Isn't it? I don't know.' He looked at the actor to avoid Camille's eyes. 'Ah, he's finished. It's funny, I could swear – '

Instead of descending from his chair, the man looked hard and straight at them. 'I'll be damned,' he said. He jumped down, wormed his way across the room, produced some cards from his pocket and thrust them at d'Anton. 'Have some free tickets,' he said. 'How are you, Georges-Jacques?' He laughed delightedly. 'You can't place me, can you? And by hell, you've grown!'

'The prizewinner?' d'Anton said.

'The very same. Fabre d'Églantine, your humble servant. Well now, well now!' He pounded d'Anton's shoulder, with a stage-effect bunched fist. 'You took my advice, didn't you? You're a lawyer. Either you're doing quite well, or you're living beyond your means, or you're blackmailing your tailor. And you have a married look about you.'

D'Anton was amused. 'Anything else?'

Fabre dug him in the belly. 'You're beginning to run to fat.'

'Where've you been? What have you been up to?'

'Around, you know. This new troupe I'm with – very successful season last year.'

'Not here, though, was it? I'd have caught up with you, I'm always at the theatre.'

'No. Not here. Nîmes. All right then. Moderately successful. I've given up the landscape gardening. Mainly I've been writing plays and touring. And writing songs.' He broke off and started to whistle something. People turned around and stared. 'Everybody sings that song,' he said. 'I wrote it. Yes, sorry, I am an embarrassment at times. I wrote a lot of those songs that go around in your head, and much good it's done me. Still, I made it to Paris. I like to come here, to this café I mean, and try out my first drafts. People do you the courtesy of listening, and they'll give you an honest opinion – you've not asked for it, of course, but let that pass. The tickets are for *Augusta*. It's at the Italiens. It's a tragedy, in more ways than one. I think it will probably come off after this week. The critics are after my blood.'

'I saw *Men of Letters*,' Camille said. 'That was yours, Fabre, wasn't it?'

Fabre turned. He took out a lorgnette, and examined Camille. 'The less said about *Men of Letters* the better. All that stony silence. And then, you know, the hissing.'

'I suppose you must expect it, if you write a play about critics. But of course, Voltaire's plays were often hissed. His first nights usually ended in some sort of riot.'

'True,' Fabre said. 'But then Voltaire wasn't always worried about where his next meal was coming from.'

'I know your work,' Camille insisted. 'You're a satirist. If you want to get on – well, try toadying to the Court a bit more.'

Fabre lowered his lorgnette. He was immensely, visibly gratified and flattered – just by that one sentence, 'I know your work.' He ran his hand through his hair. 'Sell out? I don't think so. I do like an easy life, I admit. I try to turn a fast penny. But there are limits.'

D'Anton had found them a table. 'What is it?' Fabre said, seating himself. 'Ten years? More? One says, "Oh, we'll meet again," not quite meaning it.'

'All the right people are drifting together,' Camille said. 'You can pick them out, just as if they had crosses on their foreheads. For example, I saw Brissot last week.' D'Anton did not ask who was Brissot. Camille had a multitude of shady acquaintances. 'Then, of all people, Hérault just now. I always hated Hérault, but I have this feeling about him now, quite a different feeling. Against my better judgement, but there it is.'

'Hérault is a Parlementary judge,' d'Anton told Fabre. 'He comes from an immensely rich and ancient family. He's not more than thirty, his looks are impeccable, he's well-travelled, he's pursued by all the ladies at Court – '

'How sick,' Fabre muttered.

'And we're baffled because he's just spent ten minutes talking to us. It's said,' d'Anton grinned, 'that he fancies himself as a great orator and spends hours alone talking to himself in front of a mirror. Though how would anyone know, if he's alone?'

'Alone except for his servants,' Camille said. 'The aristocracy don't consider their servants to be real people, so they're quite prepared to indulge all their foibles in front of them.'

'What is he practising for?' Fabre asked. 'For if they call the Estates?'

'We presume so,' d'Anton said. 'He views himself as a leader of reform, perhaps. He has advanced ideas. So he seems to say.'

'Oh well,' Camille said. '"Their silver and their gold will not be able to deliver them in the day of the wrath of the Lord." It's all in the Book of Ezekiel, you see, it's quite clear if you look at it in the Hebrew. About how the law shall perish from the priests and the council from the ancients. "And the King will mourn, and the Prince shall be clothed with sorrow . . ." – which I'm quite sure they will be, and quite rapidly too, if they go on as they do at present.'

Someone at the next table said, 'You ought to keep your voice down. You'll find the police attending your sermons.'

Fabre slammed his hand down on the table and shot to his feet. His thin face turned brick-red. 'It isn't an offence to quote the holy Scriptures,' he said. 'In any damn context whatsoever.' Someone tittered. 'I don't know who you are,' Fabre said vehemently to Camille, 'but I'm going to get on with you.'

'Oh God,' d'Anton muttered. 'Don't encourage him.' It was not possible, considering his size, to get out without being noticed, so he tried to look as if he were not with them. The last thing you need is encouragement, he thought, you make trouble because you can't do anything else, you like to think of the destruction outside because of the destruction inside you. He turned his head to the door, where outside the city lay. There are a million people, he thought, of whose opinions I know nothing. There were people hasty and rash, people unprincipled, people mechanical, calculating and nice. There were people who interpreted Hebrew and people who could not count, babies turning fish-like in the warmth of the womb and ancient women defying time whose paint congealed and ran after midnight, showing first the wrinkled skin dying and then the yellow and gleaming bone. Nuns in serge. Annette Duplessis enduring Claude. Prisoners at the Bastille, crying to be free. People deformed and people only disfigured, abandoned children sucking the thin milk of duty: crying to be taken in. There were courtiers: there was Hérault, dealing Antoinette a losing hand. There were prostitutes. There were wig-makers and clerks, freed slaves shivering in the squares, the men who took the tolls at the customs posts in the walls of Paris. There were men who had been gravediggers man and boy all their working lives. Whose thoughts ran to an alien current. Of whom nothing was known and nothing could be known. He looked across at Fabre. 'My greatest work is yet to come,' Fabre said. He sketched its dimensions in the air. Some confidence trick, d'Anton thought. Fabre was a ready man, wound up like a clockwork toy, and Camille watched him like a child who had been given an unexpected present. The weight of the old world is stifling, and trying to shovel its weight off your life is tiring just to think about. The constant shuttling of opinions is tiring, and the shuffling of papers across desks, the chopping of logic and the trimming of attitudes. There must, somewhere, be a simpler, more violent world.

LUCILE: inaction has its own subtle rewards, but now she thinks it is time to push a little. She had left those nursery days behind, of the china doll with the straw heart. They had dealt with her, Maître Desmoulins and her mother, as effectively as if they had smashed her china skull. Since *that* day, bodies had more reality – theirs, if not hers. They were solid all right, and substantial. Woundingly, she felt their superiority; and if she could ache, she must be taking on flesh.

Midsummer: Brienne, the Comptroller, borrowed twelve million livres from the municipality of Paris. 'A drop in the ocean,' M. Charpentier said. He put the café up for sale; he and Angélique meant to move out to the country. Annette did her duty to the fine weather, making forays to the Luxembourg Gardens. She had often walked there with the girls and Camille; this spring the blossom had smelt faintly sour, as if it had been used before.

Lucile had spent a lot of time writing her journal: working out the plot. That Friday, which began like any other, when my fate was brought up from the kitchen, superscribed to me, and put into my ignorant hand. How that night – Friday to Saturday – I took the letter from its hiding place and put it against the cold ruffled linen of my nightgown, approximately over my shaking heart: the crackling paper, the flickering candlelight, and oh, my poor little emotions. I knew that by September my life would be completely changed.

'I've decided,' she said. 'I'm going to marry Maître Desmoulins after all.' Clinically, she observed how ugly her mother became, when her clear complexion blotched red with anger and fear.

She has to practise for the conflicts the future holds. Her first clash with her father sends her up to her room in tears. The weeks wear on, and her sentiments become more savage: echoed by events in the streets.

THE DEMONSTRATION had started outside the Law Courts. The barristers collected their papers and debated the merits of staying put against those of trying to slip through the crowds. But there had been fatalities: one, perhaps two. They thought it would be safer to stay put until the area was completely cleared. D'Anton swore at his colleagues, and went out to pick his way across the battlefield.

An enormous number of people seemed to be injured. They were what you would call crush injuries, except for the few people who had fought hand-to-hand with the Guards. A respectably dressed man was walking around showing people the hole in his coat where it had been pierced by a bullet. A woman was sitting on the cobblestones saying, 'Who opened fire, who ordered it, who told them to do it?' demanding an explanation in a voice sharp with hysteria. Also there were several unexplained knifings.

He found Camille slumped on his knees by a wall scribbling down some sort of testimony. The man who was talking to him was lying on the ground, just his shoulders propped up. All the man's clothes were in shreds and his face was black. D'Anton could not see where he was injured, but beneath the black his face looked numb, and his eyes were glazed with pain or surprise.

D'Anton said, 'Camille.'

Camille looked sideways at his shoes, then his eyes travelled upwards. His face was chalk-white. He put down his paper and stopped trying to follow the man's ramblings. He indicated a man standing a few yards away, his arms folded, his short legs planted apart, his eyes on the ground. Without tone or emphasis, Camille said, 'See that? That's Marat.'

D'Anton did not look up. Somebody pointed to Camille and said, 'The French Guards threw him on the ground and kicked him in the ribs.'

Camille smiled miserably. 'Must have been in their way, mustn't I?'

D'Anton tried to get him to his feet. Camille said, 'No, I can't do it, leave me alone.'

D'Anton took him home to Gabrielle. He fell asleep on their bed, looking desperately ill.

'WELL, THERE'S ONE THING,' Gabrielle said, later that night. 'If they'd kicked *you* in the ribs, their boots would have just bounced off.'

'I told you,' d'Anton said. 'I was inside, in an office. Camille was outside, in the riot. I don't go in for these silly games.'

'It worries me, though.'

'It was just a skirmish. Some soldiers panicked. Nobody even knows what it was about.'

Gabrielle was hard to console. She had made plans, settled them, for her house, for her babies, for the big success he was going to enjoy. She feared any kind of turmoil, civil or emotional: feared its stealthy remove from the street to the door to her heart.

When they had friends to dine, her husband spoke familiarly about people in the government, as if he knew them. When he spoke of the future, he would add, 'if the present scheme of things continues'.

'You know,' he said, 'I think I've told you, that I've had a lot of work recently from M. Barentin, the President of the Board of Excise. So naturally my work takes me into government offices. And when you're meeting the people who're running the country –' he shook his head – 'you start to make judgements about their competence. You can't help making judgements.'

'But they're individuals.' (Forgive me, she wanted to say, for intruding where I don't understand.) 'Is it necessary to question the system itself? Does it follow?'

'There is really only one question,' he said. 'Can it last? The answer's no. Twelve months from now, it seems to me, our lives will look very different.'

Then he closed his mouth resolutely, because he realized that he had been talking to her about matters that women were not interested in. And he did not want to bore her, or upset her.

PHILIPPE, the Duke of Orléans, is going bald. His friends – or those who wish to be his friends – have obliged him by shaving the hair off their foreheads, so that the Duke's alopecia appears to be a fad, or whimsy. But no sycophancy can disguise the bald fact.

Duke Philippe is now forty years old. People say he is one of the richest men in Europe. The Orléans line is the junior branch of the royal family, and its princes have rarely seen eye-to-eye with their senior cousins. Duke Philippe cannot agree with King Louis, about anything.

Philippe's life up to this point had not been auspicious. He had been so badly brought up, so badly turned out, that you might well think it had been done on purpose, to debauch him, to invalidate him, to disable him for any kind of political activity. When he married, and appeared with the new Duchess at the Opéra, the galleries were packed by the public prostitutes decked out in mourning.

Philippe is not a stupid man, but he is a susceptible one, a taker-up of fads and fancies. At this time he has a good deal to complain about. The King interferes all the time in his private life. His letters are opened, and he is followed about by policemen and the King's spies. They try to ruin his friendship with the dear Prince of Wales, and to stop him visiting England, whence he has imported so many fine women and racehorses. He is continually defamed and calumniated by the Queen's party, who aim to make him an object of ridicule. His crime is, of course, that he stands too near the throne. He finds it difficult to concentrate for any length of time, and you can't expect him to read the nation's destiny in a balance-sheet; but you don't need to tell Philippe d'Orléans that there is no liberty in France.

Among the many women in his life, one stands out: not the Duchess. Félicité de Genlis had become his mistress in 1772, and to prove the character of his feelings for her the Duke had caused a device to be tattooed on his arm. Félicité is a woman of sweet and iron wilfulness, and she writes books. There are few acres in the field of human knowledge that she has not ploughed with her harrowing pedantry. Impressed, astounded, enslaved, the Duke has placed her in charge of his children's education. They have a daughter of their own, Pamela, a beautiful and talented child whom they pretend is an orphan.

From the Duke, as from his children, Félicité exacts respect, obedience, adoration: from the Duchess, a timid acquiescence to her status and her powers. Félicité has a husband, of course – Charles-Alexis Brulard de Sillery, Comte de Genlis, a handsome ex-naval officer with a brilliant service record. He is close to Philippe – one of his small, well-drilled army of fixers, organizers, hangers-on. People had once called their marriage a love-match; twenty-five years on, Charles-Alexis retains his good looks and his polish, and indulges daily and nightly his ruling passion – gambling.

Félicité has even reformed the Duke – moderated some of his wilder excesses, steered his money and his energy into worthwhile channels. Now in her well-preserved forties, she is a tall, slender woman with dark-blonde hair, arresting brown eyes, and a decisive aspect to her features. Her physical intimacy with the Duke has ceased, but now she chooses his mistresses for him and directs them how to behave. She is accustomed to be at the centre of things, to be consulted, to dispense advice. She has no love for the King's wife, Antoinette.

The consuming frivolity of the Court has left a kind of hiatus, a want of a cultural centre for the nation. It is arranged by Félicité that Philippe and *his* court shall supply that lack. It is not that she has political ambitions for him – but it happens that so many intellectuals, so many artists and scholars, so many of the people one wishes to cultivate, are liberal-minded men, enlightened men, men who look forward to a new dispensation; and doesn't the Duke have every sympathy? In this year, 1787, there are gathered about him a number of young men, aristocrats for the most part, all of them ambitious and all of them with a vague feeling that their ambitions have somehow been thwarted, that their lives have somehow become unsatisfactory. It is arranged that the Duke, who feels this more keenly than most, shall be a leader to them.

The Duke wishes to be a man of the people, especially of the people of Paris; he wishes to be in touch with their moods and concerns. He keeps court in the heart of the city, at the Palais-Royal. He has turned the gardens over to the public and leased out the buildings as shops and brothels and coffee houses and casinos: so that at the epicentre of the nation's fornication, rumour-mongering, pickpocketing and street-fighting, there sits Philippe: Good Duke Philippe, the Father of His People. Only nobody shouts that; it has not been arranged yet.

Summer of '87, Philippe is fitted out and launched for trial manoeuvres. In November the King decides to meet the obstructive Parlement in a Royal Session, to obtain registration of edicts sanctioning the raising of a loan for the state. If he cannot get his way, he will be forced to call the Estates-General. Philippe prepares to confront the royal authority – as de Sillery would have said – broadside on.

CAMILLE saw Lucile briefly outside Saint-Sulpice, where she had been attending Benediction. 'Our carriage is just over there,' she said. 'Our man, Théodore, is generally on my side, but he will have to bring it across in a minute. So let's make this quick.'

'Your mother's not in it, is she?' He looked alarmed.

'No, she's skulking at home. By the way, I heard you were in a riot.'

'How did you hear that?'

'There's this grapevine. Claude knows this man called Charpentier, yes? Well, you can imagine, Claude's thrilled.'

'You shouldn't stand here,' he said. 'Awful day. You're getting wet.'

She had the distinct impression that he would like to bundle her into the carriage, and have done with her. 'Sometimes I dream,' she said, 'of living in a warm place. One where the sun shines every day. Italy would be nice. Then I think, no, stay at home and shiver a little. All this money that my father has set aside for my dowry, I don't think I should let it slip through my fingers. It would be downright ungrateful to run away from it. We ought to be married here,' she waved a hand, 'at a time of our own choosing. We could go to Italy afterwards, for a holiday. We'll need a holiday after we've fought them and won. We could retain some elephants, and go across the Alps.'

'So you do mean to marry me then?'

'Oh yes.' She looked at him, astonished. How could it be that she had forgotten to let him know? When it was all she had been thinking about, for weeks? Perhaps she'd thought the grapevine would do that, too. But the fact that it hadn't . . . Could it be that he had *put it to the back of his mind* in some way? 'Camille . . . ' she said.

'Very well,' he said. 'But if I'm to go bespeaking elephants, I can't just do it on a promise. You'll have to swear me a solemn oath. Say "By the bones of the Abbé Terray."'

She giggled. 'We've always taken the Abbé Terray very seriously.'

'That's what I mean, a serious oath.'

'As you like. By the bones of the Abbé Terray, I swear I will marry you, whatever happens, whatever anyone says, and even if the sky falls in. I feel we should kiss but,' she extended her hand, 'this is the most I can manage. Otherwise Théodore will get a crisis of conscience, and come over right away.'

'You might take your glove off,' he said. 'It would be a start.'

She took her glove off, and gave him her hand. She thought he might kiss her fingertips, but in fact he took those fingertips, turned her hand over rather forcefully, and held her palm for a second against his mouth. And just that; he didn't kiss it; just held it there, still. She shivered. 'You know a thing or two, don't you?' she said.

By now, her carriage had arrived. The horses breathed patiently, shifted their feet; Théodore positioned his back to them, and scanned the street with deep interest. 'Now, listen,' she said. 'We come here because my mother has a *tendresse* for one of the clergy. She thinks him spiritually fine, elevated.'

Théodore turned now. He opened the door for her. She turned her back. 'His name is Abbé Laudréville. He visits us as often as my mother needs to discuss her soul, which these days is at least three times a week. And he thinks my father a man of no sensibility at all. So write.' The door slammed, and she spoke to him from the window. 'I imagine you have a way with elderly priests. You write the letters and he'll bring them. Come to evening Mass, and you'll get replies.' Théodore gathered the reins. She bobbed her head in. 'Piety to some purpose,' she muttered.

NOVEMBER: Camille at the Café du Foy, unable to get his words out fast enough. 'My cousin de Viefville actually spoke to me *in public*, he was so anxious to tell someone what had happened. So: the King came in and slumped there half-asleep, as usual. The Keeper of the Seals spoke, and said that the Estates would be convoked, but not till '92, which is a lifetime away – '

'I blame the Queen.'

'Shh.'

'And this led to some protest, and then there was discussion of the edicts that the King wants them to register. As they were approaching the vote, the Keeper of the Seals went up to the King and spoke to him privately, and the King just cut the discussion short, and said the edicts were to be registered. Just ordered it to be done.'

'But how can he – '

'Shh.'

Camille looked around at his audience. He was aware that a singular event had occurred once again: his stutter had vanished. 'Then Orléans got up, and everyone turned around and stared, and he was absolutely white, de Viefville said. And the Duke said, "You can't do that. It's illegal." Then the King became flustered, and he shouted out "It is legal, because I wish it."'

Camille stopped. There was an immediate buzz – of protest, of simulated horror, of speculation. At once he felt that hideous urge to destroy his own case; he was enough of a lawyer, perhaps, or perhaps, he wondered, am I just too honest? 'Listen, everyone, please – this is what de Viefville *says* the King said. But I'm not sure if one can believe it – isn't it too pat? I mean, if people wanted to engineer a constitutional crisis, isn't that just what they'd hope for him to say? Actually, perhaps – because he's not a bad man, is he, the King . . . I think he probably didn't say that at all, he probably made some feeble joke.'

D'Anton noted this: that Camille did not stutter, and that he talked to every person in the crowded room as if he were speaking only to them. But someone said, 'Well, get on, then!'

'The edicts were registered. The King left. As soon as he was outside the door, the edicts were annulled and struck off the books. Two members of the Parlement are arrested on *lettres de cachet*. The Duke of Orléans is exiled to his estates at Villers-Cotterêts. Oh – and I am invited to dine with my esteemed cousin de Viefville.'

AUTUMN PASSED. It's like, Annette said, if the roof fell in, you would scrabble in the debris for what valuables were left; you wouldn't sit down among the falling masonry saying 'why, oh why?' The prospect of Camille, of what he was going to do to herself and her daughter, seemed too ghastly to resist. She accepted it as people become reconciled to the long course of a terminal illness; at times, she desired death.

V. A New Profession

(1788)

NOTHING CHANGES. Nothing new. The same old dreary crisis atmosphere. The feeling that it can't get much worse without something giving way. But nothing does. Ruin, collapse, the sinking ship of state: the point of no return, the shifting balance, the crumbling edifice and the sands of time. Only the cliché flourishes.

In Arras, Maximilien de Robespierre faces the New Year truculent and disheartened. He is at war with the local judiciary. He has no money. He has given up the literary society, because poetry is becoming an irrelevance. He is trying to restrict his social life, because he finds it difficult now to be even normally courteous to the self-satisfied, the place-seekers, the mealy-mouthed – and that is a fair description of polite society in Arras. More and more, casual conversations turn to the questions of the day, and he stifles his wish to smile and let things pass; that conciliatory streak, he is fighting hard to eradicate that. So every workaday disagreement becomes an affront, every point conceded in court becomes a defeat. There are laws against duelling, but not against duelling in the head. You can't, he tells his brother Augustin, separate political views from the people who hold them; if you do, it shows you don't take politics seriously.

Somehow his thoughts ought to show on his face – but he finds himself still on the guest lists, still in demand for country drives and evenings at the theatre. They will not see that he has not enough unction left to oil the wheels of social intercourse. The pressure of their expectations forces from him again and again a little tact, the soft answer; it's so easy to behave, after all, like the nice boy you always were.

Aunt Henriette, Aunt Eulalie edge around with that stifling tact of their own, their desire always to do the very very best for you.

Aunt Eulalie's stepdaughter, Anaïs: so pretty, so fond of you: so why not? And why not make it soon? Because, he said with desperation, next year they might call the Estates, and who knows, who knows, I might be going away.

BY CHRISTMAS the Charpentiers were well settled in their new house at Fontenay-sous-Bois. They miss the café, but not the city mud, the noise, the rude people in the shops. The country air, they say, makes them feel ten years younger. Gabrielle and Georges-Jacques come out on Sundays. You can see they're happy; it's so gratifying. The baby will have enough shawls for seven infants and more attention than a dauphin. Georges-Jacques looks harassed, pale after the long winter. What he needs is a month at home in Arcis, but he can't take the time off. He now has complete charge of the Board of Excise's legal work, but he says he needs another source of income. He would like to buy some land, but he says he hasn't the capital. He says there is a limit to what one man can do, but no doubt he is worrying needlessly. We are all very proud of Georges.

AT THE TREASURY, Claude Duplessis comports himself as cheerfully as he can, given the circumstances. Last year, during a period of five months, France had three Comptrollers in succession, all of them asking the same silly questions and requiring to be fed streams of useless information. He has to think quite hard when he wakes in the morning to recall who he works for. Soon no doubt M. Necker will be invited back, to treat us to more of his glib nostrums about public confidence. If the public at large want to think of Necker as some sort of Messiah, who are we, mere clerks, mere civil servants after all ... No one at the Treasury thinks the situation can be retrieved.

Claude confides to a colleague that his lovely daughter wants to marry a little provincial lawyer who has a stutter and who hardly ever appears in court, and who seems in addition to have a bad moral character. He wonders why his colleague smirks so.

The deficit is one hundred and sixty million livres.

*

CAMILLE DESMOULINS was living in the rue Sainte-Anne, with a girl whose mother painted portraits. 'Do go and see your family,' she told him. 'Just for the New Year.' She looked at him appraisingly; she was thinking of going into her mother's line of work. Camille's not easy to put on paper; it's easier to draw the men the taste of the age admires, florid fleshy men with their conscious poise and newly barbered heads. Camille moves too quickly for even a lightning sketch; she knows he is moving on, out of their lives, and she wants if she can to make things right for him before he goes.

So now the *diligence*, not worth the name, rumbled towards Guise over roads rutted and flooded by January rains. As he approached his home, Camille thought of his sister Henriette, of her long dying. Whole days, whole weeks had gone by when they had not seen Henriette, only his mother's whey-face, and the doctor coming and going. He had gone off to school, to Cateau-Cambrésis, and sometimes he had woken in the night and thought, why isn't she coughing? When he returned home he was taken into her room and allowed to sit for five minutes by the bed. She had transparent places under her eyes, where the skin shone blue; her bony shoulders were pushed forwards by the pillows. She had died the year he went to school in Paris, on a day when the rain fell steadily and coursed in brown channels through the streets of the town.

His father had given the priest and the doctor a glass of brandy – as if they were not habituated to death, as if they needed bracing. Himself, he sat in a corner inconspicuously, and awkwardly very awkwardly the men revolved the conversation around to him: Camille, how will you like going to Louis-le-Grand? I have made up my mind to like it, he said. Won't you miss your mother and father? You must remember, he said, that they sent me to school three years ago when I was seven, so I will not miss them at all, and they will not miss me. He's upset, the priest said hurriedly; but Camille your little sister's in heaven. No, Father, he had said: we are compelled to believe that Henriette is in purgatory now, tasting torments. This is the consolation our religion allows us for our loss.

There would be brandy for him now when he arrived home, and

his father would ask, as he had done for years, how was the journey? But he was used to the journey. Perhaps the horses might fall over, or you might be poisoned *en route*, or bored to death by a fellow traveller; that was the sum of the possibilities. Once he had said, I didn't see anything, I didn't speak to anyone, I thought evil thoughts all the way. All the way? And those were the days before the *diligence*. He must have had stamina, when he was sixteen.

Before leaving Paris he had read over his father's recent letters. They were trenchant, unmagisterial, wounding. Between the lines lay the unspeakable fact that the Godards wish to break off his engagement to his cousin Rose-Fleur. It had been made when she was in her cradle; how were they to know how things would turn out?

It was Friday night when he arrived home. The next day there were calls to be paid around the town, gatherings he could not avoid. Rose-Fleur affected to be too shy to speak to him, but the pretence sat uneasily on her restless shoulders. She had darting eyes and the Godards' heavy dark hair; she ran her eyes over him from time to time, making him feel that he had been coated with black treacle.

On Sunday he went to Mass with the family. In the narrow, sleet-blown streets he was an object of curiosity. In church people looked at him as if he had come from a warmer region than Paris.

'They say you are an atheist,' his mother whispered.

'Is that what they say I am?'

Clément said, 'Perhaps you will be like that diabolic Angevin who vanished at the consecration in a puff of smoke?'

'It would be an event,' Anne-Clothilde said. 'Our social calendar has been so dull.'

Camille did not study the congregation; he was aware that they studied him. There was M. Saulce and his wife; there was the same physician, bewigged and tubby, who once assisted Henriette to her coffin.

'There's your old girlfriend,' Clément said. 'We're not supposed to know, but we do.'

Sophie was a doubled-chinned matron now. She looked through him as if his bones were glass. He felt that perhaps they were; even stone seemed to crumble and melt in the scented ecclesiastical gloom. Six points of light on the altar guttered and flared; their shadows cross-hatched flesh and stone, wine and bread. The few communicants melted away into the darkness. It was the feast of the Epiphany; when they emerged, the blue daylight scoured the burgers' skulls, icing out features and peeling them back to bone.

He went upstairs to his father's study and sifted through his filed correspondence until he found the letter he wanted, the missive from his Godard uncle. His father came in as he was reading it. 'What are you doing?' He didn't try to hide the letter. 'That's really going rather far,' Jean-Nicolas said.

'Yes.' Camille smiled, turning the page. 'But then you know I am ruthless and capable of great crimes.' He carried the paper to the light. 'Camille's known instability', he read, 'and the dangers that may be apprehended to the happiness and durability of the union'. He put the letter down. His hand trembled. 'Do they think I'm mad?' he asked his father.

'They think – '

'What else can it mean, instability?'

'Is it just their choice of words you're quibbling about?' Jean-Nicolas went over to the fireplace, rubbing his hands. 'That bloody church is freezing,' he said. 'They could have come up with other terms, but of course they won't commit them to writing. Something got back about a – relationship – you were having with a colleague whom I had always held in considerable – '

Camille stared at him. 'That was years ago.'

'I don't find this particularly easy to talk about,' Jean-Nicolas said. 'Would you like just to deny it, and then I can put people straight on the matter?'

The wind tossed handfuls of sleet against the windows, and rattled in the chimneys and eaves. Jean-Nicolas raised his eyes apprehensively. 'We lost slates in November. What's happening to the weather? It never used to be like this.'

Camille said, 'Anything that happened was – oh, back in the days when the sun used to shine all the time. Six years ago. Minimum. None of it was my fault, anyway.'

'So what are you claiming? That my friend Perrin, a family man, whom I have known for thirty-five years, a man highly respected in the Chancery division and a leading Freemason – are you claiming that one day out of the blue he ran up to you and knocked you unconscious and dragged you into his bed? Rubbish. Listen,' he cried, 'can you hear that strange tapping noise? Do you think it's the guttering?'

'Ask anyone,' Camille said.

'What?'

'About Perrin. He had a reputation. I was just a child, I – oh well, you know what I'm like, I never do quite know how I get into these things.'

'That won't do for an excuse. You can't expect that to do, for the Godards.' He broke off, looked up. 'I think it is the guttering, you know.' He turned back to his son. 'And I only bring this up, as *one* example of the sort of story that gets back.'

It had begun to snow properly now, from an opaque and sullen sky. The wind dropped suddenly. Camille put his forehead against the cold glass and watched the snow begin to drift and bank in the square below. He felt weak with shock. His breath misted the pane, the fire crackled behind him, gulls tossed screaming in the upper air. Clément came in. 'What's that funny noise, a sort of tapping?' he said. 'Is it the guttering, do you think? That's funny, it seems to have stopped now.' He looked across the room. 'Camille, are you all right?'

'I think so. Could you just tell the fatted calf it's been reprieved again?'

Two days later he was back in Paris, in the rue Sainte-Anne. 'I'm moving out,' he told his mistress.

'Suit yourself,' she said. 'If you must know, I really object to your carrying on with my mother behind my back. So perhaps it's just as well.'

So now CAMILLE woke up alone: which he hated. He touched his closed eyelids. His dreams did not bear discussion. His life is not really what people imagine, he thought. The long struggle for Annette had shredded his nerves. How he would like to be with Annette, and settled. He did not bear Claude any ill-will, but it would be neat if he could be just plucked out of existence. He did not want him to suffer; he tried to think of a precedent, in the Scriptures perhaps. Anything could happen; that was his experience.

He remembered – and he had to remember afresh every morning – that he was going to marry Annette's daughter, that he had made her swear an oath about it. How complicated it all was. His father suggested that he wrecked people's lives. He was at a loss to see this. He had not raped anybody, nor committed murder, and from anything else people ought to be able to pick themselves up and carry on, as he was always doing.

There was a letter from home. He didn't want to open it. Then he thought, don't be a fool, somone might have died. Inside was a banker's draft, and a few words from his father, less of apology than of resignation. This had happened before; they had gone through this whole cycle, of name-calling and horror and flight and appeasement. At a certain point, his father would feel he had overstepped the mark. He had an impulse, a desire to have control; and if his son stopped writing, never came home again, he would have lost control. I should, Camille thought, send this draft back. But as usual I need the money, and he knows it. Father, he thought, you have other children whom you could torment.

I'll go round and see d'Anton, he thought. Georges-Jacques will talk to me, he doesn't regard my vices, in fact perhaps he rather likes them. The day brightened.

They were busy at d'Anton's offices. The King's Councillor employed two clerks nowadays. One of them was a man called Jules Paré, whom he'd known at school, though d'Anton was younger by several years; it didn't seem odd, that he employed his seniors these days. The other was a man called Deforgues, whom d'Anton also seemed to have known for ever. Then there was a hanger-on called Billaud-Varennes, who came in when he was wanted, to draft pleas and do the routine stuff, picking up the practice's overflow. Billaud was in the office this morning, a spare, unprepossessing man with never a good word to say about anybody. When Camille came in, he was tapping papers together on Paré's desk, and at the same time complaining that his wife was putting on weight. Camille saw that he was specially resentful this morning; for here he was, down-at-heel and seedy, and here was Georges-Jacques, with his good broadcloth coat nicely brushed and his plain cravat a dazzling white, with that general money-in-the-bank air of his and that loud posh voice ... 'Why are you complaining about Anna,' Camille asked, 'when you really want to complain about Maître d'Anton?'

Billaud looked up. 'I've no complaints,' he said.

'Aren't you lucky? You must be the only man in France with no complaints. Why is he lying?'

'Go away, Camille.' D'Anton picked up the papers Billaud had brought. 'I'm working.'

'When you were received into the College of Advocates, didn't you have to go to your parish priest and ask him for a certificate to say that you were a good Catholic?' D'Anton grunted, buried in his counter-claims. 'Didn't it stick in your throat?'

'"Paris is worth a Mass,"' d'Anton said.

'Of course, this is why Maître Billaud-Varennes doesn't advance himself from his present position. He also would be a King's Councillor, but he can't bring himself to do it. He hates priests, don't you?'

'Yes,' Billaud said. 'As we're quoting, I'll quote for you – "I should like to see, and this will be the last and most ardent of my desires, I should like to see the last king strangled with the guts of the last priest."'

A short pause. Camille looks Billaud over. He can't stand him, hardly likes to be in the same room, Billaud makes his skin crawl with distaste and a sort of apprehension that he can't fathom. But that's just it – he has to be in the same room. He has to keep seeking out the company of people he can't stand, it's become a compulsion. He looks at certain people these days, and it's as if he's always known them, as if they belong to him in some way, as if they're his relatives.

'How's your subversive pamphlet?' he said to Billaud. 'Have you found a printer for it yet?'

D'Anton looked up from his papers. 'Why do you spend your

time writing things that can never be published, Billaud? I'm not asking to needle you – I just want to know.'

Billaud's face mottled. 'Because I can't compromise,' he said.

'Oh, for God's sake,' d'Anton said. 'Wouldn't it be better – no, we've had this conversation before. Perhaps you should try pamphleteering yourself, Camille. Try prose, instead of poetry.'

'His pamphlet is called "A Last Blow against Prejudice and Superstition",' Camille said. 'Doesn't look as if it will be quite the last blow, does it? Looks as if it will be about as successful as all those dismal plays he wrote.'

'The day when you – ' Billaud began.

D'Anton cut him off. 'Let's have some quiet.' He pushed the pleadings at Billaud. 'What is this rubbish?'

'You teach me my business, Maître d'Anton?'

'Why not, if you don't know it?' He tossed the papers down. 'How was your cousin Rose-Fleur, Camille? No, don't tell me now, I'm up to here.' He indicated: chin height.

'Is it hard to be respectable?' Camille asked him. 'I mean, is it really gruelling?'

'Oh, this act of yours, Maître Desmoulins,' Billaud said. 'It makes me quite ill, year after year.'

'You make me ill too, you ghoul. There must be some outlet for your talents, if the law fails. Groaning in vaults would suit you. And dancing on graves is always in request.'

Camille departed. 'What would be an outlet for his talents?' Jules Paré said. 'We are too polite to conjecture.'

AT THE THÉÂTRE DES VARIÉTÉS the doorman said to Camille, 'You're late, love.' He did not understand this. In the box-office two men were having a political argument, and one of them was damning the aristocracy to hell. He was a plump little man with no visible bones in his body, the kind that – in normal times – you see squeaking in defence of the status quo. 'Hébert, Hébert,' his opponent said without much heat, 'you'll be hanged, Hébert.' Sedition must be in the air, Camille thought. 'Hurry up,' the doorman said. 'He's in a terrible mood. He'll shout at you.'

Inside the theatre there was a hostile, shrouded dimness. Some disconsolate performers were hopping about trying to keep warm. Philippe Fabre d'Églantine stood before the stage and the singer he had just auditioned. 'I think you need a holiday, Anne,' he said. 'I'm sorry, my duck, it just won't do. What have you been doing to your throat? Have you taken to smoking a pipe?'

The girl crossed her arms over her chest. She looked as if she might be about to burst into tears.

'Just put me in the chorus, Fabre,' she said. 'Please.'

'Sorry. Can't do it. You sound as if you're singing inside a burning building.'

'You're not sorry, are you?' the girl said. 'Bastard.'

Camille walked up to Fabre and said into his ear, 'Are you married?'

Fabre jumped, whirled around. 'What?' he said. 'No, never.'

'Never,' Camille said, impressed.

'Well, yes, in a way,' Fabre said.

'It isn't that I mean to blackmail you.'

'All right. All right, I am then. She's ... touring. Listen, just wait for me a half hour, will you? I'll be through as soon as I can. I hate this hack-work, Camille. My genius is being crushed. My time is being wasted.' He waved an arm at the stage, the dancers, the theatre manager frowning in his box. 'What did I do to deserve this?'

'Everybody is disgruntled this morning. In your box-office they are having an argument about the composition of the Estates-General.'

'Ah, René Hébert, what a fire-eater. What really irks him is that his triumphant destiny is to be in charge of the ticket returns.'

'I saw Billaud this morning. He is disgruntled too.'

'Don't mention that cunt to me,' Fabre said. 'Trying to take the bread out of writers' mouths. He's got one trade, why doesn't he stick to it? It's different for you,' he added kindly. 'I wouldn't mind if you wanted to write a play, because you're such a complete and utter failure as a lawyer. I think, Camille dear, that you and I should collaborate on some project.'

'I think I should like to collaborate on a violent and bloody revolution. Something that would give offence to my father.'

'I was thinking more of something in the short-term, which would make money,' Fabre said reprovingly.

Camille took himself into the shadows, and watched Fabre losing his temper. The singer came stalking towards him, threw herself into a seat. She dropped her head, swayed her chin from side to side to relax the muscles of her neck: then pulled tight around her upper arms a fringed silk shawl that had a certain fraying splendour about it. She seemed frayed herself; her expression was bad-tempered, her mouth set. She looked Camille over. 'Do I know you?'

He looked her over in turn. She was about twenty-seven, he thought; small bones, darkish brown hair, snub nose. She was pretty enough, but there was something blurred about her features: as though at some time she'd been beaten, hit around the head, had almost recovered but would never quite. She repeated her question. 'Admire the directness of your approach,' Camille said.

The girl smiled. Tender bruised mouth. She put up a hand to massage her throat. 'I thought I really did know you.'

'I am afflicted by this, too. Lately I think I know everybody in Paris. It's like a series of hallucinations.'

'You do know Fabre, though. Can you do something for me there? Have a word, put him in a better temper?' Then she shook her head. 'No, forget it. He's right, my voice has gone. I trained in England, would you believe? I had these big ideas. I don't know what I'm going to do now.'

'Well – what have you ever done, between jobs?'

'I used to sleep with a marquis.'

'There you are, then.'

'I don't know,' the girl said. 'I get the impression that marquises aren't so free with their money any more. And me, I'm not so free with my favours. Still – move on is the best thing. I think I'll try Genoa, I've got contacts there.'

He liked her voice, her foreign accent; wanted to keep her talking. 'Where are you from?'

'Near Liège. I've – well – travelled a bit.' She put her cheek on her hand. 'My name is Anne Théroigne.' She closed her eyes. 'God, I'm so tired,' she said. She moved thin shoulders inside the shawl, trying to ease the world off her back.

AT THE RUE CONDÉ, Claude was at home. 'I'm surprised to see you,' he said. He didn't look it. 'You've had your answer,' he said. 'Positively no. Never.'

'Immortal, are you?' Camille said. He felt just about ready for a fight.

'I could almost believe you're threatening me,' Claude said.

'Listen to me,' Camille said. 'Five years from now there will be none of this. There will be no Treasury officials, no aristocrats, people will be able to marry who they want, there will be no monarchy, no Parlements, and you won't be able to tell me what I can't do.'

He had never in his life spoken to anyone like this. It was quite releasing, he thought. I might become a thug for a career.

Annette, a room away, sat frozen in her chair. It was only once in six months that Claude came home early. It followed that Camille could not have prepared for him; this was all out of his head. He wants to marry my daughter, she thought, *because someone is telling him he can't.* And she had for years nourished this rare and ferocious ego in her own drawing room, feeding it like some peculiar houseplant on mocha coffee and small confidences.

'Lucile,' she said, 'sit in your chair, don't dare leave this room. I will not condone your flouting your father's authority.'

'You mistake that for authority?' Lucile said. Frightened, she walked out of the room. Camille was white with anger, his eyes opening like dark, slow stains. She stood in his path. 'You must know,' she said, to anyone it concerned, 'I mean to have another life from the one they've worked out for me. Camille, I'm terrified of being ordinary. I'm terrified of being bored.'

His fingertips brushed the back of her hand. They were cold as ice. He turned on his heel. A door slammed. She had nothing left of him but the small chilled islands of skin. She heard her mother crying noisily out of sight, gasping and gagging. 'Never,' her father said, 'never in twenty years has there been a word said out of place in this house, there have been none of these upsets, my daughters have never heard voices raised in anger.'

Adèle came out. 'So now we are living in the real world,' she said.

Claude wrung his hands. They had never seen anyone do it before.

THE D'ANTONS' son was a robust baby, with a brown skin, a full head of dark hair, and his father's eyes, surprisingly light blue. The Charpentiers hung over the crib, pointing out resemblances and saying who he would be. Gabrielle was pleased with herself. She wanted to feed the baby herself, not send him off to a wet-nurse. 'Ten years ago,' her mother said, 'that would have been quite unthinkable for a woman in your position. An advocate's wife.' She shook her head, disliking modern manners. Gabrielle said, perhaps some changes are for the better? But apart from this one, she could not think of any.

We are now in May 1788. The King has announced that he will abolish the Parlements. Some of their members are under arrest. Receipts are 503 million, expenditure is 629 million. Out in the street, one of the local pigs pursues a small child, and jumps on it under Gabrielle's window. The incident makes her feel queasy. Since she gave birth, she does not wish to view life as a challenge.

So they moved on quarter day, to a first-floor apartment on the corner of the rue des Cordeliers and the Cour du Commerce. Her first thought was, we cannot afford this. They needed new furniture to fill it; it was the house of an established man. 'Georges-Jacques has expensive tastes,' her mother said.

'I suppose the practice is doing well.'

'This well? My dear, I've always enjoined obedience in you. But not imbecility.'

Gabrielle said to her husband, 'Are we in debt?'

He said, 'Let me worry about that, will you?'

Next day, at the front door of the new house, d'Anton stopped to admit before him a woman holding by the hand a little girl of nine or ten. They introduced themselves. She was Mme Gély, her husband Antoine was an official at the Châtelet court, M. d'Anton might know him? He did. And the baby, your first? And this is Louise – yes, I've just the one – and pray Louise, do not scowl, do you want your face to set like that? 'Please tell Mme d'Anton that if she wishes any help, she has only to ask. Next week, when you are settled, do come to supper.'

The child Louise trailed after her as she walked upstairs. She gave d'Anton a backward glance.

He found Gabrielle sitting on a packing case, fitting together the halves of a dish. 'This is all we've broken,' she said. She jumped up and kissed him. 'Our new cook is cooking. And I've engaged a maid this morning, her name's Catherine Motin, she's young and quite cheap.'

'I've just met our upstairs neighbour. Very mincing and genteel. Got a little girl, about so high. Gave me a very suspicious look.'

Gabrielle reached up and joined her hands at the nape of his neck. 'You're not reassuring to look at, you know. Is the case over?'

'Yes. And I won.'

'You always win.'

'Not always.'

'I can pretend that you do.'

'If you like.'

'So you don't mind if I adore you?'

'It's a question, I'm told, of whether you can bear the dead weight of a woman's expectations. I'm told that you shouldn't put yourself into the position with a woman where you have to be right all the time.'

'Who told you that?'

'Camille, of course.'

The baby was crying. She pulled away. This day, this little conversation would come back to him, years on: the new-born wails, her breasts leaking milk, the sweet air of inconsequentiality the whole day wore. And the smell of polish and paint and the new carpet: a sheaf of bills on the bureau: summer in the new trees outside the window.

Price inflation 1785–1789:

Wheat	66%
Rye	71%
Meat	67%
Firewood	91%

STANISLAS FRÉRON was an old schoolfriend of Camille's, a journalist. He lived around the corner and edited a literary periodical. He made waspish jokes and thought too much about his clothes, but Gabrielle found him tolerable because he was the godson of royalty.

'I suppose you call this your salon, Mme d'Anton.' He dropped into one of her new purple armchairs. 'No, don't look like that. Why shouldn't the wife of a King's Councillor have a salon?'

'It's not the way I think of myself.'

'Oh, I see, it's you that's the problem, is it? I thought perhaps we were the problem. That you saw us as second-rate.' She smiled politely. 'Of course, some of us *are* second-rate. And Fabre, for instance, is third-rate.' Fréron leaned forward and made a steeple out of his hands. 'All those men,' he said, 'whom we admired when we were young, are now dead, or senile, or retired into private life on pensions that the Court has granted them to keep the fires of their wrath burning low – though I fear it was simulated wrath in the first place. You will remember the fuss there was when M. Beauharnais wanted to have his plays performed, and how our fat, semi-literate King banned them personally because he considered them subversive of the good order of the state; it proved, didn't it, that M. Beauharnais's ambition was to have the most opulent townhouse in Paris, and now he is building it, within sight of the Bastille and within smell of some of the nastiest tenements of the city. Then again – but no, I could multiply examples. The ideas that were considered dangerous twenty years ago are now commonplaces of establishment discourse – yet people still die on the streets every winter, they still starve. And we, in our turn, are militant against the existing order only because of our personal failure to progress up its sordid ladder. If Fabre, for example, were elected to the Academy tomorrow, you would see his lust for social revolution turning overnight into the most douce and debonair conformity.'

'Very nice speech, Rabbit,' d'Anton said.

'I wish Camille would not call me that,' Fréron said with controlled exasperation. 'Now everyone calls me that.'

D'Anton smiled. 'Go on,' he said. 'About these people.'

'Well then . . . have you met Brissot? He's in America just now, I think, Camille had a letter. He is advising them on all their problems. A great theorist is Brissot, a great political philosopher, though with scarcely a shirt to his back. And all these professional Americans, professional Irishmen, professional Genevans — all the governments in exile, and the hacks, scribblers, failed lawyers — all those men who profess to hate what they most desire.'

'You can afford to say it. Your family is favoured, your paper's on the right side of the censors. A radical opinion is a luxury you may allow yourself.'

'You denigrate me, d'Anton.'

'You denigrate your friends.'

Fréron stretched his legs. 'End of argument,' he said. He frowned. 'Do you know why he calls me Rabbit?'

'I can't imagine.'

Fréron turned back to Gabrielle. 'So, Mme d'Anton, I still believe you have the makings of a salon. You have me, and François Robert and his wife — Louise Robert says she would write a novel about Annette Duplessis and the rue Condé débâcle, but she fears that as a character in fiction Camille would not be believed.'

The Roberts were newly married, soddenly infatuated with each other, and horribly impoverished. He was twenty-eight, a lecturer in law, burly and affable and open to suggestions. Louise had been Mlle de Kéralio before her marriage, brought up in Artois, daughter of a Royal Censor; her aristocratic father had vetoed the match, and she had defied him. The weight of the family displeasure left them with no money and all routes of advancement barred to François;

and so they had rented a shop in the rue Condé and opened a delicatessen, specializing in food from the colonies. Now Louise Robert sat behind her till turning the hems of her dresses, her eyes on a volume of Rousseau, her ears open for customers and for rumours of a rise in the price of molasses. In the evening she cooked a meal for her husband and laboriously checked the day's accounts, her haughty shoulders rigid as she added up the receipts. When she had finished she sat down and chatted calmly to François of Jansenism, the administration of justice, the structure of the modern novel; afterwards she lay awake in the darkness, her nose cold above the sheets, praying for infertility.

Georges-Jacques said, 'I feel at home here.' He took to walking about the district in the evening, doffing his hat to the women and getting into conversation with their husbands, returning on each occasion with some fresh item of news. Legendre the master butcher was a good fellow, and in a profitable line of business. The rough-looking man who lived opposite really was a marquis, the Marquis de Saint-Huruge, and he has a grudge against the regime; Fabre tells a tremendous story about it, all about a misalliance and a *lettre de cachet*.

It would be quieter here, Georges-Jacques had said, but the apartment was constantly full of people they half-knew; they never ate supper alone. The offices were on the premises now, installed in a small study and what would otherwise have been their dining room. During the day the clerks Paré and Deforgues would drift in to talk to her. And young men she had never seen before would come to the door and ask her if she knew where Camille lived now. Once she lost her temper and said, 'As near as makes no difference, here.'

Her mother came over once or twice in the week, to cluck over the baby and criticize the servants and say, 'You know me, Gabrielle, I'd never interfere.' She did her own shopping, because she was particular about vegetables and liked to check her change. The child Louise Gély came with her, to pretend to help her carry her heavy bags, and Mme Gély came to advise her about the local shopkeepers and pass comments on the people they met in the streets. She liked the child Louise: open-faced, alert, wistful at times, with an only-child's precocity.

'Always so much noise from your place,' the little girl said. 'So many ladies and gentlemen coming and going. It's all right, isn't it, if I come down sometimes?'

'As long as you're good and sit quietly. And as long as I'm there.'

'Oh, I wouldn't think of coming otherwise. I'm afraid of Maître d'Anton. He has such a countenance.'

'He's very kind really.'

The child looked dubious. Then her face brightened. 'What I mean to do,' she said, 'is to get married myself as soon as someone asks me. I'm going to have packs of children, and give parties every night.'

Gabrielle laughed. 'What's the hurry? You're only ten.'

Louise Gély looked sideways at her. 'I don't mean to wait until I'm old.'

On 13 July there were hail-storms; to say this is to give no idea of how the hail fell – as if God's contempt had frozen. There was every type of violence and unexplained accidents on the streets. The orchards were stripped and devastated, the crops flattened in the fields. All day it hammered on windows and doors, like nothing in living memory; on the night of the 13th to 14th, a cowed populace slept in apprehension. They woke to silence; it seemed so long before life flowed through the city; it was hot, and people seemed dazed by the splintered light, as if all France had been pushed under water.

One year to the cataclysm: Gabrielle stood before a mirror, twitching at her hat. She was going out to buy some lengths of good woollen stuff for Louise's winter dresses. Mme Gély would not contemplate such a fool's errand, but Louise liked her winter clothes in her wardrobe by the end of August; who knew what the weather would do next, she asked, and if it should suddenly turn chilly she would be stranded, because she had grown so much since last year. Not that I go anywhere in winter, she said, but perhaps you will take me to Fontenay to see your mother. Fontenay, she said, is the country.

There was someone at the door. 'Come in, Louise,' she called, but no one came. The maid Catherine was rocking the screaming baby. She ran to the door herself, hat in hand. A girl she didn't know stood there. She looked at Gabrielle, at the hat, stepped back. 'You're going out.'

'Is there anything I can do for you?'

The girl glanced over her shoulder. 'Can I come in for five minutes? I know this sounds unlikely, but I'm sure the servants have been told to follow me about.'

Gabrielle stepped aside. The girl walked in. She took off her broad-brimmed hat, shook out her dark hair. She wore a blue linen jacket, tight-fitting, which showed off her hand-span waist and the supple line of her body. She ran a hand back through her hair, lifted her jaw, rather self-conscious: caught sight of herself in the mirror. Gabrielle felt suddenly dumpy and badly dressed, a woman getting over a pregnancy. 'I imagine,' she said, 'that you must be Lucile.'

'I came,' Lucile said, 'because things are so awful and I desperately need to talk to somebody, and Camille has told me all about you, and he's told me what a kind and sympathetic person you are, and that I will love you.'

Gabrielle recoiled. She thought, what a low, mean, despicable trick: if he's told her that about me, how can I possibly tell her what I think of him? She dropped her hat on a chair. 'Catherine, run upstairs and say I'll be delayed. Then fetch us some lemonade, will you? Warm today, isn't it?' Lucile looked back at her: eyes like midnight flowers. 'Well, Mlle Duplessis – have you quarrelled with your parents?'

Lucile perched on a chair. 'My father goes around our house saying, "Does a father's authority count for nothing?" He intones it, like a dirge. My sister keeps saying it to me and making me laugh.'

'Well, doesn't it?'

'I believe in the right to resist authority when it's wrong-headed.'

'What does your mother say now?'

'Nothing much. She's gone very quiet. She knows I get letters. She pretends not to know.'

'That seems unwise of her.'

'I leave them where she can read them.'

'That makes neither of you any better.'

'No. Worse.'

Gabrielle shook her head. 'I can't condone it. I would never have defied my parents. Or deceived them.'

Lucile said, with passion, 'Don't you think women should choose who they marry?'

'Oh yes. Within reason. It just isn't reasonable to marry Maître Desmoulins.'

'Oh. You wouldn't do it then?' Lucile looked as if she were hesitating over a few yards of lace. She picked up an inch of her skirt, ran the material slowly between her fingers. 'The thing is, Mme d'Anton, I'm in love with him.'

'I doubt it. You're just going through that phase, you want to be in love with somebody.'

Lucile looked at her with curiosity. 'Before you met your husband, were you always falling in love with people?'

'To be honest, no – I wasn't that sort of girl.'

'What makes you think I am, then? All this business of going through phases, it's just a thing that older people say, they think they have the right to look at you from their mouldy perches and pass judgement on your life.'

'My mother, who is a woman of some experience, would say it is an infatuation.'

'Fancy having a mother with that sort of experience. Quite like mine.'

Gabrielle felt the first stirrings of dismay. Trouble, under her own roof. How can she make this little girl understand? Can she understand anything any more, or has common sense loosened its hold for good, or did it have a hold in the first place? 'My mother tells me,' she said, 'never to criticize my husband's choice of friends. But in this case – if I tell you that with one thing and another I don't admire him . . . '

'That becomes clear.'

Gabrielle had a mental picture of herself, in the months before the baby was born, waddling about the house. Her pregnancy, delightful in its results, had been in one way a trial and embarrassment. Even by the end of the third month she'd been quite big, and she could see people sizing her up, quite unashamedly; she knew that after the birth they would count on their fingers. As the weeks passed, Georges-Jacques treated her as interesting but alien. He talked to her even less about matters not strictly domestic. She missed the café, more than he could know; she missed that undemanding masculine company, the easy talk of the outside world.

So . . . what did it matter if Georges always brought his friends home? But Camille was always arriving or just about to leave. If he sat on a chair it was on the very edge, and if he remained there for more than thirty seconds it was because he was deeply fatigued. A note of panic in his veiled eyes struck a corresponding note in her heavy body. The baby was born, the heaviness dispersed; a rootless anxiety remained. 'Camille is a cloud in my sky,' she said. 'He is a thorn in my flesh.'

'Goodness, Mme d'Anton,' Lucile said, 'are those the metaphors you feel forced to employ?'

'To begin . . . you know he has no money?'

'Yes, but I have.'

'He can't just live on your money.'

'Lots of men live on women's money. It's quite respectable, in some circles it's always done.'

'And this business of your mother, that they may have been having – I don't know how to put it.'

'I don't either,' Lucile said. 'There are terms for it, but I'm not feeling robust this morning.'

'You must find out the truth about it.'

'My mother won't talk to me. I could ask Camille. But why should I make him lie to me? So I dismiss it from my mind. I regard the subject as closed. You see, I think about him all day. I dream about him – I can't be blamed for that. I write him letters and I tear them up. I imagine that I might meet him by chance in the street – ' Lucile broke off, raised a hand, and pushed back from her forehead an imaginary strand of hair. Gabrielle watched her with horror. This is obsession, she thought, this parody of gesture. Lucile felt herself do it; she saw herself in the glass; she thought, it is an evocation.

Catherine put her head around the door. 'Monsieur is home early.'

Gabrielle leapt up. Lucile sat back in her chair. She allowed her arms to lie along the chair's arms, and flexed her hands like a cat testing its claws. D'Anton walked in. As he was taking off his coat he was saying, 'There's a mob around the Law Courts, and here I am, you told me to stay away from trouble. They're letting off fireworks and shouting for Orléans. The Guards aren't interested in breaking it up – ' He saw Lucile. 'Ah,' he said, 'trouble has come home, I see. Camille is talking to Legendre, he will be here directly. Legendre,' he added pointlessly, 'is our butcher.'

When Camille appeared Lucile rose smoothly from her chair, crossed the room and kissed him on the mouth. She watched herself in the mirror, watched him. She saw him take her hands from his shoulders and return them to her gently, folded together as if in prayer. He saw how different she looked with her hair unpowdered, how dramatic were her strong features and perfect pallor. He saw Gabrielle's hostility towards him melt a little. He saw how she watched her husband, watching Lucile. He saw d'Anton thinking, for once he did not lie, he did not exaggerate, he said Lucile was beautiful and she is. This took one second; Camille smiled. He knows that all his derelictions can be excused if he is deeply in love with Lucile; sentimental people will excuse him, and he knows how to encourage sentiment. He thinks that perhaps he is deeply in love; after all, what else is the name for the excited misery he sees on Lucile's face, and which his own face, he feels sure, reflects?

What has put her into this state? It must be his letters. Suddenly, he remembers what Georges had said: 'Try prose.' At that, it might not be so futile. He has a good deal to say, and if he can reduce his complicated and painful feelings about the Duplessis household to a few telling and effective pages, it ought to be child's play to analyse the state of the nation. Moreover, while his life is ridiculous and inept and designed to make people smile, his writing could be stylish and heartless, and produce weeping and gnashing of teeth.

For quite thirty seconds, Lucile had forgotten to look into the mirror. For the first time, she felt she had taken a hold upon her life; she had become embodied, she wasn't a spectator any more. But how long would the feeling last? His actual physical presence, so much longed for, she now found too much to bear. She wished he would go away, so she could imagine him again, but she was unsure how to request this without appearing demented. Camille framed in his mind the first and last sentences of a political pamphlet, but his eyes did not shift from her face; as he was extremely short-sighted, his gaze gave the impression of an intensity of concentration that made her weak at the knees. Deeply at cross-purposes, they stood frozen, hypnotized, until – as moments do – the moment passed.

'So this is the creature who oversets the household and suborns servants and clergyman,' d'Anton said. 'I wonder, my dear, do you know anything of the comedies of the English writer, Mr Sheridan?'

'No.'

'I wondered if you thought that Life ought to imitate Art?'

'If it imitates life,' Lucile said, 'that's quite exciting enough for me.' She noticed the time on the clock. 'I'll be killed,' she said.

She blew them all a kiss, swept up her feathered hat, ran out on to the stairs. In her haste she almost knocked over a small girl, who appeared to be listening at the door, and who, surprisingly, called out after her, 'I like your jacket.'

In bed that night she thought, hm, that large ugly man, I seem to have made a conquest there.

ON 8 AUGUST the King fixed a date for the meeting of the Estates 1 May 1789. A week later the Comptroller-General, Brienne, discovered (or so it was said) that the state's coffers contained enough revenue for one-quarter of one day's expenditure. He declared a suspension of all payments by the government. France was bankrupt. His Majesty continued to hunt, and if he did not kill he recorded the fact in his diary: *Rien, rien, rien*. Brienne was dismissed.

ROUTINE was so broken up these days, that Claude could be found in Paris when he should have been in Versailles. Mid-morning, he strolled out into the hot August air, made for the Café du Foy. Other years, August had found him sitting by an open window at his country place at Bourg-la-Reine.

'Good morning, Maître d'Anton,' he said. 'Maître Desmoulins. I had no idea you knew each other.' The idea seemed to be causing him pain. 'Well, what do you think? Things can't go on like this.'

'I suppose we should take your word for it, M. Duplessis,' Camille said. 'How do you look forward to having M. Necker back?'

'What does it matter?' Claude said. 'I think that even the Abbé Terray would have found the situation beyond him.'

'Anything new from Versailles?' d'Anton asked.

'Someone told me,' Camille said, 'that when the King cannot hunt he goes up on the roofs at Versailles and takes pot-shots at the ladies' cats. Do you think there's anything in it?'

'Shouldn't be surprised,' Claude said.

'It puzzles a lot of people to see how things have deteriorated since Necker was last in office. If you think back to '81, to the public accounting, the books then showed a surplus – '

'Cooked,' Claude said dismally.

'Really?'

'Done to a turn.'

'So much for Necker,' d'Anton said.

'But you know, it wasn't such a crime,' Camille suggested. 'Not if he thought public confidence was the main thing.'

'Jesuit,' d'Anton said.

Claude turned to him. 'I'm hearing things, d'Anton – straws in the wind. Your patron Barentin will be moving from the Board of Excise – he's going to get the Ministry of Justice in the new government.' He smiled. He looked very tired. 'This is a sad day for me. I would have given anything to stop it coming to this. And it must give impetus to the wilder elements . . . ' His eye fell on

Camille. He had been very civil this morning, very well-behaved, but that he was a wilder element Claude had no doubt. 'Maître Desmoulins,' he said, 'I hope you aren't still entertaining notions about marrying my daughter.'

'I am, rather.'

'If you could just see it from my point of view.'

'No, I'm afraid I can see it only from my own.'

M. Duplessis turned away. D'Anton put a hand on his arm. 'About Barentin – can you tell me something more?'

Claude held up a forefinger. 'Least said, soonest mended. I hope I've not spoken out of turn. I expect I'll be seeing you before long.' He indicated Camille, hopelessly. 'Him too.'

Camille looked after him. '"Straws in the wind",' he said savagely. 'Have you ever heard such drivel? We ought to arrange him a cliché contest with Maître Vinot. Oh,' he said suddenly, 'I do see what he means. He means they're going to offer you a job.'

UPON TAKING OFFICE, Necker began to negotiate a loan from abroad. The Parlements were reinstated. The price of bread rose two sous. On 29 August, a mob burned down the guard posts on the Pont-Neuf. The King found the money to move troops into the capital. Soldiers opened fire into a crowd of six hundred; seven or eight people were killed and an unknown number injured.

M. Barentin was appointed Minister of Justice and Keeper of the Seals. The mob made a straw doll in the likeness of his predecessor, and set fire to it on the Place de Grève, to the tune of hoots and jeers, the crack and whizz of fireworks and the drunken acquiescent singing of the French Guards, who were stationed permanently in the capital and who liked that sort of thing.

D'ANTON had given his reasons precisely, without heat but without equivocation; he had worked out beforehand what he would say, so that he would be perfectly clear. Barentin's offer of a secretary's post would quickly become common knowledge around City Hall and the ministries and beyond. Fabre suggested that he take Gabrielle some flowers and break it to her gently.

When he got home, Mme Charpentier was there, and Camille. They stopped talking when they saw him. The atmosphere was ill-humoured; but Angélique came over, beaming, and kissed him on both cheeks. 'Dear son Georges,' she said, 'our warmest congratulations.'

'On what?' he said. 'My case didn't come up. Really, the process of justice is moving like treacle nowadays.'

'We understand,' Gabrielle said, 'that you have been offered a post in the government.'

'Yes, but it's of no consequence. I turned it down.'

'I told you,' Camille said.

Angélique stood up. 'I'll be off then.'

'I'll see you out,' Gabrielle said, with extreme formality. Her face glowed. She got up; they went, and whispered outside the door.

'Angélique will make her behave,' d'Anton said. Camille sat and smiled at him. 'You're easily pleased. Come back in, calm yourself, shut the door,' he said to his wife. 'Please try to understand that I am acting for the best.'

'When he said,' she pointed to Camille, 'that you'd turned it down, I said what kind of a fool did he suppose I was?'

'This government won't last a year. It doesn't suit me, Gabrielle.'

She gaped at him. 'So what are you going to do? Give up your practice because the state of the law doesn't suit you? You were ambitious before, you used to say – '

'Yes, and now he's more ambitious,' Camille cut in. 'He's far too good for a minor post under Barentin. Probably – oh, probably the Seal will be within his own gift one day.'

D'Anton laughed. 'If it ever is,' he said, 'I'll give it you. I promise.'

'That's probably treason,' Gabrielle said. Her hair was slipping down, as it tended to do at points of crisis.

'Don't confuse the issue,' Camille said. 'Georges-Jacques is going to be a great man, however he is impeded.'

'You're mad,' Gabrielle said. As she shook her head a shower of hairpins leapt out and slithered to the floor. 'What I hate, Georges, is to see you trotting along in the wake of other people's opinions.'

'Me? You think I do that?'

'No,' Camille said hurriedly, 'he doesn't do that.'

'He takes notice of you, and no notice of me whatsoever.'

'That's because – ' Camille stopped. He could not think of a tactful reason why it was. He turned to d'Anton. 'Can I produce you to the Café du Foy tonight? You may be expected to make a short speech, you don't mind, of course not.'

Gabrielle looked up from the floor, hairpin in hand. 'Do I understand that this business has glorified you, somehow?'

'I wouldn't say "glory".' Camille looked modest. 'But it's a start.'

'Would you mind?' d'Anton said to her. 'I'll not be late. When I come home I'll explain it better. Gabrielle, leave those, Catherine will pick them up.'

Gabrielle shook her head again. She would not be explained to, and if Catherine were asked to crawl around the floor after her hairpins, she would probably give notice; why did he not know this?

The men went downstairs. Camille said, 'I'm afraid it's just my existence that irks Gabrielle. Even when my desperate fiancée turns up at her door she still believes I'm trying to inveigle you into bed with me.'

'Aren't you?'

'Time to think of higher things,' Camille said. 'Oh, I am so happy. Everybody says changes are coming, everyone says the country will be overturned. They say it, but you believe it. You act on it. You are seen to act on it.'

'There was a pope – I forget which one – who told everyone that the world was going to end. They all put their estates on the market, and the pope bought them and became rich.'

'That's a nice story,' Camille said. 'You are not a pope, but never mind, I think you will do quite well for yourself.'

AS SOON AS THEY HEARD in Arras that there were going to be elections, Maximilien began to put his affairs in order. 'How do you know you'll be elected?' his brother Augustin said. 'They might form a cabal against you. It's very likely.'

'Then I'll have to sing small between now and the election,' he said grimly. 'Here in the provinces almost everyone has a vote, not just the moneyed men.' For that reason, 'They won't be able to keep me out,' he said.

His sister Charlotte said, 'They'll be ungrateful beasts if they don't elect you. After all you've done for the poor. You deserve it.'

'It isn't a prize.'

'You've worked so hard, all for nothing, no money, no credit. There's no need to pretend you don't resent it. You're not obliged to be saintly.'

He sighed. Charlotte has this way of cutting him to the bone. Hacking away, with the family knife.

'I know what you think, Max,' she said. 'You don't believe you'll come back from Versailles in six months, or even a year. You think this will alter your life. Do you want them to have a revolution just to please you?'

I DON'T CARE what the Estates-General do,' said Philippe d'Orléans, 'as long as I am there when they deal with the liberty of the individual, so that I can use my voice and vote for a law after which I can be sure that, on a day when I have a fancy to sleep at Raincy, no one can send me against my will to Villers-Cotterêts.'

Towards the end of 1788 the Duke appointed a new private secretary. He liked to embarrass people, and this may have been a major reason for his choice. The addition to his entourage was an army officer named Laclos. He was in his late forties, a tall, angular man with fine features and cold blue eyes. He had joined the army at the age of eighteen, but had never seen active service. Once this had grieved him, but twenty years spent in provincial garrison towns had endowed him with an air of profound and philosophic indifference. To amuse himself, he had written some light verse, and the libretto of an opera that came off after one night. And he had watched people, recorded the details of their manoeuvres, their power-play. For twenty years there had been nothing else to do. He became familiar with that habit of mind which dispraises what it most envies and admires: with that habit of mind which desires only what it cannot have.

His first novel, *Les Liaisons Dangereuses* was published in Paris in 1782. The first edition sold out within days. The publishers rubbed their hands and remarked that if this shocking and cynical book was what the public wanted, who were they to act as censors? The second edition was sold out. Matrons and bishops expressed outrage. A copy with a blank binding was ordered for the Queen's private library. Doors were slammed in the author's face. He had arrived.

It seemed his military career was over. In any case, his criticism of army traditions had made his position untenable. 'It seems to me I could do with such a man,' the Duke said. 'Your every affectation is an open book to him.' When Félicité de Genlis heard of the appointment, she threatened to resign her post as Governor of the Duke's children. Laclos could think of bigger disasters.

It was a crucial time in the Duke's affairs. If he was to take advantage of the unsettled times, he must have an organization, a power base. His easy popularity in Paris must be put to good use. Men must be secured to his service, their past lives probed and their futures planned for them. Loyalties must be explored. Money must change hands.

Laclos surveyed this situation, brought his cold intelligence to bear. He began to know writers who were known to the police. He made discreet inquiries among Frenchmen living abroad as to the reasons for their exile. He got himself a big map of Paris and marked with blue circles points that could be fortified. He sat up by lamplight combing through the pages of the pamphlets that had come that day from the Paris presses; the censorship had broken down. He was looking for writers who were bolder and more outspoken than the rest; then he would make overtures. Few of these fellows had ever had a bestseller.

Laclos was the Duke's man now. Laconic in his statements, his air discouraging intimacy, he was the kind of man whose first name nobody ever knows. But still he watched men and women with a furtive professional interest, and scribbled down thoughts that came to him, on chance scraps of paper.

In December 1788, the Duke sold the contents of his magnificent Palais-Royal art gallery, and devoted the money to poor relief. It was announced in the press that he would distribute daily a thousand pounds of bread; that he would defray the lying-in expenses of indigent women (even, the wits said, those he had not impregnated); that he would forgo the tithes levied on grain on his estates, and repeal the game laws on all his lands.

This was Félicité's programme. It was for the country's good. It did Philippe a bit of good, too.

RUE CONDÉ. 'Although the censorship has broken down,' Lucile says, 'there are still criminal sanctions.'

'Fortunately,' her father says.

Camille's first pamphlet lies on the table, neat inside its paper cover. His second, in manuscript, lies beside it. The printers won't touch it, not yet; we will have to wait until the situation takes a turn for the worse.

Lucile's fingers caress it, paper, ink, tape:

IT WAS RESERVED for our days to behold the return of liberty among the French ... for forty years, philosophy has been undermining the foundations of despotism, and as Rome before Caesar was already enslaved by her vices, so France before Necker was already enfranchised by her intelligence ... Patriotism spreads day by day, with the devouring rapidity of a great conflagration. The young take fire; old men cease, for the first time, to regret the past. Now they blush for it.

VI. *Last Days of Titonville*

(*1789*)

A DEPOSITION to the Estates-General:

The community of Chaillevois is composed of about two hundred persons. The most part of the inhabitants have no property at all, those who have any possess so little that it is not worth talking about. The ordinary food is bread steeped in salt water. As for meat, it is never tasted, except on Easter Sunday, Shrove Tuesday and the feast of the patron saint ... A man may sometimes eat haricots, if the master does not forbid them to be grown among the vines ... That is how the common people live under the best of Kings.

Honoré-Gabriel Riquetti, Comte de Mirabeau:

My motto shall be this: get into the Estates at all costs.

NEW YEAR. You go out in the streets and you think it's here: the crash at last, the collapse, the end of the world. It is colder now than any living person can remember. The river is a solid sheet of ice. The first morning, it was a novelty. Children ran and shouted, and dragged their complaining mothers out to see it. 'One could skate,' people said. After a week, they began to turn their heads from the sight, keep their children indoors. Under the bridges, by dim and precarious fires, the destitute wait for death. A loaf of bread is fourteen sous, for the New Year.

These people have left their insufficient shelters, their shacks, their caves, abandoned the rock-hard, snow-glazed fields where they cannot believe anything will ever grow again. Tying up in a square of sacking a few pieces of bread, perhaps chestnuts: cording a small bundle of firewood: saying no goodbyes, taking to the road. They move in droves for safety, sometimes men alone, sometimes families, always keeping with the people from their own district, whose language they speak. At first they sing and tell stories. After two days or so, they walk in silence. The procession that marched now straggles. With luck, one may find a shed or byre for the night. Old women are wakened with difficulty in the morning and are found to have lost their wits. Small children are abandoned in village doorways. Some die; some are found by the charitable, and grow up under other names.

Those who reach Paris with their strength intact begin to look for work. Men are being laid off, they're told, our own people; there's nothing doing for outsiders. Because the river is frozen up, goods do not come into the city: no cloth to be dyed, no skins to be tanned, no corn. Ships are impaled on the ice, with grain rotting in their holds.

The vagrants congregate in sheltered spots, not discussing the situation because there is nothing to discuss. At first they hang around the markets in the late afternoons, because at the close of the day's trading any bread that remains is sold off cheaply or given away; the rough, fierce Paris wives get there first. Later, there is no bread after midday. They are told that the good Duke of Orléans gives away a thousand loaves of bread to people who are penniless, like them. But the Paris beggars leave them standing again, sharp-elbowed and callous, willing to give them malicious information and to walk on people who are knocked to the ground. They gather in back courts, in church porches, anywhere that is out of the knife of the wind. The very young and the very old are taken in by the hospitals. Harassed monks and nuns try to bespeak extra linen and a supply of fresh bread, only to find that they must make do with soiled linen and bread that is days old. They say that the Lord's designs are wonderful, because if the weather warmed up there would be an epidemic. Women weep with dread when they give birth.

Even the rich experience a sense of dislocation. Alms-giving seems not enough; there are frozen corpses on fashionable streets. When people step down from their carriages, they pull their cloaks about their faces, to keep the stinging cold from their cheeks and the miserable sights from their eyes.

*

'You're going home for the elections?' Fabre said. 'Camille, how can you leave me like this? With our great novel only half finished?'

'Don't fuss,' Camille said. 'It's possible that when I get back we won't have to resort to pornography to make a living. We might have other sources of income.'

Fabre grinned. 'Camille thinks elections are as good as finding a gold-mine. I like you these days, you're so frail and fierce, you talk like somebody in a book. Do you have a consumption by any chance? An incipient fever?' He put his hand against Camille's forehead. 'Think you'll last out till May?'

When Camille woke up, these mornings, he wanted to pull the sheets back over his head. He had a headache all the time, and did not seem to comprehend what people were saying.

Two things – the revolution and Lucile – seemed more distant than ever. He knew that one must draw on the other. He had not seen her for a week, and then only briefly, and she had seemed cool. She had said, 'I don't mean to seem cool, but I – ' she had smiled painfully – 'I daren't let the painful emotion show through.'

In his calmer moments he talked to everyone about peaceful reform, professed republicanism but said that he had nothing against Louis, that he believed him to be a good man. He talked the same way as everybody else. But d'Anton said, 'I know you, you want violence, you've got the taste for it.'

He went to see Claude Duplessis and told him that his fortune was made. Even if Picardy did not send him as a deputy to the Estates (he pretended to think it likely) it would certainly send his father. Claude said, 'I do not know what sort of man your father is, but if he is wise he will disassociate himself from you while he is in Versailles, to avoid being exposed to embarrassment.' His gaze, fixed at a high point on the wall, descended to Camille's face; he seemed to feel that it was a descent. 'A hack writer, now,' he said. 'My daughter is a fanciful girl, idealistic, quite innocent. She doesn't know the meaning of hardship or worry. She may think she knows what she wants, but she doesn't, I know what she wants.'

He left Claude. They were not to meet again for some months. He stood in the rue Condé looking up at the first-floor windows, hoping that he might see Annette. But he saw no one. He went once more on a round of the publishers of whom he had hopes, as if – since last week – they might have become devil-may-care. The presses are busy day and night, and their owners are balancing the risk; inflammatory literature is in request, but no one can afford to see his presses impounded and his workmen marched off. 'It's quite simple – I publish this, I go to gaol,' the printer Momoro said. 'Can't you tone it down?'

'No,' Camille said. No, I can't compromise: just like Billaud-Varennes used to say. He shook his head. He had let his hair grow, so when he shook his head with any force its dark waves bounced around somewhat theatrically. He liked this effect. No wonder he had a headache.

The printer said, 'How is the salacious novel with M. Fabre? Your heart not in it?'

'When he's gone,' Fabre said gleefully to d'Anton, 'I can revise the manuscript and make our heroine look just like Lucile Duplessis.'

If the Assembly of the Estates-General takes place, according to the promise of the King . . . there is little doubt but some revolution in the government will be effected. A constitution, probably somewhat similar to that of England, will be adopted, and limitations affixed to the power of the Crown.

                     J. C. Villiers, MP for Old Sarum

GABRIEL RIQUETTI, Comte de Mirabeau, forty years old today: happy birthday. In duty to the anniversary, he scrutinized himself in a long mirror. The scale and vivacity of the image seemed to ridicule the filigree frame.

Family story: on the day of his birth the accoucheur approached his father, the baby wrapped in a cloth. 'Don't be alarmed . . . ' he began.

He's no beauty, now. He might be forty, but he looks fifty. One line for his undischarged bankruptcy: just the one, he's never worried about money. One line for every agonizing month in the state prison at Vincennes. One line per bastard fathered. You've lived, he told himself; do you expect life not to leave a mark?

Forty's a turning point, he told himself. *Don't look back*. The early domestic hell: the screaming bloody quarrels, the days of tight-lipped, murderous silence. There was a day when he had stepped between his mother and his father; his mother had fired a pistol at his head. Only fourteen years old, and what did his father say of him? *I have seen the nature of the beast*. Then the army, a few routine duels, fits of lechery and blind, obstinate rage. Life on the run. Prison. Brother Boniface, getting roaring drunk every day of his life, his body blowing out to the proportions of a freak at a fair. *Don't look back*. And almost incidentally, almost unnoticed, a bankruptcy and a marriage: tiny Émilie, the heiress, the little bundle of poison to whom he'd sworn to be true. Where, he wondered, is Émilie today?

Happy birthday, Mirabeau. Appraise the assets. He drew himself up. He was a tall man, powerful, deep-chested: capacious lungs. The face was a shocker: badly pock-marked, not that it seemed to put women off. He turned his head slightly so that he could study the aquiline curve of his nose. His mouth was thin, intimidating; it could be called a cruel mouth, he supposed. Take it all in all – it was a man's face, full of vigour and high breeding. By a few embellishments to the truth he had made his family into one of the oldest and noblest in France. Who cared about the embellishments? Only pedants, genealogists. People take you at your own valuation, he said to himself.

But now the nobility, the second Estate of the Realm, had disowned him. He would have no seat. He would have no voice. *Or so they thought*.

It was all complicated by the fact that last summer there had appeared a scandalous book called *A Secret History of the Court at Berlin*. It dealt in some detail with the seamier side of the Prussian set-up and the sexual predilections of its prominent members. However strenuously he denied authorship, it was plain to everyone that the book was based on his observations during his time as a diplomat. (Diplomat, him? What a joke.) Strictly, he was not at fault: had he not given the manuscript to his secretary, with orders not to part with it to anyone, especially not to himself? How could he know that his current mistress, a publisher's wife, was in the habit of picking locks and rifling his secretary's desk? But that was not quite the sort of excuse that would satisfy the government. And besides, in August he had been very, very short of money.

The government should have been more understanding. If they had given him a job last year, instead of ignoring him – something worthy of his talents, say the Constantinople embassy, or Petersburg – then he would have burned *A Secret History*, or thrown it in a pond. If they had listened to his advice, he wouldn't be getting ready, now, to teach them the hard way.

So the Nobility rejected him. Very well. Three days ago he had entered Aix-en-Provence as a candidate for the Commons, the Third Estate. What resulted? Scenes of wild enthusiasm. 'Father of his Country', they had called him; he was popular, locally. When he got to Paris those bells of Aix would still be ringing jubilee, the night sky of the south would still be criss-crossed by the golden scorch-trails of fireworks. *Living fire*. He would go to Marseille (taking no chances) and get a reception in no way less noisy and splendid. Just to ensure it, he would publish in the city an anonymous pamphlet in praise of his own character and attributes.

So what's to be done with these worms at Versailles? Conciliate? Calumniate? Would they arrest you in the middle of a General Election?

A PAMPHLET by the Abbé Sieyès, 1789:

> What is the Third Estate?
> Everything.
> What has it been, until now?
> Nothing.
> What does it want?
> To become something.

THE FIRST Electoral Assembly of the Third Estate of Guise, in the district of Laon: 5 March 1789. Maître Jean-Nicolas Desmoulins presiding, as Lieutenant-General of the Bailiwick of Vermandois: assisted by M. Saulce, Procurator: M. Marriage as Secretary: 292 persons present.

In deference to the solemnity of the occasion, M. Desmoulins's son had tied his hair back with a broad green ribbon. It had been a black ribbon earlier that morning, but he had remembered just in time that black was the colour of the Hapsburgs and of Antoinette, and that was not at all the kind of partisanship he wished to display. Green, however, was the colour of liberty and the colour of hope. His father waited for him by the front door, fuming at the delay and wearing a new hat. 'I never know why Hope is accounted a virtue,' Camille said. 'It seems so self-serving.'

It was a raw, blustery day. On the rue Grand-Pont, Camille stopped and touched his father's arm. 'Come to Laon with me, to the district assembly. Speak for me. Please.'

'You think I should stand aside for you?' Jean-Nicolas said. 'The traits which the electors will prefer in me, are not the ones you have inherited. I am aware that there are certain persons in Laon making a noise on your behalf, saying you must know your way about and so on. Just let them meet you, that's all I say. Just let them try to have a five-minute normal conversation with you. Just let them *set eyes on you*. No, Camille, in no way will I be party to foisting you on the electorate.'

Camille opened his mouth to reply. His father said, 'Do you think it is a good idea to stand about arguing in the street?'

'Yes, why not?'

Jean-Nicolas took his son's arm. Not very dignified to drag him to the meeting, but he'd do it if necessary. He could feel the damp wind penetrating his clothes and stirring aches and pains in every part. 'Come on,' he snapped, 'before they give us up for lost.'

'Ah, at last,' the de Viefville cousins said. Rose-Fleur's father looked Camille over sourly. 'I had rather hoped not to see you, but I suppose you are a member of the local Bar, and your father pointed out that we could not very well disenfranchise you. This may, after all, be your only chance to play any part in the nation's affairs. I hear you've been writing,' he said. 'Pamphleteering. Not, if I may say so, a gentleman's method of persuasion.'

Camille gave M. Godard his best, his sweetest smile. 'Maître Perrin sends his regards,' he said.

After the meeting nothing remained except for Jean-Nicolas to go to Laon to collect a formal endorsement. Adrien de Viefville, the

Mayor of Guise, walked home with them. Jean-Nicolas seemed dazed by his easy victory; he'd have to start packing for Versailles. He stopped as they crossed the Place des Armes and stood looking up at his house. 'What are you doing?' his relative asked.

'Inspecting the guttering,' Jean-Nicolas explained.

By next morning everything had fallen apart. Maître Desmoulins did not appear for breakfast. Madeleine had anticipated the festive chink of coffee cups, congratulations all round, perhaps even a little laughter. But those children who remained at home all had colds, and were coddling themselves, and she was left to preside over one son, whom she did not know well enough to talk to, and who did not eat breakfast anyway.

'Can he be sulking?' she asked. 'I didn't think he'd sulk, today of all days. This comes of apeing royalty and having separate bedrooms. I never know what the bastard's thinking.'

'I could go and find him,' Camille suggested.

'No, don't trouble. Have some more coffee. He'll probably send me a note.'

Madeleine surveyed her eldest child. She put a piece of brioche into her mouth. To her surprise, it stuck there, like a lump of ash. 'What has happened to us?' she said. Tears welled into her eyes. 'What has happened to you?' She could have put her head down on the table, and howled.

Presently word came that Jean-Nicolas was unwell. He had a pain, he said. The doctor arrived, and confined him to bed. Messages were sent to the mayor's house.

'Is it my heart?' Desmoulins inquired weakly. If it is, he was about to say, I blame Camille.

The doctor said, 'I've told you often enough where your heart is, and where your kidneys are, and what is the state of each; and while your heart is perfectly sound, to set out for Versailles with kidneys like those is mere folly. You will be sixty in two years – if, and only if, you take life quietly. Moreover – '

'Yes? While you're about it?'

'Events in Versailles are more likely to give you a heart attack than anything your son has ever done.'

Jean-Nicolas dropped his head back against the pillows. His face was yellow with pain and disappointment. The de Viefvilles gathered in the drawing room below, and the Godards, and all the electoral officials. Camille followed the doctor in. 'Tell him it's his duty to go to Versailles,' he said. 'Even if it kills him.'

'You always were a heartless boy,' said M. Saulce.

Camille turned to break into a clique of de Viefvilles. 'Send me,' he said.

Jean-Louis de Viefville des Essarts, advocate, Parlementaire, surveyed him through his pince-nez. 'Camille,' he said, 'I wouldn't send you down to the market to fetch a lettuce.'

ARTOIS: the three Estates met separately, and the assemblies of the clergy and the nobility each indicated that in this time of national crisis they would be prepared to sacrifice some of their ancient privileges. The Third Estate began to propose an effusive vote of thanks.

A young man from Arras took the floor. He was short and slightly built, with a conspicuously well-cut coat and immaculate linen. His face was intelligent and earnest, with a narrow chin and wide blue eyes masked behind spectacles. His voice was unimpressive, and half-way through his speech it died momentarily in his throat; people had to lean forward and nudge their neighbours to know what he said. But it was not the manner of his delivery that caused them consternation. He said that the clergy and the nobility had done nothing praiseworthy, but had merely promised to amend where they had abused. Therefore, there was no need to thank them at all.

Among people who were not from Arras, and did not know him, there was some surprise when he was elected one of the eight deputies for the Third Estate of Artois. He seems locked into himself, somehow not *amenable*; and he has no orator's tricks, no style, nothing about him at all.

'I NOTICE you've paid off your tailor,' his sister Charlotte said. 'And your glove-maker. And you said he was such a good glove-maker too. I wish you wouldn't go around town as if you've decided to leave for good.'

'Would you prefer it if I climbed through the window one night with all my possessions done up in a spotted handkerchief? You could tell them I'd run away to sea.'

But Charlotte was not to be mollified: Charlotte, the family knife. 'They'll want you to settle things before you go.'

'You mean about Anaïs?' He looked up from the letter he was writing to an old schoolfriend. 'She's said she's happy to wait.'

'She'll not wait. I know what girls are like. My advice to you is to forget her.'

'I am always glad of your advice.'

She threw her head up and glared, suspecting sarcasm. But his face expressed only concern for her. He turned back to his letter:

Dearest Camille,

I flatter myself you won't be very surprised to learn I'm on my way to Versailles. I can't tell you how much I'm looking forward . . .

MAXIMILIEN de Robespierre, 1789, in the case of Dupond:

The reward of the virtuous man is his confidence that he has willed the good of his fellow man: after that comes the recognition of the nations, which surrounds his memory, and the honours given him by contemporaries . . . I should like to buy these rewards, at the price of a laborious life, even at the price of a premature death.

PARIS: on 1 April, d'Anton went out to vote at the church of the Franciscans, whom the Parisians called the Cordeliers. Legendre the master butcher walked down with him – a big, raw, self-educated man who was in the habit of agreeing with anything d'Anton said.

'Now a man like you . . . ' Fréron had said, with careful flattery.

'A man like me can't afford to stand for election,' d'Anton said. 'They're giving the deputies, what, an eighteen-franc allowance per session? And I'd have to live in Versailles. I've a family to support, I can't let my practice lie fallow.'

'But you're disappointed,' Fréron suggested.

'Maybe.'

The voters didn't go home; they stood in groups outside the Cordeliers' church, gossiping and making predictions. Fabre didn't have a vote because he didn't pay enough taxes; the fact was making him spiteful. 'Why couldn't we have the same franchise as the provinces?' he demanded. 'I'll tell you what it is, they regard Paris as a dangerous city, they're afraid of what would happen if we all had votes.' He engaged in seditious conversation with the truculent Marquis de Saint-Huruge. Louise Robert closed the shop and came out on François's arm, wearing rouge and a frock left over from better days.

'Think what would happen if women had votes,' she said. She looked up at d'Anton. 'Maître d'Anton believes women have a lot to contribute to political life, don't you?'

'I do not,' he said mildly.

'The whole district's out,' Legendre said. He was pleased. He had spent his youth at sea; now he liked to feel he belonged to a place.

Mid-afternoon, a surprise visitor: Hérault de Séchelles.

'Thought I'd drop down to see how you Cordeliers wild men were voting,' he said; but d'Anton had the impression he'd come to look for him. Hérault took a pinch of snuff from a little box with a picture of Voltaire on the lid. He turned the box in his fingers, appreciatively; proffered it to Legendre.

'This is our butcher,' d'Anton said, enjoying the effect.

'Charmed,' Hérault said, not a flicker of surprise on his amiable features; but afterwards d'Anton caught him surreptitiously checking his cuffs to see if they were free of ox-blood and offal. He turned to d'Anton: 'Have you been to the Palais-Royal today?'

'No, I hear there's some trouble . . . '

'That's right, keep yourself in the clear,' Louise Robert muttered.

'So you've not seen Camille?'

'He's in Guise.'

'No, he's back. I saw him yesterday in the company of the ineffably verminous Jean-Paul Marat – oh, you don't know the doctor? Not such a loss – the man has a criminal record in half the countries in Europe.'

'Don't hold that against a man,' d'Anton said.

'But he has, you know, a long history of imposing on people. He was physician to the Comte d'Artois's household troops, and it's said he was the lover of a marquise.'

'Naturally, you don't believe that.'

'Look, I can't help my birth,' Hérault said, with a flash of irritation. 'I try to atone for it – perhaps you think I should imitate Mlle de Kéralio and open a shop? Or your butcher might take me on to scrub the floors?' He broke off. 'Oh, really, one shouldn't be talking like this, losing one's temper. It must be the air in this district. Be careful, Marat will be wanting to move in.'

'But why is this gentleman verminous? You mean it as a figure of speech?'

'I mean it literally. This man abandoned his life, walked out, chooses to live as some sort of tramp.' Hérault shuddered; the story had a horrible grip on his imagination.

'What does he do?'

'He appears to have dedicated himself to the overthrowing of everything.'

'Ah, the overthrowing of everything. Lucrative business, that. Business to put your son into.'

'What I am telling you is perfectly true – but look now, I'm getting diverted. I came to ask you to do something about Camille, as a matter of urgency – '

'Oh, Camille,' Legendre said. He added a phrase he had seldom used since his merchant navy days.

'Well, quite,' Hérault said. 'But one doesn't want to see him taken up by the police. The Palais-Royal is full of people standing on chairs making inflammatory speeches. I don't know if he is there now, but he was there yesterday, and the day before – '

'Camille is making a *speech*?'

This seemed unlikely: and yet, possible. A picture came into d'Anton's mind. It was some weeks ago, late at night. Fabre had been drinking. They had all been drinking. Fabre said, we are going to be public men. He said, d'Anton, you know what I told you about your voice when we first met, when you were a boy? I told you, you've got to be able to speak for hours, you've got to fetch up your voice from here, from here – well, you're good, but you're not that good yet. Courtrooms are one thing, but we're growing out of courtrooms.

Fabre stood up. He placed his fingertips on d'Anton's temples. 'Put your fingers here,' he said. 'Feel the resonance. Put them here, and here.' He jabbed at d'Anton's face: below the cheekbones, at the side of his jaw. 'I'll teach you like an actor,' he said. 'This city is our stage.'

Camille said: 'Book of Ezekiel. "This city is the cauldron, and we the flesh."'

Fabre turned. 'This stutter,' he said. '*You don't have to do it.*'

Camille put his hands over his eyes. 'Leave me alone,' he said.

'Even you.' Fabre's face was incandescent. 'Even you, I am going to teach.'

He leapt forward, wrenched Camille upright in his chair. He took him by the shoulders and shook him. 'You're going to talk properly,' Fabre said. 'Even if it kills one of us.'

Camille put his hands protectively over his head. Fabre continued to perpetrate violence; d'Anton was too tired to intervene.

Now, in bright sunlight, on an April morning, he wondered if this scene could really have occurred. Nevertheless, he began to walk.

THE GARDENS of the Palais-Royal were full to overflowing. It seemed to be hotter here than anywhere else, as if it were high summer. The shops in the arcades were all open, doing brisk business, and people were arguing, laughing, parading; the stockbrokers from the bourse had wrenched their cravats off and were drinking lemonade, and the patrons of the cafés had spilled into the gardens and were fanning themselves with their hats. Young girls had come out to take the air and show off their summer dresses and compare themselves with the prostitutes, who saw chances of midday trade and were out in force. Stray dogs ran about grinning; broadsheet sellers bawled. There was an air of holiday: dangerous holiday, holiday with an edge.

Camille stood on a chair, the light breeze fanning out his hair. He was holding a piece of paper, and was reading from what appeared to be a police file. When he had finished he held the piece of paper at arm's length between finger and thumb and released it to let it flutter to the ground. The crowd hooted with laughter. Two men exchanged glances and melted away from the back of the crowd. 'Informers,' Fréron said. Then Camille spoke of the Queen with cordial contempt, and the crowd hissed and groaned; he spoke of delivering the King from evil advisers, and praised M. Necker, and the crowd clapped its hands. He spoke of Good Duke Philippe and his concern for the people, and the crowd threw its hat into the air and cheered.

'They'll arrest him,' Hérault said.

'What, in the face of this crowd?' Fabre said.

'They'll pick him up afterwards.'

D'Anton looked very grave. The crowd was increasing. Camille's voice reached out to them without a trace of hesitation. By accident or design he had developed a marked Parisian accent. People were drifting over from across the gardens. From the upper window of a jeweller's shop, the Duke's man Laclos gazed down dispassionately, sipping from time to time from a glass of water and jotting down notes for his files. Hot, getting hotter: Laclos alone was cool. Camille flicked his fingers across his forehead, brushing the sweat away. He launched into grain speculators. Laclos wrote, 'The best this week.'

'I'm glad you came to tell us, Hérault,' d'Anton said. 'But I don't see any chance of stopping him now.'

'It's all my doing,' Fabre said. His face shone with pleasure. 'I told you, you have to take a firm line with Camille. You have to hit him.'

THAT EVENING, as Camille was leaving Fréron's apartment, two gentlemen intercepted him and asked him politely to accompany them to the Duc de Biron's house. A carriage was waiting. On the way, no one spoke.

Camille was glad of this. His throat hurt. His stutter had come back. Sometimes in court he had managed to lose it, when he was caught up in the excitement of a case. When he was angry it would go, when he was beside himself, possessed; but it would be back. And now it was back, and he must revert to his old tactics: he couldn't get through a sentence without the need for his mind to dart ahead, four or five sentences ahead, to see words coming that he wouldn't be able to pronounce. Then he must think of synonyms – the most bizarre ones, at times – or he must simply alter what he's going to say ... He remembered Fabre, banging his head rather painfully against the arm of a chair.

The Duc de Biron made only the briefest appearance; he accorded Camille a nod, and then he was whisked through a gallery, away, into the interior of the house. The air was close; sconces diffused the light. On walls of muffling tapestry, dim figures of goddesses, horses, men: woollen arms, woollen hooves, draperies exuding the scent of camphor and damp. The topic was the thrill of the chase; he saw hounds and spaniels with dripping jaws, dough-faced huntsmen in costumes antique: a cornered stag foundered in a stream. He stopped suddenly, gripped by panic, by an impulse to cut and run. One of his escorts took him – quite gently – by the arm and steered him on.

Laclos waited for him in a little room with walls of green silk. 'Sit down,' he said. 'Tell me about yourself. Tell me what was going through your mind when you got up there today.' Self-contained, constrained, he could not imagine how anyone could parade his raw nerves to such effect.

The Duke's friend de Sillery drifted in, and gave Camille some champagne. There was no gaming tonight, and he was bored: may as well talk to this extraordinary little agitator. 'I suppose you have financial worries,' Laclos said. 'We could relieve you of those.'

When he had finished his questions he made an imperceptible signal, and the two silent gentlemen reappeared, and the process was reversed: the chill of marble underfoot, the murmur of voices behind closed doors, the sudden swell of laughter and music from unseen rooms. The tapestries had, he saw, borders of lilies, roses, blue pears. Outside the air was no cooler. A footman held up a flambeau. The carriage was back at the door.

Camille let his head drop back against the cushions. One of his escorts drew a velvet curtain, to shield their faces from the streets. Laclos declined supper and returned to his paperwork. The Duke is well-served by crowd-pleasers, he said, by unbalanced brats like that.

ON THE EVENING of 22 April, a Wednesday, Gabrielle's year-old son refused his food, pushed the spoon away, lay whimpering and listless in his crib. She took him into her own bed, and he slept; but at dawn, she felt his forehead against her cheek, burning and dry.

Catherine ran for Dr Souberbielle. 'Coughing?' said the doctor. 'Still not eaten? Well, don't fuss. I don't call this a healthy time of year.' He patted her hand. 'Try to get some rest yourself, my dear.'

By evening there was no improvement. Gabrielle slept for an hour or two, then came to relieve Catherine. She wedged herself into an upright chair, listening to the baby's breathing. She could not stop herself touching him every few minutes – just a fingertip on cheek, a little pat to the sore chest.

By four o'clock he seemed better. His temperature had dropped, his fists unclenched, his eyelids drooped into a doze. She leaned back, relieved, her limbs turned to jelly with fatigue.

The next thing she heard was the clock striking five. Wrenched out of a dream, she jerked in her chair, almost fell. She stood up, sick and cold, steadying herself with a hand on the crib. She leaned over it. The baby lay belly-down, quite still. She knew without touching him that he was dead.

AT THE CROSSROADS of the rue Montreuil and the Faubourg Saint-Antoine there was a great house known to the people who lived there as Titonville. On the first floor were the (allegedly sumptuous) apartments occupied by one M. Réveillon. Below ground were vast cellars, where notable vintages appreciated in the dusk. On the ground floor was the source of M. Réveillon's wealth – a wallpaper factory employing 350 people.

M. Réveillon had acquired Titonville after its original owner went bankrupt; he had built up a flourishing export trade. He was a rich man, and one of the largest employers in Paris, and it was natural that he should stand for the Estates-General. On 24 April he went with high hopes to the election meeting of the Sainte-Marguerite division, where his neighbours listened to him with deference. Good man, Réveillon. Knows his stuff.

M. Réveillon remarked that the price of bread was too high. There was a murmur of agreement and a little sycophantic applause: as if the observation were original. If the price of bread were to come down, M. Réveillon said, employers could cut wages; this would lead to a reduction in the price of manufactured articles. Otherwise, M. Réveillon said, where would it all end? Prices up, wages up, prices up, wages up . . .

M. Hanriot, who owned the saltpetre works, warmly seconded these observations. People lounged near the door, and handed out scraps of news to the unenfranchised, who stood outside in the gutter.

Only one part of M. Réveillon's programme caught the public attention – his proposal to cut wages. Saint-Antoine came out on the streets.

De Crosne, the Lieutenant of Police, had already warned that there could be trouble in the district. It was teeming with migrant workers, unemployment was high, it was cramped, talkative, inflammable. News spread slowly across the city; but Saint-Marcel heard, and a group of demonstrators began a march towards the river. A drummer at their head set the pace, and they shouted for death:

> Death to the rich
> Death to the aristocrats
> Death to the hoarders
> Death to the priests.

They were carrying a gibbet knocked together in five minutes by a carpenter's apprentice anxious to oblige: dangling from it were two eyeless straw dolls with their straw limbs pushed into old clothes and their names, Hanriot and Réveillon, chalked on their chests. Shopkeepers put up their shutters when they heard them coming. The dolls were executed with full ceremony in the Place de Grève.

All this is not so unusual. So far, the demonstrators have not even killed a cat. The mock executions are a ritual, they diffuse anger. The colonel of the French Guards sent fifty men to stand about near Titonville, in case anger was not quite diffused. But he neglected Hanriot's house, and it was a simple matter for a group of the marchers to wheel up the rue Cotte, batter the doors down and start a fire. M. Hanriot got out unharmed. There were no casualties. M. Réveillon was elected a deputy.

But by Monday, the situation looked more serious. There were fresh crowds on the rue Saint-Antoine, and another incursion from Saint-Marcel. As the demonstrators marched along the embankments stevedores fell in with them, and the workers on the woodpiles, and the down-and-outs who slept under the bridges; the workers at the royal glass factory downed tools and came streaming out into the streets. Another two hundred French Guards were dispatched; they fell back in front of Titonville, commandeered carts and barricaded themselves in. It was at this point that their officers felt the stirrings of panic. There could be five thousand people beyond the barricades, or there could be ten thousand; there was no way of telling. There had been some sharp action these last few months; but this was different.

As it happened, that day there was a race-meeting at Vincennes. As the fashionable carriages crossed the Faubourg Saint-Antoine, nervous ladies and gentlemen dressed *à l'Anglais* were haled out on to the sewage and cobblestones. They were required to shout, 'Down with the profiteers,' then roughly assisted back into their seats. Many of the gentlemen parted with sums of money to ensure good will, and some of the ladies had to kiss lousy apprentices and stinking draymen, as a sign of solidarity. When the carriage of the Duke of Orléans appeared, there was cheering. The Duke got out, said a few soothing words, and emptied his purse among the crowd. The carriages behind were forced to halt. 'The Duke is reviewing his troops,' said one high, carrying aristocratic voice.

The guardsmen loaded their guns and waited. The crowd milled about, sometimes approaching the carts to talk to the soldiers, but showing no inclination to attack the barricades. Out at Vincennes the Anglophiles urged their favourites past the post. The afternoon went by.

Some attempt was made to divert the returning race-goers, but when the carriage of the Duchess of Orléans appeared the situation became difficult. Up there was where she wanted to go, the Duchess's coachman said: past those barricades. The problem was explained. The reticent Duchess did not alter her orders. Etiquette confronted expediency. Etiquette prevailed. Soldiers and bystanders began to take down the barricades. The mood altered, swung about; the idleness of the afternoon dissipated, slogans were shouted, weapons reappeared. The crowd surged through, after the Duchess's carriage. After a few minutes there was nothing left of Titonville worth burning, smashing or carrying away.

When the cavalry arrived the crowds were already looting the shops on the rue Montreuil. They pulled the cavalrymen off their horses. Infantry appeared, faces set; orders crackled through the air, there was the sudden, shocking explosion of gunfire. Blank cartridges: but before anyone had grasped that, an infantryman was grazed by a roof tile dropped from above, and as he turned his face up to see where the tile had come from the rioter who had picked him out as a target skimmed down another tile, which took out his eye.

Within a minute the mob had splintered doors and smashed locks, and they were up on the roofs of the rue Montreuil, tearing up the slates at their feet. The soldiers fell back under the barrage, hands to their faces and scalps, blood dripping between their fingers, tripping on the bodies of men who had been felled. They opened fire. It was 6.30 p.m.

By eight o'clock fresh troops had arrived. The rioters were pushed back. The walking wounded were helped away. Women appeared on the streets, shawls over their heads, hauling buckets of water to bathe wounds and give drinks to those who had lost blood. The shopfronts gaped, doors creaked off their hinges, houses were stripped to the brick; there were smashed tiles and broken glass to walk on, spilt blood tacky on the tiles, small fires running along charred wood. At Titonville the cellars had been ransacked, and the men and women who had breached the casks and smashed the necks of the bottles were lying half-conscious, choking on their vomit. The French Guards, out for revenge, bludgeoned their unresisting bodies where they lay. A little stream of claret ran across the cobbles. At nine o'clock the cavalry arrived at full strength. The Swiss Guard brought up eight cannon. The day was over. There were three hundred corpses to shovel up off the streets.

UNTIL THE DAY of the funeral, Gabrielle did not go out. Shut in her bedroom, she prayed for the little soul already burdened with sin, since it had shown itself intemperate, demanding, greedy for milk during its year's stay in a body. Later she would go to church to light candles to the Holy Innocents. For now, huge slow tears rolled down her cheeks.

Louise Gély came from upstairs. She did what the maids had not sense to do; parcelled up the baby's clothes and his blankets, scooped up his ball and his rag doll, carried them upstairs in an armful. Her small face was set, as if she were used to attending on the bereaved and knew she must not give way to their emotions. She sat beside Gabrielle, the woman's plump hand in her bony child's grasp.

'That's how it is,' Maître d'Anton said. 'You're just getting your life set to rights, then the wisdom of the bloody Almighty – ' The woman and the girl raised their shocked faces. He frowned. 'This religion has no consolation for me any more.'

After the baby was buried, Gabrielle's parents came back to sit with her. 'Look to the future,' Angélique prompted. 'You might have another ten children.' Her son-in-law gazed miserably into space. M. Charpentier walked about sighing. He felt useless. He went to the window to look out into the street. Gabrielle was coaxed to eat.

Mid-afternoon, another mood got into the room: life must go on. 'This is a poor situation for a man who used to know all the news,' M. Charpentier said. He tried to signal to his son-in-law that the women would like to be left alone.

Georges-Jacques got up reluctantly. They put on their hats, and walked through the crowded and noisy streets to the Palais-Royal and the Café du Foy. M. Charpentier attempted to draw the boy into conversation, failed. His son-in-law stared straight ahead of him. The slaughter in the city was no concern of his; he looked after his own.

As they pushed their way into the café, Charpentier said, 'I don't know these people.'

D'Anton looked around. He was surprised at how many of them he did know. 'This is where the Patriotic Society of the Palais-Royal holds its meetings.'

'Who may they be?'

'The usual bunch of time-wasters.'

Billaud-Varennes was threading his way towards them. It was some weeks since d'Anton had put any work his way; his yellow face had become an irritation, and you can't keep going, his clerk Paré had told him, all the lazy malcontents in the district.

'What do you think of all this?' Billaud's eyes, perpetually like small, sour fruits, showed signs of ripening into expectation. 'Desmoulins has declared his interest at last, I see. Been with Orléans's people. They've bought him.' He looked over his shoulder. 'Well, talk of the devil.'

Camille came in alone. He looked around warily. 'Georges-Jacques, where have you been?' he said. 'I haven't seen you for a week. What do you make of Réveillon?'

'I'll tell you what I make of it,' Charpentier said. 'Lies and distortion. Réveillon is the best master in this city. He paid his men right through the lay-offs last winter.'

'Oh, so you think he is a philanthropist?' Camille said. 'Excuse me, I must speak to Brissot.'

D'Anton had not seen Brissot until now; unless he had seen him and overlooked him, which would have been easy enough. Brissot turned to Camille, nodded, turned again to his group to say, 'No, no, no, purely legislative.' He turned back, extended a hand to Camille. He was a thin man, meagre, mousy, with narrow shoulders hunched to the point of deformity. Ill-health and poverty made him look older than his thirty-five years, yet today his wan face and pale eyes were as hopeful as a child's on its first day at school. 'Camille,' he said, 'I mean to start a newspaper.'

'You must be careful,' d'Anton told him. 'The police haven't entirely let the situation go. You may find you can't distribute it.'

Brissot's eyes travelled across d'Anton's frame, and upwards, across his scarred face. He did not ask to be introduced.

'First I thought I'd begin on 1 April and publish twice weekly, then I thought no, wait till 20 April, make it four times weekly, then I thought, no, leave it till next week, when the Estates meet — that's the time to make a splash. I want to get all the news from Versailles to Paris and out on to the streets — the police may pick me up, but what does it matter? I've been in the Bastille once, I can go again. I've not had a moment to spare, I've been helping with the elections in the Filles-Saint-Thomas district, they were desperate for my advice —'

'People always are,' Camille said. 'Or so you tell me.'

'Don't be snide,' Brissot said gently. There was impatience in the faint lines around his eyes. 'I know you think I haven't a chance of keeping a paper going, but we can't spare ourselves now. Who would have thought, a month ago, that we'd have advanced this far?'

'This man calls three hundred dead an advance,' Charpentier said.

'I think —' Brissot broke off. 'I'll tell you in private all that I think. There might be police informers here.'

'There's you,' a voice said behind him.

Brissot winced. He did not turn. He looked at Camille to see if he had caught the words. 'Marat put that about,' he muttered. 'After all I've done to further that man's career and bolster his reputation, all I get is smears and innuendos — the people I've called comrades have treated me worse than the police have ever done.'

Camille said, 'Your trouble is, you're backtracking. I heard you, saying the Estates would save the country. Two years ago you said nothing was possible unless we got rid of the monarchy first. Which is it, which is it to be? No, don't answer. And will there be an inquiry into the cause of these riots? No. A few people will be hanged, that's all. Why? Because nobody dares to ask what happened — not Louis, not Necker, not even the Duke himself. But we all know that Réveillon's chief crime was to stand for the Estates against the candidate put up by the Duke of Orléans.'

There was a hush. 'One should have guessed,' Charpentier said.

'One never anticipated the scale of it,' Brissot whispered. 'It was planned, yes, and people were paid – but not ten thousand people. Not even the Duke could pay ten thousand people. They acted for themselves.'

'And that upsets your plans?'

'They have to be directed.' Brissot shook his head. 'We don't want anarchy. I shudder when I find myself in the presence of some of the people we have to use ...' He made a gesture in d'Anton's direction; with M. Charpentier, he had walked away. 'Look at that fellow. The way he's dressed he might be any respectable citizen. But you can see he'd be happiest with a pike in his hand.'

Camille's eyes widened. 'But that is Maître d'Anton, the King's Councillor. You shouldn't jump to conclusions. Let me tell you, Maître d'Anton could be in government office. Except that he knows where his future lies. But anyway, Brissot – why so unnerved? Are you afraid of a man of the people?'

'I am at one with the people,' Brissot said reverently. 'With their pure and elevated soul.'

'Not really you aren't. You look down on them because they smell and can't read Greek.' He slid across the room to d'Anton. 'He took you for some cut-throat,' he said happily. 'Brissot,' he told Charpentier, 'married one Mlle Dupont, who used to work for Félicité de Genlis in some menial capacity. That's how he got involved with Orléans. I respect him really. He's spent years abroad, writing and, you know, talking about it. He deserves a revolution. He's only a pastry-cook's son, but he's very learned, and he gives himself airs because he's suffered so much.'

M. Charpentier was puzzled, angry. 'You, Camille – you who are taking the Duke's money – you admit to us that Réveillon has been victimized – '

'Oh, Réveillon's of no account now. If he didn't say those things, he might have done. He might have been thinking them. The literal truth doesn't matter any more. All that matters is what they think on the streets.'

'God knows,' Charpentier said, 'I like the present scheme of things very little, but I dread to think what will happen if the conduct of reform falls into hands like yours.'

'Reform?' Camille said. 'I'm not talking about reform. The city will explode this summer.'

D'Anton felt sick, shaken by a spasm of grief. He wanted to draw Camille aside, tell him about the baby. That would stop him in his tracks. But he was so happy, arranging the forthcoming slaughter. D'Anton thought, who am I to spoil his week?

VERSAILLES: a great deal of hard thinking has gone into this procession. It isn't just a matter of getting up and walking, you know.

The nation is expectant and hopeful. The long-awaited day is here. Twelve hundred deputies of the Estates walk in solemn procession to the Church of Saint-Louis, where Monseigneur de la Fare, Bishop of Nancy, will address them in a sermon and put God's blessing on their enterprise.

The Clergy, the First Estate: optimistic light of early May glints on congregated mitres, coruscates over the jewel-colours of their robes. The Nobility follows: the same light flashes on three hundred sword-hilts, slithers blithely down three hundred silk-clad backs. Three hundred white hat plumes wave cheerfully in the breeze.

But before them comes the Commons, the Third Estate, commanded by the Master of Ceremonies into plain black cloaks; six hundred strong, like an immense black marching slug. Why not put them into smocks and order them to suck straws? But as they march, the humiliating business takes on a new aspect. These mourning coats are a badge of solidarity. They are called, after all, to attend on the demise of the old order, not to be guests at a costume ball. Above the plain cravats a certain pride shows in their starched faces. We are the men of purpose: goodbye to frippery.

Maximilien de Robespierre walked with a contingent from his own part of the country, between two farmers; if he turned his head he could see the embattled jaws of the Breton deputies. Shoulders trapped him, walled him in. He kept his eyes straight ahead, suppressed his desire to scan the ranks of the cheering crowds that lined the routes. There was no one here who knew him; no one cheering, specifically, for him.

In the crowd Camille had met the Abbé de Bourville. 'You don't recognize me,' the abbé complained, pushing through. 'We were at school together.'

'Yes, but in those days you had a blue tinge, from the cold.'

'I recognized you right away. You've not changed a bit, you look about nineteen.'

'Are you pious now, de Bourville?'

'Not noticeably. Do you ever see Louis Suleau?'

'Never. But I expect he'll turn up.'

They turned back to the procession. For a moment he was swept by an irrational certainty that he, Desmoulins, had arranged all this, that the Estates were marching at his behest, that all Paris and Versailles revolved around his own person.

'There's Orléans.' De Bourville pulled at his arm. 'Look, he's insisting on walking with the Third Estate. Look at the Master of Ceremonies pleading with him. He's broken out in a sweat. Look, that's the Duc de Biron.'

'Yes, I know him. I've been to his house.'

'That's Lafayette.' America's hero stepped out briskly in his silver waistcoat, his pale young face serious and a little abstracted, his peculiarly pointed head hidden under a tricorne hat *à la* Henri Quatre. 'Do you know him too?'

'Only by reputation,' Camille muttered. 'Washington pot-au-feu.'

Bourville laughed. 'You must write that down.'

'I have.'

At the Church of Saint-Louis, de Robespierre had a good seat by an aisle. A good seat, to fidget through the sermon, to be close to the procession of the great. So close; the billowing episcopal sea parted for a second, and between the violet robes and the lawn sleeves the King looked him full in the face without meaning to, the King, overweight in cloth-of-gold; and as the Queen turned her head (this close for the second time, Madame) the heron plumes in her hair seemed to beckon to him, civilly. The Holy Sacrament in its jewelled monstrance was a small sun, ablaze in a bishop's hands; they took their seat on a dais, under a canopy of velvet embroidered with gold fleur-de-lis. Then the choir:

O salutaris hostia
If you could sell the Crown Jewels what could you buy for France?
Quae coeli pandis ostium,
The King looks half-asleep.
Bella premunt hostilia,
The Queen looks proud.
Da robur, fer auxilium.
She looks like a Hapsburg.

Uni trinoque Domino,
Madame Deficit.
Sit sempiterna gloria,
Outside, the women were shouting for Orléans.
Qui vitam sine termino,
There is no one here I know.
Nobis donet in patria.
Camille might be here somewhere. Somewhere.
Amen.

'Look, look,' Camille said to de Bourville. 'Maximilien.'

'Well, so it is. Our dear Thing. I suppose one shouldn't be surprised.'

'I should be there. In that procession. De Robespierre is my intellectual inferior.'

'What?' The abbé turned, amazed. Laughter engulfed him. 'Louis XVI by the grace of God is your intellectual inferior. So no doubt is our Holy Father the Pope. What else would you like to be, besides a deputy?' Camille did not reply. 'Dear, dear.' The abbé affected to wipe his eyes.

'There's Mirabeau,' Camille said. 'He's starting a newspaper. I'm going to write for it.'

'How did you arrange that?'

'I haven't. Tomorrow I will.'

De Bourville looked sideways at him. Camille is a liar, he thinks, always was. No, that's too harsh; let's say, he romances. 'Well, good luck to you,' he said. 'Did you see how the Queen was received? Nasty, wasn't it? They cheered Orléans though. And Lafayette. And Mirabeau.'

And d'Anton, Camille said: under his breath, to try out the sound of it. D'Anton had a big case in hand, would not even come to watch. And Desmoulins, he added. They cheered Desmoulins most of all. He felt a dull ache of disappointment.

It had rained all night. At ten o'clock, when the procession began, the streets had been steaming under the early sun, but by midday the ground was quite hot and dry.

CAMILLE had arranged to spend the night in Versailles at his cousin's apartment; he had made a point of asking this favour of the deputy when there were several people about, so that he could not with dignity refuse. It was well after midnight when he arrived.

'Where on earth have you been till this time?' de Viefville said.

'With the Duc de Biron. And the Comte de Genlis,' Camille murmured.

'Oh I *see*,' de Viefville said. He was annoyed, because he did not know whether to believe him or not. And there was a third party present, inhibiting the good row they might have had.

A young man rose from his quiet seat in the chimney corner. 'I'll leave you, M. de Viefville. But think over what I've said.'

De Viefville made no effort to effect introductions. The young man said to Camille, 'I'm Barnave, you might have heard of me.'

'Everyone has heard of you.'

'Perhaps you think I am only a troublemaker. I do hope to show I'm something more. Good-night, Messieurs.'

He drew the door quietly behind him. Camille would have liked to run after him and ask him questions, try to cement their acquaintance; but his faculty of awe had been overworked that day. This Barnave was the man who in the Dauphiné had stirred up resistance to royal edicts. People called him Tiger – gentle mockery, Camille now saw, of a plain, pleasant, snub-nosed young lawyer.

'What's the matter?' de Viefville inquired. 'Disappointed? Not what you thought?'

'What did he want?'

'Support for his measures. He could only spare me fifteen minutes, and that in the small hours.'

'So are you insulted?'

'You'll see them all tomorrow, jockeying for advantage. They're all in it for what they can grab, if you ask me.'

'Does nothing shake your tiny provincial convictions?' Camille asked. 'You're worse than my father.'

'Camille, if I'd been your father I'd have broken your silly little neck years ago.'

At the palace and across the town, the clocks began to strike one, mournfully concordant; de Viefville turned, walked out of the room, went to bed. Camille took out the draft of his pamphlet 'La France Libre'. He read each page through, tore it once across and dropped it on the fire. It had failed to keep up with the situation. Next week, *deo volente*, next month, he would write it again. In the flames he could see the picture of himself writing, the ink skidding over the paper, his hand scooping the hair off his forehead. When the traffic stopped rumbling under the window he curled up in a chair and fell asleep by the dying fire. At five the light edged between the shutters and the first cart passed with its haul of dark sour bread for the Versailles market. He woke, and sat looking around the strange room, sick apprehension running through him like a slow, cold flame.

THE VALET – who was not like a valet, but like a bodyguard – said: 'Did you write this?'

In his hand he had a copy of Camille's first pamphlet, 'A Philosophy for the French People'. He flourished it, as if it were a writ.

Camille shrank back. Already at eight o'clock, Mirabeau's antechamber was crowded. All Versailles wanted an interview, all Paris. He felt small, insignificant, completely flattened by the man's aggression. 'Yes,' he said. 'My name's on the cover.'

'Good God, the Comte's been after you.' The valet took him by the elbow. 'Come with me.'

Nothing had been easy so far: he could not believe that this was going to be easy. The Comte de Mirabeau was wrapped in a crimson silk dressing-gown, which suggested some antique drapery: as if he waited on a party of sculptors. Unshaven, his face glistened a little with sweat; it was pock-marked, and the shade of putty.

'So I have got the Philosopher,' he said. 'Teutch, give me coffee.' He turned, deliberately. 'Come here.' Camille hesitated. He felt the lack of a net and trident. 'I said come here,' the Comte said sharply. 'I am not dangerous.' He yawned. 'Not at this hour.'

The Comte's scrutiny was like a physical mauling, and designed to overawe. 'I meant to get around to waylaying you in some public place,' he said, 'and having you fetched here. Unfortunately I waste my time, waiting for the King to send for me.'

'He should send for you, Monsieur.'

'Oh, you are a partisan of mine?'

'I have had the honour of arguing from your premises.'

'Oh, I like that,' Mirabeau said mockingly. 'I dearly love a sycophant, Maître Desmoulins.'

Camille cannot understand this: the way Orléans people look at him, the way Mirabeau now looks at him: as if they had plans for him. Nobody has had plans for him, since the priests gave him up.

'You must forgive my appearance,' the Comte said smoothly. 'My affairs keep me up at nights. Not always, I am bound to say, my political ones.'

This is nonsense, Camille sees at once. If it suited the Comte, he would receive his admirers shaven and sober. But nothing he does is without its calculated effect, and by his ease and carelessness, and by his careless apologies for it, he means to dominate and outface the careful and anxious men who wait on him. The Comte looked into the face of his impassive servant Teutch, and laughed uproariously, as if the man had made a joke; then broke off and said, 'I like your writings, Maître Desmoulins. So much emotion, so much heart.'

'I used to write poetry. I see now that I had no talent for it.'

'There are enough constraints, without the metrical, I think.'

'I did not mean to put my heart into it. I expect I meant it to be statesman-like.'

'Leave that to the elderly.' The Comte held up the pamphlet. 'Can you do this again?'

'Oh that – yes, of course.' He had developed a contempt for the first pamphlet, which seemed for a moment to extend to anyone who admired it. 'I can do that . . . like breathing. I don't say like talking, for reasons which will be clear.'

'But you do talk, Maître Desmoulins. You talk to the Palais-Royal.'

'I force myself to do it.'

'Nature framed me for a demogogue.' The Comte turned his head, displaying his better profile. 'How long have you had that stutter?'

He made it sound like some toy, or tasteful innovation. Camille said, 'A very long time. Since I was seven. Since I first went away from home.'

'Did it overset you so much, leaving your people?'

'I don't remember now. I suppose it must have done. Unless I was trying to articulate relief.'

'Ah, that sort of home.' Mirabeau smiled. 'I myself am familiar with every variety of domestic difficulty, from short temper at the breakfast table to the consequences of incest.' He put out a hand, drawing Camille into the room. 'The King – the late King – used to say that there should be a Secretary of State with no other. function but to arbitrate in my family's quarrels. My family, you know, is very old. Very grand.'

'Really? Mine just pretends to be.'

'What is your father?'

'A magistrate.' Honesty compelled him to add. 'I'm afraid I am a great disappointment to him.'

'Don't tell me. I shall never understand the middle classes. I wish you would sit down. I must know something of your biography. Tell me, where were you educated?'

'At Louis-le-Grand. Did you think I was brought up by the local curé?'

Mirabeau put down his coffee cup. 'De Sade was there.'

'He's not entirely typical.'

'I had the bad luck to be incarcerated with de Sade once. I said to him, "Monsieur, I do not wish to associate with you; you cut up women into little pieces." Forgive me, I am digressing.' He sank into a chair, an unmannerly aristocrat who never sought forgiveness for anything. Camille watched him, monstrously vain and conceited, going on like a Great Man. When the Comte moved and spoke, he prowled and roared. When he reposed, he suggested some tatty stuffed lion in a museum of natural history: dead, but not so dead as he might be. 'Continue,' he said.

'Why?'

'Why am I bothering with you? Do you think I want to leave your little talents to the Duke's pack of rascals? I am preparing to give you good advice. Does the Duke give you good advice?'

'No. He has never spoken to me.'

'How pathetically you say it. Of course he has not. But myself, I take an interest. I have men of genius in my employ. I call them my slaves. And I like everyone to be happy, down on the plantation. You know what I am of course?'

Camille remembers how Annette spoke of Mirabeau: a bankrupt, an immoralist. The thought of Annette seems out of place in this stuffy little room crowded with furniture, old hangings on the walls, clocks ticking away, the Comte scratching his chin. The room is strewn with evidence of good living: why do we say good living, he wonders, when we mean extravagance, gluttony and sloth? That the bankruptcy is not discharged does not seem to hinder the Comte from acquiring expensive objects – amongst which it seems he is now numbered. As for immorality, the Comte seems only too eager to admit to it. The wild-beast collection of his ambitions crouches in the corner, hungry for its breakfast and stinking at the end of its chain.

'Well, you have had a nice pause for thought.' The Comte rose in one easy movement, trailing his drapery. He put an arm around Camille's shoulders and drew him into the sunlight that streamed in at the window. The sudden warmth seemed an effulgence of his own. There was liquor on his breath. 'I ought to tell you,' he said, 'that I like to have about me men with complicated and sordid pasts. I am then at my ease. And you, Camille, with your impulses and emotions which you have been selling at the Palais-Royal like poisoned bouquets – ' He touched his hair. 'And your interesting, faint but perceptible shadow of sexual ambivalence – '

'Do you always take people apart in this way?'

'I like you,' Mirabeau said drily, 'because you never deny anything.' He moved away. 'There is a handwritten text circulating, called "La France Libre". Is it yours?'

'Yes. You did not think that anodyne tract you have there was the whole of my output?'

'No, Maître Desmoulins, I did not, and I see that you also have your slaves and your copyists. Tell me your politics – in one word.'

'Republican.'

Mirabeau swore. 'Monarchy is an article of faith with me,' he said. 'I need it, I mean to assert myself through it. Are there many of your underground acquaintances who think as you do?'

'No, not more than half a dozen. That is, I don't think you could find more than half a dozen republicans in the whole country.'

'And why is that, do you suppose?'

'I suppose it's because people cannot bear too much reality. They think the King will whistle them from the gutter and make them ministers. But all that world is going to be destroyed.'

Mirabeau yelled for his valet. 'Teutch, lay out my clothes. Something fairly splendid.'

'Black,' Teutch said, trundling in. 'You're a deputy, aren't you.'

'Dammit, I forgot.' He nodded towards his anteroom. 'It sounds as if they're getting a bit restive out there. Yes, let them all in at once, it will be amusing. Ah, here comes the Genevan government in exile. Good morning, M. Duroveray, M. Dumont, M. Clavière. These are slaves,' he said to Camille in a carrying whisper. 'Clavière wants to be a Minister of Finance. Any country will do for him. Peculiar ambition, very.'

Brissot scuttled up. 'I've been suppressed,' he said. For once, he looked it.

'How sad,' Mirabeau said.

They began to fill the room, the Genevans in pale silk and the deputies in black with folios under their arms, and Brissot in his shabby brown coat, his thin, unpowdered hair cut straight across his forehead in a manner meant to recall the ancient world.

'Pétion, a deputy? Good day to you,' Mirabeau said. 'From where? Chartres? Very good. Thank you for calling on me.'

He turned away; he was talking to three people at once. Either you held his interest, or you didn't. Deputy Pétion didn't. He was a big man, kind-looking and fleshily handsome, like a growing puppy. He looked around the room with a smile. Then his lazy blue eyes focused. 'Ah, the infamous Camille.'

Camille jumped violently. He would have preferred it without the prefix. But it was a beginning.

'I paid a flying visit to Paris,' Pétion explained, 'and I heard your name around the cafés. Then Deputy de Robespierre gave me such a description of you that when I saw you just now I knew you at once.'

'You know de Robespierre?'

'Rather well.'

I doubt that, Camille thought. 'Was it a flattering description?'

'Oh, he thinks the world of you.' Pétion beamed at him. 'Everyone does.' He laughed. 'Don't look so sceptical.'

Mirabeau's voice boomed across the room. 'Brissot, how are they at the Palais-Royal today?' He did not wait for an answer. 'Setting filthy intrigues afoot as usual, I suppose; all except Good Duke Philippe, he's too simple for intrigues. Cunt, cunt, cunt, that's all he thinks about.'

'Please,' Duroveray said. 'My dear Comte, please.'

'A thousand apologies,' the Comte said, 'I forget that you hale from the city of Calvin. It's true though. Teutch has more notion of statesmanship. Far more.'

Brissot shifted from foot to foot. 'Quiet about the Duke,' he hissed. 'Laclos is here.'

'I swear I didn't see you,' the Comte said. 'Shall you carry tales?' His voice was silky. 'How's the dirty-book trade?'

'What are you doing here?' Brissot said to Camille, below the buzz of conversation. 'How did you get on such terms with him?'

'I hardly know.'

'Gentlemen, I want your attention.' Mirabeau pushed Camille in front of him and placed his large be-ringed hands on his shoulders. He was another kind of animal now: boisterously dangerous, a bear got out of the pit. 'This is my new acquisition, M. Desmoulins.'

Deputy Pétion smiled at him amiably. Laclos caught his eye and turned away.

'Now, gentlemen, if you would just give me a moment to dress, Teutch, the door for the gentlemen, and I will be with you directly.' They filed out. 'You stay,' he said to Camille.

There was a sudden silence. The Comte passed his hand over his face. 'What a farce,' he said.

'It seems a waste of time. But I don't know how these things are conducted.'

'You don't know much at all, my dear, but that doesn't stop you having your prim little opinions.' He bounced across the room, arms outstretched. 'The Rise and Rise of the Comte de Mirabeau. They have to see me, they have to see the ogre. Laclos comes here with his pointed nose twitching. Brissot ditto. He wears me out, that man Brissot, he never stays still. I don't mean he runs around the room like you, I mean he fidgets. Incidentally, I presume you are taking money from Orléans? Quite right. One must live, and at other people's expense if at all possible. Teutch,' he said, 'you may shave me, but do not put lather in my mouth, I want to talk.'

'As if that were anything new,' the man said. His employer leaned forward and punched him in the ribs. Teutch spilled a little hot water, but was not otherwise incommoded.

'I'm in demand with the patriots,' Mirabeau said. 'Patriots! You notice how we can't get through a paragraph without using that word? Your pamphlet will be got out, within a month or two.'

Camille sat and looked at him sombrely. He felt calm, as if he were drifting out to sea.

'Publishers are a craven breed,' the Comte said. 'If I had the ordering and disposition of the Inferno, I would keep a special circle for them, where they would grill slowly on white-hot presses.'

Camille's eyes flickered to Mirabeau's face. He found in its temper and tensions some indication that he was not the devil's only steady bet. 'Are you married?' the Comte asked suddenly.

'No, but in a way I am engaged.'

'Has she money?'

'Quite a lot.'

'I warm to you with every admission.' He waved Teutch away. 'I think you had better move in here, at least when you are in Versailles. I'm not sure you're fit to be at large.' He pulled at his cravat. His mood had altered. 'Do you know, Camille,' he said softly, 'you may wonder how you got here, but I wonder the same thing about myself . . . to be here, in Versailles, expecting daily a summons from the Palace, and this on the strength of my writings, my speeches, the support I command among the people . . . to be playing at last my natural role in this Kingdom . . . because the King must send, mustn't he? When all the old solutions have been tried and have failed?'

'I think so. But you must show him clearly how dangerous an opponent you can be.'

'Yes . . . and that will be another gamble. Have you ever tried to kill yourself?'

'It comes up as a possibility from time to time.'

'Everything is a joke,' the Comte snapped. 'I hope you're flippant when you're in the dock for treason.' He dropped his voice again. 'Yes, I take your point, it's been an option. You see, people say they've no regrets, they boast about it, but I, I tell you, I have regrets – the debts I've incurred and daily incur, the women I've ruined and let go, my own nature that I can't curb, that I've never learned to curb, that's never learned to wait and bide its time – yes, I can tell you, death would have been a reprieve, it would have given me time off from myself. But I was a fool. Now I want to be alive so – ' He broke off. He wanted to say that he had been made to suffer, had felt his face ground into his own errors, had been undermined, choked off, demeaned.

'Well, why?'

Mirabeau grinned. 'So I can give them hell,' he said.

*

THE HALL of the Lesser Pleasures, it was called. Until now it had been used for storing scenery for palace theatricals. These two facts occasioned comment.

When the King decided that this hall was a suitable meeting place for the Estates-General, he called in carpenters and painters. They hung the place with velvet and tassels, knocked up some imitation columns and splashed around some gold paint. It was passably splendid, and it was cheap. There were seats to the right and left of the throne for the First and Second Estates; the Commons were to occupy an inadequate number of hard wooden benches at the back.

It began badly. After the King's solemn entry, he surveyed them with a rather foolish smile, and removed his hat. Then he sat down, and put it on again. The brilliant robes and silk coats swept and rustled into their places. Three hundred plumes were raised and replaced on three hundred noble heads. But protocol dictates that in the presence of the monarch, commoners remain hatless and standing.

A moment later a red-faced man clamped his plain hat over his forehead and sat down with as much noise as he found he could make. With one accord, the Third Estate assumed its seat. The Comte de Mirabeau jostled on the benches with the rest.

Unruffled, His Majesty rose to make his speech. It was unreasonable, he had thought personally, to keep the poor men standing all afternoon, since they had already been waiting three hours to be let into the hall. Well, they had taken the initiative, he would not make a 'fuss. He began to speak. A moment later, the back rows leaned into the front rows. What? What did he say?

Immediately it is evident: only giants with brazen lungs will prosper in this hall. Being one such, Mirabeau smiled.

The King said – very little, really. He spoke of the debt burden of the American war. He said that the taxation system might be reformed. He did not say how. M. Barentin rose next: Minister of Justice, Keeper of the Seals. He warned against precipitate action, dangerous innovation; invited the Estates to meet separately the next day, to elect officers, draw up procedures. He sat down.

It is the earnest desire of the Commons that the Estates should meet as one body, and that the votes should be counted individually, by head. Otherwise, the churchmen and the nobles will combine against the Commons; the generous grant of double representation – their six hundred to the three hundred each of the Nobles and the Clergy – will avail them nothing. They might as well go home.

But not before Necker's speech. The Comptroller of Finances rose, to an expectant hush; and Maximilien de Robespierre moved, imperceptibly, forward on his bench. Necker began. You could hear him better than Barentin. It was figures, figures, figures.

After ten minutes, Maximilien de Robespierre's eyes followed the eyes of the other men in the hall. The ladies of the court were stacked on benches like crockery on a shelf, rigid and trapped inside their impossible gowns and stays and trains. Each one sat upright; then, when this exhausted her, leaned back for support against the knees of the lady behind. After ten minutes, those knees would twitch and flex; then the first lady would shoot upright again. Soon she would droop, stir, yawn, twitch, she would shift in the little space allowed, she would rustle and moan silently to herself, and pray for the torture to be over. How they longed to lean forward, drop their addled heads on to their knees! Pride kept them upright – more or less. Poor things, he thought. Poor little creatures. Their spines will break.

The first half hour passed. Necker must have been in here before, to test his voice in the hall, for he had been quite audible; it was just a shame that none of it made any sense. A lead was what we wanted, Max thought, we wanted some – fine phrases, I suppose. Inspiration, call it what you will. Necker was struggling now. His voice was fading. This, clearly, had been anticipated. He had a substitute by him. He passed his notes across. The substitute rose and began. He had a voice like a creaking drawbridge.

Now there was one woman Max watched: the Queen. When her husband spoke, there was some effort at a frowning concentration. When Barentin rose, she had dropped her eyes. Now she looked about her, quite frankly; she scanned the benches of the Commoners. She would watch them, watching her. She would glance down to her lap, move her fingers slightly, to catch the flash of diamonds in the light. She would raise her head, and again the stiff-jawed face would turn, turn. She seemed to be searching, searching. What was she searching for? For one face above the black coats ... An enemy? A friend? Her fan jerked in her hand, like a live bird.

Three hours later, heads reeling, the deputies stumbled out into the sun. A large group gathered at once about Mirabeau, who was dissecting for their instruction the speech of M. Necker. 'It is the speech, gentlemen, that one might expect from a banker's clerk of some small ability ... As for the deficit, it is our best friend. If the King didn't need to raise money, would we be here?'

'We may as well not be here,' a deputy observed, 'if we cannot have the voting by head.' Mirabeau slapped the man on the shoulder, unbalancing him.

Max moved well out of range. He didn't want to risk, even accidentally, being pounded on the back by Mirabeau; and the man was so free with his fists. At once, he felt a tap on his shoulder; it was no more than a tap. He turned. One of the Breton deputies. 'Conference on tactics, tonight, my rooms, eight o'clock, all right?'

Max nodded. *Strategy*, he means, he thought: the art of imposing on the enemy the time, place and conditions for the fight.

Here was Deputy Pétion, bounding up. 'Why lurk so modestly, de Robespierre? Look now – I've found you your friend.' The Deputy dived bravely into the circle around Mirabeau, and in a moment re-emerged: and with him, Camille Desmoulins. Pétion was a sentimental man; gratified, he stood aside to watch the re-union. Mirabeau stumped off in animated conversation with Barnave. Camille put his hands into de Robespierre's. De Robespierre's hands were cool, steady, dry. Camille felt his heart slow. He glanced over his shoulder at the retreating Mirabeau. For a second, he saw the Comte in quite a different light: a tawdry grandee, in some noisy melodrama. He wished to leave the theatre.

On 6 May the Clergy and the Nobility met separately, in the chambers allocated to them. But except for the Hall of the Lesser Pleasures, there was nowhere big enough for the Third Estate.

They were allowed to stay where they were. 'The King has made an error,' de Robespierre said. 'He has left us in possession of the ground.' He surprised himself: perhaps he had learned something after all from his scraps of conversation with Lazare Carnot, the military engineer. One day soon he must undertake the nervous business of addressing this great assembly. Arras seems far, very far away.

The Third Estate cannot actually transact any business, of course. To do so would be to accept their status as a separate assembly. They don't accept it. They ask the two other Estates to come back and join them. Nobility and Clergy refuse. Deadlock.

'So whatever I say next, write it down.'

The Genevan slaves sat about with scraps of paper resting on books propped on their knees. The Comte's papers covered every surface that might have been used as a writing desk. From time to time they exchanged glances, like the knowing veteran revolutionaries they were. The Comte strode about, gesturing with a sheaf of notes. He was wearing his crimson dressing-gown, and the rings on his big hairy hands caught the candlelight and flashed fire into the airless room. It was one a.m. Teutch came in.

TEUTCH: Monsieur –

MIRABEAU: Out.

[*Teutch draws the door closed behind him.*]

MIRABEAU: So, the Nobility don't wish to join us. They have voted against our proposal – by a clear hundred votes. The Clergy don't wish to join us, but their voting was, am I right, 133 to 114?

GENEVANS: You are right.

MIRABEAU: So that's close. That tells us something.

[*He begins to pace. The Genevans scribble. It is 2.15. Teutch comes in.*]

TEUTCH: Monsieur, there is a man here with a very hard name who has been waiting to see you since eleven o'clock.

MIRABEAU: What do you mean, a hard name?

TEUTCH: I can't understand what it is.

MIRABEAU: Well, get him to write it down on a piece of paper and bring it in, can't you, imbecile?

[*Teutch goes out.*]

MIRABEAU [*digressing*]: Necker. What is Necker, in the Lord's name? What are his qualifications for office? What in the name of God makes him *look so good*? I'll tell you what it is – the fellow has no debts, and no mistresses. Can that be what the public wants these days – a Swiss pinch-penny, with no balls? No, Dumont, don't write that down.

DUMONT: You make yourself sound envious of Necker, Mirabeau. Of his position as minister.

[*2.45 a.m. Teutch comes in with a slip of paper. Mirabeau takes it from him in passing and puts it in his pocket.*]

MIRABEAU: Forget Necker. Everybody will, anyway. Return to the point. It seems, then, that the Clergy are our best hope. If we can persuade them to join us . . .

[*At 3.15 he takes the slip of paper out of his pocket.*]

MIRABEAU: De Robespierre. Yes, it is a peculiar name . . . Now, everything depends on those nineteen priests. I must have a speech that will not only invite them to join us, but will inspire them to join us – no commonplace speech, but a great speech. A speech that will set their interest and duty plainly before them.

DUROVERAY: And one that will cover the name of Mirabeau in eternal glory, just by the way.

MIRABEAU: There is that.

[*Teutch comes in.*]

MIRABEAU: Oh, good heavens, am I to endure you walking in and out and slamming the door every two minutes? Is M. de Robepierre still here?

TEUTCH: Yes, Monsieur.

MIRABEAU: How very patient he must be. I wish I had that kind of patience. Well, make the good deputy a cup of chocolate, Teutch, out of your Christian charity, and tell him I will see him soon.

[*4.30 a.m. Mirabeau talks. Occasionally he pauses in front of a mirror to try out the effect of a gesture. M. Dumont has fallen asleep.*]

MIRABEAU: M. de Robinpère still here?

[*5.00 a.m. The leonine brow clears.*]

MIRABEAU: My thanks, my thanks to you all. How can I ever thank you enough? The combination, my dear Duroveray, of your erudition, my dear Dumont, of your – snores – of all your singular talents, welded together by my own genius as an orator –

[*Teutch sticks his head around the door.*]

TEUTCH: Finished, have you? He's still here, you know.

MIRABEAU: Our great work is concluded. Bring him in, bring him in.

[*Dawn is breaking behind the head of the deputy from Arras as he steps into the stuffy little room. The tobacco smoke stings his eyes. He feels at a disadvantage, because his clothes are creased and his gloves are soiled; he should have gone home to change. Mirabeau, in greater disarray, examines him – young, anaemic, tired. De Robespierre has to concentrate to smile, holding out a small hand with bitten nails.*

Bypassing the hand, Mirabeau touches him lightly on the shoulder.]

MIRABEAU: My dear M. Robispère, take a seat. Oh – is there one?

DE ROBESPIERRE: That's all right, I've been sitting for quite a time.

MIRABEAU: Yes, I'm sorry about that. The pressure of business . . .

DE ROBESPIERRE: That's all right.

MIRABEAU: I'm sorry. I try to be available to any deputy who wants me.

DE ROBESPIERRE: I really won't keep you long.

[*Stop apologizing, Mirabeau says to himself. He doesn't mind; he's just said he doesn't mind.*]

MIRABEAU: Is there anything in particular, M. de Robertspierre?

[*The deputy takes some folded papers from his pocket. He hands them to Mirabeau.*]

DE ROBESPIERRE: This is the text of a speech I hope to make tomorrow. I wondered if you'd look at it, give me your comments? Though it's rather long, I know, and you probably want to go to bed . . . ?

MIRABEAU: Of course I'll look at it. It's really no trouble. The subject of your speech, M. de Robespère?

DE ROBESPIERRE: My speech invites the Clergy to join the Third Estate.

[*Mirabeau wheels round. His fist closes on the papers. Duroveray puts his head in his hands and groans unobtrusively.*

But when the Comte turns again to face de Robespierre, his features are composed and his voice is like satin.]

MIRABEAU: M. de Robinpère, I must congratulate you. You have fixed on the very point which should occupy us tomorrow. We must ensure the success of this proposal, must we not?

DE ROBESPIERRE: Certainly.

MIRABEAU: But does it occur to you that other members of our assembly might have fixed on the same point?

DE ROBESPIERRE: Well, yes, it would be odd if no one had. That's why I came to see you, I imagined you knew the plans, we don't want a stream of people all getting up and saying the same thing.

MIRABEAU: It may reassure you to know that I have myself been drafting a little speech which touches on the topic. [*Mirabeau speaks; he also reads.*] May I suggest that the question might be better propounded by some person well-known to our fellow-deputies, some orator of experience? The Clergy may be less inclined to listen to someone who has yet – what shall we say? – who has yet to reveal his remarkable talents.

DE ROBESPIERRE: Reveal? We're not conjurers, Monsieur. We're not here to pull rabbits out of hats.

MIRABEAU: Don't be too sure.

DE ROBESPIERRE: Always supposing that one had remarkable talents, could there be a better time to reveal them?

MIRABEAU: I understand your viewpoint, but I suggest on this occasion you give way, for the common good. You see, I can be sure of carrying my audience with me. Sometimes when a famous name allies himself with a cause –

[*Mirabeau stops abruptly. He can see on the young man's delicate triangular face the pale traces of contempt. Yet his voice is still deferential.*]

DE ROBESPIERRE: My speech is quite a good speech, it makes all the relevant points.

MIRABEAU: Yes, but it is the speaker – I tell you frankly, M. de

Robertpère, that I have spent the whole night working on my speech, and I intend to deliver it, and in all possible cordiality and friendship I must ask you to find another occasion for your debut, or else to confine yourself to a few words in my support.

DE ROBESPIERRE: No, I'm not prepared to do that.

MIRABEAU: Oh, you aren't prepared? [*He sees with pleasure that the deputy flinches when he raises his voice.*] It is I who carry weight at our meetings. You are unknown. They will not even suspend their private conversations to listen to you. Look at this speech, it is prolix, it is overblown, you will be howled down.

DE ROBESPIERRE: There's no point trying to frighten me. [*Not a boast. Mirabeau scrutinizes him. Experience has taught him he can frighten most people.*] Look, I'm not trying to stop you making your speech. If you must, you make yours, then I'll make mine.

MIRABEAU: But God damn you, man, they say exactly the same thing.

DE ROBESPIERRE: I know — but I thought that since you have a name as a demagogue, they might not quite trust you.

MIRABEAU: Demagogue?

DE ROBESPIERRE: Politician.

MIRABEAU: And what are you?

DE ROBESPIERRE: Just an ordinary person.

[*The Comte's face purples, and he runs a hand through his hair, making it stand up like a bush.*]

MIRABEAU: You will make yourself a laughing-stock.

DE ROBESPIERRE: Let me worry about that.

MIRABEAU: You're used to it, I suppose.

[*He turns his back. Through the mirror, Duroveray wavers into life.*]

DUROVERAY: May one suggest a compromise?

DE ROBESPIERRE: No. I offered him a compromise, and he rejected it.

[*There is a silence. Into it, the Comte sighs heavily. Take hold of yourself, Mirabeau, he advises. Now. Conciliate.*]

MIRABEAU: M. de Robinspère, this has all been a misunderstanding. We mustn't quarrel.

[*De Robespierre takes off his spectacles and puts a finger and thumb into the corners of his itching eyes. Mirabeau sees that his left eyelid flickers in a nervous spasm. Victory, he thinks.*]

DE ROBESPIERRE: I must leave you. I'm sure you'd like to get to bed for an hour or two.

[*Mirabeau smiles. De Robespierre looks down at the carpet, where the pages of his speech lie crumpled and torn.*]

MIRABEAU: I'm sorry about that. A symptom of childish rage. [*De Robespierre bends down and picks up the papers, in an easy movement that does not seem tired at all.*] Shall I put them on the fire? [*De Robespierre hands them over, docile. The Comte's muscles visibly relax.*] You must come to dinner sometime, de Robertpère.

DE ROBESPIERRE: Thank you, I'd like that. It doesn't matter about the papers – I've got a draft copy I can read my speech from later today. I always keep my drafts.

[*Out of the corner of his eye Mirabeau sees Duroveray rise, scraping his chair, and inconspicuously put his hand to his heart.*]

MIRABEAU: Teutch.

DE ROBESPIERRE: Don't trouble your man, I can see myself out. By the way, my name is Robespierre.

MIRABEAU: Oh. I thought it was 'de Robespierre.'

ROBESPIERRE: No. Just the plain name.

D'ANTON went to hear Camille speak at the Palais-Royal. He hung to the back of the gathering and tried to find something to lean on, so that he could fold his arms and watch the proceedings with a detached smile. Camille said to him sharply, 'You can't spend all your life leering. It's time you took up an attitude.'

D'Anton asked: 'By that do you mean a pose?'

Camille was now constantly with Mirabeau. His cousin de Viefville would scarcely give him the time of day. At Versailles the deputies talked: as if there were some point in talking. When the Comte took the floor, disapproval rustled like autumn leaves. The court had not sent for him yet; in the evenings he needed much company, to keep his spirits up. The Comte had talks with Lafayette: bring over the liberal nobles, he begged. He told the Abbé Sieyès: work on the poor country curés, their hearts lie with the commoners, not with their bishops. The abbé put his fingertips together: he was a frail, still, wan man, who dropped words from his lips as though they were written in stone, who never joked, never argued: politics, he said, is a science I have made perfect.

Next the Comte pounded on the desk of M. Bailly, the Commoner's chairman, putting his forcible suggestions. M. Bailly viewed him gravely: he was a famous astronomer, and his mind, as someone had said, was more on heavenly revolutions than this terrestrial one. Because 'revolution' was the word now: not just at the Palais-Royal, but here amid the tassels and gold paint. You could hear it on Deputy Pétion's lips as he inclined his powdered head to Deputy Buzot, a personable young lawyer from Evreux. There were twenty or thirty men who always sat together, who kept up a disaffected murmur, and sometimes laughed. Deputy Robespierre's maiden speech was ruled out of order on a technicality.

People wonder what he had done to upset Mirabeau, at this early stage. Mirabeau calls him 'the rabid lamb'.

THE ARCHBISHOP OF AIX came to the Third Estate carrying a piece of stony black bread and weeping crocodile tears. He exhorted the deputies to waste no more time in futile debate. People were starving, and this was the sort of thing they were being given to eat. He held up the bread delicately, between finger and thumb, for inspection; he took out a handkerchief, embroidered with his coat of arms, and dusted from his hands the blue-and-white mould. Deputies said, disgusting. The best thing they could do, the archbishop said, was to forget the procedural wrangles and form a joint committee with the other two Estates, to discuss famine relief.

Robespierre stood up. He began to move towards the rostrum. He fancied that someone might try to stop him, saw them rising in their seats to be there first, so he put his small, neat head down like a bull's and walked as if he meant to shake them off. If they join with the other Estates for one committee session, for one vote, the Third Estate has lost its case. This was a trick, and the archbishop had come to play it. Those few steps seemed like a field, and he was walking uphill in the mud, shouting 'No, no', his voice carried off by the wind. His heart seemed to have jumped up and hardened into his throat, the exact size of the piece of black bread the archbishop held in his hand. He turned, saw below him hundreds of white, blank, upturned faces, and heard his voice in the sudden hush, blistering and coherent:

'Let them sell their carriages, and give the money to the poor . . .'

There is a moment of incomprehension. There is no applause, but a mutter, sharp and curious. People stand up to get a better view. He blushes faintly under their attention. Here everything begins: 1789, 6 June, three p.m.

JUNE 6, seven p.m., Lucile Duplessis's diary:

Must we crawl forever? When shall we find the happiness we all seek? Man is easily dazzled – when he forgets himself he thinks he is happy. No, there is no happiness on the earth, it is only a chimera. When the world no longer exists – but how can it be wiped out? They say there will be nothing any more. Nothing. The sun to lose its brightness, to shine no more. What will become of it. How will it set about becoming nothing?

Her pen hovers, about to underline *nothing*. But it doesn't really need underlining, does it?

Her father says, 'You're not eating, Lucile. You're fading away. What's happening to my pretty girl?'

She's fining down, Father. The angles of her body emerge, shoulder and wrist. There are shadows under her eyes. She refuses to put her hair up. Her eyes were once of the sharp, lively kind; but now she looks at people with a concentrated dark stare.

Her mother says: 'Lucile, I wish you would stop fiddling with your hair. It reminds me – I mean, it irritates me.'

Go out of the room then, Mother: turn your eyes away.

Her heart must be stony, for it seems that it won't break. Every morning she finds herself living, breathing, bodily present, and begins her day in the iron ring of their faces. Looking into her father's eyes she sees the reflection of a happy young woman in her mid-twenties, with two or three pretty children gathered at her knee; in the background is a stalwart, honourable man with a well-pressed coat, a nebulous area where the face should be. She'll not give them that satisfaction. She thinks of means of suicide. But that would be to make an end; and true passion, you know, is never consummated. Better to find a cloister, skewer that metaphysical lust under a starched coif. Or to walk out of the front door one day on a casual errand, into poverty and love and chance.

Miss Languish, d'Anton calls her. It is something to do with the English plays he reads.

On 12 June, three country curés come over to the Third Estate. By the 17th, sixteen more have joined them. The Third Estate now calls itself the 'National Assembly'. On 20 June, the National Assembly finds itself locked out of its hall. Closed for refurbishment, they are told.

M. Bailly is solemn amid the sardonic laughter, summer rain running down his hat. Dr Guillotin, his fellow academician, is at his elbow. 'What about that tennis court down the road?'

Those within earshot stared at him. 'It's not locked – I know it wouldn't give us a lot of room but . . . Well, anybody got a better suggestion?'

At the tennis court they stand President Bailly on a table. They swear an oath, not to separate until they have given France a constitution. Overcome by emotion, the scientist assumes an antique pose. It is, altogether, a Roman moment. 'We'll see how they stick together when the troops move in,' the Comte de Mirabeau says.

Three days later, when they are back in their own premises, the King turns up at their meeting. In an unsteady and hesitant voice he annuls their actions. He will give them a programme of reform, he alone. In silence before him, black coats, bleached cravats, faces of stone: men sitting for their own monuments. He orders them to disperse, and, gathering his sorry majesty, exits in procession.

Mirabeau is at once on his feet. Scrupulously attentive to his own legend, he looks around for the shorthand writers and the press.

The Master of Ceremonies interrupts: will they kindly break up the meeting, as the King has ordered?

MIRABEAU: If you have been told to clear us from this hall, you must ask for orders to use force. We shall leave our seats only at bayonet point. The King can cause us to be killed; tell him we all await death; but he need not hope that we shall separate until we have made the constitution.

Audible only to his neighbour, he adds, 'If they come, we bugger off, quick.'

For a moment all are silent – the cynics, the detractors the rakers-up of the past. The deputies applaud him to the echo. Later they will drop back to let him pass, staring at the invisible wreath of laurels that crowns his unruly hair.

'THE ANSWER'S THE SAME, Camille,' said Momoro the printer. 'I publish this, and we both land in the Bastille. There's no point in revising it, is there, if every version gets worse?'

Camille sighed and picked up his manuscript. 'I'll see you again. That is, I might.'

On the Pont-Neuf that morning a woman had called out to tell his fortune. She had said the usual: wealth, power, success in matters of the heart. But when he had asked her if he would have a long life she had looked at his palm again and given him his money back.

D'Anton was in his office, a great pile of papers before him. 'Come and watch me in court this afternoon,' he invited Camille. 'I'm going to drive your friend Perrin into the ground.'

'Can't you get up any malice, except against the people you meet in court?'

'Malice?' D'Anton was surprised. 'It isn't malice. I get on very well with Perrin. Though not so well as you.'

'I just can't understand how you remain wrapped up in these petty concerns.'

'The fact is,' d'Anton said slowly, 'that I have a living to make. I'd like to take a trip to Versailles and see what's going on, but there you are, I've got Maître Perrin and a snapping pack of litigants waiting for me at two o'clock sharp.'

'Georges-Jacques, what do you want?'

D'Anton grinned. 'What do I ever want?'

'Money. All right. I'll see you get some.'

CAFÉ DU FOY. The Patriotic Society of the Palais-Royal in session. News from Versailles comes in every half-hour. The clergy are going over *en masse*. Tomorrow, they say, it will be fifty of the nobles, led by Orléans.

It is established to the satisfaction of the Society that there is a Famine Plot. Hoarders in high places are starving the people to make them submissive. It must be so: the price of bread is going up every day.

The King is bringing troops from the frontier; they are on the march now, thousand upon thousand of German mercenaries. The immediate peril though are the Brigands; that is what everyone calls them. They camp outside the city walls, and no matter what precautions are taken some slip through each night. These are the refugees from the blighted provinces, from the fields stripped by the hail-storm and the winters before; hungry and violent, they stalk through the streets like prophets, knotty sticks in their hands and their ribs showing through the rags of their clothing. Unescorted women now keep off the streets. Masters arm their apprentices with pick-axe handles. Shopkeepers get new locks fitted. Housemaids going out to queue for bread slip kitchen knives into their aprons. That the Brigands have their uses is a fact noted only by the percipient: the Patriotic Society of the Palais-Royal.

'So they have heard of your exploits in Guise?' Fréron said to Camille.

'Yes, my father sends me this fat package of admonition. This letter came, too.' He proffered it to Fréron. It was from his maybe-relative, Antoine Saint-Just, the well-known juvenile delinquent from Noyon. 'Read it,' he said. 'You might read it out to everyone.'

Fréron took the letter. A minute, difficult hand. 'Why don't you do it?'

Camille shook his head. He's not up to this: speaking in small rooms. ('*Why not?*' He saw Fabre's face looming up, Fabre in the small hours getting beside himself with wrath. ('*How can it be harder than talking to a crowd? How can it possibly be?*')

'Very well,' Fréron said. It didn't suit him personally, for Camille to get too competent about ordinary things.

The letter contained interesting sorts of news: trouble all over Picardy, mobs in the streets, buildings burning, millers and landlords under threat of death. Its tone was that of suppressed glee.

'Well,' Fabre said, 'how I look forward to meeting your cousin! He sounds a most pleasant, pacific type of youth.'

'My father didn't mention all this.' Camille took the letter back. 'Do you think Antoine exaggerates?' He frowned at the letter. 'Oh dear, his spelling doesn't improve . . . He so badly wants something to happen, you see, he's not having much of a life . . . Odd way he punctuates, too, and scatters capital letters around . . . I think I shall go down to Les Halles and talk to the market men.'

'Another of your bad habits, Camille?' Fabre inquired.

'Oh, they are all Picards down there.' Fréron fingered the small pistol in the pocket of his coat. 'Tell them Paris needs them. Tell them to come out on the streets.'

'But Antoine amazes me,' Camille said. 'While you sit here, deploring undue violence in the conventional way, the blood of these tradesmen to him is like – '

'Like what it is to you,' Fabre said. 'Milk and honey, Camille. July is your promised land.'

VII. *Killing Time*

(1789)

JULY 3 1789: de Launay, Governor of the Bastille, to Monsieur de Villedeuil, Minister of State:

I have the honour to inform you that being obliged by current circumstances to suspend taking exercise on the towers, which privilege you were kind enough to grant the Marquis de Sade, yesterday at noon he went to his window and at the top of his voice, so that he could be heard by passers-by and the whole neighbourhood, he yelled that he was being slaughtered, that the Bastille prisoners were being murdered, and would people come to their aid . . . It is out of the question to allow him exercise on the towers, the cannon are loaded and it would be most dangerous. The whole staff would be obliged if you would accede to their wish to have the Marquis de Sade transferred elsewhere without delay.

(signed) De Launay

P.S. He threatens to shout again.

IN THE FIRST WEEK of July Laclos went out on a foray. There were just a few names to be added to the payroll at this last minute.

On the very day he had heard Camille Desmoulins speak at the Palais-Royal, a copy of his unpublished pamphlet, circulating in manuscript, had come into the Duke's hands. The Duke declared it made his eyes ache, but said, 'This man, the one who wrote this, he might be useful to us, eh?'

'I know him,' Laclos said.

'Oh, good man. Look him up, will you?'

Laclos could not imagine why the Duke thought Desmoulins must be some old acquaintance of his.

At the Café du Foy Fabre d'Églantine was reading aloud from his latest work. It didn't sound promising. Laclos marked him down as a man who would soon need more money. He had a low opinion of Fabre, but then, he thought, there are some jobs for which you need a fool.

Camille came up to him inconspicuously, willing to be steered aside. 'Will it be the 12th?' he asked.

Laclos was appalled by his directness: as if he did not see the infinite patience, the infinite complexity . . . 'The 12th is no longer possible. We plan for the 15th.'

'Mirabeau says that by the 13th the Swiss and German troops will be here.'

'We must take a chance on that. Communications are what worry me. You could be massacring the entire population in one district, and half a mile away they wouldn't know anything about it.' He took a sip of coffee. 'There is talk, you know, of forming a citizen militia.'

'Mirabeau says the shopkeepers are more worried about the brigands than the troops, and that's why they want a militia.'

'Will you stop,' Laclos said with a flash of irritation, 'will you stop quoting Mirabeau at me? I don't need his opinions secondhand when I can hear the man himself shouting his mouth off every day in the Assembly. The trouble with you is that you get these obsessions with people.'

Laclos has only known him a matter of weeks; already he is launched on 'the trouble with you . . . ' Is there no end to it? 'You're only angry,' Camille said, 'because you haven't been able to buy Mirabeau for the Duke.'

'I'm sure we will soon agree on an amount. Anyway, there's talk of asking Lafayette – Washington pot-au-feu, as you so aptly call him – to take charge of this citizen militia. I need hardly point out to you that this will not do at all.'

'No indeed. Lafayette is so rich that he could buy the Duke.'

'That is not for you to concern yourself with,' Laclos said coldly. 'I want you to tell me about Robespierre.'

'Forget it,' Camille said.

'Oh, he may have his uses in the Assembly. I agree he's not the most stylish performer as yet. They laugh at him, but he improves, he improves.'

'I'm not questioning that he's of use. I'm saying you won't be able to buy him. And he won't come with you for love of the Duke. He's not interested in factions.'

'Then what is he interested in? If you tell me, I will arrange it. What are the man's weaknesses, that's all I require to know. What are his vices?'

'He has no weaknesses, as far as I can see. And he certainly has no vices.'

Laclos was perturbed. 'Everyone has some.'

'In your novel, perhaps.'

'Well, this is certainly stranger than fiction,' Laclos said. 'Are you telling me the man is not in want of funds? Of a job? Of a woman?'

'I don't know anything about his bank account. If he wants a woman, I should think he can get one for himself.'

'Or perhaps – well now, you've known each other for a long time, haven't you? He isn't perhaps *otherwise* inclined?'

'Oh no. Good God.' Camille put his cup down. 'Absolutely not.'

'Yes, I agree it's difficult to imagine,' Laclos said. He frowned. He was good at imagining what went on in other people's beds – after all, it was his stock-in-trade. Yet the deputy from Artois had a curious innocence about him. Laclos could only imagine that when he was in bed, he slept. 'Leave it for now,' he said. 'It sounds as if M. Robespierre is more trouble than he's worth. Tell me about Legendre, this butcher – they tell me the man will say anything, and has a formidable pair of lungs.'

'I wouldn't have thought he was in the Duke's class. He must be desperate.'

Laclos pictured the Duke's bland, perpetually inattentive face. 'Desperate times, my dear,' he said with a smile.

'If you want someone in the Cordeliers district, there is someone much much better than Legendre. Someone with a trained pair of lungs.'

'You mean Georges d'Anton. Yes, I have him on file. He is the King's Councillor who refused a good post under Barentin last year. Strange that you should recommend to me someone who recommends himself to Barentin. He turned down another offer later – oh, didn't he tell you? You should be omniscient, like me. Well – what about him?'

'He knows everybody in the district. He is an extremely articulate man, he has a very forceful personality. His opinions are – not extreme. He could be persuaded to channel them.'

Laclos looked up. 'You do think well of him, I see.'

Camille blushed as if he had been detected in a petty deception. Laclos looked at him with his knowing blue eyes, his head tilted to one side. 'I recollect d'Anton. Great ugly brute of a man. A sort of poor man's Mirabeau, isn't he? Really, Camille, why do you have such peculiar taste?'

'I can't answer all your questions at once, Laclos. Maître d'Anton is in debt.'

Laclos smiled a simple pleased smile, as if a weight had been taken off his mind. It was one of his operating principles that a man in debt could be seduced by quite small amounts, while a man who was comfortably-off must be tempted by sums that gave his avarice a new dimension. The Duke's coffers were well-supplied, and indeed he had recently been offered a token of good will by the Prussian Ambassador, whose King was always anxious to upset a French reigning monarch. Still, his cash was not inexhaustible; it amused Laclos to make small economies. He considered d'Anton with guarded interest. 'How much for his good will?'

'I'll negotiate for you,' Camille said with alacrity. 'Most people would want a commission, but in this case I'll forgo it as a mark of my esteem for the Duke.'

'You're very cocksure,' Laclos said, needled. 'I'm not paying out unless I know he's safe.'

'But we're all corruptible, aren't we? Or so you say. Listen, Laclos, move now, before the situation is taken out of your hands. If the court comes to its senses and starts to pay out, your friends will desert you by the score.'

'Let me say,' Laclos remarked, 'that it does appear that you are less than wholly devoted to the Duke's interests yourself.'

'Some of us were discussing what plans you might have, after-wards, for the less-than-wholly-devoted.'

Camille waited. Laclos thought, how about a one-way ticket to Pennsylvania? You'd enjoy life among the Quakers. Alternatively, how about a nice dip in the Seine? He said, 'You stick with the Duke, my boy. I promise you'll do well out of it.'

'Oh, you can be sure I'll do well out of it.' Camille leaned back in his chair. 'Has it ever occurred to you, Laclos, that you might be helping me to my revolution, and not vice versa? It might be like one of those novels where the characters take over and leave the author behind.'

Laclos brought his fist down on the table and raised his voice. 'You always want to push it, don't you?' he said. 'You always want to have the last word?'

'Laclos,' Camille said, 'everyone is looking at you.' It was now impossible to go on. Laclos apologized as they parted. He was annoyed with himself for having lost his temper with a cheap pamphleteer, and the apology was his penance. As he walked he composed his face to its usual urbanity. Camille watched him go. This won't do, he thought. If this goes on I'll have no soul to sell when someone makes me a really fair offer. He hurried away, to break to d'Anton the excellent news that he was about to be offered a bribe.

JULY 11: Camille turned up at Robespierre's lodgings at Versailles. 'Mirabeau has told the King to pull his troops out of Paris,' he said. 'Louis won't; but those troops are not to be relied on. The Queen's cabal is trying to get M. Necker sacked. And now the King says he will send the Assembly to the provinces.'

Robespierre was writing a letter to Augustin and Charlotte. He looked up. 'The Estates-General is what he still calls it.'

'Yes. So I came to see if you were packing your bags.'

'Far from it. I'm just settling in.'

Camille wandered about the room. 'You're very calm.'

'I'm learning patience through listening to the Assembly's daily ration of drivel.'

'Oh, you don't think much of your colleagues. Mirabeau – you hate him.'

'Don't overstate my case for me.' Robespierre put his pen down. 'Camille, come here, let me look at you.'

'No, why?' Camille said nervously. 'Max, tell me what I should do. My opinions will go soft. The republic – the Comte laughs at it. He makes me write, he tells me what to write, and he hardly lets me out of his sight. I sit beside him each night at dinner. The food is good, so is the wine, so is the conversation.' He threw his hands out. 'He's corrupting me.'

'Don't be such a prig,' Robespierre said unexpectedly. 'He can get you on in the world, and that's what you need at the moment. You should be there, not here. I can't give you what he can.'

Robespierre knows – he almost always knows – exactly what will happen. Camille is sharp and clever, but he gives no evidence of any ideas about self-preservation. He has seen Mirabeau with him in public, one arm draped around his shoulders, as if he were some tart he'd picked up at the Palais-Royal. All this is distasteful; and the Comte's larger motives, his wider ambitions, are as clear as if Dr Guillotin had him on a dissecting table. For the moment, Camille is enjoying himself. The Comte is bringing on his talents. He enjoys the flattery and fuss; then he comes for absolution. Their relationship has fallen back into its old pattern, as if the last decade were the flick of an eyelid. He knows all about the disillusionment that Camille will suffer one day, but there's no point in trying to tell him: let him live through it. It's like disappointments in love. Everyone must have them. Or so he is told.

'Did I tell you about Anaïs, this girl I'm supposed to be engaged to? Augustin tells me I suddenly have rivals.'

'What, since you left?'

'So it seems. Hardly repining, is she?'

'Do you feel hurt?'

He considered. 'Oh, well, you know, I have always been vastly full of *amour propre*, haven't I? No . . . ' He smiled. 'She's a nice girl, Anaïs, but she's not over-bright. The truth is, it was all set up by other people anyway.'

'Why did you go along with it?'

'For the sake of a quiet life.'

Camille wandered across the room. He opened the window a little wider, and leaned out. 'What's going to happen?' he asked. 'Revolution is inevitable.'

'Oh yes. But God works through men.'

'And so?'

'Somebody must break the deadlock between the Assembly and the King.'

'But in the real world, of real actions?'

'And it must be Mirabeau, I suppose. All right, nobody trusts him, but if he gave the signal – '

'Deadlock. Signal.' Camille slammed the window shut. He crossed the room. Robespierre removed the ink from the path of his ire. 'Is a signal something you give by waving your arms?' He fell to his knees. Robespierre took his arms and tried to pull him to his feet. 'Good, this is real,' Camille said. 'I am kneeling on the floor, you are trying to get me on my feet. Not metaphorically, but actually. Look,' he said, hurling himself out of his friend's grasp, 'now I have fallen straight over on my face. This is action,' Camille said to the carpet. 'Now, can you distinguish what has just happened from what happens when somebody says "the country is on its knees"?'

'Of course I can. Please get up.'

Camille stood up and brushed himself down a little.

'You terrify me,' Robespierre said. He turned away and sat down at the table where he had been writing the letter. He took off his spectacles, rested his elbows on the table and covered his closed eyes with his fingertips. 'Metaphors are good,' he said. 'I like metaphors. Metaphors don't kill people.'

'They're killing me. If I hear another mention of rising tides or crumbling edifices I shall throw myself out of the window. I can't listen to this talk any more. I saw Laclos the other day. I was so disgusted, finally, I thought I shall have to do something by myself.'

Robespierre picked up his pen and added a phrase to his letter. 'I am afraid of civil disorder,' he said.

'Afraid of it? I hope for it. Mirabeau – he has his own interests – but if we had a leader whose name is absolutely clean – '

'I don't know if there's such a man in the Assembly.'

'There's you,' Camille said.

'Oh yes?' He applied himself to the next sentence. 'They call Mirabeau "The Torch of Provence". And do you know what they call me? "The Candle of Arras". '

'But in time, Max – '

'Yes, in time. They think I should hang around viscounts and cultivate rhetorical flourishes. No. *In time*, perhaps, they might respect me. But I don't want them ever to approve of me because if they approve of me I'm finished. I want no kickbacks, no promises, no caucus and no blood on my hands. I'm not their man of destiny, I'm afraid.'

'But are you the man of destiny, inside your own head?'

Robespierre looked down at his letter again. He contemplated a postscript. He reached for his pen. 'No more than you are.'

SUNDAY, 12 JULY: five a.m. D'Anton said, 'Camille, there are no answers to these questions.'

'No?'

'No. But look. Dawn has broken. It's another day. You've made it.'

Camille's questions: suppose I do get Lucile, how shall I go on without Annette? Why have I never achieved anything, not one damn thing? Why won't they publish my pamphlet? Why does my father hate me?

'All right,' d'Anton said. 'Short answers are best. Why should you go on without Annette? Get into both their beds, you're quite capable of it, I suppose it wouldn't be the first time in the history of the world.'

Camille looked at him wonderingly. 'Nothing shocks you these days, does it?'

'May I continue? You've never achieved anything because you're always bloody horizontal. I mean, you're supposed to be at some place, right, and you're not, and people say, God, he's so absent-minded – but I know the truth – you started the day with very good intentions, you might even have been on the way to where you're supposed to be going, and then you just run into somebody, and what's the next thing? You're in bed with them.'

'And that's the day gone,' Camille said. 'Yes, you're right, you're right.'

'So what sort of a foundation for any career – oh, never mind. What was I saying? They won't publish your pamphlet till the situation gives way a bit. As for your father – he doesn't hate you, he probably cares too much, as I do and a very large number of other people. And Christ, you wear me out.'

D'Anton had been in court all day on Friday, and had spent Saturday working solidly. His face was creased with exhaustion. 'Do me a favour.' He got up and walked stiffly to the window. 'If you're going to commit suicide, would you leave it till about Wednesday, when my shipping case is over?'

'I shall go back to Versailles now,' Camille said. 'I have to go and talk to Mirabeau.'

'Poor sod.' D'Anton slept momentarily on his feet. 'It's going to be hotter than ever today.' He swung open the shutter. The glare leapt into the room.

CAMILLE'S DIFFICULTY was not staying awake; it was catching up with his personal effects. It was some time since he had been of fixed address. He wondered, really, if d'Anton could enter into his difficulties. When you turn up unexpectedly at somewhere you used to live, it's very difficult to say to people, 'Take your hands off me, I only came for a clean shirt.' They don't believe you. They think it's a pretext.

And again, he is always in transit. It can easily take three hours to get from Paris to Versailles. Despite his difficulties, he is at Mirabeau's house for the hour when normal people have their breakfast; he has shaved, changed, brushed his hair, he is every inch (he thinks) the modest young advocate waiting on the great man.

Teutch rolled his eyes and pushed him in at the door. 'There's a new cabinet,' he said. 'And it doesn't include HIM.'

Mirabeau was pacing about the room, a vein distended in his temple. He checked his stride for a moment. 'Oh, there you are. Been with fucking Philippe?'

The room was packed: angry faces, faces drawn with anxiety. Deputy Pétion dropped a perspiring hand on his shoulder. 'Well, looking so good, Camille,' he said. 'Me, I've been up all night. You know they sacked Necker? The new cabinet meets this morning, if they can find a Minister of Finance. Three people have already turned it down. Necker's popular – they've really done it this time.'

'Is it Antoinette's fault?'

'They say so. There are deputies here who expected to be arrested, last night.'

'There's time, for arrests.'

'I think,' Pétion said sensibly, 'that some of us ought to go to Paris – Mirabeau, don't you think so?'

Mirabeau glared at him. He thinks a lot of himself, he thought, to interrupt me. 'Why don't you do that?' he growled. He pretended to have forgotten Pétion's name.

As soon as this reaches the Palais-Royal, Camille thought . . . He slid across the room to the Comte's elbow. 'Gabriel, I have to leave now.'

Mirabeau pulled him to his side, sneering – at what, was unclear. He held on to him, and with one large hand swept Camille's hair back from his face. One of Mirabeau's rings caught the corner of his mouth. 'Maître Desmoulins feels he would like to attend a little riot. Sunday morning, Camille: why aren't you at Mass?'

He pulled away. He left the room. He ran down the stairs. He was already in the street when Teutch came pounding after him. He stopped. Teutch stared at him without speaking.

'Does the Comte send me some advice?'

'He does, but I forget what it is now.' He thought. 'Oh yes.' His brow cleared. 'Don't get killed.'

IT IS MID-AFTERNOON, almost three o'clock, when the news about Necker's dismissal reaches the Palais-Royal. The reputation of the mild Swiss financier has been built up with great assiduity – and never more so than in this last week, when his fall has seemed imminent.

The whole populace seems to be out in the open: churning

through the streets and heaving through the squares in the blistering heat to the public gardens with their avenues of chestnut trees and their Orléanist connections. The price of bread has just risen. Foreign troops are camped outside the city. Order is a memory, law has a tenuous hold. The French Guards have deserted their posts and returned to their working-men's interests, and all the back-room skulkers are out in the daylight. Their closed and anaemic faces are marked by nocturnal fancies of hanging, of other public agonies and final solutions; and above this the sun is a wound, a boiling tropical eye.

Under this eye drink is spilled, tempers flash and flare. Wig-makers and clerks, apprentices of all descriptions and scene-shifters, small shopkeepers, brewers, drapers, tanners and porters, knife-grinders, coachmen and public prostitutes; these are the remnants of Titonville. The crowd moves backwards and forwards, scoured by rumour and dangerous unease, always back to the same place: and as this occurs the clock begins to strike.

Until now this has been a joke, a blood sport, a bare-knuckle contest. The crowd is full of women and chidren. The streets stink. Why should the court wait on the political process? Through these alleys the populace can be driven like pigs and massacred in back courts by Germans on horseback. Are they to wait for this to happen? Will the King profane Sunday? Tomorrow is a holiday, the people can die on their own time. The clocks finish striking. This is crucifixion hour, as we all know. It is expedient that one man shall die for the people, and in 1757, before we were born, a man called Damiens dealt the old King a glancing blow with a pocket-knife. His execution is still talked of, a day of screaming entertainment, a fiesta of torment. Thirty-two years have passed: and now here are the executioner's pupils, ready for some bloody jubilee.

Camille's precipitate entry into history came about in this fashion. He was standing in the doorway of the Café du Foy, hot, elated, slightly frightened by the press of people. Someone behind him had said that he might try to address the crowds and so a table had been pushed into the café doorway. For a moment he felt faint. He leaned against this table, bodies hemming him in. He wondered if d'Anton had a hangover. What had possessed him to want to stay up all night? He wished he were in a quiet dark room, alone but, as d'Anton said, bloody horizontal. His heart raced. He wondered if he had eaten anything that day. He supposed not. He felt he would drown in the acrid miasma of sweat, misery and fear.

Three young men, walking abreast, came carving a way through the crowd. Their faces were set, their arms were linked, they were trying to get a bit of something going, and by now he had been present at enough of these street games to understand their mood and its consequences in terms of casualties. Of these men, he recognized two, but the third man he did not know. The third man cried, 'To arms!' The others cried the same.

'What arms?' Camille said. He detached a strand of hair that was sticking to his face and threw out a hand in inquiry. Somebody slapped a pistol into it.

He looked at it as if it had dropped from heaven. 'Is it loaded?'

'Of course it is.' Somebody gave him another pistol. The shock was so great that if the man had not closed his fingers over the handle he would have dropped it. This is the consequence of intellectual rigour, of not letting people get away with a cheap slogan. The man said, 'For God's sake keep it steady, that kind are liable to go off in your face.'

It will certainly be tonight, he thought: the troops will come out of the Champs-de-Mars, there will be arrests, round-ups, exemplary dealings. Suddenly he understood how far the situation had moved on from last week, from yesterday – how far it had moved in the last half-hour. It will certainly be tonight, he thought, and they had better know it; we have run out to the end of our rope.

He had so often rehearsed this moment in his mind that his actions now were automatic; they were fluid and perfectly timed, like the actions of a dream. He had spoken many times from the café doorway. He had to get the first phrase out, the first sentence, then he could get beside himself and do it, and he knew that he could do it better than anyone else: because this is the scrap that God has saved up for him, like the last morsel on a plate.

He put one knee on to the table and scrambled up on to it. He scooped up the firearms. Already he was ringed about by his audience, like the crowds in an amphitheatre. Now he understood the meaning of the phrase 'a sea of faces'; it was a living sea, where panic-striken faces nosed for air before the current pulled them under. But people were hanging out of the upstairs windows of the café and of the buildings around, and the crowd was growing all the time. He was not high enough, or conspicuous. Nobody seemed to be able to see what he needed, and until he began to speak properly he would not be able to make himself heard. He transferred both the pistols to one hand, bundling them against his body, so that if they go off he will be a terrible mess; but he feels uncurably reluctant to part with them for an instant. With his left arm he waved to someone inside the café. A chair was passed out, and planted on the table beside him. 'Will you hold it?' he said. He transferred one of the pistols back to his left hand. It is now two minutes past three.

As he stepped on to the chair he felt it slide a little. He thought it would be amazing if he fell off the chair, but people would say it was typical of him. He felt it being gripped by the back, steadied. It was an ordinary straw-bottomed chair. What if he were Georges-Jacques? He would go straight through it.

He was now at a dizzying height above the crowd. A fetid breeze drifted across the gardens. Another fifteen seconds had passed. He was able to identify certain faces, and surprise at this made him blink: ONE WORD, he thought. There were the police, and there were their spies and informers, men who have been watching him for weeks, the colleagues and accomplices of the men who only a few days before had been cornered and beaten by the crowds and half-drowned in the fountains. But now it is killing time; there were armed men behind them. In sheer fright, he began.

He indicated the policemen, identified them for the crowd. He defied them, he said: either to approach any further, to shoot him down, to try to take him alive. What he is suggesting to the crowd, what he is purveying, is an armed insurrection, the conversion of the city to a battlefield. Already (3.04) he is guilty of a long list of capital offences and if the crowd let the police take him he is finished, except for whatever penalty the law provides. Therefore if they do make the attempt he will certainly shoot one policeman, and he will certainly shoot himself, and hope that he dies quickly: and then the Revolution will be here. This decision takes one half-second, plaited between the phrases he is making. It is five past three. The exact form of the phrases does not matter now. Something is happening underneath his feet; the earth is breaking up. What does the crowd want? To roar. Its wider objectives? No coherent answer. Ask it: it roars. Who are these people? No names. The crowd just wants to grow, to embrace, to weld together, to gather in, to melt, to bay from one throat. If he were not standing here he would be dying anyway, dying between the pages of his letters. If he survives this – death as a reprieve – he will have to write it down, the life that feeds the writing that feeds the life to come, and already he fears he cannot describe the heat, the green leaves of the chestnut trees, the choking dust and the smell of blood and the blithe savagery of his auditors; it will be a voyage into hyperbole, an odyssey of bad taste. Cries and moans and bloody promises circle his head, a scarlet cloud, a new thin pure element in which he floats. For a second he puts his hand to his face and feels at the corner of his mouth the place caught that morning by the Comte's ring; only that tells him, and nothing else, that he inhabits the same body and owns the same flesh.

The police have received a check. A few days ago, on this spot, he said, 'The beast is in the snare: finish it off.' He meant the animal of the old regime, the dispensation he had lived under all his life. But now he sees another beast: the mob. A mob has no soul, it has no conscience, just paws and claws and teeth. He remembers M. Saulce's dog in the Place des Armes, slipped out to riot in the sleepy afternoon; three years old, he leans from the window of the Old House and sees the dog toss a rat into the air and snap its neck. No one will pull him away from this spectacle. No one will chain this dog, no one will lead it home. Suitably he addressed it, leaning out towards the mob, one hand extended, palm upwards, charming it and coaxing it and drawing it on. He has lost one of the pistols, he does not know where, it does not matter. The blood has set like marble in his veins. He means to live forever.

By now the crowd was hoarse and spinning with folly. He jumped down into it. A hundred hands reached for clothes and hair and skin and flesh. People were crying, cursing, making slogans. His name was in their mouths; they knew him. The noise was some horror from the Book of Revelations, hell released and all its companies scouring the streets. Although the quarter-hour has struck, no one knows this. People weep. They pick him up and carry him round the gardens on their shoulders. A voice screams that pikes are to be had, and smoke drifts among the trees. Somewhere a drum begins to beat: not deep, not resonant, but a hard, dry, ferocious note.

CAMILLE DESMOULINS to Jean-Nicolas Desmoulins, at Guise:

You made an error when you would not come to Laon to recommend me to the people who would have had me nominated. But it doesn't matter now. I have written my name on our Revolution in letters larger than those of all our deputies from Picardy.

AS THE EVENING DREW ON, M. Duplessis walked out with a couple of friends who wished to satisfy their curiosity. He took a stout cane, with which he intended to repel working-class bully-boys. Mme Duplessis asked him not to go.

Annette's face was pinched with anxiety. The servants had brought in disgusting rumours, and she was afraid there might be substance to them. Lucile seemed sure there was. She sat conspicuously quietly and modestly, like a lottery winner.

Adèle was at home. She usually was now, unless she was at Versailles paying calls and picking up gossip. She knew deputies' wives and deputies, and all the café talk, and all the voting strategies in the National Assembly.

Lucile went to her room. She took pen and ink, and a piece of paper, and on the paper she wrote, 'Adèle is in love with Maximilien Robespierre.' She tore the strip off the sheet, and crumpled it in her palm.

She picked up some embroidery. She worked slowly, paying close attention to what she was doing. Later she intended to show people the meticulous work she had done that afternoon between a quarter past five and a quarter past six. She thought of practising some scales. When I am married, she thought, I will have a piano: and there will be other innovations.

When Claude got home, he walked straight into his study, coat, cane and all, and slammed the door. Annette understood that he might need a short time to recover himself. 'I'm afraid your father may have received some bad news,' she said.

'How could he,' Adèle said, 'just by going out to see what's happening? I mean, it's not anyone's personal bad news, is it?'

Annette tapped at the door. The girls stood at her elbows. 'Come out,' she said. 'Or shall we come in?'

Claude said, 'The minister has been made a pretext.'

'Necker,' Adèle corrected. 'He's not the minister any more.'

'No.' Claude was torn between his loyalty to his departmental chief and his desire to have his thoughts out in the open. 'You know I never cared for the man. He is a charlatan. But he deserves better than to be made a pretext.'

'My dear,' Annette said, 'there are three women here in considerable agony of mind. Do you think you could bring yourself to be a little more particular in your description of events?'

'They are rioting,' Claude said simply. 'The dismissal of M. Necker has caused a furore. We are plunged into a state of anarchy, and anarchy is not a word I use.'

'Sit down, my dear,' Annette said.

Claude sat, and passed a hand over his eyes. From the wall the old King surveyed them: the present Queen in a cheap print, feathers in her hair and her chin flattered into insignificance: a plaster bust of Louis, looking like a wheelwright's mate: the Abbé Terray, both full-face and in profile.

'There is a state of insurrection,' he said. 'They are setting the customs barriers on fire. They have closed the theatres and broken into the waxworks.'

'Broken into the waxworks?' Annette was conscious of the idiot grin growing on her face. 'What did they want to do that for?'

'How do I know?' Claude raised his voice. 'How should I know what they are doing things for? There are five thousand people, six thousand people, marching on the Tuileries. That is just one procession and there are others coming up to join them. They are destroying the city.'

'But where are the soldiers?'

'Where are they? The King himself would like to know, I'm sure. They might as well be lining the route and cheering, for all the use they are. I thank God the King and Queen are at Versailles, for who knows what might not happen, as at the head of these mobs there is – ' Words failed him. 'There is that person.'

'I don't believe you.' Annette's voice was matter-of-fact. She only said it in courtesy to form; she knew it was true.

'Please yourself. You can read it in the morning paper – if there is one. It appears that he made a speech at the Palais-Royal and that it had a certain effect and that he has now become some sort of hero to these people. To the mob, I should say. The police moved in to arrest him and he unwisely held them off at gunpoint.'

'I'm not sure it was unwise,' Adèle said, 'given the result it seems to have produced.'

'Oh, I should have taken measures,' Claude said. 'I should have sent you both away. I ask what I have done to deserve it, one daughter hobnobbing with radicals and the other planning to plight herself to a criminal.'

'Criminal?' Lucile sounded surprised.

'Yes. He has broken the law.'

'The law will be altered.'

'My God,' Claude said, 'do you tell me? The troops will flatten them.'

'You seem to think that all this is accidental,' Lucile said. 'No, Father, let me speak, I have a right to speak, since I know better than you what is going on. You say there are thousands of rioters, how many thousands you are not sure, but the French Guards will not attack their own people, and most of them indeed are on our side. If they are properly organized they will soon have enough arms to engage the rest of the troops. The Royal Allemand troops will be swamped by sheer force of numbers.'

Claude stared at her. 'Any measures you might have taken are too late,' his wife said in a low voice. Lucile cleared her throat. It was almost a speech she was making, a pale drawing-room imitation. Her hands shook. She wondered if he had been very frightened: if pushed and driven by the crowds he had forgotten the calm at the eye of the storm, the place of safety at the living heart of all the close designs.

'All this was planned,' she said. 'I know there are reinforcements, but they have to cross the river.' She walked to the window. 'Look. No moon tonight. How long will it take them to cross in the dark, with their commanders falling out amongst themselves? They only know how to fight on battlefields, they don't know how to fight in the streets. By tomorrow morning – if they can be held now at the Place Louis XV – the troops will be cleared out of the city centre. And the Paris Electors will have their militia on the streets; they can ask for arms from City Hall. There are guns at the Invalides, forty thousand muskets – '

'Battlefield?' Claude said. 'Reinforcements? How do you know all this? Where did you learn it?'

'Where do you suppose?' she said coolly.

'Electors? Militia? Muskets? Do you happen to know,' he asked, with hysterical sarcasm, 'where they will get the powder and shot?'

'Oh yes,' Lucile said. 'At the Bastille.'

GREEN WAS THE COLOUR they had picked for identification – green, the colour of hope. In the Palais-Royal a girl had given Camille a bit of green ribbon, and since then the people had raided the shops for it and yards and yards of sage-green and apple and emerald and lime stretched over the dusty streets and trailed in the gutters. In the Palais-Royal they had pulled down leaves from the chestnut trees, and now wore them sad and wilting in their hats and buttonholes. The torn, sweet vegetable smell lay in clouds over the afternoon.

By evening they were an army, marching behind their own banners. Though darkness fell, the heat did not abate; and sometime during the night the storm broke, and the crack of thunder overhead vied with the sting and rumble of gunfire and the crash of splintering glass; people sang, orders were bawled into the darkness, all night long there was the thud of boots on cobblestones and the ring of steel. Jagged flashes from the sky lit the devastated streets, and smoke billowed on the winds from the burning barriers. At midnight a drunken grenadier said to Camille, 'I've seen your face somewhere before.'

At dawn, in the rain, he met Hérault de Séchelles; but then he was beyond surprise by now, and would not have passed any comment if he had found himself shoulder to shoulder with Mme du Barry. The judge's face was dirty, his coat was ripped half off his back. In one hand he had a very fine duelling pistol, one of a valuable pair made for Maurice de Saxe: and in the other a meat-cleaver.

'But the waste, the irresponsibility,' Hérault said. 'They've plundered the Saint-Lazare monastery. All that fine furniture, my God, and the silver. Yes, they've raided the cellars, they're lying in the streets vomiting now. What's that you say? Versailles? Did you say "finish it off" or "finish them off"? If so I'd better get a change of clothes, I'd hate to turn up at the palace looking like this. Oh yes,' he said, and he gripped the cleaver and charged back into the crowds, 'it beats filing writs, doesn't it?' He had never been so happy: never, never before.

DUKE PHILIPPE had spent the 12th at his château of Raincy, in the forest of Bondy. On hearing of the events in Paris, he expressed himself 'much surprised and shocked'. 'Which,' says his ex-mistress Mrs Elliot, 'I really thought he was.'

At the King's levee on the morning of the 13th, Philippe was first ignored; then asked by His Majesty (rudely) what he wanted; then told, 'Get back where you came from.' Philippe set off for his house at Mousseaux in a very bad temper, and swore (according to Mrs Elliot) 'that he would never go near them again'.

IN THE AFTERNOON Camille went back to the Cordeliers district. The drunken grenadier was still dogging his footsteps saying, 'I know you from somewhere.' There were four murderous but sober French Guardsmen who were under threat of lynching if anything happened to him; there were several escaped prisoners from La Force. There was a raucous market-wife with a striped skirt, a woollen bonnet, a broad-bladed kitchen knife and a foul tongue; I've taken a fancy to you, she kept saying, you aren't going anywhere from now on without me. There was a pretty young woman with a pistol in the belt of her riding-habit, and her brown hair tied back with a red ribbon and a blue one.

'What happened to the green?' he asked her.

'Somebody remembered that green is the Comte d'Artois's colour. We can't have that – so now it's the Paris colours, red and blue.' She smiled at him with what seemed like old affection. 'Anne Théroigne,' she said. 'We met at one of Fabre's auditions. Remember?'

Her face seemed luminous in the watery light. Now he saw that she was very cold, drenched and shivering. 'The weather has broken,' she said. 'And so much else.'

At the Cour du Commerce the concierge had the doors barred, so he talked to Gabrielle through a window. She was pasty-faced and her hair was in a mess. 'Georges went out with our neighbour, M. Gély,' she said, 'to recruit for the citizens' militia. A few minutes ago Maître Lavaux came by – you know him, he lives across the way? – and he said, "I'm very worried about Georges, he's standing on a table yelling his head off about protecting our homes from the military and the brigands."' She gaped at the people standing behind him. 'Who are these? Are they with you?'

Louise Gély appeared, her face bobbing at Gabrielle's shoulder. 'Hallo,' she said. 'Are you coming in, or are you just going to stand in the street?'

Gabrielle put an arm around her and held her tight. 'I've got her mother in here having the vapours. Georges said to Maître Lavaux, "Come and join us, you've lost your position anyway, the monarchy's finished." Why, why, why did he say that?' Her distraught hand clutched the sill. 'When will he be back? What shall I do?'

'Because it's true,' he said. 'He'll not be long, not Georges. Keep the door locked.'

The drunken grenadier dug him in the ribs. 'That your wife, then?'

He stepped back and looked at the man in amazement. At that point something seemed to snap very loudly inside his head, and they had to prop him against a wall and pour brandy into him, so that soon after that nothing made much sense at all.

Another night on the streets: at five o'clock, the tocsin and the alarm cannon. 'Now it begins in earnest,' Anne Théroigne said. She pulled the ribbons from her hair, and looped them into the button-hole of his coat. Red and blue. 'Red for blood,' she said. 'Blue for heaven.' The colours of Paris: blood-heaven.

At six, they were at the Invalides barracks, negotiating for arms. Someone turned him around gently and pointed out to him where the rays of the early sun blazed on fixed bayonets on the Champs-de-Mars. 'They'll not come,' he said, and they didn't. He heard his own voice saying calming, sensible things, as he looked upwards into the mouths of the cannon, where soldiers stood with lighted tapers in their hands. He was not frightened. Then the negotiation was over, and there was running and shouting. This is called storm-ing the Invalides. For the first time he was frightened. When it was finished he leaned against the wall, and the brown-haired girl put a bayonet into his hands. He put his palm against the blade, and asked in simple curiosity, 'Is it hard to do?'

'Easy,' the drunken grenadier said. 'I've remembered you, you know. It was a matter of a little riot outside the Law Courts, couple of years back. Good day out. Sort of dropped you on the ground and kicked you in the ribs. Sorry about that. Just doing the job. Not done you any harm, by the look of it.'

Camille looked up at him steadily. The soldier was covered in blood, dripping with it, his clothes sodden, his hair matted, grinning through a film of gore. As he watched him he spun on his heels and executed a little dance, holding up his scarlet forearms.

'The Bastille, eh?' he sang. 'Now for the Bastille, eh, the Bastille, the Bastille.'

*

DE LAUNAY, the governor of the Bastille, was a civilian, and he made his surrender wearing a grey frock-coat. Shortly afterwards he tried to stab himself with his sword-stick, but was prevented.

The crowd who pressed around de Launay shouted, 'Kill him.' Members of the French Guard attempted to protect him, shielding him with their bodies. But by the Church of Saint-Louis, some of the crowd tore him away from them, spat at him, and clubbed and kicked him to the ground. When the Guards rescued him, his face was streaming blood, his hair had been torn out in handfuls, and he was barely able to walk.

As they approached City Hall their path was blocked. There was an argument between those who wanted to put the man on trial before hanging him and those who wanted to finish him right away. Crushed and panic-striken, de Launay flung out his arms wide; they were grasped at both sides, so that he no longer had a free hand to wipe away the blood that ran from his scalp wounds into his eyes. Tormented, he struggled and lashed out with his foot. It made contact with the groin of a man named Desnot. Desnot – who was an unemployed cook – screamed in shock and agony. He fell to his knees, clutching himself.

An unknown man stepped from behind him and eyed the prisoner. After one second's hesitation, he took a pace forward and pushed his bayonet into de Launay's stomach. As it was withdrawn, de Launay stumbled forward on to the points of six more weapons. Someone hammered repeatedly at the back of his head with a big piece of wood. His protectors stepped back as he was dragged into the gutter, where he died. Several shots were fired into his smashed and twitching body. Desnot hobbled forward and pushed his way to the front. Somebody said, 'Yours.' He fished in his pocket, his face still twisted in pain, and knelt down by the body. Threading his fingers into the remaining strands of de Launay's hair, he flicked open a small knife, and straining back the corpse's head began to hack away at the throat. Someone offered him a sword, but he was not confident of his ability to manage it; his face betrayed little more than his own discomfort, and he continued digging with his pocket-knife until de Launay's head was quite severed.

CAMILLE SLEPT. His dreams were green, rural, full of clear water. Only at the end the waters ran dark and sticky, the open sewers and the gashed throats. 'Oh, Christ,' a woman's voice said. Choked with tears. His head was held against a not very maternal bosom. 'I am in the grip of strong emotions,' Louise Robert said.

'You've been crying,' he said. He stated the obvious. How long had he slept? An hour, or half a day? He could not understand how he came to be lying on the Roberts' bed. He did not remember how he had got there. 'What time is it?' he asked her.

'Sit up,' she said. 'Sit up and listen to me.' She was a little girl, pallid, with tiny bones. She walked about the room. 'This is not our revolution. This is not ours, or Brissot's or Robespierre's.' She stopped suddenly. 'I knew Robespierre,' she said. 'I suppose I might have been Mme Candle of Arras, if I'd taken trouble. Would that have been a good thing for me?'

'I really don't know.'

'This is Lafayette's revolution,' she said. 'And Bailly's, and fucking Philippe's. But it's a start.' She considered him, both hands at her throat. 'You of all people,' she said.

'Come back.' He held out a hand to her. He felt that he had drifted out on a sea of ice, far far beyond human contact. She sat down beside him, arranging her skirts. 'I have put the shutters of the shop up. No one is interested in delicacies from the colonies. No one has done any shopping for two days.'

'Perhaps there will be no colonies. No slaves.'

She laughed. 'In a while. Don't divert me. I have my job to do. I have to stop you going anywhere near the Bastille, in case your luck runs out.'

'It's not luck.' Barely awake, he is working on his story.

'You may think not,' Louise said.

'If I went to the Bastille, and I were killed, they'd put me in books, wouldn't they?'

'Yes.' She looked at him oddly. 'But you're not going anywhere to be killed.'

'Unless your husband comes home and kills me,' he said, with reference to their situation.

'Oh, yes.' She smiled grimly, eyes elsewhere. 'Actually, I mean to be faithful to François. I think we have a future together.'

We all have a future now. It was not an accident, he thinks, it was not luck. He sees his body, tiny and flat, his hands groping for handholds against the blinding white chalk face of the future, feels his face pressed against the rock, and the giddy lurch of vertigo inside; he has always been climbing. Louise held him tightly. He sagged against her, wanting to sleep. 'Such a *coup de théâtre*,' she whispered. She stroked his hair.

She brought him some coffee. Stay quite, quite still, she said. He watched it go cold. The air around him was electric. He examined the palm of his right hand. Her finger traced the cut, thin as a hair. 'How would you think I got that? I don't remember, but in the context it seems, with people being crushed to death and trampled on –'

'I think you lead a charmed life,' she said. 'Though I never suspected it until now.'

François Robert came home. He stood in the doorway of the room and kissed his wife on the mouth. He took off his coat and gave it to her. Then deliberately he stood in front of a mirror and combed his curly black hair, while Louise waited by him, her head not quite up to his shoulder. When he finished he said, 'The Bastille has been taken.' He crossed the room and looked down at Camille. 'Despite the fact that you were here, you were also there. Eye-witnesses saw you, one of the mainstays of the action. The second man inside was Hérault de Séchelles.' He moved away. 'Is there some more of that coffee?' He sat down. 'All normal life has stopped,' he said, as if to an idiot or small child. He pulled off his boots. 'Everything will be quite different from now on.'

You think that, Camille said tiredly. He could not entirely take in what was said to him. Gravity has not been abolished, the ground below has been spiked. Even at the top of the cliff there are passes and precipices, blank defiles with sides like the sides of the grave. 'I dreamt I was dead,' he said. 'I dreamt I had been buried.' There is a narrow path to the heart of the mountains, stony, ambivalent, the slow-going tedious country of the mind. Still your lies, he says to himself. I did not dream that, I dreamt of water; I dreamt that I was bleeding on the streets. 'You would think that my stutter might have vanished,' he said. 'But life is not as charmed as that. Can you let me have some paper? I ought to write to my father.'

'All right, Camille,' François said. 'Tell him you're famous now.'

PART THREE

Tell many people that your reputation is great; they will repeat it, and these repetitions will make your reputation.

I want to live quickly . . .

'The Theory of Ambition', an essay:
Jean-Marie Hérault de Séchelles

I. *Virgins*

(*1789*)

MONSIEUR SOULÈS, Elector of Paris, was alone on the walls of the Bastille. They had come for him early in the evening and said, Lafayette wants you. De Launay's been murdered, they said, so you're governor *pro tem*. Oh no, he said, why me?

Pull yourself together, man, they'd said; there won't be any more trouble.

Three a.m. on the walls. He had sent back his weary escort. The night's black as a graceless soul: the body yearning towards extinction. From Saint-Antoine, lying below him, a dog howled painfully at the stars. Far to his left a torch licked feebly at the blackness, burning in a wall-bracket: lighting the clammy stones, the weeping ghosts.

Jesus, Mary and Joseph, help us now and in the hour of our deaths.

He was looking into a man's chest, and the man had a musket.

There should be, he thought wildly, a challenge, you are supposed to say, who goes there, friend or foe? What if they say 'foe', and keep coming?

'Who are you?' the chest said.

'I am the governor.'

'The governor is dead and all chopped up into little pieces.'

'So I've heard. I am the new governor. Lafayette sent me.'

'Oh really? Lafayette sent him,' the chest said. There were sniggers from the darkness. 'Let's see your commission.'

Soulès reached inside his coat: handed over the piece of paper that he had kept next to his heart all these nervous hours.

'How do you expect me to read it in this light?' He heard the sound of paper crumpling. 'Right,' the chest said with condescension. 'I am Captain d'Anton, of the Cordeliers Battalion of the citizens' militia, and I am arresting you because you seem to me a very suspicious character. Citizens, carry out your duty.'

Soulès opened his mouth.

'No point shouting. I have inspected the guard. They're drunk and sleeping like the dead. We're taking you to our district headquarters.'

Soulès peered into the darkness. There were at least four armed men behind Captain d'Anton, perhaps more in the shadows.

'Please don't think of resisting.'

The captain had a cultured and precise voice. Small consolation. Keep your head, Soulès told himself grimly.

THEY RANG THE TOCSIN at Saint-André-des-Arts. A hundred people were on the streets within minutes. A lively district, as d'Anton had always said.

'Can't be too careful,' Fabre said. 'Perhaps we should shoot him.'

Soulès said, over and over again, 'I demand to be taken to City Hall.'

'Demand nothing,' d'Anton said. Then a thought seemed to strike him. 'All right. City Hall.'

It was an eventful journey. They had to take an open carriage, as there was nothing else available. There were people already (or still) in the streets, and it was obvious to them that the Cordeliers citizens needed help. They ran along the side of the carriage and shouted, 'Hang him.'

When they arrived, d'Anton said, 'It's much as I thought. The government of the city is in the hands of anyone who turns up and says, "I'm in charge."' For some weeks now, an unofficial body of Electors had been calling itself the Commune, the city government; M. Bailly of the National Assembly, who had presided over the Paris elections, was its organizing spirit. True, there had been a Provost of Paris till yesterday, a royal appointee; but the mobs had murdered him, when they had finished with de Launay. Who runs the city now? Who has the seals, the stamps? This is a question for the daylight hours. The Marquis de Lafayette, an official said, had gone home to bed.

'A fine time to be asleep. Get him down here. What are we to think? A patrol of citizens leaves their beds to inspect the Bastille, wrested from tyrants at enormous cost – they find the guard the worse for drink, and this person, who cannot explain himself, claiming to be in charge.' He turned to his patrol. 'Someone should account to the people. There are skeletons to be counted, one would think. Why, there may be helpless victims chained in dungeons still.'

'Oh, they're all accounted for,' the official said. 'There were only seven people in there, you know.'

Nevertheless, d'Anton thought, the accommodation was always available. 'What about the prisoners' effects?' he asked. 'I myself have heard of a billiard table that went in twenty years ago and has never come out.'

Laughter from the men behind. A blank wild stare from the official. D'Anton's mood was suddenly sober. 'Get Lafayette,' he said.

Jules Paré, released from clerking, grinned into the darkness. Lights flared in the Place de Grève. M. Soulès eyes were drawn irresistibly to the Lanterne – a great iron bracket from which a light swung. At that spot, not many hours earlier, the severed head of the Marquis de Launay had been kicked around like a football among the crowd. 'Pray, M. Soulès,' d'Anton suggested pleasantly.

DAWN HAD BROKEN when Lafayette appeared. D'Anton saw with disappointment that his turn-out was immaculate; but his newly shaven face was flushed along the cheek bones.

'Do you know what time it is?'

'Five o'clock?' d'Anton said helpfully. 'Just guessing. I always thought that soldiers were ready to get up at any time of the night.'

Lafayette turned away for a second. He clenched his fists, and cast up his eyes to the red-fingered sky. When he turned back his voice was crisp and amiable. 'Sorry. That was no way to greet you. Captain d'Anton, isn't it? Of the Cordeliers?'

'And a great admirer of yours, General,' d'Anton said.

'How kind.' Lafayette gazed wonderingly at the subordinate this new world had brought him: this towering, broad-shouldered, scar-faced man. 'I don't know that this was necessary,' he said, 'but I suppose you're only doing your – best.'

'We'll try to make our best good enough,' Captain d'Anton said doggedly.

For an instant, a suspicion crossed the general's mind: was it possible that he was the victim of a practical joke? 'This is M. Soulès. I formally identify him. M. Soulès has my full authority. Yes, of course I'll give him a new piece of paper. Will that do?'

'That will do fine,' the captain said promptly. 'But your word alone will do for me, any time, General.'

'I'll get back home now, Captain d'Anton. If you've quite finished with me.'

The captain didn't understand sarcasm. 'Sleep well,' he said. Lafayette turned smartly, thinking, we really must decide if we're going to salute.

D'Anton wheeled his patrol back to the river, his eyes glinting. Gabrielle was waiting for him at home. 'Why ever did you do it?'

'Shows initiative, doesn't it?'

'You've only annoyed Lafayette.'

'That's what I mean.'

'It's just the sort of game people around here like,' Paré said. 'I should think they really will make you a captain in the militia, d'Anton. Also, I should think they'll elect you president of the district. Everybody knows you, after all.'

'Lafayette knows me,' d'Anton said.

WORD FROM VERSAILLES: M. Necker is recalled. M. Bailly is named Mayor of Paris. Momoro the printer works through the night setting up the type for Camille's pamphlet. Contractors are brought in to demolish the Bastille. People take it away, stone by stone, for souvenirs.

The Emigration begins. The Prince de Condé leaves the country in haste, lawyers' bills and much else unpaid. The King's brother Artois goes; so do the Polignacs, the Queen's favourites.

On 17 July, Mayor Bailly leaves Versailles in a flower-bedecked coach, arrives at City Hall at ten a.m., and immediately sets off back again, amid a crowd of dignitaries, to meet the King. They get as far as the Chaillot fire-pump: mayor, Electors, guards, city keys in silver bowl – and there they meet three hundred deputies and the royal procession, coming the other way.

'Sire,' says Mayor Bailly, 'I bring Your Majesty the keys of your good city of Paris. They are the very ones that were presented to Henri IV; he had reconquered his people, and here the people have reconquered their King.'

It sounds tactless, but he means it kindly. There is spontaneous applause. Militiamen three deep line the route. The Marquis de Lafayette walks in front of the King's coach. Cannon are fired in salute. His Majesty steps down from the coach and accepts from Mayor Bailly the nation's new tricolour cockade: the monarchy's white has been added to the red and the blue. He fastens the cockade to his hat, and the crowd begins to cheer. (He had made his will before he left Versailles.) He walks up the staircase of City Hall under an arch of swords. The delirious crowd pushes around him, jostling him and trying to touch him to see if he feels the same as other people. 'Long live the King,' they shout. (The Queen had not expected to see him again.)

'Let them be,' he says to the soldiers. 'I believe they are truly fond of me.'

Some semblance of normal life takes hold. The shops re-open. An old man, shrunken and bony, with a long white beard, is paraded through the city to wave to the crowds who still hang about on every street. His name is Major Whyte – he is perhaps an Englishman, perhaps an Irishman – and no one knows how long he has been locked up in the Bastille. He seems to enjoy the attention he is getting, though when asked about the circumstances of his incarceration he weeps. On a bad day he does not know who he is at all. On a good day he answers to Julius Caesar.

EXAMINATION of Desnot, July 1789, in Paris:

Being asked if it was with this knife that he had mutilated the head of the Sieur de Launay, he answered that it was with a black knife, a smaller one; and when it was observed to him that it was impossible to cut off heads with so small and weak an instrument, he answered that, in his capacity as cook, he had learned how to handle meat.

*

18 August 1789

At Astley's Amphitheatre, Westminster Bridge
(*after rope-dancing by Signior Spinacuta*)
An Entire New and Splendid Spectacle

THE FRENCH REVOLUTION

From Sunday 12 July to Wednesday 15 July (inclusive)
called

PARIS IN AN UPROAR

displaying one of the grandest and most extraordinary
entertainments that ever appeared
grounded on
Authentic Fact

BOX 3s., PIT 2s., GAL 1s., SIDE GAL 6d.
The doors to be opened at half-past five, to begin at
half-past six o'clock precisely.

CAMILLE WAS NOW *persona non grata* at the rue Condé. He had to rely on Stanislas Fréron to come and go, bring him the news, convey his sentiments (and letters) to Lucile.

'You see,' Fréron told him, 'if I grasp the situation, she loved you for your fine spiritual qualities. Because you were so sensitive, so elevated. Because – as she believed – you were on a different planet from us more coarse-grained mortals. But now what happens? You turn out to be the kind of man who goes storming round the streets covered in mud and blood, inciting butchery.'

D'Anton said that Fréron was 'trying to clear the field for himself, one way or another'. His tone was cynical. He quoted the remark Voltaire had made about Rabbit's father: 'If a snake bit Fréron, the snake would die.'

The truth was – but Fréron was not about to mention this – Lucile was more besotted than ever. Claude Duplessis remained convinced that if he could introduce his daughter to the right man she'd get over her obsession. But he'd have a hard job finding anyone who remotely interested her; if he found them suitable, it followed she wouldn't. Everything about Camille excited her: his unrespectability, his *faux-naïf* little mannerisms, his skittish intellect. Above all, the fact that he'd suddenly become famous.

Fréron – the old family friend – had seen the change in Lucile. A pretty curds-and-whey miss had become a dashing young woman, with a mouth full of political jargon and a knowing light in her eye. Be good in bed, Fréron thought, when she gets there. He himself had a wife, a stay-at-home who hardly counted in his scheme of things. Anything's possible, these days, he thought.

Unfortunately, Lucile had taken up this ludicrous fashion for calling him 'Rabbit'.

CAMILLE didn't sleep much: no time. When he did, his dreams exhausted him. He dreamt, *inter alia*, that the whole world had gone to a party. The scene, variously, was the Place de Grève: Annette's drawing room: the Hall of the Lesser Pleasures. Everyone in the world was at this party. Angélique Charpentier was talking to Hérault de Séchelles; they were comparing notes about him, exploding his fictions. Sophie from Guise, whom he had slept with when he was sixteen, was telling everything to Laclos; Laclos had his notebook out, and Maître Perrin was at his elbow, demanding attention in a lawyer's bellow. The smirking, adhesive Deputy Pétion had linked arms with the dead governor of the Bastille; de Launay flopped about, useless without his head. His old schoolfriend, Louis Suleau, was arguing in the street with Anne Théroigne. Fabre and Robespierre were playing a children's game; they froze like statues when the argument stopped.

He would have worried about these dreams, except that he was going out to dinner every night. He knew they contained a truth; all the people in his life were coming together now. He said to d'Anton, 'What do you think of Robespierre?'

'Max? Splendid little chap.'

'Oh no, you mustn't say that. He's sensitive about his height. He used to be, anyway, when we were at school.'

'Good God,' d'Anton said. 'Then just take it that he's splendid. I haven't time to pussyfoot around people's vanities.'

'And you accuse me of having no tact.'

'Are you trying to start an argument?'

So he never found out what d'Anton thought of Robespierre.

He said to Robespierre, 'What do you think of d'Anton?' Robespierre took off his spectacles and polished them. He mulled over the question. 'Very pleasant,' he said at length.

'But what do you think, really? You're being evasive. I mean you don't just think that someone is pleasant, and that's all you think, surely?'

'Oh, you do, Camille, you do,' Robespierre said gently.

So he never found out what Robespierre thought of d'Anton, either.

THE EX-MINISTER FOULON had once remarked, in a time of famine, that if the people were hungry they could eat grass. Or so it was believed. That was why – and reason enough – on 22 July he was in the Place de Grève, with an audience.

He was under guard, but it seemed likely that the small but ugly crowd, who had plans for him, would tear him away. Lafayette arrived and spoke to them. He had no wish to stand in the way of the people's justice; but at least Foulon should have a fair trial.

'What's the use of a trial,' someone called out, 'for a man who's been convicted these thirty years?'

Foulon was old; it was many years since he had ventured his *bon mot*. To escape this fate he had hidden, and put about rumours of his own death. It was said that a funeral had been conducted over a coffin packed with stones. Tracked down, arrested, he now looked beseechingly at the general. From the narrow streets beyond City Hall, there came the low rumble which Paris now identified as marching feet.

'They're converging,' an aide reported to the general. 'From the Palais-Royal on one hand, and from Saint-Antoine on the other.'

'I know,' the general said. 'I can hear on both sides of my head. How many?'

No one could estimate. Too many. He looked at Foulon without much sympathy. He had no forces on hand; if the city authorities wanted to protect Foulon, they would have to do it themselves. He glanced at his aide, gave a minute shrug.

They pelted Foulon with grass, tied a bunch of it on his back, stuffed his mouth with it. 'Eat up the nice grass,' they urged him. Gagging on the sharp stalks, he was dragged across the Place de Grève, where a rope was tossed over the iron projection of the Lanterne. For a few moments the old man swung where at dusk the great light would swing. Then the rope snapped; he plummeted into the crowd. Mauled and kicked, he was hoisted back into the air. Again the rope broke. The mob's hands grasped him, careful not to deliver the *coup de grâce*. A third noose was placed about the livid neck. This time the rope held. When he was dead, or nearly so, the mob cut off his head and speared it on a pike.

At the same time, Foulon's son-in-law Berthier, the Intendant of Paris, had been arrested in Compiègne and conveyed, glassy-eyed with terror, to City Hall. He was bundled inside, through a crowd that peppered him with crusts of sour black bread. Shortly afterwards he was bundled out again, on his way to the Abbaye prison; shortly after that, he was bundled to his death – strangled perhaps, or finished with a musket-ball, for who knew the moment? And perhaps he was not dead either when a sword began to hack at his neck. His head in turn was stabbed on to a pike. The two processions met and the pikes swayed together, bringing the severed heads nose-to-nose. 'Kiss Daddy!' the mob called out. Berthier's chest was sawn open, and the heart was wrenched out. It was skewered on to a sword, marched to City Hall, and flung down on Bailly's desk. The mayor almost collapsed. The heart was then taken to the Palais-Royal. Blood was squeezed out of it into a glass, and people drank it. They sang:

> A party isn't a party
> When the heart's not in it.

THE NEWS OF THE LYNCHINGS at Paris caused consternation at Versailles, where the Assembly was absorbed in a debate on human rights. There was shock, outrage, protest: where was the militia while this was going on? It was generally believed that Foulon and his son-in-law had been speculators in grain, but the deputies, moving between the Hall of the Lesser Pleasures and the well-stocked larders of their lodgings, had lost touch with what is often called popular sentiment. Disgusted at their hypocrisy, Deputy Barnave asked them, 'This blood that has been shed, was it so pure?' Revolted, they shouted him down, marking him in their minds as dangerous. The debate would resume; they were intent on framing a 'Declaration of the Rights of Man'. Some were heard to mutter that the Assembly should write the constitution first, since rights exist in virtue of laws; but jurisprudence is such a dull subject, and liberty so exciting.

Night of 4 August, the feudal system ceases to exist in France. The Vicomte de Noailles rises and, voice shaking with emotion, gives away all he possesses – not a great deal, as his nickname is 'Lackland'. The National Assembly surges to its feet for a saturnalia of magnanimity; they slough off serfs, game laws, tithes in kind, seigneural courts – and tears of joy stream down their faces. A member passes a note to the President – 'Close the session, they have lost control of themselves.' But the hand of heaven can't hold them back – they vie in the pandemonium to be each more patriotic than the last, they gabble to relinquish what belongs to them and with eagerness even greater what belongs to others. Next week, of course, they will try to backtrack; but it will be too late.

And Camille moves around Versailles spreading a scatter of crumpled paper, generating in the close silence of the summer nights the prose he no longer despises . . .

It is on that night, more so than on Holy Saturday, that we came forth from the wretched bondage of Egypt . . . That night restored to Frenchmen the rights of man, and declared all citizens equal, equally admissable to all offices, places and public employ; again, that night has snatched all civil offices, ecclesiastical and military from wealth, birth and royalty, to give them to the nation as a whole on the basis of merit. That night has taken from Mme d'Epr— her pension of 20,000 livres for having slept with a minister . . . Trade with the Indies is now open to everyone. He who wishes may open a shop. The master tailor, the master shoemaker, the master wig-maker will weep, but the journeymen will rejoice, and there will be lights in the attic windows ... O night disastrous for the Grand Chamber, the clerks, the bailiffs, the lawyers, the valets, for the secretaries, for the under-secretaries, for all plunderers ... But O wonderful night, *vera beata nox*, happy for everyone, since the barriers that excluded so many from honour and employment have been hurled down for ever, and today there no longer exist among the French any distinctions but those of virtue and talent.

A DARK CORNER, in a dark bar: Dr Marat hunched over a table. August 4 was a sick joke, he said.

He scowled at the manuscript in front of him. '*Vera beata nox* – I wish it were true, Camille. But you're myth-making, do you see? You're making a legend of what is happening, a legend of the Revolution. You want to have artistry, you see, where there's only the necessity – ' He broke off. His small body seemed to contract in pain.

'Are you ill?'

'Are you?'

'No, I've just been drinking too much.'

'With your new friends, I suppose.' Marat shuffled back on the bench, the same expression of tension and discomfort on his face; then he considered Camille, his fingers tapping arhythmically on the table top. 'Feeling safe, are we?'

'Not especially. I've been warned I might be arrested.'

'Don't expect the Court to stand on formalities. A man with a knife could do a nice job on you. Or on me for that matter. What I'm going to do is move into the Cordeliers district. Somewhere I can shout for help. Why don't you move in there too?' Marat grinned, showing his dreadful teeth. 'All neighbours together. Very cosy.' He bent his head over the papers, scrabbling through them, stabbing with his forefinger. 'What you say next, I approve. It would have taken the people years of civil war, at any other time, to rid themselves of such enemies as Foulon. And in wars, thousands of people die, don't they? Therefore the lynchings are quite acceptable. They are the humane alternative. You may be made to suffer

for that sentiment, but don't be afraid to take it to the printer.'
Thoughtfully the doctor rubbed the bridge of his flat nose: so
prosaic, the gesture, the tone. 'You see what we must do, Camille,
is to cut off heads. The longer we delay, the more we will have to
decapitate. Write that. The necessity is to kill people, and to cut off
their heads.'

FIRST TENTATIVE SCRAPE of the bow on gut. One, two: d'Anton's
fingers tapped the pommel of his sabre. His neighbours stamped
and shrilled under his window, flourishing seating plans. The
orchestra of the Royal Academy of Music was tuning up. Good idea
of his, hiring them, gives the occasion a bit of tone. There'd also, of
course, be a military band. As president of the district and a captain
in the National Guard (as the citizens' militia now called itself) he
was responsible for all parts of the day's arrangements.

'You're fine,' he said to his wife, not looking at her. He was
sweating inside his new uniform: white breeches, black top-boots,
blue tunic faced with white, scarlet collar proving too tight. Outside,
the sun blistered paint.

'I asked Camille's friend Robespierre to come over for the day,'
he said. 'But he can't take time off from the Assembly. Very conscientious.'

'That poor boy,' Angélique said. 'I can't think what kind of a
family he comes from. I said to him, my dear, aren't you homesick?
Don't you miss your own people? He said – serious as may be –
"Well, Mme Charpentier, I miss my dog."'

'I rather liked him,' Charpentier said. 'How he ever got mixed up
with Camille I can't imagine. Now,' he rubbed his hands, 'what's
the order of the day?'

'Lafayette will be here in fifteen minutes. We all go to Mass, the
priest blesses our new battalion flag, we file out, run it up, march
past, Lafayette stands about looking like a commander-in-chief. I
assume he will expect to be cheered. I should think there'll be
enough oafs to make a respectable din, even in this cynical district.'

'I'm still not sure I understand.' Gabrielle sounded aggrieved. 'Is
the militia on the King's side?'

'Oh, everybody is on the King's side,' her husband said. 'It's just his ministers and his servants and his brothers and his wife we can't stand. Louis is all right, silly old duffer.'

'But why do people say that Lafayette's a republican?'

'In America he's a republican.'

'Are there any republicans here?'

'Very few.'

'Would they kill the King?'

'Heavens, no. We leave that sort of thing to the English.'

'Would they keep him in prison?'

'I don't know. Ask Mme Robert when you see her. She's one of the extremists. Or Camille.'

'So if the National Guard is on the King's side -'

'On the King's side,' he interrupted her, 'as long as he doesn't try to go back to where we were before July.'

'Yes, I understand that. It's on the King's side, and against republicans. But Camille and Louise and François are republicans, aren't they? So if Lafayette told you to arrest them, would you do it?'

'Good God, no. I'm not going to do his dirty work.'

And he thought, we could be a law unto ourselves in this district. I might not be the battalion commander, but he's under my thumb.

Camille arrived, breathless and ebullient. 'The news couldn't be better,' he said. 'In Toulouse my new pamphlet has been burned by the public executioner. It's too kind of them, the publicity will certainly mean a second edition. And in Oléron a bookshop that was selling it has been attacked by *monks*, and they threw out all the stock and started a fire and carved up the bookseller.'

'I don't think that's very funny,' Gabrielle said.

'No. Quite tragic really.'

A pottery outside Paris was turning out his picture on thick glazed crockery in a strident yellow and blue. This is what happens when you become a public figure; people eat their dinners off you.

There was not a breath of wind when they ran up the new flag; it lay around its pole like a lolling tricolour tongue. Gabrielle stood between her father and mother. Her neighbours the Gélys were on her left, little Louise wearing a new hat of which she was insufferably proud. She was conscious of people's eyes upon her: there, they were saying, that's d'Anton's wife. She heard someone say, 'How handsome she is, have they children?' She looked up at her husband, who stood on the church steps, his prize-fighter bulk towering over the ramrod figure of Lafayette. She worked up some contempt for the general, because of her husband's contempt. She could see that they were being polite to each other. The commander of the battalion waved his hat in the air, raised the shout for Lafayette. The crowd cheered; the general acknowledged them with a spare smile. She half closed her eyes against the sun. Behind her she could hear Camille's voice running on, talking to Louise Robert exactly as if she were a man. The deputies from Brittany, he was saying, and the initiative in the Assembly. I wanted to go to Versailles as soon as the Bastille was taken – she heard Mme Robert's muffled agreement – but it should be done as soon as possible. He's talking about another riot, she thought: another Bastille. Then from behind her, there was a shout: '*Vive d'Anton.*'

She turned, amazed and gratified. The cry was taken up. 'It's only a few Cordeliers,' Camille said, apologetically. 'But soon it will be the whole city.'

A few minutes later, the ceremony was over and the party could begin. Georges was down among the crowd, hugging her. 'I was thinking,' Camille said. 'It's time you took out that apostrophe from your name. It doesn't suit the times.'

'You may be right,' her husband said. 'I'll do it gradually – no point making an announcement.'

'No, do it suddenly,' Camille said. 'So that everyone knows where you stand.'

'Bully,' Georges-Jacques said fondly. He was acquiring it too: this appetite for confrontation. 'Do you mind?' he asked her.

'I want you to do whatever you think best,' she said. 'I mean, whatever you think right.'

'Suppose they did not coincide?' Camille asked her. 'I mean, what he thought best and what he thought right?'

'But they would,' she said, flustered. 'Because he is a good man.'

'That is profound. He will suspect you of thinking while he is not in the house.'

Camille had spent the previous day at Versailles, and in the evening had gone with Robespierre to a meeting of the Breton Club. It was the forum now for the liberal deputies, those inclined to the popular cause and suspicious of the Court. Some of the nobles attended; the frenzied Fourth of August had been calculated quite carefully there. Men who were not deputies were welcomed, if their patriotism was well known.

And whose patriotism was better known than his? Robespierre urged him to speak. But he was nervous, had difficulty making himself heard. The stutter was bad. The audience were not patient with him. He was just a mob-orator, an anarchist, as far as they could see. All in all it was a miserable, deflating occasion. Robespierre sat looking at his shoe-buckles. When Camille came down from the rostrum to sit beside him, he didn't look up; just flicked his green eyes sideways, and smiled his patient, meditative smile. No wonder he had no encouragement to offer. Whenever he stood up in the Assembly, unruly members of the nobility would pretend to blow candles out, with a great huffing and puffing; or a few of them would get together and orchestrate their imitation of a rabid lamb. No point him saying, 'You were fine, Camille.' No point in comforting lies.

After the meeting was closed, Mirabeau took the rostrum, and performed for his well-wishers and sycophants an imitation of Mayor Bailly trying to decide whether it was Monday or Tuesday: of Mayor Bailly viewing the moons of Jupiter to find the answer, and finally admitting (with an obscene flourish) that his telescope was too small. Camille was not much entertained by this; he felt almost tearful. Finishing to applause, the Comte strode down from the rostrum, slapped a few backs, and wrung a few hands. Robespierre touched Camille's elbow: 'Let's get off, shall we?' he suggested.

Too late. The Comte spied Camille. He caught him up in a rib-cracking hug. 'You were grand,' he said. 'Ignore these provincials. Leave them to their poxy little standards. None of them could have done what you did. None of them. The fact is, you terrify them.'

Robespierre had faded to the back of the meeting room, trying to get out of the way. Camille looked so cheered up, so delighted at the prospect of terrifying people. Why couldn't he have said what Mirabeau had said? It was all perfectly true. And he wanted to make things right for Camille, he wanted to look after him. Nearly twenty years ago he'd promised to look after him, and he saw nothing to suggest he'd been relieved of the duty. But there it was – he didn't have the gift of saying the right thing. Camille's needs and wishes were a closed book, largely: a volume written in a language he'd never learned. 'Come to supper,' he heard the Comte say. 'And let's tow the lamb along, why don't we? Give him some red meat to fall on.'

There were fourteen at table. Tender beef bled on to the plates. Turbot's slashed flesh breathed the scent of bay leaves and thyme. Blue-black shells of aubergines, seared on top, yielded creamy flesh to the probing knife.

The Comte was living very well these days. It was hard to tell if he was just running up more debts or if he could suddenly afford it; if the latter, one wondered how. He had a secret correspondence with a variety of sources. His public utterances had an air both sonorous and cryptic, and he had bought a diamond on credit for his mistress, the publisher's wife. And how pleasant he was, that evening, to young Robespierre. Why? Politeness costs nothing, he thought. But over these last weeks he had been watching the deputy, noting the frequent dryness of his tone, noting his (apparent) indifference to other people's opinion of him, noting the flicker of ideas through the lawyer's brain that is no doubt, he thought, sufficient unto the day.

All that evening he talked to the Candle of Arras, in a low confidential tone. When you get down to it, he thought, there's not much difference between politics and sex; it's all about power. He didn't suppose he was the first person in the world to make this observation. It's a question of seduction, and how fast and cheap you can effect it: if Camille, he thought, approximates to one of those little milliners who can't make ends meet – in other words, an absolute pushover – then Robespierre is a Carmelite, mind set on becoming Mother Superior. You can't corrupt her; you can wave your cock under her nose, and she's neither shocked nor interested: why should she be, when she hasn't the remotest idea what it's for?

They talked about the King, and whether he should have a veto on the legislation passed by the Assembly. Robespierre thought no. Mirabeau thought yes – or thought he could think yes, if the price were right. They talked about how these things were managed in England; Robespierre corrected his facts in a hurried, half-amused way. He accepted the correction, softened him up; when he was rewarded by a precise triangular smile, he felt a most extraordinary flood of relief.

Eleven o'clock: the rabid lamb excused himself, slipped out of the room. It's something to know he's mortal, that he has to piss like other men. Mirabeau felt strange, unwontedly sober, unwontedly cold. He looked across the table at one of his Genevans. 'That young man will go far,' he said. 'He believes everything he says.'

Brulard de Sillery, Comte de Genlis, stood up, yawned, stretched. 'Thanks, Mirabeau. Time to get down to the serious drinking now. Camille, you coming back with us?'

The invitation seemed to be general. It excluded two people: the Candle of Arras (who was at that moment absent) and the Torch of Provence. The Genevans, self-excluded, stood up and bowed and said their good-nights; they began to fold their napkins and pick up their hats, to adjust their cravats, to twitch at their stockings. Suddenly Mirabeau detested them. He detested their grey silk frock-coats and their exactitude and their grovelling attention to all his demands, he wanted to squash their hats over their eyes and roar out into the night, one comradely arm around his milliner and the other around a bestselling novelist. And this was odd, really; if there was anyone he couldn't stand, it was Laclos, and if there was anyone he would have hated to get drunk with, it was Camille. These wild feelings could only be, he thought, the product of a well-mannered and abstemious evening spent cultivating Maximilien Robespierre.

By the time Robespierre got back, the room would have emptied. They'd be left to exchange a dry little English handshake. Take care of yourself, Candle. Mind how you go, Torch.

THEY HAD TO GET the cards out, of course; de Sillery would never go to bed at all if they didn't. After he had indulged his losing streak, he sat back in his chair and started laughing. 'How annoyed Mr Miles and the Elliots would be, if they knew what I did with the King of England's money.'

'I imagine they have a pretty good idea what you do with it.' Laclos shuffled the pack. 'They don't suppose you devote it to charitable work.'

'Who is Mr Miles?' Camille asked.

Laclos and de Sillery exchanged a glance. 'I think you should tell him,' Laclos said. 'Camille should not live like a careless king, in gross ignorance of where the money comes from.'

'It's very complicated.' Reluctantly, de Sillery laid his cards face-down on the table. 'You know Mrs Elliot, the charming Grace? No doubt you've seen her flitting around the town gathering the political gossip. She does this because she works for the English government. Her various liaisons, you see, have put her in such an interesting position. She was the Prince of Wales's mistress before Philippe brought her to France. Now, of course, Agnès de Buffon is mistress – my wife Félicité arranges these things – but Grace and the Duke are still on the best of terms. Now,' he paused, and rubbed his forehead tiredly, 'Mrs Elliott has two brothers-in-law, Gilbert and Hugh. Hugh lives in Paris, Gilbert comes over every few weeks. And there is another Englishman with whom they associate, a Mr Miles. They are all agents for the British Foreign Office. They are here to observe events, make reports and convey funds to us.'

'Well done, Charles-Alexis,' Laclos said. 'Admirably lucid. More claret?'

Camille said, 'Why?'

'Because the English are deeply interested in our Revolution,' de Sillery said. 'Yes, go on Laclos, push the bottle over. You may think they want us to enjoy the blessings of a Parliament and a con-stitution like theirs, but it is hardly that; they are interested in anything that undermines Louis's position. As is Berlin. As is Vienna. It might be an excellent thing for the English if we dispensed with King Louis and replaced him by King Philippe.'

Deputy Pétion looked up slowly. His large handsome face was

creased with scruple. 'Did you bring us here to burden us with this information?'

'No,' Camille said. 'He is telling us because he has had too much to drink.'

''Tisn't a burden,' Charles-Alexis said. 'It's pretty well generally known. Ask Brissot.'

'I have a great deal of respect for Brissot,' Deputy Pétion insisted.

'Have you so?' Laclos murmured.

'He doesn't seem to me to be the type of man who would engage in this sort of deviousness.'

'Dear Brissot,' Laclos said. 'So unworldly is he that he thinks money appears in his pocket by spontaneous generation. Oh, he knows – but he doesn't admit he knows. He takes care never to make inquiries. If you want to give him a fright, Camille, just walk up to him and say in his ear "William Augustus Miles".'

'If I may make a point,' Pétion interposed, 'Brissot has not the air of a man receiving money. I only ever see him in the one coat, and that is almost out at elbows.'

'Oh, we don't pay him much,' Laclos said. 'He wouldn't know what to do with it. Unlike present company. Who have a taste for the finer things in life. You still don't believe it, Pétion? Tell him, Camille.'

'It's probably true,' Camille said. 'He used to take money from the police. Have casual chats with his friends and report on their political opinions.'

'Now you shock me.' But no: Pétion's tone was controlled.

'How else was he to make a living?' Laclos asked.

Charles-Alexis laughed. 'All these writers and people, they have enough on each other to live by blackmail and get rich. Not so, Camille? They only desist out of fear of being blackmailed back.'

'But you are drawing me into something . . . ' For a moment Pétion looked sober. He rested his forehead in the palm of his hand. 'If I could only think straight about this.'

'It doesn't permit straight thinking,' Camille said. 'Try some other kind.'

Pétion said, 'It will be so difficult to keep any kind of . . . integrity.' '

Laclos poured him another drink. Camille said, 'I want to start a newspaper.'

'And whom did you envisage as your backer?' Laclos said smoothly. He liked to hear people admit they needed the Duke's money.

'The Duke's lucky I'll take his money,' Camille said, 'when there are so many other sources. We may need the Duke, but how much more does the Duke need us.'

'Collectively, he may need you,' Laclos said in the same tone. 'Individually he does not need you at all. Individually you may all jump off the Pont-Neuf and drown your sorry selves. Individually, you can be replaced.'

'Oh, you think so?'

'Yes, Camille, I do think so. You have a prodigiously inflated idea of your own place in the scheme of things.'

Charles-Alexis leaned forward, put a hand on Laclos's arm. 'Careful, old thing. Change of subject?' Laclos swallowed mutinously. He sat in silence, brightening only a little as de Sillery told stories of his wife. Félicité, he said, had kept stacks of notebooks under the marital bed. Sometimes she groped for them as you lay on top of her, labouring in pursuit of ecstasy. Did the Duke find this, he wondered, as off-putting as he always had?

'Your wife's a tiresome woman,' Laclos said. 'And Mirabeau says he's had her.'

'Very likely, very likely,' de Sillery said. 'He's had everybody else. Still, she doesn't do much these days. She's happier organizing it for other people. When I think, my God, when I think back on my life . . . ' He fell into a short reverie. 'Could I ever have imagined I'd end up married to the best-read procuress in Europe?'

'By the way, Camille,' Laclos said, 'Agnès de Buffon was twittering on about your last pamphlet. The prose. She thinks she's a judge. We must introduce you.'

'And to Grace Elliot,' de Sillery said. He and Laclos laughed.

'They'll eat him alive,' Laclos said.

At dawn Laclos opened a window and draped his elegant body

out over the town, breathing in the King's air in gasps. 'No persons in Versailles,' he announced, 'are so inebriated as we. Let me tell you, my pirate crew, every dog has his day, and Philippe's is at hand, soon, soon, August, September, October.'

CAMILLE's new pamphlet came out in September. It bore the title 'A Lecture to Parisians, by the Lanterne' and this epigraph from St Matthew: '*Qui male agit odit lucem.*' Loosely translated by the author: scoundrels abhor the Lanterne. The iron gibbet on the Place de Grève announced itself ready to bear further burdens. It suggested their names. The author's name did not appear; he signed himself 'My Lord Prosecutor to the Lanterne'.

At Versailles, Antoinette read the first two pages only. 'In the normal way of things,' she said to Louis, 'this writer would be put in prison for a very long time.'

The King was reading a geography book. He glanced up. 'Then we must consult Lafayette, I suppose.'

'Are you out of your mind?' his wife asked him coldly: they had developed, in these exigencies, a fairly ordinary manner of talking. 'The Marquis is our sworn enemy. He pays creatures such as this to slander us.'

'So does the Duke,' the King said in a low voice. He found it hard to pronounce Philippe's name. 'Our red cousin,' the Queen called him. 'Which is the more dangerous?'

They pondered. The Queen thought it was Lafayette.

LAFAYETTE read the pamphlet and hummed tunelessly under his breath. He took it to Mayor Bailly. 'Too dangerous,' the mayor said.

'I agree.'

'I mean, to arrest him would be too dangerous. The Cordeliers section, you know. He's moved in.'

'With respect, M. Bailly, I say this writing is treasonable.'

'I can only say, General, that it came pretty near the bone last month when the Marquis de Saint-Huruge sent me an open letter telling me to oppose the King's veto or be lynched. As you're aware, when we arrested the man the Cordeliers made so much trouble I thought it best to let him go again. I don't like it, but there you are. That whole district is spoiling for a fight. Do you know this man Danton, the Cordeliers' president?'

'Yes,' Lafayette said. 'I do indeed.'

Bailly shook his head. 'We must exercise caution. We can't handle any more riots. We mustn't make martyrs, you see.'

'I'm compelled to admit,' Lafayette said, 'that there's sense in what you say. If all the people Desmoulins threatens were strung up tomorrow, it would hardly be a Massacre of the Innocents. So we do nothing. But then our position becomes impossible, because we shall be accused of countenancing mob law.'

'So what would you like to do?'

'Oh, I would like . . . ' Lafayette closed his eyes. 'I would like to send three or four stout fellows across the river with instructions to reduce My Lord Prosecutor to a little red stain on the wall.'

'My dear Marquis!'

'You know I don't mean it,' Lafayette said regretfully. 'But sometimes I wish I were not such an Honourable Gentleman. I often wonder how civilized methods will answer, in dealing with these people.'

'You are the most honourable gentleman in France,' the mayor said stiffly. 'That is generally known.' Universally, he would have said, had he not been an astronomer.

'Why do you think we have such trouble with the Cordeliers section?' Lafayette asked. 'There's this man Danton, and that abortion Marat, and this – ' he indicated the paper. 'By the way, when this is at Versailles it stays with Mirabeau, which may tell us something about Mirabeau.'

'I will make a note of it. You know,' the mayor said mildly, 'considered as literature, the pamphlet is admirable.'

'Don't tell me about literature,' Lafayette said. He was thinking of Berthier's corpse, the bowels trailing from the gashed abdomen. He leaned forward and flicked up the pamphlet with his fingertips. 'Do you know Camille Desmoulins?' he asked. 'Have you seen him? He's one of these law-school boys. Never used anything more dangerous than a paperknife.' He shook his head wonderingly. 'Where do they come from, these people? They're virgins. They've never been to war. They've never been on the hunting field. They've never killed an animal, let alone a man. But they're such *enthusiasts* for murder.'

'As long as they don't have to do it themselves, I suppose,' the mayor said. He remembered the dissected heart on his desk, a shivering lump of butcher's meat.

In Guise: 'How am I to hold my head up on the street?' Jean-Nicolas asked rhetorically. 'The worse of it is, he thinks I should be proud of him. He's known everywhere, he says. He dines with aristocrats every day.'

'As long as he's eating,' Mme Desmoulins said. Proceeding out of her own mouth, the comment surprised her. She had never been one for taking a maternal interest. And equally, Camille had never been one to eat.

'I don't know how I'm to face the Godards. They'll all have read it. There's one thing, though – I bet Rose-Fleur's glad now that they made her break it off.'

'How little you understand women!' his wife said.

Rose-Fleur Godard kept the pamphlet on her sewing-table and quoted it in and out of season, to annoy M. Tarrieux de Tailland, her new fiancé.

D'Anton had read the pamphlet and given it to Gabrielle to read. 'You'd better,' he said. 'Everybody will be talking about it.'

Gabrielle read half, then left it aside. Her reasoning was this: she had, in a manner of speaking, to live with Camille, and she would therefore prefer not to know too much of his opinions. She was quiet now; feeling her way from day to day, like a blind woman in a new house. She never asked Georges what had happened at the meetings of the District Assembly. When new faces appeared at the supper table she simply laid extra places, and tried to keep the conversation light. She was pregnant again. No one expected much of her. No one expected her to bother her head about the state of the nation.

*

THE FAMOUS WRITER, Mercier, introduced Camille into the salons of Paris and Versailles. 'In twenty years time,' Mercier predicted, 'he will be our foremost man of letters.' Twenty years? Camille can't wait twenty minutes.

His mood, at these gatherings, would swing violently, from moment to moment. He would feel exhilarated; then he would feel he was there under false pretences. Society hostesses, who had taken such pains to get him, often felt obliged to pretend not to know who he was. The idea was that his identity should seep and creep out, gradually, so that if anyone wanted to walk out they could do it without making a scene. But the hostesses must have him; they must have the *frisson*, the shock-value. A party isn't a party . . .

His headache had come back; too much hair-tossing, perhaps. The one constant, at these parties, was that he didn't have to say anything. Other people did the talking, around him. About him.

Friday evening, late, the Comtesse de Beauharnais's house: full of young poets to flatter her, and interesting rich Creoles. The airy rooms shimmered: silver, palest blue. Fanny de Beauharnais took his arm: a proprietorial gesture, so different from when no one wanted to own him.

'Arthur Dillon,' she whispered. 'You've not met? Son of the eleventh Viscount Dillon? Sits in the Assembly for Martinique?' A touch, a whisper, a rustle of silk: 'General Dillon? Here is something to pique your curiosity.'

Dillon turned. He was forty years old, a man of singular and refined good looks; almost a caricature aristocrat, with his thin beak of a nose and his small red mouth. 'The Lanterne Attorney,' Fanny whispered. 'Don't tell everybody. Not all at once.'

Dillon looked him over. 'Damned if you're what I expected.' Fanny glided away, a little cloud of perfume billowing in her wake. Dillon's gaze had become fixed, fascinated. 'The times change, and we with them,' he remarked in Latin. He slid a hand on to Camille's shoulder, took him into custody. 'Come and meet my wife.'

Laure Dillon occupied a *chaise-longue*. She wore a white muslin dress spangled with silver; her hair was caught up in a turban of white-and-silver silk gauze. Reclining, Laure was exercising her foible: she carried round with her the stump of a wax candle and, when unoccupied, nibbled it.

'My dear,' Dillon said, 'here's the Lanterne Attorney.'

Laure stirred a little crossly: 'Who?'

'The one who started the riots before the Bastille fell. The one who has people strung up and their heads cut off and so forth.'

'Oh,' Laure looked up. The silver hoops of her earrings shivered in the light. Her beautiful eyes wandered over him. 'Sweet,' she said.

Arthur laughed a little. 'Not much on politics, my wife.'

Laure unglued from her soft lips the warm piece of wax. She sighed; absent-mindedly she fondled the ribbon at the neck of her dress. 'Come to dinner,' she said.

As Dillon steered him back across the room, Camille caught sight of himself: his wan, dark, sharp face. The clocks tinkled eleven. 'Almost time for supper,' Dillon said. He turned, and saw on the Lanterne Attorney's face a look of the most heart-rending bewilderment. 'Don't look like that,' he said earnestly. 'It's *power*, you see. You've got it now. It changes things.'

'I know. I can't get used to it.'

Everywhere he went there was this covert scrutiny, the dropped voices, the glances over shoulders. Who? That? Really?

The general observed him, only minutes later, in the centre of a crowd of women. It seemed that his identity was now known. There was colour in their cheeks, their mouths were slightly ajar, their pulses fluttered at proximity merely. An unedifying spectacle, the general thought: but that's women for you. Three months ago, they'd not have given the boy a second glance.

The general was a kind man. He had undertaken to worry and wonder about Camille, and from that night on – at intervals, over the next five years – he would remember to do so. When he thought about Camille he wanted – stupid as it might seem – to protect him.

SHOULD KING LOUIS have the power to veto the actions of the National Assembly?

'Mme Veto' was the Queen's new name, on the streets.

If there were no veto, Mirabeau said obscurely, one might as well live at Constantinople. But since the people of Paris were solidly opposed to the veto (by and large they thought it was a new tax) Mirabeau cobbled together for the Assembly a speech which was all things to all men, less the work of a statesman than of a country-fair contortionist. In the end, a compromise emerged: the King was left with the power not to block but to delay legislation. Nobody was happy.

Public confusion deepened. Paris, a street-corner orator: 'Only last week the aristocrats were given these Suspensive Vetoes, and already they're using them to buy up all the corn and send it out of the country. That's why we're short of bread.'

OCTOBER: no one quite knew whether the King was contemplating resistance, or flight. In any event, there were new regiments at Versailles, and when the Flanders Regiment arrived the King's Bodyguard gave a banquet for them at the palace.

It was a conspicuous affair, lacking in tact: though the pamphleteers would have bawled Bacchanalia at a packed lunch in the grounds.

When the King appeared, with his wife and the little Dauphin, he was cheered to the echo by inebriated military voices. The child was lifted on to the tables, and walked down them, laughing. Glasses were raised to the confusion of rebels. The tricolour cockade was thrown to the floor and ground under the gentlemen's heels.

That is Saturday, 3 October: Versailles banqueting while Paris starves.

Five o'clock that evening, President Danton was roaring at his District Assembly, his doubled fist pounding the table. The Cordeliers citizens will placard the city, he said. They will revenge this insult to the patriots. They will save Paris from the royal threat. The battalion will call out its brothers-in-arms in every district, they will be the first on the road. They will hale the King to Paris, and have him under their eye. If all else fails it is clear that President Danton will march there himself, and drag Louis back single-handed. I have finished with the King, said the King's Councillor.

Stanislas Maillard, an officer of the Châtelet court, preached to the market-women. He referred, needlessly, to their hungry children. A procession formed. Maillard was a long, gaunt figure, like Death in a picture-book. On his right was a tinker woman, a tramp, known to the down-and-outs as the Queen of Hungary. On his left was a brain-damaged escapee from an asylum, clutching in his hand a bottle of the cheapest spirits. The liquor ran from his nerveless mouth down his chin, and in his flint-coloured eyes there was no expression at all. Sunday.

Monday morning: 'I suppose you think you are going somewhere?' Danton asked his clerks.

They had thought of a day at Versailles, actually.

'Is this a legal practice, or a field headquarters?'

'Danton has an important shipping case,' Paré told Camille, later in the morning. 'He is not to be disturbed. You weren't really thinking of going there yourself, were you?'

'It was just that he gave the impression, at the District Assembly – well, no, I wasn't, not really. By the way, is this the same shipping case he had when the Bastille was taken?'

'The appeal,' Danton said, from behind his bolted door.

SANTERRE, a National Guard battalion commander, leads an assault on City Hall; some money is stolen and papers are torn up. The market-women run through the streets, sweeping up the women they meet, exhorting and threatening them. In the Place de Grève the crowd is collecting arms. They want the National Guard to go to Versailles with them, Lafayette at their head. From nine a.m. to eleven a.m. the Marquis argues with them. A young man tells him, 'The government is deceiving us – we've got to go and bring the King to Paris. If, as they say, he's an imbecile, then we'll have his son for King, you'll be Regent, everything will be better.'

At eleven a.m., Lafayette goes to argue with the Police Committee. All afternoon he is barricaded in, gets the news only in snatches. But by five o'clock he is on the road to Versailles, at the head of fifteen thousand National Guardsmen. The number of the mob is uncounted. It is raining.

An advance party of women have already invaded the Assembly. They are sitting on the deputies' benches, with sodden skirts hitched up and legs spread out, jostling the deputies and making jokes, calling for Mirabeau. A small delegation of the women is admitted to the King's presence, and he promises them all the bread that can be found. Bread or blood? Théroigne is outside, talking to soldiers. She wears a scarlet riding-habit. She is in possession of a sabre. The rain is spoiling the plumes on her hat.

A message to General Lafayette, on the road: the King has decided after all to accept the Declaration of the Rights of Man. Oh really? To the general, weary and dispirited, his hands frozen on the harness and rain running down his pointed nose, it is not the most relevant piece of news.

PARIS: Fabre talking round the cafés, making opinion. 'The point is,' he said, 'one initiates something like this, one should take the credit. Who can deny that the initiative was seized by President Danton and his district? As for the march itself, who better than the women of Paris to undertake it? They won't fire on women.'

Fabre felt no disappointment that Danton had stayed at home; he felt relief. He began to sense dimly the drift of events. Camille was right; in public, before his appropriate audience, Danton had the aura of greatness about him. From now on, Fabre would always urge him to think of his physical safety.

NIGHT. Still raining. Lafayette's men waiting in the darkness, while he is interrogated by the Assembly. What is the reason for this unseemly military demonstration?

In his pocket Lafayette has a desperate note from the president of this same Assembly, begging him to march his men to Versailles and rescue the King. He would like to put his hand in his pocket, to be sure that the message is not a dream, but he cannot do that in front of the Assembly; they would think he was being disrespectful. What would Washington do? he asks himself: without result. So he stands, mud-spattered up to his shoulders, and answers these strange questions as best he can, pleading with the Assembly in an increasingly husky voice – could the King, to save a lot of trouble, be persuaded to make a short speech in favour of the new national colours?

A little later, exhausted, he is assisted into the presence of the King and, still covered in mud, addresses himself to His Majesty, His Majesty's brother the Comte de Provence, the Archbishop of Bordeaux and M. Necker. 'Well,' the King says, 'I suppose you've done what you could.'

Become semi-articulate, the general clasps his hands to his breast in an attitude he has hitherto seen only in paintings, and pledges his life as surety for the King's – he is also the devoted servant of the constitution, and someone, someone, he says, has been paying out a great deal of money.

The Queen stood in the shadows, looking at him with dislike.

He went out, fixed patrols about the palace and the town, watched from a window the low burning of torches and heard drunken singing on the night wind. Ballads, no doubt, relating to Court life. Melancholy swept him, a sort of nostalgia for heroism. He checked his patrols, visited the royal apartments once more. He was not admitted; they had retired for the night.

Towards dawn, he threw himself down fully clothed and shut his eyes. General Morpheus, they called him later.

Sunrise. Drumbeats. One small gate is left unguarded, by negligence or treachery; shooting breaks out, the Bodyguard are overwhelmed, and within minutes there are heads on pikes. The mob are in the palace. Women armed with knives and clubs are sprinting through the galleries towards their victims.

The general awake. Move, and at the double. Before he arrives the mob have reached the door of the Salon de la Œuil de Boeuf, and the National Guardsmen have driven them back. 'Give me the Queen's liver,' a woman screams. 'I want it for a fricassee.' Lafayette – on foot, no time to wait for a horse to be saddled – is not yet inside the château, for he is caught up in a screaming mob who have already got nooses round the necks of members of the Bodyguard. The royal family are safe – just – inside the salon. The royal children are crying. The Queen is barefoot. She has escaped death by the thickness of a door.

Lafayette arrives. He meets the eyes of the barefoot woman – the woman who drove him from Court, who once ridiculed his manners and laughed at his dancing. Now she requires of him more than a courtier's skills. The mob seethes beneath the windows. Lafayette indicates the balcony. 'It is necessary,' he says.

The King steps out. The people shout, 'To Paris.' They wave pikes and level guns. They call for the Queen.

Inside the room, the general makes a gesture of invitation to her. 'Don't you hear what they are shouting?' she says. 'Have you seen the gestures they make?'

'Yes.' Lafayette draws his finger across his throat. 'But either you go to them, or they come for you. Step out, Madame.'

Her face frozen, she takes her children by the hands, steps out on to the balcony. 'No children!' the mob call. The Queen drops the Dauphin's hand; he and his sister are drawn back inside the room.

Antoinette stands alone. Lafayette's mind is racing to consequences – all hell will be let loose, there will be total war by nightfall. He steps out beside her, hoping to shield her with his body if the worst . . . and the people howl . . . and then – O perfect courtier! – he takes the Queen's hand, he raises it, he bows low, he kisses her fingertips.

Immediately, the mood swings around. '*Vive* Lafayette!' He shivers at their fickleness; shivers inside. And '*Vive la reine*,' someone calls. '*Vive la reine!*' That cry has not been heard in a decade. Her fists unclench, her mouth opens a little; he feels her lean against him, floppy with relief. A Bodyguard steps out to assist her, a tricolour cockade in his hat. The crowd cheer. The Queen is handed back inside. The King declares he will go to Paris.

This takes all day.

On the way to Paris Lafayette rides by the King's carriage, and speaks hardly a word. There will be no bodyguards after this, he thinks, except those I provide. I have the nation to protect from the King, and now the King to protect from the people. I saved her life, he thinks. He sees again the white face, the bare feet, feels her sag against him as the crowd cheer. She will never forgive him, he knows. The armed forces are now at my disposal, he thinks, my position should be unassailable . . . but slouching along in the half-dark, the anonymous many, the People. '*Here we have them,*' they cry, '*the baker, the baker's wife, and the baker's little apprentice.*' The National Guardsmen and the Bodyguards exchange hats, and thus make themselves look ridiculous: but more ridiculous still are the bloody defaced heads that bob, league upon league, before the royal carriage.

That was October.

THE ASSEMBLY followed the King to Paris, and took up temporary lodgings in the archbishop's palace. The Breton Club resumed its meetings in the refectory of an empty conventual building in the rue Saint-Jacques. The former tenants, Dominicans, were always called by the people 'Jacobins', and the name stuck to the deputies and journalists and men of affairs who debated there like a second Assembly. They moved, as their numbers grew, into the library; and finally into the old chapel, which had a gallery for the public.

In November the Assembly moved to the premises of what had formerly been an indoor riding-school. The hall was cramped and badly lit, an inconvenient shape, difficult to speak in. Members faced each other across a gangway. One side of the room was broken by the president's seat and the secretaries' table, the other by the speaker's rostrum. The stricter upholders of royal power sat on the right of the gangway; the patriots, as they often called themselves, sat on the left.

Heat was provided by a stove in the middle of the floor, and ventilation was poor. At Dr Guillotin's suggestion, vinegar and herbs were sprinkled twice daily. The public galleries were cramped too, and the three hundred spectators they held could be organized and policed – not necessarily by the authorities.

From now on the Parisians never called the Assembly anything but 'the Riding-School'.

RUE CONDÉ: towards the end of the year, Claude permitted a thaw in relations. Annette gave a party. His daughters asked their friends, and the friends asked their friends. Annette looked around: 'Suppose a fire were to break out?' she said. 'So much of the Revolution would go up in smoke.'

There had been, before the guests arrived, the usual row with Lucile; nothing was accomplished nowadays without one. 'Let me put your hair up,' Annette wheedled. 'Like I used to? With flowers?'

Lucile said vehemently that she would rather die. She didn't want pins, ribbons, blossoms, devices. She wanted a mane that she could toss about, and if she was willing to torture a few curls into it, Annette thought, that was only for greater verisimilitude. 'Oh really,' she said crossly, 'if you're going to impersonate Camille, at least get it right. If you go on like that you'll get a crick in your neck.' Adèle put her hand over her mouth, and snorted with mirth. 'You've got to do it like this,' Annette said, demonstrating. 'You don't *simultaneously* toss your head back and shake the hair out of your eyes. The movements are actually quite separate.'

Lucile tried it, smirking. 'You could be right. Adèle, you have a go. Stand up, you have to stand up to get the effect.'

The three women jostled for the mirror. They began to splutter with laughter, then to shriek and wail. 'Then there's this one,' Lucile said. 'Out of my way, minions, while I show you.' She wiped the smile from her face, stared into the mirror in a rapture of wide-eyed narcissism, and removed an imaginary tendril of hair with a delicate flick.

'Imbecile,' her mother said. 'Your wrist's at quite the wrong angle. Haven't you eyes to see?'

Lucile opened her eyes very wide and gave her a Camille-look. 'I was only born yesterday,' she said pitifully.

Adèle and her mother staggered around the room. Adèle fell on to Annette's bed and sobbed into the pillow. 'Oh, stop it, stop it,' Annette said. Her hair had fallen down and tears were running through her rouge. Lucile subsided to the floor and beat the carpet with her fist. 'I think I'll die,' she said.

Oh, the relief of it! When for months now, the three of them had hardly spoken! They got to their feet, tried to compose themselves; but as they reached for powder and scent, great gouts of laughter burst from one or the other. All evening they're not safe: 'Maître Danton, you know Maximilien Robespierre, don't you?' Annette said, and turned away because tears were beginning to well up in her eyes and her lips were twitching and another scream of laughter was about to be born. Maître Danton had this exceedingly aggressive habit of planting a fist on his hip and frowning, while he was talking about the weather or something equally routine. Deputy Maximilien Robespierre had the most curious way of not blinking, and a way of insinuating himself around the furniture; it would be marvellous to see him spring on a mouse. She left them to their self-importance, guffawing inside.

'So where are you living now?' Danton inquired.

'On the rue Saintonge in the Marais.'

'Comfortable?'

Robespierre didn't reply. He couldn't think what Danton's standard of comfort might be, so anything he said wouldn't mean much. Scruples like this were always tripping him up, in the simplest conversations. Luckily, Danton seemed not to want a reply. 'Most of the deputies don't seem very happy about moving to Paris.'

'Most of them aren't there half the time. When they are they don't pay attention. They sit gossiping to each other about clarifying wine and fattening pigs.'

'They're thinking of home. After all, this is an interruption to their lives.'

Robespierre smiled faintly. He was not supercilious, he just thought that was a peculiar way of looking at things. 'But this is their life.'

'But you can understand it – they think about the farm going to seed and the children growing up and the wife hopping into bed with all and sundry – they're only human.'

Robespierre flicked a glance up at him. 'Really, Danton, the times being what they are, I think we could all do with being a bit more than that.'

Annette moved amongst her guests, trying to discipline her grin to a social smile. Somehow it no longer seemed possible to see her male guests as they wished to be seen. Deputy Pétion (self-regarding smirk) seemed amiable; so did Brissot (a whole set of little tics and twitches). Danton was watching her across the room. Wonder what he's thinking? She had a shrewd idea. She imagined Maître Danton's

drawl: 'Not a bad-looking woman, considering her age.' Fréron
stood alone, conspicuously alone; his eyes followed Lucile.

Camille, as usual these days, had an audience. 'All we really have
to do is decide on a title,' he said. 'And organize the provincial
subscriptions. It's going to come out every Saturday, though more
often when events require it. It will be in octavo, with a grey paper
cover. Brissot is going to write for us, and Fréron, and Marat. We
shall invite correspondence from readers. We shall carry particularly
scathing theatre reviews. The universe and all its follies shall be
comprehended in the pages of this hyper-critical journal.'

'Will it make money?' Claude asked.

'Oh, not at all,' Camille said happily. 'I don't even expect to
cover costs. The idea is to keep the cover price as low as possible,
so that nearly everybody will be able to afford it.'

'How are you going to pay your printer, then?'

Camille looked mysterious. 'There are sources,' he said. 'The idea
really is to let people pay you to write what you were going to
write anyway.'

'You frighten me,' Claude said. 'You appear to have no moral
sense whatever.'

'The end result will be good. I won't have to spend more than a
few columns paying compliments to my backers. The rest of the
paper I can use to give some publicity to Deputy Robespierre.'

Claude looked around fearfully. There was Deputy Robespierre,
in conversation with his daughter Adèle. Their conversation seemed
confidential – intimate almost. But then – he had to admit it – if
you could separate Deputy Robespierre's speeches at the Riding-
School from the deputy's own person, there was nothing at all
alarming about him. Quite the reverse really. He is a neat, quiet
young man; he seems equable, mild, responsible. Adèle is always
bringing his name into the conversation; she must, obviously, have
feelings towards him. He has no money, but then, you can't have
everything. You have to be glad simply to have a son-in-law who
isn't physically violent.

Adèle had found her way to Robespierre by easy conversational
stages. What were they talking about? Lucile. 'It's fearful,' she was
saying. 'Today – well, today was different, actually we had a good

laugh.' I won't tell him what about, she decided. 'But normally the atmosphere's quite frightening. Lucile's so strong-willed, she argues all the time. And she's really made her mind up on him.'

'I thought that, as he'd been asked here today, your father was softening a little.'

'So did I. But now look at his face.' They glanced across the room at Claude, then turned back and nodded to each other gloomily. 'Still,' Adèle said, 'they'll get their way in the end. They're the kind of people who do. What worries me is, what will the marriage be like?'

'The thing is,' Robespierre said, 'that everyone seems to regard Camille as a problem. But he isn't a problem to me. He's the best friend I've ever had.'

'Aren't you nice to say so?' And yes, isn't he, she thought. Who else would venture so artless a statement, in these complicated days? 'Look,' she said. 'Look over there. Camille and my mother are talking about us.'

So they were; heads together, just like in the old days. 'Matchmaking is the province of elderly spinsters,' Annette was saying.

'Don't you know one you could call in? I like things done correctly.'

'But he'll take her away. To Artois.'

'So? One may travel there. Do you think there's a steep cliff around Paris, and at Chaillot you drop off into hell? Besides, I don't think he'll ever go back home.'

'But what about when the constitution's made, and the Assembly dissolves?'

'I don't think it will work like that, you see.'

Lucile watched. Oh, mother, she thought, can't you get any closer? Why don't you just grapple him to the carpet, and have done with it? The earlier bonhomie had evaporated, as far as she was concerned. She didn't want to be in this room, with all these chattering people. She looked around for the quietest possible corner. Fréron followed her.

She sat; managed a strained smile. He stretched a proprietorial arm along the back of her chair; lounging, making small-talk, his eyes on the room and not on her. But from time to time his eyes flickered downwards. Finally, softly, insinuatingly, he said, 'Still a virgin, Lucile?'

Lucile blushed deeply. She bent her head. Not so far from the proper little miss, then? 'Most emphatically,' she said.

'This is not the Camille I know.'

'He's saving me till I'm married.'

'That's all very well for him, I suppose. He's got – outlets, hasn't he?'

'I don't want to know this,' she said.

'Probably better not. But you're a grown-up girl now. Don't you find the delights of your maiden state begin to pall?'

'What do you suggest I do about it, Rabbit? What opportunities do you think I have?'

'Oh, I know you find ways to see him. I know you slip out now and again. I thought, at the Danton's place perhaps. He and Gabrielle are not excessively moral.'

Lucile gave him a sideways glance, as devoid of expression as she could make it. She would not have taken part in this conversation – except that it was a painful relief to talk about her feelings to anyone, even a persecutor. Why must he slander Gabrielle? Rabbit will say anything, she decided. Even he realized he had gone too far – she could see it in his face. Just *imagine*, she thought – 'Gabrielle, can we come round tomorrow and borrow your bed?' Gabrielle would die sooner.

The thought of the Dantons' bed gives her, she admits, a very strange feeling. An indescribable feeling, really. The thought crosses her mind that, when that day comes, Camille won't hurt her *but Danton will* – and her heart bounds, she blushes again, more furiously, because she doesn't know where the idea came from, she didn't ask for it, she didn't want to think that thought at all.

'Has something upset you?' Fréron says.

She snaps: 'You ought to be ashamed of yourself.' Still, she can't erase the picture from her mind: that belligerent energy, those huge hard hands, that weight. A woman must thank God, she says to herself, that she has a limited imagination.

*

THE NEWSPAPER went through various changes of name. It began
as the *Courier du Brabant* – they were having a revolution over the
border, too, and Camille thought it worth a mention. It became the
Révolutions de France et du Brabant, ended up simply as the *Révolutions
de France*. Of course, Marat was the same, always changing his title,
for various shady reasons. He had been the *Paris Publicist*, was now
the *People's Friend*. A title, they thought at the *Révolutions*, of risible
naïveté; it sounded like a cure for the clap.

Everyone is starting newspapers, including people who can't
write and who, says Camille, can't even think. The *Révolutions*
stands out; it makes a splash; it also imposes a routine. If the staff is
small, temporary and a bit disorganized, this hardly matters; at a
push, Camille can write a whole issue himself. What's thirty-two
pages (in octavo) to a man with so much to say for himself?

Monday and Tuesday they were in the office early, working on
the week's edition. By Wednesday the greater part was ready for the
printer. On Wednesday, also, the writs came in from the previous
Saturday's libels, though it had been known for the victims to drag
their lawyers back from the country on a Sunday morning and get
writs served by Tuesday. Challenges to duels came in sporadically,
throughout the week.

Thursday was press day. They made the last-minute corrections,
then a menial would sprint around to the printer, M. Laffrey, whose
premises were on the Quai des Augustins. Thursday midday brought
Laffrey and the distributor, M. Garnery, both tearing their hair. Do
you want to see the presses impounded, do you want us in gaol? Sit
down, have a drink, Camille would say. He rarely agreed to changes;
almost never. And they knew that the bigger the risk, the more
copies they'd sell.

René Hébert would come into the office: pink-skinned, unpleasant. He made snide jokes all the time about Camille's private life; no
sentence lacked its *double-entendre*. Camille explained him to his assistants; he used to work in a theatre box-office, but he was sacked for
stealing from the petty cash.

'Why do you put up with him?' they said. 'Next time he comes,
shall we throw him out?'

They were like that at the *Révolutions*; always hoping for a less sedentary occupation.

'Ah, no, leave him alone,' Camille said. 'He's always been offensive. It's his nature.'

'I want my own newspaper,' Hébert said. 'It will be different from this.'

Brissot was in that day, perched on a desk, twitching. 'Shouldn't be too different,' he said. 'This one is a pre-eminent success.'

Brissot and Hébert didn't like each other.

'You and Camille write for the educated,' Hébert said. 'So does Marat. I'm not going to do that.'

'You are going to start a newspaper for the illiterate?' Camille asked him sweetly. 'I wish you every success.'

'I'm going to write for the people in the street. In the language they speak.'

'Then every other word will be an obscenity,' Brissot said, sniffing.

'Precisely,' Hébert said, tripping out.

Brissot is the editor of the *French Patriot* (daily, four pages in quarto, boring). He is also a most generous, painstaking, endlessly inventive contributor to other people's papers. He quivers into the office most mornings, his narrow, bony face shining with his latest good idea. I've spent all my life grovelling to publishers, he would say; and tell how he had been cheated, how his ideas had been stolen and his manuscripts pirated. He didn't seem to see that there was any connection between this sad record of his, and what he was doing now – 11.30 in the morning, in another editor's office, turning his dusty, Quaker-style hat in his hands and talking his substance away. 'My family – you understand, Camille? – was very poor and ignorant. They wanted me to be a monk, that was the best life they could envisage. I lost my faith – well, in the end, I had to break it to them, didn't I? Of course, they didn't understand. How could they? It was as if we spoke different languages. Say, they were Swedes, and I was Italian – that's how close I was to my family. So then they said, you could be a lawyer, we suppose. Now, I was walking along the street one day, and one of the neighbours said,

"Oh, look, there's M. Janvier on his way back from court." And he pointed to this lawyer, stupid-looking man with a paunch, trotting along with his evening's work under his arm. And he said, "You work hard, you'll be like that someday." And my heart sank. Oh, I know, that's a figure of speech – but, do you know, I swear it did, it bunched itself up and thudded into my belly. I thought no, any hardship – they can put me in gaol – but I don't want to be like that. Now, of course, he wasn't that stupid-looking, he had money, he was looked up to, didn't oppress the poor or anything, and he'd just got married for the second time, to this very nice young woman . . . so why wasn't I tempted? I might have thought – well, it's a living, it's not too bad. But – there you are – steady money, easy life – it's never quite been enough, has it?'

One of Camille's volatile assistants put his head around the door. 'Oh, Camille, here's a woman after you. Just by way of a change.'

Théroigne swept in. She wore a white dress, and a tricolour sash about her waist. A National Guardsman's tunic, unbuttoned, was draped over her slim, square shoulders. Her brown hair was a breeze-blown waterfall of curls; she had employed one of those expensive hairdressers who make you look as if you've never been near a hairdresser in your life. 'Hallo, how's it going?' she said. Her manner was at variance with this democratic greeting; she radiated energy and a quasi-sexual excitement.

Brissot hopped up from the desk, and considerately lifted the jacket from her shoulders, folded it carefully and laid it over a vacant chair. This reduced her to – what? A pretty-enough young woman in a white dress. She was displeased. There was a weight in the pocket of the tunic. 'You carry firearms?' Brissot said, surprised.

'I got my pistol when we raided the Invalides. Remember, Camille?' She swished across the room. 'You're not seen much on the streets, these last weeks.'

'Oh, I couldn't cut the figure,' Camille murmured. 'Not like you.'

Théroigne took his hand and turned it palm-up. You could still just see the bayonet-cut, not much thicker than a hair, that he had got on 13 July. Théroigne, meditatively, drew her forefinger along it. Brissot's mouth became slightly unhinged. 'Look, am I in your way?'

'Absolutely not.' The last thing he wanted was any rumours about Théroigne coming to Lucile's ears. As far as he knew, Anne was leading a chaste and blameless life; the strange thing was, that she seemed dedicated to giving the contrary impression. The royalist scandal-sheets were not slow to pick anything up; Théroigne was a gift from God, as far as they were concerned.

'Can I write for you, my love?' she said.

'You can try. But I have very high standards.'

'Turn me down, would you?' she said.

'I'm afraid I would. The fact is, there's just too much on offer.'

'As long as we know where we stand,' she said. She scooped up her jacket from the chair where Brissot had disposed it, and – out of some perverse form of charity – placed a kiss on his sunken cheek.

When she'd gone, an odour trailed behind her – female sweat, lavender-water. 'Calonne,' Brissot said. 'He used lavender water. Remember?'

'I didn't move in those circles.'

'Well, he did.'

Brissot would know. He would know everything, really. He believed in the Brotherhood of Man. He believed that all the enlightened men in Europe should come together to discuss good government and the development of the arts and sciences. He knew Jeremy Bentham and Joseph Priestley. He ran an anti-slavery society, and wrote about jurisprudence, the English parliamentary system and the Epistles of Saint Paul. He had arrived at his present cramped apartment on the rue de Grétry by way of Switzerland, the United States, a cell in the Bastille and a flat on Brompton Road. Tom Paine was a great friend of his (he said) and George Washington had more than once asked for his advice. Brissot was an optimist. He believed that common sense and love of liberty would always prevail. Towards Camille he was kind, helpful, faintly patronizing. He liked to talk about his past life, and congratulate himself on the better days ahead.

Now Théroigne's visit – perhaps the kiss, particularly – put him into a regular fit of how-did-we-get-here and ain't-life-strange. 'I had a hard time,' he said. 'My father died, and shortly afterwards my mother became violently insane.'

Camille put his head down on his desk, and laughed and laughed, until they really thought he would make himself quite ill.

On Fridays Fréron would usually be in the office. Camille would go out to lunch for several hours. Then they would have a writ conference, to decide whether to apologize. Since Camille would not be entirely sober, they never apologized. The staff of the *Révolutions* was never off duty. They were committed to leaping out of bed in the small hours with some hair-raising bright idea; they were doomed to be spat at in the street. Each week, after the type was set, Camille would say, never again, this is the last edition, positively. But next Saturday the paper would be out again, because he could not bear anyone to think that THEY had frightened him, with their threats and insults and challenges, with their money and rapiers and friends at Court. When it was time to write, and he took his pen in his hand, he never thought of consequences; he thought of style. I wonder why I ever bothered with sex, he thought; there's nothing in this breathing world so gratifying as an artfully placed semi-colon. Once paper and ink were to hand, it was useless to appeal to his better nature, to tell him he was wrecking reputations and ruining people's lives. A kind of sweet venom flowed through his veins, smoother than the finest cognac, quicker to make the head spin. And, just as some people crave opium, he craves the opportunity to exercise his fine art of mockery, vituperation and abuse; laudanum might quieten the senses, but a good editorial puts a catch in the throat and a skip in the heartbeat. Writing's like running downhill; can't stop if you want to.

A FEW LOW INTRIGUES to wrap up the *annus mirabilis* . . . Lafayette tells Duke Philippe that he is seeking proofs of his involvement in the October riots and that if he finds them he will . . . proceed. The general wants the Duke out of the country; Mirabeau, finding him essential to his schemes, wants him in Paris. 'Tell me who is pressuring you,' Mirabeau begs; not that he can't guess.

The Duke is confused. He should have been King by now, but he isn't. 'You set these things afoot,' he complains to de Sillery, 'and other people take them out of your hands.'

Charles-Alexis is sympathetic: 'Not exactly plain sailing, is it?'

'Please,' the Duke says, 'I am not in the mood for your naval metaphors this morning.'

The Duke is frightened – frightened of Mirabeau, frightened of Lafayette, and marginally more frightened of the latter. He is even frightened of Deputy Robespierre, who sits in the Assembly opposing everyone and everything, never raising his voice, never losing his temper, his gentle eyes implacable behind his spectacles.

After the October days, Mirabeau conceives a plan for the escape of the royal family – you have to talk, now, in terms of 'escape'. The Queen loathes him, but he is trying to manipulate the situation so that he seems to the Court a necessary man. He despises Lafayette, but believes he might be turned to some account; the general has his fingers on the purse-strings of the Secret Service funds, and that is no small matter, if one has to entertain, to pay one's secretaries, to help out needy young men who happen to put their talents at your disposal.

'They may pay me,' the Comte says, 'but they have not bought me. If someone would trust me, I wouldn't need to be so devious.'

'Yes, Monsieur,' Teutch says stonily. 'I wouldn't go marketing that epigram, if I were you, Monsieur.'

AND MEANWHILE, General Lafayette brooded: 'Mirabeau,' he said coldly, 'is a charlatan. If I cared to expose his schemes I could bring the sky around his ears. The idea of him in the ministry is unthinkable. He is massively corrupt. It is wonderful how the man's popularity survives. I might say it grows. It does, it grows. I will offer him a place, some embassy, get him out of France ... ' Lafayette ran his fingers through his scanty blond hair. It was fortunate that Mirabeau had once said – said in public – that he wouldn't have Philippe as his valet. Because if they should ally themselves ... no, it's unthinkable. Orléans must leave France, Mirabeau must be bought off, the King must be guarded day and night by six National Guardsmen, likewise the Queen, tonight I dine with Mirabeau and I will offer . . . He had lapsed into silent thought. It didn't matter where his sentences began and ended, because he was talking to himself – who else could he trust? He glanced up once to a mirror, to the thin, fair face and receding hairline that the Cordeliers' pamphleteers found so risible; then, sighing, walked out of the empty room.

THE COMTE DE MIRABEAU to the Comte de la Marck:

Yesterday, late, I saw Lafayette. He spoke of the place and the pay; I refused; I should prefer a written promise of the first major embassy; a part of the pay is to be advanced to me tomorrow. Lafayette is very anxious about the Duke of Orléans . . . If a thousand louis seems to you indiscreet, do not ask for it, but that is the amount I urgently need . . .

ORLÉANS left for London, with a sulky expression and Laclos. 'A diplomatic mission,' the official announcement said. Camille was with Mirabeau when the bad news came. The Comte strode about, he said, swearing.

And another disappointment for the Comte: early November, the Assembly passed a motion debarring deputies from office as ministers.

'They unite to ostracize me,' Mirabeau howled. 'This is Lafayette's doing, Lafayette's.'

'We fear for your health,' said the slave Clavière, 'when you get into these rages.'

'That's right, slight me, sneer, abandon me,' the Comte roared. 'Place-seekers. Fair-weather friends. Toadying swine.'

'The measure was aimed at you, there is no doubt.'

'I'll break that bastard. Who does he think he is? Cromwell?'

DECEMBER 3 1789: Maître G.-J. Danton paid over to Maître Huet de Paisy and Mlle Françoise Duhauttoir the sum of 12,000 livres, with 1,500 livres interest.

He thought he'd tell his father-in-law; it would be a weight off his mind. 'But that's sixteen months early!' Charpentier said. He was adding up in his head, calculating income and expenditure. He smiled, swallowed. 'Well, you'll feel more settled,' he said.

Privately, he thought: it's impossible. What in God's name is Georges-Jacques up to?

II. *Liberty, Gaiety, Royal Democracy*

(1790)

'OUR CHARACTERS make our destiny,' Félicité de Genlis says. 'Ordinary people for that reason do not have destinies, they belong to chance. A pretty, intelligent woman who has original ideas should have a life full of extraordinary events.'

WE ARE NOW IN 1790. Certain events befall Gabrielle – a few of them extraordinary.

IN MAY THIS YEAR, I gave my husband a son. We called him Antoine. He seems strong; but so did my first baby. We never talk about our first son now. Sometimes, though, I know that Georges thinks about him. Tears come into his eyes.

I will tell you what else has happened, in the larger world. In January my husband was elected to the Commune, along with Legendre, our butcher. I did not say so – I never say anything now – but I was surprised that he put himself up for office, because he criticizes the Commune all the time, and Mayor Bailly most of all.

Just before he went to take his seat, there was the business of Dr Marat. Marat insulted the authorities so much that an order was put out for his arrest. He was staying at the Hôtel de la Fautrière, within our district. They sent four officers to arrest him, but a woman ran to warn him, and he got away.

I didn't understand why Georges should be so concerned about Marat. He usually brings Dr Marat's paper into the house, then in the middle of reading it cries, 'Scum, scum, scum!' and throws it across the room, or into the fire if he happens to be standing near it. But anyway, he said it was a matter of principle. He told the District Assembly that no one was going to be arrested in our district without his permission. 'My writ runs here,' he said.

Dr Marat went into hiding. I thought, that will be the end of the newspaper for a while, we shall have some peace. But Camille said, 'Well, I think we should help each other, I'm sure I can get the next issue out on time.' The next issue of the paper insulted the people at City Hall still worse.

On 21 January M. Villette, who is our battalion commander now, came round and asked to see Georges urgently. Georges came out of his office. M. Villette waved a piece of paper and said, 'Order from Lafayette. Arrest Marat, top priority. What do I do?'

Georges said, 'Put a cordon round the Hôtel de la Fautrière.'

The next thing that happened was that the sheriff's officers came again with the warrant – and a thousand men.

Georges was in a fury. He said it was an invasion by foreign troops. The whole district turned out. Georges found the commander and walked up to him and said, 'What the hell is the use of these troops, do you think? I'll ring the tocsin, I'll have Saint-Antoine out. I can put twenty thousand armed men on the streets, just like *that*.' And he snapped his fingers under the man's nose.

'PUT YOUR HEAD out of the window,' Marat said. 'See if you can hear what Danton is saying. I'd put my own head out, but somebody might shoot it off.'

'He is saying, where is that fucking battalion commander.'

'I wrote to Mirabeau and Barnave.' Marat turned to Camille his tired, gold-flecked eyes. 'I thought they needed enlightenment.'

'I expect they didn't reply.'

'No.' He thought. 'I renounce moderation,' he said.

'Moderation renounces you.'

'That's all right.'

'Danton is sticking his neck out for you.'

'What an expression,' Marat said.

'Yes, I don't know where I pick them up.'

'Why don't they ever try arresting you? I've been on the run since October.' Marat wandered around the room, pursuing a muttered monologue and scratching himself occasionally. 'This affair could be the making of Danton. We lack good men. We could blow the Riding-School up, it would be no great loss. There are only half a dozen deputies who are any use at all. Buzot has some of the right ideas, but he's too bloody high-minded. Pétion is a fool. I have some hopes for Robespierre.'

'Me too. But, I don't think a single measure he has proposed has ever been passed. Just to know that he supports a motion is enough to make most of the deputies vote against it.'

'But he has perseverance,' Marat said sharply. 'And the Riding-School is not France, is it? As for you, your heart is in the right place, but you are mad. Danton I esteem. He will do something. What I should like to see – ' he stopped, and pulled at the filthy kerchief knotted around his neck, 'I should like to see the people dispense with the King, the Queen, the ministers, Bailly, Lafayette, the Riding-School – and I should like to see the country governed by Danton and Robespierre. And I should be there to keep an eye on them.' He smiled. 'One may dream.'

GABRIELLE: It was like this for the rest of the day, our men ringing the building, Dr Marat inside, and the troops Lafayette had sent drawn up around the cordon. Georges came home to check that we were safe, and he seemed quite calm, but every time he went out on to the streets he seemed to be in a towering rage. He made a speech to the troops, he said, 'You can stay here till tomorrow if you want, but it won't bloody get you anywhere.'

There was a great deal of bad language that day.

As the morning wore on, our men and their men started talking to each other. There were regular troops, and volunteers too, and people said, after all, these are our brothers from other districts, of course they're not going to fight us. And Camille went around saying, of course they're not going to arrest Marat, he's the People's Friend.

Then Georges went down to the Assembly. They wouldn't let him speak at the bar of the House, and they passed a motion saying that the Cordeliers district must respect the law. He seemed to be away for hours. I just kept finding things to do. Picture it. You marry a lawyer. One day you find you're living on a battlefield.

*

'So here are the clothes, Dr Marat,' François Robert said. 'M. Danton hopes they fit.'

'Well, I don't know,' Marat said. 'I was hoping to make my escape by balloon. I've wanted for such a long time to ascend in a balloon.'

'We couldn't get one. Not in the time we had.'

'I bet you didn't try,' Marat said.

After he had washed, shaved, dressed in a frock-coat, combed his hair, François Robert said, 'Amazing.'

'One was always well-dressed,' Marat said, 'in one's days in high society.'

'What happened?'

Marat glowered. 'I became the People's Friend.'

'But you could still dress normally, couldn't you? For instance, you mention Deputy Robespierre as a patriot, and he is always wonderfully turned-out.'

'There is perhaps a strain of frivolity in M. Robespierre,' Marat said drily. 'For myself, I have no time for the luxuries, I think of the Revolution for twenty-four hours of the day. If you wish to prosper, you will do the same. Now,' he said, 'I am going to walk outside, through the cordon, and through Lafayette's troops. I am going to smile, which I admit you do not often see, and affecting a jaunty air I am going to swing this elegant walking-cane with which M. Danton has so thoughtfully provided me. It's like a story-book, isn't it? And then I am off to England, just until the fuss dies down. Which will be a relief to you all, I know.'

GABRIELLE: When there was a knock at the door I didn't know what to do. But it was only little Louise from upstairs. 'I went out, Mme Danton.'

'Oh, Louise, you shouldn't have done that.'

'I'm not frightened. Besides – it's all over. The troops are dispersing. Lafayette has lost his nerve. And I'll tell you a secret, Mme Danton, that M. Desmoulins told me to tell you. Marat isn't even in there any more. He got out an hour ago, disguised as a human being.'

A few minutes later Georges came home. That night we threw a party.

Next day my husband went to take his seat at City Hall. There was another row. Some people tried to stop him and said he had no right to be a member of the Commune because he had no respect for law and order. They said that in his own district he was acting like a king. They said a lot of terrible things about Georges at that time – that he was taking money from the English to stir up the Revolution and that he was taking money from the Court not to make the Revolution any worse. One day Deputy Robespierre came, and they talked about who was slandering Georges. Deputy Robespierre said he shouldn't feel he was alone. He brought a letter from his brother Augustin, from Arras, which he gave to Georges to read. It seemed that people in Arras were saying Robespierre was a godless man who wanted to kill the King – which absolutely can't be true, because I've never met a more mild-mannered human being. I felt sorry for him; they had even printed in what Georges calls 'the royalist rags' some stupid claim that he was descended from Damiens, the man who tried to kill the old King. They deliberately spell his name wrong, to insult him. When he was elected for a term as president of the Jacobin Club, Lafayette walked out in protest.

After Antoine was born, Georges's mother came up from the country for a few days to see the baby. Georges's stepfather would have come with her but he couldn't spare any time from inventing spinning machines – at least, that was the story, but I should think the poor man was glad to be on his own for a few days. It was terrible. I hate to say it, but Mme Recordain is the most disagreeable woman I have ever met.

The first thing she said was, 'Paris is filthy, how can you bring a child up here? No wonder you lost your first. You'd better send this one to Arcis when he's weaned.'

I thought, yes, what a good idea, let him be gored by bulls and scarred for life.

Then she looked around and said, 'This wallpaper must have cost a pretty penny.'

At the first meal she complained about the vegetables, and asked how much I paid our cook. 'Far too much,' she said. 'Anyway, where does all the money come from?' I explained to her how hard Georges worked, but she just snorted, and said that she had an idea of how much lawyers earned at his age and it wasn't enough to keep a house like a palace and a wife in the lap of luxury.

That's where she thinks I am.

When I took her shopping, she thought the prices were a personal insult. She had to admit we got good meat, but she said Legendre was common, and that she didn't bring up Georges *with all the care she'd lavished on him* to see him associate with someone who ran a butcher's shop. She amazed me – it isn't as if Legendre stands there wrapping up bleeding parcels of beef these days. You never see him in an apron. He puts on a black coat like a lawyer and sits beside Georges at City Hall.

Madame Recordain would say, in the mornings: 'Of course, I don't require to go anywhere.' But if we didn't, she would say in the evening, 'It's a long way to come and sit and see four walls.'

I thought I'd take her to visit Louise Robert – seeing as Madame is such a snob, and Louise is so well-born. Louise couldn't have been more charming. She didn't say a single word about the republic, or Lafayette, or Mayor Bailly. Instead she showed Madame all her stock and explained to her where all the spices came from and how they were grown and prepared and what they were for, and offered to make her up a parcel of nice things to take home. But after ten minutes Her Ladyship was looking like thunder, and I had to make my excuses to Louise and follow her out. In the street she said, 'It's a disgrace for a woman to marry beneath her. It shows low appetites. And it wouldn't surprise me if I found out they weren't married at all.'

Georges said, 'Look, because my mother comes, does it mean I can't see my friends? Invite some people to supper. Somebody she'll like. How about the Gélys? And little Louise?'

I knew this was a sacrifice on his part, because he's not over-fond of Mme Gély; in fact, the strain was showing in his face already. And I had to say, 'Well, no, they've already met. Your mother thinks Mme Gély is mincing and ridiculous and mutton dressed as lamb. And Louise is precocious and needs a stick taking to her.'

'Oh dear,' Georges said: which was quite mild for him, don't you think? 'We must know somebody nice. Don't we?'

I sent a note to Annette Duplessis, saying, please please could Lucile come to supper? Georges's mother would be there, it would be perfectly proper, she'd never be alone with etc. So Lucile was allowed to come; she wore a white dress with blue ribbons, and she behaved like an angel, asking Madame all sorts of intelligent questions about life in Champagne. Camille was so polite – as, indeed, he almost always is, except in his newspaper – I had hidden the back-numbers, of course. I asked Fabre too, because he's so good at keeping a conversation going – and he tried really hard with Madame. But she kept snubbing him, and in the end he gave up and started to look at her through his lorgnette, which I had given him strict instructions not to do.

Madame walked out as we were having coffee, and I found her in our bedroom running her finger under the windowsill, looking for dust. I said to her very politely, 'Is there anything the matter?' and she said in the most sour tone you can imagine, 'There'll be plenty the matter with you if you don't watch that girl with your husband.'

For a minute I didn't even know what she meant.

'And I can tell you something else,' she said. 'You'd better watch that boy with your husband as well. So they're going to be married, are they? They'll suit each other.'

Once we got admission tickets for the public gallery at the Riding-School, but the debate was very dull. Georges says that any time now they will be discussing taking over the church's lands for the nation, and that if she'd been present for that debate she'd have caused a commotion and got us thrown out. As it was, she called them villains and ingrates, and said no good would come of it. M. Robespierre saw us and came over for a few minutes, and was very kind. He pointed out the important people, including Mirabeau. Madame said, 'That man will go straight to hell when he dies.'

M. Robespierre looked at me sideways and smiled and said to

Madame, 'You're a young lady after my own heart.' This set her up for the day.

All summer the consequences of that business of Dr Marat seemed to be hanging over us. We knew there was a warrant for Georges's arrest, drawn up and ready, gathering dust in a drawer at City Hall. And I'd think, every morning, what if today is the day they decide to take it out and blow the dust off? We had plans – if he was arrested, I was to pack a bag and go at once to my mother, give the keys of the apartment to Fabre and leave everything else to him. I don't know why Fabre – I suppose because he's always around.

At this time Georges's affairs were very complicated. He didn't seem to spend much time in his own office. I suppose Jules Paré must be competent, because the money keeps coming in.

Early in the year something happened that Georges said showed the authorities were very frightened of him. They abolished our district, and all the others, and re-organized the city into voting areas. From now on there weren't to be any public meetings of the citizens in a particular district unless it was for an election. Already they had stopped us calling our National Guard battalion 'the Cordeliers'. They said we were just to be called 'Number 3'.

Georges said it would take more than this to kill the Cordeliers. He said we were going to have a club, like the Jacobins but better. People from any part of the city could attend, so no one could say it was illegal. Its real name was the Club of the Friends of the Rights of Man, but from the beginning everybody called it the Cordeliers Club. At first they had meetings in a ballroom. They wanted to hold them in the old Cordeliers monastery, but City Hall had the building sealed up. Then one day – no explanation – the seals came off, and they moved in. Louise Robert said it was done by the influence of the Duke of Orléans.

It's hard to get into the Jacobin Club. The yearly subscription is high, and you have to have a lot of members to back your application, and their meetings are very formal. When Georges went to speak there once he came home annoyed. He said they treated him like dirt.

At the Cordeliers anyone could come and speak. So you would

get a lot of the actors and lawyers and tradesmen from around here, but you'd also get quite rough-looking types who'd walk in off the street. Of course, I never went there when there was a meeting, but I saw what they'd done with the chapel. It was very bleak and bare. When some windows got broken it was weeks before they were mended. I thought, how odd men are, at home they like to be comfortable but outside they pretend they don't care.. The president's desk was a joiner's bench that happened to be lying about when they moved in. Georges really wouldn't have much to say to a joiner, if it weren't for the present upheavals. The speaker's rostrum at the club was made of four rough beams with a plank running between them. On the wall somebody had nailed a strip of calico with a slogan in red paint. It said *Liberty, Equality, Fraternity.*

After the bad time I had with Georges' mother I was miserable when he said he wanted to spend some time in Arcis. To my great relief, we stayed with his sister Anne Madeleine, and to my surprise we were received everywhere with great deference and respect. It was uncanny really – unnerving. Anne Madeleine's friends were practically curtseying to me. At first I thought the local people must have heard of Georges's successes as president of the district, but I soon realized that they don't get the Paris newspapers and they don't much care what goes on there anyway. And people kept asking me strange questions, like, what's the Queen's favourite colour, what does she like to eat. So one day it came to me: 'Georges,' I said, 'they think that because you're a King's Councillor, he asks you in every day to give him advice.'

For a moment he looked amazed. Then he laughed. 'Do they? Bless them. And I have to live in Paris, with all these cynics and wits. Give me four or five years, Gabrielle, and I'll come back here and farm. We'll get out of Paris for good. Would you like that?'

I didn't know how to answer. On the one hand, I thought, how wonderful to be away from the newspapers and the fishwives and the crime rate and the shortages of things in the shops. But then I thought of the prospect of Mme Recordain calling on me every day. So I didn't say anything, because I saw it was just a whim of his. I mean, is he going to give up the Cordeliers Club? Is he going to give up the Revolution? I watched him start to get restless. And one evening he said, 'We're going back tomorrow.'

All the same, he spent a long time with his stepfather, looking at properties, and arranging with the local notary about buying a piece of land. M. Recordain said, 'Doing nicely, son, are you?' Georges only smiled.

I think that summer will always be clear in my memory. In my heart I was uneasy, because I believe in my heart that whatever is happening we should be loyal to the King and Queen and to the church. But soon, if some people have their way, the Riding-School will be more important than the King, and the church will be just a goverment department. I know that we are bound to obey authority, and that Georges has often flouted it. That is in his nature, because at school, Paré tells me, they used to call him 'the Anti-Superior'. Of course you must try to overcome the worst things in your nature, but meanwhile where am I? – because I am bound to obey my husband, unless he counsels me to commit sin. And is it a sin to cook supper for people who talk about sending the Queen back to Austria? When I asked my confessor for guidance, he said that I should maintain an attitude of wifely obedience and try to bring my husband back to the Catholic faith. That was no help. So outwardly I defer to all Georges's opinions, but in my *heart* I make reservations – and every day I pray that he will change some of them.

And yet – everything seems to be going so well for us. There's always something to celebrate. When it came to the anniversary of the taking of the Bastille, every town in France sent delegations to Paris. A great amphitheatre was built on the Champs-de-Mars, and an altar was set up which they called the Altar of the Fatherland. The King went there, and took an oath to uphold the constitution, and the Bishop of Autun said High Mass. (It is a pity he is an atheist.) We didn't go ourselves; Georges said he couldn't stand to see the people kiss Lafayette's boots. There was dancing where the Bastille used to be, and in the evening we had celebrations throughout our own district, and we went from one party to another, and stayed out all night. I got quite tipsy, everyone laughed at me. It had poured with rain all day, and somebody made a verse saying it proved that God was an aristocrat. I'll never forget the ludicrous business of trying to let off fireworks in a downpour; or Georges bringing me back home, me leaning on his arm, the cobbles wet and slick and dawn breaking over the streets. Next day I saw that my new satin shoes had got a water-mark; they were completely ruined.

You should see us now; you wouldn't know us from last year. Some quite fashionable ladies have given up powdering their hair; instead of pinning it up, they wear it down, in loose curls. Many gentlemen have also given up powder, and far less lace is worn. It's quite unfashionable for a woman to paint her face; I don't know what they do at Court now, but Louise Robert is the only woman I know who still wears rouge. Admittedly, she has not a good colour without it. We make our dresses from the simplest of fabrics, and the fashionable colours are the national colours, red, white and blue. Mme Gély says the new fashions are not flattering to older women, and my mother agrees with her. 'But you,' my mother says, 'can take your chance to get out of laces and stays.' I don't agree with her. I haven't got my figure back since Antoine was born.

The modish jewellery this year is a chip of stone from the Bastille, made into a brooch or worn on a chain. Félicité de Genlis has a brooch with the word LIBERTY spelled out in diamonds – Deputy Pétion described it to me. We have given up our elaborate fans, and now have them made out of cheap sticks and pleated paper, with bright colours portraying some patriotic scene. I have to be very careful to have a scene that fits in with my husband's views. I can't have a portrait of Mayor Bailly crowned with laurels, or of Lafayette on his white horse, but I can have Duke Philippe, or the taking of the Bastille, or Camille making his speech in the Palais-Royal. But why should I want his portrait when I see too much of the original?

I remember Lucile at our apartment, the morning of the Bastille celebrations, her tricolour ribbons all bedraggled, wringing out the hem of her dress. The muslin clung to her figure in the most startling way, and she didn't seem to be possessed of much in the way of underwear. Think what Georges's mother would have said! I was quite severe with her myself – I had a fire lit, and I took away her clothes, and wrapped her in the warmest blanket I could find. I'm sorry to report that Lucile looks quite exquisite in a blanket. She sat with her bare feet drawn up beneath her, like a cat.

'What a child you are,' I said. 'I'm surprised your mother let you go out dressed like that.'

'She says I must learn from my mistakes.' She put out two white arms from her blanket. 'Let me have the baby.'

I gave her my little Antoine. She billed and cooed at him for a bit. 'Camille has been famous for a whole year now,' she said dejectedly, 'and we're no nearer getting married. I thought it would be neat if I got pregnant, it would hurry things up. But – there you are – can't get him into bed. You've no idea what Camille's like when he's got one of his fits of rectitude. John Knox was merely a beginner.'

'You wicked girl,' I said. More for form's sake, than anything. I like her; you can't help it. Oh, I'm not a perfect fool, I know that Georges looks at her, but so do all the men. Camille lives just around the corner now. He's actually got a really nice apartment, and a rather fierce-looking woman called Jeanette to do the housekeeping. I don't know where he found her, but she's a good cook, and quite happy to come round here and help when we have a lot of people to dine. Hérault de Séchelles comes quite often these days, and of course then I make a special effort. Very fine manners he has; it makes a change from Fabre's theatrical friends. Various deputies and journalists come, and I have various opinions about them, which I do not usually express. Georges's viewpoint is that if somebody is a patriot, it doesn't matter about their personality too much. He says that, but I notice he doesn't spend any time with Billaud-Varennes if he can help it. You remember Billaud, don't you? He used to work for Georges, here and there. Since the Revolution he looks marginally cheered-up. It seems, in some way, to give him steady employment.

One evening in July, a man called Collot d'Herbois came to supper. What would you think – they must have Christian names, these people? Yes, but 'Collot' was what we were to call him. He was rather like Fabre, in that he was an actor and a playwright, and had been a theatre manager – and he was about the same age, too. At that time he had a play called *The Patriotic Family* at the Théâtre de Monsieur. It was the kind of play that had suddenly become very popular, and we spent all evening hedging around the fact that we hadn't actually seen it. It was a great success at the box-office, but that didn't make Collot agreeable company. He insisted on telling us the story of his life, and it appeared that nothing had ever gone right for him till now, and even this he was suspicious about. When he was young – he said – he used to be baffled at the way people were always cheating him and doing him down – but then he realized they were jealous of his gifts. He used to think he just had no luck, but then he realized that people were conspiring against him. (When he said this Fabre made signs to me that he was a lunatic.) Every topic we raised had some bitter association for Collot, and at the smallest thing his face would become congested with anger and he would make violent sweeping gestures, as if he were speaking at the Riding-School. I feared for my crockery.

Later I said to Georges, 'I don't like Collot. He's sourer than your mother. And I'm sure the play is dreadful.'

'A typical feminine remark,' Georges said. 'I don't see what's wrong with him, except he's a bore. His opinions are – ' He paused and smiled. 'I was going to say they're correct, but of course I mean they're mine.'

Next day, Camille said: 'This hideous Collot. Much the worst person in the world. Play I suppose is unbearable.'

Georges said meekly, 'I'm sure you're right.'

Towards the end of the year Georges addressed the Assembly. A few days later the Ministry fell. People said that Georges had brought it down. My mother said, you are married to a powerful man.

THE NATIONAL ASSEMBLY in session: Lord Mornington, September 1790:

They have no regular form of debate on ordinary business; some speak from their seats, some from the floor, some from the table and some from their tribune or desk ... the riot is so great that it is very difficult to collect what is being said. I am certain I have seen above a hundred in the act of addressing the Assembly together, all persisting to speak, and as many more replying in different parts of the House; then the President claps his hands on both ears and roars Order, as if he were calling a coach ... he beats his table, his breast ... wringing his hands is quite a common action, and I really believe he swears ... the galleries approve and disapprove by groaning and clapping.

I went to court this morning at the Tuileries, and a very gloomy court it was ... The King seemed well, but I thought his manner evidently humbled since I was introduced to him before; he now bows to everybody, which was not a Bourbon fashion before the Revolution.

LUCILE'S YEAR: I keep two sets of notebooks now. One's for pure and elevated thoughts, and the other's for what really goes on.

I used to live like God, in different Persons. The reason for this was, life was so dull. I used to pretend to be Maria Stuart, and to be quite honest I must say I still do, for old time's sake. Its not easy to break yourself of these habits. Everybody else in my life would be assigned a role – usually as a lady-in-waiting, or something – and I would hate them when they wouldn't play it properly. If I got tired of Maria S. I would play at being Julie from *La Nouvelle Héloïse*. These days I wonder what is my relationship to Maximilien Robespierre. I'm living inside his favourite novel.

You have to employ some fantasy to keep brute reality at bay. The year began with Camille being sued for libel by M. Sanson, the public executioner. Strange – you don't think of executioners having recourse to law, in the normal way, you don't think of them having any animosity to spare.

Fortunately, the law is slow, its processes are cumbersome, and when damages are awarded the Duke is ready to pick up the bill. No, it's not the courts that worry me. Every morning I wake up and think to myself: is he still alive?

Camille is attacked on the street. He is denounced in the Assembly. He is challenged to duels – though the patriots have made a pact never to respond. There are lunatics going round the city, boasting that they're waiting for a chance to put a knife in him. They write him letters, these lunatics – letters so demented and so revolting that he won't read them himself. You can tell, he says, by a quick scan, what sort of letter it is. Sometimes you can tell by the handwriting on the outside of the packet. He has a box that he throws them into. Then other people have to look through them, in case any of the threats are very specific – I will kill you, at such a time and place.

My father's odd. About twice a month he'll forbid me ever to see Camille again. But every morning he's making a grab for the papers – 'Any news, any news?' Does he want to hear that Camille's been found across the river with his throat cut? I don't think so. I don't think my father would find any joy in his life if it weren't for Camille. My mother teases him in the most cold-blooded way. 'Admit it, Claude,' she says. 'He's the son you've never had.'

Claude brings home young men for supper. He thinks I might like them. Civil servants. Dear God.

Sometimes they write me poems, lovely civil service sonnets. Adèle and I read them out with suitable sentimental expressions. We turn up our eyes, slap our hands on our ribcages, and sigh. Then we make them into paper darts and bombard each other. Our spirits, you see, are high. We roll through our days in a sort of unwholesome glee. It's either this, or a permanent welter of sniffles and tears, forebodings and fears – and we prefer to be hilarious. We prefer to make blood-curdling jokes.

My mother, by contrast, is strained, sad; but fundamentally, I think she suffers less than I do. Probably it's because she's older, and she's learned to ration these things. 'Camille will survive,' she says. 'Why do you think he goes around in the company of such large men?' There are guns, I say, knives. 'Knives?' she says. 'Can you imagine someone trying to get a knife past M. Danton? Hacking through all that muscle and flesh?' That's to imagine, I say, that he would interpose himself. She says, 'Isn't Camille rather good at exacting human sacrifices? After all,' she says, 'look at me. Look at you.'

We expect, quite soon, to hear of Adèle's engagement. Max came here, and quite gratuitously praised the Abbé Terray. Much that the abbé had done, he said, had not been generally understood. Claude has consequently ceased to mind that Max has only his deputy's salary, and that he is supporting a younger brother and a sister out of it.

What will Adèle's life be like? Robespierre gets letters too, but they're not the same as the ones Camille gets. They come from all over the city; they're letters from little people, who have fallen foul of the authorities or got themselves into some form of trouble, and they think he can take up their case and put everything right. He has to get up at five a.m. to answer these letters. Somehow I think his standards of domestic comfort are rather low. His requirements for recreation, amusement, diversion seem to be nil. Now, ask yourself – will that suit Adèle?

ROBESPIERRE: It's not just Paris he must consider. Letters come from all over the country. Provincial towns have set up their Jacobin Clubs, and the Correspondence Committee of the Paris club sends them news, assessments, directives; back come their letters, distinguishing among the Paris brethren the deputy Robespierre, marking him out for their praise and thanks. This is something, after the vilification of the royalists. Inside his copy of *The Social Contract* he keeps a letter from a young Picard, an enthusiast called Antoine Saint-Just: 'I know you, Robespierre, as I know God, by your works.' When he suffers, as he does increasingly, from a distressing tightness of the chest and shortness of breath, and when his eyes seem too tired to focus on the printed page, the thought of the letter urges the weak flesh to more Works.

Every day he attends the Assembly, and every evening the Jacobin Club. He calls when he can at the Duplessis house, dines occasionally with Pétion – working dinner. He goes to the theatre perhaps twice in the season, with no great pleasure, and regret at the time lost. People wait to see him outside the Riding-School, outside the club, outside the door of his lodgings.

Each night he is exhausted. He sleeps as soon as his head touches the pillow. His sleep is dreamless, a plummeting into blackness: like falling into a well. The night world is real, he often feels; the mornings, with their light and air, are populated by shadows, ghosts. He rises before dawn, to have the advantage of them.

*

WILLIAM AUGUSTUS MILES, observing the situation on behalf of His (English) Majesty's government:

The man held of least account in the National Assembly . . . will soon be of the first consideration. He is a stern man, rigid in his principles, plain, unaffected in his manners, no foppery in his dress, certainly above corruption, despising wealth, and with nothing of the volatility of a Frenchman in his character. Nothing the King could bestow . . . could warp this man from his purpose. I watch him closely every night. He is really a character to be contemplated; he is growing every hour into consequence, and strange to relate, the whole National Assembly hold him cheap, consider him insignificant; when I said he would be the man of sway in a short time, and govern the million, I was laughed at.

EARLY IN THE YEAR, Lucile was taken to meet Mirabeau. She would never forget the man, standing squarely on a good Persian rug in a room decorated in appalling taste. He was thin-lipped, scarred and massive. He looked her over. 'I believe your father's a civil servant,' he said. He thrust his face forward and leered at her. 'Do you come in duplicate?'

Mirabeau, in a room, seemed to use up all the available air. He seemed, too, to use up all Camille's brains. It was extraordinary, the set of delusions Camille could entertain; no, *of course* Mirabeau was not in the pay of the Court, that was slander. *Of course* Mirabeau was the perfect patriot. Come the day Camille can no longer sustain these eccentric beliefs, he is practically suicidal. There is almost no newspaper that week.

'Max warned him,' Adèle said. 'He wouldn't listen. Mirabeau has called that half-educated Austrian baggage "a great and noble woman". And yet, to the people in the streets, Mirabeau is a god still. It shows how easily they can be misled.'

Claude put his head in his hands. 'Must we have this every hour, every hour of the day and night, this blasphemy and sedition from the mouths of young women? In our own house?'

'I was thinking,' Lucile said, 'that Mirabeau must have his own reasons for talking to the Court. But he has lost his credit with the patriots now.'

'His reason? Money is his reason, and greed for power. He wants to save the monarchy so that they will be grateful to him and bound to him for ever more.'

'Save the monarchy?' Claude said. 'From what? From whom?'

'Father, the King has asked the Assembly for a civil list of twenty-five million, and the grovelling fools have granted it. You know the state of the nation. They want to drain its blood. Consider, can this last?'

He looked at his daughters to discern, if he could, the children they had once been. He felt impelled to plead with them. 'But if you had not the King, or Lafayette, or Mirabeau, or the ministers – and I have heard you speak against them all – who would there be left to rule the nation?'

They exchanged glances. 'Our friends,' the sisters said.

Camille attacked Mirabeau in print, with a savagery he had not known himself to command. He did command it; abuse moves in the bloodstream, anger is better than food. For a time Mirabeau continued to speak out for him, defending him against the Right when they tried to silence him. 'My poor Camille,' he called him. In time, he would pass over to the ranks of his enemies. 'I am truly Christian,' Camille said. 'I *love* my enemies.' And indeed, his enemies gave him definition. He could read his purpose in their eyes.

Moving away from Mirabeau, he became closer to Robespierre. This made for a different life – evenings spent pushing papers across a desk, silence broken only by the odd murmur of consultation, the scratching of quills, the ticking of a clock. To be with Robespierre, Camille had to put on gravity like a winter cloak. 'He is all I should be,' he told Lucile. 'Max doesn't care for failure or success, it all evens out in his mind. He doesn't care what other people say about him, or what opinion they hold of his actions. As long as what he does feels right, inside, that's enough for him, that's his guide. He's one of the few men, the very few men, to whom only the witness of their own conscience is necessary.'

Yet just the day before, Danton had said to her, 'Ah, young Maximilien, he's too good to be true, that one. I can't work him out.'

But after all, Robespierre had been quite right about Mirabeau. Whatever you thought about him, you had to admit that he was almost always right.

In May, Théroigne left Paris. She had no money, and she was tired of the royalist papers calling her a prostitute. One by one, the murky layers of the past had been peeled away. Her time in London with a penniless milord. Her more profitable relationship with the Marquis de Persan. Her sojourn in Genoa with an Italian singer. A silly few weeks, when she was new in Paris, when she introduced herself to people as the Comtesse de Campinado, a great lady fallen on hard times. Nothing criminal, or madly hyperbolic: just the sort of thing we've all done when necessity has pressed. It left her open, though, to ridicule and insult. Whose life, she asked as she did her packing, would stand up to the sort of scrutiny mine has received? She meant to be back in a few months. The press will have moved on to new targets, she thought.

She left a gap, of course. She'd been a familiar figure at the Riding-School, lounging in the public gallery in a scarlet coat, her claque around her; strolling through the Palais-Royal, with a pistol in her belt. News came that she'd disappeared from her home in Liège; her brothers thought she'd gone off with some man, but before long rumours seeped through that she'd been abducted, that the Austrians had got her.

Hope they keep her, Lucile said. She was jealous of Théroigne. What gave her the right to be a pseudo-man, turning up at the Cordeliers and demanding the rostrum? It made Danton mad. It was funny to see what a rage it put him into. The kind of woman he liked was the kind he met at the Duke's dinner table: Agnès de Buffon, who gave him the most ridiculous languishing looks, and the blonde Englishwoman, Grace Elliot, with her mysterious political connections and her mechanical, eye-flashing flirtatiousness. Lucile had been to the Duke's house; she had watched Danton there. She supposed he knew what was happening; he knew that Laclos was setting him up, dangling these women under his nose. The procuress, Félicité, he left to Camille. Camille didn't mind having to have intelligent conversations with women. He seemed to enjoy them. One of his perversions, Danton said.

That summer Camille's old school-enemy, Louis Suleau, came to Paris. He came from Picardy under arrest, charged with seditious, anti-constitutional writings. He had a different brand of sedition from Camille, being more royalist than the King. Louis was acquitted; on the night of his release he and Camille sat up and argued until dawn. It was a very good argument – very articulate, very erudite, and its patron saint was Voltaire. 'I have to keep Louis away from Robespierre,' Camille said to Lucile. 'Louis is one of the best people in the world, but I'm afraid Max doesn't understand that.'

Louis was a gentleman, Lucile thought. He had dash, he had flair, he had presence. Soon he had a platform, too; he joined the editorial board of a royalist scandal-sheet called the *Acts of the Apostles*. The deputies who sat on the left were fond of calling themselves 'the apostles of liberty', and Louis thought such pomposity ought to be punished. Who were the contributors? A cabal of exhausted roués and defrocked priests, said the patriots whose noses were out of joint. How did it get written at all? The *Acts* held 'evangelical dinners' at the Restaurant du Mais and at Beauvillier's, where they'd exchange gossip and plot the next edition. They would invite their opponents and ply them with drink, to see what they'd say. Camille understood the principle: a titbit here, a trade-off there, a screamingly good time at the expense of the fools and bores who tried to occupy the middle-ground. Often a witticism for which the *Révolutions* had no use would find its home in the *Acts*. 'Dear Camille,' Louis said, 'if only you would throw in your lot with us. One day we are sure to see eye-to-eye. Never mind this "Liberty, Equality, Fraternity" rot. Do you know our manifesto? "Liberty, Gaiety, Royal Democracy". When it comes down to it, we both want the same – we want people to be happy. What's the use of your Revolution if it breeds long faces? What's the use of a revolution run by miserable little men in miserable little rooms?'

Liberty, Gaiety, Royal Democracy. The Duplessis women give orders to their dressmakers for the autumn of 1790. Black silks with

scarlet sashes and cut-away coats piped with the tricolour take them
to first nights, supper parties, private views. Take them to meet
new people . . .

It was still summer, though, when Antoine Saint-Just came to
Paris. Not to stay, just to visit; Lucile was avid to get a sight of
him. She'd heard the stories, about how he'd absconded with the
family silver and had run through the money in a fortnight. She was
highly prepared to like him.

He was twenty-two now. The episode with the silver was three
years ago. Had Camille perhaps made it up? It was hard to believe a
person could change so much. She looked up at Saint-Just – he was
tall – and noted the awesome neutrality of his expression. Introductions were made, and he looked at her as if he were not interested
in her at all. He was with Robespierre; it seemed they'd exchanged
letters. It was quite strange, she thought – most men seemed to fall
over themselves in their eagerness to get more out of her than her
normal workaday affability. Not that she held it against him: it
made a change.

Saint-Just was handsome. He had velvet eyes and a sleepy smile;
he moved his fine body carefully, as big men sometimes do. He had
a fair skin and dark brown hair – if there was any fault in his face, it
was that his chin was too large, too long. It saved him from
prettiness, she thought, but seen from certain angles his face had an
oddly overbalanced look.

Camille was with her, of course. He was in one of those precarious
moods; teasing, but quite ready for a fight. 'Done any more poems?'
he asked. Last year, Saint-Just had published an epic, and sent it for
his opinion; it was interminable, violent, faintly salacious.

'Why? Would you read them?' Saint-Just looked hopeful.

Camille slowly shook his head. 'Torture has been abolished,' he
said.

Saint-Just's lip curled. 'I suppose it offended you, my poem. I
suppose you thought it was pornographic.'

'Nothing so good,' Camille said, laughing.

Their eyes met. Saint-Just said, 'My poem had a serious point.
Do you think I would waste my time?'

'I don't know,' Camille said, 'whether you would or not.'

Lucile's mouth went dry. She watched the two men try to face each other down: Saint-Just waxen, passive, waiting for results, and Camille nervously aggressive, his eyes bright. This is nothing to do with a poem, she thought. Robespierre, too, looked faintly alarmed. 'You're a little severe, Camille,' he said. 'Surely the work had some merit?'

'None, none,' Camille said. 'But if you like, Antoine, I could bring you some specimens of my own early efforts, and let you mock them at your leisure. You are probably a better poet than I was, and you will certainly be a better politician. Because look at you, you have self-control. You would like to hit me, but you aren't going to.'

Saint-Just's expression had deepened; it was not fathomable.

'Have I really offended you?' Camille tried to sound sorry.

'Oh, deeply.' Saint-Just smiled. 'I am wounded to the core of my being. Because isn't it obvious that you are the one human being whose good opinion I crave? You without whom no aristocrat's dinner party is complete?'

Saint-Just turned his back to speak to Robespierre. 'Why couldn't you be kind?' Lucile whispered.

Camille shrugged. 'As a friend, I'd have been kind. But he was talking to an editor, not to a friend. He wanted me to put a piece in the paper crying up his talents. He didn't want my personal opinion, he wanted my professional opinion. So he got it.'

'What's happened? I thought you liked him?'

'He was all right. He's changed. He used to be always thinking up mad schemes and getting into difficulties with women. But look at him, he's become so solemn. I wish Louis Suleau could see him, he's a fine example of a miserable revolutionary. He's a republican, he says. I wouldn't like to live in his republic.'

'Perhaps he wouldn't let you.'

Later she heard Saint-Just tell Robespierre, 'He is frivolous.'

She contemplated the word. She associated it with giggly summer picnics, or gossipy theatre suppers with champagne: the rustling hot still-painted actresses sitting down beside her and saying, I see you are much in love, he is beautiful, I hope you will be happy. She had never before heard it uttered as an indictment, charged with menace and contempt.

THAT YEAR the Assembly made bishops and priests into public officials, salaried by the state and subject to election, and in time also required of them an oath of loyalty to the new constitution. To some it seemed a mistake to force the priests to a stark choice; to refuse was to be counted disloyal, and dangerous. Everybody agreed (at her mother's little afternoon salons) that religious conflict was the most dangerous force that could be unleashed in a nation.

From time to time her mother would sigh over the new developments. 'Life will be so prosaic,' she complained. 'The constitution, and the high-mindedness, and the Quaker hats.'

'What would you have, my dear?' Danton asked her. 'Plumes and grand passions at the Riding-School? Mayhem among the Municipality? Love and death?'

'Oh, don't laugh. Our romantic aspirations have received a shock. Here is the Revolution, the spirit of Rousseau made flesh, we thought – '

'And it is only M. Robespierre, with defective eyesight and a provincial accent.'

'It is only a lot of people discussing their bank balances.'

'Who has been gossiping to you about my affairs?'

'The walls and gateposts talk of you, M. Danton.' She paused, touched his arm. 'Tell me something, will you? Do you dislike Max?'

'Dislike him?' he seemed surprised. 'I don't think so. He makes me a bit uneasy, that's all. He does seem to set everyone very high standards. Will you be able to scrape up to them when you're his mother-in-law?'

'Oh, that's – not settled yet.'

'Can't Adèle make up her mind?'

'It's more that the question hasn't been asked.'

'Then it's what they call an understanding,' Danton said.

'I'm not sure whether Max thinks he has asked her – well, no, I must decline to comment. You need not raise your eyebrows in that way. How can a mere woman say what a deputy understands?'

'Oh, we don't have "mere women" any more. Last week your two prospective sons-in-law defeated me in argument. I am told that women are in every respect the equal of men. They only want opportunity.'

'Yes,' she said. 'All this is set in motion by that opinionated little creature Louise Robert, who doesn't know what she's starting. I don't see why men should spend their time arguing that women are their equals. It seems against their interests.'

'Robespierre is disinterested, you see. As always. And Camille tells me we shall have to give women the vote. We shall have them at the Riding-School soon, wearing black hats and lugging document cases and droning on about the taxation system.'

'Life will be even more prosaic.'

'Don't worry,' he said. 'We may yet have our grubby little tragedies.'

So has this revolution a philosophy, Lucile wanted to know, has it a future?

She dared not ask Robespierre, or he would lecture her for the afternoon on the General Will: or Camille, for fear of a thoughtful and coherent two hours on the development of the Roman republic. So she asked Danton.

'Oh, I think it has a philosophy,' he said seriously. 'Grab what you can, and get out while the going's good.'

December 1790: Claude changed his mind. He changed it on an ominous December day, when iron-coloured clouds, pot-bellied with snow, grazed among the city's roofs and chimneys.

'I just can't take it any more,' he said. 'Let them get married, before I die of the fatigue of it all. Threats, tears, promises, ultimata ... I couldn't take another year of it, I couldn't take another week. I should have been much firmer, long ago – but it's too late now. We'll have to make the best of it, Annette.'

Annette went to her daughter's room. Lucile was scribbling away at something. She looked up, startled and guilty, put her hand over her work. An ink blot grew on the page.

When Annette gave her the news, she stared into her mother's face, her dark eyes wide, hardly comprehending. 'So simple?' she whispered. 'Claude simply changes his mind, and everything comes right? Somehow I'd started thinking it was very much more complicated than that.' She turned her head. She began to cry. She put her head down on to her diary and let tears flow over the forbidden words: let them salt her paragraphs, let them turn the letters liquid. 'Oh, it's relief,' she said. 'It's relief.'

Her mother stood behind her, took her by the shoulders, gave her an incidental but vindictive pinch. 'So, you've got what you wanted. Let's have no more of your nonsense with M. Danton, either. You behave yourself, now.'

'I'll be a paragon.' She sat upright. 'Let's get organized then.' She scrubbed the back of her hand across her cheeks. 'We'll be married right away.'

'Right away? But think what people will say! And besides, it's Advent. You can't get married in Advent.'

'We'll get a dispensation. As for what people will say, that is a matter for them. I shall not be worrying about it. It is beyond my control.'

Lucile leapt up. She seemed no longer able to contain herself within civilized bounds. She ran through the house, laughing and crying at the same time, slamming the doors. Camille arrived. He seemed mystified. 'Why has she got ink on her forehead?' he asked.

'I suppose you might see it as a second baptism,' Annette said. 'Or the republican equivalent of anointing with holy oil. After all, my dear, there's so much ink in your lives.'

There was in fact a spot of it on Camille's cuff. He had very much the air of a man who has just written an editorial, and is worrying about what the typesetter will do to it. There was the time he'd referred to Marat as 'an apostle of liberty' and it had come out as 'an apostate of liberty'. Marat had arrived in the office, foaming with rage . . .

'Look, M. Duplessis are you sure about this?' Camille said.

'Good things like this don't happen to me. Could it be some mistake? A sort of printing error?'

Annette couldn't stop the images – didn't want them, but couldn't stop them. The swish of her skirts as she strode about this room, telling Camille to get out of her life. The rain pattering against the windows. And that kiss, that ten-second kiss that would have ended, if Lucile had not walked in, with a locked door and some undignified gratification on the *chaise-longue*. She cast her eye on it, that same item of furniture, upholstered in fading blue velvet. 'Annette,' Claude said, 'why are you looking so angry?'

'I'm not angry, dear,' Annette said. 'I'm having a lovely day.'

'Really? If you say so. Ah, women!' he said fondly, looking at Camille for complicity. Camille gave him a cool glance; said the wrong thing again, Claude thought, forgotten his Views. 'Lucile seems equally confused about her feelings. I hope – ' He approached Camille. He seemed to be about to put a hand on his shoulder, but it wavered in the air and dropped loosely at his side. 'Well, I hope you'll be happy.'

Annette said, 'Camille, dear, your apartment is very nice, but I expect you'll be moving to somewhere bigger? You'll need some more furniture – would you like the *chaise-longue*? I know you've always admired it.'

Camille dropped his eyes. 'Admired it? Annette, I've dreamt of it.'

'I could get it re-upholstered.'

'Please don't think of it,' Camille said. 'Leave it exactly as it is.'

Claude looked faintly bemused. 'Well, I'll leave you to it then, if you want to talk about furniture.' He smiled, gallantly. 'I must say, my dear boy, you never cease to surprise.'

THE DUKE OF ORLÉANS said: 'Are they? Isn't that wonderful? Do you know, I never get any nice news nowadays?' Some months previously Lucile had been brought for his inspection; he had passed her. She had style, almost the style of an Englishwoman; be good to see her on the hunting field. That toss of the head, that supple spine. I'll give them a good present, he decided. 'Laclos, what's that town-house of mine standing empty, the one with the garden, bit shabby, twelve bedrooms? Corner of thing street?'

'OH, WONDERFUL!' Camille said. 'I can't wait to hear what my father says! We're going to have this amazing house! Plenty of room for the *chaise-longue.*'

Annette put her head in her hands. 'Sometimes I lose hope,' she said. 'What would happen to you if you didn't have so many people to look after you? Camille, think. How can you accept from the Duke a house, which is the largest, most visible bribe he could come up with? Wouldn't it be a shade compromising? Wouldn't it lead to a little paragraph or two in the royalist press?'

'I suppose so,' Camille said.

She sighed. 'Just ask him for the cash. Now, speaking of houses, come and look at this.' She unfolded a plan of her property at Bourg-la-Reine. 'I have been making some sketches for a little house I should like to build for you. I thought here,' she indicated, 'at the bottom of the linden avenue.'

'Why?'

'Why? Because I value my holidays, and I don't intend to have you and Claude in the same house sneering at each other and having meaningful silences. It would be like taking weekend excursions to Purgatory.' She bent over her drawings. 'I've always wanted to design a sweet little cottage. Of course, I may in my amateur enthusiasm leave a few vital bits out. Don't worry, I'll remember to put in a nice bedroom for you. And of course, you'll not be exiles. No, I'll come tripping down to see you, when the mood takes me.'

She smiled. How ambivalent he looked. Caught between terror and pleasure. The next few years will be quite interesting, she thought, one way and another. Camille has the most extraordinary eyes: the darkest grey, as near-black as the eyes of a human being can be, the iris almost merging with the pupil. They seem to be looking at the future now.

'AT SAINT-SULPICE,' Annette said, 'confessions are at three o'clock.'

'I know,' Camille said. 'Everything's arranged. I sent a message to Father Pancemont. I thought it was only fair to warn him. I told him to expect me on the dot of three, and that I don't do this sort of thing every day and I don't expect to be kept waiting. Coming?'

'Order the carriage.'

OUTSIDE THE CHURCH Annette addressed her coachman. 'We'll be – how long will we be? Do you favour a long confession?'

'I'm not actually going to confess anything. Perhaps just a few token peccadilloes. Thirty minutes.'

A man in a dark coat was pacing in the background, a folder of documents tucked under his arm. The clock struck. He advanced on them. 'Just three, M. Desmoulins. Shall we go in?'

'This is my solicitor,' Camille said.

'What?' Annette said.

'My solicitor, notary public. He specializes in canon law. Mirabeau recommended him.'

The man looked pleased. How interesting, she thought, that you still see Mirabeau. But she was having trouble with this notion: 'Camille, you're taking your solicitor to confession with you?'

'A wise precaution. No serious sinner should neglect it.'

He swept her through the church at an unecclesiastical pace. 'I'll just kneel down,' she said, lurching sideways to get away from him. It was quiet; a gaggle of grannies praying for the old days to come back, and a small dog curled up, snoring. The priest seemed to see no reason to lower his voice. 'It's you, is it?' he said.

Camille said to the notary, 'Write that down.'

'I didn't think you'd come, I must say. When I got your message I thought it was a joke.'

'It's certainly not a joke. I have to be in a state of grace, don't I, like everybody else?'

'Are you a Catholic?'

A short pause.

'Why do you ask?'

'Because if you're not a Catholic I can't confer on you the sacraments.'

'All right then. I'm a Catholic.'

'Have you not said – ' Annette heard the priest clearing his throat ' – have you not said in your newspaper that the religion of Mahomet is quite as valid as that of Jesus Christ?'

'You read my newspaper?' Camille sounded gratified. A silence. 'You won't marry us, then?'

'Not until you have made a public profession of the Catholic faith.'

'You have no right to ask that. You have to take my word for it. Mirabeau says – '

'Since when has Mirabeau been a Church Father?'

'Oh, he'll like that, I'll tell him. But do change your mind, Father, because I am dreadfully in love, and I cannot abide even as you abide, and it is better to marry than to burn.'

'Whilst we are on the subject of Saint Paul,' the priest said, 'may I remind you that the powers that be are ordained of God? And whosoever resisteth the power resisteth the ordinance of God, and that they that resist shall receive unto them damnation?'

'Yes, well, I'll have to take my chances on that,' Camille said. 'As you know very well – see verse fourteen – the unbelieving husband is sanctified by the wife. If you're going to be obstructive, I'll have to take it to an ecclesiastical commission. You are just putting a stumbling block or an occasion to fall in your brother's way. You're not supposed to go to law, you're supposed to rather suffer yourself to be defrauded. See chapter six.'

'That's about going to law with unbelievers. The Vicar-General of the Diocese of Sens is not an unbeliever.'

'You know you're wrong,' Camille said. 'Where do you think I was educated? Do you think you can get away with talking this sort of rubbish to me? No,' he said to his lawyer, 'you needn't write that down.'

They emerged. 'Strike that out,' Camille said. 'I was being hasty.' The notary looked cowed. 'Write at the top of the page, "In the matter of the solemnization of the marriage of L. C. Desmoulins, barrister-at-law". That's right, put some lines under it.' He took Annette's arm. 'Were you praying?' he said. 'Get it to the commission right away,' he said over his shoulder.

*

'No church,' Lucile said. 'No priest. Marvellous.'

'The Vicar-General of the Diocese of Sens says I am responsible for the loss of half of his annual revenue,' Camille said. 'He says it was because of me that his château was burned to the ground. Adèle, stop giggling.'

They sat around Annette's drawing room. 'Well, Maximilien,' Camille said, 'you're good at solving people's problems. Solve this.'

Adèle tried to compose herself. 'Haven't you a tame priest? Someone you were at school with?'

Robespierre looked up. 'Surely Father Bérardier could be persuaded? He was our last principal,' he explained, 'at Louis-le-Grand, and he sits in the Assembly now. Surely, Camille . . . he was always so fond of you.'

'When he sees me now, he smiles, as if to say, "I predicted how you would turn out". They say he will refuse the oath to the constitution, you know.'

'Never mind that,' Lucile said. 'If there's any chance . . .'

'On these conditions,' Bérardier said. 'That you make a public profession of faith, in your newspaper. That you cease to make anti-clerical gibes in that publication, and that you erase from it its habitually blasphemous tone.'

'Then what am I to do for a living?' Camille asked.

'It was foolish of you not to foresee this when you decided to take on the church. But then, you never did plan your life more than ten minutes ahead.'

'On the conditions stipulated,' Father Pancemont said, 'I will let Father Bérardier marry you at Saint-Sulpice. But I'm damned if I'll do it myself, and I think Father is making a mistake.'

'He is a creature of impulse,' Father Bérardier said. 'One day his impulses will lead him in the right direction; isn't that so, Camille?'

'The difficulty is that I wasn't thinking of bringing an issue out before the New Year.'

The priests exchanged glances. 'Then we will expect to see the statement in the first issue of 1791.'

Camille nodded.

'Promise?' Bérardier said.

'Promise.'

'You always lied with amazing facility.'

'HE WON'T DO IT,' Father Pancemont said. 'We should have said, statement first, marriage after.'

Bérardier sighed. 'What is the use? Consciences cannot be forced.'

'I believe Deputy Robespierre was your pupil too?'

'For a little while.'

Father Pancemont looked at him as one who said, I was in Lisbon during the earthquake year. 'You have given up teaching now?' he asked.

'Oh, look – there are worse people.'

'I can't think of any,' the priest said.

THE WITNESSES to the marriage: Robespierre, Pétion, the writer Louis-Sébastien Mercier, and the Duke's friend, the Marquis de Sillery. A diplomatically chosen selection, representing the left wing of the Assembly, the literary establishment and the Orléanist connection.

'You don't mind, do you?' Camille said to Danton. 'Really I wanted Lafayette, Louis Suleau, Marat and the public executioner.'

'Of course I don't mind.' After all, he thought, I shall be a witness to everything else. 'Are you going to be rich now?'

'The dowry is a hundred thousand livres. And there's some quite valuable silver. Don't look at me like that. I've had to work for it.'

'And are you going to be faithful to her?'

'Of course.' He looked shocked. 'What a question. I love her.'

'I only wondered. I thought it might be nice to have a statement of intent.'

THEY TOOK a first-floor apartment on the rue des Cordeliers, next door to the Dantons; and on 30 December they held their wedding breakfast for a hundred guests, the dark, icy day nuzzling in hostile curiosity at the lighted windows. At one o'clock in the morning

they found themselves alone. Lucile was still in her pink wedding dress, now crumpled, and with a sticky patch where she had spilled a glass of champagne over herself some hours earlier. She sank down on to the blue *chaise-longue*, and kicked off her shoes. 'Oh, what a day! Has there been anything like it in the annals of holy matrimony? My God, rows of people sniffing and groaning, and my mother crying, and my father crying, and then old Bérardier publically lecturing you like that, and you crying, and the half of Paris that wasn't weeping in the pews standing outside in the streets shouting slogans and making lewd comments. And – '
Her voice tailed off. The day's sick excitement washed over her, wave on wave of it. Probably, she thought, this is what it's like to be at sea. Camille seemed to be talking to her from a long way off:

' . . . and I never thought that happiness like this could have anything to do with me, because two years ago I had nothing, and now I have you, and I've got the money to live well, and I'm famous . . . '

'I've had too much to drink,' Lucile said.

When she thought back on the ceremony, everything appeared to be a sort of haze, so that she felt that perhaps even by then she had had too much to drink, and she wondered in momentary panic, are we properly married? Is drunkenness an incapacity? What about last week, when we looked over the apartment – was I quite sober then? Where is the apartment?

'I thought they'd never go,' Camille said.

She looked up at him. All the things she'd been going to say, all the rehearsals she'd had for this moment, four years of rehearsals; and now, when it came to it, she could only manage a queasy smile. She forced her eyes open to stop the room spinning, and then closed them again, and let it spin. She rolled face down on the *chaise-longue*, drew up her knees comfortably, and gave a little grunt of contentment, like the dog at Saint-Sulpice. She slept. Some kind person slid a hand under her cheek, and then replaced the hand by a cushion.

*

'LISTEN to what I will be,' said the King, 'if I do not uphold the constitutional oath on the poor bishops.' He adjusted his spectacles and read:

'. . . enemy of the public liberty, treacherous conspirator, most cowardly of perjurers, prince without honour, without shame, lowest of men . . .' He broke off, put down the newspaper and blew his nose vigorously into a handkerchief embroidered with the royal arms – the last he had, of the old sort. 'A happy new year to you too, Dr Marat,' he said.

III. *Lady's Pleasure*

(*1791*)

'91: 'LAFAYETTE,' Mirabeau suggests to the Queen, 'is walking more closely in the footsteps of Cromwell than becomes his natural modesty.'

We're done for, Marat says, it's all up with us; Antoinette's gang are in league with Austria, the monarchs are betraying the nation. It is necessary to cut off 20,000 heads.

France is to be invaded from the Rhine. By June, the King's brother Artois will have an army at Coblenz. Maître Desmoulins's old client, the Prince de Condé, will command a force at Worms. A third, at Colmar, will be under the command of Mirabeau's younger brother, who is known, because of his shape and proclivities, as Barrel Mirabeau.

The Barrel spent his last few months in France pursuing the Lanterne Attorney through the courts. He now hopes to pursue him, with an armed force, through the streets. The *émigrés* want the old regime back, not one jot or one tittle abated: and a firing squad for Lafayette. They call, as of right, for the support of the powers of Europe.

The powers, however, have their own ideas. These revolutionaries are dangerous, beyond doubt; they menace us all in the most horrible fashion. But Louis is not dead, nor deposed; though the furnishings and appointments at the Tuileries may not measure up to those at Versailles, he is not even seriously inconvenienced. In better times, when the revolution is over, he may be inclined to admit that the sharp lesson has done him good. Meanwhile it is a secret, unholy pleasure to watch a rich neighbour struggle on with taxes uncollected, a fine army rent by mutiny, Messieurs the Democrats making themselves ridiculous. The order established by God must be maintained in Europe; but there is no need, just at present, to re-gild the Bourbon lilies.

As for Louis himself, the *émigrés* advise him to begin a campaign of passive resistance. As the months pass, they begin to despair of him. They remind each other of the maxim of the Comte de Provence: 'When you can hold together a number of oiled ivory balls, you may do something with the King.' It infuriates them to find that Louis's every pronouncement bows to the new order – until they receive his secret assurance that everything he says means the exact opposite. They cannot understand that some of those monsters, those blackguards, those barbarians of the National Assembly, have the King's interests at heart. Neither can the Queen comprehend it:

'If I see them, or have any relations with them, it is only to make use of them; they inspire me with a horror too great for me to ever become involved with them.' So much for you, Mirabeau. It is possible that Lafayette is penetrated with a clearer idea of the lady's worth. He has told her to her face (they say) that he intends to prove her guilty of adultery and pack her off home to Austria. To this end, he leaves every night a little door unguarded, to admit her supposed lover, Axel von Fersen. 'Conciliation is no longer possible,' she writes. 'Only armed force can repair the damage done.'

Catherine, the Tsarina: 'I am doing my utmost to spur on the courts of Vienna and Berlin to become entangled in French affairs so that I can have my hands free.' Catherine's hands are free, as usual, for choking Poland. She will make her counter-revolution in Warsaw, she says, and let the Germans make one in Paris. Leopold, in Austria, is occupied with the affairs of Poland, Belgium, Turkey; William Pitt is thinking of India, and financial reforms. They wait and watch France weakening herself (as they think) by strife and division so that she is no longer a threat to their schemes.

Frederick William of Prussia thinks a little differently; when war breaks out with France, as he knows it will, he intends to come out best. He has agents in Paris, directed to stir up hatred of Antoinette and the Austrians: to urge the use of force, to unbalance the situation, and tilt it to violent conclusions. The real enthusiast for counter-revolution is Gustavus of Sweden, Gustavus who is going to wipe Paris off the face of the earth: Gustavus who was paid one and a half million livres per annum under the old regime, Gustavus and his imaginary army. And from Madrid, the fevered reactionary sentiments of an imbecile King.

These revolutionaries, they say, are the scourge of mankind. I will move against them – if you will.

From Paris the future looks precarious. Marat sees conspirators everywhere, treason on the breeze drifting the new tricolour flag outside the King's windows. Behind that façade, patrolled by National Guardsmen, the King eats, drinks, grows stout, is seldom out of countenance. 'My greatest fault,' he had once written, 'is a sluggishness of mind which makes all my mental efforts wearisome and painful.'

In the left-wing press, Lafayette is now referred to not by his title, but by his family name of Mottié. The King is referred to as Louis Capet. The Queen is called 'the King's wife'.

There is religious dissension. About one-half of the curés of France agree to take the constitutional oath. The rest we call refractory priests. Only seven bishops support the new order. In Paris, nuns are attacked by fishwives. At Saint-Sulpice, where Father Pancemont is obdurate, a mob tramps through the nave singing that wholesome ditty: 'Ça ira, ça ira, les aristocrats à la Lanterne'. The King's aunts, Mesdames Adelaide and Victoire, leave secretly 'for Rome. The patriots have to be assured that the two old ladies have not packed the Dauphin in their luggage. The Pope pronounces the civil constitution schismatic. The head of a policeman is thrown into the carriage of the Papal Nuncio.

In a booth at the Palais-Royal, a male and female 'savage' exhibit themselves naked. They eat stones, babble in an unknown tongue and for a few small coins will copulate.

Barnave, summer: 'One further step towards liberty must destroy the monarchy, one further step towards equality must destroy private property.'

Desmoulins, autumn: 'Our revolution of 1789 was a piece of business arranged between the English government and a minority of the nobility, prepared by some in the hopes of turning out the Versailles aristocracy, and taking possession of their castles, houses and offices: by others to saddle us with a new master: and by all, to give us two Houses, and a constitution like that of England.'

'91: eighteen months of revolution, and securely under the heel of a new tyranny.

'That man is a liar,' Robespierre says, 'who claims I have ever advocated disobedience to the laws.'

JANUARY AT BOURG-LA-REINE. Annette Duplessis stood at the window, gazing into the branches of the walnut tree that shaded the courtyard. From here, you could not see the foundations of the new cottage; just as well, for they were as melancholy as ruins. She sighed in exasperation at the silence welling from the room behind her. All of them would be beseeching her, inwardly, to turn and make some remark. If she were to leave the room, she would come back to find it alive with tension. Taking chocolate together mid-morning: surely that should not be too much of a strain?

Claude was reading the *Town and Court Journal*, a right-wing scandal-sheet. He had a faintly defiant air. Camille was gazing at his wife, as he often did. (Two days married, she discovered with a sense of shock that the black soul-eating eyes were short-sighted. 'Perhaps you should wear spectacles.' 'Too vain.') Lucile was reading *Clarissa*, in translation and with scant attention. Every few minutes her eyes would flit from the page to her husband's face.

Annette wondered if this were what had plunged Claude so deeply into disagreeableness – the girl's air of sexual triumph, the high colour in her cheeks when they met in the mornings. You wish she were nine years old, she thought, kept happy with her dolls. She studied her husband's bent head, the strands of grey neatly dressed and powdered; rural interludes wrung no concessions from Claude. Camille, a few feet away, looked like a gypsy who had mislaid his violin and had been searching for it in a hedgerow; he frustrated daily the best efforts of an expensive tailor, wearing his clothes as a subtle comment on the collapsing social order.

Claude let his paper fall. Camille snapped out of his reverie and turned his head. 'What now? I told you, if you read that thing you must expect to be shocked.'

Claude seemed unable to articulate. He pointed to the page; Annette thought he whimpered. Camille reached forward for it; Claude clasped it to his chest. 'Don't be silly, Claude,' Annette said, as one does to a baby. 'Give the paper to Camille.'

Camille ran his eyes down the page. 'Oh, you'll enjoy this. Lolotte, will you go away for a minute?'

'No.'

Where did she get this pet-name? Annette had some feeling that Danton had given it to her. A little too intimate, she thought; and now Camille uses it. 'Do as you're told,' she said.

Lucile didn't move. I'm married now, she thought; don't have to do what anybody says.

'Stay then,' Camille said, 'I was only thinking to spare your feelings. According to this, you're not your father's daughter.'

'Oh, don't say it,' Claude said. 'Burn the paper.'

'You know what Rousseau said.' Annette looked grim. '"Burning isn't answering."'

'Whose daughter am I?' Lucile asked. 'Am I my mother's daughter, or am I a foundling?'

'You're certainly your mother's daughter, and your father's the abbé Terray.'

Lucile giggled. 'Lucile, I am not beyond slapping you,' her mother said.

'Hence the money for the dowry,' Camille said, 'comes from the abbé's speculation in grain at times of famine.'

'The abbé did not speculate in grain.' Claude held Camille in a red-faced inimical stare.

'I do not suggest he did. I am paraphrasing the newspaper.'

'Yes . . . of course.' Claude looked away miserably.

'Did you ever meet Terray?' Camille asked his mother-in-law.

'Once, I think. We exchanged about three words.'

'You know,' Camille said to Claude, 'Terray did have a reputation with women.'

'It wasn't his fault.' Claude flared up again. 'He never wanted to be a priest. His family forced him into it.'

'Do calm yourself,' Annette suggested.

Claude hunched forward, hands pressed together between his knees. 'Terray was our best hope. He worked hard. He had energy. People were afraid of him.' He stopped, seeming to realize that for the first time in years he had added a new statement, a coda.

'Were you afraid of him?' Camille asked: not scoring a point, simply curious.

Claude considered. 'I might have been.'

'I'm quite often afraid of people,' Camille said. 'It's a terrible admission, isn't it?'

'Like who?' Lucile said.

'Well, principally I'm afraid of Fabre. If he hears me stutter, he shakes me and takes me by the hair and bangs my head against the wall.'

'Annette,' Claude said, 'there have been other imputations. In other newspapers.' He looked covertly at Camille. 'I have contrived to dismiss them from my mind.'

Annette made no comment. Camille hurled the *Town and Court Journal* across the room. 'I'll sue them,' he said.

Claude looked up. 'You'll do what?'

'I'll sue them for libel.'

Claude stood up. 'You'll sue them,' he said. 'You. You'll sue someone for libel.' He walked out of the room, and they could hear his hollow laughter as he climbed the stairs.

FEBRUARY, Lucile was furnishing her apartment. They were to have pink silk cushions; Camille wondered how they would look a few months on, when grimy Cordeliers had mauled them. But he confined himself to an unspoken expletive when he saw her new set of engravings of the Life and Death of Maria Stuart. He did not like to look at these pictures at all. Bothwell had a ruthless, martial expression in his eye that reminded him of Antoine Saint-Just. Bulky retainers in bizarre plaids waved broadswords; kilted gentlemen, showing plump knees, helped the distressed Queen of Scots into a rowing boat. At her execution Maria was dressed to show off her figure, and looked all of twenty-three. 'Crushingly romantic,' Lucile said. 'Isn't it?'

Since they had moved, it was possible to run the *Révolutions* from home. Inky men, short-tempered and of a robust turn of phrase, stamped up and down the stairs with questions to which they expected her to know the answers. Uncorrected proofs tangled about table legs. Writ-servers sat around the street door, sometimes playing cards and dice to pass the time. It was just like the Danton house, which was in the same building round the corner – complete strangers tramping in and out at all hours, the dining room colonized by men scribbling, their bedroom an overflow sitting room and general thoroughfare.

'We must order more bookcases made,' she said. 'You can't have things in little piles all over the floor, I skid around when I get out of bed in the morning. Do you need all these old newspapers, Camille?'

'Oh yes. They're for searching out the inconsistencies of my opponents. So that I can persecute them when they change their opinions.'

He lifted one from a pile. 'Hébert's,' she said. 'That is dismal trash.'

René Hébert was peddling his opinions now through the persona of a bluff, pipe-smoking man of the people, a fictitious furnace-maker called Père Duchesne. The paper was vulgar, in every sense – simple-minded prose studded with obscenity. 'Père Duchesne is a great royalist, isn't he?' Camille swiftly marked a passage. 'I may have to hold that one against you, Hébert.'

'Is Hébert really like Père Duchesne? Does he really smoke a pipe and swear?'

'Not at all. He's an effete little man. He has peculiar hands that flutter about. They look like things that live under stones. Listen, Lolotte – are you happy?'

'Absolutely.'

'Are you sure? Do you like the apartment? Do you want to move?'

'No, I don't want to move. I like the apartment. I like everything. I am very happy.' Her emotions now seemed to lie just below the surface, scratching at her delicate skin to be hatched. 'Only I'm afraid something will happen.'

'What could happen?' (He knew what could happen.)

'The Austrians might come and you'd be shot. The Court might have you assassinated. You could be abducted and shut up in prison somewhere, and I'd never know where you were.'

She put up her hand to her mouth, as if she could stop the fears spilling out.

'I'm not that important,' he said. 'They have more to do than arrange assassins for me.'

'I saw one of those letters, threatening to kill you.'

'That's what comes of reading other people's mail. You find out things you'd rather not know.'

'Who obliges us to live like this?' Her voice muffled against his shoulder. 'Someday soon we'll have to live in cellars, like Marat.'

'Dry your tears. Someone is here.'

Robespierre hovered, looking embarrassed. 'Your housekeeper said I should come through,' he said.

'That's all right,' Lucile gestured around her. 'Not exactly a love-nest, as you see. Sit on the bed. Sit in the bed, feel free. Half of Paris was in here this morning while I was trying to get dressed.'

'I can't find anything since I moved,' Camille complained. 'And you've no idea how time-consuming it is, being married. You have to take decisions about the most baffling things – like whether to have the ceilings painted. I always supposed the paint just grew on them, didn't you?'

Robespierre declined to sit. 'I won't stay – I came to see if you'd written that piece you promised, about my pamphlet on the National Guard. I expected to see it in your last issue.'

'Oh Christ,' Camille said. 'It could be anywhere. Your pamphlet, I mean. Have you another copy with you? Look, why don't you just write the piece yourself? It would be quicker.'

'But Camille, it's all very well for me to give your readers a digest of my ideas, but I expected something more – you could say whether you thought my ideas were cogent, whether they were logical, whether they were well-expressed. I can't write a piece praising myself, can I?'

'I don't see the difficulty.'

'Don't be flippant. I haven't time to waste.'

'I'm sorry.' Camille swept his hair back and smiled. 'But you're our editorial policy, didn't you know? You're our hero.' He crossed the room, and touched Robespierre on the shoulder, very lightly, with just the tip of his middle finger. 'We admire your principles in general, support your actions and writings in particular – and will therefore never fail to give you good publicity.'

'Yet you have failed, haven't you?' Robespierre stepped back. He was exasperated. 'You must try to keep to the task in hand. You are so heedless, you are unreliable.'

'Yes, I'm sorry.'

She felt a needlepoint of irritation.

'Max, he isn't a schoolchild.'

'I'll write it this afternoon,' Camille said.

'And be at the Jacobins this evening.'

'Yes, of course.'

'You are terribly dictatorial,' she said.

'Oh, no, Lucile.' Robespierre looked at her earnestly. His voice suddenly softened. 'It's just that one has to use exhortation with Camille, he's such a dreamer. I'm sure,' he dropped his eyes, 'if I had just been married to you, Lucile, I'd be tempted to spend time with you and I wouldn't give such attention to my work as I ought. And Camille is no use at fighting temptation on his own, he never has been. But I'm not dictatorial, don't say that.'

'All right,' she said, 'you have the licence of long acquaintance. But your tone. Your manner. You should save that for berating the Right. Go and make *them* flinch.'

His face tightened: defensive, distressed. She saw why Camille preferred always to apologize. 'Oh,' he said, 'Camille quite likes being pushed around. It's something in his character. So Danton says. Goodbye. Write it this afternoon, won't you?' he added gently.

'Well,' she said. They exchanged glances. 'That was pointed, wasn't it? What does he mean?'

'Nothing. He was just shaken because you criticized him.'

'Must he not be criticized?'

'No. He takes things to heart, it undermines him. Besides, he was right. I should have remembered about the pamphlet. You mustn't be hard on him. It's shyness that makes him abrupt.'

'He ought to have got over it. Other people don't get allowances made for them. Besides, once you said he had no weaknesses.'

'Day to day he has weaknesses. In the end he has no weaknesses.'

'You might leave me,' she said suddenly. 'For someone else.'

'What makes you imagine that?'

'Today I keep thinking. I keep thinking of what could happen. Because I never supposed that one could be so happy, that everything could come right.'

'Do you think you have had an unhappy life?'

Appearances were against her; but truthfully she answered, 'Yes.'

'I also. But not from now on.'

'You could be killed in an accident in the street. You might die. Your sister Henriette died of a consumption.' She scrutinized him as if she wanted to see the tissue beneath the skin, and provide against contingencies.

He turned away; he didn't feel he could bear it. He was terribly afraid that happiness might be a habit, or a quality knitted into the temperament; or it might be something you learn when you're a child, a kind of language, harder than Latin or Greek, that you should have a good grasp on by the time you're seven. What if you haven't got that grasp? What if you're in some way happiness-stupid, happiness-blind? It occurred to him that there are some people, ashamed of being illiterate, who always pretend to others that they can read. Sooner or later they get found out, of course. But it is always possible that while you are valiantly pretending, the principles of reading strike you for the first time, and you are saved. By analogy, it is possible that while you, the unhappy person, are trying out some basic expressions – the kind of thing you get in phrasebooks for travellers – the grammar and syntax of this neglected language are revealing themselves, somewhere at the back of your mind. That's all very well, he thought, but the process could take years. He understood Lucile's problem: how do you know you will live long enough to be fluent?

*

THE PEOPLE'S FRIEND, No. 497, J.-P. Marat, editor:

... name immediately a military tribunal, a supreme dictator ... you are lost beyond hope if you continue to heed your present leaders, who will continue to flatter you and lull you until your enemies are at your walls ... Now is the time to have the heads of Mottié, of Bailly ... of all the traitors in the National Assembly ... within a few days Louis XVI will advance at the head of all the malcontents and the Austrian legions ... A hundred fiery mouths will threaten to destroy your town with red shot if you offer the least resistance ... all the patriots will be arrested, the popular writers will be dragged away to dungeons ... a few more days of indecision, and it will be too late to shake off your lethargy; death will overtake you in your sleep.

DANTON at Mirabeau's house.

'So how goes it?' the Comte said.

Danton nodded.

'I mean, I really want to know.' Mirabeau laughed. 'Are you totally cynical, Danton, or do you harbour some guilty ideals? Where do you stand, really? Come, I'm taken with a passion to know. Which is it to be for King, Louis or Philippe?'

Danton declined to answer.

'Or perhaps neither. Are you a republican, Danton?'

'Robespierre says that it is not a government's descriptive label that matters, but its nature, the way it operates, whether it is government by the people. Cromwell's republic, for instance, was not a popular government. I agree with him. It seems to me of little importance whether we call it a monarchy or a republic.'

'You say its nature matters, but you do not say which nature you would prefer.'

'My reticence is considered.'

'I'm sure it is. You can hide a great deal behind slogans. *Liberty, Equality, Fraternity*, indeed.'

'I subscribe to that.'

'I hear you invented it. But freedom comprehends – what?'

'Do I have to define it for you? You should simply know.'

'That is sentimentality,' Mirabeau said.

'I know. Sentimentality has its place in politics, as in the bedroom.'

The Comte looked up. 'We'll discuss bedrooms later. Let's, shall we, descend to practicalities? The Commune is to be reshuffled, there will be elections. The office ranking below mayor will be that of administrator. There will be sixteen administrators. You wish to be one of them, you say. Why, Danton?'

'I wish to serve the city.'

'No doubt. I myself am assured of a place. Amongst your colleagues you may expect Sieyès and Talleyrand. I take it from the expression on your face that you think it a company of tergiversators in which you will be quite at home. But if I am to support you, I must have an assurance as to your moderate conduct.'

'You have it.'

'Your moderation. You understand me?'

'Yes.'

'Fully?'

'Yes.'

'Danton, I know you. You are like myself. Why else have they started calling you the poor man's Mirabeau, do you suppose? You haven't an ounce of moderation in your body.'

'I think our resemblances must be superficial.'

'Oh, you think you are a moderate?'

'I don't know. I could be. Most things are possible.'

'You may wish to conciliate, but it is against your nature. You don't work *with* people, you work *over* them.'

Danton nodded. He conceded the point. 'I drive them as I wish,' he said. 'That could be towards moderation, or it could be towards the extremes.'

'Yes, but the difficulty is, moderation looks like weakness, doesn't it? Oh yes, I know, Danton, I have been here before you, crashing down this particular trail. And speaking of extremism, I do not care for the attacks on me made by your Cordeliers journalists.'

'The press is free. I don't dictate the output of the writers of my district.'

'Not even the one who lives next door to you? I rather thought you did.'

'Camille has to be running ahead of public opinion all the time.'

'I can remember the days,' Mirabeau said, 'when we didn't have public opinion. No one had ever heard of such a thing.' He rubbed his chin, deep in thought. 'Very well, Danton, consider yourself elected. I shall hold you to your promise of moderation, and I shall expect your support. Come now – tell me the gossip. How is the marriage?'

LUCILE looked at the carpet. It was a good carpet, and on balance she was glad she had spent the money on it. She did not particularly wish to admire the pattern now, but she could not trust the expression on her face.

'Caro,' she said, 'I really can't think why you are telling me all this.'

Caroline Rémy put her feet up on the blue *chaise-longue*. She was a handsome young woman, an actress belonging to the Théâtre Montansier company. She had two arrangements, one with Fabre d'Églantine and one with Hérault de Séchelles.

'To protect you,' she said, 'from being told all this by unsympathetic people. Who would delight in embarrassing you, and making fun of your *naïveté*.' Caroline put her head on one side, and wrapped a curl around her finger. 'Let me see – how old are you now, Lucile?'

'Twenty.'

'Dear, dear,' Caroline said. 'Twenty!' She couldn't be much older herself, Lucile thought. But she had, not surprisingly, a rather well-used look about her. 'I'm afraid, my dear, that you know nothing of the world.'

'No. People keep telling me that, lately. I suppose they must be right.' (A guilty capitulation. Camille, last week, trying to educate her: 'Lolotte, nothing gains truth by mere force of repetition.' But how to be polite, faced with such universal insistence?)

'I'm surprised your mother didn't see fit to warn you,' Caro said. 'I'm sure she knows everything there is to know about Camille. But if I'd had the courage – and believe me I reproach myself – to come to you before Christmas, and tell you, just for instance, about Maître Perrin, what would your reaction have been?'

Lucile looked up. 'Caro, I'd have been riveted,'

It was not the answer Caro had expected. 'You are a strange girl,' she said. Her expression said clearly, strangeness doesn't pay. 'You see, you have to be prepared for what lies ahead of you.'

'I try to imagine,' Lucile said. She wished for the door to smash open, and one of Camille's assistants to come flying in, and start firing off questions and rummaging for a piece of paper that had been mislaid. But the house was quiet for once: only Caro's well-trained voice, with its tragedienne's quaver, its suggestion of huskiness.

'Infidelity you can endure,' she said. 'In the circles in which we move, these things are understood.' She made a gesture, elegant fingers spread, to indicate the laudable correctness, both aesthetic and social, of a little well-judged adultery. 'One finds a *modus vivendi*. I have no fear of your not being able to amuse yourself. Other women one can cope with, provided they're not too close to home – '

'Just stop there. What does that mean?'

Caro became a little round-eyed. 'Camille is an attractive man,' she said. 'I know whereof I speak.'

'I don't see what it has to do with anything,' Lucile muttered, 'if you've been to bed with him. I could do without that bit of information.'

'Please regard me as your friend,' Caro suggested. She bit her lip. At least she had found out that Lucile was not expecting a child. Whatever the reason for the hurry about the marriage, it was not that. It must be something even more interesting, if she could only make it out. She patted her curls back into place and slid from the *chaise-longue*. 'Must go. Rehearsal.'

I don't think you need any rehearsal, Lucile said under her breath. I think you're quite perfect.

WHEN CARO had gone, Lucile leaned back in her chair, and tried to take deep breaths, and tried to be calm. The housekeeper, Jeanette, came in, and looked her over. 'Try a small omelette,' she advised.

'Leave me alone,' Lucile said. 'I don't know why you think that food solves everything.'

'I could step around and fetch your mother.'

'I should just think,' Lucile said, 'that I can do without my mother at my age.'

She agreed to a glass of iced water. It made her hand ache, froze her deep inside. Camille came in at a quarter-past five, and ran around snatching up pen and ink. 'I have to be at the Jacobins,' he said. That meant six o'clock. She stood over him watching his scruffy handwriting loop itself across the page. 'No time ever to correct . . . ' He scribbled. 'Lolotte . . . what's wrong?'

She sat down and laughed feebly: nothing's wrong.

'You're a terrible liar.' He was making deletions. 'I mean, you're no good at it.'

'Caroline Rémy called.'

'Oh.' His expression, in passing, was faintly contemptuous.

'I want to ask you a question. I appreciate it might be rather difficult.'

'Try.' He didn't look up.

'Have you had an affair with her?'

He frowned at the paper. 'That doesn't sound right.' He sighed and wrote down the side of the page. 'I've had an affair with everybody, don't you know that by now?'

'But I'd like to know.'

'Why?'

'Why?'

'Why would you like to know?'

'I can't think why, really.'

He tore the sheet once across and began immediately on another. 'Not the most intelligent of conversations, this.' He wrote for a minute. 'Did she say that I did?'

'Not in so many words.'

'What gave you the idea then?' He looked up at the ceiling for a synonym, and as he tipped his head back the flat, red winter light touched his hair.

'She implied it.'

'Perhaps you mistook her.'

'Would you mind just denying it?'

'I think it's quite probable that at some time I spent a night with her, but I've no clear memory of it.' He had found the word, and reached for another sheet of paper.

'How could you not have a clear memory? A person couldn't just not remember.'

'Why shouldn't a person not remember? Not everybody thinks it's the highest human activity, like you do.'

'I suppose not remembering is the ultimate snub.'

'I suppose so. Have you seen Brissot's latest issue?'

'There. You've got your paper on it.'

'Oh, yes.'

'What, you mean you really can't remember?'

'I'm very absent-minded, anyone will tell you. It needn't have been so much as a night. Could have been an afternoon. Or just a few minutes, or not at all. I might have thought she was someone else. My mind might have been on other things.'

She laughed.

'I'm not sure you ought to be amused. Perhaps you ought to be shocked.'

'She thinks you very attractive.'

'What heartening news. I was consumed with anxiety in case she didn't. The page I want is missing. I must have thrown it on the fire in a rage. A literary jockey, Mirabeau calls Brissot. I'm not quite sure what that means but I expect he thinks it's very insulting.'

'She was telling me something, about a barrister you once knew.'

'Which of the five hundred?'

But he was on the defensive now. She didn't answer. He wiped his pen carefully, put it down. He looked at her sideways, cautiously, from under his eyelashes. He smiled, slightly.

'Oh God, don't look at me like that,' she said. 'You look as if you're going to tell me what a good time you had. Do people know?'

'Some people, obviously.'

'Does my mother know?'

No answer.

'Why didn't I know?'

'I can't think. Possibly because you were about ten at the time. We hadn't met. I can't think how people would have broached the topic.'

'Ah. She didn't tell me it was so long ago.'

'No, I'm sure she just told you exactly what suited her. Lolotte, does it matter so much?'

'Not really. I suppose he must have been nice.'

'Yes, he was.' Oh, the relief of saying so. 'He was really extremely nice to me. And somehow, oh, you know, it didn't seem much to do.'

She stared at him. He's quite unique, she thought. 'But now – ' and suddenly she felt she had the essence of it – 'now you're a public person. It matters to everybody what you do.'

'And now I am married to you. And no one will ever have anything to reproach me with, except loving my wife too much and giving them nothing to talk about.' Camille pushed his chair back. 'The Jacobins can wait. I don't think I want to listen to speeches tonight. I should prefer to write a theatre review. Yes? I like taking you to the theatre. I like walking around in public with you. I get envied. Do you know what I really like? I like to see people looking at you, and forming ideas, and people saying, is she married? – yes – and their faces fall, but then they think, well, still, even so, and they say, to whom? And someone says, to the Lanterne Attorney, and they say oh, and walk away with a glazed look in their eye.'

She raced off to get dressed for the theatre. When she looked back, she had to admire it, as a way of getting off the subject.

A LITTLE WOMAN – Roland's wife – came out of the Riding-School on Pétion's arm. 'Paris has changed greatly,' she said, 'since I was here six years ago. I shall never forget that visit. We were night after night at the theatre. I had the time of my life.'

'Let's hope we can do as well for you this time,' Pétion said, with gallantry. 'And yet you are a Parisian, my friend Brissot tells me?'

You're overdoing the charm, Jérôme, his friend Brissot thought.

'Yes, but my husband's affairs have kept us so long in the

provinces that I no longer lay claim to the title. I have so often wished to return – and now here I am, thanks to the affairs of the Municipality of Lyon.'

Brissot thought, she talks like a novel.

'I'm sure your husband is a most worthy representative,' Pétion said, 'yet let us cherish a secret hope that he does not conclude Lyon's business too quickly. We should hate to lose, so soon, the benefit of your advice – and the radiance of your person.'

She glanced up at him and smiled. She was the type he liked – petite, a little plump, hazel eyes, dark auburn ringlets about an oval face – style perhaps a little bit young for her? What would she be, thirty-five? He pondered the possibility of burying his head in her opulent bosom – on some later occasion, of course.

'Brissot has often told me,' he said, 'of his Lyon correspondent, his "Roman Lady" – and of course I have read all her articles and come to admire both her elegant turn of phrase and the noble cast of mind which inspires it; but never, I confess, did I look to see beauty and wit so perfectly united.'

A slight rigidity in her ready smile showed that this was just a little too fulsome. Brissot was rolling his eyes in a rather obvious manner. 'So what did you think of the National Assembly, Madame?' he asked her.

'I think perhaps it has outlived its usefulness – that is the kindest thing one can say. And such a disorderly set of people! Today's session can't be typical?'

'I'm afraid it was.'

'They waste so much time – scrapping like schoolboys. I had hoped for a higher tone.'

'The Jacobins pleased you better, I think. A more sober gathering.'

'At least they seem concerned with the matter in hand. I am sure that there are patriots in the Assembly, but it shocks me that grown men can be so easily duped.' They could see the unwelcome conclusion darkening her eyes. 'I'm afraid some of them must be willing dupes. Some of them, surely, have sold themselves to the Court. Otherwise our progress would not be so slow. Do they not understand that if there is to be any liberty in Europe we must rid ourselves of all monarchs?'

Danton was walking by, in pursuit of the city's business; he turned, raised an eyebrow, removed his hat and passed them with a laconic, 'Good morning, Mme Revolutionary, Messieurs.'

'Good heavens. Who was that?'

'That was M. Danton,' Pétion said smoothly. 'One of the curiosities of the capital.'

'Indeed.' Reluctantly she dragged her eyes from Danton's retreating back. 'How did he come by those scars?'

'No one cares to speculate,' Brissot said.

'What a brute he looks!'

Pétion smiled. 'He is a man of culture,' he said, 'a barrister by profession, and a very staunch patriot. One of the City Administrators, in fact. His exterior belies him.'

'I should hope it does.'

'Whom did Madame see at the Jacobins?' Brissot asked. 'Which of our friends has she met?'

'She has met the Marquis de Condorcet – I beg your pardon, I shouldn't say Marquis – and Deputy Buzot – oh, Madame, do you recall that little fellow at the Jacobins that you took such a dislike to?'

How rude, Brissot thought: I am a little fellow myself, which is better than you, who are running to fat.

'That vain, sarcastic man, who looked at the company through a lorgnette?'

'Yes. Now he is Fabre d'Églantine, a great friend of Danton.'

'What an odd pair they must make.' She turned. 'Ah, here is my husband at last.' She made the introductions. Pétion and Brissot stared at M. Roland in ill-concealed bewilderment, taking in his bald dome, his grave face with its yellow ageing skin, his tall, spare, dessicated body. He could have been her father, each thought: and exchanged glances to that effect.

'Well, my dear,' Roland said, 'I hope you've been amusing yourself?'

'I have prepared the abstracts you asked for. The figures are all checked, and I have drafted several possibilities for your deposition to the Assembly. It is up to you to tell me which you prefer, and then I will cast it in its final form. Everything is in order.'

'My little secretary.' He lifted her hand and kissed it. 'Gentlemen – see how lucky I am. I'd be lost without her.'

'So, Madame,' Brissot said, 'perhaps you would like to have a little salon? No, don't blush, you are not unqualified. We who debate the great questions of the hour need to do so under some gentle feminine influence.' (Pompous arsehole, Pétion thought.) 'To lighten the tone, perhaps a few gentlemen from the world of the arts?'

'No.' Brissot was surprised by the firmness of tone. 'No artists, no poets, no actors – not for their own sake. We must establish our seriousness of purpose. If they were also patriots, of course they would be welcome.'

'You are penetrating, as always,' Pétion said. (You'd be penetrating if you could, Brissot thought.) 'You should ask Deputy Buzot – you liked him, didn't you?'

'Yes. He seemed to me to be a young man of singular integrity, a most valuable patriot. He has moral force.'

(And such a handsome, pensive face, Pétion thought, which no doubt has something to do with his appeal; God help poor plain Mme Buzot if this determined little piece sinks her claws into François-Léonard.)

'And shall I bring Louvet?'

'I'm not sure of Louvet. Has he not written an improper book?' Pétion looked down at her pityingly. 'You are laughing at me because I am a provincial,' she said. 'But one has standards.'

'Of course. But *Faublas* was really a very harmless book.' He smiled involuntarily, as people always did when they tried to imagine whey-faced Jean-Baptiste writing a risqué bestseller. It was all autobiographical, people said.

'And Robespierre?' Brissot persisted.

'Yes, bring Robespierre. He interests me. So reserved. I should like to draw him out.'

Who knows, Pétion thought, perhaps you're the girl who will? 'Robespierre's always busy. He has no time for a social life.'

'My salon will not form part of anyone's social life,' she corrected sweetly. 'It will be a forum for serious discussion of the issues confronting patriots and republicans.'

I wish she would not talk so much about the republic, Brissot thought. That's an issue to be tiptoed around. I will teach her a lesson, he thought. 'If you wish republicans, I shall bring Camille.'

'Who is that?'

'Camille Desmoulins – did nobody point him out at the Jacobins?'

'Dark, sulky boy with long hair,' Pétion said. 'Has a stutter – but no, he didn't speak, did he?' He looked at Brissot. 'He sat next to Fabre, whispering.'

'Thick as thieves,' Brissot said. 'Great patriots, of course, but not what you'd call examples of the civic virtues. Camille's only been married for weeks, and already – '

'Gentlemen,' Roland interposed, 'is this fit for the ears of my wife?' They had forgotten he was there – so vague and grey a presence beside his blithe, vivacious spouse. He turned to her: 'M. Desmoulins, my dear, is a clever and scandalous young journalist who is sometimes known as the Lanterne Attorney.'

A faint blush again on the soft, fresh skin: how quickly the smile could vanish, leaving her mouth a hard, decisive line. 'I see no need to meet him.'

'But it is fashionable to know him, you see.'

'What has that to do with anything?'

'After all,' Pétion said, 'one has standards.'

Brissot chuckled. 'Madame doesn't find much to commend in Danton's clique.'

'She's not alone.' Pétion spoke for Roland's benefit. 'Danton has some qualities, but there is a certain lack of scruple in evidence – he is careless with money, extravagant, and of course one wonders at its source. Fabre's antecedents are dubious in the extreme. Camille – well, he's clever, I grant you, and he's popular, but he'll never stay the course.'

'I suggest,' Brissot continued, 'that Madame open her apartment to the patriots between the close of business in the Assembly –

about four o'clock on a normal day – and the meeting of the Jacobins at six.' (She can open her legs to the patriots a little later, Pétion thought.) 'People will come and go, it will be pleasant.'

'And useful,' she added.

'I think, gentlemen,' Roland said, 'that you will congratulate yourselves on this initiative. As you see, my wife is a woman of culture and sensibility.' He looked down at her, gratified, as if she were an infant daughter taking her first steps.

Her face glowed with excitement. 'To be here – at last,' she said. 'For years I've watched, studied, fulminated, argued – with myself, of course; I've waited, longed, if I had any faith I would have prayed; all my concern has been that a republic should be established in France. Now here I am – in Paris – and it is going to happen.' She smiled at the three men, showing her even white teeth, of which she was very proud. 'And soon.'

DANTON saw Mirabeau at City Hall. It was three o'clock, an afternoon in late March. The Comte was leaning against the wall, his mouth slightly ajar as if he were recovering from some exertion. Danton stopped. He saw that the Comte had changed since their last meeting – and he was not one to notice such things. 'Mirabeau – '

Mirabeau smiled dolefully. 'You must not call me that. Riquetti is my name now. Titles of nobility have been abolished by the Assembly. The decree was supported by Marie Joseph Paul Yves Roch Gilbert du Mottié, *ci-devant* Marquis de Lafayette, and opposed by the Abbé Maury, who is the son of a shoemaker.'

'Are you quite well?'

'Yes,' Mirabeau said. 'No. No, to tell the truth, Danton, I am ill. I have a pain – here – and my eyesight is failing.'

'Have you seen a doctor?'

'Several. They speak of my choleric disposition, and advise compresses. Do you know what I think of, Danton, these days?' There was agitation in his face.

'You should rest, at least find yourself a chair.' Danton heard himself speak, unwittingly, as if to a child or an old man.

'I don't need a chair, just listen to me.' He put a hand on Danton's arm. 'I think about the old King's death. When he died, they tell me,' he passed the other hand across his face, 'they couldn't find anyone willing to shroud the corpse. The stench was so atrocious, it was so horrible to look at – none of the family dared risk contagion, and the servants just plain refused. In the end they brought in some poor labouring men, paid them I don't know what – and they put it in the coffin. That's how a king ends. They say one of the men died. I don't know if that's true. When they were taking the coffin to the crypt the people stood by the roadside spitting and shouting obscenities. "There goes Lady's Pleasure!" they said.' He raised his outraged face to Danton. 'Dear God, and they think they are invulnerable. Because they reign by the grace of God they think they have God in their pockets. They ignore my advice, my honest, considered, well-meant advice; I want to save them, and I am the only man who can do it. They think they can ignore all common sense, common humanity.' Mirabeau looked old; his pitted face had reddened with emotion, but beneath the blush it was like clay. 'And I feel so mortally tired. The time has all got used up. Danton, if I believed in slow poisons I should say that someone has poisoned me, because I feel as if I am dying by degrees.' He blinked. There was a tear in his eye. He seemed to shake himself like a big dog. 'My regards to your dear wife. And to that poor little Camille. Work,' he said to himself. 'Get back to work.'

ON 27 MARCH the *ci-devant* Comte de Mirabeau collapsed suddenly in great pain and was taken to his house on the rue Chaussée-de-l'Antin. He died in a coma on 2 April, at 8.30 in the morning.

LATELY CAMILLE had retreated to the blue *chaise-longue*, fenced in by books, his long legs curled up beneath him as if to disassociate himself from Lucile's taste in carpets. It was late afternoon. The light was failing, and the street was almost deserted. Today the shops were shut, as a mark of respect. The funeral was tonight, by torchlight.

He had been to Mirabeau's house. He's in great pain, they said, he can't see you. He had begged: just for a moment, please, please. Put your name in the book of well-wishers, they said. There, by the door.

Then a Genevan, in passing, too late: 'Mirabeau asked for you, at the last. But we had to say you were not there.'

The Court had sent twice a day to inquire: time was, when Mirabeau could have helped them, that they did not send at all. All forget now, the distrust, the evasions, the pride: the grasping egotist's hand on the nation's future, rifling through circumstance as through a greasy sheaf of promissory notes. Strangers stop each other in the streets, to commiserate and express dread of the future.

On Camille's desk, a scribbled-over sheet, almost illegible. Danton picked it up. ' "Go then, witless people, and prostrate yourself before the tomb of this god" – what does it say then?'

'This god of liars and thieves.'

Danton put down the paper, appalled. 'You can't write that. Every newspaper in the country is given over to panegyrics. Barnave, who was his staunch opponent, has pronounced his eulogy at the Jacobins. Tonight the Commune and the whole Assembly will walk in his funeral procession. His most obdurate enemies are praising him. Camille, if you write that, you may be torn to pieces the next time you appear in public. I mean, literally.'

'I can write what I like,' he snapped. 'Opinion is free. If the rest of the world are hypocrites and self-deluders, does it therefore follow – am I bound to alter my views because the man is dead?'

Danton said, 'Jesus Christ' in an awestruck way, and left.

It was now almost dark. Lucile was at the rue Condé. Ten minutes passed; Camille sat in the unlit room. Jeanette put her head in at the door. 'Don't you want to talk to anybody?'

'No.'

'Only Deputy Robespierre is here.'

'Oh yes, I want to talk to Robespierre.'

He could hear the woman's tactful lower-class voice outside the door. I am forever coming into mothers, he thought: mothers and friends.

Robespierre looked haggard and uneasy, a sallow tinge on his fair skin. He pulled up a hard chair uncertainly, and sat facing Camille. 'Are you not sleeping?' Camille asked.

'Not very well, these last few nights. I have a nightmare, and when I wake up it is difficult to breathe.' He put his hand tentatively against his ribcage. He dreaded the summer ahead, the suffocating blanket of walls and streets and public buildings. 'I wish I had better health. My hours at the moment are trying my strength.'

'Shall we open a bottle of something and drink to the glorious dead?'

'No thanks. I've been drinking too much,' he said apologetically. 'I have to try to keep off it in the afternoons.'

'I don't call this afternoon,' Camille said. 'Max, what's going to happen next?'

'The Court will be looking for a new adviser. And the Assembly for a new master. He was their master, and they have a slavish nature – or so Marat would say.' Robespierre brought his chair an inch or two forward. The complicity was total; they had understood Mirabeau, and they alone. 'Barnave will loom large now. Though he is hardly a Mirabeau.'

'You hated Mirabeau, Max.'

'No.' He looked up quickly. 'I don't hate. It blurs the judgement.'

'I have no judgement.'

'No. That's why I try to guide you. You can judge events, but not men. You were too much attached to Mirabeau. It was dangerous for you.'

'Yes. But I liked him.'

'I know. I accept that he was generous to you, he built your confidence. I almost think – he wished to be a father to you.'

Goodness, Camille thought: is that the impression you carried away? I think perhaps my sentiments were not entirely filial. 'Fathers can be deceptive creatures,' he said.

Max was silent for a moment. Then he said, 'In the future, we must be careful of personal ties. We may have to break free of them – ' He stopped, conscious that he had suddenly said what he came to say.

Camille looked at him without speaking. After a moment: 'Perhaps you did not come to discuss Mirabeau,' he said. 'Perhaps I am quite wrong, but perhaps you have chosen this evening to tell me that you don't intend to marry Adèle.'

'I don't want to hurt anybody. That's the reason, really.'

Robespierre avoided his eyes. They sat for a moment in silence. Jeanette came in, smiled at them both, and lit the lamps. When she had gone, Camille flung himself to his feet. 'You'll have to do better than that.' He was very angry.

'It's hard to explain. Have patience for a minute.'

'And I'm to tell her. Is that it?'

'I hoped you would. I honestly don't know what I would say. You must realize, I feel I hardly know Adèle.'

'You knew what you were doing.'

'Don't yell at me. There was no definite arrangement of any kind, nothing was settled. And I can't go on with it. The longer it goes on the worse it gets. There are plenty of people for her to marry, better than me. I don't even know how the whole thing got started. Am I in a position to marry?'

'Why shouldn't you?'

'Because – because I work all the time. I work because it's my duty, so it seems to me. I have no time to devote to a family.'

'But you have to eat, Max, you have to sleep somewhere, you have to have a home. Even you have to take an hour off occasionally. Adèle knows what to expect.'

'That's not the whole point. You see, I might have to make sacrifices for the sake of the Revolution. I'd be very happy to do it, it's what I – '

'What kind of sacrifices?'

'Suppose it were necessary for me to die?'

'What are you talking about?'

'It would leave her a widow for the second time.'

'Have you been talking to Lucile? She has it all worked out. How there might be an outbreak of bubonic plague. Or one might be run over by a carriage. Or be shot by the Austrians, which I admit is quite likely. All right – one day you're going to die. But if everybody proceeded on your assumptions, the human race would come to an end, because no one would have children.'

'Yes, I know,' he said awkwardly. 'It's right for you to marry, even though your life may be in danger. But not for me. It's not right for me.'

'Priests now marry. You campaigned in the Assembly for their right to do so. You run contrary to the spirit of the times.'

'What the priests do and what I do are two separate questions. Most of them couldn't remain celibate, we ended an abuse.'

'Do you find celibacy so easy?'

'The easiness of it isn't the question.'

'What about the girl in Arras – Anaïs, wasn't it? Would you have married her, if things had gone differently?'

'No.'

'Then it's not Adèle?'

'No.'

'You just don't want to be married?'

'That's right.'

'But not for the reasons you give me.'

'Don't browbeat me, you haven't got me in court.' He got up, in great distress. 'Oh, you think I'm callous, but I'm not. I want everything that people do want – but it just doesn't work out, for me. I can't commit myself, knowing – I mean, fearing – what the future may hold.'

'Are you afraid of women?'

'No.'

'Give the question your honest consideration.'

'I try always to be honest.'

'As a practical matter,' Camille said scathingly, 'life will be difficult for you now. You may not like the fact, but it seems that you're attractive to women. In company they pin you against walls and heave their bosoms at you. There is a positive rustle of carnality from the public galleries when you make an intervention. The belief that you had an attachment has held them back so far, but what now? They'll be pursuing you in public places and ripping your clothes off. Think of that.'

Robespierre had sat down again, his face frozen by consternation and distaste.

'Go on. Tell me your real reason.'

'You have it already. I can't explain any more.' At the back of his mind, something moved, full of dread. A woman, her pinched mouth, her hair scraped back into a band; the crackle of firewood, the drone of flies. He looked up, helpless. 'Either you understand or you don't. I think there was something I wanted to say ... but you shouldn't have flown into a rage because now I can't remember what it was. But I need your help.'

Camille dropped into a chair. He looked at the ceiling for a while, his arms hanging loose over the chair's arms. 'It's all right,' he said softly. 'I'll sort it out. Don't think about it any more. Your fear is, that if you marry Adèle, you will love her. If you have children, you will love them more than anything else in the world, more than patriotism, more than democracy. If your children grow up, and prove traitors to the people, will you be able to demand their deaths, as the Romans did? Perhaps you will, but perhaps you will not be able to do it. You're afraid that if you love people you may be deflected from your duty, but it's because of another kind of love, isn't it, that the duty is laid upon you? It is really my fault, this business, mine and Annette's. We liked the idea, so we set it up. You were too polite to upset our arrangements. You've never so much as kissed her. Of course, you wouldn't. I know, there is your work. No one else is going to do what you are going to do, and you come to the point of renouncing, as much as you can, human needs and human weaknesses. I wish – I wish I could help you more.'

Robespierre searched his face for some evidence of malice or levity; saw none. 'When we were children,' he said, 'life wasn't particularly easy for either of us, was it? But we kept each other going, didn't we? The years in Arras were the worst, the years in between. I'm not so lonely, now.'

'Mm.' Camille was looking for a formula, a formula to contain what his instinct rejected. 'The Revolution is your bride,' he said. 'As the Church is the Bride of Christ.'

*

'OH WELL,' ADÈLE SAID. 'Now I shall have Jérôme Pétion look-ing down the front of my dress and breathing sentimental slogans in my ear. Look, Camille, I've understood the situation for weeks. Let this be a lesson to you not to scheme.'

He was amazed, that she was taking it so well. 'Will you go away and cry?'

'No, I'll just – do a bit of rethinking.'

'There are lots of men, Adèle.'

'Don't I just know it?' she said.

'Will you not feel able to see him now?'

'Of course I'll feel able to see him. People can be friends, can't they? I presume that's what he wants?'

'Yes, of course. I'm so glad. Because it would be difficult for me, otherwise.'

She looked at him fondly. 'You're a self-centred little bastard, aren't you, Camille?'

DANTON began to laugh. 'Eunuch,' he said. 'The girl should be glad he didn't carry the farce any further. Oh, I should have guessed.'

'No need for such unholy jubilation.' Camille was gloomy. 'Try to understand.'

'Understand? I understand perfectly. It's easy.'

He went to hold forth at the Café des Arts. He had it on good authority, he told everyone, that Deputy Robespierre was sexually impotent. He told his cronies at City Hall, and a few score deputies of his acquaintance; he told the actresses backstage at the Théâtre Montansier, and almost the entire membership of the Cordeliers Club.

APRIL 1791, Deputy Robespierre opposed a property qualification for future deputies, defended freedom of speech. May, he upheld press freedom, spoke against slavery, and asked for civil rights for the mulattos in the colonies. When the organization of a new legislature was discussed, he proposed that members of the existing Assembly should not be eligible for re-election; they must give way to new men. He was heard for two hours in a respectful silence, and his motion was carried. In the third week of May, he fell ill from nervous strain and overwork.

Late May, he demanded without success the abolition of the death penalty.

June 10, he was elected Public Prosecutor. The city's Chief Magistrate resigned rather than work with him. Pétion took the vacant place. Gradually, you see, our people are coming into the power they have always thought is their due.

IV. *More Acts of the Apostles*

(*1791*)

IT IS THE END of Lent. The King decides that he does not wish, on Easter Sunday, to take holy communion from a 'constitutional' priest. Nor does he wish to cause protest and outrage the patriots.

He decides therefore to spend Easter quietly at Saint-Cloud, away from the censorious eye of the city.

His plans become known.

PALM SUNDAY: City Hall.

'Lafayette.'

This was the voice the general now associated with calamity. Danton stood close when he spoke to him, forcing him to look up into the battered face.

'Lafayette, this morning a refractory priest, a Jesuit, said Mass at the Tuileries.'

'You are better informed than I,' Lafayette said. His mouth felt dry.

'We won't have it,' Danton said. 'The King has accepted the changes in the church. He has put his signature to them. If he cheats, there will be reprisals.'

'When the royal family leave for Saint-Cloud,' Lafayette said, 'the National Guard will cordon off the area for their departure, and if necessary I shall give them an escort. Don't get in the way, Danton.'

Danton took out of his coat – not a firearm, as Lafayette had half-feared, but a rolled piece of paper. 'This is a wall-poster drafted by the Cordeliers Battalion. Would you like to read it?'

Lafayette held out his hand. 'Some of M. Desmoulins's instant invective?'

Lafayette's eyes swept over the paper. 'You call upon the National

Guard to prevent the King's departure from the Tuileries.' His eyes now searched Danton's face. 'I shall order otherwise. Therefore, it is a kind of mutiny you are urging.'

'You could say that.'

Danton watched him steadily, waiting for a slight flush along the cheekbones to tell him that the general's inner forces were in disarray. In a moment, the capillaries obliged. 'I shouldn't have thought religious intolerance was amongst your vices, Danton. What is it to you who ministers to the King's spiritual needs? As he conceives of it, he has a soul to save. What is it to you?'

'It is something to me when the King breaks his promises and flouts the law. It is something that he leaves Paris for Saint-Cloud, and Saint-Cloud for the border, where he can put himself at the head of the *émigrés*.'

'Who told you that was his intention?'

'I can divine it.'

'You sound like Marat.'

'I am sorry if you think so.'

'I shall ask for an emergency meeting of the Commune. I shall ask for martial law to be declared.'

'Go ahead,' Danton said contemptuously. 'Do you know what Camille Desmoulins calls you? The Don Quixote of the Capets.'

EMERGENCY session. M. Danton obtained a majority against martial law, working on the peaceable and the pliable. Lafayette, in a passion, offered Mayor Bailly his resignation. M. Danton pointed out that the mayor was not competent to accept it; if the general wanted to resign, he would have to visit each of the forty-eight Sections in turn and tell them.

Further, M. Danton called General Lafayette a coward.

THE TUILERIES, Monday of Holy Week, 11.30 a.m.

'It is a piece of folly,' Mayor Bailly said, 'to have the Cordeliers Battalion here.'

'You mean Battalion No. 3,' said Lafayette. He closed his eyes. He had a small tight pain behind them.

The royal family were allowed to enter their coach, and there they stayed. The National Guard were disobeying orders. They would not allow the gates to be opened. The crowd would not allow the carriage to proceed. The National Guard would not disperse the crowd. The 'Ça Ira' was sung. The First Gentleman of the Bedchamber was assaulted. The Dauphin burst into tears. Last year, or the year before, it might have aroused some compunction. But if they didn't want to subject the child to the ordeal, they should have taken him back into the palace.

Lafayette swore at his men. He was quivering with fury as he sat his white horse, and the animal twitched restively and shifted its feet.

The mayor appealed for order. He was shouted down. Inside the carriage, the royal couple gazed into each other's faces.

'You pig,' a man shouted at the King. 'We pay you twenty-five million a year, so do what we tell you.'

'Proclaim martial law,' Lafayette told Bailly.

Bailly did not look him in the face.

'Do it.'

'I cannot.'

Now patience was required. An hour and three-quarters, and the King and Queen had had enough. As they re-entered the Tuileries, the Queen turned to speak to Lafayette above the jeers of the mob. 'At least you must admit that we are no longer free.'

It was 1.15 p.m.

EPHRAIM, AN AGENT in the service of Frederick William of Prussia, to Laclos, in the service of the Duke of Orléans:

For some hours our position was brilliant. I even thought your dear employer was about to replace his cousin on the throne; but now my expectations have altered. The only thing that gives me pleasure in all this is that we have ruined Lafayette, which is a great deal achieved. Our 500,000 livres have been spent more or less for nothing, which is what I find so unfortunate; we shall not have such sums at our disposal every day, and the King of Prussia will get tired of paying out.

*

ON A FINE DAY in June, Philippe was on the Vincennes road, driving Agnès de Buffon in his English dog-cart. Bearing down on him pretty fast was a smart, very large, very new equipage of the type known as a 'berlin'.

The Duke flagged it down with a flourish of his whip. 'Hallo there, Fersen. Trying to break your neck, old chap?'

The Queen's lover, the thin-faced, supple Swedish count: 'Trying out my new travelling-carriage, my lord.'

'Really?' Philippe noted the elegant lemon wheels, the dark-green coachwork and the walnut fittings. 'Going on a trip, are you? Bit big, isn't it? Are you taking all the girls from the Opéra chorus?'

'No, my lord.' Fersen inclined his head respectfully. 'I leave them all for you.'

The Duke looked after the carriage as it gathered speed along the road. 'I wonder,' he said to Agnès. 'It would be just like Louis to choose a get-up like that for a quick sprint to the border.'

Agnès turned away with an uncomfortable half-smile; it made her afraid to think that Philippe might soon be King.

'And you can keep that damned pious expression off your face, Fersen,' the Duke announced to the dust on the road. 'We all know how you spend your time when you're not at the Tuileries. His latest woman is a circus acrobat, if you please. Not that I'd wish that Austrian scrag-end to be any man's sole consolation.' He gathered up the reins.

THE BABY, ANTOINE, woke up at six o'clock and lay watching the sunlight filter through the shutters. When this bored him, he yelled for his mother.

In a few moments Gabrielle stood over him. Her face was soft with sleep. 'Tyrant child,' she whispered. He put up his arms to be lifted. Shushing him, a finger over his lips, she carried him to the big bedroom. A curtained alcove sheltered twin beds, marked off their private territory from the patriotic circus that their bedroom had become. Lucile had this problem, she said. Perhaps we should move, get somewhere bigger? But no, everybody knows Danton's house, he'll not want to move. And such an upheaval it would be.

She climbed into her bed, settled down with the warm little body against hers. In the other bed, his father slept with his face pushed into the pillow.

Seven o'clock, the doorbell jangled. Her heart jolted with apprehension. It's too early for it to be anything good. She heard Catherine, protesting; then the bedroom door was flung open. 'Fabre!' she said. 'My God, what's happened? Are the Austrians here?'

Fabre pounced on her husband, pummelled him into life. 'Danton, they've gone in the night. The King, his wife, his sister, the Dauphin, the whole bloody bunch.'

Danton stirred, sat up. Immediately, he was wide awake; perhaps he had never been asleep? 'Lafayette was in charge of security. Either he's sold out to the Court, betrayed us, or he's an incompetent dolt.' He punched Fabre's shoulder. 'I've got him where I want him. Organize me some clothes, girl, would you?'

'Where to?'

'The Cordeliers first – find Legendre, tell him to get people together. Then City Hall, then the Riding-School.'

'What if they're not caught?' Fabre said.

Danton drew his hand across his chin. 'Does it matter? As long as enough people see them running away.'

Very ready, his answers; very neat. Fabre said, 'Did you know this was going to happen? Did you want it to happen?'

'Anyway, they will be caught. They'll be dragged back within the week. Louis messes everything up. Poor devil,' he said ruminatively. 'I feel sorry for him at times.'

GRACE ELLIOT: 'I have no doubt that Lafayette was privy to the attempt, and afterwards, through fear, betrayed them.'

GEORGES-JACQUES DANTON, to the Cordeliers Club: 'By upholding a hereditary monarchy, the National Assembly has reduced France to slavery. Let us abolish, once and for all, the name and function of King; let us turn this kingdom into a republic.'

*

ALEXANDRE DE BEAUHARNAIS, President of the Assembly: 'Gentlemen, the King has fled in the night. Let us proceed to the Order of the Day.'

WHEN DANTON ARRIVED at the Riding-School, with a small military escort, the packed, rumour-ridden crowd cheered him. 'Long live our father, Danton,' someone called. He was momentarily astonished.

Later that day, M. Laclos arrived at the rue des Cordeliers. He looked Gabrielle over carefully – not with lecherous intent, but as if he were assessing her suitability for something. She flushed slightly, and twitched away from his gaze. She thought, these days, that everyone was noticing that she had put on weight. A small sigh escaped Laclos. 'Warm weather we're having, Mme Danton.' He stood in the drawing room and removed his gloves, easing them off finger by finger, raising his eyes to Danton's. 'There are things we must discuss,' he said pleasantly.

Three hours later he replaced his gloves by a similar careful process, and left.

PARIS WITHOUT THE KING. Some wit hung a placard on the railing of the Tuileries: PREMISES TO LET. All over town, Danton talked about the republic. At the Jacobins Robespierre rose to reply to him, adjusting his cravat minutely with his small fingers with the bitten nails. 'What is a republic?' he asked.

Danton must define his terms, he sees. Maximilien Robespierre takes nothing on trust.

THE DUKE brought his fist down hard on a fragile table, inlaid with a pattern of roses, ribbons and violins.

'Don't talk to me as if I were a three-year-old,' he snarled.

Félicité de Genlis was a patient woman. She smiled faintly. She was prepared to argue, if necessary, all day.

'The Assembly have asked you to accept the throne, should it become vacant,' she said.

'There you are,' the Duke bellowed. 'You're doing it again.

We've established that, haven't we? We all know that. You are a tiresome woman.'

'Don't bluster, dear. Firstly, may I point out that it is unlikely that the throne will become vacant? I hear that your cousin's journey has been interrupted. He is on his way back to Paris.'

'Yes,' the Duke said with relish. 'The booby. Let himself get caught. They've sent Barnave and Pétion to fetch them back. I hope Deputy Pétion is bloody rude to them all the way.'

Félicité did not doubt that he would be. 'You know,' she went on, 'that now the Assembly has the new constitution framed and ready for the King's signature, it – I mean the Assembly – is most anxious for stability. Change has gone so far and so fast, and I believe people are aching for a return to good order. It is possible that a month from now Louis will be replaced firmly-on the throne. It will be as if all this had never happened.'

'But dammit, he *ran away*. He's supposed to be King of this country, and he was *running away* from it.'

'The Assembly may not put that construction on his actions.'

'What other is there? Forgive me, I'm a simple man – '

'They aren't. They're really quite ingenious. Lawyers, mostly.'

'Don't trust 'em,' Philippe said. 'As a breed.'

'Think then, my dear – if Louis is restored – think how it will antagonize him if you appear so anxious to step into his shoes.'

'But I am, aren't I?' Philippe gaped at her. What was she trying to do to him? Wasn't this what all the fuss was about, over the last three years and more? Wasn't it to be King that he had endured the company of people who weren't gentlemen, who didn't hunt, who didn't know the nose of a racehorse from its tail? Wasn't it in order to be King that he had allowed himself to be patronized by that fish-eyed Laclos? Wasn't it to be King that he had endured that scar-faced thug Danton at his own dinner table, quite blatantly eyeing up his mistress Agnès and his ex-mistress Grace? Wasn't it to be King that he had paid, paid, paid?

Félicité closed her eyes. Carefully, she thought. Speak carefully, but do speak: for the nation, for this man's children, whom I have brought up. And for our lives.

'Think,' she said.

'Think!' The Duke exploded. 'Very well, you don't trust my supporters. Neither do I. I have their measure, I tell you.'

'I doubt it.'

'You think I'd let those low types push me around?'

'Philippe, you're not the man to set limits to their ambition. They'll swallow you up, you and your children – and everything, everybody that is close to your heart. Don't you realize that the men who can destroy one King can destroy another? Do you think they'd have any scruple, if you didn't do everything exactly as they wished? And you'd only be, at best, a stop-gap for them – until they felt they could get along without you, till they felt they didn't need any King at all.' She took a breath. 'Think back, Philippe – think back to before the Bastille fell. Louis used to tell you, go here, go there – come back to Versailles, keep away from Versailles – you know how it was? Your life wasn't your own, you used to say. You had no freedom. Now, from the moment you say, "Yes, I want to be King," you give your freedom away again. From that day on, you will be in prison. Oh, not a prison with bars and chains – but a pleasant gaol that M. Danton will make for you. A gaol with a civil list and protocol and precedent and the most charming social occasions, ballets and masked balls and yes, even horse-racing.'

'Don't like ballet,' the Duke said. 'Bores me.'

Félicité smoothed her skirt, glanced down at her hands. A woman's hands show her age, she thought; they give everything away. Once there'd been hope. Once there'd been the promise of a fairer, cleaner world; and no one had hoped harder, no one had worked for it more assiduously than she had. 'A gaol,' she said. 'They'll trick you, amuse you, occupy you – while they carve up the country between them. That is their object.'

He looked up at her, this middle-aged child of hers. 'You think they're cleverer than me, do you?'

'Oh, much, my darling: much, much, much.'

He avoided her eye now. 'I've always known my limitations.'

'Which makes you wiser than most men. And wiser than these manipulators give you credit for.'

That pleased him. It came to him vaguely that he might outsmart them. She had spoken so softly, as if the thought were his own. 'What's the best thing to do? Tell me, Félicité, please.'

'Disassociate yourself. Keep your name clear. Refuse to be their dupe.'

'So you want me – ' he struggled – 'to go to the Assembly, and say no, I don't want the throne, you may have thought I did but that was not what I meant at all?'

'Take this paper. Look. Sit here. Write as I dictate.'

She leaned against the back of his chair. The words were prepared, in her head. Precarious, she thought. This was a near thing. If I could shut him away from all counter-persuasion, all other influence – but that's impossible. I was lucky to get him for an hour alone.

Quickly now – before he changed his mind. 'Put your signature. There, it's done.'

Philippe threw his pen down. Ink spattered the roses, the ribbons, the violins. He clapped a hand to his head. 'Laclos will kill me,' he wailed.

Félicité made soothing noises, as if to a child with colic, and took the paper from Philippe to amend his punctuation.

WHEN THE DUKE told Laclos of his decision, Laclos bowed imperceptibly from the shoulder. 'As you wish, Milord,' he said, and withdrew. Why he had spoken in English he never afterwards understood. In his apartment he turned his face to the wall and drank a bottle of brandy with a thoughtful but murderous expression.

At Danton's apartment he worked around to a comfortable chair, handing himself from one piece of furniture to the next in a manner faintly nautical. 'Have patience,' he said. 'Any moment now I shall deliver myself of a profound observation.'

'I shall go,' Camille said. He wasn't sure he wanted to hear what Laclos had to say. He preferred not to know the finer details of Danton's entanglements; and, though he knew they were supposed to regard Philippe only as a means to an end, it was very difficult when somebody had been so nice to you. Every time some

Cordeliers oaf came tramping though his apartment, yelling from room to room, he thought of the Duke's twelve-bedroomed wedding-present. He could have wept.

'Sit down, Camille,' Danton said.

'You may stay,' Laclos said, 'but keep confidences, or I shall kill you.'

'Yes, of course you will,' Danton said. 'Now – go on.'

'My observations fall into three parts. One, Philippe is a pea-brained, yellow-livered imbecile. Two, Félicité is a nasty, poxy, vomit-inducing whore.'

'All right,' Danton said. 'And the third part of your observations?'

'A *coup d'état*,' Laclos said. He looked at Danton without lifting his head.

'Come now. Let's not get over-excited.'

'Force Philippe's hand. Make him see his duty. Put him in a position where – ' Laclos's right hand made languid chopping motions.

Danton stood over him. 'What exactly is it you have in mind?'

'The Assembly will debate, decide to restore Louis. Because they need him to make their pretty constitution work. Because they're King's men, Danton, because bloody Barnave has been bought. Alliteration.' He hiccuped. 'Or if he hadn't, he has been by now, after his knee-to-knee trip back from the border with the Austrian slut. I tell you, even now they are working on the most risible set of fictions. You've seen the proclamation that Lafayette put out – "the enemies of the Revolution have seized the person of the King". They are speaking of *abduction*,' he smashed the heel of his hand into the arm of his chair, 'they are saying that the fat fool was carried to the border against his will. They will say anything, anything, to save their faces. Now tell me, Danton, when such lies are sold to the people, isn't it time to spill a little blood?'

Laclos now looked at his feet. His manner became sober and discursive. 'The Assembly should be influenced, must be influenced by the people's will. The people will never forgive Louis for abandoning them. Therefore *dignum et justum est, aequum et salutare* that the Riding-School should do what we tell them. Therefore we will make a petition. Some hack such as Brissot may draft it. It will ask for the deposition of Louis. The Cordeliers will sponsor it. The Jacobins might be persuaded to sign it, I say they might. The 17th of July, the whole city assembles on the Champs-de-Mars for the Bastille celebrations. We get our petition signed, thousands and thousands of names. We take it to the Assembly. If they refuse to act on it, the people invade the Assembly – in pursuance of their Sacred Will, all that. The doctrine behind the action we'll work out when we have leisure.'

'You suggest that we employ armed force against the Assembly?'

'Yes.'

'Against our representatives?'

'Representatives nothing.'

'Bloodshed, possibly?'

'Damn you,' Laclos said. Scarlet flowed into his fine-boned face. 'Have we come all this way to throw up our hands now, to turn into some sort of puling humanitarians – now, when everything's ours for the taking?' He splayed out his fingers, palms upwards. 'Can you have a revolution without blood?'

'I never said you could.'

'Well, then. Not even Robespierre thinks you could.'

'I just wanted to have your meaning clear.'

'Oh. I see.'

'And then, if we succeed in deposing Louis?'

'Then, Danton, divide the spoils.'

'And do we divide them with Philippe?'

'Right, he's refused the throne once. But he will see his duty, if I have to strangle Félicité with my own hands – and that would be a thrill, I can tell you. Look, Danton, we'll run the country between us. We'll make Robespierre our Minister of Finance, he's honest they say. We'll repatriate Marat and let him give fleas to the Swiss. We'll –'

'Laclos, this is not serious.'

'Oh, I know.' Laclos got unsteadily to his feet. 'I know what you want. One month after the ascension of Philippe the Gullible, M.

Laclos found in a gutter, deceased. Blamed on a traffic accident. Two months after, King Philippe found in a gutter, deceased – it really is a bad stretch of road. Philippe's heirs and assigns having coincidentally expired, end of the monarchy, reign of M. Danton.'

'How your imagination runs away with you.'

'They do say that if you keep drinking you start to see snakes,' Laclos said. 'Great serpent things, dragons and similar. Would you do it, Danton? Would you risk it with me?'

Danton didn't answer.

'You would, you would.' Laclos stood up, swaying a little, and held out his arms. 'Triumph and glory.' He dropped his arms to his side. 'And then perhaps you'll kill me. I'll risk it. For a footnote in the history books. I dread obscurity, do you see? The meagre and unrewarded old age, the piddling end of mediocrity, *sans* everything, as the English poet says. "There goes poor old Laclos, he wrote a book once, the title escapes me." I'm going away now,' he said with dignity. 'All I ask is that you think it over.' He lurched towards the door, and met Gabrielle coming in. 'Nice little woman,' he said under his breath. They heard him stumble on the stairs.

'I thought you'd want to know,' she said. 'They're back.'

'The Capet family?' Camille asked.

'The royal family. Yes.' She withdrew from the room, closing the door softly behind her. They listened. Heat and silence lay over the city.

'I like a crisis,' Camille said. A short pause. Danton looked not at him, but through him. 'I'll keep you to the spirit of your recent republican mouthings. I was thinking about it, when Laclos was ranting – and I'm sorry for it, but I think Philippe will have to go. You can use him and dispense with him later.'

'Oh, you are as cold-blooded – ' Danton stopped. He couldn't think what was as cold-blooded as Camille, pushing his hair back with a flick of his wrist and saying *use him and dispense with him later*. 'Were you born with that gesture,' he asked, 'or did you pick it up from some prostitute?'

'First get rid of Louis, then we can battle it out.'

'We might lose everything,' Danton said. But he had made his calculations: always, when he seemed to flare up for a moment into some unreasoning, sneering aggression, his mind was moving quite coldly, quite calmly, in a certain direction. Now his mind was made up. He was going to do it.

THE ROYAL PARTY had been intercepted at Varennes; they had travelled 165 miles from inept beginning to blundering end. Six thousand people surrounded the two carriages on the first stage of their journey home. A day later the company was joined by three deputies of the National Assembly. Barnave and Pétion sat with the family inside the berlin. The Dauphin took a liking to Barnave. He chattered to him and played with the buttons on his coat, reading out the legend engraved there: 'Live free, or die'. 'We must show character,' the Queen repeated, over and over again.

By the end of the journey, the future for Deputy Barnave was plain. Mirabeau dead, he would replace him as secret adviser to the court. Pétion believed that the King's plump little sister, Mme Elisabeth, had fallen in love with him; it was true that, on the long road back, she had fallen asleep with her head on his shoulder. Pétion burbled incessantly about it, for a month or two.

On a day of blazing heat, the King re-entered Paris. Vast silent crowds lined the routes. The berlin was filled with choking dust from the road, and there appeared at the window the lined, harried face of a grey-haired woman: Antoinette. They arrived at the Tuileries. When they were installed, Lafayette placed his guards and hurried to the King. 'Your Majesty's orders for the day?'

'It appears,' Louis said, 'that I am more at your orders than you at mine.'

As they passed through the city, the ranks of soldiers lining the route had presented arms with the butts reversed, as if it were a funeral: which, in a manner of speaking, it was.

CAMILLE DESMOULINS, *Révolutions de France*, No. 83

When Louis XVI re-entered his apartment at the Tuileries, he threw himself into an armchair, saying 'It's devilish hot,' then, 'That was a — journey. However, I have had it in my head to do it for a long time.'

Afterwards, looking towards the National Guardsmen who were present, he said, 'I have done a foolish thing, I admit. But must I not have my follies, like other people? Come along, bring me a chicken.' One of his valets came in. 'Ah, there you are,' he said, 'and here I am.' They brought the chicken, and Louis XVI ate and drank with an appetite that would have done honour to the King of Cockayne.

AND HÉBERT has changed his royalist opinions:

We will stuff you into Charenton and your whore into the Hôpital. When you are finally walled up, both of you, and when you no longer have a civil list, put an axe in me if you get away.

Père Duchesne, No. 61

FROM HERE, sprawled in this chair, Danton could see Louise Robert, arguing, wanting to cry and just managing not to. Her husband had been arrested, was in prison. 'Demand his release,' she was saying. 'Force it.'

He spoke to her across the room. 'Not much of the big tough republican now, are you?'

She gave him a glance that surprised him by its intensity of dislike. 'Let me think,' he said. 'Just let me think.'

His eyes half-closed, he watched the room. Lucile sat fiddling with her wedding ring, signs of strain on her child's face. He found her, these days, always on his mind; hers was the first face he saw when he came into a room. He spent time chiding himself; called it remarkable disloyalty to the mother of his children.

(FRÉRON: I've loved her for years.

DANTON: Rubbish.

FRÉRON: You may say so. What do you know?

DANTON: I know you.

FRÉRON: But you seem to entertain certain expectations yourself. At least, everybody remarks on it.

DANTON: Ah, well, I don't tell her I love her. It might be something far more crude than that. I might be more honest than you.

FRÉRON: Would you, if you could –?

DANTON: Naturally.

FRÉRON: But Camille –

DANTON: I could keep Camille quiet. Look, you have to seize the opportunities to get what you want in life.
FRÉRON: I know.)

Fréron was now watching him, trying to read his face and anticipate him. It had gone wrong. Their plans were known at City Hall; Félicité, who always found out what was going on, had probably dropped a word in the ear of Lafayette. Lafayette was moving troops up to the Tuileries; the blond holy fool still had the men, the guns, the whip-hand. He had thrown a cordon round the Riding-School, to protect the deputies from any incursion; he had rung the tocsin, he had set a curfew. The Jacobins – parading their moderation, their timidity – had refused their support. Fréron would have liked to forget the whole thing, and that was why he was saying, 'Danton, I don't think we can pull back now.'

'Is it so hard to convince yourself, Rabbit? Do you have to keep making the point?' The whole room turned at the sound of his voice. They stiffened, shifted their positions. 'Camille, go back to the Jacobins.'

'They won't listen,' Camille said. 'They say the law doesn't allow them to support such a petition, they say the deposition of the King is a matter for the Assembly. So what's the point? Robespierre is in the chair, but the place is packed with Lafayette's supporters, so what can he do? Even if he wanted to support us, which is . . .' His voice tailed off. 'Robespierre wants to work within the law.'

'And I have no particular relish for breaking it,' Danton said. Two days of close argument have come to nothing. The petition had been carried about between the Assembly and the Jacobins and the Cordeliers, it had been printed, amended (sometimes covertly) and printed again. They were waiting: three women, and Fréron, Fabre, Legendre, Camille. He remembered Mirabeau at City Hall: you don't work *with* people, Danton, you work *over* them. But how could he have known, he asked himself, that people would be so ready to take orders? Earlier in life, he had never suspected it.

'This time we'll give you some support,' he said to Camille. 'Fréron, get together a hundred men. They should be armed.'

'The citizens of this district are never far from their pikes.'

Danton glared at the interruption. Camille was embarrassed by the things Fréron said, his false bonhomie, his suspect eagerness.

'Pikes,' Fabre murmured. 'I hope he intends it as a figure of speech. I am very far from my pike. I do not have a pike.'

'Do you think, Rabbit,' Camille asked him, 'that we are going to skewer the Jacobins to their benches?'

'Call it a show of determination,' Danton said. 'Don't call it a show of force. We don't want to upset Robespierre. But Rabbit – ' Danton's voice called him back from the door. 'Give Camille fifteen minutes to try to persuade them. A decorous interval, you know.'

Around him the room eddied into activity. The women stood up, smoothing their skirts, their eyes forlorn and their lips pinched. Gabrielle tried to meet his eyes for a moment. Apprehension gives a yellow cast to her skin, he has observed. One day he noticed – as one notices rain clouds, or the time on the face of a clock – that he doesn't love her now.

EVENING, the National Guard cleared people off the streets. The volunteer battalions were out, but a lot of Lafayette's regular companies were in evidence too. 'You wonder,' Danton said. 'There are patriots among the soldiers, but that old habit of blind obedience dies hard.' And we may need to count on the old habit, he thought, if the rest of Europe moves against us. He tried not to think of that; for now it was someone else's problem. He had to narrow his thinking, to the next twenty-four hours.

Gabrielle went to bed after midnight. It was difficult to sleep. She heard the tread of horses in the streets. She heard the gate bell, in the Cour du Commerce, and the murmur of voices as people were let in and out. It might have been two o'clock, half-past two, when she gave up the unequal battle; sat up, lit a candle, looked across at Georges's bed. It was empty and had not been disturbed. It was very hot still; her nightdress clung to her. She slid out of bed, stripped her nightdress off, washed in water that should have been cold but was lukewarm. She found a clean nightdress. She went to her dressing-table, sat down, dabbed her temples and her throat with cologne. Her breasts ached. She pulled her long dark hair from its plait, combed out the rippling wave, re-plaited it. Her face seemed hollow, sombre in the candlelight. She went to the window. Nothing: the rue des Cordeliers was empty. She pulled on her soft slippers, and left the bedroom for the dark dining room. She opened the shutter. The light shone in from the Cour du Commerce below. Shadows seemed to move, behind her; the room was an octagon, paper-strewn, and the papers lifted a little in a merciful night breeze. She leaned out, to feel it on her face. There was no one to be seen, but she could hear a dull thump and clatter. It is Guillaume Brune's printing press, she thought: or it is Marat's. What are they doing at this hour? They live by words, she thought; they don't need sleep.

She closed the shutter, made her way towards the bedroom in the dark. She heard her husband's voice, from behind the closed door of his study. 'Yes, I understand what you are saying. We try our strength, Lafayette tries his. He is the one with the guns.'

The other man spoke. She did not know his voice. 'Just a warning,' he said. 'Well-intentioned. Well-meant.'

Georges said, 'Well, it's three o'clock. I'm not going to scramble off now like a debtor on quarter day. We meet here at dawn. Then we'll see.'

THREE O'CLOCK. François Robert was sunk into a miserable lethargy. It wasn't the worst kind of cell – there was no evidence of rats, and at least it was cool – but he would rather have been elsewhere. He could not see why he was here – he had only been about the business of the petition. He and Louise had a broadsheet to publish; the *Mercure Nationale* must be on the streets, no matter what. Probably Camille would see if she needed help. She'd never ask for it.

God in heaven, what is this? Someone with steel-tipped boots must be kicking the door. Other boots, tramping; then a voice, startlingly loud: 'Some of these shits have knives.' Then the tramp of feet again, and a flat and drunken voice singing a few bars of one of Fabre's popular songs: forgetting the words, starting again. The steel-tipped boots on his door, then a few seconds of silence, then a slogan-shouter: To the Lanterne.

François Robert shivered. Lanterne Attorney, you should be here, he thought.

'Death to the Austrian bitch,' said the drunken singer. 'Hang up Louis Capet's whore. Hang up the beast of Babylon, cut off her tits.'

A chilling cackle ran along the walls. A young voice laughed, high-pitched, tinged with hysteria. 'Long live the People's Friend.'

Then a voice he couldn't make out; then a voice near at hand: 'He says he's got seventeen prisoners and nowhere to put them.'

'Well, well,' said the young voice. 'A laugh a minute.'

A second later the cell was flooded by orange torchlight. He scrambled to his feet. A few heads appeared around the door; to his relief, they were still joined to bodies. 'You can come out now.'

'Can I really go?'

'Yes, yes.' A sober, irritated voice. 'I've more than a hundred persons to accommodate, persons on the street without lawful excuse. We can always pick you up again in a few days' time.'

'What did you do anyway?' asked the high-pitched young man.

'A professor of law,' Steel Tips announced. He was also the drunk. 'Aren't you, professor? A big mate of mine.' He draped an arm around Robert's shoulder and leaned on him, breathing sourly into his face. 'What about Danton then? He's the lad.'

'If you say so,' Robert said.

'I seen him,' Steel Tips told his colleagues. 'He says to me, seeing as you know all about the prisons, when I get to be boss of this city I'm going to put you in charge of rounding up all the aristos and cutting off their heads. For which you'll get a good wage, he says, because you'll be doing a public service.'

'Go on,' the boy said. 'Danton never spoke to you. You drunken old sot. M. Sanson's the public executioner. His father was the executioner and his father before him. You going to put him out of a job, are you? Danton never said that to you.'

FRANÇOIS ROBERT at home. The coffee cup wouldn't stay still in his grasp; it was chinking and chinking against the saucer. 'Who would have thought it would put me in this state?' He was trying to smile, but his face would only contort. 'Being released was as bad as being arrested. Louise, we forget what the people are like, their ignorance, their violence, the way they jump to conclusions.'

She thought of Camille, two years ago; the Bastille heroes on the streets, the coffee going cold by their bed, the aftermath of panic in his chilling, wide-set eyes. 'The Jacobins have split apart,' she said. 'The Right has walked out. They're going to form another club. All Lafayette's friends have gone, all the people who used to support Mirabeau. Pétion remains, Buzot, Robespierre – a handful.'

'What does Robespierre say?'

'That he's glad the divisions are out in the open. That he'll start again, with patriots this time.'

She took the cup out of his hands and pulled his head into her waist, stroking his hair and the back of his neck. 'Robespierre will go to the Champs-de-Mars,' she said. 'He'll show his face, you can be sure. But they, they won't go. Danton's lot.'

'Then who's going to take the petition? Who's going to represent the Cordeliers?'

Oh no, he thought.

Dawn, Danton was slapping him on the back. 'Good boy,' he was saying. 'Don't worry, we'll look after your wife. And François, the Cordeliers won't forget this.'

AT DAWN THEY HAD MET in Danton's red-walled study. The servants were still asleep on the mezzanine floor. Sleeping their servant's sleep, Gabrielle thought. She brought coffee to the men, avoiding their eyes. Danton handed Fabre a copy of the *People's Friend*, stabbing at it with his forefinger. 'It says – God knows with what foundation – that Lafayette intends to fire on the people. "Therefore," says Marat, "I intend to have the general assassinated." Now as it happens, in the night we have been tipped off – '

'Can't you stop it?' Gabrielle said. 'Can't you stop the whole thing happening?'

'Send the crowds home? Too late. They're out to celebrate. To them, the petition is only part of it. And I cannot answer for Lafayette.'

'Then are we to be ready to leave, Georges? I don't mind, but just tell me what to do. Just tell me what's happening.'

Danton looked shifty. His instinct said, today will go badly – so cut and run. He glanced around the room, for someone to serve as the voice of his instinct. Fabre was about to open his mouth, when Camille said, 'You know, two years ago, Danton, it was all right for you to lock your door and work on your shipping case. But it's a different matter now.'

Danton looked at him: considered: nodded. So they waited. It was fully light, another day beginning in sunshine and moving towards a sultry, growling, hardly bearable heat.

CHAMPS-DE-MARS, the day of celebration: a crowd of people in Sunday clothes. Women with parasols, pet dogs on leads. Sticky-fingered children pawing at their mothers; people who have bought coconuts and don't know what to make of them. Then the glint of light on bayonets, people clutching hands, whirling children off their feet, pushing and calling out in alarm as they are separated from their families. Some mistake, there must be some mistake. The red flag of martial law is unfurled. What's a flag, on a day of celebration? Then the horrors of the first volley. And back, losing footing, blood blossoming horribly on the grass, fingers under stampeding feet, the splinter of hoof on bone. It is over within minutes. An example has been made. A soldier slides from his saddle and vomits.

MID-MORNING the news came; perhaps fifty dead, though this was the highest estimate. Whatever the tally, it's hard to take in. The red-walled room seemed so small now, and close. There was the very bolt on the door, the one that was locked two years ago: the one that was locked when the women marched on Versailles.

'Not to put too fine a point on it,' Danton said, 'it's time we were elsewhere. When the National Guard realize what they have done, they will be looking for someone to blame. It will occur to them to blame the authors of the petition, and they,' he finished heavily, 'and they, the authors, that's us.' He looked up. 'Did someone fire a shot from the crowd? Was that it? A panic?'

'No,' Camille said. 'I believe Marat. I believe your tip-offs, I think this was planned.'

Danton shook his head. Still hard to take it in. All the phrase-making, the trimming and teasing of clauses, the drafting and redrafting of the petition, the to-ing and fro-ing to the Jacobins and the Assembly, to end in this – swift, stupid, bloody. He had thought, lawyer's tactics can win this; violence maybe but *only as a last resort*. He'd played by the rules – mostly. He'd kept within the law, just. He'd expected Lafayette and Bailly to play by the rules; to contain the crowds, let them be. But we are moving, now, into a world where the rules are being redefined; it is as well to expect the worst.

Camille said, 'The patriots saw the petition as an opportunity. So, it seems, did Lafayette. He saw it as an opportunity for a massacre.'

This, they knew, was a journalist talking. Real life is never so clear and crisp. But that would always be the word for it, in the years ahead: 'The Massacre on the Champs-de-Mars.'

Danton felt a huge surge of anger. Next time, he thought, bull's tactics, lion's tactics; but for now the tactics of a rat in a run.

LATE AFTERNOON: Angélique Charpentier was in her garden at Fontenay-sous-Bois, a flower basket over her arm. She was trying to behave decorously; really she would have liked to dive to her knees in the salad beds and do some violence to the slugs. Hot weather, thunder in the air: we're not ourselves.

'Angélique?' Slim black shape against the sun.

'Camille? What are you doing here?'

'Can we go into the house? There are several others who will be here within an hour. You may not thank Georges-Jacques, but he thought this would be a place of safety. There has been a massacre. Lafayette has fired on the people celebrating the Bastille.'

'Georges – he's not hurt?'

'Of course not. You know Georges. But the National Guard are looking for us.'

'Won't they come here?'

'Not for a few hours. The city is in confusion.'

Angélique took his arm. This is not, she thought, the life I meant to have; this is not the life I meant for Gabrielle.

As they hurried to the house, she pulled off the white linen square that she wore to keep the sun off the back of her neck. She tried to pat her hair into place. How many for dinner? she wondered; people have to be fed. The city might have been a thousand miles away. It was that time of the afternoon when the birds are silent; heavy, undisturbed scents lay over the gardens.

Here was her husband François, hurrying out, his face alarmed. Despite the temperature he looked as he always used to - dapper, particular. He was in shirt-sleeves, but his cravat was knotted neatly; his round brown wig was on his head; you could almost imagine the napkin over his arm. 'Camille?' he said.

For a moment Camille thought half a decade might roll away. He wished he were back at the Café de l'École, cool and echoing; the coffee strong, Angélique svelte, Maître Vinot boring on about his Life Plan. 'Oh, fuck this,' he muttered. 'I don't know where we go from here.'

ONE BY ONE they straggled in through the afternoon. Camille seemed somehow to have got the advantage of them; by the time Danton arrived, he was sitting on the terrace, reading the New Testament and drinking lemonade.

Fabre brought news that François Robert had been seen alive. Legendre had seen patrols swarming over the Cordeliers district, and printing presses smashed, and a quantity of carcases carried away from his shop by the vultures who came in the wake of the patrols. 'Do you know,' he said, 'there are days when my love of the sovereign people abates a bit?' He had seen a young journalist, Prudhomme, beaten up by National Guardsmen, dragged off somewhere looking quite bad. 'I'd have gone back for him,' he said. 'But you told us not to risk it, didn't you, Danton?' His eyes appealed, dog-like, for approval.

Danton nodded once, without comment. 'What did they want Prudhomme for?'

'Because,' Fabre said, 'heat of the moment, they thought they had Camille.'

'I'd have gone back for Camille,' Legendre said.

Camille looked up from Saint Matthew. 'The hell you would.'

Gabrielle, looking sallow and scared, arrived with enough baggage to withstand a siege. 'Into the kitchen,' Angélique said, ripping the bags from her hands. 'There are vegetables to be prepared. Five minutes to clean yourself up and then report for active service.' Cruel to be kind, she said under her breath; keep her busy, make small-talk.

But Gabrielle was not fit even to string beans. She sat down at the kitchen table, Antoine on her knees, and dissolved into tears. 'Look, he's safe,' her mother said. 'He's making plans right now. The worst is over.' Still tears ran out of Gabrielle's eyes. 'You're pregnant again, aren't you?' Angélique said. She held her daughter, hiccupping and sobbing, against her chest, smoothing her hair and feeling the skin of Gabrielle's cheek burning beneath her hand, as if she had a fever. What a time to find out, she thought. The baby Antoine began to wail. She could hear the men laughing, out on the terrace.

Gallows humour, she supposed; except Georges, who could be relied on, none of them had much appetite. The duck went to waste; the sauce congealed; the vegetables went cold in their dishes. Fréron was the last to arrive; he was a wreck, bruised, trembling, incoherent. Alcohol was needed, before he could get his story straight. He had been caught on the Pont-Neuf, beaten to the ground. Some men from the Cordeliers' Battalion had come by. They had recognized him, waded in, caused a diversion while he scrambled away. Otherwise, he said, he would have been dead.

'Has anyone seen Robespierre?' Camille asked. Heads were shaken. Camille picked up a table knife, and ran his finger round the edge of it reflectively. Lucile, he presumed, would be at the rue Condé; she would not have stayed in their apartment alone, for she was not without sense. Two days ago she had been saying, you know we really have to decide about this wallpaper, shall we have treillage? He'd said, *Lucile, ask me a real question.* He had a feeling that this was the real question, now. 'I'm going back to Paris,' he said, and stood up.

There was a short silence. 'Why don't you just go in the kitchen and cut your own throat?' Fabre inquired. 'We'll bury you in the garden.'

'Now Camille,' Angélique said reproachfully. She leaned across the table and took him by the wrist.

'One speech,' he said. 'To the Jacobins, what's left of them. Just to lay down our line. Give us some sort of grasp on the situation. Besides, I have to find my wife, and I have to find Robespierre. I'll be away again before anything goes wrong. I know Marat's escape routes.'

They looked at him, dumbstruck, jaw-dropped. It is really hard for these people to remember – between crises – that he ever held the police at bay in the Palais-Royal, that he ever waved a pistol about and threatened to shoot himself. Even he finds it hard to comprehend – between crises. But there it is. He is the Lanterne Attorney now. He is locked into a role, he is cast in a part, he won't stutter if he keeps to the script. Danton said, 'A word with you, alone.' He nodded his head towards the door that led to the garden.

'Secrets among the brotherhood?' Fréron said archly.

No one answered. Silent, respectful of the gloom, Angélique began to gather the dishes towards her. Gabrielle muttered something and slipped from the room.

'WHERE WILL YOU GO?' Camille said.

'Arcis.'

'They'll come after you.'

'Yes.'

'So then?'

'England.'

'And when will you be back?'

'As soon as – ' Danton swore softly. 'Let's face it, possibly never. Don't go back to Paris. Stay here tonight – we'll have to risk it, because we need the sleep. Write to your father-in-law, tell him to put your affairs in order. Have you made your will?'

'No.'

'Well, make one now, and write to Lucile. Tomorrow at dawn we'll leave for Arcis. We can hide out for a week or so, until it's safe to make a dash for the coast.'

'My geography's not up to much,' Camille said, 'but wouldn't it be better to dash from here?'

'I have things to see to, papers to sign.'

'If you're not coming back, I can see you would have.'

'Now don't waste time arguing with me. The women can come after us as soon as is practicable. You can even ship your mother-in-law over if you really feel you can't do without her.'

'And do you think the English will be glad to see us? Do you think they'll meet us at Dover with a civic banquet and a military band?'

'We have contacts.'

'So we have, but,' Camille said with mock-bitterness, 'where is Grace Elliot when you need her?'

'We don't have to travel under our own names. I have papers already, I can get some for you. We'll pretend to be businessmen – what I don't know about cotton-spinning isn't worth knowing. Once in the country we can make contact with our sympathizers, look for somewhere to live – money shouldn't be a problem – what's the matter?'

'When did you work this out?'

'On the way here.'

'But it's all settled in your mind – oh, for God's sake, this has always been your idea, hasn't it? Profit from the smooth patches and skip out as soon as it gets rough? Do you want to live in Hampshire as a gentleman-farmer? Is that the latest of your lofty ambitions?'

'What's the alternative?' Danton had a headache, and Camille was making it worse. I knew you, he wanted to say: I knew you when you were shaking in your shoes.

'I can't believe' – and Camille's voice was shaking now – 'that you would run away.'

'But if we go to England we can start again. Plan.'

Camille looked at him in sorrow. The expression was more

complex than sorrow, but Danton could not analyse it, because he was so mentally weary at the thought of starting again.

'You go then,' Camille said. 'I'll stay. I'll hide for as long as I have to. When I think it's safe, I'll get word to you. Then I hope you'll come back. I don't know if you will, but if you say you will I'll have to believe you. There's no other way to do it. If you don't come back, I suppose I'll come to England. I have no intention of carrying on here without you.'

'I have a wife, and a child, and I –'

'Yes, I know. And another child soon.'

'She told you that?'

'No. Gabrielle and I are not on such terms.'

'Good. Because she didn't tell me.'

Camille indicated the house. 'I'll go back in now and talk at that lot and make them thoroughly ashamed of themselves. They'll whimper back to Paris tonight, you may be sure. They can form a diversion – it will give you a chance, and you're the important one. I quite see that, I shouldn't have said what I said just then. I'll get Fabre to take Lucile to Bourg-la-Reine, and he can lurk there out of the way for a week or two.'

'I'm not sure I'd trust my wife to Fabre as an escort.'

'Who then? Rabbit? Our butcher brave and bold?'

They grinned at each other. Their eyes met. 'You know what Mirabeau used to say,' Camille said. '"We live at a time of great events and little men."'

'Take care, then,' Danton said. 'Oh, and do make your will anyway. And Camille, leave me your wife.'

Camille laughed. Danton turned his back. He didn't want to see him go.

ROBESPIERRE had been crushed against a barrier when the fighting started. The shock had been greater than the pain. He had seen dead bodies; after the troops had pulled back, he had watched as the wounded were carried away, and he had noted the absurd detritus of the civilian battlefield: flowered hats, single shoes, dolls and spinning tops.

He began walking. Perhaps he had walked for hours. He was not sure of the route he had taken, but it seemed to him necessary to get back to the rue Saint-Honoré, to the Jacobins, to take possession of the ground. He had almost made it. But now someone was blocking his path.

He looked up. The man had a shirt torn open at the neck, a dusty bonnet and the remnants of a National Guardsman's uniform.

What was strangest, he was laughing: his teeth were bared, like a dog's.

He had a sabre in his hand. There was a tricolour ribbon tied around the hilt.

Behind him were three other men. Two had bayonets.

Robespierre stood quite still. He had never carried a pistol, despite the number of times Camille had told him to. 'Camille,' he'd said, 'I'd never use it anyway. I'd never shoot anybody.'

Well, that was true. And it was too late now.

Would he die quickly or slowly? That was a question for someone else to decide; he could not influence it. His efforts were over.

In a moment, he thought, I shall rest. In a moment I shall sleep.

The dreadful calm in his heart invaded his face.

With a leisurely movement, the dog-man reached out. He took him by the front of his coat.

'Down on your knees,' he said.

Someone pushed him from behind. He was jerked off his feet.

He closed his eyes.

Like this, he thought.

In the public street.

THEN HE HEARD his name called: not across eternity, but in his very physical and temporal ear.

Two pairs of hands hauled him to his feet.

He heard the cloth of his coat tear. Then oaths, a scream, the contact of a fist with the precarious arrangements of the human face. But when he opened his eyes he saw the dog-man, blood streaming from his nose, and a woman, as tall as dog-man, with blood running from her mouth. She said, 'Attack women, would you?

Come on then, sonny, let's see what I can cut off with these.' From her skirts she produced what looked like a pair of tailor's shears. Another woman, behind her, had the kind of little axe you use for splitting kindling.

By the time he had drawn breath, a dozen more women had swarmed out of a doorway. One had a crowbar, one a pikestaff, and they all had knives. They were shouting '*Robespierre*' and people were running out of the shops and houses to see.

The men with bayonets had been beaten away. Dog-man spat; blood and saliva hit the face of the woman general. 'Spit, aristocrat,' she yelled. 'Show me Lafayette, I'll slit his belly and have him stuffed with chestnuts. *Robespierre*,' she yelled. 'If we've got to have a King, we'll have him.

'King Robespierre,' the women yelled. 'King Robespierre.'

The man was tall and balding, with a clean calico apron and a hammer in his hand. He was flailing with his other arm as he forced himself through the crowd. 'I'm for you,' he bawled. 'My house is here.' The women dropped back: 'The carpenter Duplay,' one said, 'a good patriot, a good master.'

Duplay shook the hammer at the Guardsmen and the women cheered: 'Scum,' he said to the men. 'Get back, scum.' He took Robespierre by the arm. 'My house is here,' he repeated, 'here, good citizen, quickly. This way.'

The women parted their ranks, reaching out, touching Robespierre as he passed. He followed Duplay, stooping through a little door cut in a high solid gate. Bolts slammed home.

In the yard, workmen stood in a knot. Another minute, it was clear, and they would have joined their master on the streets. 'Back to work, my good lads,' Duplay said. 'And put your shirts on. I'm not sure that you show respect.'

'Oh no.' He tried to catch Duplay's eye. They must not alter things because he had come. A thrush sang in a scrubby bush by the gate. The air smelt sweetly of new wood. Over there was the house. He knew what he would find behind that door. The carpenter Duplay put out a hand. It gripped his shoulder. 'You're safe now, boy,' Duplay said. He did not pull away.

A tall, plain woman in a dark dress came out of the side door. 'Father,' she said, 'what is the matter, we heard shouting, is there some trouble in the street?'

'Eléonore,' he said, 'go in, and tell your mother that Citizen Robespierre has come to stay with us at last.'

ON 18 JULY, a detachment of police marched down the rue des Cordeliers, with orders to close down the *Révolutions de France*. They did not find the editor, but they found an assistant of his, who produced a gun. Shots were exchanged. The editor's assistant was overpowered, beaten up and thrown into prison

When the police arrived at the Charpentiers' house at Fontenay-sous-Bois, they found only one man who – being the right age – might have been Georges-Jacques Danton. He was Victor Charpentier, Gabrielle's brother. He was lying injured in a pool of blood by the time they discovered their mistake, but these were not the days to stand on niceties of conduct. Warrants for the arrest of one Danton, advocate: Desmoulins, journalist: Fréron, journalist: Legendre, master butcher.

Camille Desmoulins was in hiding near Versailles. In Arcis Danton arranged his affairs. He had given his brother-in-law a power of attorney, authorizing him *inter alia* to sell his furniture and cancel the lease of his Paris apartment, if he deemed fit. He signed the deeds of purchase for a manor house by the river, and installed his mother in it, arranging for her at the same time a life annuity. In early August, he left for England.

LORD GOWER, the British Ambassador, in dispatches:

Danton is fled, and M. Robespierre the great *denunciateur* and by office *Accusateur Publique* is about to be *denoncé* himself.

RÉVOLUTIONS de Paris:

What will become of liberty? Some say it is finished . . .

PART FOUR

Camille Desmoulins:

The King has aimed a pistol at the nation's head; he has misfired, and it is the nation's turn now.

Lucile Desmoulins:

We want to be free; but oh God, the cost of it.

I. *A Lucky Hand*

(1791)

MANON ROLAND sat by the window, turning her cheek to catch the fading warmth of the late October sun. Slowly, with deliberation, she dipped her needle through worn cloth. Even in our circumstances, there are domestic servants for such tasks. But nothing is ever done quite so well as when you do it yourself. Then again – she bent her head over the work – what could be more soothing, more ordinary than a linen sheet? In a fractious world? There will be more need to darn and patch, to mend and make do, now that, as her husband puts it, 'the blow has fallen'.

What is it with these metaphors of domestic work? Does she resist them, or do they resist her? The centre is frayed, worn, gone to threads; so, turn edges to middle. 'Ça Ira'. She smiles. She is not, she likes to think, without humour.

Her husband, late fifties now, ulcer, liver complaint, is prevented by her nursing and her strength of will from sinking into invalidity. He had been an Inspector of Manufactures; now under the new dispensation, September 1791, his post is abolished. They had applauded the death of the old regime; they were not self-interested people. But the applause must be muted, when you have no retirement pension, and nothing ahead but genteel poverty.

You have been ill, she thought, fevered and drained by the Paris summer, sickened by the blood of the Champs-de-Mars. 'It has been too much for you, my dear; see how excitable you have become. We must leave everything and go home, because nothing is more important than your health, and at Le Clos you were always so serene.' Serene? She serene? Since '89?

That was why they had come back to the run-down little estate in the Beaujolais hills, to the vegetable beds and faded hangings, and the poor women coming to the back door for advice and herb poultices. Here (she had read a great deal of Rousseau) one lived in harmony with nature and the seasons. But the nation was choking to death, and she wanted . . . she wanted . . .

Impatiently she hitched her chair away from the window. All her life she has been a spectator, an onlooker; the role has brought her nothing, not even the gift of philosophical detachment. And study has not brought it, nor self-analysis, nor even, she thought wryly, gardening. Some would think that it ought to come in the course of nature to a woman of thirty-six, a wife and mother. A little calm, a little quiet within – little chance. Even after childbearing, there is blood in your veins, not milk. I am not passive in the face of life, and I do not think I ever will be, and – considering recent events – why should I be?

This latest misfortune, for instance; of course she will not lie down under it. They have just come from Paris; they must go back. Either they must obtain a pension, or a new position under the new order.

Roland did not look forward to the trip. But she thought, Paris calls me. I was born there.

HER FATHER'S SHOP was on the Quai d'Horloge, near the Pont-Neuf. He was an engraver – fashionable trade, fashionable customers – and he had the manner shaped to go with it, assertive yet sufficiently obsequious, artist and artisan, both and neither.

She had been baptised Marie-Jeanne, always called Manon. Her brothers and sisters all died. There must be some reason (she thought at eight or nine) why the good God spared me: some particular purpose? She looked narrowly at her parents, measuring with callous child's eyes their limitations, their painstaking veneer of refinement. They were over-careful of her; held her, perhaps, a little in awe. She had a great number of music lessons.

When she was ten her father bought her several treatises on the education of the young, reasoning that any book with 'education' in the title was the kind of thing she needed.

This clever child, this pretty child, this child for whom nothing was too good; what carelessness of theirs was it to leave her alone

one day in the workshop? Yet the boy, the apprentice (fifteen, too tall for his age, raw-handed, freckled) had always seemed well-mannered, harmless. It was evening, he was working under a lamp, and she stood at his elbow to look at his work. She was not disturbed when he took her hand. He held it for a moment, playing with her fingers, smiling up at her, his head tilted; then forced it under the workbench.

There she touched strange flesh, a damp swollen spike of flesh, quivering with its own life. He tightened his grip on her wrist, then turned in the chair to face her. She saw what she had touched. 'Don't tell,' he whispered. She tore her hand away. Her eyebrows flew up to the curls bouncing on her forehead, and she strode away, slamming the door of the workroom behind her.

On the stairs she heard her mother calling her. There was some small errand or task to perform – she could never remember afterwards what exactly it had been. She carried out her mother's request, her face dazed, her stomach churning. Said nothing. Did not know what to say.

But in the weeks that followed – and this was what, later, she found hard to understand, because she could not believe that she was a child of vicious inclination – she went back to the workshop. Yes: she took the occasion. She made little excuses to herself; it was as if she had decided, in those days, to walk around with eyes half-closed to her own nature. It was only curiosity, her grown-up self said: the natural curiosity of the over-protected child. But then her grown-up self would say, you made excuses then and you are making them now.

Each evening the boy ate with the family; because he was so young, and far away from his own people, her mother was anxious about him. She couldn't afford to be different, in his presence; they would wonder about it, might ask questions. After all, if they do – I did nothing wrong, she would tell herself. But she began to wonder if life were fair; if people were not often blamed when they were not at fault. Of course, it was so in childhood; every day there were careless slaps and nursery injustices. Grown-up life, she'd thought, would be different, more rational – and she was on the verge of grown-up life now. The closer she came, the more risky it all looked, the less it seemed that people were amenable to reason. A nagging inner voice told her: you are not at fault, but you can be made to appear at fault.

Once he whispered to her: 'I didn't show you anything your mother hasn't seen.' She flung her chin up, opened her mouth to quell his impertinence; but then her mother came in with a plate of bread and a bowl of salad, and there they were side by side, good children, shy children, eyes on the tablecloth, thanking God for salad and cheese and bread.

In the workshop, where she lurked around, there was tension between them, an invisible wire drawn tight. Had she perhaps tormented him a little, scampering in and out when the presence of other people protected her? She kept thinking of that strange flesh, blind and white and quivering, like something new-born.

One day they had of course found themselves alone. She kept a distance from him; she was not to be trapped in that way again. This time he had approached from behind her, while she stood looking out of the window. He slipped his hands up under her arms, then pulled her backwards on to his knees, folding into a chair strategically placed. Her skirt was rucked up; he touched her once, between her legs. Then his freckled arm, full of its scrawny nascent strength, was locked across her body; the hand formed a fist. She gazed down at that fist; he held her there like a doll, inanimate like a doll, her pretty lips parted, whilst he wheezed and puffed his way to satisfaction. Not that she knew it was satisfaction: only that some kind of climax to this activity had been reached, for he released her, and muttered a few distracted kindnesses, and never once (she thought later) did he look at her face, he had held her quite deliberately backwards so that he did not need to see whether she was pleased or horrified, whether she was laughing or whether she was too stunned to scream.

She ran; and soon after – at the first, rapid request to know what was wrong with her – she began to splutter out her story. Tears poured out of her eyes as she told it, and her legs felt weak, so she allowed herself to totter to a chair. Her mother's face seemed to fly apart in horror. She reached for her, dragging her back to her feet; her mother's hands gripped her arms with a crushing pressure. She had shaken her – her, the precious child – shrieking questions: what did he do, where did he touch you, tell me every word he said, every word, don't be afraid, tell your mother (and all the time she was shaking her, distorted face inches from her own): did he make you touch him, are you bleeding, Manon, tell me, tell me, tell.

Dragged along the street, she wailed like a three-year-old; inside the church her mother snatched at the bell-pull that brings the priest quickly if you have done a murder or are dying, then the priest comes at once and he gives you absolution so that you won't be damned. And he did come ... Her mother pushed her in the small of the back and left her alone in the dimness with the asthmatical breathing of the elderly man. Father listened, turning his one good ear, to the convulsive sobbing of what he took to be a violated child.

The curious thing was this: they did not dismiss the boy. They were afraid of scandal. They were afraid that should the business become known the mischief might be attributed to her. She had to see the boy every day, though he no longer ate with the family. She knew she was to-blame now; it was not a question of what other people said or thought, it was a question of an inner reconciliation, and one that could not take place. It could, her mother said, have been very much worse; she was *intact*, her mother said, whatever that meant. Try not to think about it, her mother advised; one day, when you're grown up and married, it won't seem so bad. But however hard she tried – and perhaps trying so hard was part of the problem – she did think about it. She would blush and begin to shake inside, and she would jerk her head with a little involuntary movement, a flinching.

When she was twenty-two, her mother was dead; in the mornings she attended to the running of the household, in the afternoons she studied – mastering Italian and botany, rejecting the systems of Helvetius, progressing with her mathematics. In the evening she read classical history, and sat with closed eyes over the books, her hands still on the pages, dreaming of Liberty. She dwelled – forced herself to dwell – on what was great in Man, on progress and nobility of spirit, on brotherhood and self-sacrifice: on all the disembodied virtues.

She read Buffon's *Histoire Naturelle*; there were passages she felt forced to omit, and pages she turned quickly, because they contained information that she did not want.

Seven or eight years after the boy had left her father's employment, she met him again. He had just married; he was, she saw, a perfectly ordinary young man. It was a brief meeting, no time for private talk, not that she'd have wished it – but he whispered to her, 'I hope you don't still blame me. I did you no harm.'

In 1776 her life altered. It was the year the Americans proclaimed their independence, and she brought her affections to be bound. There had been offers of marriage – from tradesmen mainly, in their twenties and early thirties. She had been polite to them but very, very discouraging. Marriage was something she avoided thinking about. The family began to despair.

But in January that year, Jean-Marie Roland appeared on the scene. He was tall, well-educated, well-travelled, with the kindness of a father and the gravity of a teacher. He belonged to the minor nobility, but he was the youngest of five sons; he had a little land and the money he earned, nothing more. He was an administrator: to that estate born. In his capacity as inspector, he had travelled Europe. He knew about bleaching and dyeing and making lace and using peat for fuel: about the manufacture of gunpowder, the curing of pork and the grinding of lenses; about physics, free trade and ancient Greece. At once, he sensed her own voracity for knowledge – for a certain type of knowledge, at least. At first she did not notice his strange, dusty coats, his frayed linen, his shoes fastened not with buckles but with old scraps of ribbon; when she did, she thought how refreshing it was to meet a man quite without vanity. Their talk was earnest, full of a kind of quibbling, wary courtesy.

He had kissed her fingertips, but that was politeness. He sat across the room from her. He attempted nothing. It would have been as if a statue of Saint Paul had leaned down and chucked you under the chin.

They exchanged letters, long, absorbing letters that took half a day to compose and an hour to read. At first they penned judicious essays on subjects of general interest. After some months they wrote of marriage – its sacramental aspect, its social usefulness.

He went to Italy for a year, and reported his travels in a published work of six volumes.

In 1780, after four thoughtful and diffident years, they married.

On the night of their wedding it had not been possible to communicate by letter. She did not know what she thought might happen; she would not allow herself to think of the apprentice and his fumbling, or to construct a theory about what, after all, had taken place behind her back. So she was unprepared for his body, for the hollow chest with its sparse, greying hair; she was unprepared for the haste with which he pulled her against that body, and for the pain of penetration. His breathing changed, and jerking her head up over his shoulder she asked, 'Is that . . . ?' But he had already rolled away from her into sleep, his open mouth breathing in the darkness.

The next day he had woken to lean over her with apology and concern: 'Were you entirely ignorant? My poor dear Manon, had I known . . .'

One child (both thought) justifies a marriage: Eudora, born 4 October 1781.

She had an ability – she was proud of it – to grasp the essentials of a complicated matter within minutes. Name her a topic – the Punic Wars, let us say, or the manufacture of tallow candles – and within a day she will give you a satisfactory account of it; within a week she will be capable of setting up her own factory, or drawing up a battle plan for Scipio Africanus. She liked to help him in his work, it was a pleasure to her. She began on the humblest level, copying passages he wished to study. Then she tried her hand at indexing, proved careful and competent; then she applied her retentive memory and dogged curiosity to his research projects. Finally – since she wrote with such fluency and grace and ease – she began to help him out with his reports and letters. Oh, let me have that, she'd say, I'll polish it off while you're humming and hawing over the first paragraph. My dear, clever girl, he'd say, how did I ever manage without you?

But I want, she thought, more than a meed of praise; I want a quiet life, and yet, I want to move on to a larger stage. Knowing the place allotted to a woman, and content, respecting it, I want the respect of men. I want their respect and their approbation; for I too make schemes, I reason, I have my ideas about the state of France. She wished she could feed them, by some imperceptible process, into the heads of the nation's legislators: as she feeds them into her husband's.

She recalled a July day: flies clustering and buzzing about the casement of a sickroom, her husband's yellow face above the white sheets, and her mother-in-law, a tyrant of eighty-five, nodding in a corner, breath whistling. She saw herself, in a grey dress: grey-minded by age and sickness and heat, creeping through the rooms with herb tea: the summer going obdurately on outside the windows.

'Madame?'

'Quietly. What is it?'

'Madame, the news from Paris.'

'Has someone fallen ill?'

'Madame, the Bastille has fallen.'

She dropped the cup at her feet and let it shatter. Later she thought: I did it on purpose. Startled from his doze, Roland lifted his head from the pillow. 'Manon, has some dreadful calamity occurred?'

In the corner the Old Regime woke up, clucking at the disturbance, and fixed with a baleful eye the intemperate joy of her son's wife.

She began to write for the press now: first for the *Lyon Courier* then for Brissot's paper the *French Patriot*. (Her husband and Brissot had corresponded at length, these two years.) She signed herself 'A Lady from Lyon' or 'A Roman Lady'. In June 1790 she received a charming if not very legible letter, seeking permission for the *Révolutions de France et du Brabant* to reprint one of her articles. She agreed at once: not knowing, then, the character of the paper's editor.

In Paris the great opportunity had come, and she had taken it; she had made herself useful to the patriots. Waking and sleeping, she had dreamed of such a chance; dreamed of it in her lonely hours of study, dreamed of it pregnant with Eudora, watching the grave-diggers at work in an Amiens cemetery. *The salon of Mme Roland.* So, perhaps in detail the dream had disappointed; the men were lightweight, frivolous, wrong-headed, and she had to bite her lips to keep from interventions that would cut them down to size. Yet, it was a beginning; and soon they would be on their way to Paris again.

She had not divorced herself from the situation, these last months. In a locked drawer she kept letters from Brissot, from Robespierre, from that grave and prepossessing young deputy François-Léonard Buzot. From these letters she had learned of the aftermath of the Champs-de-Mars. They had told her (she would hate to be synoptic, but events press so fast) how Louis, restored to the throne, had sworn to uphold the constitution: how Lafayette, no longer com-mander of the National Guard, had left Paris for an army post. The new Legislative Assembly was called, former deputies barred from it; so Buzot had returned to his home in Evreux. Never mind; they could still exchange letters, and no doubt one day they'd meet again.

Their friend Brissot was a deputy now: dear Brissot, who worked so hard. And Robespierre had not left for his home town; he remained in Paris, rebuilding the Jacobin Club, bringing in the new deputies, inducting them into the rules and procedures of the debates that shadowed the Assembly's own. A diligent man, Robespierre; but he had disappointed her all the same.

On the day of the massacre she had sent a message to him, offering to hide him in their apartment. She got no answer; she heard later that he had been taken in by a tradesman's family, and was living with them now. She felt flat, let-down, when the moment of danger never came. She saw herself out-facing a regiment; she saw herself talking down the National Guard.

During this exile, also, she had followed with some interest the career of M. Danton and his friends. She had been relieved to learn that he was in England, and hoped he would stay there. Yet still, she sought information; and as soon as there was rumour of an amnesty, M. Danton came bouncing back. He had the nerve to put himself up for the Legislative Assembly; and in the middle of one of the election meetings (she had heard) an officer had arrived with a warrant for his arrest. Abused verbally and physically by the mob that seemed to attend the lawyer in all his activities, the officer was carried off to the Abbaye prison, where he was shut up for three days in the cell reserved for Danton.

The amnesty had been passed; but the Electors had seen through the lout's pretensions. Rejected, Danton had retired to his province to brood; and now he had decided he would like to become Deputy Public Prosecutor. With luck, there too he would be thwarted; the time was far distant (she hoped) when France would be governed by thugs.

For the future ... It irked her to think that in Paris the silly people were once more cheering the King and Queen, simply because they had put their names to the constitution: as if they had forgotten the years of tyranny and rapacity, the betrayal on the road to Varennes. Louis was plotting with the foreign powers, that much was clear to her; there will be war, and we would be foolish not to strike the first blow. (She turned the cloth in her hands and caught a loop of thread with the needle to make a knot.) And we must fight as a republic, as Athens did and Sparta. (She reached for her scissors.) Louis must be deposed. Preferably, killed.

Then the reign of the aristocrats would be over for ever.

And such a reign it had been ...

Once, long ago, her grandmother had taken her to a house in the Marais, to call on a noblewoman with whom she had some acquaintance. There was a footman to bow them in; on a sofa reclined an old woman, opulently gowned, with a stupid, rouged face. A small dog rose from among her draperies and yapped at them, bouncing on stiff legs; the noblewoman swatted at it, perfunctory, and motioned her grandmother to a low stool. For some reason, in this household, her grandmother was addressed by her maiden name.

She herself was left to stand, hot and silent. Her scalp still burned from the tortures which her grandmother, early that morning, had inflicted on her hair. The old woman shifted on her cushions, rasping on in her dictatorial, oddly uncultivated voice. Urged forward, Manon had bobbed a curtsey inside her stiff best dress. Thirty years later she had not forgiven herself for that curtsey.

Watery eyes regarded her. 'Religious, is she?' the noblewoman said.

The dog subsided, snuffled by her side; a discarded tapestry lay over the arm of the sofa. She had dropped her eyes. 'I try to perform my duties.'

Her grandmother shifted painfully on the stool. The old woman patted at her lace bonnet, as if she were before a mirror; then she turned her hard eyes on Manon again, and began to ask her questions, schoolbook questions. When she answered correctly, with studied politeness, the creature sneered. 'Little scholar isn't she? Do you think that's what a man requires?'

The catechism over – still standing, feeling faint in the airless room – she had to hear her merits and faults enumerated. A good figure *already*, the noblewoman said; as if to imply that when she was grown-up she would be fat. Sallow complexion, the noblewoman said; *might* freshen up, in time. 'Tell me, my darling,' she said, 'have you ever bought a ticket in the lottery?'

'No, Madame, I don't believe in games of chance.'

'What a prig she is,' the old creature drawled. A hand shot out; grasped her little wrist in a vice of bone. 'I want her to buy a lottery ticket for me. I want her to pick the number, you understand, then bring it here to me and give it to me herself. I think she has a lucky hand.'

In the street she gulped in God's clean air. 'Please, I needn't go back, need I?' She wanted to race home, back to her books and the reasonable people inside them.

Even now, when someone said the word 'aristocrat' – when they spoke of 'a noblewoman' or 'a titled lady' – it called to her mind the picture of that malignant gambler. It was not just the lace cap, the hard eyes, nor the crushing words. It was the pervasive odour of a heavy musk, it was the reek of scent which overlay (she knew) the sweetness of bodily decay.

Lottery ticket, indeed. There would be no gambling under the republic, she thought; it would not be permitted.

PARIS: 'Look,' said the judge to the Clerk of the Court, 'I don't care if they're retaining John the Baptist. They've infringed the gaming laws and I'm giving them six months. Why do you suppose Desmoulins has come back to the Bar, anyway?'

'Money,' said the clerk.

'I thought Orléans paid well.'

'Oh, the Duke is finished,' the clerk said cheerfully. 'Mme de Genlis is in England, Laclos has gone back to his regiment, and the Mistresses are making up to Danton. Of course, they get money from the English.'

'What, you think the English have bought Danton's people?'

'I think they are paying them, but that's a different matter. They're an unscrupulous lot. Time was in this country when you paid a man a bribe and you could rely on his honesty.'

The judge shifted uneasily in his chair. The clerk was becoming aphoristic; when that happened, they always got home late. 'Still,' he said. 'To the matter in hand.'

'Ah yes, Maître Desmoulins. He took his father-in-law's investment advice and went in for City of Paris bonds. And we all know what's happened to them.'

'Indeed,' said the judge feelingly.

'And now the authorities have closed the newspaper he wants another source of income.'

'He can hardly be poor.'

'He has money, but wants more. In that, if in no other particular, he resembles the rest of us. I understand he's playing the stock market. While he waits for that to pay off he intends to recoup his fortunes from the handsome fees he can now command at the Bar.'

'I was told he hated the business.'

'But it's different now, isn't it? Now if he gets in difficulties we have to sit and wait for him to finish his sentences. We're a bit afraid – '

'Not I,' said the judge stoutly.

'And he is able.'

'I don't deny it.'

'And when milords find the police interfering with their pleasures, how convenient for them to have one of their own to argue the case. Arthur Dillon, de Sillery, that lot, they've put him up to this.'

'And he associates with them quite openly – you'd think the patriots –'

'Will tolerate most things from him. After all, in a manner of speaking he *is* the Revolution. I believe there are mutterings, though. Yet after all – this is Paris, not Geneva.'

'I take it you're a gambling man yourself.'

'That's by the way,' the clerk said breezily. 'Perhaps, like Maître Desmoulins, I am interested in limiting the interference of the state in the private life of the individual.'

'You agree with him?' the judge said. 'I shall see you soon with your boots up on the table, sansculotte in homespun trousers, a red cap on your reverend pate, and a pike against the wall behind you.'

'Every possibility,' said the clerk. 'Such are the times.'

'I shall tolerate much, but I shall not permit you to smoke a pipe, like Père Duchesne.'

CAMILLE made a small gesture to his clients, of rueful apology, then turned his smile on the judge. The man and woman looked at each other, allowing their shoulders to sag a little. 'You will not escape imprisonment,' their counsel had told them, 'so we may as well use your case to discuss some wider issues.'

'I wish to ask the court –'

'Stand up.'

The lawyer hesitated, did so, wandered across to the judge to stare at him at close range. 'I wish to ask for permission to publish my opinion.'

The judge dropped his voice. 'Are you intending to start some sort of public controversy?'

'Yes.'

'You could do that without my permission.'

'It's a formality, isn't it? I'm polite.'

'Have you any quarrel with the verdict on the facts?'

'No.'

'On the law?'

'No.'

'Then?'

'I object to the use of the courts as instruments of the intrusive moralizing state.'

'Really?' The judge leaned forward; he liked to argue generalities. 'As you seem to have the wiped the church out of the picture, who is going to make men what they ought to be, if the laws do not do it?'

'Who is to say what men ought to be?'

'If the people elect their lawmakers – which, nowadays, they do – don't they depute that task to them?'

'But if the people and their deputies were formed by a corrupt society, how are they to make good decisions? How are they to form a moral society when they have no experience of one?'

'We really are going to get home late,' the judge said. 'We shall be here for six months if we are to do justice to the question. You mean, how are we to become good when we're bad?'

'We used to do it through the agency of divine grace. But the new constitution doesn't provide for that.'

'How wrong can you be?' the judge said. 'I thought all you fellows were on course for the moral regeneration of humankind. Doesn't it worry you that you're out of step with your friends?'

'Since the Revolution you're allowed to dissent, aren't you?'

He seemed to be waiting for an answer. The judge was disconcerted.

II. *Danton: His Portrait Made*

(1791)

GEORGES-JACQUES Danton: 'Reputation is a whore, and people who talk about posterity are hypocrites and fools.'

NOW WE HAVE a problem. It wasn't envisaged that he should have part of the narrative. But time is pressing; the issues are multiplying, and in a little over two years he will be dead.

Danton did not write. He may have gone into court with a sheaf of notes; we have represented such occasions, fictitious but probable. The records of these cases are lost. He kept no diaries, and wrote few letters: unless perhaps he wrote the kind of letters that are torn up on receipt. He distrusted the commitments he might make on paper, distrusted the permanent snare for his temporary opinions. He could lay down his line at the tricolour-draped committee tables; others kept the minutes. If there were points to press at the Jacobins, patriotic wrath to vent at the Cordeliers, the public would wait till Saturday for recapitulation, and find his invective, a good deal polished up, between the grey paper covers of Camille Desmoulins's journal. In times of excitement – and there are many such times – extempore editions of the paper are thrown together, to appear twice weekly, sometimes daily. As Danton sees it, the most bizarre aspect of Camille's character is his desire to scribble over every blank surface; he sees a guileless piece of paper, virgin and harmless, and persecutes it till it is black with words, and then besmirches its sister, and so on, through the quire.

Since the massacre, of course, the paper no longer appears. Camille says he is sick of deadlines and printers' tantrums and errors; his compulsion has gone freelance. This is no drawback, as long as he writes, every week, about as many words as Danton speaks. Between now and the end of his career, Danton will make scores of speeches, some of them hours long. He makes them up in his head, as he goes. Perhaps you can hear his voice.

I CAME BACK from England in September. The amnesty was the last act of the old National Assembly. We were supposed to inaugurate the new era in a spirit of reconciliation – or some such sanctimonious twaddle. You will see how that worked out.

The summer's events had injured the patriots – literally, in many cases – and I returned to a royalist Paris. The King and his wife once more appeared in public, and were cheered. I saw no reason for pique; I am all for amiability. I need not tell you that my strong-minded friends at the Cordeliers felt differently. We have come a long way since '88, when the only republicans I knew were Billaud-Varennes and my dear irrepressible Camille.

There was some jubilation – premature – about Lafayette's departure from the capital. (I'm sorry, I can't get used to calling him Mottié.) Had he emigrated, I would personally have ordained three days of fireworks and free love on our side of the river; but the man is now with the armies, and when we have war, which will be in six or nine months, we shall need to turn him into a national hero again.

In October our fulsome patriot Jérôme Pétion was elected Mayor of Paris. The other candidate was Lafayette. So deeply does the King's wife detest the general, that she moved heaven and earth to secure Pétion's election – Pétion, mark you, a republican. I hold it my best example yet of the political ineptitude of women.

It is just possible, of course, that Pétion is on some royalist payroll that I don't know about. Who can keep track these days? He is still convinced that the King's sister fell in love with him on their journey back from Varennes. He has made himself ridiculous over that. I am surprised that Robespierre, who countenances no antics, has not reproved him. The new popular slogan, by the way, is 'Pétion or death!' Camille earned some filthy looks at the Jacobins by remarking audibly, 'Not much of a choice.'

His sudden elevation has made Jérôme quite dizzy, and he erred when he received Robespierre in state and forced him to sit through a banquet. Recently Camille said to Robespierre, 'Come to supper, we have this marvellous champagne.' Robespierre replied, 'Champagne is the poison of liberty.' What a way to talk to your oldest friend!

My failure to gain election to the new Assembly disappointed me. It occurred – forgive me if I sound like Robespierre – becáuse of the number of people working against me; and because of our failure to amend the restrictive franchise. If I sought a mandate from the man in the street, I could be King if I wanted to.

And I never make claims I can't substantiate.

I was disappointed for myself, and also for my friends. They had worked hard for me – Camille, of course, and especially Fabre – I am, nowadays, the single channel for the genius that was to inundate our age. Poor Fabre: but he is useful, and able in his way. And dedicated to the advancement of Danton, which is the trait in him I prefer above others.

I wished, in my turn, to obtain office so that I could be of service to them. I mean, by that, that I could help them to fulfil their political ambitions and augment their incomes. Don't pretend to be shocked, or not more than is necessary for form's sake. I assure you, as our wives say, it is always done. No one will seek office, unless there are proper rewards.

After the elections I went to Arcis for a while. Gabrielle is expecting her baby in February, and was in need of rest. There is nothing to do in Arcis unless one is fond of agricultural labour, and to my certain knowledge she is not. It seemed a good time to be away. Robespierre was in Arras (recruiting his provincial accent, I presume) and I thought that if he could leave the pot unwatched I could do the same. Paris was not particularly pleasant. Brissot, who has a lot of friends in the new Assembly, was busy collecting support for a policy of war against the European powers – a policy so staggeringly dangerous and inept that I became quite incoherent when I tried to argue with him.

I have now, under my roof at Arcis, my mother and my stepfather, my unmarried sister Pierrette, my old nurse, my great aunt, my sister Anne Madeleine, her husband Pierre and their five children.

The arrangement is a noisy one, but it gives me satisfaction to think that I can provide for my people in this way. I have concluded five purchases of land, including some woodland; I have leased out one of my farms, and bought more livestock. When I am in Arcis, you know, I never want to see Paris again.

Very soon my friends in the city decided that I should seek public office. Precisely, they wanted me to stand for the post of First Deputy Public Prosecutor. It is not that the post is of great intrinsic importance. My candidature is a way of announcing myself: of saying, '*Danton is back.*'

To expound this plan to me, Camille and wife arrived in Arcis, with several weeks accumulated gossip and bags overflowing with newspaper cuttings, letters and pamphlets. Gabrielle greeted Lucile with something less than enthusiasm. She was then six months into her pregnancy, ungainly and easily tired. Lucile's visit to the country had of course required a whole new wardrobe of very artful simplicity; she is becoming even more beautiful but, as Anne Madeleine says, oh so thin.

The family, who regard Parisians as something akin to Red Indians, received them with guarded politeness. Then after a day or two, Anne Madeleine simply added them to the number of her five children, who are fed on sight and conducted through the countryside on forced marches in an effort to subdue their spirits. After dinner one day Lucile remarked in conversation that she thought she might be pregnant. My mother slid her eyes round to Camille and said she would be surprised, very. I thought perhaps it was time to go back to Paris.

'WHEN WILL you be home again?' Anne Madeleine asked her brother.

'A few months – show you the baby.'

'I meant, for good.'

'Well, the state of the country – '

'What has that to do with us?'

'In Paris, you see, I have a certain position.'

'Georges-Jacques, you only told us that you were a lawyer.'

'Essentially, I am.'

'We thought that fees must be very high in Paris. We thought that you must be the top lawyer in the country.'

'Not quite that.'

'No, but you're an important man. We didn't realize what you did.'

'What do I do? If you've been talking to Camille, he exaggerates.'

'Aren't you frightened?'

'What should I be frightened of?'

'You had to run away once. What happens next time things go wrong? People like us, we have our day – we might get to the top of the heap for a year or two, but it doesn't last, it's not in the nature of things that it should.'

'We are trying, you see, to alter the nature of things.'

'But couldn't you come home now? You have land, you have what you want. Come back with your wife and let your children grow up with mine, as they ought, and bring that little girl and let her have her baby here – Georges, is it yours?'

'Her baby? Good heavens, no.'

'It's just the way you look at her. Well, how am I to know what goes on in Paris?'

So I stood for election, and was beaten by a man named de Gerville. Within days, this de Gerville was appointed Minister of the Interior, and thus removed from my path. There were fresh elections. My opponent this time was Collot d'Herbois, the none-too-successful playwright, whom I suppose I must regard as a revolutionary comrade. The electors may question my fitness for office, but Collot has all the gravitas of a mad dog. My majority was very large.

Make of this what you will. My opponents made much of it, to my discredit. They said that 'the Court had a hand in it'. Since Louis Capet retains the prerogative of ministerial appointment, it would be strange if it were otherwise.

Let me spell it out for you: they say I am 'in the pay of the Court'. Now that is a very vague allegation, an imprecise charge, and unless you could be more definite about names, dates, amounts, I would not feel obliged to make any statement. But if you ask Robespierre, he will vouch for my integrity. Nowadays that is the highest guarantee; because he is afraid of money, he is known as 'the Incorruptible'.

If you feel well-disposed to me, regard de Gerville's removal as a happy coincidence. If not, console yourself that my friend Legendre was recently offered a very large sum to slit my throat. However, he told me of it; he obviously sees some long-term advantage in turning down a good cash offer.

My new salary was useful, and status as a prominent public official does no harm. I thought that now we might be seen to spend a little money without incurring criticism (oh, I was wrong of course) and so I kept Gabrielle busy during the last tedious weeks in choosing carpets, china and silver for our apartment, which we have just had redecorated.

But I suppose you will not want to know about our new dining-table – you will want to know who is sitting in the new Assembly. Lawyers, naturally. Propertied men, like myself. On the right, Lafayette's supporters. In the centre, a huge uncommitted many. On the left – now, this is what concerns us. My good friend Hérault de Séchelles is a deputy, and we have a few recruits for the Cordeliers Club. Brissot is amongst those elected for Paris, and many of his friends seem likely to lay claim to the public's attention.

I must explain something about 'Brissot's friends'; it is a misnomer, as many of them can't stand him. But to be 'one of Brissot's people' is a kind of tag, a label, one which we find useful. In the old Assembly, Mirabeau used to point to the Left and shout, 'Silence, those thirty voices.' Robespierre said to me one day, it would be convenient if all 'Brissot's people' would sit together in the Jacobin Club, so that we could do the same.

Do we want them silent? I don't know. If we could get over this absurd matter of war or peace – and it is a lot to get over – there wouldn't be much to divide us. They're just, somehow, not our sort – and don't they let us know it! There are a number of outstanding men from the Gironde region, amongst them the leading lights of the Bordeaux Bar. Pierre Vergniaud is a polished orator, the best in the House – if you like that antique type of oratory, which is a bit different from the fire-eating style we affect on our side of the river.

'Brissot's people' are of course outside the Assembly as well as in it. There is Pétion – now mayor, as I said – and Jean-Baptiste Louvet, the novelist, who now writes for the papers – and of course you'll remember François-Léonard Buzot, the humourless young fellow who sat with Robespierre on the far Left of the old Assembly. They have several newspapers between them, and assorted positions of influence in the Commune and the Jacobin Club. Why they rally round Brissot I can never grasp, unless they need his nervous energy as a driving force. He is here, there, an instant opinion, a lightning analysis, an editorial in the blink of an eye. He is forever setting up a committee, launching a project; he is forever hatching a plan, blazing a trail, putting his machinery in motion. I saw Vergniaud, who is a large, calm man, regarding him from under his thick eyebrows; as Brissot chattered, a small sigh escaped him, and a look of pained exhaustion grew on his face. I understood. Camille can wear me out in the same way. But one thing you must say about Camille – even in the direst circumstances, he can make you laugh. He can even make the Incorruptible laugh. Yes, I have seen it with my own eyes and Fréron says he has seen it too – unseemly tears of mirth streaming down the Incorruptible's face.

I don't wish to suggest that Brissot's people are anything so definite as a party. Yet they see a good deal of each other – salon life, you know. Last summer they used to meet at the apartment of an ageing nonentity called Roland, a provincial married to a much younger woman. The wife would be passably attractive, if it were not for her incessant Fervour. She is the type who always wants to surround herself with young men, and play them off against each other. She probably cuckolds the old husband, but I doubt if that is the point for her – it's not her body that she wants to gratify. Well, so I suppose. To my relief, I don't know her very well.

Robespierre used to go to supper there, so I gather they're a high-minded lot. I asked him did he contribute much to the conversation; he said, 'Not a word do I speak, I sit in a corner and bite my nails.' He has his moments, does Maximilien.

He called on me in early December, soon after he got back from Arras. 'Am I disturbing you?' he asked – anxious as usual, peering into our drawing room to make sure there was no one he didn't wish to meet. I waved him in airily. 'Only do you mind the dog?'

I hastily removed the hand I had placed on his shoulder.

'I don't mean to take him everywhere,' he said, 'but he will follow.'

The dog – which was the size of a small donkey – disposed itself at his feet, its head on its paws and its eyes on his face. It was a great brindled creature, and its name was Brount. 'He is my dog at home,' he explained. 'I thought I should bring him because – well, Maurice Duplay wants me to have a bodyguard, and I don't like the idea of people following me about. I thought the dog –'

'I'm sure it will,' I said.

'He's very well-behaved. Do you think it's a good idea?'

'Well, after all,' I said, 'I have Legendre.'

'Yes.' He moved uneasily, causing the dog to twitch its ears. My wit is lost on Maximilien. 'Is it true that there was an assassination plot against you?'

'More than one, I understand.'

'But you don't let them intimidate you. Danton, I have great respect for you.'

I was nonplussed: I had not expected a testimonial. We talked a little about his visit to Arras. He told me about his sister Charlotte, who is his warmest supporter in public, but tiresome in private. It was the first time he had spoken to me about his personal life. What I know of him, I know from Camille. I suppose that, returning to find Paris full of new men running things, he looks on me as an old comrade-in-arms. I comforted myself that he had forgiven me for the jokes I made at his expense when he broke off his engagement to Adèle.

'So what do you make of the new Assembly?' I asked him.

'I suppose they're an improvement on the last lot.' A lack of warmth in his tone.

'But?'

'These people from Bordeaux – they have a great opinion of

themselves. I wonder about their motives, that's all.' Then he began to talk about Lazare Carnot, a military man he's known for years, who is now a deputy; Carnot was the first soldier I heard him praise, and probably the only one. 'And Couthon,' he said, 'have you met him?'

I had. Couthon is a cripple, and has an attendant who wheels him about in a special chair; when there are steps, the attendant lifts him on to his back and carries him, his withered legs trailing. Some helpful person brings the chair up, the poor man is dropped back in and off they go. Despite being crippled he has enjoyed, like Robespierre, a sparkling career as a poor man's lawyer. Couthon's spine is diseased, he has constant pain. Robespierre says this does not embitter him. Only Robespierre could believe this.

He was worried, he said, about the war-mongers — in other words, 'Brissot's people'.

'You've just come from England, Danton. Do they mean to fight us?'

I was able to assure him that only extreme provocation would bring them to it.

'Danton, a war would be disastrous, wouldn't it?'

'Beyond doubt. We have no money. Our army is led by aristocrats whose sympathy might well be with the enemy. Our navy's a disgrace. We've political dissension at home.'

'Half our officers, perhaps more, have emigrated. If we have a war, it will have to be fought by peasants with pitchforks. Or pikes, if we can stand the expense.'

'It might benefit some people,' I said.

'Yes, the Court. Because they think that the chaos war brings will force us to turn back to the monarchy, and that when our Revolution is crippled and brought to its knees we'll come crawling to them, begging them to help us forget that we were ever free. If that were attained, what would they care if Prussian troops burn our homes and slaughter our children? It would be meat and drink to them to see that day.'

'Robespierre —'

But he could not be stopped. 'So the Court will support war, even if it is against Antoinette's own people. And there are men who sit in the Assembly, calling themselves patriots, who will grasp any chance to distract attention from the real revolutionary struggle.'

'You mean Brissot's people?'

'Yes.'

'Why do you suppose that they want to, as you put it, distract attention?'

'Because they're afraid of the people. They want to contain the Revolution, hold it back, because they're afraid of the real exercise of the people's will. They want a revolution to suit their own ends. They want to line their pockets. I'll tell you why people always want war – it's because there's easy money to be made out of it.'

I was amazed at this grim conclusion: not that I had not come to it, but that Robespierre should come to it, Robespierre of the clean mind and the noble motive.

'They talk,' I said, 'of a crusade to bring liberty to Europe. Of how it's our duty to spread the gospel of fraternity.'

'Spread the gospel? Well, ask yourself – who loves armed missionaries?'

'Who indeed?'

'They speak as if they had the interests of the people at heart, but the end of it will be military dictatorship.'

I nodded. I felt he was right, but I didn't like the way he spoke; he spoke, if you follow me, as if it were beyond dispute. 'Don't you think,' I said, 'that Brissot and his friends might be given credit for good intentions? They think a war would pull the country together and make the Revolution secure and get the rest of Europe off our backs.'

'Do you think that?'

'Personally, no.'

'Are you a fool? Am I?'

'No.'

'Isn't the reasoning clear? With France as she is, poor and unarmed, war means defeat. Defeat means either a military dictator who will salvage what he can and set up a new tyranny, or it means a total collapse and the return of absolute monarchy. It could mean both, one after the other. After ten years not a single one of our achievements will remain, and to your son liberty will be an old man's daydream. This is what will happen, Danton. No one can sincerely maintain the contrary. So if they do maintain it, they are not sincere, they are not patriots, and their war policy is a conspiracy against the people.'

'You are saying, in effect, they are traitors.'

'In effect. Potentially. And so we must strengthen our own position against them.'

'If we could win the war, would you favour it?'

'I hate all war.' A forced smile. 'I hate all unnecessary violence. I hate quarrels, even dissension among people, but I know I am doomed to live with that.' He made a small gesture, as if putting the controversy aside. 'Tell me, Georges-Jacques – do I seem unreasonable?'

'No, what you say is logical ... it's just ... ' I couldn't think how to finish my sentence.

'The Right try to present me as a fanatic. They'll end up by making me one.'

He got up to go, and the dog jumped up and glared at me when I took his hand.

'I should like to talk to you, informally,' I said. 'I'm tired of speaking at you in public places, of never getting to know you any better. Come to supper tonight?'

'Thank you, but,' he shook his head, 'too much work. Come and see me at Maurice Duplay's.'

So he went downstairs, the reasonable person, with his dog padding after him and growling at the shadows.

I felt depressed. When Robespierre says he dislikes the whole idea of war, it is an emotional reaction – and I am not immune to those. I share his distrust of soldiers; we are suspicious, envious perhaps, as only pen-pushers can be. Day by day, the movement for war gains momentum. We must strike first, they say, before we are stricken. Once they begin to beat the big drum, there's no reasoning with them. Now, if I have to stand against the tide, I would rather do it with Robespierre than anyone. I may make jokes at his expense – no, not 'may', I do – but I know his energy, and I know his honesty.

And yet . . . he feels something, in his heart, and then he sits down and works out the logic of it, in his head. Then he says that the head part came first; and we believe him.

I did visit him at Duplay's, but first I let Camille reconnoitre. The master carpenter had hidden him when he was in danger, and we all assumed that when things got back to normal, etcetera – but he stayed.

Once you shut the gate from the rue Saint-Honoré, the place seems quiet, almost rural. The yard is full of Duplay's workmen, but the noise is muted and the air is fresh. He has a room on the first floor, plain but pleasant enough. I did not notice the furniture, I suppose it is not anything special. When I called on him he waved at a large bookcase, new and well-finished if not stylish. 'Maurice made that for me.' He was pleased with it. As if he were pleased someone would take the trouble.

I looked at his books. Jean-Jacques Rousseau by the yard; few other modern authors. Cicero, Tacitus, the usual: all well-thumbed. I wonder – if we go to war with England, will I have to hide my books of Shakespeare, and my Adam Smith? I guess that Robespierre reads no modern language but his own, which seems a pity. Camille, by the way, thinks modern languages beneath his notice; he is studying Hebrew, and looking for someone to teach him Sanskrit.

He had warned me what to expect of the Duplays. 'There . . . are . . . these . . . dreadful . . . people,' he had said. But that day he was engaged in pretending to be Hérault de Séchelles, so I did not take him too seriously. 'There is, first, the paterfamilias Maurice. He is fifty or fifty-five, balding and very, very earnest. He can bring out only the worst in our dear Robespierre. Madame is a homely sort, and can never have been even tolerably good-looking. There is a son, also called Maurice, and a nephew, Simon – these last both young, and apparently quite witless.'

'But tell me about the three daughters,' I said. 'Are they worth calling on?'

Camille gave an aristocratic groan. 'There is Victoire, who cannot easily be distinguished from the furniture. She never opened her mouth –'

'Not surprising, if you were in this mood,' Lucile said. (She was, however, vastly entertained.)

'There is the little one, Elisabeth – they call her Babette – who is tolerable, if you like goose-girls. And then the eldest – words fail me.'

They didn't, of course. Eléonore, it appeared, was an unfortunate girl, plain, drab and pretentious; she was an art student under David, and preferred to her own perfectly adequate name the classical appellation 'Cornélia'. This detail, I confess, I found risible.

To dispel any remaining illusions, he opined that the bed-curtains in Robespierre's room were made out of one of Madame's old dresses, because they were just the kind of ghastly fabric she would choose for her personal adornment. Camille goes on like this for days on end, and it's impossible to get any sense out of him.

They are good people, I suppose; have struggled to get to their present comfortable position. Duplay is a staunch patriot: goes in for plain-speaking at the Jacobins, but is modest with it. Maximilien seems at home there. It probably, when I think of it, helps him financially to live with them. He gave up his post as Public Prosecutor as soon as he decently could, saying that it interfered with his 'larger work'. So he has no office, no salary, and must be living on savings. I understand that wealthy but disinterested patriots send him drafts on their bankers. And what do you think? Yes, he writes polite notes and sends them back.

The daughters – the shy one is nothing worse than that, and Babette has a certain schoolroom appeal. Eléonore, I admit . . .

They do their best to make him comfortable: God knows, it's time somebody did that. It is a rather spartan comfort, by our refurbished standards; I'm afraid it brings out the worst in us when we sneer at the Duplays, with what Camille calls their 'good plain food and good plain daughters'.

Later, I became aware of something odd in the atmosphere of the house. Some of us began to jib when the family began to collect portraits of their new son to decorate their walls, and Fréron asked me if I did not think it was prodigiously vain of Robespierre to allow it. I suppose we have all had our portrait made: even I, at whom any artist might baulk. But this was different; you sat with Robespierre in the little parlour where he sometimes received visitors, and found him meeting your eyes not just in person but in oils, in charcoal, three-dimensionally in terracotta. Every time I called – which perhaps was not often – there was a new one. It made me uneasy – not just the portraits and busts, but the way all the family looked at him. They're grateful he turned up on their doorstep at all, but that's no longer enough. They fasten their eyes on him, Father, Mother, young Maurice, and Simon, Victoire, Eléonore, Babette. In his place I should ask myself: what do these people really want? What will I lose if I give it them?

Any gloom we might have felt at the end of '91 was dispelled by the continuing comedy of Camille's return to the Bar.

They do contrive to spend a lot of money, he and Lucile – although, like most patriots, they avoid public censure by keeping few servants and no carriage. (I keep a carriage; I place personal comfort above the plaudits of the masses, I fear.) But where does anyone's money go? They entertain, and Camille gambles, and Lolotte spends money on the things women do spend money on. But all in all, Camille's venture was prompted less by shortage of cash than by the need of a new arena for self-advertisement.

In the old days, he claimed that his stutter was a complete obstacle to successful pleading. Of course, until one is used to it, it might discomfit, irritate or embarrass. But Hérault has pointed out that Camille has wrung some extraordinary verdicts from distraught judges. Certainly I have observed that Camille's stutter comes and goes. It goes when he is angry or wishes forcibly to make a point; it comes when he feels put-upon, and when he wishes to show people that he is in fact a nice person who is really not quite able to cope. It says much for his natural optimism that after some eight years of acquaintance he sometimes assumes the latter pose with me and expects me to believe in it. Not entirely without success: there are days when I am so bemused by Camille's helplessness that I go around opening doors for him.

All went smoothly until the New Year. Then he took on the defence of the couple concerned in the affair of the gambling house in the Passage Radziwill. Camille deplores the intervention of the state in what he sees as a matter of private morality; he not only published his opinion, but placarded it all over the city. Now Brissot – who is a man with a regrettable busybody tendency, both in his political philosophy and in his private life – was outraged by the whole affair. He attacked Camille verbally and set one of his hacks to assail him in the press. As a result, Camille said he would 'ruin Brissot. I shall simply write his autobiography,' he said. 'I shall not need to embroider the facts. He is a plagiarist and a spy, and if I have refrained so far from making these revelations it is out of sentimentality over the length of our acquaintance.'

'Nonsense,' I said, 'it has been out of fear of what he might reveal about you.'

'When I have finished with him . . .' Camille said. It was at this point I felt I must intervene. We may not see eye-to-eye on the war question, but if we are to achieve any political power of the formal kind, our natural allies are Brissot and the men of the Gironde.

I wish I could cast more light for you on Camille's private life. The long-promised fidelity to Lucile lasted, oh, all of three months – yet from his disconnected statements at various times I gather that he doesn't care for anyone else and would go through the whole business again to get her. There is nothing about them of the ironical coldness of people who are bored with each other; in fact, they give a lively impression of a well-heeled young couple with a great deal of energy who are having a very good time. It amuses Lucile to try out her powers on any personable man – and even on those who, like me, could never be described as personable. She has Fréron on a string, and now Hérault too. And you remember General Dillon, that romantic Irishman who is so attached to Camille? Camille brings him home from wherever they have been playing cards that night – for the general shares that addiction – and presents him to Lucile as if he were bringing her the most

wonderful present – which indeed he is, because Dillon, along with
Hérault, is widely spoken of as the most handsome man in Paris,
and is in addition quite wonderfully poised and polished and gallant,
and all that rubbish. Quite apart from the gratification she gets
from flirting, I imagine that someone – the minx Rémy perhaps –
has advised her that one way to keep an errant husband is to make
him jealous. If this is her idea, she is having a great failure. Witness
a recent conversation:

LUCILE: Hérault tried to kiss me.

CAMILLE: Well, you have been raising his hopes. Did you let him?

LUCILE: No.

CAMILLE: Why not?

LUCILE: He has a double chin.

What are they then – just an amiable, cool, amoral pair who have
decided to make life easy for each other? That is not what you
would think if you lived on our street, not what you would think if
you lived next door. They are playing for high stakes, it seems to
me, and each of them is watching the other for a failure of nerve;
each waits for the other to throw down the hand. The truth is, the
more enmeshed Lucile becomes with her various beaux, the more
Camille seems to enjoy himself. Why should this be? I'm afraid your
imagination will have to supply the deficiencies of mine. After all,
you know them well enough by now.

And I? Well, now, I suppose you like my wife, most people do.
Our little actresses – Rémy and her friends – are so accommodating,
so pleasant and so easy for my Gabrielle to ignore. They never cross
the threshold of this house; what would she have to say to them?
They are not whores, these girls, far from it; they would be shocked
if you offered them money. What they like are outings and treats
and presents, and to be seen on the arm of the men whose names are
in the papers. As my sister Anne Madeleine says, people like us, we
have our day; and when our day is over, and we are forgotten, they
will be on the arms of other men. I like them, these girls. Because I
like people who live without illusions.

I must get round to Rémy herself some day soon – if only as a
gesture of fellowship to Fabre and Hérault and Camille.

I should say, in my defence, that I was faithful to Gabrielle for a long time; but these are not the days for fidelity. I think of all that has passed between us, the strong and sincere attachment I felt and do feel; I think of the kindness of her father and mother, and of the little child we buried. But I think too of her tone of cold disapproval, of her withdrawn silences. A man has his work in this world, and must do it as he sees fit, and (like the actresses) he must accommodate himself to the times in which he lives; Gabrielle does not see this. What irks me most is her downtrodden air. God knows, I never trod on her.

So I am seeing – oh, this girl and that girl – and from time to time the Duke's ladies. Come now, you will say, surely not; this fellow is boasting again. With Mrs Elliot, I would merely say that I have a business relationship. We discuss politics, English politics: English politics as applied to French affairs. But there is, nowadays, much warmth in Grace's tone, in her eyes. She is an arch-dissimulator; I do believe she finds me perfectly loathsome.

Not so Agnès. I visit Agnès when the Duke is out of town. If the Duke thinks I might want to see Agnès, he is usually out of town. It works so smoothly that I would have credited Laclos with the arrangements, if that unfortunate had not disgraced himself by failure and slunk off into provincial oblivion. But why should the mistress of a Prince of the Blood – who might be a character in a novel, don't you think? – bend herself to the conquest of a lawyer with an unsavoury reputation, overweight and as ugly as sin?

Because the Duke foresees a future where he will need a friend; and I am the friend he will need.

But I find it hard, I tell you, to keep my thoughts away from Lucile. So much passion there, so much wit and flair. She is, of course, getting herself a reputation. It is widely believed already that she is my mistress, and soon of course she will be; unlike her other suitors, I am not a man to tease.

In a matter of weeks Gabrielle will give me another son. We shall celebrate, and be reconciled – which means that she will accept the situation. After Lucile's child is born – by the way, it is her husband's – Camille and I will arrive at an understanding, which will not be immensely difficult for us to do. I think perhaps 1792 is my year.

In January I took up my post as Deputy Public Prosecutor.

I shall be speaking to you again, no doubt.

III. *Three Blades, Two in Reserve*

(1791–1792)

LOUIS XVI to Frederick William of Prussia:

Monsieur my brother . . . I have just written to the Emperor, the Empress of Russia, the Kings of Spain and Sweden, and proposed to them a congress of the major powers of Europe, supported by an armed force, as the best means of checking the factions here, of re-establishing a more desirable order of things, and of preventing the evil which torments us from gaining hold on other states in Europe . . . I hope that Your Majesty . . . will keep this step on my part in the most absolute secrecy . . .

J.-P. BRISSOT to the Jacobin Club, 16 December 1791:

A people which has just gained its liberty after twelve centuries of slavery needs a war to consolidate itself.

MARIE-ANTOINETTE to Axel von Fersen:

The fools. They do not see that it is in our interests.

GABRIELLE'S pains began in the night, a week earlier than they had expected. He heard her lurch from her bed, and when he opened his eyes she stood over him. 'It's begun,' she said. 'Call Catherine for me, would you? I don't think it will be many hours this time.'

He sat up, put his arms around her bulky body. Candlelight flickered wetly on her dark hair. She cradled his head against her. 'Please, after this,' she whispered, 'let it be all right.'

How did it come to this? He doesn't know.

'You're cold,' he said, 'you're very cold.' He eased her back into her bed, tucked the counterpane around her. Then he went into the drawing room, to put some wood on the embers of the fire.

This was not the place for him now; this was the place for the surgeon and the midwife, for Angélique, for Mme Gély from upstairs. He spoke to her once more, hovering at the door of the room. Louise Gély sat on the bed, braiding his wife's hair tightly. He asked her mother in a low voice, was it suitable for the little girl to be here? But Louise heard him and looked up. 'Well, M. Danton,' she said, 'it is suitable. Or even if it is not, we all have to go through it, and I am fourteen now.'

'And when you are forty,' her mother told her, 'it will be time enough for you to be pert. Back to your bed.'

He leaned over Gabrielle, kissed her, squeezed her hand. He stood back to let Louise pass, but she brushed against him, and looked up for a second into his face.

The dawn was late, late and very chill, and his son cried pitifully when he came into the world, with the frost riming the windows, and the icy winds of battle scything the empty streets.

On 9 March the Emperor Leopold died. For a day or two, until the views of the new Emperor became known, peace seemed possible.

'Stock market's up,' Fabre said.

'Are you interested in the stock market?'

'I dabble, when I have the cash.'

'In the name of God,' said the Queen. 'Escape in the carriage of Necker's daughter? Take refuge in Lafayette's camp? One could almost laugh.'

'Madame,' said the King, 'Madame, they say it is our last chance. My ministers advise me –'

'Your ministers are mad.'

'It could be worse. We are still dealing with gentlemen.'

'It could not be worse,' the Queen said, in frank disbelief.

The King looked at her sadly. 'If this administration falls . . .' It fell.

March 21: 'So, Dumouriez,' said the King, 'you think you can hold a government together?' Nagging in the back of his mind, the thought: this man was two years in the Bastille. Charles Dumouriez bowed. 'Let us not . . .' the King said hurriedly. 'I know you are a Jacobin. I know it.' (But who else is there, Madame? Who else?)

'Sire, I am a soldier,' Dumouriez said. 'I am fifty-three years old. I have always served Your Majesty faithfully. I am Your Majesty's truest subject and I . . .'

'Yes, yes,' said the King.

' . . . and I will take the Foreign Office. After all, I know Europe. I have served as Your Majesty's agent – '

'I don't query your abilities, General.'

Dumouriez allowed himself a very small sigh. Time was when Louis heard his ministers out. Louis had less and less appetite for the business of state, no relish for the distasteful details; this was the day of the incomplete statement and the quick pay-off. If the King and Queen were to be saved, it was a good thing for them not to know too much: or they would reject his help, as they had rejected Lafayette's.

'For Finance, Clavière,' he said.

'He was a crony of Mirabeau's.' The King's face was expressionless; Dumouriez did not know whether it commended the man or not. 'For the Interior?'

'This is difficult. The really able men are in the Assembly, and deputies may not be ministers. Give me a day's grace, if you please.'

The King nodded curtly. Dumouriez bowed. 'General . . .' The unregal voice trailed after him. The dapper little man turned on his heel. 'You aren't against me, are you . . . ?'

'Against Your Majesty? Because I attend at the Jacobins?' He tried to catch Louis's eye, but Louis had fixed it at some point to the left of his head. 'Factions rise and fall. The tradition of loyalty endures.'

'Oh yes,' Louis said absently. 'I don't so much call the Jacobins a faction, more a power . . . as once we had the church within the state, now we have the club. This man Robespierre, where does he come from?'

'Artois, sire, or so I understand.'

'Yes, but you know, in a deeper sense . . . where does he *come* from?' Louis shifted his heavy body uncomfortably in his chair. Of the two men, he looked rather older. 'Like you, I recognize you. You are what we call an adventurer. And M. Brissot is a faddist – he is a man who holds all the ideas of his time, just because they are current. And M. Danton I recognize – for he is one of those brutal demagogues we find in our history books. But M. Robespierre . . . You see, if only I knew what the man wanted. Perhaps I could give it him, and that would be an end of it.' He slumped. 'Something of a mystery there, don't you think?'

General Dumouriez bowed again. Louis did not notice him go.

A CORRIDOR AWAY, Brissot waited for his favourite general. 'You have your government,' Dumouriez told him.

'You seem depressed,' Brissot said sharply. 'Something gone wrong?'

'No – just the epithets His Majesty has been hanging on me.'

'He was offensive? He is not in a position to be.'

'I did not say he was offensive.'

Their eyes rested on each other, just for a second. They did not trust each other, even slightly. Then Dumouriez touched Brissot on the shoulder, with a sportive air. 'A Jacobin ministry, my dear fellow. Seemed unthinkable, only a short while ago.'

'And on the question of war?'

'I did not press him. But I think I can guarantee you hostilities within the month.'

'There must be war. The greatest possible disaster would be peace. You agree?'

Dumouriez turned his cane about in his fingers. 'How not? I'm a soldier. I have my career to think of. Wonderful opportunity for all sorts of things.'

'TRY IT,' said Vergniaud. 'Give the Court the fright of its life. Can't resist the idea.'

'Robespierre – ' Brissot called.

Robespierre stopped. 'Vergniaud,' he said. 'Pétion. Brissot.' Having named them, he seemed satisfied.

'We have a proposal.'

'I know your proposal. You propose to make us slaves again.'

Pétion held up a placating hand. He was a larger, stouter man than when Robespierre had first known him, and satin success had settled in his face.

'I think we need not traffic in the small change of the debating chamber,' Vergniaud suggested. 'We could have private talks.'

'I want no private talks.'

'Believe me,' Brissot said, 'believe me, Robespierre, we wish you would come with us on the war question. The intolerable meddling in our internal affairs – '

'Why do you think of fighting Austria and England, when your enemy is here at home?'

'You mean there?' With a motion of his head, Vergniaud indicated the direction of the King's apartments in the Tuileries.

'There, yes – and all around us.'

'With our friends in the ministry,' Pétion said, 'we can take care of them.'

'Let me go.' Robespierre pushed past them.

'He is becoming morbidly suspicious,' Pétion said. 'I used to be his friend. Not to mince matters, I fear for his sanity.'

'He has a following,' Vergniaud said.

Brissot pursued Robespierre, took him by the elbow. Vergniaud watched them. 'A good ratting dog,' he observed.

'Eh?' Pétion said.

Brissot was still at Robespierre's heels.

'Robespierre, we were speaking of the ministry – we are offering you a situation.'

Robespierre broke away. He pulled down the sleeve of his coat. 'I want no situation,' he said sombrely. 'And there is no situation suitable for me.'

'FOURTH FLOOR?' said Dumouriez. 'Is he poverty-stricken, this Roland, that he lives on the fourth floor?'

'Paris costs money,' Brissot said defensively. His chest heaved.

'Really,' Dumouriez was irritated, 'you don't have to run after me if you can't stand the pace. I would have waited; I have no intention of going in alone. Now: are you quite sure about this?'

'Proven administrator – ' Brissot gasped, – 'and record of service – and sound attitudes – and wife – great capabilities – utter dedication – to our aims.'

'Yes, I think I followed that,' Dumouriez said. He did not think they had many aims in common.

Manon answered the door herself. She was a little dishevelled, and she had been very, very bored.

General Dumouriez kissed her hand with an excess of old regime politeness. 'Monsieur?' he inquired.

'He is just now sleeping.'

'I think you could put it to Madame,' Brissot suggested.

'And I think not,' Dumouriez muttered. He turned to her. 'Be so good as to rouse him. We have a proposition which may be of interest.' He looked around the room. 'It would mean your moving house. Perhaps, m'dear, you'd like to pack your china or something?'

'BUT NO,' MANON SAID. She looked very young, and on the verge of frustrated tears. 'You are teasing me. How can you do this?'

There was a slight abeyance of the greyness on her husband's face. 'I hardly think, my sweet, that M. Brissot would joke about so serious a subject as the composition of the government. The King offers the Ministry of the Interior. We – I – accept.'

VERGNIAUD had also been asleep, in his apartment at Mme Dodun's house, No. 5 Place Vendôme. But one got out of bed for Danton. What he knew of Danton compelled his reluctant admiration, but he had one glaring fault – he worked too hard.

'But why this Roland?' Danton said.

'Because there was no one else,' Vergniaud said, listless. He was bored with the subject. He was tired of people asking him who Roland was. 'Because he's pliable. Believed to be discreet. Who would you have us take up? Marat?'

'They call themselves republicans, the Rolands. So do you, I think.'

Vergniaud nodded impassively. Danton studied him. A year under forty, he was not quite tall or broad enough to cut an impressive figure. His pale, heavy face was slightly marked from smallpox, and his large nose seemed to have slight acquaintance with his small, deep-set eyes, as if either feature would just as soon belong in some other face. He was not a man who would be noticed in a crowd; but at the tribune of the Assembly or the Jacobins – his audience silent, the galleries craning – he was a different man. He became handsome, with an assured graceful integrity of smooth voice and commanding body. There he had the presence supposed to belong only to aristocrats; a spark kindled in his brown eyes. 'Note that,' Camille said. 'That is the spark of self-regard.'

'Oh, but I like to see a man doing what he is good at,' Danton had answered warmly.

Of Brissot's friends, he decided, this man was much the best. I like you, he thought; but you are lazy. 'A republican in the ministry – ' he said.

'– is not necessarily a republican minister,' Vergniaud finished. 'Well, we shall see.' Carelessly he turned over a few papers on his desk. Danton saw in it a reflection of some slight contempt for the people they spoke of. 'You will have to call on them, Danton, if you want to get on in life. Pay your compliments to the lady.' He chuckled at Danton's expression. 'Beginning to think you're out on a limb? With Robespierre for company? He'd better reconcile himself to war. His popularity has never been lower.'

'Popularity is not the issue.'

'Not with Robespierre, no. But you, Danton, where do you go from here?'

'Up. Vergniaud, I wish you would throw in your lot with us.'

'Who exactly is "us"?'

Danton began to speak, then paused, struck for the first time by the disreputable quality of the names he had to offer. 'Hérault de Séchelles,' he said at length.

Vergniaud raised a heavy eyebrow. 'Just the two of you? Messieurs Camille and Fabre d'Églantine suddenly excluded from your confidence? Legendre too busy butchering? Well, I dare say these people are useful to you. But I don't seek to attach myself to a faction. I favoured the war, so I sat with the others who favoured it. But I am not a Brissotin, whatever that may be. I am my own man.'

'I wish we all were,' Danton said. 'But you will find it does not work out like that.'

ONE MORNING, late March, Camille woke up with a certain thought going around in his head. He had been talking to soldiers – General Dillon amongst others – and they said if there is going to be a war anyway, what is the point of standing out against public opinion and the tide of the times? Was it not better to put yourself at the head of an irresistible movement, rather than be trampled in the rush?

He roused his wife and told her. 'I feel sick,' she said.

At 6.30 a.m. he was in Danton's drawing room, pacing the carpet. Danton called him a fool.

'Why do I always have to agree with you? I'm not allowed any independent thoughts. I can think what I like as long as it happens to be what you think.'

'Go away,' Danton said. 'I am not your father.'

'What does that mean?'

'I mean that you sound like a fifteen-year-old and what you are trying to do is pick a fight, so why don't you go home for a few days and quarrel with your father? We would be spared political consequences.'

'I shall write – '

'You will not put pen to paper. You do try my temper, exceed-ingly. Go away, before I make you the first Brissotin martyr. Go to Robespierre, and see if you get a better reception.'

ROBESPIERRE was ill. The raw spring weather hurt his chest, and his stomach rejected what he fed it.

'So you desert your friends,' he said, wheezing a little.

'This need not affect our friendship,' Camille said grandly.

Robespierre looked away.

'You remind me – what's the name of that English King?'

'George,' Robespierre snapped.

'I think I mean Canute.'

'You will have to go away,' Robespierre said. 'I can't argue with you this morning. I have to conserve my strength for important things. But if you commit yourself to paper, I shall never trust you again.'

Camille backed out of the room.

Eléonore Duplay was standing outside. He knew she had been listening, because of the sudden vivacity in her dreary eyes. 'Ah, it's Cornélia,' he said. He had never in his life spoken to a woman in that tone; she would have excited cruelty in a mouse.

'We wouldn't have let you in if we'd known you were going to upset him. Don't come again. In any case, he won't see you.'

She ran her eyes over him. I hoped you would quarrel, they said.

'You and your ghastly family, Eléonore. Do you think you own him? Do you think because he condescends to stay under your roof you have the right to decide who comes and goes? Do you think you are going to keep him away from his oldest friend?'

'You are so sure of yourself, aren't you?'

'With reason,' Camille said. 'Oh, Cornélia, you are so transparent. I know exactly what your plans are. I know exactly what you think. You think he'll marry you. Forget it, my dear. He won't.'

THAT WAS THE ONLY SPARK of satisfaction in the day. Lucile sat waiting for him sadly, her little hands resting on the draped bulk of the child. Life was no fun now. She had reached the stage when women looked at her with lively sympathy: when men's eyes passed over her as if she were an old sofa.

'There's a note from Max,' she said. 'I opened it. He says he regrets what happened this morning, he spoke hastily, and he begs you to forgive him. And Georges called. He said "Sorry."'

'I had a wonderful row with Eléonore. They're predatory, those people. I wonder, you know, what would happen to me if Danton and Robespierre ever disagreed?'

'You have a mind of your own.'

'Yes, but you will find it doesn't work out like that.'

*

ON 26 MARCH the Queen passed to the enemy full details of France's war plans. On 20 April, France declared war on Austria.

APRIL 25 1792 – Scientific and Democratic Execution of Nicolas-Jacques Pelletier, highway robber.

There are bigger crowds than for any ordinary execution, and an air of anticipation. The executioners, of course, have been practising with dummies; they look quite buoyant, and they are nodding to each other, putting each other on their honour not to make a blunder. Yet there's nothing to fear, the machine does everything. It is mounted on a scaffold, a big frame with a heavy blade. The criminal ascends with his guards. He is not to suffer, because in France the age of barbarism is over, superseded by a machine, approved by a committee.

Moving quickly, the executioners surround the man, bind him to a plank and slide it forward; swoop of the blade, a soft thud, and a sudden carpet of blood. The crowd sighs, its members look at each other in disbelief. It is all over so soon, there is no spectacle. They cannot see that the man can be dead. One of Sanson's assistants looks up at him, and the master executioner nods. The young man lifts the leather bag into which the head has fallen, and picks out the dripping contents. He holds the head up to the crowd, turning slowly to each quarter to show the empty, expressionless face. Good enough. They are placated. A few women pick up their children so that they can see better. The dead man's trunk is cut free and rolled into a big wicker basket to be taken away; the severed head is placed between the feet.

All in all, including holding up the head (which will not always be necessary), it has taken just five minutes. The master executioner estimates that the time could be cut almost by half, if time were ever important. He and his assistants and apprentices are divided over the new device. It is convenient, true, and humane; you cannot believe that the man feels any pain. But it looks so easy; people will be thinking that there is no skill in it, that anyone can be an executioner. The profession feels itself undermined. Only the previous year, the Assembly had debated the question of capital punishment, and the popular deputy Robespierre had actually pleaded for it to be abolished. They said he still felt stongly about the question, was hopeful of success. But that deep-thinking man, M. Sanson, feels that M. Robespierre is out of step with public opinion, on this point.

An estimate by M. Guérdon, formerly master carpenter to the Parlement of Paris:

> To the steps ....1,700 livres
> To three blades (two in reserve)........................600 livres
> To pulley and copper grooves ....300 livres
> To the iron drop-weight (for the blade)............300 livres
> To rope and rigging ....60 livres
> To constructing the whole, testing it,
>   and time spent discussing it........................1,200 livres
> To a small scale model for demonstrations,
>   to prevent accidents ....1,200 livres
>
> TOTAL   5,360 livres

WARMLY RECOMMENDING the new invention to the Assembly, the public health expert Dr Guillotin said: 'With this machine I can have your head off in a flash and you won't suffer at all.' (Laughter.)

DANTON: Robespierre called at Camille's apartment late at night, looking for him. I was there with Lucile. It was harmless enough. The servant Jeanette was about the place, sitting up rather pointedly. Though what they all think I would be doing, with the girl six months pregnant ... And where was Camille? Everybody must be in when Robespierre calls. Young Maximilien was faintly annoyed. Lucile caught my eye. She didn't know where he was.

'I can suggest some places,' I said. 'But I wouldn't advise you to try them, Max, not personally.'

He blushed. What it is to be evil-minded, I thought. In fact I had an idea that Camille was across the river, addressing one of these freakish women's groups with which he and Marat are involved –

Society of Young Ladies for Maiming Marquises, Fishwives for Democracy, you know the sort of thing. And I really thought that, as the Incorruptible has such a large female following, if he walked in while they were already adoring Camille the ladies might lose all restraint and begin attacking people on the streets.

He asked if he might wait. It was important.

'What won't keep till morning?'

'I don't keep conventional hours,' he explained to me. 'Neither, as you know, does Camille. When I need him he is usually available.'

'Not this time,' I said. Lucile looked at me beseechingly.

So we sat for an hour or more, and how hard it is to make small-talk with Maximilien. It was then that Lolotte asked him to be godfather to the child. He was pleased. She reminded him that it was his privilege to choose the name. He felt somehow it would be a boy, he said; we should give him a name that was inspiring, the name of a great man, someone distinguished for his possession of the republican virtues; for we already talked of the republic, not as a political phenomenon but as a state of mind. He mulled over in his mind the Greeks and Romans, and decided that he should be named for the poet, Horace. I said, 'What if it's a girl?'

Lucile said gently that it was a most suitable name, and I could see her calculating already, we won't use it, that's not what he'll actually be called. Perhaps, she said, for a second name we could call him Camille? Robespierre smiled, saying, 'And there is much honour in that too.'

Then we sat and looked at each other; by this time I had made him uncomfortably suspicious that the honourable original was out whoring.

He slipped in about two o'clock, inquired which of us had arrived first; being told, looked knowing but not put out. Lucile did not ask where he had been. Ah, I thought, for such a wife. I said goodnight, Robespierre began to talk of some business of the Commune's, as if it were two in the afternoon, and harsh words had never been invented.

*

ROBESPIERRE: There were such people as Lucile. Rousseau said so. Robespierre laid the book aside, but marked the passage.

One proof of the amiable woman's character is that all who loved her loved each other, jealousy and rivalry submitting to the more powerful sentiment with which she inspired them; and I never saw those who surrounded her entertain the least ill-will among themselves. Let the reader pause a moment, and if he can recollect any other woman who deserves this praise, let him attach himself to her if he would obtain happiness.

It must be applicable. Life was strangely calm in the Desmoulins household. Of course, they might be keeping things from him. People did tend to keep things from him.

They had asked him to be godfather to the child – or whatever was the equivalent, because he did not suppose it would be baptised within the Roman rite. It was Lucile who had asked him one evening when he called (late, almost midnight) and found her alone with Danton. He hoped those rumours were not true. He hoped to be able to believe that they were not.

The servant removed herself as soon as he appeared: at which Danton, unaccountably, laughed.

There were things he needed to talk over with Danton, and he could have spoken freely in front of her; she understood situations, and her opinions were worth having. But Danton seemed to be in some singular mood – half-aggressive, half-joking. He had not been able to find the key to this mood, and they had fallen back on desultory conversation. Then at one point he felt an almost physical force pushing against him. That was Danton's will. He wanted him to go. Ridiculous as it seemed, in retrospect, he had to put out a hand to grip the arm of his chair and steady himself. It was just then that Lucile raised the topic of the baby.

He was pleased. Of course, it was right, because he was Camille's oldest friend. And he thought it unlikely now that he would have children of his own.

They had spent some time discussing a name. Perhaps it was sentimental of him, but he remembered all the poetry that Camille used to write. Did he write any now? Oh no, Lucile said. She laughed edgily. In fact, whenever he found some of the old stuff, he'd exclaim, 'worse than Saint-Just, worse than Saint-Just,' and burn it. For a moment Robespierre felt deeply affronted, wounded: as if his judgement had been called into question.

Lucile excused herself, to go and speak with Jeanette.

'Horace-Camille,' Danton said speculatively. 'Do you think it will bring him luck in life?'

Robespierre smiled his thin smile. He was conscious of the thinness of it. If he were remembered into the next generation, people would speak of his thin, cold smile, as they would speak of Danton's girth, vitality, scarred face. He wanted, always, to be different – and especially with Danton. Perhaps the smile looked sarcastic, or patronizing or disapproving. But it was the only one available to his face.

'I think Horace . . .' he said. 'A great poet, and a good republican. If one discounts the later verse, where I think he was probably forced to flatter Augustus.'

'Yes . . .' Danton said. 'Camille's writings flatter you – though probably I shouldn't say *flatter*, I am choosing the wrong word.'

He had to grit his teeth; that is, he thought of gritting them, and the action usually suffices.

'As I said, it is an honourable name.'

Danton sat back in his chair. He stretched out his long legs. He drawled. (It is a commonplace, but there is no other word for it, he drawled.) 'I wonder what the honourable original is doing now.'

'I don't know.'

'You don't know.'

'Why, what do you imagine he is doing?'

'Probably something unthinkable in a whorehouse.'

'I don't know what right you have to think that. I don't know what you mean.'

'My dear Robespierre, I don't expect you to know what I mean. I should be very shocked if you did know. Disillusioned.'

'Then why must you pursue the subject?'

'I really believe you haven't an idea of half the things that Camille gets up to. Have you?' He sounded interested.

'It is a private concern.'

'You surprise me. Isn't he a public concern? A public man?'

'Yes, that's true.'

'Therefore he should be good. Virtuous. According to you. But he's not.'

'I don't want to know – '

'But I ought to insist on telling you. For the public welfare, you know. Camille – '

Lucile came back into the room. Danton laughed. 'I promise you the details at another time, Maximilien. For your intimate consideration.'

[THE JACOBIN CLUB in session, M. Robespierre speaking.]
FROM THE FLOOR: Despot!
M. DANTON [*president*]: Silence. Order. M. Robespierre has never exercised any despotism here but the despotism of pure reason.
FROM THE FLOOR: The demagogue's awake!
M. DANTON: I am not a demagogue, and for a long time now I have kept silent with great difficulty. I shall unmask those who boast of having served the people. The time has come when there is a grave need to speak out against those who, for the past three months, have been impugning the courage of a man to whose bravery the whole Revolution bears witness . . .

ROBESPIERRE to the Jacobins, 10 May 1792: The more you isolate me, the more you cut off all my human contacts, the more justification I find in my own conscience, and in the justice of my cause.

PASSAGES from the life of the Brissotin ministry:

General Dumouriez appeared at the Jacobin Club, of which he was a member. He had a proper soldierly bearing, and the workings of a questioning and restless mind showed in his otherwise unremarkable face. On hair lately powdered, he wore a red woollen bonnet, the Cap of Liberty. He had come to pay his respects at the shrine of patriotism (or some such flimsy metaphor) and he besought fraternal advice and guidance.

Ministers had never behaved like this before.

With anxiety, the patriots watched Robespierre's face. It expressed contempt.

M. Roland, the Minister of the Interior, turned up at the Tuileries to be presented to the King. The courtiers fell back from him in horrified silence. He did not know what was the matter; his stockings had recently been mended. The Master of Ceremonies took Dumouriez aside and spoke in a chilling whisper: 'How can he be presented? He has no buckles on his shoes.'

'No buckles?' said the general humorously. 'Alas, Monsieur, then all is lost.'

'My dear Mme Danton,' Hérault de Séchelles said, 'such an excellent dinner. And now would it be unpardonable if we talked politics?'

'My wife is a realist,' Danton said. 'She knows that politics pays for the dinners.'

'I am used to it,' Gabrielle said.

'Do you take an interest in public affairs, my dear? Or do you find they weary you?'

She could not think what to say, but she smiled to remove any provocation from the only answer she could give: 'I make the best of it.'

'Which is what we all must do.' Hérault turned to Danton. 'If Robespierre insists on making the worst of it, that's his affair. These people – Brissotins, Rolandins, Girondins, call them what you will – are running things for the present. They have – what? – hardly cohesion. Hardly a policy, except for the war – which has begun rather disastrously, they must agree.'

'They have zeal,' Danton said. 'They are talented debaters. Have a certain lack of dogmatism. And that awful woman.'

'Ah, how has the little creature taken to celebrity?'

Danton snorted with disgust. 'We dined. Must I be reminded?'

On the previous evening, he and Fabre had spent two painful hours over a wretched meal with the Minister of the Interior. Dumouriez had been there. From time to time he had muttered, 'I should like a private word with you, Danton, you understand?' But he had not found opportunity It was the minister's wife who had orchestrated the occasion. The minister was propped into a chair at the head of the table; he ventured few remarks, and Danton had the impression that the real minister was scribbling at a desk elsewhere in the building, while a wax model sat before them, sewn into an ancient black coat. He was possessed by a temptation to lean over and stick a fork in him to see if he would scream, but he resisted it, and dragged his eyes back glumly to his plate. There was a nameless soup, at once both watery and floury; there was a meagre portion of a tough fowl, and some turnips which, though small, were past their first youth.

Manon Roland walked now down grand marble staircases, caught the reflection of her plump and pretty person mirrored in walls of Venetian glass. But the dress she wore that Monday evening was three years old, and an ample fichu covered her shoulders. No surrender.

She had let it be known that she would retain the habits of a private person. The trappings of aristocracy were foreign to her. She would not dispense patronage, and her visitors (strictly by invitation) would observe her rules. The grand salons could stay shrouded, unlit, for she did not aspire to hold court there; she had set up for herself a neat, humble little study, quite near the minister's office. There she would spend her days, at her desk, making herself useful to the minister; and if anyone wished to see the minister privately, without the nuisance of a crowd of civil servants and petitioners, nothing could be easier than for her to send a message, and for the minister to step through to her tiny sanctum, and confer there with his visitor while she · sat unobtrusively, listening hard, her hands folded in her lap.

She had made her rules, the rules by which the ministry would be conducted. Dinner would be given twice weekly. The food would be simple and no alcohol would be served. Guests would leave by 9 p.m. – we'll volunteer to start the exodus, Fabre whispered. No women would be received; with their chatter, their petty rivalries over their clothes, they detracted from the high tone and purpose of Mme Roland's gatherings.

This particular Monday had been a difficult one. Robespierre had declined her invitation. Pierre Vergniaud had accepted it. She did not like the man, personally; and these days her personal likes counted for a good deal. She could find no political point on which she differed from him, but he was lazy, reserving his oratory for grand themes and grand occasions. That night his eyes were glazed with boredom. Dumouriez was lively enough – but he was not lively in the right direction. He had told at least one scandalous anecdote, and then begged her pardon. She accorded it with the merest movement of her head; and the general knew that his work tomorrow would be mysteriously obstructed. Soon and easily, she had slipped into the habits of power.

Fabre d'Églantine had tried to draw the conversation round to the theatre, but she had firmly returned it to its proper subject – the manoeuvres, both military and political, of the *ci-devant* Marquis de Lafayette. She had seen Fabre catch Danton's eye, and cast his own momentarily to the naked goddesses prancing across the ceiling. She had been glad of Jean-Baptiste Louvet, sitting beside her. It was true that she had once been suspicious of him, because of the novel he had written. But she understood what the position of patriots had been, under the old regime, and a great deal could be excused to such a promising journalist. His thinning blond hair flopped forward as he leaned over to listen to her. A partisan. A friend of Mme Roland.

She talked to Louvet, but her eyes had been drawn, against her will, to Danton. It was Dumouriez who insisted she invite him: 'He is a man we ought to cultivate. He has a following on the streets.'

'Among the mob,' she had said scornfully.

'Do you think we shall have no dealings with the mob?'

So here the man sat. He made her shudder. That air of joviality, that affectation of frankness and bonhomie: it covered – just barely – the man's evident, monstrous ambition. Oh, he was just a good fellow, he was just a simple fellow, his heart was in the farmland of his province – oh was it? She glanced down at the confident hands resting on the cloth, the thick fingers outstretched. He could kill with those hands; he could snap a woman's neck, or squeeze the breath from a man's throat.

And that scar, faded to a dead white, slashed across his mouth; how did he get that scar? It twisted his lips, so that his smile was not really a smile, more a kind of sneer. What would it feel like to touch that scar? What would be the texture, under the fingertips? This man had a wife. He had, they said, a bevy of mistresses. Some women's fingers had touched that scar, traced its course, its edges.

He caught her eyes resting on him. She looked away quickly, but then she couldn't bear not to look up again, and spend the rest of the night wondering what he had thought. Cautiously, her glance crept back. Yes, take a good look, his face said; you have never in your safe little life seen a man like me.

AND ON TUESDAY MORNING, all Danton could say, with tired exasperation: 'Well, which one of us is going to sleep with the bitch, because clearly that's what she wants?'

'Why ask?' Fabre said. 'She didn't take her eyes off you for two hours.'

'Women are peculiar,' Danton said.

'And talking of peculiar women, I understand Théroigne is back. The Austrians have let her go. I can't imagine why, unless they thought she was the sort to bring the Revolution into disrepute.'

'No such subtlety,' Danton said. 'I expect they were afraid she'd cut off their balls.'

'But to return to the subject, Georges-Jacques – if Madame has her eye on you, you might as well, you really might as well. No point oiling around, "My dear Mme Roland, how we all esteem your talents" – why don't you offer her some solid evidence? Then she might bring all her gentlemen friends into line with our line. Do it, Georges-Jacques – she'll be easy. I don't suppose she gets much from that old husband of hers. He looks as if he's going to die at any minute.'

'I think he probably died years ago,' Camille said. 'I think she's had him embalmed and stuffed, because at heart she's sentimental. Also I think the whole Brissotin ministry is in the pay of the Court.'

'Robespierre,' Fabre said, nodding significantly.

'Robespierre does not think it,' Camille said.

'Don't lose your temper.'

'He thinks they are fools and dupes and unintentional traitors. I think it is worse than that. I think we should have nothing to do with them.'

'They certainly think they should have nothing to do with you. Dumouriez said, "Where's your little Camille tonight, why have you left him at home when he could be here sharing the excitement with us?" Madame heaved her bosom and inhaled most disdainfully.'

'I think you're wrong,' Danton said. They saw that he was very serious. 'I don't say anything about Dumouriez and the rest, but that woman couldn't be bought. That woman hates Louis and his wife as if they had done her some desperate injury.' He laughed sourly. 'Marat thinks he has a monopoly on hate?'

'You trust them, then?'

'I didn't say that. I don't think they're bad people. That's all I'm prepared to say.'

'What do you think Dumouriez wanted with you?'

The question seemed to cheer Danton. 'No doubt he wants me to do something, and is anxious to know my prices.'

IV. *The Tactics of a Bull*

(1792)

GABRIELLE: You see, I can only say what I've heard, what people have told me. I can only be sure about the people I know, and not so very sure about them. Looking back over the summer – what can I say to you that won't seem ridiculously naïve?

You can grow up, not what you would call a person of iron conviction; but you think there are things about you that won't change, beliefs you will always hold, things happening that will go on happening: a world that will do you for as long as you need it. Don't be deceived.

I must go back to when our new baby was born. The birth was easier than the first two – quicker, anyway. It was another boy; healthy, bonny, with good lungs and the same head of thick dark hair that Antoine had, and the little one I lost. We called him François-Georges. My husband kept buying me things – flowers and china and jewellery, lace and scent and books that I never read. So one day this made me cry. I shouted at him, it's not as if I've done anything clever, anyone can have a baby, stop trying to buy me off. A kind of storm of crying overtook me, and when it was over I was left with stinging eyes and a heaving chest and an aching throat. My memory seemed to have been wiped clean; if Catherine my maid had not told me that I said such things I wouldn't have believed it.

Next day Dr Souberbielle came. He said, 'Your husband tells me you're not very well.' I was simply tired, he said. Child-bearing was a great strain. Soon I would feel much better. But no, doctor, I said to him, very politely, I don't think I'll ever feel better again.

Whenever I put my baby to my breast, whenever I felt the flow of milk, I felt tears begin to leak out of my eyes; and my mother came, looking business-like and serious, and said that he should be put out to nurse, because we were making each other unhappy. It is better for children to be out of Paris, she said, and not to be crying at night and waking their fathers.

Of course, she said, when you get married, you live your first year or two in another world. As long as you've got a good man, a man you like, you feel so smug and pleased with yourself. You manage to keep all your problems at bay for that year or two – you think you're not subject to the rules that govern other people.

'Why should there be rules?' I said. I sounded just like Lucile. That's what she'd say – why should there be rules?

'And *she* will have her baby,' I said. 'And then what?'

My mother didn't need to ask for clarification. She just patted my arm. She said I was not the sort of girl to make a fuss. I had to be told that often these days – or who knows, I might have forgotten, and made one? My mother patted me once more – my hand this time – and said things about girls today. Girls today are romantic, she reckons. They have these strange illusions that when a man takes his marriage vows he means them. In her day, girls understood what was what. You had to come to a practical arrangement.

She found the wet-nurse herself, a pleasant, careful woman out at l'Isle-Adam. Pleasant she may be, careful she may be, but I didn't like to leave my baby. Lucile came with me, to meet the woman, to see if she would do for her own child; and yes, she would. What a neat arrangement! How practical! Lucile has only weeks to go now. How they fuss over her; you've never seen such a fuss. No question, though, of her feeding the mite herself. Her husband and her mother have forbidden it. She has sterner duties; there are parties to go to, after all. And General Dillon will prefer her bosom a discreet, agreeable size.

I don't really blame Lucile, though I make it sound as if I do. It isn't true that she is Fréron's mistress, though he has this slow, dragging obsession with her that makes him miserable and makes everybody else miserable too. With Hérault, as far as I can see, she simply goes through the usual social routine – leading him on, then pulling away. Hérault looks slightly weary sometimes, as though he has had rather too much experience of this sort of thing – I suppose he got it at Court. And part of the reason Lucile has fixed on him is that she wants to get back at Caroline Rémy, who made her so confused when she was just married and hadn't learned all the tricks. Oh, I was relieved when I knew that Lucile was pregnant! I thought, this at least postpones things. But I didn't hope for more than a postponement. I watch Georges. I watch his eyes following her. I wouldn't expect anyone to refuse him. If you think that's an impossible attitude for me to take, then it just shows that you don't know him well enough. Perhaps you've only heard him making a speech once. Or passed him in the street.

Only once I did blunder in, talking to Lucile's mother, trying to ease the situation because I thought it needed easing. 'Does she – ' I wasn't sure what I meant to say. 'Does she have a very hard time with Camille?'

Mme Duplessis raised her eyebrows in that way she has, that makes her seem clever. 'No harder than she wants,' she said.

But then, just as I was turning away, feeling rather sick about it all and apprehensive about what my future was to be, Mme Duplessis put out her little be-ringed hand and took me by the sleeve – I remember this, it was like a little pinch, cloth not skin – and said to me one of the few real things that this artificial woman has ever said. 'You do believe, I hope, that all this now is out of my control?'

I wanted to say, Madame, you have brought up a monster, but it would not have been fair to her. Instead I said, 'It is as well she is pregnant.'

Mme Duplessis murmured, *'Reculer pour mieux sauter.'*

All this summer, as in the summers since '88, our apartment was full of people coming and going; strange names, strange faces, some of them becoming less strange as the weeks went on, and some of them, frankly, more. Georges was out a good deal, keeping odd hours; he gave dinners at the Palais-Royal, at restaurants as well as at home. We entertained the people they call Brissotins, though not often Brissot himself. There was a lot of uncharitable talk about the wife of the Minister of the Interior, whom they call 'Queen Coco' – some joke that Fabre started off. Other people came late at night, after the meetings of the Jacobins and the Cordeliers. There was René Hébert – Père Duchesne, people call him, from the name of his foul news-sheet. Georges said, 'We have to put up with these people.' There was a man called Chaumette, scruffy and sharp-featured. He hated the aristocrats and he also hated prostitutes, and the two things used to get quite confused in his mind. They talked of the need to arm the whole city, against the Austrians and against the royalists. 'When the time comes,' Georges said.

I thought – he talks like a man who has circumstance by the throat, but really he is making his calculations, he is carefully weighing the odds. He has only once made a mistake – last summer, when we had to run away. You will say, what was it, after all? A few weeks skulking out of Paris, and then an amnesty, and things go on as before. But picture me, that summer night at Fontenay, saying goodbye, trying to keep my self-control and put a good face on things, knowing that he was going to England and fearing that he might never come back. It just shows, doesn't it, how much worse things can get when you think you've hit rock-bottom? Life has more complications in store than you can ever formulate or imagine. There are many ways of losing a husband. You can do it on several levels, the figurative and the actual. I operate on all of them, it seems.

Faces come and go . . . Billaud-Varennes, who was once Georges's part-time clerk, has met up with this actor Collot, whom Camille calls 'much the worst person in the world'. (He says that about a lot of people these days.) A well-suited pair they are, wearing their identical dyspeptic expressions. Robespierre avoids Hébert, is cool to Pétion, just civil to Vergniaud. Brissot twitters, 'We must try to avoid personalities.' Chaumette will not speak to Hérault, which Hérault declares no loss. Fabre examines everyone through his lorgnette. Fréron talks about Lucile. Legendre, our butcher, says he makes nothing of the Brissotins. 'I have no education,' he says, 'and I am as good a patriot as you could find.' François Robert is agreeable to everybody, thinking that he has a career to make; all the fight has gone out of him since last summer, when he was thrown into gaol.

M. Roland never comes. Neither does Marat.

The second week in June, there was a crisis in the government. The King was not cooperating with the ministers, he was holding out against them, and Roland's wife wrote him a terrible letter, lecturing him on his duty. I don't say anything about the rights and wrongs of it – not my place, is it? – but one can see, surely, that there are insults that a King can't accept, lie down under, without no longer being a King. Louis must have thought so, because he dismissed the ministry.

My husband's friends talked about the Patriotic Ministry. They said it was a national calamity. They have a way of turning calamities to their own account.

General Dumouriez was not dismissed. We understood he was on rather different terms with the Court. But he called on us. I was ashamed. Georges strode about and shouted at him. He said that he was going to put the fear of God into the Court, and that the King must divorce the Queen and pack her off back to Austria. When the general left he was white to the lips. The day after this he resigned, and went back to the armies. Georges was a good deal more frightening than the Austrians, Camille said.

Then came the letter from Lafayette to the Assembly, telling them to suppress the clubs, close down the Jacobins and the Cordeliers, or else . . . or else what? He would march his army on Paris? 'Let him show his face,' Georges said. 'I'll tear him in little pieces and dump the remains in the Queen's bedroom.'

The Assembly would not dare to act against the clubs – but, even for the suggestion, I knew that the patriots would have some revenge. There seems to be a pattern to these crises. Louise Gély said to my husband, 'Is there going to be a "day", M. Danton?'

'Well, what do you think?' He seemed amused. 'Perhaps we should have a second Revolution?'

She turned to me with a mock-shudder. 'Does your husband want to be King?'

The comings and goings in our apartment had to be worked out carefully, so that Chaumette never met Vergniaud, Hébert's path never crossed Legendre's. It is a trial to me; it is a trial to the servants. I became aware of the tension in the air that says, tomorrow, or the day after . . . Robespierre came; sat making general conversation. He looked as ever, like a tailor's model taken out of a box, so formal, so well-barbered, so polite. But he wore, besides his striped olive-green coat, a little smile that never seems to leave his face now; it's full of tension, it's his way (Camille says) of stopping himself swearing at people. He asked after the baby; he began to tell Antoine a story, and said he'd finish it in a day or two. So that's not too bad, I thought, we are going to survive . . . What is strange, in such a clean, precise man, is how much M. Robespierre likes children, and cats, and dogs. It's only the rest of us that put this worrying smile on his face.

It was quite late now. Pétion was the last to leave. I was keeping out of the way. I heard the study door open. My husband slapped him on the shoulder. 'Timing,' he said.

'Don't be afraid I'll nip anything in the bud,' the mayor said. 'I'll show my face, but not too early. There'll be time for events to take their natural course.'

He's alone now, I thought, they've gone. But as I approached the study door – closed again – I heard Camille's voice: 'I thought you were going to adopt the tactics of a bull. The tactics of a lion. That's what you said.'

'Yes, I am. But only when I'm ready.'

'You don't hear bulls saying, when I'm ready.'

'Hey you – I'm the expert on bulls. You don't hear them saying anything, that's why they're so successful.'

'Don't they bellow a bit?'

'Not the really successful ones.'

There was a pause. Then Camille said: 'But you don't leave it to chance. If you want someone killed, you don't leave it to chance.'

'What business is it of mine to want the King killed? If the district of Saint-Antoine wants him killed, the district will do it. Tomorrow, or at some future date.'

'Or not at all. All this sudden fatalism. Events can be controlled.' Camille sounded calm and very tired.

'I'd prefer not to rush things,' Georges said. 'I'd like to settle matters with Lafayette. I don't want to have to fight on all fronts at once.'

'But we can't let this chance go.'

Georges yawned. 'If they kill him,' he said, 'they kill him.'

I walked away. My courage failed. I didn't want to listen. I opened a window. I never remember the summers being so hot. There was some noise on the street, nothing you don't get every night. A patrol of National Guardsmen swung up the street. They slowed down as they approached. One of them said quite clearly, 'Danton's place.' There must be somebody new, that they were pointing it out. I pulled my head back, and heard them march away.

I went back to the door of Georges's study and pushed it open. He and Camille were sitting at either side of the empty fireplace, not speaking, just staring into each other's faces.

'Am I interrupting you?'

'No,' Camille said, 'we were just staring into each other's faces. I hope you weren't discomfitted by what you heard when you were listening at the door just now?'

Georges laughed. 'Was she? I didn't know.'

'It is like Lucile. She opens my letters, then gets into a terrible state. It is my poor cousin, Rose-Fleur Godard, who causes problems at the moment. She writes every week from Guise. Her marriage is not happy. She now wishes she were married to me.'

'I think I'd advise her to be reconciled to her lot,' I said. We laughed: surprising, how one can. The tension was broken. I looked at Georges. I never see the face that horrifies people. To me it is really a kind face. Camille looked no different from the boy Georges had brought to the café six years before. He stood up, leaned forward quickly, kissed my cheek. I have misheard, I thought, I have misunderstood. There is a distance between a politician and a killer. But then, 'Think of the poor fools,' Georges said to him in parting.

'Yes,' Camille replied. 'Sitting there, waiting to be murdered.'

THE DAY OF THE RIOT I did not go out, and neither did Georges. No one came until the middle of the evening. Then I heard the stories the day had produced.

The people from Saint-Antoine and Saint-Marcel, led by agitators from the Jacobins and the Cordeliers, had entered the Tuileries, armed and in their thousands. Legendre was one of the leaders; he insulted the King to his face, and came back here to sit in my drawing room and boast about it. Perhaps the King and Queen should have died under their staves and pikes, but it didn't happen like that. I was told that they stood for hours in a window embrasure, with the little Dauphin and his sister, and the King's own sister Mme Elisabeth. The crowd filed past them and laughed at them, as if they were the freaks at a country fair. They made the King put on a 'cap of liberty'. These people – people out of the gutter – passed the King cheap wine and made him drink from the bottle to the health of the nation. This went on for hours.

At the end of it they were still alive. A merciful God protected them; and as for the man who should have protected them – Pétion, I mean, the Mayor of Paris – he didn't show his face until the evening. When he could not decently wait any longer, he went to the Tuileries with a group of deputies and got the mob out of the palace. 'And then, do you know what?' Vergniaud said. I handed him a glass of cold white wine. It was ten p.m. 'When they had all gone, the King snatched the red cap off his head, threw it on the floor and stamped on it.' He nodded his thanks to me, urbanely. 'The curious thing is that the King's wife behaved with what can only be called dignity. It is unfortunate, but the people are not so opposed to her as they were before.'

Georges was in a rage. It is a spectacle to contemplate, his rage. He tore off his cravat, strode about the room, his throat and chest glistening with sweat, his voice shaking the windows. 'This bloody so-called Revolution has been a waste of time. What have the patriots got out of it? Nothing.' He glared around the room. He looked as if he would hit anyone who contradicted him. Outside there was some far-off shouting, from the direction of the river.

'If that's true – ' Camille said. But he couldn't manage it, he couldn't get his words out. 'If this one's done for – and I think it always was done for – ' He put his face into his hands, exasperated with himself.

'Come on, Camille,' Georges said, 'there's no time to wait around for you. Fabre, please bang his head against the wall.'

'That's what I'm trying to say, Georges-Jacques. We have no more time left.' I don't know whether it was the threat, or because he suddenly saw the future, that Camille recovered his voice: but he began to speak in short, simple sentences. 'We must begin again. We must stage a coup. We must depose Louis. We must take control. We must declare the republic. We must do it before the summer ends.'

Vergniaud looked uneasy. He ran his finger along the arm of his chair. He looked from face to face.

Camille said, 'Georges-Jacques, you said you weren't ready, but you must be ready now.'

MANON OUT OF OFFICE. A phrase of Danton's kept coming back to her: 'France's natural frontiers'. She spent hours these days poring over the maps of the Low Countries, the Rhine. Properly: had she not been one of the foremost advocates of the war policy? Less easy to find the natural frontiers of a human being . . .

They blamed her, of course, the feather-brained patriots; they said it was because of her letter that Louis had dismissed the ministry. It was nonsense: Louis just wanted a pretext, that was all. She had to brace herself against their accusations, accusations that she had interfered, that she had meddled, that she dictated policy to Roland. It was so unfair; they had always worked together, she and her husband, pooling their talents and energy; she knew his thoughts before he knew them himself. 'Roland loses nothing,' she said, 'by being interpreted through me.' Glances were exchanged. *Always*, glances exchanged. She would have liked to slap their complacent male faces.

Buzot alone seemed to understand. He took her hand, pressed it. 'Don't regard them, Manon,' he whispered. 'True patriots know your worth.'

They would regain office; this was her opinion. But they would have to fight for it. 20 June, the so-called 'invasion' of the Tuileries – it had been a fiasco, it had been a joke. It had been mismanaged from start to finish; and mismanagement seemed to be the rule.

Afternoons, these days, she was in the public gallery at the Riding-School, listening through gritted teeth to the debate. One day a young woman strode in, wearing a scarlet riding-habit, a pistol stuck in her belt. Alarmed, Manon looked around for the usher; but no one except herself took the spectacle amiss. The young woman was laughing; she was surrounded by a pack of supporters; she disposed herself on a bench, proprietorially, and ran her hand back through brown curls cropped short like a man's. Her claque applauded Vergniaud; they called out his name; they called out to other deputies, and then they tossed apples along the rows and ate them and threw down the cores.

Vergniaud came up to speak to her and she congratulated him on his speech, but in reserved tones; he got too much praise. To the strange, scarlet girl, he merely inclined his head. 'That is Théroigne,' he said. 'Can it be that you have not seen her before? She spoke to the Jacobins in spring, telling of her ordeal among the Austrians. They yielded the tribune to her. Not many women can say the same.'

He stopped then, with the air of a man who had talked himself into a corner. A hunted, vaguely mutinous expression crossed his face. 'Don't trouble yourself,' Manon murmured. 'I shall not ask you to arrange it. I am not one of these viragos.'

'What are they, after all?' Vergniaud said. 'Street-girls.'

She could, of course, have punched him on the jaw. But look what he was offering – a sweet readmission to the conspiracy, a reinstatement. She smiled. 'Street-girls,' she said.

LUCILE'S BABY had taken a lurch to the left, and was kicking her with vigour. She could hardly push herself into an approximately upright position, let alone be civil to a visitor. 'Hell,' she said, staring at Théroigne's outfit. 'Aren't you hot in that scarlet attire? Isn't it time you put it into honourable retirement?' She could see, in fact, that the hem was frayed, that the dust of the streets was upon it, that even the red was not so red as it used to be.

'Camille's avoiding me,' Théroigne complained. She paced the room. 'He's hardly exchanged two words with me since I came back to Paris.'

'He's busy,' Lucile said.

'Oh yes, I'm sure he's busy. Busy playing cards at the Palais-Royal, busy dining with aristocrats. How can anyone think of passing the time of day with an old friend when there's so much champagne to be drunk and so many silly, empty-headed bitches to be screwed?'

'Including you,' Lucile murmured.

'No, not including me.' Théroigne stopped pacing. '*Never* including me. I have never slept with Camille, or with Jérôme Pétion, or with any of the other two dozen men the newspapers have named.'

'The papers will print anything,' Lucile said. 'Sit down, please. You're making me wild and frantic with your red pacing.'

Théroigne didn't sit. 'Louis Suleau will print anything,' she said. 'This filthy *Acts of the Apostles*. Why is Suleau at large, that's what I want to know? Why isn't he *dead*?'

Lucile thought, perhaps I can pretend to go into labour. She essayed a small moan. Théroigne took no notice. 'Why is it,' she said, 'that Camille can get away with anything? When Suleau laughed at me he just laughed with him, they had their heads together making up more libels, inventing more lovers for me, plotting to expose me to derision and scorn – but no one says to Camille, look, you hang around with Suleau, so how can you be a patriot? Tell me, Lucile, how does it happen?'

'I don't know.' Lucile shook her head. 'It's a mystery. I suppose – you know how in families there's usually one child who gets away with more than the others? Well, perhaps it's like that in revolutions as well.'

'But I've suffered, Lucile. I've been a prisoner. Does no one understand that?'

Oh Lord, Lucile thought, it looks as if Théroigne has set in for the afternoon. She tottered to her feet. She could see that Théroigne was about to cry. She made clucking noises, laid a hand upon her upper arm, pressed her gently to the blue *chaise-longue*. 'Jeanette,' she called, 'have we some ice? Bring me something cool, bring me something sweet.' Inside the scarlet cloth the girl's skin was hot and damp. 'Are you ill?' Lucile asked her. 'Dear little Anne, what have they done to you?' As she pressed a folded handkerchief against the girl's temples, she saw herself, as if from an angel's height, and thought, what a saintly young woman I am, mopping up this liar.

Théroigne said, 'I tried to speak to Pétion yesterday, and he pretended not to have seen me. I want to give Brissot's people my support, but they pretend I don't exist. I do exist.'

'Of course,' Lucile said. 'Of course you do.'

Théroigne dropped her head. The tears dried on her cheeks. 'When will your baby be born?'

'Next week, the doctor says.'

'I had a child.'

'What? Did you? When?'

'She's dead.'

'I'm sorry.'

'She would have been – oh, I don't know. The years go by. You lose track. She died the spring before the Bastille. No, that's not right – '88, she died, I never saw her, hardly ever. I left her with a foster-mother, I paid every month, I sent money for her from wherever I was, Italy, England. But it doesn't mean I'm hard, Lucile, it doesn't mean I didn't love her. I did. She was my little girl.'

Lucile eased herself back into her chair. She rested her hands on the writhing, hidden form of her own baby. Her face showed strain. Something in Théroigne's tone – something very hard to place – suggested that she might be making this up. 'What was your little girl's name?' she asked.

'Françoise-Louise.' Théroigne looked down at her hands. 'One day I would have come for her.'

'I know you would,' Lucile said. A silence. 'Do you want to tell me about the Austrians? Is that it?'

'Oh, the Austrians. They were strange.' Théroigne threw back her head. She laughed, her laugh uncertain, forced; alarming, how she snapped from topic to topic, from mood to mood. 'They wanted to know the course of my life, my whole life from the time I was born. Where were you on such a date, month, year? – I can't remember, I'd say – then, "Allow us to assist your memory,

Mademoiselle," and out would come some piece of paper, some little chit I'd signed, some receipt, some laundry list or some pawnbroker's ticket. They frightened me, those bits of paper; it was as if all my life, from the time I learned to write, these blessed Austrians had set spies to follow me about.'

Lucile thought: if half of this is fact, what do they know about Camille? Or Georges-Jacques? She said, 'Well, you know that can't be true.'

'How do you account for it then? They had a piece of paper from England, a contract I'd signed with this Italian singing teacher, this man who said he'd promote me. And yes, I had to agree with them, that's my handwriting – I remembered signing it – the idea was, he'd give me lessons, to improve my technique, then I'd pay him back out of my concert fees. Now, I signed that paper, Lucile, on a foggy afternoon, in London, in Soho, in my teacher's house on Dean Street. So tell me, tell me, if you can work it out at all – how did that piece of paper get from Dean Street, Soho, on to the desk of the commandant of the prison at Kufstein? How can it have got there, unless someone has been following me all these years?' Suddenly she laughed again, that disturbing, stupid giggle. 'On this paper, you know, I'd signed my name, and underneath it said "Anne Théroigne, Spinster". The Austrians said, "Who is he, this Englishman, this Mr Spinster? Did you make a secret marriage to him?"'

'So there you are,' Lucile said. 'They don't know all about you, do they? This Kufstein, what was it like?'

'It grows out of the rocks,' Théroigne said. Her mood had swung again; she spoke softly, calmly, like a nun looking back on her life. 'From the windows of my room I could see the mountains. I had a white table and a white chair.' She frowned, as if trying to recollect. 'When they shut me up at first I sang. I sang every song I knew, every aria, every little ditty. When I came to the end of them I started again.'

'Did they hurt you?'

'Oh, no. Nothing like that. They were polite, they were . . . tender. Each day they brought me food, they asked me what I'd like to eat.'

'But what did they want from you, Anne?' She wanted to add, 'because you aren't important'.

'They said I organized the October days, and they wanted to know who paid me to do it. They said I rode to Versailles astride a cannon, and that I led the women into the palace and that I had a sword in my hand. It's not true, you know. I was there already, in Versailles. I'd rented a room, so I could go to the National Assembly every day and listen to the debates. Yes, I went out and talked to the women, I talked to the National Guard. But when they broke into the palace I was in my bed, asleep.'

'I suppose someone could testify to that,' Lucile said. Théroigne stared at her, uncomprehending. 'Never mind,' Lucile said. 'I was making a joke. The thing is, Anne – you must have realized by now – since the Bastille fell, it doesn't matter what you actually did, it's what people say you did. You can't pick the past apart in this way, it doesn't avail you. Once you start to live in the public eye people attribute actions and words to you, and you have to live with that. If they say you rode astride a cannon, then I'm afraid you did.'

Théroigne looked up at her. 'Did I? I did.'

'No, I mean – ' Oh, curse God, Lucile thought, she's not very bright, is she? 'No, you *didn't* – oh, can't you understand?'

Théroigne shook her head. 'They asked me about the Jacobin Club. Asked who was paid to say what. I don't know anything about the Jacobins. But there it is. They didn't like my answers.'

'Some of us thought, you know, that we would never see you again.'

'People say that I ought to write a book about it. But I've no education, Lucile, I could no more write a book than I could land on the moon. Do you think Camille would write it for me?'

'Why did the Austrians let you go, Anne?'

'They took me to Vienna. I saw the chancellor, the Emperor's chief minister, in his private rooms.'

'Yes, but you are not answering my question.'

'Then they took me back to Liège. To where I was born. I thought I was used to travelling, but they were hell, these journeys – oh, they tried to be kind to me, but I wanted to lie by the roadside and die. When we got to Liège they gave me some money, they said I could go where I liked. I said, even Paris? They said, yes, of course.'

'We knew this,' Lucile said. 'It was reported in *Le Moniteur*, last December. We kept the paper, I have it somewhere. We said, "So, she's on her way home." We were surprised. There were rumours, from time to time, that the Austrians had hanged you. But instead of that, they let you go, gave you money, didn't they? Do you wonder Camille keeps away from you now?'

A good lawyer, she has closed her case. And yet it is hard to believe that – as everyone thinks but doesn't say – the girl has agreed to act as a spy. Take away the firearms, strip the scarlet away, and she seems harmless, hopeless, not even quite sane. 'Anne,' she said. 'You ought to think of getting out of Paris. Somewhere quiet. Till you get your health back.'

Théroigne looked up at her quickly. 'You forget, Lucile. I once let the journalists drive me out, I let Louis Suleau kick me out of Paris. Then what happened? I had a room at an inn, Lucile, miles from anywhere, the birds singing, just what you need to recuperate. I ate well, and I slept so soundly, those nights. Then one night I woke up, and there were men in my room, and they were men I didn't know, and they dragged me out, into the dark.'

'I think you should go now,' Lucile said. Fear touched the base of her throat; fear touched the pit of her stomach, and laid its cold finger on her child.

'LAFAYETTE is in Paris,' Fabre said.

'So I hear.'

'You knew, Danton?'

'I know everything, Fabre.'

'So when are you going to tear him in little pieces?'

'Restrain yourself, Fabre.'

'But you said – '

'A bit of bombast has its uses. It encourages others. I am thinking of visiting my in-laws in Fontenay for a day or two.'

'I see.'

'The general has plans. For marching on the Jacobins, closing them down. Reprisals for 20 June. He hopes to carry the National Guard with him. In the event, no one can prove that I had anything to do with 20 June – '

'Mm,' Camille said.

'– but I prefer to avoid inconvenience. It will come to nothing.'

'But surely this is serious.'

Danton was patient. 'It isn't serious, as we know his plans.'

'How *do* we know?'

'Pétion told me.'

'Who told Pétion?'

'Antoinette.'

'Dear God.'

'Yes, stupid, aren't they? When Lafayette is the only person still willing to do anything for them. It makes you wonder about the wisdom of dealing with them at all.'

Camille looked up. 'Dealing with them?'

'Dealing with them, child. Grabbing what you can.'

'You don't mean it. You don't *deal* with them.'

'Fabre, do I mean it?'

'Yes, you mean it.'

'Now, does it worry you, Fabre?'

'Not in the sense of having scruples. I think it frightens me. Worrying about the possible complications.'

'Not in the sense of having scruples,' Danton repeated. 'Frightens him. Scruples. What a beautiful concept. Mention this conversation to Robespierre, Camille, and I'm finished with you. My God,' he said. He went away, shaking his head vigorously.

'Mention what?' Camille said.

LAFAYETTE'S PLAN: a grand review of the National Guard, at which the general will inspect the troops and the King himself will be present to take the salute. The King will withdraw, Lafayette will harangue the battalions; for is he not their first, most glorious commander, does he not have the natural authority to take control again? Then in the name of the constitution, in the name of the monarchy, in the name of public order, General Lafayette will proceed to put the capital to rights. Not that he has the King's enthusiastic backing; for Louis is afraid of failure, afraid of the consequences of it, and the Queen says coldly that she would rather be murdered than be saved by Lafayette.

Pétion can move quickly, when he likes. An hour before the review is due to begin, he simply cancels it: leaving the arrangements to cannon into each other, and relying on natural confusion to undo any larger schemes. The general is left to trail through the streets with his aides, cheered on by patriots of the old-fashioned sort. He is left to assess his situation; to take the road out of Paris to his army command the frontier. At the Jacobins, Deputy Couthon is wheeled to the tribune, to denounce the general as a 'great scoundrel'; Maximilien Robespierre calls him 'an enemy of the Fatherland'; Messieurs Brissot and Desmoulins vie with each other in heaping the hero with abuse. The Cordeliers come back from the short holiday many of them had found it wise to take, and burn the general in effigy, coining slogans for the future above the cracking and spitting of the uniformed doll.

ANNETTE SAID, 'If she survives this, will you be good?' July morning, sunshine, a fresh breeze. Camille looked out of the window, saw the rue des Cordeliers, his neighbours busying about, life going on in its achingly usual way; heard the printing presses at work in the Cour du Commerce, saw women stopping to chat on the corner, tried hard to imagine any other kind of life or any kind of death. 'I've stopped striking bargains with God,' he said. 'So don't *you* try to wring a bargain from me, Annette.'

He looked, Annette thought, utterly wretched; pale, shaky, quite unable to come to terms with the fact that his wife must give birth and that it was going to hurt her. It's remarkable, really, how many quite ordinary things Camille can't or won't come to terms with. I'll put the knife in just a bit, Annette thought, just an inch or two; not often that you have him at a disadvantage these days. 'You're just playing at marriage,' she said. 'Both of you. This is the bit that isn't a game.' She waited.

'I would die,' Camille said, 'if anything happened to her.'

'Yes.' Annette got up wearily from her chair. She had gone to bed at midnight, but been roused at two o'clock. 'Yes, I almost believe you would.'

She would go back to her daughter now. Lucile was still quite cheerful; that was because she didn't know how bad it was going to get. She thought, could I have saved her from this? Of course she could. She could have followed her inclinations seven years ago; in that case, she would now be remembered by Camille, if he ever thought of her at all, as just a woman in his past, a woman he'd had to work extra hard for; and he would no longer be part of her life, he would be someone she read about in the newspapers. Instead, she had clung to her precious virtue, her daughter was married to the Lanterne Attorney and was now in labour, and she was observing daily – shuttling between the rue Condé and the rue des Cordeliers – the sort of sickeningly destructive love affair that you only read about in books. Of course, people could call it different things, but she called it a love affair. And she thought she had lived long enough to know what she was talking about.

'We must have you out of here,' she said. 'Go for a walk. Get some fresh air. Why don't you go and see Max? He's full of reassuring good sense and homely wisdom.'

'Mm,' Camille looked ill with tension. 'Bachelors always are. Send to me immediately, won't you. The very minute?'

'ANNETTE SAID I must go away, she said I disseminated panic. I hope you don't mind my arriving at this hour.'

'I expected it,' Robespierre said. 'We should be together, you and me. I have to go and get the day under way, but I'll be back in an hour or two. The family will look after you. Would you like to go down and talk to one of the girls?'

'Oh no,' Camille said. 'I've given up talking to girls. Look what it leads to.'

It was hard for Robespierre to smile. He reached forward and squeezed Camille's hand. Odd, that; he usually avoided touching people. Camille divined that some kind of psychic emergency was taking place. 'Max,' he said, 'you're almost in a worse state than I am. If I am disseminating panic, you are communicating disaster.'

'It will be all right,' Robespierre said, in a tone deeply unconvinced. 'Yes, yes, it will be, I feel it. She's a healthy girl, she's strong, there's no reason to believe, is there, that anything could go wrong?'

'Desperate, isn't it?' Camille said. 'Can't even *pray* for her.'

'Why can't you?'

'I don't believe God listens to those sorts of prayers. They're self-serving, aren't they?'

'God accepts all kinds of prayers.'

They looked at each other, vaguely alarmed. 'We are here under Providence,' Robespierre said. 'I am sure of that.'

'I couldn't say that I'm sure of it. Though I do find the idea consoling.'

'But if we are not under Providence, what is everything for?' Robespierre now looked wildly alarmed. 'What is the Revolution for?'

For Georges-Jacques to make money out of, Camille thought. Robespierre answered himself. 'Surely it is to bring us to the kind of society that God intends? To bring us to justice and equality, to full humanity?'

Oh good heavens, Camille thought. This Max, he believes every word he says. 'I wouldn't presume to know what kind of society God intends. It sounds to me as if you've gone to a tailor to order your God. Or had him knitted, or something.'

'A knitted God.' Robespierre shook his head, amazed. 'Camille, you are a fount of original notions.' He put his hands on Camille's shoulders. In a cautious way, they hugged each other. 'Under Providence, we shall go on being silly,' Robespierre said. 'I will be back in two hours, and then I will sit with you and we will discuss theology and whatever else will while away the time. If *anything happens*, get a message to me.'

Camille was left alone. Conversations do take the most amazing turn, he thought. He looked around Robespierre's room. It was plain, quite small, with an insomniac's hard bed and a plain whitewood table that served as Robespierre's very tidy desk. There was only one book on it – a small copy of Rousseau's *Social Contract* – and he recognized it as the one that Robespierre always carried with him, in the inside pocket of his coat. Today he had forgotten it. His routine was broken; he had been overset.

He picked up the book and looked at it closely. It had some special magic, which had communicated itself to Robespierre; this volume and no other will do. An idea struck him. He flourished the book before an imaginary audience. He said, in Robespierre's Artesian accent: 'Victim of an assassin's musket-ball, this copy of the *Social Contract* saved my life. Remark, fellow-patriots, how the fatal bullet was deflected by the immortal cheap cloth binding of the immortal words of the immortal Jean-Jacques. Under Providence –' He was going to go on to speak about the plots that menaced the nation, plots, plots, plots, plots, plots, but he felt suddenly weak and jittery and knew that he ought to sit down. He pulled up to the table a straw-bottomed chair. It was exactly like the chair he had stood on when he spoke to the mob at the Palais-Royal. I don't think I could live with such a chair, he thought. It frightens me too much.

He had a speech to write. What stupendous self-control, he thought, if I could write any of it, but I don't suppose I will. He got up and looked out of the window for a while. Maurice Duplay's workmen were fetching and carrying in the yard below. Seeing him watching them, they raised hands in greeting. He could go down and talk to them, but he might meet Eléonore. Or he might meet Mme Duplay, and she would trap him in that drawing room of hers, and expect him to make conversation, and eat things. He had a dread of that room, with its vast *articles* – you could only call them that – of mahogany furniture, and its dark-red draperies of Utrecht velvet, with its old-fashioned hangings and its enamelled stove that gave off a fume-laden heat. It was a room for hopes to die in; he imagined picking up a crimson cushion, and placing it decisively over Eléonore's face.

He wrote. He tried a paragraph. He deleted it. He began again. Time passed, he supposed. Then a little scratch at the door: 'Camille, can I come in?'

'You may.'

Oh, why be like that? On edge.

Elisabeth Duplay. 'Are you busy?'

He put the pen down. 'I'm supposed to be writing a speech, but I'm not concentrating. My wife – '

'I know.' She closed the door softly. Babette. The goose-girl. 'So would you like it if I stayed and talked to you?'

'That,' Camille said, 'would be very nice.'

She laughed. 'Oh, Camille, you are sour. You don't really think it would be very nice, you think it would be a bore.'

'If I thought it would be a bore, I would say so.'

'You have such a reputation for charm, but we don't see much of it in this house. You're never charming to my sister Eléonore. Although – I must admit – I'd often like to be rude to Eléonore myself, but I'm the youngest, and in our family we've been brought up to be polite to our elders.'

'Quite right,' Camille said. He was perfectly serious. He couldn't understand why she kept laughing. Then suddenly he could. When she laughed she was quite pretty. She was quite pretty anyway. An improvement on her sisters.

She sat down on the edge of the bed. 'Max talks about you a lot,' she said. 'It would be lovely to know you better. I think you're the person in the world he cares about most. And yet you're very different – so why do you think that is?'

'It must be my charm,' Camille said. 'Obvious, isn't it?'

'He's very nice to us, you know. He's like a brother. He stands up to our father for us. Our father's a tyrant.'

'All children think that.' He was struck by what he had said. How would he treat this child of his, when it grew a will of its own? The child in its teens, he in middle age: there seemed something unlikely about it. He thought, I wonder what my father did while my mother was having me? I bet he worked on the *Encyclopaedia of Law*. I bet he did a bit of indexing while my mother screamed in agony.

'What are you thinking?' she asked.

He couldn't suppress a smile. How well was she suggesting she might get to know him? Women had a special time for that question, usually after the sexual act; but he supposed they had to rehearse it, even as schoolgirls. 'Oh, nothing,' he said. (She may as well get used to the usual reply.) He felt uneasy. 'Elisabeth, does your mother know you're up here?'

'You should call me Babette. That's my pet-name.'

'Does she, though?'

'I don't know whether she knows or not. I think she's gone out for the bread.' She ran a hand over her skirt, sat further back on the bed. 'Does it matter?'

'People might wonder where you are.'

'They could call out, if they wanted me.'

A pause. She watched him steadily. 'Your wife is very beautiful,' she said.

'Yes.'

'Did she like being pregnant?'

'She liked it at first, but then she found it was tedious.'

'I expect you found it was tedious too.'

He closed his eyes. He was almost sure he was right. He opened them again. He wanted to be sure that she didn't move. 'I think I must go now,' he said.

'But Camille.' Her eyes became round. 'If you leave, a message might come about the baby. You'd want to know right away, wouldn't you?'

'Yes. Yes. Then perhaps we ought not to stay here.'

'Why not?'

Because I think you are trying to seduce me. Short of taking your clothes off, you couldn't be much more plain about it. And you will probably do that in a minute. 'You know damn well why not,' he said.

'People can have conversations in bedrooms. People can have whole parties in bedrooms. Whole conferences.'

'Yes, of course they can.' I should be gone by now.

'But you're afraid of doing something wrong? You find me attractive?'

You can't say, I didn't say that. She might weep, become

permanently diffident, die a spinster. All right, you can't say that, but there are worse things that you can say. 'Elisabeth, do you do this often?'

'I don't come up here often. Max is so busy.'

Oh, a neat wit, he thought. This is a sort of standard-bearer in the army of round-faced, middle-class virgins, the sort of girl you got into a lot of trouble over when you were sixteen. And might again.

'I don't want you,' he said gently.

'That's not the point.'

'What did you say?'

'I said that's not the point.' She jumped from the bed and came towards him; her little slippered feet made no sound at all. Standing over him, she rested a hand lightly on his shoulder. 'You're here. I'm here.' She put a hand up, pulled at her hair, releasing it from its pins and shaking it out. Mouse-brown hair, dishevelled now. And colour in her cheeks . . . 'Want to go now?' she said. Because then she would crash downstairs after him, and there would be (he knew these awful assemblies) Eléonore and the nephew and Maurice Duplay – as he stood up he caught sight of his face in the mirror, and saw that it was irate, guilty and confused. She moved backwards and leaned against the door, laughing up into his face: no longer the least significant member of the household.

'Oh, this is ridiculous,' he said. 'This is incredible.'

She watched him narrowly. She had a poacher's face, inspecting the early-morning traps.

'No romantic interlude you had in mind,' he said. 'You just want to see the blood.'

'Ah,' she said, 'then have we nothing in common?'

She was a little girl, but she was built on solid lines; she made herself into dead-weight resistance. As he pulled her away from the door, the fichu that covered her shoulders slipped and unknotted and floated to the floor. I wonder, he thought, what Mme Duplay's dressmaker thought she was about. Such a quantity of white swelling adolescent bosom. 'Look,' she said, 'at the state I'm in.' She caught his hand and held it at the base of her bared throat. He could feel the pulse quiver beneath her skin. 'You've touched me *now*,' she said. Her face invited violence. He wanted to hit her. Then she would scream. Dear God, I must warn people about her, he thought. He made a mental list of the people he must warn.

'You might as well, now,' she said. 'We're quite safe. There's a lock on the door. Might as well go a little bit further.'

He scooped up the fichu from the floor, slid it around her shoulders, held her tight while he did it, his fingers digging into her arm above the elbow. 'I shall call your sisters,' he said. 'Perhaps you are not well.'

She gaped at him. 'You're hurting me,' she said faintly.

'No, I'm not. Pin your hair up.'

Strange, the expression he had time to notice on her face – not hesitation or anger, but disgruntlement. She tore herself out of his grip and lunged towards the window. Her face was flushed and she was taking deep breaths, great gulps of air. He came up behind her, shaking her a little: 'Stop it. You'll make yourself ill, you'll faint.'

'Yes, then you explain that. Or I could call out now. No one would believe you.'

In the yard below them, the sound of sawing had stopped, and the men were looking up at the house. Their faces were a blur to Camille, but he could imagine every furrow on their brows. Maurice Duplay was walking slowly towards the house, and a second later he heard a woman's voice raised, sharply questioning: Duplay's voice, muffled but urgent: a sharp little feminine cry: the advance of footsteps, footsteps climbing the stairs.

He went cold. She can say what she likes, he thought, they'll believe her. Below the window now, something like a small crowd. All of them Duplay's people, and all looking up; and their faces, he thought, were expectant.

The door was flung open. Maurice Duplay filled it; energetic master, shirt-sleeves rolled up. He threw out his arms, the good Jacobin Duplay, and formed a sentence totally original, something which had never been uttered in the history of the world: 'Camille, you have a son, and your wife is very well, and is asking you to be at home, right now.'

A sea of smiles in the doorway. Camille stood fighting down his fright. You need not speak, a voice said inside, they will think you are too pleased and surprised to speak. Elisabeth had turned her back to them. With deft unobtrusive movements, she was straightening her clothes. 'Congratulations,' she said lightly. '*What* an achievement for you.'

'Maximilien has a godchild,' Madame Duplay said, beaming. 'Please God one day he will have a fine son of his own.'

Maurice Duplay locked his arms about Camille. It was a horrible, brisk, patriotic hug, Jacobin to Jacobin, Camille's face pressed to the beefy flesh of Duplay's shoulder. He rehearsed this sentiment, to the dampish white skin barely veiled by coarse linen: your youngest daughter's a practising rapist. No, he thought. It really won't do. The best thing to do is not to mention it to anybody, they'll only laugh. The best thing to do is to get home to Lucile and after this be very very careful and very very good.

THE FIRST CONSOLATION was that it had taken less time than people feared – twelve hours from when it began; the second consolation was this tiny, black-haired child, lying along her arm. She felt such an access, such a purity of love that she could hardly speak; they warn you of all sorts of things, she thought, but no one ever warns you of this. She could hardly speak anyway; she was weary, deadly weary, hardly able to hold up her head.

What different opinions people had! Through each contraction her mother had held her hands, wincing at the strength of her grip, saying, be a *brave* girl, Lucile, be *brave*. The midwife had said, you have a good scream, flower, you scream the ceiling down if you feel like it, I'm sure your husband can afford the plaster. You can't please everybody. Every time she'd thought of trying a scream, the next crashing pain had knocked the breath right out of her. Gabrielle Danton had leaned over her, saying something – something sensible, no doubt – and surely at one point Angélique had been there too, muttering spells in Italian? But for minutes at a time – whole strings of seconds, anyway – she had not known who was there. She had been living in another world: an unyielding world, with crimson walls.

Deliberately, consciously, Camille set the morning's other events to the back of his mind. Holding the fragile scrap of being against his shoulder, he breathed promises: I shall be very very nice to you; whatever strange or stupid sorts of thing you want to do will be all right by me. Claude peered at the baby, hoping that Camille would not offer to hand him over. 'I wonder who he will look like,' he said.

Camille said, 'There's a lot of money on that.'

Claude closed his mouth on the heartfelt congratulations he had been about to offer his son-in-law.

'Why don't we overthrow Louis on 14 July?' inquired the *ci-devant* Duke of Orléans.

'Oh-hum,' said the *ci-devant* Comte de Genlis. 'You're so fond of the sentimental gesture. I'll speak to Camille and see if he could trouble to arrange it.'

The Duke did not spot sarcasm easily. He groaned. 'Every time you speak to Camille these days it costs me a small fortune.'

'You don't know where rapacity begins. How much have you given Danton, over these last three years?'

'I couldn't say. But if we fail this time, even a small riot will be beyond my means. When Louis falls – you don't think, do you, that they'll cheat me out of the throne this time?'

De Sillery would have liked to point out that he had thrown away his chance once already (by listening, he would have said, to my wife Félicité, the procuress); but Félicité and her daughter Pamela had left for England last autumn, seen safely across the channel by the ever-useful, ever-obliging Jérôme Pétion. 'Let me think,' he said. 'Have you bought up the Brissotins, the Rolandins, the Girondins?'

'Aren't they all the same?' Philippe looked alarmed. 'I thought they were.'

'Are you quite sure that you can offer Georges Danton more than the Court can? More than he stands to make out of a republic?'

'Has it come to that?' The Duke sounded disgusted; he quite forgot for a moment his own part in bringing it there.

'I don't mean to be discouraging. I understand though that Danton thinks we should wait for the volunteers from Marseille.'

They are hand-picked, staunch patriots, these Marseille men, marching to the capital for the Bastille celebrations; they march singing their new patriotic song, and their minds and jaws are set. A neat spearhead for the Sections, when the day comes.

'The Marseille men . . . who do I pay in their case?'

'Young local politician called Charles Barbaroux.'

'How much will he want? Can we secure him?'

'Oh, dammit all.' De Sillery closed his eyes. He felt tired. 'He's been in Paris since 11 February. He had a meeting with the Rolands on 24 March.' Laclos would have had a little file on Barbaroux's burgeoning self-importance, would have tabulated him in his 'womanizer' column, with a little star for emphasis. 'Do you ever wonder if it's worth it?' de Sillery said.

It was a question Philippe couldn't get his mind around. Anything had been worthwhile, any connivance, any shame, any slaughter, if at the end of it you were King of France. Then Félicité had come along and muddled him – and truly she was right, for it wasn't worthwhile to be King and rapidly dead. But for years now he had been set on a course by the people around him; he had been chivvied and steered, willing or unwilling. There was no time to set another; and he was nearly bankrupt.

'But damn Danton,' he said, 'I even let him have Agnès.'

'No one "lets" him have anything,' Charles-Alexis said. 'Danton just takes.'

'But he must give too,' Philippe said. 'The people will want something from him. What will he give them?'

'He'll give them one-man, one-vote. That's something they've never had before.'

'They'll like that, I suppose. They'll come out on the streets for that.' The Duke sighed. 'All the same, the 14th would have been nice.' When he looked back on '89, he thought, those were my halcyon days. He voiced the thought.

'Your salad days,' Charles-Alexis said.

*

JULY 10, a state of emergency was declared. All over the city there were military bands, and recruiting booths decked with tricolour bunting. From the window of her bedroom Lucile could hear Danton pursuing his own recruiting drive, the noisiest for miles. The first clear expression she saw on the baby's face looked very like exasperation. When she was well enough to travel she went out to the farm at Bourg-la-Reine. Camille came at the weekend and wrote a very long speech.

The General Council of the Commune met on 24 July to hear it. It was Danton's manifesto – universal suffrage and universal responsibility, the citizens of every Section empowered to assemble at any hour, to arm themselves, to mobilize themselves against subversion and imminent attack. When Camille predicted that the monarchy would fall within days, Danton folded his arms, exchanged glances with his nearest colleagues, and affected surprise.

'Thank you,' said Pierre Chaumette. 'That was what we wanted to hear.'

René Hébert nodded to him. He rubbed his fat white hands together, expressing satisfaction with the way things were going.

Outside City Hall there was a big crowd. It cheered deafeningly when Camille came out. Danton dropped a heavy hand on his shoulder, believing that such popularity should be shared around. 'This is different from a year ago,' Camille said, 'when we were on the run.' He waved to his well-wishers and blew them a kiss. The crowd laughed and jostled and pushed forward to touch him, as if he were lucky, a lucky charm. They threw up their red caps and began to sing the 'Ça Ira' in one of its bloodier versions. Then they sang this new song, the 'Marseillaise'.

'Strange beasts,' Danton said mildly. 'Let's hope they perform in a week or two.'

THE DUKE OF BRUNSWICK, the commander-in-chief of the Allies, issued a document, a manifesto, a statement of intent. He called upon the French people to lay down their arms and offer no resistance to the invading forces, which came to restore proper authority.

Any city that resisted would be laid waste. Every deputy, every National Guardsman and every public official in Paris should consider themselves personally responsible for the safety of the King and Queen. If any violence were offered to the royal family, all such persons would be court-martialled as soon as the allies entered Paris – and they need not hope for pardon. If June's attack on the Tuileries were repeated, the city of Paris would be utterly destroyed, and its inhabitants exterminated·by firing squads.

Danton stood with Caroline Rémy at an upper window at the Palais-Royal. Below, Camille was reading the allies' declaration to the crowd. 'Isn't he good?' Caroline said. 'I must say, Fabre has done a marvellous job there.'

'Brunswick has given us what we needed,' Danton said. 'Tell people that they're to be shot in mass executions, tell people that the Germans are going to pitch them into mass graves – then what have they got to lose?'

He slipped a hand around Caroline's waist, and she stroked the back of it with her fingers. Below, the people began to shout, chanting their decision at Europe, wave after wave of hilarity and defiance and rage.

[ZOPPI's, *on the rue des Fossés-Saint-Germain. One day in the long history of coffee house conspiracy.*]

DANTON: I think you all know each other.

LEGENDRE: Get on with it. 'Tisn't a dinner party.

DANTON: If anyone was in doubt, this is Legendre. This large gentleman's name is Westermann. He comes from Alsace originally, and we have been acquainted for some time. He is a former army officer.

FABRE [*to Camille*]: Long time since he was in the army. Small-time Palais-Royal crook.

CAMILLE: Just our sort.

DANTON: This is Antoine Fouquier-Tinville.

LEGENDRE: You remind me of somebody.

DANTON: Fouquier-Tinville is Camille's cousin.

LEGENDRE: Maybe a very slight resemblance.

FABRE: I don't see it myself.

HÉRAULT: Perhaps they're very distant cousins.

FABRE: You don't have to look like your relations.

HÉRAULT: Perhaps he can speak.

FABRE: Perhaps you have an opinion to offer, Camille's cousin?

FOUQUIER: Fouquier.

HÉRAULT: Good heavens, you don't expect us to learn your name? We shall always call you 'Camille's cousin'. It will be easy for us, and humiliating for you.

FRÉRON [*to Fouquier*]: Your cousin's weird.

FABRE: He's a mass-murderer.

FRÉRON: He's a satanist.

FABRE: He's learning poisoning.

HÉRAULT: And Hebrew.

FRÉRON: He commits adultery.

HÉRAULT: He's a bloody disgrace.

[*Pause.*]

FABRE: See? He hasn't a spark of cousinly feeling.

FRÉRON: Where's your family pride?

FOUQUIER [*indifferently*]: It might all be true. I haven't seen Camille for a long time.

FRÉRON: Some of it is true. The adultery, and the Hebrew.

FABRE: He might be a satanist. I saw him talking to de Sade once.

HÉRAULT: De Sade isn't a satanist.

FABRE: Oh, I thought he was.

HÉRAULT: Why are you learning Hebrew, Camille?

CAMILLE: It has to do with my work on the Church Fathers.

DANTON: Oh God.

CAMILLE [*whispering to Hérault*]: Notice how close together his eyes are. His first wife died in mysterious circumstances.

HÉRAULT [*whispering*]: Is that true?

CAMILLE: I never make things up.

DANTON: M. Fouquier expresses himself ready to do anything.

HÉRAULT: He's definitely related to Camille.

LEGENDRE: Can we get on with the planning? [*To Fouquier*] They treat me like an imbecile. It's because I've got no formal education.

Your cousin makes snide remarks about me in foreign languages.

FOUQUIER: Ones you don't speak?

LEGENDRE: Yes.

FOUQUIER: How do you know then?

LEGENDRE: Are you a lawyer?

FOUQUIER: Yes.

DANTON: I'd say about a week now.

MOUSSEAUX, the residence of the Duke of Orléans: a lack of conviviality, not to say a bleakness, at the Duke's supper table. Charles-Alexis looked discomfited – whether because of the pâté, or royalist intimidation, the Duke could not say. His unhappy eyes travelled over the pigeon breasts, boned, stuffed with asparagus and morels; they travelled over his guests, and alighted on Robespierre. He looked much as he had in '89, the Duke thought: same impeccably cut coat (same coat in fact), same correctly powdered hair. It must be rather different, Philippe thought, from the carpenter's dinner table. Did he sit so upright there, did he eat so little, did he make mental notes? By his glass of wine there was a glass of water. The Duke leaned forward almost timidly, and touched his arm.

PHILIPPE: I feel . . . perhaps things have gone wrong . . . the royalists are very strong . . . the danger is immediate. I mean to leave for England, I beg you to come with me.

DANTON: I'll cut the throat of any bastard that pulls out now. The fucking thing's organized. We're going through with it.

PÉTION: My dear Danton, there are certain problems.

DANTON: And you're one. Your people just want the King to give them their ministries back, then they'll be happy. That's as far as they're interested in going.

PÉTION: I don't know what you mean by 'my people'. I am not a member of any faction. Factions and parties are injurious to democracy.

DANTON: Tell Brissot. Don't tell me.

PÉTION: The defence of the palace is being organized right now. There are three hundred gentlemen ready to defend it.

DANTON: Gentlemen? I'm terrified.

PÉTION: I'm just telling you.

DANTON: The more the merrier. They'll be tripping over each other when they faint.

PÉTION: We haven't enough cartridges.

DANTON: I'll get you some from the police.

PÉTION: What, officially?

DANTON: I am First Deputy Public Prosecutor. I can manage a simple thing like cartridges, for God's sake.

PÉTION: There are nine hundred Swiss Guard at the palace, and I'm told they're very good fighting men and loyal to Capet and that they won't give up.

DANTON: Make sure they're not allowed to stock up on ammunition. Come on, Pétion, these are just technicalities.

PÉTION: There is the problem of the National Guard. We know that many individual Guardsmen support us, but they won't just break ranks, they have to act under orders, or we're in a totally unpredictable situation. We made a mistake when we allowed the Marquis de Mandat to take over as commander. He's an out-and-out royalist.

[*Philippe thinks, we'll have to stop using the word in that condemnatory sense, when I become King.*]

PÉTION: We'll have to remove Mandat.

DANTON: What do you mean, remove him? Kill him, man, kill him. The dead can't come back.

[*Silence.*]

DANTON: Technicalities.

CAMILLE DESMOULINS:

For the establishment of liberty and the safety of the nation, one day of anarchy will do more than ten years of National Assemblies.

MME ELISABETH:

There's nothing to worry about. M. Danton will look after us.

V. *Burning the Bodies*

(1792)

AUGUST 7: 'Gone?' Fabre said. 'Danton's gone?'

Catherine Motin rolled her eyes. 'Listen to me once more, Monsieur. Mme Danton has gone to Fontenay to her parents, and M. Danton has gone to Arcis. If you don't believe me you can step around the corner and ask M. Desmoulins. Because I've already had the same conversation with him.'

Fabre tore out of the street door and through the Cour du Commerce and on to the rue des Cordeliers, then into the other door of the same building and up the stairs. He thought, why don't Georges-Jacques and Camille knock a hole through the wall? Really, it would be easier if we lived under one roof.

Lucile was sitting with her feet up, reading a novel and eating an orange. 'Here you are,' she said, offering him a segment.

'Where is he?' Fabre demanded.

'Georges-Jacques? Gone to Arcis.'

'But why, why, why? Mother of God! Where's Camille?'

'He's lying on our bed. I think he's crying.'

Fabre burst into the bedroom, stuffing the segment of orange into his mouth. He hurled himself at the bed and Camille. 'No, please, don't, please,' Camille said. He covered his head with his hands. 'Don't beat me up, Fabre, I feel ill. I can't take this.'

'What's Danton up to? Come on, you must know.'

'He's gone to see his mother. His mother. I didn't know till this morning. No message, no letter, nothing. I can't cope.'

'The fat bastard,' Fabre said. 'I bet he's planning to stay away.'

'I'm going to kill myself,' Camille said.

Fabre rolled from the bed. He propelled himself back into the drawing room. 'I can't get any sense out of him. He says he's going to kill himself. What shall we do?'

Lucile inserted her bookmark and laid her novel aside. It was clear that she would get no further with it. 'Georges told me he would be back, and I have no reason to disbelieve him – but perhaps you'd like to sit down here and write him a letter? Tell him you can't manage the thing without him, which is true. Tell him *Robespierre says* he can't get along without him. And when you're done, you might go and find Robespierre and ask him to call. He is such a steadying influence when Camille is killing himself.'

SURE ENOUGH, 9 August, nine a.m., Danton is back. 'No point in being in a temper with me. A man must settle his affairs. It's a dangerous business, this.'

'Your affairs have been settled more times than I can count,' Fabre said.

'Well, you see, I keep on getting richer.'

He kissed his wife on top of her head. 'Will you unpack for me, Gabrielle?'

'You have got that right?' Fabre said. 'Unpack, not pack?'

Camille said, 'We thought you'd run out on us again.'

'What do you mean, again?' He grabbed Camille by the wrist and pulled him across the room, scooped up his small son Antoine in one arm. 'Oh, I have missed you, my loves,' he said. 'It's been all of two days. Why are you here, hm?' he asked the child. 'You should be out of town.'

'He cried to come home,' Gabrielle said. 'I couldn't settle him last night till I promised he'd see you today. My mother is coming to fetch him this afternoon.'

'Splendid woman, splendid. Child-minding in the cannon's mouth.'

'Will you stop being so bloody hearty?' Camille asked. 'You make me feel sick.'

'Country air,' Danton said. 'Got lots of energy now. You should get out of Paris more often. Poor Camille.' Danton pulled Camille's head into his shoulder and stroked his hair. 'He's scared, scared, scared.'

*

TWELVE NOON. 'Only twelve hours now,' Danton said. 'I give you my word.'

TWO P.M. Marat came. He looked dirtier than ever. As if in sympathy with his work, his skin had taken on the colour of poor-quality newsprint.

'There are other places we could have met,' Danton said. 'I didn't ask you here. I don't want my wife and child given nightmares.'

'You will be pleased to invite me, afterwards. Besides, who knows – I might clean myself up under the republic. Now,' he said briskly. (He always allowed a certain amount of time for personal abuse.) 'Now. I suspect the Brissotins of trying to make a deal with the Court. They have been talking to Antoinette, and this I can prove. Nothing they do at this stage can harm us, but the question arises of what we do with them afterwards.'

This word keeps intruding into conversations: *afterwards*.

Danton shook his head. 'I find it hard to believe. Roland's wife wouldn't be party to a deal. She got them kicked out of office, remember? I can't see her talking to Antoinette.'

'Lying, am I?' Marat said.

'I admit that some of them would be willing to negotiate. They want their positions back. It just goes to show that there's no such thing as a Brissotin.'

'Only when it suits us,' Marat said.

FOUR P.M., the rue des Cordeliers: 'But you can't just say "Goodbye".' Camille was aghast. 'You can't turn up in the middle of a sunny afternoon and say, I've enjoyed knowing you for twenty years, now I'm off to get killed.'

'Well, you can,' Louis Suleau said, unsteadily. 'It seems that you can.'

He'd had a kind of luck, the chronicler of the *Acts of the Apostles*. In '89, '90, the mobs might have killed him; they were the mobs the Lanterne Attorney had driven on. 'Whenever I pass a lamppost,' he had written, 'I see it stretch out towards me, covetously.'

Camille looked at him in silence, stunned – though he must have known, must have expected it. Louis had been over the border, in

the *émigré* camps; why would he be back in Paris now, if he were
not bent on some suicidal gesture?

'You have taken risks yourself,' Louis said. 'I don't need to tell
you why one does it. I've given up trying to make you a royalist.
At least we have that in common – we stick to our principles. I am
prepared to die in the defence of the palace, but who knows, the
King may have the best of it. We may have a victory yet.'

'Your victory would be my death.'

'I don't want that,' Louis said.

'You're a hypocrite. You must want it. You can't pursue a course
and then disown the natural consequences of it.'

'I'm not pursuing a course. I'm keeping faith.'

'With that sad fat fool? Nobody who aspires to be taken seriously
could be dying for Louis Capet. There's something ludicrous about
it.'

Louis looked away. 'I don't know . . . perhaps in the end I agree
with you. But it can't be avoided any longer.'

Camille made a gesture of irritation. 'Of course it can be avoided.
Go back to your apartment and burn anything you think might be
incriminating. Be very careful, because you notice that as the Revolution goes on there are new crimes. Pack only what you need, you
mustn't look as if you're going anywhere. Later you can give me
your keys and I'll see to everything after – I mean, next week.
Don't come back here, we have several of the Marseille men invited
for an early supper. Go to Annette Duplessis, stay there till I come.
When you get there sit down and prepare for me a very clear
statement of how you want your financial affairs to be handled. But
dictate it, it shouldn't be in your own hand, my father-in-law will
take it down for you and he will give you his advice. Don't sign it,
and don't leave it lying around. Meanwhile I'll get you a passport
and some papers. You speak English, don't you?'

'You've really got into the habit of giving orders. One would
suppose you were used to banishing people.'

'For God's sake, Louis.'

'Thank you, but no.'

'Then –' he was pleading – 'if you won't do that – just come back here at nine o'clock this evening, I'll divert people tomorrow. You won't be seen. At least you'll have a chance.'

'But Camille, the risk to you – you could get into trouble, terrible trouble.'

'You won't come, will you?'

'No.'

'Then why enlarge on the theme?'

'Because I'm afraid of what may happen to you. You have no duty to me. We found ourselves – no, we *put* ourselves – on opposite sides. I never expected, I never dreamed, that our friendship could last so long with circumstances as they are.'

'You didn't think that once – you laughed, and said people were above politics.'

'I know. "Liberty, Gaiety, Royal Democracy". I believed in my slogan, but I don't any more. There won't be any royalty and personally I think precious little liberty and there'll always be war and civil war, so I don't give gaiety much of a chance either. You must see that from now on – after tomorrow, I mean – personal loyalty will count for very little in people's lives.'

'You are asking me to accept that because of the Revolution – because of what you suppose the Revolution to be – I must stand by while someone I love is destroyed by his own stupidity.'

'I don't want you to think about it, afterwards.'

'I'll stop you doing this. I'll have you arrested tonight. I won't let you kill yourself.'

'You wouldn't be doing me a favour. I've cheated the Lanterne so far, and I don't want to be dragged out of prison and lynched. That's not a death fit for a human being. I know that you could have me arrested. But it would be a betrayal.'

'Of?'

'Of principle.'

'Am I a principle to you, and are you a principle to me?'

'Ask Robespierre,' Louis said wearily. 'Ask the man with the conscience which is more important, your friend or your country – ask him how he weighs an individual in the scheme of things. Ask him which comes first, his old pals or his new principles. You ask him, Camille.' He stood up. 'I wondered whether I should come here at all – whether it might make difficulties for you.'

'No one can make difficulties for me. There is no authority that can do it.'

'No, I suppose it is coming to that. Camille, I'm sorry I never saw your little boy.'

He held his hand out. Camille turned away from it. Louis said, 'Father Bérardier is in prison, love. Will you see if you can get him out?'

His face averted, Camille said, 'This supper with the Marseille people will be over by 8.30, always assuming that they don't sing. After that I'll be with Danton, wherever he is. You could go to his apartment at any time. Neither he nor his wife would give you away.'

'I don't know Danton. I've seen him, of course, but I've never spoken with him.'

'You don't have to have *spoken* with him. Just tell him I want you safe. That you're one of my whims.'

'Would you look at me?'

'No.'

'Are you pretending to be Lot's wife?'

Camille smiled, turned. The door closed.

'I DON'T THINK I should try to get back to Fontenay,' Angélique said. 'Victor will put me up. Would you like to go and see your uncle?'

'No,' Antoine said.

Danton laughed. 'He's a fighter, he wants to stay.'

'Will they be safe at Victor's?' Gabrielle looked ill, sallow with strain.

'Yes, yes, yes. Would I let them go otherwise? Ah, Lolotte, there you are.'

Lucile swirled across the room, put her hands on Danton's shoulders. 'Stop looking worried,' she said. 'We'll win. I know it.'

'You've had too much champagne.'

'I am indulged.'

He dropped his head to whisper into her hair, 'I wish you were mine to indulge.' She pulled away, laughing.

'How can you?' Gabrielle demanded. 'How can you laugh?'

'Why not, Gabrielle? I'm sure we'll all be crying soon enough. Perhaps tonight.'

'What do you want to take?' Angélique asked the little boy loudly. 'Do you want to take your spinning-top? Yes. I think perhaps you do.'

'Keep him warm,' Gabrielle said automatically.

'My dear girl, it's stifling, he's more likely to suffocate than take cold.'

'All right, Mother. I know.'

'Walk a little way with her,' Danton said. 'It's still light.'

'I don't want to.'

'Oh, come.' Lucile hauled her bodily from her chair. Angélique was faintly annoyed. All these years, and her daughter had still not learned when men wanted to get rid of women. Was it an incapacity, or a constantly stated objection to the situation? At the door Angélique turned. 'I suppose it's needless to say take care, Georges?' She nodded to Camille, and shepherded the younger women out.

'What a way to put it,' Danton said. From the window they watched the child's progress across the Cour du Commerce, great leaps sustained by the arms of his mother and grandmother. 'He wants to get round the corner without his feet touching the ground.'

'What a good idea,' Camille said.

'You don't look happy, Camille.'

'Louis Suleau came.'

'Ah.'

'He intends to join the resistance at the palace.'

'More fool him.'

'I told him to come here if he changes his mind. Was that the right thing to do?'

'Risky, but morally impeccable.'

'Any problems?'

'None so far. Seen Robespierre?'

'No.'

'If you do, keep him out of my way. I don't want him at my elbow tonight. I may have to do things that will offend his delicate sense of propriety.' He paused. 'We can count the hours now.'

AT THE TUILERIES the courtiers prepared for the ceremony of the King's *coucher*. They greeted each other formally, in the time-honoured way. Here was the blue-blood who received the royal stockings, warm from the royal calf; here was the grandee whose task was to turn down the royal coverlet; here was the thoroughbred who handed – as his father did before him, his father before that – the royal nightshirt, and assisted Louis Capet to settle it about his blue-white, corpulent torso.

They followed Louis's slumped shoulders, arranging themselves to enter the bedchamber in the due order. But the King turned to them his pale, full, anxious face – and slammed the door on them.

The aristocrats stood looking at each other. Only then did the enormity of events become plain. 'There is no precedent for it,' they whispered.

LUCILE touched Gabrielle's hand, for comfort. There were a dozen people in the apartment, and a stack of firearms on the floor. 'Bring more lights,' Danton said, and Catherine brought them, dough-faced, eyes averted, so that new shadows danced across the ceiling and walls.

Louise Robert said, 'Can I stay here, Gabrielle?' She wound her shawl about her, as if she were cold.

Gabrielle nodded. 'Must these guns stay here?'

'Yes, they must. Don't go tidying them up, woman.'

Lucile threaded her way across the room to her husband. They spoke in low, small voices. Then she turned away, calling Georges, Georges; her head ached now, that fuzzy champagne kind of headache that you feel you could brush away, and there was a knot of tension in her throat. Without looking at her Danton broke off his conversation with Fréron, put an arm around her and pulled her close to him. 'I know, I know,' he said. 'But you must be strong, Lolotte, you are not a silly girl, you must look after the others.' His face was distant, and she wanted all his attention, to fix herself finally in his mind, her priority, her need. But he might have been down the street somewhere; his mind was at the Tuileries, at City Hall, and his mouth issued automatic words of comfort.

'Please take care of Camille,' she said. 'Please don't let anything happen to him.'

He looked down at her now, sombre, giving her request consideration; he wanted to give her an honest answer.

'Keep him with you,' she said. 'I beg of you, Georges.'

Fréron put a hand on her elbow, tentative; her arm shrank away from it. 'Lolotte, we all look out for each other,' he said. 'It's the best we can do.'

She said, 'I want nothing from you, Rabbit. You just take care of yourself.'

'Listen now.' Danton's blue eyes fixed her, and she thought she heard those familiar words, I am going to speak to you as if you were grown up. But he did not say that. 'Listen now, when you married Camille you knew what it meant. You have to choose, a safe life, or a life in the Revolution. But do you think I would ask him to take any unnecessary risk?' His eyes travelled to the clock, and she followed them. We shall measure our survival by that clock, she thought. It had been a wedding-gift to Gabrielle; its hands were pointed, delicate fleur-de-lis. '86, '87. Georges had been King's Councillor. Camille had been in love with her mother. She had been sixteen. Danton touched her forehead with his scarred lips. 'Victory would be ashes,' he said. He could of course have driven a bargain with her. But he was not that sort of man.

Fréron picked up a gun. 'For my part,' he said, 'I wouldn't be sorry if it ended tonight.' He glanced at Lucile. 'I see little point in my life as I live it now.'

Camille's voice across the room, acidly solicitous: 'Rabbit, I didn't realize you felt like that, is there anything I can do?'

Someone sniggered. Lucile thought, I can't help it if you're in love with me, you should have more sense, you do not hear Hérault saying his life is over, you do not hear Arthur Dillon say it, they know when a game is a game. This is no game, now; this has nothing to do with love. She raised her hand to Camille. She felt she ought to salute. Then she turned away and walked into the bedroom. She left the door slightly ajar; a little light penetrated from other rooms, and the odd muted syllable of conversation. She sat down on a couch, leaned back, and began to doze – a post-party doze, full of fragmentary dreams.

'THE GREAT COUNCIL CHAMBER, Monsieur.' Pétion was making for the royal apartments, sash of office round substantial chest. The aristocrats removed themselves from his path as he walked.

He reached the outer galleries. 'May I inquire why all you gentlemen are standing around?' His tone suggested that he was addressing performing apes, and did not expect an answer.

The first ape who stepped forward was at least eighty years old – a quavering, paper-tissue ape, with orders of chivalry, which Pétion could not identify, gleaming on his breast. He made a courteous little bow. 'M. Mayor, one does not *sit* in or near the royal apartments. Unless specifically commanded to do so. Did you not know this?'

He cast a glance of distress at his companions. A small ceremonial sword hung at his withered shank. They all wore them, all the trained apes. Pétion snorted and strode on.

The King looked dazed; he was accustomed to a long sleep, to his regular hours. Antoinette sat very upright, her Hapsburg jaw clenched; she looked precisely as Pétion had expected her to look. Pierre-Louis Roederer, a high official of the Seine *département*, was standing by her chair. He was holding three massive bound volumes and talking to the Marquis de Mandat, commander-in-chief of the National Guard.

Pétion bowed, but not profoundly; not in any sense obsequiously.

PÉTION: What's that you have there, Roederer? You're not going to need law books tonight.

ROEDERER: I wondered, if it became necessary to declare martial

law within the city boundaries, whether the *département* has the
authority to do it.

MME ELISABETH: Has it?

ROEDERER: I don't think so, Madame.

PÉTION: I have that authority.

ROEDERER: Yes, but I thought I'd check in case you were – detained
in some way.

KING [*heavily*]: As on 20 June.

PÉTION: Forget your law books. Throw them away. Burn them.
Eat them. Or you might like to keep them to hit people over the
head with. Better than those toothpicks they're all wearing.

MANDAT: Pétion, you do grasp the fact that you're legally
responsible for the defence of the palace?

PÉTION: Defence against what?

QUEEN: The insurrection is being organized under your very eyes.

MANDAT: We have no ammunition.

PÉTION: What, none at all?

MANDAT: Not nearly enough.

PÉTION: How improvident.

GABRIELLE sat down with a rustle of skirts. Lucile woke with a
gasp. 'It's only me,' Gabrielle said. 'They've gone.'

Louise Robert sank to the floor in front of her, took both her
hands and squeezed them. 'Will they ring the tocsin?' Lucile asked.

'Yes. Very soon.'

Anticipation tightened the back of her neck. She put up a hand
to her face and tears spilled between her fingers.

AT MIDNIGHT Danton came back. Gabrielle jumped up in alarm
when they heard his footsteps, and they scurried after her into the
drawing room.

'Why are you back so soon?'

'I told you I would be. If everything's going smoothly, I said, I'll
be back for midnight. Why do you never believe anything I say?'

'Then it is going smoothly?' Louise demanded. He looked at
them, irritated. They were his problems.

'Of course. Or would I be here?'

'Where's François? Where have you sent him?'

'How the hell do I know where he is? If he's where I left him, he's at City Hall. And the place isn't on fire, and there's no shooting.'

'But what are you *doing*?'

He resigned himself. 'There is a large body of patriots at City Hall. They are shortly going to take over from the existing Commune and call themselves the Insurrectionary Commune. Then the patriots will have *de facto* control of the city.'

Gabrielle: 'What does *de facto* mean?'

'It means they'll do it now and make it legal later,' Lucile said.

Danton laughed. 'Your turn of phrase, these days, Madame! We can tell what marriage has done for you.'

Louise Robert said, 'Don't patronize us, Danton. We understand what the plan is, we just want to know whether it's working or not.'

'I'm going to get some sleep,' Danton said. He walked into the bedroom they had just left and slammed the door. Fully clothed, he lay down: staring at the ceiling, waiting for the tocsin to ring, waiting for the alarm signal that would bring the people surging out into the streets. The clock struck; it was 10 August.

PERHAPS TWO HOURS LATER, they heard someone at the door; and Lucile shadowed Gabrielle as she answered it.

There was a little group of men outside. They had been very quiet on the stairs. One stepped forward: 'Antoine Fouquier-Tinville. For Danton, if you please.' His courtesy was automatic and very brisk; courtroom politeness.

Gabrielle stood aside. 'Must I wake him?'

'Yes, we need him now, my dear. It's time.'

She indicated the bedroom. Fouquier-Tinville inclined his head to Lucile. 'Good morning, cousin.'

She nodded nervously. Fouquier had Camille's thick dark hair and dark skin; but the hair was straight, the face was hard, the lips were thin and set for crises, for bad situations becoming worse.

Possible, yes, to trace a family likeness. But when you saw Camille you wanted to touch him; when you saw his cousin, that was not your reaction.

Gabrielle followed the men into the bedroom. Lucile turned to Louise Robert, opened her mouth to make some usual kind of remark: was shocked by the violence in her face. 'If anything happens to François, I'll put a knife in that pig myself.'

Lucile's eyes widened. The King? No: Danton was the pig she meant. She could not think of an answer.

'Did you see that man? Fouquier-Tinville? Camille says all his relations are like that.'

They heard Danton's voice, intermittently, between the others: 'Fouquier — first thing tomorrow — but WAIT — and getting to the Tuileries at the right time, Pétion should know — cannon on the bridges — tell him to hurry it up.

He came out, hauling his cravat into place, skimming his fingers over his blueish chin. 'Georges-Jacques,' Lucile said, 'what an unregarding tough you look. A proper man of the people, I do declare.'

Danton grinned. He put a hand on her shoulder, squeezed it; so jovially, so painfully, that she almost cried out. 'I'm going now. City Hall. Otherwise they'll keep running up here —' He paused at the door. He was not going to kiss his wife and have her start crying. 'Lolotte, you look after things here. Try not to worry too much.' They heard him striding down the stairs.

'ALL RIGHT, little man?'

'I am impervious,' Jean-Paul Marat said, 'to bullets and your wit.'

'You look even worse at this hour.'

'The Revolution does not value me for my decorative qualities, Danton. Nor you, I believe. Men of action, that's what we are, aren't we?' As usual, Marat seemed to be deeply entertained by some private joke. 'Get Mandat here,' he said.

'Is he still at the palace? Message to Mandat,' Danton said over his shoulder. 'My compliments to him, and the Commune requests his presence urgently at City Hall.'

From the Place de Grève, the roar of the growing crowd. Danton splashed some brandy into a glass and stood cradling it in his palm. He reached up to loosen the cravat he had wasted his time in tightening, at home in the Cour du Commerce. The pulse jumped at the side of his neck. His mouth was dry. A wave of nausea welled inside him. He took another sip from the glass. The nausea abated.

THE QUEEN extended her hand and Mandat kissed it. 'I shall never come back,' he said. It was the sort of thing to say. 'Order to the commander of the Place de Grève duty battalion. Attack from the rear and disperse the mob marching on the palace.' He scrawled a signature. His horse was waiting. The duty commander had the order within minutes. At City Hall, Mandat went straight to his own office. He was ordered to make his report, but so far as he could discern there was no proper authority to report to. He toyed with the notion of locking his door. But it seemed an unsoldierly thing to do.

'Rossignol,' said Danton, 'thank you.' He glanced over Mandat's order, which the district police commissioner had put into his hand. 'Let us step along the corridor, and ask Mandat to explain to the new Commune why he has deployed armed force against the people.'

'I REFUSE,' Mandat said.

'You refuse.'

'Those people are not the municipal government. They are not the Commune. They are rebels. They are criminals.'

'I shall compound their crimes,' Danton said. He reached forward and took Mandat by the front of his coat, hauling him by physical force from the room. Rossignol leaned forward and deftly confiscated the Marquis's rapier; he turned its hilt in his fingers and grimaced.

Outside the room Mandat looked up into a ring of hostile faces. He became limp with terror. 'Not now,' Danton said. 'Not yet, my friends. You can leave this to me, I don't need help.' He tightened his grip. 'Keep refusing, Mandat,' he said, and began to drag him towards the Throne Room, where the new Commune had assembled. He laughed. It was like being a child again – the licensed brutality, when the issues are simple.

FIVE A.M. Antoinette: 'There is no hope.'

FIVE A.M. Gabrielle began to tremble and shiver. 'I'm going to be sick,' she said. Louise Robert sprinted off for a basin, and held it while Lucile lifted Gabrielle's hair from her shoulders and smoothed it back from her brow. When she had finished her unproductive retching they eased her back on to a sofa, placed the basin inconspicuously at hand, tucked cushions under the small of her back and dabbed her temples with handkerchiefs soaked in lavender-water. 'Well, you probably guessed,' Gabrielle said. 'I'm pregnant again.'

'Oh, Gabrielle!'

'People usually say congratulations,' she said mildly.

'Oh, but so soon,' Lucile moaned.

'Well, what do you do?' Louise Robert shrugged. 'It's either you get pregnant, or you use English overcoats, don't you, take your choice.'

'What are English overcoats?' Gabrielle said, looking glassily from one to the other.

'Oh really!' Louise was scornful. 'What does *de facto* mean? What are English overcoats? Right little noble savage we've got here, Lucile.'

'I'm sorry,' Gabrielle said. 'I can't keep up with your conversation.'

'No point trying,' Lucile said. 'Rémy knows all about English overcoats, but they are not things that married men will entertain. Especially Georges-Jacques, I imagine.'

'I don't think we really want to know what you imagine, Mme Desmoulins,' Louise said. 'Not in this context.'

A tear quivered on the end of Gabrielle's lashes. 'I don't mind being pregnant, really. He's always very pleased. And you get used to it.'

'The way things are going,' Louise said, 'you'll have eight, nine, ten. When's it due?'

'February, I think. It seems such a long way off.'

'Go home. Sleep. Two hours.'

The hideous flare of the torches at three o'clock: the oaths of the fighting men above the creak and rumble of the cannon on the move.

'Sleep?' Camille said. 'It would be a novelty. Shall I find you at the palace?'

Danton breathed spirits into his face. 'No, why at the palace? Santerre is in control of the National Guard, we have Westermann, he's a professional, leave it to him. Can I never impress upon you that there is no need to take these personal risks?'

Camille slumped against the wall and covered his face with his hands. 'Fat lawyers sitting in rooms,' he said. 'It is very exciting.'

'It's quite exciting enough for any normal person,' Danton said. He wanted to beg, will it be all right, will we make it, will we see sunrise? 'Oh Christ, Camille, go home,' he said. 'What I violently object to is your hair tied up with that piece of string.'

THE MARQUIS DE MANDAT had been interrogated by the new Commune, and locked up in a room at City Hall. At first light, Danton suggested that he should be taken to the Abbaye prison. He stood by a window to watch him led down the steps, flanked by a strong guard.

He nodded to Rossignol. Rossignol leaned out of the window and shot Mandat dead.

'COME ON,' Lucile said. 'Change of scene.' The three women picked up their effects, locked the doors, went downstairs and out into the Cour du Commerce. They would walk around to Lucile's apartment, to the prison of waiting in another place. No one around; and the air was fresh, even chilly. An hour from now, there would be the promise of heat. Lucile thought, I have never been so alive as I am now: this poor betrayed cow, leaning on my right shoulder, this bird-boned virago leaning on my left. The dead weight, the flyer; she had to coordinate their steps up the stairs.

The servant Jeanette did her best to look shocked when she saw them. 'Make up a bed for Mme Danton,' Lucile said. Jeanette tucked her under a quilt, on one of the drawing-room sofas; Gabrielle, willing to be babied for once, let her head fall back on to the cushions while Louise Robert took out her hairpins and let the warm dark cloak of hair spread over the sofa's arm and tumble to the carpet. Lucile brought her hairbrush, and knelt like a penitent, smoothing long easy strokes through the electric mane; Gabrielle lay with her eyes closed, *hors de combat*. Louise Robert edged on to the blue *chaise-longue*, inched to the back of it, drew her feet up. Jeanette brought her a blanket. 'Your mother is rarely fond of this piece of furniture,' she told Lucile. 'She always said, you never know when you'll be glad of it.'

'If you want anything, call me.' Lucile trailed towards her bedroom; did a detour, to pick up a bottle that contained three inches of flat champagne. She was tempted to drink it, but then reflected that there was nothing more unpleasant. It seemed a week since these bottles were opened.

The very thought made her queasy. Jeanette came up behind her; she jumped violently. 'Lie down now, my sweetheart,' the woman said. 'You won't make any difference by trying to stay upright.' The grim set of her mouth said: I love him too, you know.

AT 6 A.M. THE KING decided to inspect the National Guard. He descended to the courtyards of the palace. He wore a sad purple coat, and carried his hat under his arm. It was an unhappy business. The noblemen outside his suite dropped to their knees as he approached and murmured their words of allegiance; but the National Guardsmen insulted him, and a gunner shook a fist in his face.

RUE SAINT-HONORÉ: 'Some breakfast?' said Eléonore Duplay.

'I don't think so, Eléonore.'

'Max, why not eat?'

'Because I never eat at this hour,' Robespierre said. 'At this hour I answer my letters.'

Babette at the door. Round morning face. 'Father sent this up. Danton is signing proclamations at City Hall.'

Robespierre let the document lie on his desk. He did not touch it, but ran his eyes to the signature. 'In the name of the nation – DANTON.'

'So Danton claims to speak for the nation?' Eléonore said. She watched his face.

'Danton is an excellent patriot. Only – I thought he would have sent for me by now.'

'They dare not risk your life.'

Robespierre looked up. 'Oh no, that's not it. I think Danton doesn't want me to – what shall we say? – study his methods.'

'That may be so,' Eléonore agreed. What did it matter? She would say anything: anything that would keep him safe behind Duplay's wall, that would keep his heart beating till tomorrow and tomorrow and the day after that.

IT WAS PERHAPS 7.30 in the morning when the patriots trained their big guns on the palace. Behind those guns were all the weapons the Insurrectionary Commune could find: muskets, sabres, cutlasses, and rank upon rank of the sacred pike. The rebel thousands sang the 'Marseillaise'.

Louis: What do they want?

Camille slept for an hour with his head on his wife's shoulder.

'DANTON.' Roederer looked up at the apparition blocking the doorway. 'Danton, you're drunk.'

'I've been drinking to keep awake.'

'What do you want?' With me, Roederer meant. His fright showed clearly on his face. 'Danton, I am not a royalist, whatever you may think. I was at the Tuileries because I was commanded there. But I hope you and your commanders know what you're doing. You must understand that the carnage will be terrible. The Swiss will fight to the last man.'

'So I'm told,' Danton said. 'I want you to go back there.'

'Back?' Roederer gaped at him.

'I want you to get the King out.'

'Out?'

'Stop repeating what I say, imbecile. I want you to get the King out and in doing so force him to abandon the defence. I want you to go back now and tell Louis and tell Antoinette that they'll be dead within hours unless they leave the palace, call off the resistance and put themselves under the protection of the Assembly.'

'You want to save them? Do I understand you?'

'I believe I'm making myself plain.'

'But how am I to do it? They won't listen to me.'

'You must tell them that once the mob gets into the palace there is nothing I can do. The devil himself won't be able to save them then.'

'But you *want* to save them?'

'This is becoming tedious. We must have the King and the Dauphin at all costs. The others matter less, though I dislike seeing women harmed.'

'Costs,' the lawyer repeated. Something seemed to take shape in his tired brain. 'Costs, Danton. Now I see.'

Danton launched himself across the room. He grabbed Roederer's coat-front and wrapped a hand round the man's throat. 'You will bring them out or you will answer to me. I shall be watching you, Roederer.'

Choking, Roederer put out a hand, clawing at Danton's arm. The room was spinning. I shall die, he thought. He struggled for breath and his ears roared. Danton flung him to the floor. 'That was the first cannon fire. They are attacking the palace now.'

Roederer looked up, propping himself weakly on one arm, along the column of Danton's heavy body to his savage face. 'Now get them out for me.'

'A CLOTHESBRUSH, I think,' Camille said. 'We are supposed to be distinguishing ourselves from the rabble. So Danton says.' He looped the tricolour sash over his shoulder. 'Am I presentable?'

'Oh, you could take your morning chocolate with a duchess. Supposing there were one left to take it with. But what now?' Lucile could not keep the fear off her face for long.

Louise and Gabrielle were waiting for news. He had been uncommunicative, when he came in.

'Georges-Jacques intends to remain at City Hall, in control of operations. François is there too, working away in the next office.'

Louise: 'Will he be safe?'

'Well, apart from a great earthquake, and the sun going black, and the moon becoming as blood, and the heavens departing as a scroll when it is rolled together, and the coming of the seven last angels with the seven last plagues – all of which is an ever-present risk, I agree – I can't see much going wrong for him. We'll all be safe, as long as we win.'

'And at the palace?' Gabrielle said.

'Oh, at the palace they'll be killing people by now.'

ANTOINETTE: We still have a defence here.

ROEDERER: Madame, all Paris is marching on you. Do you wish to be responsible for the massacre of the King, of yourself and your children?

ANTOINETTE: God forbid.

ROEDERER: Time presses, Sire.

LOUIS: Gentlemen, I beg you to abandon a futile defence, and withdraw. There's nothing to be done here, either for you or for me. Let's go.

THE ACCOUNT of Thomas Blaikie, a Scottish gardener employed at the French court:

But all seemed to prepaire for the great catostrophe of the 10th August and many people wished a Change and they talked of people come from Marsielles to attact the Thuilleries; this seemed a projected affaire and the Thuileries was garded by the Suisse gardes and many more in Suisse dress was expecting to take part with the King. The night before we was nearly informed of what was to happen although non could emagine how it was to turn; the evening of the 9 by the fall of a Bottle from the wall which happened to cut my leg and render me lame so that I was forced to sit on our Terrasse which was opposite the Champs Elize and the Thuileries, where I could hear the first coup de Cannon about 9 and then the other firing and tumult continued. I could see the people running to and fro in the Champs Elize and the horror of the misacre increased and as the King left his gardes and went to the Nationalle assembly, so that those poor wretches that had come to defend him being deserted by him was left to be misacred by the rabble, whereas if the King had stopt there was the greatest part of the Sections ready to defend him; but when they found he had gone to the Assembly they all turned to the mesacre of the poor Suisse gardes ... Many of these anthrophages passed in the Street and stoppt to show us parts of the Suisses they had misacred some of whom I knew ... every one seemed to glory in what he had done and to show even their fury on the dead body by cutting them or even tearing their clothes as monuments of triumph, so that this seemed as if the people were struck with a sort of Madness ... But it was impossible to describe all the acts of wanten horor that happened this day ...

'CAMILLE.' A young National Guardsman whom he'd never seen before, pop-eyed with nervousness and expecting to be slapped down. 'We have taken a royalist patrol, they were dressed in our uniforms, we have them shut in our guardroom at the Cour de Feuillants. Some people are trying to take them off us. Our commander has asked for reinforcements to clear the courtyard but no one has come. We can't hold them back much longer – can you talk to this rabble, can you talk some sense into them?'

'What is the point?' Fréron said.

'People shouldn't be killed like dogs, Monsieur,' the boy said to Fréron. His mouth trembled.

'I'm coming,' Camille said.

WHEN THEY REACHED the courtyard, Fréron pointed: 'Théroigne.'

'Yes,' Camille said calmly. 'She'll get killed.'

Théroigne had taken charge; here was her own, her little Bastille. A hostile, unfocused rabble had a leader now; and already it was too late for the prisoners in the guardroom, for above the shouts, above the woman's own voice, you could hear the crash of glass and the splinter of wood. She had driven them on, as they stoved in the door and pitted their strength, like goaded beasts in a cage, at the iron bars of the windows. But they were breaking in, not breaking out; confronted by bayonets in a narrow passage, they had dropped back for a moment, but now they were tearing the building apart.

They were stone-eating beasts, and it was not meant for a siege; they had pick-axes, and they were using them. Behind the front rank of attackers the courtyard was swarming with their well-wishers, shouting, shaking their fists, waving weapons.

Seeing the guardsman's uniform, the tricolour sashes, sections of the crowd gave way to them, letting them pass. But before they reached the front of the crowd, the boy put a hand on Camille's arm, holding him back. 'Nothing you can do now,' he said.

Théroigne wore black; she had a pistol in her belt, a sabre in her hand, and her face was incandescent. A cry went up: 'The prisoners are coming out.' She had stationed herself before the doorway, and as the first of the prisoners was dragged out she gave the signal to the men beside her and they raised their swords and axes. 'Can't someone stop her?' Camille said. He shrugged off the guardsman's restraining hand and began to push forward, yelling at people to get out of his way. Fréron forced a path after him and took him by the shoulder. Camille pushed him violently away. The crowd fell back, diverted by the prospect of two patriotic officials about to take each other apart.

But the few seconds of grace had passed; from the front rank there was an animal scream. Théroigne had dropped her arm, like a public executioner; the axes and swords were at work, and the prisoners were being kicked and hauled, one by one, to the deaths prepared for them.

Camille had made headway; the National Guardsman was at his back. Louis Suleau was the fourth prisoner to emerge. At a shout from Théroigne the crowd held off; they even moved back, and as they did so they crushed the people behind them, so that Camille was helpless, immobile, arms pinioned to his sides, when he saw Théroigne approach Louis Suleau and say to him something that only he could have heard; Louis put up a hand, as if to say, what's the point of going into all this now? The gesture etched itself into his mind. It was the last gesture. He saw Théroigne raise her pistol. He did not hear the shot. Within seconds they were surrounded by the dying. Louis's body – perhaps still breathing, no one could know – was dragged into the crowd, into a vortex of flailing arms and blades. Fréron yelled into the National Guardsman's face, and the young man, red with anguish and bewilderment, drew his sabre and shouted for a way out. Their feet splashed through fresh blood.

'There was nothing you could do,' the young man kept saying. 'Please, Camille, I should have come before, they were royalists anyway and there was really nothing you could do.'

LUCILE HAD BEEN OUT to buy some bread for breakfast. No point in asking Jeanette to go; with daylight, the woman's nerve had snapped, and she was running round the apartment, as Lucile said, like a hen without a head.

Lucile put her basket over her arm. She draped a jacket around her, though it was warm, because she wanted to put her little knife into the pocket. No one knew she had this little knife; she hardly allowed herself to know, but she kept it on her person in case of need. Just think, she said to herself. I could be living on the Right Bank. I could be married to a senior clerk at the Treasury. I could be sitting with my feet up, embroidering a linen handkerchief with a rambling-rose design. Instead I'm on the rue des Cordeliers in pursuit of a baguette, with a three-inch blade for comfort.

She looked into the eyes of her familiar neighbours. Who would have thought our Section contained so many royalists? 'You murderer's whore,' a man said to her. She kept a smile on her face, a particularly maddening smile that she had learned from Camille, a smile that taunted and said, all right, *just try it*. In imagination, she eased the knife's smooth handle into her palm, pressed its point against yielding flesh. As she was on her way back, and outside her own front door, another man recognized her and spat in her face.

She stopped inside the front door, to wipe the saliva away, then wafted up the stairs, sat down, the bread in her lap. 'Are you going to eat that?' Jeanette said, wringing her apron between her hands in a pantomime of anguish.

'Of course I am, since I went to such trouble to get it. Pull yourself together, Jeanette, put some coffee on.'

Louise called from the drawing room, 'I think Gabrielle is going to faint.'

So possibly she never got her breakfast; afterwards she didn't remember. They got Gabrielle on to the bed, loosened her clothes, fanned her. She opened a window, but the noise from the street was agitating Gabrielle even more; so she closed it again, and they endured the heat. Gabrielle dozed; she and Louise took turns at reading to each other, and gossiped and bickered gently, and told each other their life stories. The hours crept on, until Camille and Fréron came home.

Fréron flopped into a chair. 'There are bodies – ' he indicated a height from the ground. 'I'm sorry to have to tell you this, Lucile, but Louis Suleau is dead. Yes, we saw it, we saw it happen, we saw him killed before our eyes.'

He wanted Camille to say, Fréron saved my life; or at least to say, Fréron stopped me doing something very very stupid. But Camille only said, 'For the love of Christ, Rabbit, save it for your memoirs If I hear any more about this morning I'll do you an injury. And not a trivial one, either.'

At the sight of him, Jeanette pulled herself together. The coffee was produced at last. Gabrielle came staggering from the bedroom doorway, fastening the bodice of her dress. 'I haven't seen François since early morning,' Camille told Louise. His voice was unnaturally flat, without the trace of a stutter. 'I haven't seen Georges-Jacques, but he is signing decrees from City Hall so clearly he is alive and well. Louis Capet and all his family have deserted the palace and are at the Riding-School. The Assembly is in permanent session. I don't think even the Swiss Guard knows the King has gone and I'm sure the people attacking the palace don't know. I'm not sure if we're supposed to tell them.' He stood up, held Lucile in his arms for a moment. 'I am going to change my clothes once more, because I have got dried blood on them, and then I am going out again.'

Fréron looked after him gloomily. 'I'm afraid the reaction will set in later,' he said. 'I know Camille. He's not cut out for all this.'

'You think not?' Lucile said. 'I think he thrives on it.' She wants to ask how Louis Suleau died, how and why. But now is not the time. As Danton had said, she is not a silly girl; no, no, she is the voice of common sense. Maria Stuart, on the wall, approaches the headsman; nubile, shapely, Maria wears a sickly Christian smile. The pink silk cushions are looking the worse for wear, as Camille could have predicted but didn't; the blue *chaise-longue* has a knowing air, like a piece of furniture that's seen a lot in its time. Lucile Desmoulins is twenty-two years old, wife, mother, mistress of her house. In the August heat – a fly buzzing against glass, a man whistling in the street, a baby crying on another floor – she feels her soul set into its shape, small and stained and mortal. Once she might have said the prayers for the dead. Now she thought, what the fuck's the use, it's the living I have to worry about.

WHEN GABRIELLE felt strong enough, she said that she would like to go back to her own house. The streets were packed and noisy. The porter had panicked and closed the big gate to the Cour du Commerce; Gabrielle hammered and banged and rang the bell, yelling to be let into her own home. 'We can go in through the baker's if he'll let us,' she said, 'in at his front door and out through his back kitchen.'

But the baker wouldn't even let them into his shop; he shouted into their faces and pushed Gabrielle in the chest, bruising her and winding her and sending her flying back into the road. Dragging her between them, they retreated to the big gate, huddled against it. As a group of men crowded around them Lucile reached into her pocket and felt that the knife was there and caressed it with her fingertips; she said, 'I know you, I know your names, and if you approach one step nearer your heads will be on pikes before nightfall and I will take the greatest pleasure in helping to put them there.'

And then the gate opened for them; hands pulled them inside; bolts slammed home; they were inside the front door, they were on the stairs, they were in the Dantons' house, and Lucile was saying crossly, 'This time we're staying put.'

Gabrielle was shaking her head – lost, utterly exhausted. From across the river the gunfire was heavy and constant. 'Mother of God, I look as if I've been three days in the tomb,' Louise Robert said, catching sight of herself as they once again plumped pillows and disposed Gabrielle to the horizontal.

'Why do you think the Dantons have separate beds?' she whispered to Lucile, when she thought they were out of earshot.

Lucile shrugged. Gabrielle said in a drugged voice, 'Because he lashes his arms about, dreams he's fighting – I don't know who.'

'His enemies? His creditors? His inclinations?' Lucile said.

Louise Robert raided Gabrielle's dressing-table. She found a pot of rouge, and applied it in round scarlet spots, as they used to do at Court. She offered some to Lucile, but Lucile said, 'Come, you minx, you know I am beyond improvement.'

MIDDAY PASSED. The streets fell silent. This is what the last hours will be like, Lucile thought; this is what it will be like when the world ends, and we are waiting for the death of the sun. But the sun did not fail; it beat down, and beat down at last on the blazing tricolour, on the heads of the Marseille men, on the singing victory processions and the loyal lurking Cordeliers who'd had the sense to stay indoors all day and who now poured on to the streets, chanting for the republic, calling for the death of tyrants, calling for their man Danton.

There was a pounding at the door. Lucile threw it open; nothing could worry her now. A big man stood propping himself in the doorway, swaying a little. He was a man from the streets: 'Forgive me, Monsieur,' Louise Robert said, laughing. 'I don't think we've been introduced.'

'They're smashing the mirrors at the palace,' the man said. 'The Cordeliers are kings now.' He tossed something to Gabrielle. She caught it awkwardly. It was a hairbrush, heavy, silver-backed. 'From the Queen's dressing-table,' the man said.

Gabrielle's forefinger traced the embossed monogram: 'A' for Antoinette. The man lurched forward and caught Lucile around the waist, spinning her off her feet. He smelled of wine, tobacco and blood. He kissed her throat, a sucking, greedy, proletarian kiss; he set her on her feet again, clattered back into the street.

'Goodness,' Louise said. 'What a legion of admirers you have, Lucile. He's probably been waiting two years for the chance to do that.'

Lucile took out her handkerchief and dabbed at her neck. It wasn't my admirers I met this morning, she thought. She wagged a finger and dropped her voice a tone, for her well-rehearsed Rémy imitation: 'I just say to them, now boys, stop quarrelling over me – liberty, equality, fraternity, remember?'

The Queen's hairbrush lay where Gabrielle had dropped it, on the drawing-room carpet.

DANTON CAME HOME. It was late afternoon. They could hear his voice out in the street. He came home with Fabre the genius of our age, with Legendre the butcher, with Collot d'Herbois much-the-worst-person-in-the-world; with François Robert, with Westermann. He came home with his arms around the shoulders of Legendre and Westermann, unsteady on his feet, unshaven, exhausted, reeking of brandy. 'We won!' they shouted. It was a simple chant – as slogans go it was right to the point. He gathered Gabrielle into his arms, hugged her fiercely, protectively; once again she felt her knees give way.

He propped her into a chair. 'She's had terrible trouble staying upright at all,' Louise Robert said. Her skin glowed now, beneath the rouge; François was back at her side.

'Get out, the lot of you!' Danton said. 'Haven't you beds to go to?' He crashed into his own bedroom, threw himself down on his bed. Lucile followed him. She touched the back of his neck, took him by the shoulders. He groaned. 'Try me some other time,' he advised. He flopped on to his back, grinning. 'Oh, Georges-Jacques, Georges-Jacques,' he said to himself, 'life's just a series of wonderful opportunities. What would Maître Vinot make of you now?'

'Tell me where my husband is.'

'Camille?' His grin broadened. 'Camille's at the Riding-School, fixing the next bit of the Life Plan. No, Camille's not like humans, he doesn't need sleep.'

'When I last saw him,' she said, 'he was in a state of shock.'

'Yes.' The grin faded. His eyelids fluttered closed, then opened again. 'That bitch Théroigne slaughtered Suleau within twenty yards of where he stood. You know, we never saw Robespierre all day.

Perhaps he was hiding in Duplay's cellar.' His voice began to tail off. 'Suleau was at school with Camille. Small world, so was Max. Camille is a hard-working boy, and will go far. Tomorrow we shall know . . .' His eyes closed. 'That's it,' he said.

THE ASSEMBLY had begun its current sitting at two a.m. The debate was attended by some inconveniences: drowned out intermittently by gunfire, and thrown into confusion by the arrival of the royal family at about 8.30 in the morning. Only yesterday it had voted to suspend any further discussion on the future of the monarchy, yet it did seem now that the vestiges of the institution had been left behind in the smashed and devastated palace. The Right said that the adjournment of the debate had been the signal for insurrection; the Left said that when the deputies abandoned the issue they also abandoned any claim to be leaders of public opinion.

The King's family and a few of their friends were squashed into a reporters' box which looked down on the deputies from behind the President's dais. From mid-afternoon onwards, a constant procession of petitioners and delegates jostled through the corridors and overflowed the debating chamber. The rumours from outside were frightful and bizarre. All the bolsters and mattresses in the palace had been slashed, and the air was thick with flying feathers. Prostitutes were plying their trade on the Queen's bed: though how this fitted with the earlier story, no one could say. A man had been seen playing the violin over the corpse of someone whose throat he had cut. A hundred people had been stabbed and clubbed to death in the rue de l'Échelle. A cook had been cooked. The servants were being dragged from under beds and up chimneys and tossed out of windows to be impaled on pikes. Fires had been started, and there were the usual dubious reports of cannibalism.

Vergniaud, the current president of the Assembly, had long ago given up trying to distinguish truth from fantasy. Below him, on the floor of the House, he counted rather more invaders than deputies. Every few minutes the doors would burst open to admit begrimed and weary men staggering under the weight of what, if it had not been brought straight to the Riding-School, would have been loot. Really, Vergniaud thought, it was going too far to place inlaid night-stools and complete sets of Molière at the feet of the Nation. The place had begun to resemble an auction room. Vergniaud tried unobtrusively to loosen his cravat.

In the cramped, airless reporters' box, the royal children were falling asleep. The King, who believed in keeping his strength up, was gnawing at the leg of a capon. From time to time he wiped his fingers on his sad purple coat. On the benches below him a deputy put his head in his hands.

'Went out for a piss,' he said. 'Camille Desmoulins ambushed me. Pushed me against the wall, made me support Danton for Pope. Or something. Seems Danton might stand for God, they haven't decided yet, but I'm told I'd better vote for him or else I might wake up with my throat cut.'

A few benches away, Brissot conferred with ex-minister Roland. M. Roland was yellower in the face than he used to be; he hugged his dusty hat to his chest, as if it were his last line of defence.

'The Assembly must be dissolved,' Brissot said, 'there will have to be fresh elections. Before this session breaks up, we must nominate a new cabinet, a new Council of Ministers. Yes, now, we must do it now – someone must govern the country. You will return to your post as Minister of the Interior.'

'Really? And Servan, Clavière?'

'Yes, indeed,' Brissot said. He thought, this is what I was born to do: shape governments. 'Back to the situation as it was in June, except that you won't have the royal veto to hamper you. And you'll have Danton for a colleague.'

Roland sighed. 'Manon won't like this.'

'She must make her mind up to it.'

'Which ministry do we want Danton to have?'

'It hardly matters,' Brissot said bleakly, 'as long as he has the whip-hand.'

'Has it come to that?'

'If you'd been on the streets today, you couldn't doubt it.'

'Why, have you been on the streets?' Roland rather doubted that.

'I'm informed,' Brissot said. 'Very fully informed. I'm told he's their man. They're yelling their throats out for him. What do you think of that?'

'I wonder,' Roland said, 'whether this is a proper beginning for the republic. Shall we be chivvied by the rabble?'

'Where is Vergniaud going?' Brissot asked.

The president had signalled for his substitute. 'Please make way for me,' he was asking pleasantly.

Brissot followed Vergniaud with his eyes. It was entirely possible that alliances, factions, pacts would be proposed, framed, broken – and, if he were not everywhere, party to every conversation – the dreadful possibility arose that he might forfeit his status as the best-informed man in France.

'Danton is a complete crook,' Roland said. 'Perhaps we should ask him to take over as Minister of Justice?'

By the door Vergniaud, faced with Camille, had been unable to get into his proper oratorical sweep and stride. One quite sees, he said, and one does appreciate, and one fully understands. For the first time in his three-minute tirade, Camille faltered. 'Tell me, Vergniaud,' he said, 'am I beginning to repeat myself?'

Vergniaud released his indrawn breath. 'A little. But really what you have to say is all so fresh and interesting. Finish what you've started, you say. In what way?'

Camille made a sweeping gesture, encompassing both the Riding-School and the howling streets outside. 'I don't understand why the King isn't dead. Plenty of better people are dead. And these super-fluous deputies? The royalists they've crammed into the prisons?'

'But you can't kill them all.' The orator's voice shook.

'We do have the capacity.'

'I said "can't" but I meant "ought not to". Danton wouldn't require a superfluity of deaths.'

'Would he not? I don't know. I haven't seen him for hours. I think he arranged for the Capet family to be brought out of the palace.'

'Yes,' Vergniaud said. 'That seems a reasonable supposition. Now, why do you think he did that?'

'I don't know. Perhaps he's a humanitarian.'

'But you're not sure.'

'I'm not even sure if I'm awake.'

'I think you should go home, Camille. You are saying all the wrong things.'

'Am I? You are kind. If you were saying the wrong things I'd be, you know, making mental notes.'

'No,' Vergniaud said reassuringly. 'You wouldn't.'

'Yes,' Camille insisted. 'We don't trust you.'

'So I see. But I doubt you need spend any more energy frightening people. Did you not think that we might want Danton anyway? Not because of what he might do if he were denied power – which I am sure would be quite as distasteful as you imply – but because of a belief that he's the only man who can save the country?'

'No,' Camille said. 'That never occurred to me.'

'Don't you believe it?'

'Yes, but I've got used to believing it by myself. It's been such a long time. And the greatest obstacle has been Danton himself.'

'What is he expecting?'

'He isn't expecting anything. He's asleep.'

'Now listen. I intend to address the Assembly. It would be an advantage if the rabble were removed.'

'They were the sovereign people until they put you into power this afternoon. Now they're the rabble.'

'There are petitioners here asking for the suspension of the monarchy. The Assembly will decree it. And the calling of a National Convention, to draw up a constitution for the republic. I think now you can go and get some sleep.'

'No, not until I hear it for myself. If I went away now everything might fall apart.'

'Life takes on a persecutory aspect,' Vergniaud murmured. 'Let us try to remain rational.'

'It isn't rational.'

'It will be,' Vergniaud said smoothly. 'My colleagues intend to remove government from the sphere of chance and prejudice and make it into a reasoned process.'

Camille shook his head.

'I assure you,' Vergniaud said. He broke off. 'There's a horrible smell. What is it?'

'I think – ' Camille hesitated – 'I think they're burning the bodies.'

'Long live the republic,' Vergniaud said. He began to walk towards the president's dais.

PART FIVE

Terror is nothing other than justice, prompt, stern and inflexible; it is not so much a particular principle as a consequence of the general principle of democracy applied to the most urgent needs of our country ... The government of the Revolution is the despotism of liberty against the tyrants.

Maximilien Robespierre

In a word, during these reigns, the natural death of a famous man was so rare that it was gazetted as an event and handed down to posterity by the historians. Under one consulate, says the annalist, there was a Pontiff called Pisonius, who died in his bed; this was regarded as a marvel.

Camille Desmoulins

I. *Conspirators*

(1792)

'FATHER-IN-LAW!' Camille gives a cry of delight. He points to Claude. 'You see,' he invites the company, 'never throw anything away. Any object, however outworn and old-fashioned, may prove to have its uses. Now, Citizen Duplessis, tell me, in short simple sentences, or verse, or comic song, how to run a ministry.'

'This is beyond my nightmares,' Claude says.

'Oh, they haven't given me my own ministry – not quite yet – there will have to be a few more catastrophes before that happens. The news is this – Danton is Minister of Justice and Keeper of the Seals, and Fabre and I are his secretaries.'

'An actor,' Claude says. 'And you. I do not like Danton. But I am sorry for him.'

'Danton is leader of the Provisional Government, so I must try to run the ministry for him, Fabre will not bother. Oh, I must write and tell my father, give me some paper quick. No, wait, I'll write to him from the ministry, I'll sit behind my big desk and send it under seal.'

'Claude,' Annette says, 'where are your manners? Say congratulations.'

Claude shudders. 'One point. A technicality. The Minister of Justice is also Keeper of the Seals, but he is only one person. He has always had the one secretary. Always.'

'Cheeseparing!' Camille says. 'Georges-Jacques is above it! We shall be moving to the Place Vendôme! We shall be living in a palace!'

'Dear Father, don't take it so badly,' Lucile begs.

'No, you don't understand,' Claude tells her. 'He has arrived now, he is the Establishment. Anyone who wants to make a revolution has to make it against him.'

Claude's sense of dislocation is more acute than on the day the

Bastille fell. So is Camille's, when he thinks about what Claude has said. 'No, that's not true at all. There are plenty of good battles ahead. There's Brissot's people.'

'You like a good battle, don't you?' Claude says. Briefly, he imagines an alternative world: into café conversation he drops the phrase 'my son-in-law, the secretary'. The reality is, however, that his life has been wasted; thirty years of diligence have never made him intimate with a secretary, but now he is forced into intimacy by his mad womenfolk and the way they have decided to run their lives. Look at them all, rushing to give the secretary a kiss. He could, he supposes, cross the room and pat the secretary on the head; has he not seen the secretary sit, neck bent, while the minister-elect, discoursing on some patriotic theme, runs *distrait* strangler's fingers through his curls? Will the minister do this in front of his civil servants? Claude takes an easy decision against any such display of affection. He glares at his son-in-law. Look at him – couldn't you just commit violence? There he sits, lashes lowered, eyes on the carpet. What is he thinking? Is it anything a secretary should be thinking, at all?

Camille regards the carpet, but imagines Guise. The letter that he means to write is, in his mind, already written. Invisible, he floats across the Place des Armes. He melts through the closed front door of the narrow white house. He insinuates his presence into his father's study. There, on the desk, lies the *Encyclopaedia of Law*; by now, surely, we are in the lower reaches of the alphabet?

Yes, indeed – this is Vol. VI. On top of it lies a letter from Paris. In whose handwriting? In his own! In the handwriting his publishers complain of, in his own inimitable script! The door opens. In comes his father. How does he look? He looks as when Camille last saw him: he looks spare, grey, severe and remote.

He sees the letter. But wait, stop – how did it get there, how did it come to be lying on top of the *Encyclopaedia of Law*? Implausible, this – unless he is to imagine a whole scene of the letter's arrival, his mother or Clément or whoever carrying it up and managing not to slide their fingers and eyes into it.

All right, start again.

Jean-Nicolas climbs the stairs. Camille (in ghost form) drifts up behind him. Jean-Nicolas has a letter in his hand. He peers at it; it is the familiar, semi-legible handwriting of his eldest son.

Does he want to read it? No – not especially. But the rest of the household is calling up the stairs, what's the news from Paris?

He unfolds it. With a little difficulty, he reads – but he will not mind the difficulty, when he comes to the news his son has to impart.

Amazement, glory! My son's best friend (well, one of his two best friends) is made a Minister! My son is to be his secretary! He is to live in a palace!

Jean-Nicolas clasps the letter to his shirt front – an inch above his waistcoat, and to the left, above his heart. We have misjudged the boy! After all, he was a genius! I will run at once, tell everyone in town – they will be sick with spleen, they will look green, and puke with unadorned jealousy. Rose-Fleur's father will be ill with grief. Just think, she might now be the secretary's wife.

But no, no, Camille thinks – this is not at all how it will be. Will Jean-Nicolas seize his pen, dash off his congratulations? Will he toss his hat upon his severe grey locks, and dash out to waylay the neighbours? The hell he will. He'll stare at the letter – going, oh no, oh no! He'll think, what unimaginable form of behaviour has procured this favour for my son? And pride? He'll not feel pride. He'll just feel suspicious, aggrieved. He'll get a vague nagging pain in his lower back, and take to his bed.

'Camille, what are you thinking?' Lucile says.

Camille looks up. 'I was thinking there's no pleasing some people.'

The women give Claude poison-dart glances, and gather round and adore Camille.

'IF I HAD FAILED,' Danton said, 'I would have been treated as a criminal.'

It was twelve hours since Camille and Fabre had woken him up and told him to take charge of the nation. Dragged out of a disjointed dream of rooms and rooms, of doors and doors opening into other rooms, he had clutched Camille in incoherent gratitude – though perhaps it wasn't the thing, perhaps a touch of *nolo episcopari* was in order? A touch of humility in the face of destiny? No – he was too tired to pretend reluctance. He commanded France, and this was a natural thing.

Across the river the urgent problem was the disposal of the bodies, both living and dead, of the Swiss Guard. Fires still smoked in the gutted palace.

'KEEP THE SEALS?' Gabrielle had said. 'Do you know what you're doing? Camille couldn't keep two white rabbits in a coop.'

Here Robespierre sat, very new, as if he had been taken out of a box and placed unruffled in a velvet armchair in Danton's apartment. Danton called out to admit no one – 'no one but my Secretaries of State' – and prepared to defer to the opinions of this necessary man.

'I hope you'll help me out?' he said.

'Of course I will, Georges-Jacques.'

Very serious, Robespierre, very attentive; superlatively himself this morning when everyone should have woken up different. 'Good,' Georges-Jacques said. 'So you'll take a post at the ministry?'

'Sorry. I can't.'

'What do you mean, you can't? I need you. Very well, you've got the Jacobins to run, you've a seat on the new Commune, but we've all got to – ' the new minister broke off, and made a consolidating, squeezing gesture with his huge fists.

'If you want a Head of Civil Service, François Robert would do the job very well for you.'

'I'm sure he would.' Did you imagine, Danton thought, that I wanted to make you into a functionary? Of course I didn't; I wanted to attach you in some highly paid but highly unofficial capacity, as my political adviser, my third eye, my third ear. So what's the problem? Perhaps you are one of those people who's made for opposition, not for government. Is that it? Or is it that you don't want to work under me?

Robespierre looked up; light eyes, just touching his would-be master's. 'Let me off?' He smiled.

'As you wish.' So often he's aware, these days, of his pseudo-refined barrister's drawl, of the expressions that go with it; and of his other voice, his street voice, just as much the product of cultivation. Robespierre has only one voice, rather flat, unemphatic, ordinary; he's never in his life seen the need to pretend. 'But now, at the Commune, you'll be taking hold of things there?' He tried to soften the tone to one of suggestion. 'Fabre is a member, you should consider him at your orders.'

Robespierre seemed amused. 'I'm not sure I've your taste for giving them.'

'Your first problem is the Capet family. Where are you going to keep them?'

Robespierre inspected his fingernails. 'There was some suggestion that they should be kept under guard at the Minister of Justice's palace.'

'Oh yes? And I suppose they'll give me some attic, or perhaps a broom-cupboard, to transact affairs of state from?'

'I said you wouldn't like it.' Robespierre seemed interested to have his suspicions confirmed.

'They should be shut up in the old Temple tower.'

'Yes, that's the view of the Commune. It's a bit grim for the children, after what they've been used to.' Maximilien, Danton thought, were you once a child? 'I'm told they'll be made comfortable. They'll be able to walk in the gardens. Perhaps the children would like to have a little dog they could take out?'

'Don't ask me what they'd like,' Danton said. 'How the hell would I know? Anyway, there are more pressing matters than the Capets. We have to put the city on a war footing. We have to take search powers, requisition powers. We have to round up any royalists who are still armed. The prisons are filling up.'

'That's inevitable. The people who opposed us, this last week – we now define them as criminals, I suppose? They must have some status, we must define them somehow. And if they are defendants, we must offer them a trial – but it is rather puzzling this, because I am not sure what the crime would be.'

'The crime is being left behind by events,' Danton said. 'And, of course, I am not some jurisprudential simpleton, I see that the ordinary courts will not do. I favour a special tribunal. You'll sit as a judge? We'll settle it later today. Now, we have to let the provinces know what's happening. Any thoughts?'

'The Jacobins want to issue an agreed – '

'Version?'

'Is that your choice of word? Of course . . . People need to know what has happened. Camille will write it. The club will publish and distribute it to the nation.'

'Camille is good at versions,' Danton said.

'And then we must think ahead to the new elections. As things stand I don't see how we can stop Brissot's people being returned.'

His tone made Danton look up. 'You don't think we can work with them?'

'I think it would be criminal to try. Look Danton, you must see where their policies tend. They are for the provinces and against Paris – they are federalists. They want to split the nation into little parts. If that happens, if they get their way, what chance have the French people against the rest of Europe?'

'A greatly reduced chance. None.'

'Just so. Therefore their policies tend to the destruction of the nation. They are treasonable. They conduce to the success of the enemy. Perhaps – who knows – perhaps the enemy has inspired them?'

Danton raised a finger. 'Stop there. You're saying, first they start a war, then they make sure we lose it? If you want me to believe that Pétion and Brissot and Vergniaud are agents of the Austrians, you'll have to bring me proper proofs, legal proofs.' And even then, he thought, I won't believe you.

'I'll do my best,' Robespierre said: earnest schoolboy, pitting himself at the task. 'Meanwhile, what are we going to do about the Duke?'

'Poor old Philippe,' Danton said. 'He deserves something. I think we should encourage the Parisians to elect him to the new Assembly.'

'National Convention,' Robespierre corrected. 'Well, if we must.'

'And then there's Marat.'

'What does he want?'

'Oh, he doesn't ask anything, not for himself – I simply mean that he's someone we must come to terms with. He has an enormous following among the people.'

'I accept that,' Robespierre said.

'You will have him with you at the Commune.'

'And the Convention? People will say Marat's too extreme, Camille, too – but we must have them.'

'Extreme?' Danton said. 'The times are extreme. Armies are extreme. This is a crisis point.'

'I don't doubt it. God is with us. We have that comfort.'

Danton rolled around in his mind this astonishing statement. 'Unfortunately,' he said at last, 'God has not yet furnished us with any pikes.'

Robespierre turned his face away. It is like playing with a hedgehog, Danton thought, you just touch its nose and in it goes and all you've got to negotiate with is spikes. 'I didn't want this war,' Robespierre said.

'Unfortunately, we've got it, and we can't keep insisting it belongs to somebody else.'

'Do you trust General Dumouriez?'

'He's given us no reason not to.'

Robespierre's mouth set in a wry line. 'That's not enough, is it? What has he done to convince us he's a patriot?'

'He's a soldier, there's a presumption of loyalty to the government of the day.'

'That presumption was ill-founded in '89, when the French Guards came over to the people. They followed their natural interests. Dumouriez and all our other dashing aristocratic officers will soon follow theirs. I wonder about Dillon, Camille's friend.'

'I didn't say the loyalty of the officers is assured, I said that the government takes it for granted till they show otherwise. On any other terms, it would be impossible to have an army.'

'May I give you a word of advice?' Robespierre's eyes were fixed on Danton's face, and Danton thought, this is not advice I shall like. 'You begin to talk too much of "the government". You are a revolutionary, the Revolution made you, and in revolution the old presumptions do not hold good. In times of stability and peace it may be possible for a state to deal with its enemies by ignoring them, but in times such as these we have to identify them and take them on, tackle them.'

Tackle them how? Danton wondered. Reason with them? Convert them? Kill them? But you won't have killing, will you, Max? You don't hold with it. Out loud, he said, 'Diplomacy can limit the war. While I'm in office I shall do what I can to keep England out. But when I'm not in office – '

'You know what Marat would say? He'd say, why should you ever be out of office?'

'But I intend to sit in the Convention. That's my stage, that's where I'll be effective – you can't mean to tie me to a desk. And as you know quite well, a deputy can't be a minister.'

'Listen.' Robespierre eased out of a pocket his little volume of *The Social Contract*.

'Oh good, story time,' Danton said.

Robespierre opened it at a marked page. 'Listen to this. "The inflexibility of the laws can in some circumstances make them dangerous and cause the ruin of a state in a crisis . . . if the danger is such that the machinery of the laws is an obstacle, then a dictator is appointed, who silences the laws."' He closed the book, raised his eyes questioningly.

'Is that a statement of fact,' Danton inquired, 'or is it prescriptive?'

Robespierre said nothing.

'I am afraid I am not impressed by that, just because you have read it out of a book. Even out of Jean-Jacques.'

'I want to prepare you for the arguments that people will throw at you.'

'You had the passage marked, I see. In future, don't bother to draw the conversation round. Just ask me straight off what you want to know.'

'I didn't come here to tempt you. I marked the passage because I have been giving the matter much thought.'

Danton stared at him blankly. 'And your conclusion?'

'I like . . . ' Robespierre hesitated. 'I like to think around all the possible circumstances. We mustn't be doctrinaire. But then, pragmatism can so easily degenerate into lack of principle.'

'They kill dictators,' Danton said. 'In the end.'

'But if, before that happens, you have saved your country? "It is expedient that one man should die for the people."'

'Forget it. I've no desire to be a martyr. Have you?'

'It's all hypothetical anyway. But you and I, Danton . . . You and I,' he said thoughtfully, 'are not alike.'

'I WONDER WHAT Robespierre really thinks of me?' Danton said to Camille.

'Oh, he thinks you're wonderful.' Camille smiled as best he could in his rather nervous and distracted state. 'He can't praise you too highly.'

'I'd like to know how Danton really regards me,' Robespierre said.

'Oh, he can't praise you too highly.' Camille's smile was a little strained. 'He thinks you're wonderful.'

LIFE'S GOING to change. You thought it already had? Not nearly as much as it's going to change now.

Everything you disapprove of you'll call 'aristocratic'. This term can be applied to food, to books and plays, to modes of speech, to hairstyles and to such venerable institutions as prostitution and the Roman Catholic Church.

If 'Liberty' was the watchword of the first Revolution, 'Equality' is that of the second. 'Fraternity' is a less assertive quality, and must creep in where it may.

All persons are now plain 'Citizen' or 'Citizeness'. The Place Louis XV will become the Place de la Révolution, and the scientific beheading machine will be set up there; it will become known as the 'guillotine', in tribute to Dr Guillotin the noted public-health expert.

The rue Monsieur-de-Prince will become the rue Liberté, the Place de la Croix-Rouge will become the Place de la Bonnet-Rouge. Notre Dame will become the Temple of Reason. Bourg-la-Reine will become Bourg-la-République. And in the fullness of time, the rue des Cordeliers will become the rue Marat.

Divorce will be very easy.

For a time, Annette Duplessis will continue to walk in the Luxembourg Gardens. A cannon factory will be set up there; the patriotic din and stench will be beyond belief, and the patriotic waste-products will be tipped into the Seine.

The Luxembourg Section will become the Section Mutius Scaevola. The Romans are very fashionable. So are the Spartans. The Athenians less so.

In at least one provincial town, Beaumarchais's *Marriage of Figaro* will be banned, just as the King once banned it. It depicts a style of life now outlawed; also, it requires the wearing of aristocratic costumes.

'Sansculottes', the working men call themselves, because they wear trousers not breeches. With them, a calico waistcoat with broad tricolour stripes: a hip-length jacket of coarse wool, called a *carmagnole*. On the sansculotte head, the red bonnet, the 'cap of liberty'. Why liberty is thought to require headgear is a mystery.

For the rich and powerful, the aim is to be accepted as sansculotte in spirit, without assuming the ridiculous uniform. But only Robespierre and a handful of others keep hope alive for the unemployed hairdressers of France. Many members of the new Convention will wear their hair brushed forward and cut straight across their foreheads, like the statues of heroes of antiquity. Riding-boots are worn on all occasions, even at harp recitals. Gentlemen have the air of being ready to run down a Prussian column after dinner, any day of the week.

Cravats grow higher, as if they mean to protect the throat. The highest cravats in public life will be worn by Citizen Antoine Saint-Just, of the National Convention and the Committee of Public Safety. In the dark and harrowing days of '94, an obscene feminine inversion will appear: a thin crimson ribbon, worn round a bare white neck.

There will be economic controls, price maximums imposed by

the government. There will be coffee riots and sugar riots. One month there will be no firewood, then it will be no soap, or no candles. The black market will be a flourishing but desperate business, with the death penalty for hoarders and traffickers.

There will be persistent rumours about *ci-devant* lords and ladies, returned *émigrés*. Someone has seen a marquis working as a bootblack, his wife taking in sewing. A duke is employed as a footman in his own house, which now belongs to a Jewish banker. Some people like to think these things are true.

In the National Assembly there were deplorable occasions when overwrought gentlemen placed hands on rapier-hilts. In the Convention and the Jacobin Club, fist-fights and knife-fights will be quite common. Duelling will be replaced by assassination.

For the rich – the new rich, that is – it is possible to live as well as one would have liked to under the old regime. Camille Desmoulins, in semi-private conversation at the Jacobins, one evening in '93: 'I don't know why people complain about not being able to make money nowadays. I have no trouble.'

Churches will be despoiled, statues disfigured. Stone-eyed saints raise stumps of fingers in truncated benediction. If you want to save a statue of the Virgin, you put a red cap on her head and turn her into a Goddess of Liberty. And that's the way all the virgins save themselves; who wants these ferocious political women?

Because of the changes in the street names, it will become impossible to direct people around the city. The calendar will be changed too; January is abolished, goodbye to aristocratic June. People will ask each other, 'What's today in real days?'

'92, '93, '94. Liberty, Equality, Fraternity or Death.

DANTON's first action at the Ministry of Justice was to call together his senior civil servants. He surveyed them. A grin split his broken face. 'I advise you gentlemen,' he said, 'to take up the option of early retirement.'

'I'LL MISS YOU terribly,' Louise Gély said to Gabrielle. 'Shall I come and see you at the Place Vendôme?'

'The Place des Piques,' Gabrielle corrected. She smiled: a very small smile. 'Yes, of course you must come. And we will be back soon, because Georges has only taken office for the Emergency, and when the Emergency is over – ' She bit the words back. Tempting fate, she called it.

'You shouldn't be frightened,' Louise said, hugging her gently. 'You should have a look in your eyes which says, I know that while my husband is in the city the enemy cannot come.'

'Well, Louise . . . you are brave.'

'Danton believes it.'

'But can one man do so much by himself?'

'It's not a question of one man.' She moved away. Hard sometimes not to be irritated by Gabrielle. 'It's a question of many men with the best leader.'

'I didn't think you liked my husband.'

Louise raised her eyebrows. 'When did I say I did? All the same, it is good of him to do something for my father.'

M. Gély had a new post at the Ministry of Marine.

'Oh, it's nothing,' Gabrielle said. 'He's found places for all the people who used to be his clerks, and – oh, everybody really. Even Collot d'Herbois, whom we don't like.'

'And are they duly grateful?' Probably not, Louise thought. 'People he likes, people he doesn't like, people of no importance whatever – I think he'd give the whole city a job, if he could. It's interesting. I was wondering why he has sent Citizen Fréron off to Metz?'

'Oh,' she said uneasily, 'it's to do with the Executive Council there – they need some help running their revolution, I suppose.'

'Metz is on the frontier.'

'Yes.'

'I was wondering if he'd done it as a favour to Citizeness Desmoulins. Fréron was always following her around, wasn't he? And giving her soulful glances, and paying her compliments. Danton doesn't like it. It will make life easier for him, now that Fréron's away.'

Gabrielle wouldn't, out of choice, be having this conversation

Even this child notices, she thinks, even this child of fourteen knows all about it.

WHEN THE NEWS of the coup of 10 August reached his military headquarters, General Lafayette tried to organize his armies to march on Paris and bring down the Provisional Government. Only a handful of officers were prepared to back him. On 19 August he crossed the border near Sedan, and was promptly taken prisoner by the Austrians.

THE MINISTRY of Justice had taken to having breakfast together, to work out the plan for the day. Danton greeted everyone except his wife, but after all, he had seen her before that morning. This would have been the time to make the change to separate rooms, they both thought; but neither had the heart to mention it first. Consequently, the usual conjugal arrangements were made; they woke up beneath a coronet and a canopy, stifled by velvet bed-curtains thicker than Turkey carpets.

Lucile was wearing grey this morning. Dove-grey: piquantly puritanical, Danton thought. He imagined leaning across and kissing her savagely on the mouth.

Nothing affected Danton's appetite – not a sudden seizure of lust, not the national emergency, not the historic dust of the state bed-curtains. Lucile ate nothing. She was starving herself, trying to get back pre-pregnancy angles. 'You'll fade away, girl,' Danton told her.

'She's trying to look like her husband,' Fabre explained. 'She will not admit to it, but for some reason best known to herself that is what she is doing.'

Camille sipped a small cup of black coffee. His wife watched him covertly as he opened their letters – nasty little slits with a paperknife, and his long elegant fingers. 'Where are François and Louise?' Fabre asked. 'Something must be detaining them. How quaint they are, always waking up side by side and always in the bed they started off in.'

'Enough!' Danton said. 'We shall have a rule, no lubricious gossip before breakfast.'

Camille put down his coffee cup. 'For you it may be before breakfast, but some of us are anxious to begin on our daily ration of scandal, backbiting and malice.'

'We must hope the gracious atmosphere of the place will seep into us in time. Even into Fabre.' Danton turned to him. 'It won't be like living among the Cordeliers, with your every little depravity applauded as soon as you step out of doors.'

'I'm not depraved,' Fabre complained. 'Camille's depraved. Incidentally, I suppose it will be all right for Caroline Rémy to move in?'

'No,' Danton said. 'It won't be all right at all.'

'Why not? Hérault won't mind, he can call round.'

'I don't give a damn whether he minds or not. Do you think you're going to turn the place into a brothel?'

'Are you serious?' Fabre demanded. He looked at Camille for support, but Camille was reading his letters.

'Divorce your Nicole, marry Caroline, and she'll be welcome.'

'Marry her?' Fabre said. 'You're certainly not serious.'

'Well, if it's so unthinkable, she shouldn't be in the company of our wives.'

'Oh, I see.' Fabre was belligerent. Quite right, too; he can't believe what he's hearing. The minister and his colleague the other secretary have both availed themselves of Caro quite frequently, this summer. 'There's one law for you,' he said, 'and quite another for me.'

'I don't know what you mean. Am I proposing to keep a mistress on the premises?'

'Yes,' Fabre muttered.

Camille laughed out loud.

'Please realize,' Danton said, 'that if you move Caro in here, the ministries and the Assembly will know about it in an hour, and it will bring down on us – on me – some very severe and justified criticism.'

'Very well,' Fabre said resentfully. 'Change the subject. Do you want to hear what Condorcet has to say about your elevation, Minister, in today's paper?'

'I hope you won't edify us with Brissotin ramblings every morning,' Lucile said. 'However. Go on.'

Fabre unfolded the sheet. '"The Chief Minister had to be someone who possessed the confidence of the agitators lately responsible for overthrowing the monarchy. He had to be a man with sufficient personal authority to control this most advantageous, glorious and necessary Revolution's most contemptible instruments." That's us, Camille. "He had to be a man of such eloquence, spirit and character that he would demean neither the office he held nor those members of the National Assembly called upon to have dealings with him. Danton only combined these qualities. I voted for him, and I do not regret my decision."' Fabre leaned over to Gabrielle. 'There now – aren't you impressed by that?'

'Something grudging in the middle,' Camille said.

'Patronizing.' Lucile reached out to take the paper from Fabre. '"Called upon to have dealings with him." It sounds as if you'd be in a cage and they'd poke you with a long stick through the bars. And their teeth would chatter.'

'As if it mattered,' Camille said, 'whether Condorcet regretted his decision. As if he had a choice, in the first place. As if Brissotin opinion mattered to anyone.'

'You will find it matters when the National Convention is elected,' Danton said.

'I like that bit about your character,' Fabre said. 'What if he'd seen you dragging Mandat through City Hall?'

'Let's try and forget that,' Danton said.

'Oh – and I thought it was one of your better moments, Georges-Jacques.'

Camille had sorted his letters into little piles. 'Nothing from Guise,' he said.

'Perhaps they're overawed by the new address.'

'I think they simply don't believe me. They think it's one of my elaborate lies.'

'Don't they get the newspapers?'

'Yes, but they know better than to believe what they read in the newspapers, thank goodness. Now that I write for them. You know, my father thinks I shall be hanged.'

'You may be yet,' Danton said, jocular.

'This may interest you. A letter from my dear cousin Fouquier-Tinville.' Camille cast an eye over his relative's best handwriting. 'Squirm, flattery, abasement, squirm, dearest sweetest Camille, squirm squirm squirm . . . "the election of the Patriot Ministers . . . I know them all by reputation, but I am not so happy as to be known by them" – '

'He's known by me,' Danton said. 'Useful fellow. Does as he's told.'

' "I flatter myself that you will put forward my interests to the Minister of Justice to procure me a situation . . . you know I am the father of a large family and not well-off" . . . There.' He dropped the letter in front of Danton. 'I put forward the interest of my humble and obedient servant Antoine Fouquier-Tinville. He is spoken of in the family as a perfectly competent lawyer. Employ him if you choose.'

Danton picked up the letter. He laughed. 'The servility, Camille! Just think – three years ago this spring, would he have given you the time of day?'

'Absolutely not. Wouldn't have been related to me even remotely, until the Bastille fell.'

'Still,' Danton said, reading the letter, 'your cousin might be useful for our special tribunal that we are setting up to try the losers. Leave it with me, I'll find him something to do.'

'What are those?' Lucile indicated the other pile of letters.

'Those were ingratiating.' Camille waved a hand. 'These are obscene.' Her attention fastened on the hand; it looked almost transparent. 'You know, I used to give such correspondence to Mirabeau. He kept a file.'

'Can I see?' Fabre asked.

'Later,' Danton said. 'Does Robespierre get these things?'

'Yes, a few. Maurice Duplay sifts them out. Of course, the household is wonderful prey for the avid imagination. All those daughters, and the two young boys. Maurice gets very cross. I'm often mentioned, it seems. He complains to me. As if I could do anything about it.'

'Robespierre should get married,' Fabre said.

'It doesn't seem to help.' Danton turned to his wife, mock-uxurious. 'What are you going to do today, my love?' Gabrielle didn't reply. 'Your zest for life is unbounded, isn't it?'

'I miss my home,' Gabrielle said. She looked down at the table-cloth. She did not care to have her private life in public.

'Why don't you go and spend some money?' her husband suggested. 'Take your mind off it. Go to the dressmakers, or whatever it is you do.'

'I'm three months pregnant. I'm not interested in dresses.'

'Don't be horrible to her, Georges-Jacques,' Lucile said softly.

Gabrielle threw back her head and glared at her. 'I don't need your protection, you little slut.' She got up from the table. 'Excuse me, please.' They watched her go.

'Forget about it, Lolotte,' Danton said. 'She's not herself.'

'Gabrielle has the temperament of these letter-writers,' Fabre said. 'She views everything in the worst possible light.'

Danton pushed the letters towards Fabre. 'Quench your burning curiosity. But take them away.'

Fabre made Lucile an extravagant bow, and left the room with alacrity.

'He won't like them,' Danton said. 'Not even Fabre will like them.'

'Max has marriage proposals,' Camille said unexpectedly. 'He gets two or three a week. He keeps them in his room, tied up with tape. He files everything, you know.'

'This is one of your fantasies,' Danton said.

'No, I assure you. He keeps them under his mattress.'

'How do you know?' Danton said narrowly.

They began to laugh. 'Don't go spreading this story,' Camille said, 'because Max will know where it comes from.'

Gabrielle reappeared, standing in the doorway, sullen and tense. 'When you are finished, I'd like to speak to my husband, just for one moment. If you can spare him?'

Danton got up. 'You can be Minister of Justice today,' he said to Camille, 'and I shall deal with what Gabrielle calls "the foreign business". Yes, my love, what was it you wanted?'

'Oh, hell,' Lucile said, when they'd gone. 'Slut, am I?'

'She doesn't mean anything. She's very unhappy, she's very confused.'

'We don't help, do we?'

'Well, what do you suggest?'

Their hands touched, lightly. They were not going to give up the game.

THE ALLIES were on French soil. 'Paris is so safe,' Danton told the Assembly, 'that I have brought my infant sons and my aged mother to Paris, to my apartment in the Place des Piques.'

He met Citizen Roland in the Tuileries garden; they strolled among the trees. A green, dappled light fretted his colleague's face. Citizen Roland's voice shook. 'Perhaps this is the time to go. The government must stay together, at all costs. If we were to move beyond the Loire, then perhaps, when Paris is taken – '

Danton turned on him ferociously. 'Take care when you talk about running away, Roland – the people might hear you. Go on then, old man, you run. If you've no stomach for a fight you take yourself off. But I go nowhere, Roland, I stay here and govern. Paris taken? It'll never be taken. We'll burn it first.'

You know how fear spreads? Danton thinks there must be a mechanism for it, a process that is part of the human brain or soul. He hopes that, by the same process, along the same pathways, courage can spread; he will stand at the centre, and it can go out from him.

Mme Recordain sat in a high-backed chair and surveyed the opulence of the Minister of Justice's palace. She sniffed.

They began digging trenches round the city walls.

IN THE FIRST WEEKS of the ministry, Dr Marat often called. He disdained to bathe for these occasions, and refused to make an appointment; hopping through the galleries with his nervous, contorted stride, he would enunciate 'The minister, the secretary', with a sort of disgust, and physically grapple with anyone who tried to stop him.

This morning two senior officials were conferring outside Secretary Desmoulins's door. Their faces were aggrieved, their tones indignant. They made no effort to stop Marat. He deserves you, their expressions said.

It was a large and splendid room, and Camille was the least conspicuous thing in it. The walls were lined with portraits, aged to the colours of tallow and smoke; the grave ministerial faces, under their wigs and powder, were all alike. They gazed without expression at the occupant of a desk which had once perhaps been theirs: it is all one to us, we are dead. It seemed to give them no trouble to overlook Camille, no trouble whatsoever.

'Longwy has fallen,' Marat said.

'Yes, they told me. There is a map over there, they gave it to me because I don't know where anything is.'

'Verdun next,' Marat said. 'Within the week.' He sat down opposite Camille. 'What's the problem with your civil servants? They're standing out there muttering.'

'This place is stifling. I wish I were running a newspaper again.'

Marat was not, at this time, publishing his own newspaper in the ordinary way; instead, he was writing his opinions on wall-posters, and posting them up through the city. It was not a style to encourage subtlety, close argument; it made a man, he said, economical with his sympathies. He surveyed Camille. 'You and I, sunshine, are going to be shot.'

'That had occurred to me.'

'What will you do, do you think? Will you break down and beg for mercy?'

'I expect so,' Camille said realistically.

'But your life is worth something. Mine, too, though I wouldn't expect many people to agree. We have a duty to the Revolution, at this point. Brunswick is fully mobilized. What does Danton say? The position is desperate, not hopeless. He is not a fool, I take him to have some grounds for hope. But Camille, I am afraid. The enemy say they will devastate the city. People will suffer, you know, as perhaps they never have in all our history. Can you imagine the revenge the royalists will take?'

Camille shook his head, meaning, I try not to.

'Provence and Artois will be back. Antoinette. She will resume her state. The priests will be back. Children now in their cradles will suffer for what their fathers and mothers did.' Marat leaned forward, his body hunched, his eyes intent, as he did when he spoke from the tribune at the Jacobins. 'It will be an abattoir, an abattoir of a nation.'

Camille put his elbows on the desk, and watched Marat. He could not imagine what Marat expected him to say.

'I don't know how the enemy advance may be stopped,' Marat said. 'I leave that to Danton and to the soldiers. It is this city that is my business, it is the traitors within, the subversives, the royalists packed into our prisons. These prisons are not secure – you know very well, we have people shut up in convents, in hospitals, we have not places enough for them, or any way of keeping them secure.'

'Pity we knocked the Bastille down,' Camille said. 'I suppose.'

'And if they break out?' Marat said. 'No, I am not being fanciful – the weapon of imprisonment, the whole notion of it, demands some assent from the victim, some cooperation. Suppose that co-operation is withdrawn? As our troops join battle, leaving the city to women and children and politicians, the aristocrats pour out of the prisons, locate their arms caches – '

'Arms caches? Don't be stupid. Why do you think the Commune has been making house-to-house searches?'

'And can you swear to me that they've missed nothing?'

Camille shook his head. 'So what do you want us to do? Go into the prisons and kill them all?'

'At last,' Marat said. 'I thought we should never arrive.'

'In cold blood?'

'However you like.'

'And you'll organize this, will you, Marat?'

'Oh no, it would just happen spontaneously. The people, you see, being in such terror, being so inflamed against their enemies – '

'Spontaneously?' Camille said. 'Oh, very likely.' And yet, he thought: we have a city that is in immediate peril, we have a populace that is enraged, we have a sea of futile unfocused hatred slapping at the institutions of state and washing through the public squares, and we have victims, we have the focus for that hate, we have traitors ready, to hand – yes, it became more likely, by the minute.

'Oh, come on, man,' Marat said. 'We both know how these things are done.'

'We have already begun putting the royalists on trial,' he said.

'Have we got a year or two, do you think? Have we got a month? Have we got a week?'

'No. No, I see what you mean. But Marat, we've never – I mean, we never contracted ourselves for this sort of thing. It's murder, whichever way you look at it.'

'Take your hands away from your face. Hypocrite. What do you think we did in '89? Murder made you. Murder took you out of the back streets and put you where you sit now. Murder! What is it? It's a word.'

'I shall tell Danton what you advise.'

'Yes. You do that.'

'But he will not connive at it.'

'Let him suit himself. It will happen anyway. Either we control it as far as we can or it happens outside and beyond our control. Danton must be either master or servant – which will he be?'

'He will lose his good name. His honour.'

'Oh, Camille,' Marat said softly. 'His honour!' He shook his head. 'Oh, my poor Camille.'

Camille threw himself back in his chair, looked at the ceiling, looked at the faces that lined the room; the ministers' eyes were dull beneath their patina, the whites pickled by age. Had they wives, children? Had they feelings at all? Beneath their embroidered waistcoats, had the ribs moved, had the hearts ever beat? The portraits stared back at him; they made no sign. The officials had removed themselves from beyond the door. He could hear a clock, hear the minutes ticking away. 'The people have no honour,' Marat said. 'They have never been able to afford it. Honour is a luxury.'

'Suppose the other ministers prevent it?'

'Other ministers? Spare me that. What are the other ministers? Eunuchs.'

'Danton will not like this.'

'He doesn't have to like it,' Marat said fiercely, 'he has to see the necessity. That would be easy for him, I should think – a child can see the necessity. Like it? Do you think I like it?' Camille didn't answer. Marat paused for thought. 'Well, I don't mind it,' he said. 'I don't mind it at all.'

THE PRELIMINARIES for elections to the Convention have already begun. It seems, then, that life is going forward. Bread is being baked for the next day, plays are in rehearsal.

Lucile has her baby back; infant cries echo through the grand suites, under the painted ceilings, among the documents and the leather-bound law books, where no baby has ever cried before.

Verdun falls on 1 September. The enemy, if they choose now to advance on Paris, are two days' march away.

ROBESPIERRE: he kept thinking of Mirabeau now, of how that man had always said, with a great sweep of his arm, 'Mirabeau will do this', or, 'the Comte de Mirabeau will answer . . . ': speaking of himself like a character in a play he was directing. He is conscious now of eyes upon him: Robespierre acts. Or, Robespierre does not act. Robespierre sits still and watches them watching him.

He had refused to sit as a judge on Danton's special tribunal. He caught the flash of annoyance on Danton's face: 'You are still against the death penalty then, my friend?' And yet, Danton himself had been merciful. There had been very little work for Citizen Sanson. An officer of the National Guard had been executed – by the new beheading machine – and so had the Secretary of the Civil List, but there was an aristo journalist whose death sentence had not been carried out. Camille had slid his hands on to Danton's tired shoulders and said coaxingly that it was a bad precedent to execute journalists. Danton had laughed: 'As you wish. You can't rescind the verdict, so keep postponing the execution. We'll lose the man in the system somewhere. Do what you think best, you have my signature stamp.'

It was, in other words, arbitrary: the man's life depending, Fabre said, on Camille remembering a victory in some exchange of insults with him in '89, and so feeling magnanimous, and then putting on his cheap-tart act to amuse Danton and cajole him back into a good humour at the end of a hard day. (A secret, Fabre said, that Camille could profitably sell to Danton's wife.) Fabre was sour about the incident: not, Robespierre thought, because he had a passion for justice, but because he had no similar means of getting his own way. Was he, Robespierre, alone in feeling that the law should not be used and abused like this? It caused a minute revulsion in him, an intellectual flinching. But this feeling came from the old days, before the Revolution. Justice was the servant of policy now; no other position was compatible with survival. Yet it would have sickened him to hear Danton bellowing for heads, like that devil Marat. If anything, Danton lacked energy: was susceptible to individual blandishments, and not just from Camille.

Brissot. Vergniaud. Buzot. Condorcet. Roland. Roland, and Brissot again. In his dreams they wait, laughing, to catch him in a net. And Danton will not act . . .

These are the conspirators: why, he asked (since he is a reasonable man), does he fear conspiracy where no one else does?

And answered, well, I fear what I have past cause to fear. And these are the conspirators within: the heart that flutters, the head that aches, the gut that won't digest, and eyes that, increasingly, cannot bear bright sunlight. Behind them is the master conspirator, the occult part of the mind; nightmares wake him at half-past four, and then there is nothing to do but lie in a hopeless parody of sleep until the day begins.

To what end is this inner man conspiring? To take a night off and read a novel? To have more friends, to be liked a bit more? But people said, have you seen how Robespierre has taken to those tinted spectacles? It certainly gives him a sinister air.

DANTON WORE a scarlet coat. He stood before the Assembly. People cheered; some wept. The noise from the galleries could be heard across the river.

Huge, resonant voice in easy command: breathing as Fabre taught him. Two trains of thought running quietly in his head: plans laid, armies deployed, diplomatic manoeuvres set afoot: my generals can hold them for a fortnight, and after that (he said in his head), after that I do something else, after that I sell them the Queen if they would buy, or my mother, or I surrender, or I slit my throat.

The second train of thought: actions are being manufactured out of speech. How can words save a country? Words make myths, it seems, and for their myths people fight to win. Louise Gély: 'You have to direct them what to do. Once they know what attitude to take, how to face the situation, it is easy for them.' She is so right, the child . . . the situation is simple. Even a fourteen-year-old can grasp it. Simple words are needed. Few, and short. He draws himself up, puts out a hand to his audience. 'Dare,' he says. 'Always dare. And again, dare. In this way you will save France.'

At that moment, someone wrote, that hideous man was beautiful.

He felt then like a Roman emperor, present at his own deification. Living gods walk in the streets now: avatars load the cannon, icons load the dice.

LEGENDRE: 'The enemy was at the gates of Paris. Danton came, and he saved the country.'

IT IS VERY LATE. Marat's face, in candlelight, looks livid, drowned. Fabre has found things to laugh at. He has a bottle of brandy at his elbow. At this stage there are perhaps a dozen people in the room. They did not greet each other by name, and try to avoid each other's eyes. Perhaps a year from now they won't be able to swear to who was there and who wasn't. An affectedly plebeian Section leader sits by an open window, because the meeting doesn't like the smell of his pipe.

'It won't be arbitrary,' a man from the Commune says. 'We'll have trusted patriots, men from the Sections, and we'll equip them with the full lists. They'll be able to interview each prisoner, release any innocent persons who we've not already let go, and pass sentence on the others. What do you think?'

'I think it's fine,' Marat says. 'As long as there is only one possible sentence.'

'Do you think it will do any good, this travesty?' Camille asks the man from the Commune. 'Don't you think you may as well just wade in and slaughter people indiscriminately?'

Marat says, 'No doubt that is what will happen in the end, anyway. We must have the semblance of form. But quickly, citizens, we have to move quickly. The people are hungry and thirsty for justice.'

'Oh, Marat,' Camille says. 'Let us have an end to your slogans.'

The sansculotte with the pipe takes it out of his mouth. 'You're not really very good at this, Camille, are you? Why don't you just go home?'

Camille's finger stabs at the papers on the table. 'This is my business, it's the minister's business.'

'Look, if it helps you,' the sansculotte says, 'just think of it as an extension of what we did on 10 August. On that day we started something; now we're finishing it. What's the point of founding a republic if you can't take the action needed to maintain it?'

'I tell him this and tell him this,' Marat says quietly. 'I tell him and tell him. Stupid boy.'

At the centre of the table, like a prize, is the Minister of Justice's signature stamp. This is all that is needed to release a man or a woman from prison. It's true that Citizen Roland, as Minister of the Interior, should have some say in what happens in the gaols. But the feeling is that Roland neither knows nor cares; cares, but doesn't know; knows, but doesn't care; cares, but doesn't dare do anything about it. What does Roland matter anyway? One more pressing decision might give him a heart attack.

'To our lists,' says Citizen Hébert.

The lists are very long. There are about two thousand people in the prisons, after all; it's difficult to establish an exact number, there are a lot of people unaccounted for. Whoever is struck from the lists will be let out tonight; the others must take their chances, stand before their impromptu judges.

They come to a priest, one Bérardier. 'I want him released,' Camille says.

'A refractory priest, who has refused the oath to the constitution –'

'Released,' Camille says fiercely. They shrug, stamp the order. Camille is unpredictable, it does not do to frustrate him too much; besides, there is always the possibility that a given person is a government agent, an undercover man. Danton has scribbled his own list of people to be released, and given it to Fabre. Camille asks to see it; Fabre refuses. Camille suggests that Fabre has altered it. Fabre asks what he is taken for. No one answers. Fabre insinuates that a middle-aged barrister whose release Camille has obtained had been one of his lovers in the early '80s when he was very pretty and not very prosperous. Camille snaps back that it might be so but that is better than saving somebody's life for a fat fee, which Fabre is probably doing. 'Fascinating,' Hébert says. 'Shall we go on to the next sheet?'

Messengers wait outside the door, to carry urgent orders for release. It is difficult, when the pen skips over a name, to associate it with the corpse it might belong to, tomorrow or the day after that. There is no sense of evil in the room, just tiredness and the aftertaste of petty squabbling. Camille drinks quite a lot of Fabre's brandy. Towards daybreak, a kind of dismal camaraderie sets in.

THERE HAD BEEN, of course, the matter of who should do the killing, and it would obviously not be the men with the lists, not even the sansculotte with the pipe. It was thought advisable to recruit a number of butchers, and promise them a rate for the job. The intention was not mocking or macabre, but sound and humane.

Unfortunately, as the rumours of an aristo plot spread panic through the city, enthusiastic beginners joined in. They lacked skill, and the butchers tut-tutted over their small knowledge of anatomy. Unless it was their intention to torture and mutilate.

Exasperation at midday: 'We might as well not have bothered sitting up all night over those lists,' Fabre says. 'I'm sure the wrong people are being killed.'

Camille thinks of what Marat said: either we control it ourselves or it happens outside and beyond our control. It seems, as the unspeakable news comes in, hour by hour, that we have got the worst of both worlds. We will never, now, know an hour free from guilt; we will never, now, recover such reputation as we possessed; yet we neither planned nor willed the whole of it, the half of it. We simply turned away, we washed our hands, we made a list and we followed an agenda, we went home to sleep while the people did their worst and the people (Camille thinks) were translated from heroes to scavengers, to savages, to cannibals.

In the early stages at least, there was some attempt at order, some pretence, however risible, of legality. A group of sansculottes, red-capped, armed, behind the largest table they can find, the suspect before them: outside, the courtyard where the executioners wait, with cutlasses, axes, pikes. They set half of the suspects free – for a reason, or out of sentimentality, or because a mistake of identity has been found out just in time. The whole question of identification becomes more muddled as the day wears on, people claiming to have lost their papers or to have had them stolen; but anyone in prison must be there for a reason, isn't that so, and that reason must be against the public good, and as one man said, all aristos look the same to me, I can't tell their faces apart.

Some people know they are condemned; some have time to pray, and others die struggling and screaming, fighting to their last breath. An irate killer stamps in to the tribunal – 'Use your heads, give us a bloody chance, can't you? We can't keep up.' So the prisoners are waved away airily by their judges – 'Go, you're free.' Outside the door a steady man waits to fell them. Freedom is the last thing they know.

MID-AFTERNOON: Prudhomme, the young journalist, waited for Danton's meeting to break up. He did not know that Danton had laughed at the representations of the Supervisor of Prisons, or that he had sworn at Roland's private secretary. Since that day in '91, when a pack of National Guardsmen had thought he was Camille and nearly killed him, Prudhomme had felt himself entitled to take an interest in Danton and his friends.

Danton's eyes took him in: somewhat blankly. 'The prisoners are being massacred,' Prudhomme said to him.

'Fuck the prisoners. They must look after themselves.' He strode away. Camille looked closely at Prudhomme, failing, as he always did, to transpose Prudhomme's fading scars on to his own face.

'It's all right,' he said. He looked nervously guilty; it was the effect of Prudhomme, rather than the larger situation. He brushed one of Prudhomme's clenched hands with his own. 'It's all organized. No one who is innocent will be touched. If his Section vouch for a prisoner, he'll be set free. It's – '

'Camille.' Danton stopped, turned around and bellowed at him. 'For God's sake, come here, hurry up.'

He would have liked to hit him. Or hit Prudhomme. His official attitude was: I don't know anything about this.

THE PRINCESSE de Lamballe was murdered at La Force prison. Possibly she was raped. When the mob had torn out most of her internal organs and stuck them on pikes, they cut off her head and carried it to a hairdresser. At knife-point they forced the nauseated man to curl and dress the Princesse's pretty fair hair. Then they marched in procession to the Temple, where the Capet family were locked up. They put the head on a pike and hoisted it up to sway outside the high windows. 'Come and say hallo to your friend,' they exhorted the woman inside.

VOLTAIRE:

Reason must first be established in the minds of the leaders; then gradually it descends and at length rules the people, who are unaware of its existence, but who, perceiving the moderation of their rulers, learn to imitate them.

Nine ways by which one may share in the guilt of another's sin:

By counsel
By command
By consent
By provocation
By praise or flattery
By concealment
By being a partner in the sin
By silence
By defending the ill deed.

*

WHEN ROBESPIERRE spoke, the members of the Commune's Watch Committee put down their pens and looked straight at him. They did not fidget with their papers, blow their noses or allow their eyes to wander. If they had coughs, they suppressed them. They squared their shoulders and put conscientious expressions on their faces. He expected their attention, so he got it.

There was a plot, Robespierre told them, to put the Duke of Brunswick on the throne of France. Incredible as it might seem – he looked around the room, and no one allowed incredulity to show on his face – the allied commander had such ambitions, and Frenchmen were furthering them. He named Brissot.

Billaud-Varennes, Danton's former clerk, spoke at once to back him up. Whined rather, Max thought; he did not like Billaud. The man claimed a startling ability: he said he could recognize a conspirator by looking him straight in the eye.

The officials of the Commune drew up warrants for the immediate arrest of Brissot and Roland. Robespierre went home.

Eléonore Duplay caught him as he crossed the courtyard. 'Is it true that everyone in the prisons is being killed?'

'I don't know,' he said.

Aghast: 'But you'd have to know, they can't do anything without asking you.'

He put out a hand and pulled her to his side, not in intimacy, but because he wanted to influence the expression on her face. 'Supposing it were true, my dear Eléonore, my dear Cornélia, would you cry about it? If you think of the people the Austrians are killing now, driving them out of their farms, burning their roofs over their heads – well, which would you cry for?'

'I don't question it,' she said. 'You couldn't be wrong.'

'Well, which would you cry for?' He answered himself. 'Both.'

DANTON SIFTED through the papers on the Public Prosecutor's desk. He allowed himself this much familiarity with everyone's business. In the end it all came back to him.

When he saw the two warrants, he lifted them, and dropped them again. Brissot. Roland. He let them lie, and stared at them, and as his mind moved, slowly, he began to shake from head to foot, as he had on the morning when he was told of the death of his first child. Who had been at the Commune all day? Robespierre. Whose word was law there? His, and Robespierre's. Who had caused these warrants to be issued? Robespierre. One could call for the minutes, no doubt, one could read and judge the exact words that had brought it to this, one could apportion blame. But it was no more possible that the Commune had done this without Robespierre than that Roland and Brissot should be arrested and survive the night. I must move, he told himself; I must move from this spot.

It was Louvet, Manon Roland's fair frail novelist friend, who touched his elbow. 'Danton,' he said, 'Robespierre denounced Brissot by name . . . '

'So I see.' He picked up the warrants. He turned on Louvet, his voice savage. 'Jesus, how could you be such fools? How could I?' He pushed the papers under the man's nose. 'For God's sake, man, go and hide yourself somewhere.'

He folded the warrants, slipped them into an inside pocket of his coat. 'Now then. The little fellow will have to knock me down if he wants these back.'

Colour had rushed into Louvet's face. 'There's another war on now,' he said. 'Either we will kill Robespierre, or he will kill us.'

'Don't ask me to save you.' Danton's hand in his chest skidded him across the room. 'I have my own hide to think of, and the bloody Germans too.'

PÉTION PICKED UP the warrants and dropped them, just as Danton had done. '*Robespierre* authorized them?' Well, he kept saying, well; and again, well. 'Danton, does he know? Can he know? That they would be killed?'

'Of course he knows.' Danton sat down and put his head in his hands. 'By tomorrow there would have been no government. God knows what he thought he could pull out of it. Has he lost his mind, since I saw him yesterday, or was it intended, calculated – and in that case he is setting himself up as some sort of power, and since '89 he has been lying to us, not outright, I grant you, but by implication – Pétion, which is it?'

Pétion seemed to be talking to himself, in his rising panic. 'I think . . . that he is better than most of us, yes, certainly better, but now with the pressure of events . . .' He stopped. He himself was called Brissot's friend; his natural antipathy to the man had not stopped people sticking the label on him. Since 10 August, the Brissotins had governed on sufferance. The pretence was that they had invited Danton into the government; the truth was that he had given them their posts back, and that it was he who imposed his will at every cabinet meeting, sprawling in the great chair once occupied by Capet's softer bulk. 'Danton,' Pétion said, 'does Robespierre want my life too?' Danton shrugged; he did not know. Pétion looked away; he seemed ashamed of his thoughts. 'Manon said this morning, "Robespierre and Danton hold the big knife over us all."'

'And what answer did you give to the dear woman?'

'We said, after all, Citizeness, Robespierre is only a little clerk.'

Danton stood up. 'I don't hold a knife over you. You can tell her that. But there is a knife. And I'm not going to put my neck under it.'

'I don't see what we did to deserve this,' Pétion said.

'I do. I mean, if I were Robespierre, I would see. You people have studied your own political advantage for so long that you've forgotten what you ever wanted the power for. Look, I'll not defend you – not in public. Camille has been working on me for months about Brissot. So has Marat, in his different way. And Robespierre – oh yes, he's talked. We thought talking was all he ever did.'

'Robespierre must find out – that you have blocked him.'

'He's not a dictator.'

Pétion's affable features were still blank with shock. 'Would he be grateful to you, do you think, for saving him from the consequences of an ill-considered action? A moment of wrath?'

'Wrath? He's never had a moment of wrath. I was wrong to say he must be going mad. You could lock him up in a dungeon for fifty years and he wouldn't go mad. He's got everything he needs inside his head.' For a moment he put an outstretched hand on Pétion's shoulder. 'I bet he lives longer than we do.'

*

WHEN DANTON ENTERED his own apartment, massive inside his scarlet coat, his wife gave him one swollen glance of beaten betrayal; she pulled away from his outstretched hands and crossed her arms over her body, as if to hide from him the shape of the child she was carrying.

'You, Gabrielle?' he said. 'If only you knew. If only you knew how many people I've saved.'

'Get away from me,' she said. 'I can hardly bear to be in the same room.'

He rang for one of the maids. 'Attend to her,' he said.

He crashed his way into the Desmoulins's apartment. There was only Lucile, sitting quietly with her cat curled up in her lap. Everything had come to the Place des Piques: baby, cat, piano. 'I wanted to find Camille – ' he said. 'No, no, it doesn't matter.' He dropped to a knee beside her chair. The cat cleared the opposite arm, in one neat, fearful leap. He thought, I've seen that cat approach Robespierre, purring: animals can't know much.

Lucile put out a delicate hand; she touched his cheek, stroked his forehead, so gently that he hardly felt it.

'Lucile,' he said, 'let me take you to bed.' God knows, it was not what he meant to say.

She shook her head. 'I'd be frightened of you, Georges. And besides, would it be your bed, or ours? The beds themselves are so intimidating. You have the coronet, but we have such a number of gilt cherubim to cope with. We're always falling foul of their little gilt fists and feet.'

'Lucile, I beg of you. I need you.'

'No, I don't think you'd like the break with routine. You ask politely, I say no – isn't that the way it is? Today is not the day. Afterwards you'd confuse it all in your mind with Robespierre. You'd hate me, which I really couldn't bear.'

'No, no, I wouldn't.' His tone changed abruptly. 'What do you know about Robespierre?'

'It's surprising what you find out if you just sit still and listen.'

'Camille knew then – he knew, he must have known what Robespierre was going to do?'

Again she touched his face; that touch, and the softness of her voice, were almost reverential. 'Don't ask, Georges. Better not to ask.'

'Don't you mind? Don't you mind what we've done?'

'Perhaps I mind – but I know I'm part of it. Gabrielle, you see, she can't bear it – she thinks you've damned your soul and hers too. But for myself – I think possibly that when I first saw Camille, I was twelve then, twelve or thirteen – I thought, oh, here comes hell. It doesn't become me to start squealing now. Gabrielle married a nice young lawyer. I didn't.'

'You can't persuade me of that – you can't say you knew what you were getting.'

'One can know. And not know.'

He took her hand, her wrist, gripped it hard. 'Lolotte, this cannot go on for much longer. I am not Fréron, I am not Dillon, I am not a man you flirt with, I will not allow you to enjoy yourself at my expense.'

'So, then?'

'And I do mean to have you, you know.'

'Georges, are you threatening me?'

He nodded. 'I suppose I am,' he said thoughtfully. 'I suppose I must be.' He stood up.

'Well, this is quite a new phase of my existence,' she said. She looked up at him, with a sweet, confident smile. 'But you have neglected all the orthodox arts of persuasion, Georges. Is this the best you can do by way of seduction? All you do is glare at me and make the occasional grab. Why don't you languish? Why don't you sigh? Why don't you write me a sonnet?'

'Because I've seen where it gets your other beaux,' he said. 'Oh, dammit all, girl, this is ridiculous.'

He thought, she wants me really, the bitch. She thought, it takes his mind off things.

He picked up his papers, and went back to his own suite. The cat crept back, and jumped on to her knee and curled up; Lucile stared into the hearth, like an old spinster lady.

Perhaps fourteen hundred people are dead. Compared to the

average battlefield, it is a trifle. But think – (Lucile does): one life is everything to its possessor, one life is all we have.

THE ELECTIONS for the National Convention were conducted by the usual two-tier system, and, as the nine hundred second-stage Electors walked to their meeting in the hall of the Jacobins, they passed heaps of fresh corpses piled in the street.

There were repeated ballots, until a candidate got an absolute majority. It took a long time. A candidate could offer himself for election in more than one part of the country. It was not necessary to be a French citizen. The variety of candidates was so great that the Electors might have become confused, but Robespierre was always ready to offer guidance. He embraced Danton, tentatively, when Danton was returned with a 91 per cent poll in his favour; at least, if you could not say he embraced him, you could say he patted his sleeve. He relished the applause when he himself defeated Pétion in a direct contest, and forced him to seek a provincial seat; it was important to him that the Paris deputies form a solid anti-Brissotin bloc. He was both pleased and anxious when the Paris electors returned his younger brother Augustin; he worried a little in case his family name carried undue influence, but after all, Augustin had worked hard for the revolution in Arras, and it was time for him to make the move to the capital. Help and support for me, he thought. He managed a dazzled smile at the way things were going. He looked younger, for a minute or two.

The journalist Hébert did not receive more than six votes in any one ballot; again Robespierre's face seemed to open, the tense muscles of his jaw relaxed. Hébert has a certain sansculotte following, although he is known to keep a carriage; Hébert *in propria persona* is not so important as the image he shelters behind, and thankfully, Père Duchesne the furnace-maker will not be puffing his democratic pipe on the Convention's benches.

But not everything went smoothly . . . The English scientist Priestley seemed to be gathering support, in an Electors' rebellion against Marat. 'The need now is not for exceptional talent,' Robespierre advised, 'and certainly not for foreign talent. It is for men who have hidden in cellars for the sake of the Revolution. And,' he added, 'for butchers even.'

He intended no irony. Legendre was safely elected next day. So was Marat.

His protégé Antoine Saint-Just would be in Paris at last, and the Duke of Orléans would be sitting beside the men he had once paid and patronized. Having cast about for a surname, the Duke had adopted the one the people had stuck on him, half in mockery; he was now Philippe Égalité.

A hint of trouble on 8 September: 'Some jumped-up Brissotin intellectual,' Legendre said, 'this Kersaint, has polled enough votes to stop Camille coming through on the first ballot. What are we going to do about it?'

'Don't upset yourself,' Danton said soothingly. 'Better the jumped-up intellectual you know, eh?' He had quite expected the Electors to resist handing the nation's affairs over to Camille. Kersaint wasn't, anyway, what he called an intellectual; he was a naval officer from Brittany, had sat in the last Assembly.

Robespierre said, 'Citizen Legendre, if there is a conspiracy to stop Camille's election, I shall quash it.'

'Now wait a minute . . . ' Legendre said. His objection tailed off, but he looked uneasy. He hadn't mentioned a *conspiracy*; but Citizen Robespierre has this hair-trigger mechanism. 'What will you do?' he asked.

'I shall propose that until the elections are over, an hour a day be given to a public discussion of the candidates' merits.'

'Oh, a discussion,' Legendre said, relieved. For a moment he'd thought Robespierre might be planning to put a warrant out for Kersaint. Last week, you'd known what kind of a man you were dealing with; this week, you didn't know. It put him up in your estimation, in a way.

Danton grinned. 'You'd better make a list of Camille's merits, and circulate it. We aren't all so inventive as you. I don't know how you'd justify Camille, except under the heading "exceptional talent".'

'You do want him elected?' Robespierre demanded.

'Of course. I want someone to talk to during the boring debates.'

'Then don't sit there laughing.'

Camille said, 'I wish you wouldn't discuss me as if I weren't here.'

On the next ballot, Citizen Kersaint, who before had received 230 votes, now mysteriously found that he had only thirty-six. Robespierre shrugged. 'One does try to persuade people, of course. There's no more to it than that. Congratulations, my dear.' For some reason, an image comes into his head, of Camille at twelve or thirteen years old: a violent, whimsical child, given to stormy outbreaks of tears.

Meanwhile the volunteers, in their thousands, march to the front singing. They have sausages and loaves of bread stuck on the end of their bayonets. Women give them kisses and bunches of flowers. Do you remember how it used to be when the recruiting sergeant came to a village? No one hides now. People are scraping the walls of their cellars for saltpetre to make gunpowder. Women are giving their wedding rings to the Treasury to be melted down. Many of them, of course, will be taking advantage of the new laws to get divorced.

'PIKES?' Camille said.

'Pikes,' Fabre said sullenly.

'I don't wish to appear legalistic, a pettifogger as it were, but is it the business of the Minister of Justice to purchase pikes? Does Georges-Jacques know we've got a bill for pikes?'

'Oh, come on, do you think I can go running to the minister with every trifling expense?'

'When you add it all up,' Camille pushed his hair back, 'we've spent a lot of money over the past few weeks. It worries me to think that now we're all deputies there'll be new ministers soon, and they'll want to know where the money has gone. Because really, I haven't the least idea. I don't suppose you have?'

'Anything that causes difficulty,' Fabre said, 'you just put down as "Secret Fund". Then nobody asks any questions, because they can't, you see – it's secret. Don't worry so much. Everything's all right as long as you don't lose the Great Seal. You haven't lost it, have you?'

'No. At least, I saw it somewhere this morning.'

'Good – now look, shall we reimburse ourselves a bit? What

about that money Manon Roland is supposed to be getting for her ministry to issue news-sheets?'

'Oh yes. Georges told her that she'd better ask me nicely to edit them.'

'He did, I was there. She said perhaps her husband would see you, and decide if you were suitable. Our minister, he began to bellow and paw the ground.'

They laughed. 'Well, then,' Camille said. 'One Treasury warrant . . . ' His hands moved over his desk. '. . . Claude taught me this . . . they never query anything, you know, if it has Danton's signature.'

'I know,' Fabre said.

'What did I do with the signature stamp? I lent it to Marat. I hope he brings it back.'

'Speaking of Queen Coco,' Fabre said, 'have you noticed anything different in her manner lately?'

'How could I? You know I'm forbidden the presence.'

'Oh yes, of course you are. Well, let me tell you . . . There's a certain lightness in the step, a certain bloom on the cheek – what does that betoken?'

'She's in love.'

FABRE IS NOW around forty years years old. He is neat, pale, built on economic lines: actor's eyes, actor's hands. Bits of his autobiography emerge, late at night, in no particular chronological order. No wonder nothing fazes him. In Namur once, aided by army-officer friends, he eloped with a fifteen-year-old girl called Catiche; he did it, he explains, to preserve her virginity from the girl's own father. Better that he should have it . . . They had been apprehended; Catiche had been hastily married off, he had been sentenced to hang. How is it, then, that he lives to tell the tale? All these years on, and with so much excitement in between, he can hardly remember. Camille says, 'Georges-Jacques, we have lived sheltered lives, you and me.'

'Monk-like,' the minister agrees.

'Oh, I don't know,' Fabre says modestly.

Fabre follows the minister as he stamps through public buildings, his large hands slapping backs and desk tops, wringing the necks of all compromise solutions, all the tried and tested methods, all the decent ways of doing things. Power becomes him, fits him like an old top-coat; his little eyes glitter if anyone tries to dispute with him. Fabre feeds his ego in all the unsubtle ways he likes best; they are comfortable together, sit up drinking and discussing shady inter-departmental deals. When dawn comes, Danton finds himself alone with the map of Europe.

Fabre is limited, he complains, he makes me waste my time. But his company is never exacting, and the minister is used to him, and he is always there when he's wanted.

This morning the minister was thoughtful, chin on fist. 'Fabre, have you ever planned a robbery?'

Fabre darted at him a look of alarm.

'No,' Danton said good-humouredly, 'I know petty criminality is a pastime of yours. We'll come to that later. No, I need your help, because I want to steal the Crown Jewels. Yes, do sit down.'

'Perhaps, Danton, a word of explanation?'

'You're entitled to that – but I want no ifs or buts or exclamations of incredulity. Use your imagination. I do. Now, consider the Duke of Brunswick.'

'Brunswick – '

'Spare me your Jacobin diatribe – I've heard it. The truth is that Brunswick, as a man, is not wholly unsympathetic to us. The July manifesto wasn't his – the Austrians and the Prussians made him sign it. Think about him. He's an intelligent man. He's a forward-looking man. He has no tears to waste on the Bourbons. He is also a very rich man. He is a great soldier. But to the allies he is – what? A mercenary.'

'What does he aspire to be?'

'Brunswick knows as well as I do that France isn't ready for republican government. The people may not want Louis or his brothers, but they want a King, because Kings are what they understand, and sooner or later the nation will fall to a King, or to a dictator who will make himself King. Ask Robespierre, if you don't think I'm right. Now there might have been circumstances in which

– having established a constitution – we were scouring Europe for some reasonably regal old buffer to come and uphold it. Brunswick would perhaps word it differently – but there is no doubt that he wished to play that role.'

'Robespierre alleged this.' (And you, Fabre thought, pretended not to believe it.) 'But then in July, with the manifesto – '

'Brunswick wrecked his chances. We use him as a swear-word. Why did the allies make him put his name on their manifesto? Because they need him. They wanted to make him hated here, so that his personal ambitions were quashed, and he was secured to their service.'

'They succeeded. So what about it?'

'The situation's not – irretrievable. You see, I've considered whether Brunswick might be bought off. I've asked General Dumouriez to open negotiations.'

Fabre drew in his breath. 'You're reckless with our lives. We're in Dumouriez's hands now.'

'That's possible, but that's not the issue. The issue is the result for France, not the unfinished business between me and the general. Because . . . it appears that Brunswick can be bought off.'

'Well, he's human, isn't he? He isn't Robespierre, or even the Virtuous Roland, as the newspapers call the Minister of the Interior.'

'Don't banter,' Danton said. Suddenly he grinned. 'I take your point. We do have a few saints on our side. Well, when they're dead, the French will be able to march into battle with their relics for protection. In lieu of cannon, of which we are rather short.'

'What does Brunswick want? How much?'

'His requirements are specific. He wants diamonds. Did you know he collects them? We know, don't we, what lust diamonds can inspire? We have the example, dear to our hearts, of the woman Capet.'

'But I can hardly believe – '

Danton cut him off with a gesture. 'We steal the Crown Jewels. We convey to Brunswick the stones he especially covets, and we allow the others to be recovered. For use on future occasions.'

'Can the thing be done?'

Danton scowled. 'Do you think I'd have got so deep in, if it couldn't? The theft itself would pose very few problems, for professionals, if they have a bit of help from us. A few slip-ups on the security side. A few blunders with the investigation.'

'But all that – the security of the jewels, the investigation – all that would come under Roland's jurisdiction.'

'The Virtuous Roland will fall in with our scheme. After he's been told a certain amount about it, after he's implicated, he won't be able to betray us without betraying himself. I will bring him to that point, I will make sure he has the knowledge he doesn't want to have – you can leave that to me. But in fact, what he knows will be very little – we'll wrap the affair up so that he has to guess who is involved and who isn't. If things get difficult, we'll stick him with the blame. After all, as you say, his department is responsible.'

'But he'd simply say, Danton originated this – '

'If he lived long enough.'

Fabre stared. 'You are a different man, Danton.'

'No, Fabre, I am a filthy patriot, as I always have been. What I am buying from Brunswick is one battle, one battle for our poor, underfed, barefoot soldiers. Is that wrong?'

'The means . . . '

'The means I will set out to you, and I have no time to waste discussing ends. I want no cant about justification. The justification is the saving of the country.'

'For what?' Fabre looked stupefied. 'Saving it for what?'

Danton's face darkened. 'If this day fortnight an Austrian soldier takes you by the throat and says, "Do you want to live?" will you say, "For what?"'

Fabre looked away. 'Yes . . . ' he muttered. 'To survive at all will be the thing now. And Brunswick is willing to lose a battle – with his reputation at stake?'

'It will be managed so that he doesn't lose face. He knows what he's doing. So do I. Now, Fabre, some professional criminals. I have contacts already, which you must follow up. They mustn't know who they're working for. They will all be,' he waved a hand, 'dispensable. We can allow Roland to direct the police in a certain amount of inept investigation. Of course, we can expect the matter to be taken very seriously. Death penalty.'

'What's to stop them talking at their trial? Because we may need to let the police catch *somebody*.'

'As far as you can, make sure they have nothing to talk about. We shall have a blanket of obfuscation between each stratum of this conspiracy, and between each conspirator. So see to that. Obfuscate. If anyone should begin to suspect government involvement, the trail should lead to Roland. Now, there are two people in particular who must know nothing of this. One is Roland's wife. The woman is innocent of practical politics, and very loud-mouthed. The trouble is, he doesn't seem able to keep anything from her.'

'The other person is Camille,' Fabre said. 'Because he would tell Robespierre, and Robespierre would call us traitors for talking to Brunswick at all.'

Danton nodded. 'I can't divide Camille's loyalties. Who knows? He might make the wrong choice.'

'But both of them are in a position to find out so much.'

'That's a risk we take. Now, I can buy one battle – and by doing so, I can hope to turn the tide of the war. But after that I can't remain in office. I would be open to blackmail, by Brunswick or more likely by – '

'General Dumouriez.'

'Quite. Oh, I know you don't like the odds, Fabre. But consider yourself. I don't know how much you've embezzled from the ministry in the past few weeks, but I take it to be more than a trifle. I – let us say as long as your ambitions remain on a reasonable scale – I won't thwart them. You are thinking, what use will Danton be to me out of office? But Fabre, war is so lucrative. You'll never be far from power now. Inside information . . . just imagine. I know what you're worth to me.'

Fabre swallowed. He looked away. His eyes seemed unfocused. 'Do you ever think, does it ever bother you . . . that everything is founded on lies?'

'That's a dangerous thing to say. I don't like that.'

'No, I didn't mean on your part, I was asking . . . on my own account . . . to see if one might compare experiences.' He smiled wanly; for the first time in all the years he'd known him Danton saw him at a loss, mystified, a man whose life has been taken out of his control. He looked up. 'It's nothing,' he said lightly. 'I didn't mean anything, Danton.'

'You can't afford to speak without thinking. No one must know the truth about this, not in a thousand years. The French are going to win a battle, that's all. Your silence is the price of mine, and neither of us breaks the silence, even to save our own lives.'

II. *Robespierricide*

(*1792*)

'I FELL IN LOVE with you the first time I saw you.' Oh, Manon thought, not before that? It seemed to her that her letters, her writings, should have prompted some quickening of sensibility in the man who – she now knew – was the only one who could ever have made her happy.

This was no hasty process. Rivers of ink had flowed between them, when they'd been apart; when they've been together – or, let us say, in the same city – they have seldom had a private moment. Salon conversation, hours of it, had been their lot; they spoke the language of legislators, before they spoke the language of love. Even now, Buzot did not say much. He seemed perplexed, torn, tormented. He was younger than she was, less tutored in his emotions. He had a wife: a plain woman, older.

Manon ventured this: her fingertips on his shoulder, as he sat with his head in his hands. It was consolatory; and it stopped her fingers from trembling.

There was a need for secrecy. The newspapers nominated lovers for her – Louvet, often. Until now she's reacted with public scorn; have they no arguments, have they not even a higher form of wit? (In private, though, these skits and squibs brought her near to tears; she asked herself why she was meted out the same treatment as that peculiar, wild young woman Théroigne, the same treatment – when she thought about it – as the Capet woman used to get.) The newspapers – just – she could bear; what was harder to bear was the activity of the gossip circus that centred on the Ministry of Justice.

Danton's comments were relayed to her; he claimed her husband had been a cuckold for years, in every moral sense if not the physical one. But how could he imagine her situation; how could he appreciate, acknowledge the delicate satisfactions of a relationship between a chaste woman and an honourable man? It was impossible to think of him in any context but that of the grossly physical. She had seen his wife; since he became a minister he had brought her once to the Riding-School, to sit in the public gallery and hear him roaring at the deputies. She was a dull type of woman, pregnant, probably with no thought in her head beyond gruel and baby-mush. Still, she's a woman – how could she bear it, she asked out loud, how could she bear to have that bully's overweight body stretched on top of hers?

It was an unguarded remark, a remark almost shocked out of her by the strength of her own repulsion; next day it was of course repeated all over town. She went scarlet at the thought of it.

Citizen Fabre d'Églantine called. He crossed his legs and put his fingertips together. 'Well, my dear,' he said.

This ghastly assumption of familiarity was what she resented. This unserious person, who associated with females who trembled on the outer fringes of polite society: this creature with his theatrical affectations and his snide remarks out of earshot; they sent him here to watch her, and he went back and made reports. 'Citizen Camille is saying,' he told her, 'that your now-famous remark suggests that you are in fact greatly attracted to the minister – as he has always suspected.'

'I can't imagine how he presumes to divine the state of my feelings. As we have never met.'

'No, I realize this: why won't you meet him?'

'We would have nothing to say to each other.'

She had seen Camille Desmoulins's wife at the Riding-School, and at the public gallery of the Jacobins; she looked an accommodating sort of girl, and they said she accommodated Danton. They said Camille condoned it, or did rather more ... Fabre noticed that little, flinching movement of the head, that flinching away from knowledge. And yet, what a cesspit the woman's mind must be; even we, he thought, do not speculate *in public* about what our colleagues do in bed.

Manon asked herself: why do I have to put up with this man? If I must communicate with Danton, couldn't there be some other go-between? Apparently not. Perhaps, she thought, Danton doesn't trust as many people as his expansive manner suggests?

Fabre looked at her quizzically. 'Your loss,' he said. 'Really, you have the wrong impression; you'd like Camille much better than you like me. Incidentally, he believes that women should have been allowed to vote in the elections.'

She shook her head. 'I disagree. Most women know nothing of politics. They do not reason – ' she thinks of Danton's women – 'they have no constructive thoughts at all. They would simply be influenced by their husbands.'

'Or their lovers.'

'In your circles, perhaps.'

'I'll tell Camille what you say.'

'Please don't bother. I've no wish to carry on a debate with him, at first- or second-hand.'

'He'll be devastated to know that your opinion of him has sunk even lower.'

'Do you take me for a fool?' she said harshly.

He raised an eyebrow: as he always did, when he had provoked her to an outburst. Day after day he watched her, reaping her moods and garnering her expressions.

Secrecy then. Yet there's a need for honesty, and François-Léonard admitted it. 'We are both married, and I see that it's impossible . . . for you, anyway . . . to do anything to dishonour those vows. . . . '

But it *feels* so right, she cried. My instinct tells me it can't be wrong.

'Instinct?' He looked up. 'Manon, this is suspect. You know, we have no absolute right to be happy . . . or rather, we need to think carefully about what the nature of happiness might be . . . We have no right to please ourselves, at the expense of others.' Still those steady fingers rested upon his shoulder; but her face was unconvinced, her face was . . . greedy. 'Manon?' he said. 'Have you read Cicero? "On Duty"?'

Has she read Cicero? Does she know her Duty? 'Oh, yes . . . ' she moaned. 'Oh, I'm well-read. And I know that obligations must be weighed, that no one can be happy at the expense of other people. Don't you think I've been through all this, in my head?'

'Yes.' He looked abashed. 'I've underestimated you.'

'Do you know, if I have a fault – ' she paused minutely, waiting for the polite rejoinder – 'if I have a fault, it's that I speak to the point, I can't bear hypocrisy, I can't bear this politeness that detracts from honesty – I must speak to Roland.'

'Speak to him? Of what?'

Fair question. Nothing has happened between them – in the sense that Danton and his friends think of *something happening*. (She pictured Lucile Desmoulins's little breasts, crushed between Danton's fingers.) Only his precipitate declaration, her precipitate answer: but since then, he had barely touched her, barely touched her hand.

'My dear'– she dropped her head – 'this goes so far beyond the realms of the physical. As you say – in that sense, nothing is possible for us. And, of course, I must support Roland – this is a time of crisis, I am his wife, I cannot abandon him. And yet – I cannot allow him to live in doubt about the true nature of things. This is part of my character, you must understand it.'

He looked up. He frowned. 'But Manon, you have nothing to say to your husband. Nothing has occurred. We have simply spoken of our feelings – '

'Yes, we have spoken of them! Roland has never spoken to me of his feelings – but I respect them, I know he has feelings, he must have, everybody has them. I must say to him: here is the truth. I have met the man I was meant to love; our situation is thus, and thus; I shall not mention his name; nothing has occurred; nothing shall occur; I shall remain a faithful wife to you. He will understand me; he will know my heart has gone elsewhere.'

Buzot cast his eyes down. 'You are implacable, Manon. Has there ever been a woman like you?'

I doubt it, she thought. She said, 'I cannot betray Roland. I cannot leave him. My body, you may think, was meant for pleasure. But pleasure is not of the first account.' Still, she thought of Buzot's hands; rather robust hands for so elegant, so well-kept a man. Her breasts are not like the Desmoulins woman's; they are breasts that have fed a child, they are responsible breasts.

Buzot said, 'Do you think it's a good idea to tell him? Do you think – ' (God help me) – 'that there's any point?'

He had an intimation that he had gone about this the wrong way. But then, he had no experience. He was a virgin, in these matters; and his wife, whom he had married for her money, was older, and plain.

'Yes, yes, yes!' Fabre said. 'There's certainly someone! How pleasant to find that people are no better than you are.'

'Not Louvet?'

'No. Barbaroux, perhaps?'

'Oh no. Reputation bad. Attractions obvious. Rather,' Camille sighed, 'rather florid and showy for Madame.'

'I wonder how the Virtuous Roland will take it?'

'At her age,' Camille said with disgust. 'And she so plain, too.'

'Are you ill?' Manon asked her husband. It was hard to keep the sharpness out of her voice. Her husband had slumped in his chair, and as he dragged his eyes to her face his expression was certainly that of physical pain.

'I'm sorry.' Sorry for him, she meant. She did not feel any further need to apologize; she was simply setting out the situation for him, so that there should be no need for demeaning behaviour, for pretences, for anything that could be construed as deceit.

She waited for him to speak. When he did not, she said, 'You understand why I won't tell you his name.'

He nodded.

'Because it would produce impediments to our work. Obstacles. Even though we are reasonable people.' She waited. 'I am not a woman who can bridle my emotions. My conduct, though, will be above reproach.'

At last he broke the silence.

'Manon, how is Eudora, our daughter?'

She was amazed, angry at the irrelevance. 'You know she's well. You know she's well looked after.'

'Yes, but why do we never have her here?'

'Because the ministry is no place for a child.'

'Danton has his children at the Place des Piques.'

'His children are infants, they can be left to nursemaids. Eudora is a different matter – she would need my attention, and at present that is taken up elsewhere. You know she is not pretty, she has no accomplishments – what would I do with her?'

'She is only twelve, Manon.'

She looked down at him. She saw his sinewy hand, clenching and unclenching; then she saw that he had begun to cry, that tears were running silently down his cheeks. She thought, he would not want me to witness this. With a look of puzzled sadness she left the room, closing the door quietly, as she did when he was sick, when he was her patient and she his nurse.

He listened until the clip of her footsteps died away, and then at last permitted himself to make a sound, a sound that seemed to him to be natural, as natural as speech: it was a stifled animal bleat, a bleat of mourning, from a narrow chest. On and on it went; unlike speech, it went nowhere, it had no necessary end. It was for himself; it was for Eudora; it was for all the people who had ever got in her way.

ELÉONORE: She had thought, when all this is over, Max will marry me. She had hinted it to her mother. 'Yes, I think so,' Mme Duplay had said comfortably.

A few days later her father took her aside. With a thoughtful, embarrassed gesture, he smoothed his thinning hair over his scalp. 'He's a great patriot,' he said. It seemed to be worrying him. 'I should think he's very fond of you. He's very reserved, isn't he, in his private capacity? Not that one would wish him any different. A great patriot.'

'Yes.' She was irritated. Did her father imagine that her pride in him needed to be bolstered in this way?

'It's a great honour that he lives here with us, and so of course we ought to do all we can . . . The fact is, you're already married, in my eyes.'

'Oh,' she said. 'I see what you mean.'

'I'd rely on you ... if there were anything you could do to make his life more comfortable – '

'Father, didn't you hear me, I said, I see what you mean.'

FINALLY, she let her hair down, so that it tumbled over her square shoulders and down her back. She pushed it away from her small breasts and leaned into the mirror to scrutinize herself. Perhaps it is folly to imagine that with my plain face ... Lucile Desmoulins had come yesterday, bringing the baby for them to see. They fussed around her and chattered, and she had passed the baby to Victoire and sat alone: one hand drooping over the arm of her chair, like a winter flower touched with ice. When Max had come in, she had turned her head, smiled; and sudden pleasure lit his face. It ought to be called brotherly affection, what he felt for Lucile; but for me, she thought, if there were any justice it ought to be more than that.

She smoothed her hand down over her flat belly and hips. She began to take pleasure in the softness of her own skin; she felt what his hands would feel. But when she turned away from the mirror, she saw for a second the square, solid lines of her body, and, as she eased herself into the bed and put her head on his pillow, only a residue of disappointment remained. As she lay and waited, her whole body locked rigid in anticipation.

She heard him climbing the stairs; turned her face resolutely to the door. For one dreadful half-second she imagined that – O God, is it possible – the dog might burst in, hurl himself upon her, panting and grinning, whining and slurping, snatching up (as he was prone to do) jawfuls of her very clean and well-brushed hair.

But the door handle turned, and nothing and no one entered. He hesitated on the threshold of the room, and looked as if he might back out, and down the stairs again. Then, deciding, he stepped in. Eyes met; of course, they would. He had a sheaf of loose papers in his hands, and as he reached out to put them down, his eyes still on her face, some of them went fluttering to the floor.

'Shut the door,' she said. She hoped it would be all that she would need to say, perfect understanding then; but emerging from her mouth it sounded just a practical suggestion, as if she were incommoded by a draught.

'Eléonore, are you sure about this?'

An expression of impatience and self-mockery crossed his face; it did seem that she had made up her mind. He lifted her hands, kissed her fingertips. He wanted to say, very clearly, we can't do this; as he bent to retrieve the scattered papers, blood rushed into his face, and he realized the total impossibility of asking her to get up and go.

When he turned back to her she was sitting up. 'No one will complain,' she said. 'They understand. We're not children. They're not going to make things difficult for us.'

Are they not, though, he thought. He sat down on the bed and stroked her breast, the nipple hardening into the palm of his hand. His face expressed concern for her.

'It's all right,' she said. 'Really.'

No one had ever kissed her before. He did it very gently, but still, she seemed surprised. He thought that he had better take his clothes off because in a minute she would start advising it, telling him that was all right too. He touched alien flesh, soft, strange; there was a girl he used to see when he came to Versailles at first, but she was not a good girl, not in any sense, and it had been easier to drift apart, and since then it had been easier not to do anything, celibacy is easy but half-celibacy is very hard, women don't keep secrets and the papers are avid for gossip . . . Eléonore did not seem to expect or want any delay. She pushed her body against his, but it was stiff with the anticipation of pain. She knows the mechanics, he thought, but no one has introduced her to the art. Does she know she might begin to bleed? He felt a sharp, nauseous pang.

'Eléonore, close your eyes,' he whispered to her. 'You should try to relax, just a minute until you feel – ' Better, he had almost said; as if it were a sick bed. He touched her hair, kissed her again. She didn't touch him; she hadn't thought of it. He pushed her legs apart a little. 'I don't want you to be frightened,' he said.

'It's all right,' she said.

But it wasn't. He couldn't force his way into her dry and rigid body without using a brutality he couldn't call up. After a minute or two he propped himself on his elbow and looked down at her. 'Don't try to rush,' he said. He slipped a hand under her buttocks. Eléonore, he would have liked to say, I'm not practised at this, and I wouldn't describe you as a natural. She arched her body against his. Someone's told her to work hard for what she wants in life, to grit her teeth and never give up . . . poor Eléonore, poor women. Rather unexpectedly, and at a faintly peculiar angle, he penetrated her. She did not make a sound. He gathered her head against his shoulder so that he did not have to see her face and would not know if it hurt her. He eased himself around – not that there was much ease about it – into a more agreeable position. He thought again, it's been too long, you do this often or not at all. And so, of course, it was over quickly. He buried in her neck a faint sound of release. He let her go, and her head dropped back against the pillow

'Did I hurt you?'

'It's all right.'

He rolled over on his side and closed his eyes. She would be thinking, so that's it, is it, is that what the fuss is about? Of course she would think that. It was his own disappointment he couldn't get over, a kind of bitter, stained feeling in his throat. There's a lesson somewhere, he thought; when pleasures you deny yourself turn out not to be pleasures, you're doubly destroyed, for not only do you lose an illusion, you also feel futile. It had been much better, of course, with the Versailles girl, but there was no going back to that situation, there was no conquering one's spiritual distaste for the casual encounter. Should he say to Eléonore, I'm sorry it was so quick, I realize you didn't enjoy it? But what was the point, since she didn't have a standard of comparison, and would only say 'it was all right' anyway.

'I'll get up now,' she said.

He put an arm around her. 'Stay.' He kissed her breasts.

'All right. If you want.'

He made tentative exploration. There was no blood, at least he didn't think so. He thought, presumably she will actually know that there is more to it, that it gets better with practice, because she will understand that for some people it is such an important part of their lives.

Now at last she relaxed a little. She smiled. It was a smile of accomplishment. Who can guess what she's thinking? 'This bed's not very big,' she said.

'No, but – ' If it came to that, he would just have to tell her. He would have to say Eléonore, Cornélia, much as I appreciate the free and generous offer of your body, I have no intention of spending my nights with you, even if your whole family helps us to move the furniture. He closed his eyes again. He tried to think what excuse he could make to Maurice when he left the house, how he would cope with Madame's questions, no doubt tears. He thought then of the recrimination that would descend on Eléonore's muddled and guiltless head, and the feminine spite. And besides, he didn't want to go, to cold and unfrequented rooms in another district, and meet Maurice Duplay at the Jacobins, and nod to him, and refrain from asking after the family. And he knew, quite certainly, that this would happen again. When Eléonore decided that it was time she'd just trip upstairs and wait for him, and he wouldn't be able to send her away, any more than he had the first time. He wondered who she'd confide in, because she'd need advice on how often to expect it; and the disastrous possibilities came tumbling in on his head, as he tried to delimit the circle of her female friends. It was fortunate that she hardly knew Mme Danton.

He must have gone to sleep then, and when he woke up she had gone. It was nine p.m. Tomorrow, he thought, she will go bouncing along the street, smiling at people, and paying calls for no real reason.

IN THE DAYS afterwards he became sick with guilt. The second time she was easier, less tense, but she never gave any sign of experiencing pleasure. It came to him that if she found herself pregnant they would have to be married very quickly. Perhaps, he thought, when the Convention meets new people will come to the house, and perhaps someone will like her, and I can be generous and release her from any promise or tie.

But in his heart, he knew that this wouldn't happen. No one would like her. The family wouldn't let them like her. The people who're married, he thought, can get divorced now. But the only thing that will release us is if one of us dies.

AT THE MINISTRY, Camille sat at his desk, and irrelevant thoughts flitted through his head. He thought of the night he had spent in his cousin de Viefville's apartment, before he had gone to see Mirabeau. Barnave had called. Barnave had spoken to him as if he were someone worthy of consideration. He had liked Barnave, personally. He was in prison now, accused of conspiring with the Court; of this charge he was, of course, utterly guilty. Camille sighed. He drew little ships at sea in the margin of the encouraging letter he was drafting to the Jacobins of Marseille.

The members of the Convention were gathering now in Paris. Augustin Robespierre: Camille, you haven't changed a bit. And Antoine Saint-Just ... he would have to be patient about Saint-Just, stop that disastrous, illogical animosity flaring up ...

'I have the feeling he harbours loathsome thoughts in his head,' he told Danton.

And Danton, preoccupied with solidarity: 'Do try, do try,' he said, in his tired barrister's voice, 'to keep the peace, you know, not be a constant disappointment to Maximilien? You do make work for him, tidying up your indiscretions.'

'Saint-Just will not have indiscretions, I suppose.'

'He doesn't look as if he would.'

'That will endear him to everyone, I'm sure.'

'Endear,' Danton laughed. 'The boy alarms me. That chilly, purposive smirk.'

'Perhaps he's trying to look pleasant.'

'Hérault will be jealous. The women will be interested in someone else.'

'Hérault need not worry. Saint-Just isn't interested in women.'

'You used to say that about Saint Maximilien, but now he has the delightful Cornélia. Yes, isn't it so?'

'I don't know.'

'I do.'

So that was common gossip now, besides the supposed infidelity of Roland's wife and the ménage here at the Place des Piques. What things for people to occupy themselves with, he thought.

Perhaps Danton would leave office soon. For himself he would be pleased. Yet it seemed certain that Roland's supporters would try to arrange for him to stay on at the Interior, though he had been elected to the Convention. Even after the scandal about the Crown Jewels, the dusty old bureaucrat was riding high. And if he stayed in office, why not Danton, so much more necessary to the nation?

I don't want to be here much longer, he thought. I shall turn into Claude. I don't much want to speak to the Convention either, they won't be able to hear me. Then again, he said to himself, it isn't a question of what I want.

It was more troubling to think that Danton himself wanted to leave office. Even now he hadn't thrown over his dreams – his delusions – of getting out of Paris for good. In the small hours, Camille had found him solitary in a pool of yellow candlelight, poring over the deeds to his Arcis property, each boundary stone, water course, right of way. As he lifted his head Camille had seen in his eyes a picture of mellow buildings, fields, copses and streams.

'Ah,' he had said, startled. 'I thought my assassin had come at last.' He laid a hand, palm down, on the deeds. 'To think of the Prussians here, perhaps.'

Fabre had been evasive lately, Camille thought. Not that he was given to plain speaking. If Fabre had to choose, between money and revolutionary fame . . . No, he'd refuse to choose, he'd go on dizzily demanding both.

'What interpretation are we to put on the removal of the Crown Jewels?' Camille asked Danton.

What are we to think? Or – what are we to say? He watched Danton digest the ambiguity.

'I think we must say that Roland's carelessness is much to blame.'

'Yes, he should have made better security arrangements, should he not? Fabre was with the Citizeness Roland the day after. He went at half-past ten and came back at one. Do you think he had been castigating her?'

'How do I know?'

Camille gave him an amused, sideways glance. 'And after he left the Citizeness, she went straight to her husband and told him that the man who stole the Crown Jewels had just called.'

'How do you know that?'

'Perhaps I'm making it up. Do you think I am?'

'You could be,' Danton said unhappily.

'Don't trust Dumouriez.'

'No. Robespierre says it. I am sick of him saying it.'

'Robespierre is never wrong.'

'Perhaps I should go to the front myself. See a few people. Get a few things straightened out.'

So – perhaps when these pastoral moods came upon him, it was really a kind of fear. God knows he was vulnerable enough, though it seemed strange to apply the word to him. He was vulnerable to Dumouriez, and to supporters of the Bourbons too, seeking fulfilment of promises made ... 'There's nothing to worry about. M. Danton will look after us.'

Camille swept the thought away hastily, pushing his hair back in nervous agitation, as if someone were in the room with him. He seemed to hear Robespierre's voice drifting across a cold spring day in 1790: 'Once you bestow affection on a person, reason flies out of the window. Look at the Comte de Mirabeau – objectively, if you can, for a moment. The way he lives, his words, his actions, put me on my guard immediately – then I apply a little thought, and I discover that the man is wholly given over to self-aggrandizement. Now why can't you come to this conclusion, because it's plain enough? You don't yield to your feelings in other respects, when they run counter to your larger aims; for instance, you're frightened of speaking in public, but you don't let it stop you. Then, like that – you have to be ruthless with your feelings.'

Suppose he found that persistent unsparing voice at his elbow one day, claiming that Danton lacked probity; he had an answer, pat, not a logical one, but one sufficiently chilling to put logic in abeyance. To question Danton's patriotism was to cast in doubt the whole Revolution. A tree is known by its fruits, and Danton made 10 August. First he made the republic of the Cordeliers, then he made the Republic of France. If Danton is not a patriot, then we have been criminally negligent in the nation's affairs. If Danton is not a patriot, we are not patriots either. If Danton is not a patriot, then the whole thing – from May '89 – must be done again.

It was a thought to make even Robespierre tired.

WHEN THE NEWS of the victory at Valmy reached Paris, the city was delirious with relief and joy, and it was only later that a few people began to wonder why the French had not pursued their immediate advantage, chased up Brunswick and cut his retreat to pieces. The National Convention, meeting for the first time, had officially proclaimed the French Republic; it was the best of omens. Before long there will be no enemies on French soil – or no foreign enemies at least. The generals will push on to Mainz, Worms, Frankfurt; Belgium will be occupied, England, Holland and Spain will enter the war. In time defeats will occur, and betrayal, conspiracy and mere half-heartedness receive a ghastly reward; as the numbers of the Convention dwindle, one can seem to see every day on the empty benches a figure of Death, smiling, familiar and spry.

For the moment the Convention's most startling phenomenon was Danton's voice; it was heard every day, on every question, but its arrogant power never ceased to surprise. Shunning the ministerial bench, he sat in the high tier of seats to the left of the chamber, with the other Paris deputies and the fiercer of the provincials. These seats, and by extension those who occupy them, will be called the Mountain. The Girondins, Brissotins – whatever you please to call them – drift to the right of the hall, and between them and the Mountain lies the area called the Plain, or the Swamp, in accordance with the quaking natures of those who sit there. Now that the split was visible, wide open, there seemed no reason for discretion or restraint. Day after day, Buzot poured out into the airless, stifling, sweating chamber Manon Roland's suspicions of Paris, tyrant city, leech, necropolis. Sometimes she watched him from the public gallery, rigidly impersonal in her applause; in public they behaved like polite strangers, and in private, though less strange, they were not less polite. Louvet carried in his pocket a speech, kept for the right time, which he called a *Robespierricide*.

Because the crux of the matter – September, October, November – was the Brissotin attempt to rule; their private army of 16,000, brought from the provinces, singing in the streets, demanding the blood of would-be dictators – Marat, Danton, Robespierre – whom they called the Triumvirate. The War Minister shuttled that army to the front before there were pitched battles on the streets; but the battle-lines of the Convention were not within his jurisdiction.

Marat sat alone, hunched over his bloody preoccupations. When he got up to speak, the Brissotins hurried out of the chamber, or stayed to stare with fascinated distaste, murmuring among themselves; but as time passed they stayed to listen, because his words concerned them intimately. He spoke with one arm crooked before him and resting on the tribune, his head flung back on his short, muscular neck, prefacing his remarks with the demonic chuckle he cultivated. He was ill, and no one knew the name of his disease.

Robespierre met him – in passing, of course, he had always known him, but he had shrunk from closer contact. There was the danger that, if you talked with Marat, you would be blamed for him, accused of dictating his writings and fanning his ambition. And yet, one can't pick and choose; in the present climate one must count up one's friends. Perhaps from this point of view the meeting was not wholly successful, serving only to show how the patriots were divided. Robespierre's body, young and compact, had a neat, feline tension inside his well-cut clothes; his emotions, or those emotions that might be worn on his face, were buried with the victims of September. Marat twitched at him across a table, coughing, a dirty kerchief wrapped around his head. He spluttered with passion, his grubby fist pumped, frustration blotched and mottled his skin. 'Robespierre, you don't understand me.'

Robespierre watched him dispassionately, his head tilted a little to one side. 'That is possible.'

October 10: two months since the coup. Under Robespierre's eyes (he spoke there every night) the Jacobin Club 'purged' itself. Brissot and his colleagues were expelled; they were cast out from the body of patriotism, as filthy waste matter. October 29: the Convention, Roland on his feet. His supporters clapped and cheered him; but the old man seemed a bloodless marionette, duty and habit jerking the strings. Robespierre, he suggested, would like to see the September massacres over again. At the name of Robespierre, the Gironde broke out into groans and cries.

Robespierre rose from his place on the Mountain. He made for the rostrum, his small head lowered in a way that suggested belliger-ence. Gaudet, the Girondist who was president of the Convention, tried to stop him speaking. Danton's voice was audible above the uproar. 'Let him speak. And I demand to speak, when he's done. It's time a few things were put straight around here.'

VERGNIAUD [*his eyes on Danton*]: I was afraid of this ... of their alliance. I have feared it for some time.

GAUDET [*beside him*]: One can deal with Danton.

VERGNIAUD: Up to a point.

GAUDET: Where the money runs out.

VERGNIAUD: It's more complicated than that. God help you if you can't see it's more complicated than that.

GAUDET: Robespierre has the rostrum.

VERGNIAUD: As usual. [*He closes his eyes; his pale heavy face settles into attentive folds.*] The man cannot speak.

GAUDET: Not in your sense.

VERGNIAUD: There is no show.

GAUDET: The people like it well enough. His style.

VERGNIAUD: Oh yes, the people. The People.

Robespierre was unusually angry. It was the insult of Roland as an opponent, this dotard with his trollop of a wife and his incessant, obsessive muttering about the accounts of Danton's ministry. That, and the gnat-bites of their insinuations, whispers behind hands, stray voices in the street that call September and pass on. Danton has heard them too. It sometimes shows in his face.

Robespierre's voice, above the low muttering which filled the body of the hall, was dripping with contempt: 'Not one of you dares accuse me to my face.'

There was a pause, a little silence for the Gironde to contemplate their cowardice.

'I accuse you.'

Louvet walked forward, fumbling inside his coat for the pages of the Robespierricide. 'Ah, the pornographer,' Philippe Égalité said. The Duke's voice rolled down, from the height of the Mountain. There was an outbreak of sniggering. Then the silence welled back.

Robespierre stepped aside, and yielded Louvet the rostrum. He wore a patient, hesitant smile; he glanced up towards the Paris deputies, then took a seat, in Louvet's line of sight, and waited for him to begin his tirade.

'I accuse you of persistently slandering the finest patriots. Of having spread your slanders in the first week of September, when rumours were death-blows. I accuse you of having degraded and proscribed the representatives of the nation.' He paused – the Mountain were yelling, baying at him – it was difficult to continue – Robespierre twisted his head, looked up at them, and the noise subsided, dwindled, tailed off, into another silence.

In it, Louvet resumed; but his voice, pitched for opposition, for a shouting-match, had the wrong timbre now, and as he heard it – as he heard what was wrong, as he said to himself, this will not do – his voice shook a little. To brace himself, he put his hands on the rostrum; he found he could not take a grip, because his palms were slippery with sweat.

His quarry's head was turned to him; but the light struck across his face, so that he was eyeless behind his tinted lenses. He seemed to wear no expression at all. Louvet launched himself forward, physically, as if he were going to jump: 'I accuse you of having set yourself up as an object of idolatry: of having allowed people to name you in your presence as the only man who could save the nation – and of having said it yourself. I accuse you of aiming at being the supreme power.'

Whether he had finished, or he had simply paused – whatever the truth, the Mountain were yelling again, redoubling their volume, and he saw Danton shoot upwards from his seat and start forward as if to stride down the hall and settle the matter with his fists; he saw Danton's friends on their feet, and Fabre holding his chief back in a theatrical parade of restraint. Louvet stepped down from the tribune. His shoulders had bowed, he had developed a consumptive stoop; Robespierre was on his feet lightly, bouncily. He was back at the tribune, indicating by his manner that he'd not detain them; in his cool, even, voice, he asked the House for time to prepare his defence. Danton would have strode to the rostrum, struck terror into them, torn the case to pieces, there and then; this was not Robespierre's method. He made a sign to Danton, an inclination of the head, almost a bow; then left the chamber, a knot of Montagnards clustering about him, his brother Augustin clutching at his arm and saying the Gironde would murder him.

'A bad moment,' Legendre said. 'Who would have expected it? I would not.'

Danton was very pale. The scar stood out on his face. 'They are baiting me,' he said.

'Baiting *you*, Danton?'

'Yes, me. If they strike at Robespierre they strike at me, if they take him on they must take me on too. Tell them this. Tell Brissot.'

They told Vergniaud, later. 'I am not Brissot,' he said. 'I am not a Brissotin. At least, I think not. They fling the word about like largesse to the poor. Still – we have not been kind to Danton. We have resented his power in the ministry, we have been rude about his friends. Some of us have allowed our wives to make personal remarks. We have demanded to see his accounts, which naturally makes him nervous. We have, take it all in all, failed to bang our foreheads on the floor. Yet I hardly thought he bore us a grudge. How dangerously naïve.' He spread his hands. 'But surely, in private, he and Robespierre have an antipathy for each other? Does that matter? Oh yes, it will matter, in the end.'

And Louvet: that was his big moment, and he met it damp with fright, trailing the Duke's plaudits like a bad memory. He was just

Louvet the novelist after all, lightweight, inconsiderable, the little tiger's practice prey. Now they will be wondering why they let him do it, his friends who are vehement against Robespierre. The Plain saw only how Robespierre stepped aside, how he took his seat, how he signalled silence: no despot, that. But only I, Louvet thought, will know that I ended before I began, at the foot of the tribune – held in a look that turned my stomach above the sweet, encouraging, Judas smile.

'WE REGARD HIM,' Mme Duplay said, 'as our son.'

'But in point of fact,' Charlotte Robespierre said, 'he is my brother. Which is why, I am afraid, my claim on him takes precedence over any that you and your daughters imagine yourself to have.'

Mme Duplay – mother of so many – could claim that she understood girls. She understood her mortally shy Victoire, her serious and awkward Eléonore and her pretty child-like Babette. She also understood Charlotte Robespierre. But she didn't know what to do with her.

When Maximilien had said that his brother Augustin would be coming to Paris, he had asked her advice on the matter of his sister. At least, that's what she thought he had done. He seemed to find it difficult to talk about the girl.

'What is she like?' She had been so curious, naturally. He never talked about his family. 'Is she quiet, like you? What shall I expect?'

'Not too much,' he said, looking worried.

Maurice Duplay had insisted that the house had space for them all. And, indeed, there were two rooms, unfurnished at present, never used. 'Could we let your brother and sister go to strangers?' Maurice said. 'No, we should all be together, as one family.'

The day came. They arrived at the gate. Augustin made a good first impression – a pleasant, capable boy, Madame thought, and he clearly couldn't wait to see his brother. She opened her arms to receive the sweet-faced, lissom young thing that Max's sister would be. Charlotte's cold stare stabbed her with deadly equality. Her arms dropped.

'Perhaps we might go straight to our rooms,' Charlotte said. 'We're tired.'

The older woman's cheeks burned as she led the way. Neither proud nor exacting, she was still used to deference – from her daughters, from her husband's workmen. Charlotte had taken with her the tone used to an underservant.

She turned on the threshold. 'Everything is very simple. Ours is a simple house.'

'So I see,' Charlotte said.

The floor was polished, the curtains were new, dear little Babette had arranged a vase of flowers. Mme Duplay stood back, allowing Charlotte to walk in before her. 'If there is any way in which we can make you more comfortable, please tell me.'

You could make me more comfortable, Charlotte's face said, by dropping dead.

MAURICE DUPLAY filled his pipe and addressed himself to the aroma of the tobacco. When Citizen Robespierre was in the house, or likely to come home soon, he never smoked, out of respect for his patriotic lungs. However, Augustin didn't mind.

'Of course,' Duplay said at length, 'she's your sister. I shouldn't criticize.'

'You can if you want,' Augustin said. 'I suppose I ought to try to explain Charlotte to you. Max never will. He's too good. He's always trying to avoid thinking ill of people.'

'Is that so?' Duplay was mildly surprised, put it down to a proper fraternal blindness. Citizen Robespierre was open, just, equitable – but charity – no, that was not his strong point.

'I don't remember our mother at all,' Augustin said. 'Max does, but he never seemed to want to talk about her.'

'Your mother's dead? I had no notion that your mother was dead.'

Augustin was taken aback. 'He never told you about our family?' He shook his head. 'How odd.'

'We presumed, you know, a quarrel. A serious quarrel. We didn't want to pry.'

'She died when I was a baby. Our father went away. We don't know if he's dead or alive. I wonder, now – if he's alive, would he have heard of Max?'

'I think so, if he's anywhere in the civilized world. If he can read.'

'Oh yes, he can read.' Augustin was literal-minded. 'I wonder what he thinks, then? Our grandfather brought us up, the girls went to our aunts. Until we got away to Paris. Charlotte, of course, she couldn't get away. Then Henriette died, oh yes, we had another sister, and she and Max, when they saw each other, they got on very well, and I think Charlotte was probably jealous, a bit. She was only a child when she started to keep house for us. It aged her, I suppose. But she's not thirty yet. She could still get married.'

Duplay drew on his pipe. 'Why doesn't she give it a go?'

'She had a disappointment over someone. You know him, in fact – he lodges down the road – Deputy Fouché. Can you call him to mind? He has no eyelashes and a sort of green face.'

'Was it a big disappointment?'

'I don't think she liked him much actually, but she did take the view that she'd been . . . Well, you know how it is, some people are born with sour temperaments and they use the misfortunes in their lives as an excuse for them. I've been engaged three times, you know? When it came down to it, they couldn't face the thought of Charlotte for a sister-in-law. She's made us her life's work. She doesn't want any other women around. Nobody's allowed to do anything for us, except her.'

'Mm. Do you think that's why your brother hasn't married yet?'

'I don't know. He's had plenty of chances. Women like him. But then again . . . perhaps he's not the sort of person who marries.'

'Don't talk about it round the town,' Duplay suggested. 'About him not being the sort of person who marries.'

'Perhaps he's afraid that most families end up like ours. Not superficially . . . I mean in some deeper way. There ought to be a law against families like ours.'

'Perhaps we shouldn't speculate about what he thinks. If he wanted us to know, he'd tell us. Plenty of children lose their parents. We hope you will regard us as your family now.'

'I agree, plenty of children lose their parents – but the difficulty with my father is that we don't know whether we've lost him or not. It's very odd, the thought that he's probably living somewhere, perhaps even here in Paris, reading about Max in the papers. Suppose he turns up one day? He might. He could come to the Convention, sit in the gallery, watch over us ... If I passed him on the street I wouldn't know him. When I was a boy I used to hope he'd come back ... and at the same time I was a bit afraid of what it would be like if he did. Grandfather talked about him a lot, when he was in a bad mood. "Expect your father's drunk himself to death," that sort of thing. And people were always watching us, looking for signs. People in Arras now, the ones who don't like the way Max's career has gone, they say, "The father was a drunk and a womanizer, and the mother was no better than she should be." They use, you know, worse terms than that.'

'Augustin, you must put all this behind you. You're in Paris now, you have a chance at a fresh start. I hope your brother will marry my eldest girl. She'll give him children.' Augustin silently demurred. 'And for now, he has good friends.'

'Do you think so? I haven't been here long, of course, but I get the impression that mainly he has associates. Yes, he has a great mass of admirers – but he's not supported by a group of friends, like Danton.'

'Well of course, there is a difference in style. He has the Desmoulins. Camille's baby is his godchild, you know.'

'If it is Camille's. There, you see ... I feel sorry for my brother. Nothing he has is ever quite what it seems.'

'I HAVE A SENSE of duty,' Charlotte said. 'It's not a common thing, I find.'

'I know, Charlotte.' Her elder brother always spoke to her gently, if he possibly could. 'What am I not doing that you think I should be doing?'

'You shouldn't be living here.'

'Why not?' He knew one good guilty reason why not; probably, he thought, so did she.

'You are an important man. You are a great man. You should behave as if you know that. Appearances count. They do. Danton has it right. He puts on a show. People love it. I haven't been here long, but I've noticed that much. Danton –'

'Charlotte, Danton spends too much money. And nobody quite knows where he gets it from.' There was a hint in his voice, that she should change the subject.

'Danton has some style about him,' she insisted. 'They say he doesn't scruple to sit in the King's chair at the Tuileries, when the cabinet meets.'

'And fills it to the inch, no doubt,' Robespierre said drily. 'And if there were such a thing as the King's table, Danton would put his feet up on it. Some people, Charlotte, are more equipped by nature for that sort of thing. And it makes enemies, too.'

'How long have you worried about making enemies? I can't remember the day when you gave a damn. Do you imagine people think any better of you for living in a garret?'

'I don't know why you have to make it sound so much worse than it is. I'm perfectly comfortable. There's nothing I want that I haven't got here.'

'You would be much better off if I were taking care of you.'

'Charlotte, my dear, you've always taken care of us – couldn't you just for a while take a rest?'

'In another woman's house?'

'All houses belong to somebody, and most of them have women in them.'

'We could have privacy. A nice convenient apartment of our own.'

It would solve some problems, he thought. Her face darkened as she watched him, expecting contradiction. He opened his mouth to agree. 'And there's another thing,' she said.

He stopped short. 'And what is that?'

'These girls. Maximilien, I've seen Augustin ruining himself with women.'

So she knew. Did she? 'How is he ruined?'

'Well, he would have been, if it weren't for me. And that wretched old woman has no other aim in life but to get those girls into your bed. Whether she's succeeded I leave to your conscience. That little horror Elisabeth looks at men as if – I can't describe it. If any harm ever came to her, it wouldn't be the man I'd blame.'

'Charlotte, what are you talking about? Babette's just a child. I've never heard anyone say a word against her.'

'Well, you have now. What about it then? Shall I look for an apartment for us?'

'No. We'll stay as we are. I can't bear to live with you. You're just as bad as you ever were.' And just as mad, he thought.

NOVEMBER 5: people have queued all night for a place in the public galleries. If they expect to see on Robespierre's face a sense of personal crisis, they will be disappointed. How familiar now, these streets and these slanders. Arras seems twenty years ago; even in the Estates-General, wasn't he there singled out for attack? It is his nature, he thinks.

He is careful to deny responsibility for September, but he does not, you notice, condemn the killings. He also refrains from killing words, sparing Roland and Buzot, as if they were beneath his notice. August 10 was illegal, he says; so too was the taking of the Bastille. What account can we take of that, in revolution? It is the nature of revolutions to break laws. We are not justices of the peace; we are legislators to a new world.

'Mm,' Camille says, up on the Mountain. 'This is not an ethical position. It is an excuse.'

He is speaking quietly, almost to himself; he is surprised by the violence with which his colleagues turn round on him. 'He is in politics, practical politics,' Danton says. 'What the fuck does he want with an ethical position?'

'I don't like this idea of ordinary crimes and political crimes. Our opponents can use it to murder us, just as we can use it to murder them. I don't see what good the idea does. We ought to admit that all crimes are the same.'

'No,' Saint-Just said.

'And you talk, Lanterne Attorney.'

'But when I was the Lanterne Attorney, I said, right, let's have some violence, it's our turn. I never excused myself by saying I was a legislator to the world.'

'He is not making excuses,' Saint-Just said. 'Necessity does not have to be excused or justified.'

Camille turned on him. 'Where did you read that, you half-wit? Your politics are like those improving fables they give to children, each one with a little moral tag on the end. What does it mean? You don't know. Why do you say it? You have to say something.'

He watched a flush of rage wash over Saint-Just's pale skin. 'Whose side are you on?' Fabre hissed into his ear.

Stop now, he told himself. You are antagonizing everybody. 'Whose side? That's what we say about the Brissotins, that their judgement is destroyed by factional interest. Isn't it?'

'My God, you are a liability,' Saint-Just snapped. Camille got to his feet, more frightened by the words coming out of his own mouth than of theirs, thinking that in minutes he could be among the black branches and indifferent faces in the Tuileries gardens. It was Orléans who put out a hand and detained him, a slight social smile on his face. 'Must you go now?' the Duke said, as if a party were breaking up early. 'Don't go. You can't do a walk-out in the middle of Robespierre's speech.'

His actions at variance with his manner, the Duke reached out and pulled Camille to the bench beside him. 'Sit still,' he said. 'If you go now, people will read things into it.'

'Saint-Just hates me,' Camille said.

'He certainly isn't a very friendly young man, but you shouldn't feel singled out. I myself am on his list, I feel.'

'His list?'

'He would have one, wouldn't you think? Looks the type.'

'Laclos had lists,' Camille said. 'O God, I sometimes wish it were '89 again. I miss Laclos.'

'So do I. So do I.'

Hérault de Séchelles was in the president's chair. He glanced up at his Montagnard colleagues and flicked an eyebrow, a request for later explanation. They seemed to be holding some private parliamentary session up there; and now Camille was having some sort of tussle with Égalité. Robespierre had reached his peroration. He had left his opponents with nothing to say and nowhere to go. Camille was going to miss the end of the speech, he would not be there for the applause. The Duke seemed to have released him. He was on his way to the door. Hérault remembered Camille running out of a courtroom, years ago, long long before they had been introduced: his chin lifted, his expression a compound of contempt and glee. Winter 1792, still running; his expression now a compound of contempt and fear.

ANNETTE wasn't at home; he attempted retreat, but Claude heard his voice, came out. 'Camille? You look upset. No, don't try escaping, I have to talk to you.'

He looked upset himself – a discreet, semi-official agitation. There were a couple of Girondist newspapers draped around the room. 'Really,' Claude said. 'The tone of public life these days! The lowness of it! Need Danton say such things? Deputy Philippeaux asks the Convention to request Danton to stay on in the ministry – reasonable. Danton refuses – reasonable. Then he has to add that if the Convention wants Roland to stay in office it had better ask his wife first. That was a sharp, personal thing to say, in front of so many people, and naturally they make personal attacks in their turn. Now they are talking about Lucile and Danton.'

'That's nothing new.'

'Why do you allow it to be said? Is it true?'

'I thought you were immune to the newspapers, after the business of Annette and the Abbé Terray.'

'That was the most preposterous fabrication – this is something that people believe. Can you possibly like what it implies about you?'

'What is that?'

'Simply that Danton can do what he likes, that you can't stand up to him.'

'I can't,' Camille muttered.

'They mention other men besides Danton. I don't want this said of Lucile. You should make her see . . . '

'She likes to live up to a certain reputation, without ever quite deserving it.'

'Why? If it is not true, why does she give cause for such rumours? You neglect her, I think.'

'No, that's not it. We quite enjoy ourselves, really. But Claude, please don't shout at me. I've had a terrible day. During Robespierre's speech – '

A head appeared round the door; servants were so casual these days. 'Monsieur, Citizen Robespierre's here.'

Robespierre had not called often, since his farcical engagement to Adèle. But he was welcome; Monsieur retained his good opinion. Claude hurried forward to greet him; the servant, having thoroughly muddled the forms of address, ducked out and slammed the door. 'Robespierre,' Claude said, 'I am glad to see you. Would you help us re-establish some communication?'

'My father-in-law is possessed by a horror of scandal.'

'I think you,' Claude said simply, 'are possessed by a devil.'

'Let me see,' Robespierre said. He was in a high old mood, quite unexpected, so elevated that he was near to smothered giggles. 'Asmodeus?'

'Asmodeus was a seraphim, when he started,' Camille said.

'So were you. Now, let's have it – what was it made you run out on my speech?'

'Nothing. I mean, I misunderstood something you said, and I made a remark, and they all jumped on me.'

'Yes, I know. They're all very sorry.'

'Not Saint-Just.'

'No – well – Saint-Just is very decided in his views, he won't permit any wavering.'

'Permit? For Christ's sake, I don't need any permission from him. He said I was a liability. What right has someone to walk into a revolution that was made before he came and call other people a liability?'

'Don't yell at me, Camille. He had a right to express his opinion, I suppose.'

'But I haven't?'

'No one has taken your right away – they've just shouted at you for exercising it. Camille is morbidly sensitive,' he said cheerfully to Duplessis.

'I could wish he were more sensitive on certain matters.' He nodded towards the newspapers. Robespierre seemed confused. He took off his glasses. His eyes were red-rimmed. Claude wondered at his patience, his equanimity: at his finding time for all this.

'Try to – suppress this gossip, of course,' Robespierre said. 'Well, not suppress, exactly. That sounds as if there were some truth in it. Must all behave very discreetly.'

'So as not to attract attention to our sins,' Camille said.

'I must take Camille away,' Robespierre said to Claude. 'Don't let the newspapers spoil your peace of mind.'

'Do you imagine I have any great amount to spoil?' He rose to see them out. 'Will you be at Bourg-la-Reine this weekend?'

'Bourg-la-République,' Camille said. 'Good patriots don't have weekends.'

'Oh, you can have a weekend if you want to,' Robespierre said.

'I wish you'd join us,' Claude said. 'But I suppose not.'

'I *am* very busy just now. This business with Louvet has wasted my time.'

And you would not be allowed to come, Camille thought, not without Eléonore and Mother as chaperone to Eléonore and Charlotte as chaperone to Mother, and Babette because she would scream if denied the treat, and Victoire because it wasn't fair to leave her at home. 'Shall I come?' he asked his father-in-law.

'Yes. Lucile needs the fresh air, and you, I suppose, need a pause from contention.'

'And you are offering me one?'

Claude raised the ghost of a smile for him.

'WHAT ARE we going to do now?' Camille asked.

'We are going to walk a little, and see if anyone recognizes us. You know, I think your father-in-law is almost fond of you.'

'You think that?'

'He is growing used to you. At his age, one likes to have something to complain about. Nevertheless, I think – '

'Why do you want to know if people will recognize you?'

'It is an idea I have. I have heard people say that I am vain. Do you think I am vain?'

'No, it's not a word I would have applied.'

'To myself I seem an obscure person.'

'Obscure?' This is the prelude, Camille thought, to a shocking outbreak of diffidence; Robespierre had never reconciled himself to fame, and his modesty, if not placated, took a ferocious turn. 'I'm sorry if I upset your concentration, when you were making your speech.'

'It's nothing. Louvet's quashed. They'll think twice now before they make another attack on me. I have the Convention – ' he cupped his hand – 'beautiful.'

'You look very tired, Max.'

'I shall be, when I think about it. Never mind. Something is achieved. You, you look well. You look as if you have plenty of appetite left for revolution.'

'It must be the life of debauchery Brissot's friends say I lead. It suits me.'

A man checked his pace to look into their faces. He frowned. 'Not sure,' Camille said. 'Do you want people to recognize you?'

'No. But I wanted a quiet word. There's almost nowhere one can go without being overheard.'

The exuberance was draining away; often now he had a pinched look, his mouth drawn into a thin, apprehensive line.

'Do you really think that? That people are always listening to your conversations?'

'I know they are.' (If you lived with my sister Charlotte, he thought, you'd not doubt it.) 'Camille, I want you to consider more seriously the Brissotin newspapers. We know that they are motivated by malice, but you don't give them the trouble of inventing things. It looks so bad, especially with Citizeness Danton unwell, that her husband is so seldom at home, and that you are both seen around the town, with women.'

'Max, I spend most of my evenings with the Jacobin correspondence committee. And Gabrielle is not unwell, she is expecting a baby.'

'Yes, but when I spoke with her, earlier this week, I thought she was unwell. And she and Georges are never seen together, they never accept invitations together.'

'They quarrel.'

'What about?'

'Politics.'

'I didn't think she was that sort of woman.'

'It isn't an abstract argument. It's a matter of the way we live our lives now.'

'I don't want to lecture you, Camille – '

'Yes you do.'

'Very well, then, I do. Stop gambling. Try to get Danton to stop. Stay at home more. Make your wife behave respectably. If you must have a mistress, pick someone discreet, and make a proper arrangement.'

'But I don't want a mistress.'

'That's all to the good then. The way you've been living is in some sense a reproach to our ideals.'

'Stop there. I never volunteered for these ideals.'

'Listen – '

'No, you listen, Max. For as long as we've known each other you've been trying to keep me out of trouble. But you've known better than to exercise your pompous side with me. A few months ago, you wouldn't have been talking about "a reproach to our ideals". You looked the other way. You have a great capacity for ignoring what doesn't suit you. But now you want to make an issue of it. Or rather, I know who does. Saint-Just.'

'What is going on in your head about Saint-Just?'

'I have to fight him now, while it can do me some good. He called me a liability. So I deduce he wants to get rid of me.'

'Get rid?'

'Yes, get rid of me, disable me, pack me off to Guise, oh my God, where fierce indignation can no longer tear his heart at the sound of my silly little stutter.'

They almost halted for a moment, to look into each other's faces. 'There's very little I can do about your personal disagreements. Is there?'

'Except not take his side.'

'I don't want to take a side. I don't need to. I have a high regard for both of you, personally, politically – don't the streets look shabby now?'

'Yes. Where are we going?'

'Will you come and see my sister?'

'Will Eléonore be at home?'

'She'll be at her drawing class. I know she doesn't like you.'

'Are you going to marry her?'

'I don't know. How can I? She's jealous of my friends, of my occupations.'

'Won't you have to marry her?'

'Eventually, perhaps.'

'Also – no, never mind.'

Very often, he had come close to telling Robespierre what had happened with Babette on the morning his son was born. But Max was so fond of the girl, so much more at ease with her than with most people, and it seemed cruel to hunt out trust from where he had reposed it. And it would be horrible to be disbelieved; he might be disbelieved. Again, how to retell exactly what had been said and done, without putting your own interpretation on it, and submit it to another judgement? It wasn't possible. So at the Duplay house he was very polite to everybody – except Eléonore – and very careful; and still the incident preyed upon his mind. He had once begun to tell Danton, then abandoned the subject; Danton would certainly say he was making it up, and tease him about his fantasy life.

Beside him, Robespierre's voice was running on: ' . . . and I sometimes think that the fading out of the individual personality is what one should desire, not the status of a hero – a sort of effacement of oneself from history. The entire record of the human race has been falsified, it has been made up by bad governments to suit themselves, by kings and tyrants to make them look good. This idea of history as made by great men is quite nonsensical, when you look at it from the point of view of the people. The real heroes are those who have resisted tyrants, and it is in the nature of tyranny not only to kill those who oppose it but to wipe their names out of the record, to obliterate them, so that resistance seems impossible.'

A passer-by hesitated, stared. 'Excuse me –' he said. 'Good citizen – are you Robespierre?'

Robespierre didn't look at the man. 'Do you understand what I say about heroes? There is no place for them. Resistance to tyrants means oblivion. I will embrace that oblivion. My name will vanish from the page.'

'Good citizen, forgive me,' the patriot said doggedly.

Eyes rested on him briefly. 'Yes, I'm Robespierre,' he said. He put his hand on Citizen Desmoulins's arm. 'Camille, history is fiction.'

ROBESPIERRE: . . . you see, you can't understand how things were for me then. For the first two years at school I wasn't exactly miserable, I was happy in a way, but I was cut off from people, sealed off by myself in a cell – then Camille came – do you think I'm being sentimental?

SAINT-JUST: I do rather.

ROBESPIERRE: You don't understand how it was.

SAINT-JUST: Why all this preoccupation with the past? Why not look to the future?

ROBESPIERRE: A lot of us would like to forget the past, but you can't, well, you can't put it out of your head entirely. You're younger than I am, naturally you think about the future. You haven't got any past.

SAINT-JUST: A little.

ROBESPIERRE: Before the Revolution, you were a student, you were preparing for your life. You've never had any other job. You're a professional revolutionary. You're an entirely new breed.

SAINT-JUST: I had thought of that.

ROBESPIERRE: If I can explain – when Camille came – I myself, I find it difficult to get along with people sometimes, people don't take to me so easily. I didn't understand why Camille bothered with me, but I was glad. He was like a magnet to people. He was just the same as he is now. When he was ten years old he had that sort of – black radiance.

SAINT-JUST: You are fanciful.

ROBESPIERRE: It made things easier for me. Camille's always complained that his family don't care about him. I could never see that. And I couldn't see how it mattered, when other people love him so much.

SAINT-JUST: So what are you saying – that because of some association in your past life, everything he does is all right?

ROBESPIERRE: Oh no. I'm just saying, he's an extremely complicated person, and whatever he gets up to, the fact remains, we're very close. Camille's clever, you know. He's also a very good journalist.

SAINT-JUST: I have doubts about the value of journalists.

ROBESPIERRE: You just don't like him, really, do you?

III. *The Visible Exercise of Power*

(1792–1793)

DANTON THOUGHT: ambassadors give me a headache. For part of the day, every day, he had stared mutely at maps, turning the continent over in his mind, Turkey, Sweden, England, Venice . . . Keep England out of this war. Beg and pray neutrality. Keep the English fleet out of it . . . and yet with English agents everywhere, talk of sabotage and forgery . . . Yes, of course Robespierre is right, England is fundamentally hostile. But if we get into that sort of war, will we get out, within our natural lifetimes? Not, he thinks sourly, that we expect to have those.

Since he left office, some of this is no longer his direct concern. But there is enough to occupy him: the pressure for the King's trial, the stupidity and divisiveness of the Brissotins. Even after the Robespierricide, he clings to a half-faith in their good intentions. He had not wanted to be pulled into the struggle; but they have taken all his choices away.

Soon, perhaps within a year, he hopes to be out of Paris. Perhaps he is deluding himself, but he hopes to leave it all in the hands of other people. With the Prussians driven out, those houses and farms are secured to him. And the children – Antoine is growing up sturdily, and François-Georges is a fat, contented baby, he's not going to die. Also the new child. In Arcis, Gabrielle will begin to understand him better. Whatever he has done, whatever their differences of opinion, he is committed to her, he feels. In the country, they are going to be ordinary people again.

It is when he's had too much to drink that he imagines this simple future for himself. It is a pity that it is so often Camille who is around at these times to disabuse him of his dreams, leaving him lachrymose, or raging against the trap of power he thinks he has fallen into. Whether at other times he believes in this future . . . He can hardly understand his pursuit of Lucile, because of the complications it makes. Yet it continues . . .

'I DON'T LIKE PALACES. I'm glad to be home.' So Gabrielle says. Some version of the feeling seems to be general. Camille is glad to be parting from his staff, and his staff are glad to be parting from Camille. As Danton says, now we can find a lot of other things to worry about. Lucile does not entirely share the general feeling. She has enjoyed sweeping down grand staircases, the visible exercise of power.

At least in returning home she is relieved of Gabrielle's company, and of Louise Robert's. In recent weeks Louise has been applying her novelist's imagination to their ménage – and what a lot of imagination novelists have! 'Observe,' she says, 'the expression of pleasure and interest Camille wears when Danton deigns to maul his wife about in his presence! Why don't you three set up house together when you leave here? Isn't that what it's coming to?'

'And,' said Fabre, 'may I come to breakfast?'

'I'm sick,' Louise said, 'of this drama you're playing out, man falls in love with best friend's wife, how tragic etc., how terrible to be human. Tragic? You can hardly keep the grins off your faces.'

Yes, it was true; they hardly could, and that included Danton. Luckily Gabrielle had been elsewhere for the gifted writer's outburst. Gabrielle had been kind to her, in the past; but in the present, she is relentlessly morose. She's put on a lot of weight, with this pregnancy; she moves slowly, says she can't breathe, says the city stifles her. Luckily, Gabrielle's parents have just sold their house at Fontenay and moved to Sèvres, bought two properties set in parkland. One house they'll live in; one is for their daughter and son-in-law to use when they like. The Charpentiers have never been poor, but the likelihood is that Georges-Jacques has put up the money; he just doesn't want people to know how much cash he's laying out these days.

So, Lucile thinks, Gabrielle has the prospect of escape; but in her apartment at the rue des Cordeliers, she sits still and silent, in the conscious postures of pregnant women. Sometimes she cries; this chit Louise Gély trips down the stairs to join her in a few sniffles. Gabrielle is crying for her marriage, her soul and her king; Louise is crying, she supposes, for a broken doll or a kitten run over in the street. Can't stand it, she thinks. Men are better company.

Fréron was safely home from his mission in Metz. You would never know, from his journalism, that Rabbit had once been a gentleman. He was a good writer – the trade was in his blood – but his opinions grew steadily more violent, as if it was a contest and he badly wanted to win; at times you couldn't distinguish his work from Marat's. Despite his new ferocity, her other beaux considered him the one from whom they had nothing to fear. Yet she had been heard to ask him once, earnestly: 'Will you always be there, in case I need you?' He had replied that he would be there for time and eternity: things like that. The problem – week to week – was that he had the status of Old Family Friend. So at weekends he could come out to the farm at Bourg-la-République. There he would follow her around, and try to get her alone. Poor Rabbit. His chances were nil.

It was difficult, sometimes, to remember that there was a Mme Fréron, and a Mme Hérault de Séchelles.

Hérault called in the evenings, when the Jacobins were in session. Bores, he called them, dreadful bores. In fact politics fascinated him; but he did not suppose it could fascinate her, and so he set out to strike a sympathetic chord. 'They are discussing economic controls,' he would say, 'and how to quiet these ludicrous sansculotte agitators, with their continual whine about the price of bread and candles. Hébert does not know whether to ridicule them or take them up.'

'Hébert is prospering,' she would suggest sweetly, and he would say, 'Yes, at the Commune, Hébert and Chaumette are such a force – ' and then he would break off, feeling foolish, realizing he'd been sidetracked again.

Hérault was Danton's friend, he sat with the Mountain, but he could not mend a single aristocratic way. 'It is not just your speech, your manner, but your whole way of thinking that is profoundly aristocratic,' she told him.

'Oh, no, no. Surely not. Very modern. Very republican.'

'Your attitude to me, for instance. You can't put it out of your mind that before the Revolution I would have fallen flat on my back in simulated adoration if you had even glanced in my direction. If I hadn't, my family would have given me a push. And at that, it might not have been simulated. The way women thought then.'

'If that's true,' he said, 'and of course it is true, how does it affect our situation today?' (He thinks, women don't change.) 'I'm not trying to exercise any prerogative over you. I simply want to see you have some pleasure in your life.'

She folded her hands over her heart. 'Altruism!'

'Dear Lucile. The worst thing your husband has done to you is to make you sarcastic.'

'I was always sarcastic.'

'I find it too hard to believe. Camille manipulates people.'

'Oh, so do I.'

'He is always trying to convince people that he is harmless, so that the stab in the back will be a greater shock to them. Saint-Just, whom I do not unreservedly admire – '

'Oh, change the subject. I don't like Saint-Just.'

'Why is that, I wonder?'

'I don't think I like his politics. And he frightens me.'

'But his politics are Robespierre's – which means they are your husband's, and Danton's.'

'We shall have to see about that. Saint-Just's main aim seems to be to improve people, along the lines of some plan that he has in his head, and which – I must say – he has difficulty articulating to the rest of us. Now, you cannot accuse Camille and Georges-Jacques of trying to improve people. In fact quite the opposite, most of the time.'

Hérault looked thoughtful. 'You're not stupid, are you, Lucile?'

'Well, I used to be. But intelligence rubs off.'

'The trouble is, with Saint-Just, Camille sets out to antagonize him.'

'Of course he does – and on every level. We may be tainted with pragmatism, but it only needs a clash of personalities to remind us of our principles.'

'Oh dear,' Hérault said. 'I was planning a seduction, tonight. We seem to have got sidetracked.'

'You might as well have gone to the Jacobins.' She gave him a nice smile. Hérault looked depressed.

Whenever he was in Paris, General Dillon called. It was a pleasure to see him, with his splendid height and his chestnut head and his knack of looking younger and younger. Valmy did him good, no doubt; there's nothing like Victory to perk a man up. Dillon never talked about the war. He'd call in the afternoons, when the Convention was in session. His approach was so interesting that it had to be elevated to a strategy; she was moved to discuss it with Camille, and he agreed that it was marvellously oblique. For whereas Rabbit dropped mournful hints about Camille's infidelities, and Hérault raged at her that she must be unhappy and he could change that, the general simply sat and told her stories, about life in Martinique, or about the splendid silliness of Court life before the Revolution; he told her how his little daughter, Lucile's age exactly, had been advised never to stand in a strong light, in case her glowing complexion made the fading Queen spiteful. He told her the history of his mad, distinguished Franco-Irish family. He retailed the idiosyncrasies of his second wife, Laure, and of various pretty, vacuous mistresses from the past. He described the fauna of the West Indies, the heat, the blue of the sea, the green tangled hillsides that tumbled into the sea, the flowers that blew and rotted in the bud; he described the imbecile ceremonial that attended the Governor of Tobago, alias himself. In sum, he told her how pleasant life had been for a member of an old and distinguished family who had never worried about money or anything else and who was extremely good-looking and polished and in addition highly adaptable.

From there he would go on to tell her what a truly special young man she had married. He could quote at admiring length from Camille's writings: with some accuracy. He explained to her – to her – that sensitive people like Camille should be allowed to do exactly as they liked, provided it was not criminal, or not too criminal at any rate.

Then, every so often, he would put an arm round her and try to kiss her, and say to her, dear little Lucile, let me make love to you properly. When she said no, he would look incredulous, and ask her why she didn't enjoy life more. Surely she didn't think Camille would mind?

What they did not know, these gentlemen, what they did not understand, was – well, anything about her, really. They did not know about the exquisite torture she had devised for herself, the rack upon which her days and weeks were stretched. Quite coldly, she puts herself to the question, and the question is this: what if anything happened to Camille? What if – not to put too fine a point on it – someone assassinated him? (God knows, if she were an assassin, she'd be tempted.) Of course, she has asked herself this before, since '89 it has been her preoccupation; but now she is more obsessed with him, not less. Nothing had prepared her for this; the received wisdom about a love-match was that, after a year's delirium, the emotions settle down. Nobody had even hinted to her that you could go on falling in love and falling in love, till you felt quite ill with it, spiritually sick and depleted, as if you were losing your essence day by day. If Camille were not here – if he were permanently not here – what would lie before her would be a sort of semi-demi-half-life, dragged out for duty, sick and cold and stumbling towards death; the important part of her would be dead already. If anything happened to him I'd kill myself, she thought; I'd make it official, so at least they could bury me. My mother would look after the baby.

Of course, she didn't speak about this torture programme. People would think she was foolish. Camille, these days, was almost knitting his weaknesses into strengths. Legendre reproached him for not speaking more in the Convention. 'My dear Legendre,' he said, 'everyone has not your lungs.' You are, his smile suggested, blundering, crass, self-important. His colleagues on the Mountain relied on him for interpreting the ravings of Marat, with whom only he and Fréron were on terms. (Marat has a new opponent, a loud-mouthed sansculotte ex-priest who calls himself Jacques Roux.)

'You are two centuries ahead of your time,' Camille told him. Marat, more livid and reptilian by the day, blinked at him. It might have been appreciation.

What Camille wanted now was a Convention without the Brissotins, and the King and Queen on trial. He went avid and bright-eyed into the winter of '92. When he was at home, she was happy; she could work on her imitations, which (her mother and sister agree) now approach perfection. When he was not at home, she sat by the window and watched for him. She talked to everybody about him, in a very bored tone.

No one was frightened of the allies, for this year at least: or only the quartermasters, supervising the issue of mouldy bread and paper-soled boots, watching the peasants spit on the government's banknotes and hold out their paws for gold. The Republic was younger than her child. This child, his view still largely supine, watched the world with round, obsidian eyes, and smiled indiscriminately. Robespierre called to see how his godson did, and her mother's old friends came in the afternoons, and gave him their fingers to hold, and told pointless stories about their own children as babies. Camille carried him around and whispered to him, assuring him that his path in life should be made smooth, that his every whim should be attended to, that because of his evident natural wisdom he would never need to go away to any unspeakable school. Her mother fussed over the little thing, showed him the cat and the sky and the trees. But she felt, though she was ashamed of the feeling, that she didn't want to furnish the baby's mind; she was a tenant with a short lease.

To reach the house where Marat lives, you walk through a narrow passage between two shops and across a small courtyard with a well in the corner. On the right is a stone staircase with an iron handrail. Go up to the first floor.

After you have knocked, you must withstand the inspection of one, perhaps both of the Marat women. This will take time. Albertine, the sister from some unimaginable childhood, is a fierce, starved scrap of a woman. Simone Evrard has a serene oval face, brown hair, a grave and generous mouth. Today they are not suspicious of their visitor. The way is clear; the People's Friend sits in his parlour. 'I like the way you come running to me,' he says, meaning that he doesn't like it at all.

'I am not running,' Camille said. 'I came here at a furtive slouch.'

Marat at home. Simone, the common-law wife, put in front of them a pot of coffee, bitter and black. 'If it is a matter of discussing the crimes of the Brissotins,' she said, 'you will be here for some time. Let me know if you need a candle.'

'Are you here on your own behalf,' Marat said, 'or have you been sent?'

'Anyone would think you didn't like having visitors.'

'I want to know whether Danton or Robespierre has sent you, or who.'

'I think they'd both welcome your help with Brissot.'

'Brissot makes me sick.' Marat always said this: such a person makes me sick. And they did, they had. 'He's always acted as if he ran the Revolution, as if it were something of his making – setting himself up as an expert on foreign affairs, just because he's had to skip the country so many times to avoid the police. If it were a matter of that, I would be the expert.'

'We have to attack Brissot on every front,' Camille said. 'His life before the Revolution, his philosophy, his associates, his conduct in every patriotic crisis from May '89 to last September –'

'He cheated me, you know, over the English edition of my *Chains of Slavery*. He conspired with his publishers to pirate my work, and I never saw a penny.'

Camille looked up. 'Good God, you don't want us to allege that against him?'

'And ever since he made this trip to the United States –'

'Yes, I know, personally he's insufferable, but that's not the point.'

'For me it is. I suffer enough.'

'He was a police spy, before the Revolution.'

'Yes,' Marat said. 'He was.'

'Put your name on a pamphlet with me.'

'No.'

'Cooperate, for once.'

'Geese go in flocks,' Marat said, precisely.

'All right, I'll do it by myself. I only want to know if he has anything on you, anything really destructive.'

'My life has been conducted on the highest principles.'

'You mean nobody knows anything about you.'

'Try not to offend me,' Marat said. It was a plain, useful piece of advice.

'Let's get on,' Camille said. 'We can hold up his actions before the Revolution, which were deliberate betrayals of old future comrades, his monarchist pronouncements, which I have newspaper cuttings to verify: his vacillation in July '89 –'

'Which was?'

'Well, he has that jumpy look about him all the time, someone will be sure to remember that he vacillated. Then his involvement with Lafayette, his part in the attempted escape of the Capet family and his secret communication afterwards with the Capet woman and the Emperor.'

'Good, good,' Marat said. 'Very good so far.'

'His efforts to sabotage the Revolution of 10 August and his false accusation that certain patriots were involved in the killings in the prisons. His advocacy of destructive federalist policies. Remembering, of course, that in the early days he was closely involved with certain aristocrats – Mirabeau, for instance, and Orléans.'

'You have a touching faith in the shortness of people's memories. I dare say it is justified. However, though Mirabeau is dead, Orléans is still sitting beside us in the Convention.'

'But I was thinking ahead, to next spring, say. Robespierre feels Philippe's position is untenable. He recognizes that he has been of some service to the people, but he would rather that all the Bourbons were out of France. He would like Philippe to take his whole family to England. We could give them a pension, he says.'

'What, we could give Philippe money? How novel!' Marat said. 'But yes – next spring – you are right. Let the Brissotins run out their rope for another six months. Then – snap.' Marat looked satisfied.

'I hope we will be able to accuse them all – Brissot, Roland, Vergniaud – of creating obstacles and delays to the King's trial. Even perhaps of voting to keep him alive. Again, I'm thinking ahead.'

'Of course, there might be other people who will wish delays, obstacles, what have you. In this matter of Louis Capet.'

'I think we can get Robespierre over his horror of the death sentence.'

'Yes, but I don't mean Robespierre. I think you will find Danton absenting himself at that time. I think it entirely possible that the activities of General Dumouriez in Belgium will call him away.'

'What activities, particularly?'

'There is sure to be a crisis in Belgium soon. Are our troops liberating the country, or are they annexing it, or are they somehow doing both? Who is General Dumouriez making his conquests for? The Republic? Or the defunct monarchy? Or perhaps for himself? Someone will have to go and sort the situation out, and it will have to be someone with the ultimate personal authority. I can't see Robespierre leaving his paperwork to go wallowing about in the mud with the armies. Much more Danton's sort of thing – high-level skulduggery, loot, military bands, and all the women of an occupied territory.'

The slow, wheezy drawl in which Marat articulated all this had a chilling effect of its own. 'I'll tell him,' Camille said.

'You do that. As for Brissot – looked at in a certain way, it becomes obvious that he was conspiring against the Revolution all along. Yet he and his cronies, they have entrenched themselves – and it will need vigour to expel them from public life.'

His habituation, now, to the current of Marat's speech made him look up. 'You do mean that, I suppose – expel them from public life? You don't mean anything worse, do you?'

'Just when one imagined you were beginning to face reality,' Marat said. 'Or is this some hope of your two queasy masters? Robespierre knew in September what had to be done, in the crisis; but since then, oh, he has grown very nice.'

Camille sat with his head resting on his hand. He twisted a curl of hair around his finger. 'I've known Brissot a long time.'

'We have known evil since the moment of our births,' Marat said, 'but we do not tolerate it on that account.'

'That is just phrase-making.'

'Yes. Cheapskate profundity.'

'It is a pity. Kings have always killed their opponents, but we were supposed to reason with ours.'

'At the front, people die for their mistakes. Why should politicians be more gently treated? They made the war. They deserve a dozen deaths, each of them. What can we try them for, except for treason, and how can you punish treason, except by death?'

'Yes, I see.' Camille began drawing patterns with his fingernail on the dusty table before them, but stopped when he realized what he was doing.

Marat smiled. 'There was a time, Camille, when aristocrats flocked to my house, wanting my cure for the consumption. Their carriages sometimes blocked the streets. I kept a handsome equipage myself. My dress was immaculate, and I was known for the calm graciousness of my manner.'

'Of course,' Camille said.

'You were a schoolchild, you know nothing about it.'

'Did you cure consumption?'

'Sometimes. When there was enough faith. Tell me, do you people who began the Cordeliers ever go there now?'

'Sometimes. Other people run it. That's not a problem.'

'The sansculottes have taken over.'

'In effect.'

'While you move in higher spheres.'

'I know what you are saying. But we are still quite able to handle a street meeting. We aren't drawing-room revolutionaries. One doesn't have to live in squalor – '

'Enough,' Marat said. 'It is just that I am exercised about our sansculottes.'

'Jacques Roux, this priest – but that's not really his name?'

'Oh no – but then perhaps you think Marat is not mine?'

'It doesn't matter, does it?'

'No. But idiots like Roux divert the minds of the people. When they should be thinking of purifying the Revolution, they encourage them to loot grocers' shops.'

'There is always someone ready to pose as the champion of the oppressed poor,' Camille said. 'I don't know what is the use of it. The situation of the poor does not change. It is just that the people who think it can change are admired by posterity.'

'Just so. What they will not realize, what they will not accept, is that the poor are going to be driven like pack-animals through this Revolution and every other. Where would we have been in '89 if we had waited for the sansculottes? We made the Revolution in the cafés and took it out on to the streets. Now Roux wants to kick it into the gutter. And every one of them – Roux and all that mob – are agents of the allies.'

'Knowingly, you mean?'

'What does it matter if they serve the enemy interests because they're wicked, or because they're stupid? They do it. They sabotage the Revolution from within.'

'Even Hébert is beginning to speak out against them. *Enragés*, people are calling them. Ultra-revolutionaries.'

Marat spat on the floor. Camille jumped violently. 'They are not ultra-revolutionaries. They are not revolutionaries at all. They are atavists. Their idea of social betterment is a god in the sky who throws down bread every day. But a fool like Hébert wouldn't see that. No, I have no more affection for Père Duchesne than you have.'

'Perhaps Hébert is a secret Brissotin?'

Marat laughed sourly. 'Camille, you progress, you progress. Hébert has defamed you, I think – and yes, you'll have his head, when the time comes. But a few others will fall, before that one. Let's, as the women say, let's get Christmas over, and then we'll see what we can do to put this Revolution on the right lines. I wonder if our masters realize what assets we are? You with your sweet smile, and me with my sharp knife.'

HÉBERT, Le Père Duchesne, on the Rolands:

Some days ago a half-dozen of the sansculottes went in deputation to the house of the old humbug Roland. Unfortunately they arrived just as dinner was being served . . . Our sansculottes pass along the corridor and arrive in the antechamber of the virtuous Roland. They are unable to make their way through the crowd of lackeys that fill it. Twenty cooks bearing the finest fricassees cry, 'Take care, clear the way, these are the virtuous Roland's entrées.' Others carry the virtuous Roland's hors-d'œuvres, others carry the virtuous Roland's roasts, others again the virtuous Roland's side-dishes. 'What do you want?' the virtuous Roland's valet asks the deputation.

'We want to speak with the virtuous Roland.'

The valet goes to take the message to the virtuous Roland, who comes out, looking sulky, his mouth full, with a napkin over his arm. 'The republic must surely be in danger,' says he, 'for me to be obliged to leave my dinner like this' . . . Louvet with his papier mâché face and hollow eyes was casting lascivious glances at the virtuous Roland's wife. One of the deputation tries to pass through the pantry without a light, and overturns the virtuous Roland's dessert. At the news of the loss of the dessert, the virtuous Roland's wife tears her false hair with rage.

'HÉBERT is getting very silly,' Lucile said. 'When I think of those notorious turnips that were served to Georges-Jacques!' She passed the newspaper to Camille. 'Will the sansculottes believe this?'

'Oh yes. They believe every word. They don't know that Hébert keeps a carriage. They think he is Père Duchesne, that he smokes a pipe and makes furnaces.'

'Can no one enlighten them?'

'Hébert and I are supposed to be allies. Colleagues.' He shakes his head. He does not mention his afternoon with Marat. Mostly, he would not like his wife to know what is going on in his head.

'SO YOU MUST GO?' Maurice Duplay said.

'What can I do? She is my sister, she feels that we should have a home of our own.'

'But this is your home.'

'Charlotte doesn't understand that.'

'Mark my words, he'll be back,' says Mme Duplay.

CONDORCET, the Girondist, on Robespierre:

One wonders why there are so many women who follow Robespierre. It is because the French Revolution is a religion, and Robespierre is a priest. It is obvious that his power is all on the distaff side. Robespierre preaches, Robespierre censures . . . He lives on nothing and has no physical needs. He has only one mission – to talk – and he talks almost all the time. He harangues the Jacobins when he can attract some disciples there, he keeps quiet when he might damage his authority . . . He has given himself a reputation for austerity that borders on saintliness. He is followed by women and weak people, he soberly receives their adoration and their homage.

ROBESPIERRE: We've had two revolutions now. '89 and last August. It doesn't seem to have made much difference to people's lives.

DANTON: Roland and Brissot and Vergniaud are aristocrats.

ROBESPIERRE: Well –

DANTON: In the new sense of the word, I mean. Revolution is a great battlefield of semantics.

ROBESPIERRE: Perhaps we need another revolution.

DANTON: Not to pussyfoot about.

ROBESPIERRE: Quite.

DANTON: But with your well-known views, your scruples about taking life . . . ?

ROBESPIERRE [*without much hope*]: Cannot change be profound without being violent?

DANTON: I can't see my way to it.

ROBESPIERRE: Innocent people suffer. But then perhaps there are no innocent people. Possibly it's just a cliché. It rolls off the tongue.

DANTON: What about all these conspirators?

ROBESPIERRE: They are the ones who should be suffering.

DANTON: How do you tell a conspirator?

ROBESPIERRE: Put them on trial.

DANTON: What if you *know* they're conspirators, but you haven't enough evidence to convict them? What if you as a patriot just *know*?

ROBESPIERRE: You ought to be able to make it stand up in court.

DANTON: Suppose you can't? You might not be able to use your strongest evidence. It might be state secrets.

ROBESPIERRE: You'd have to let them go, in that case. But it would be unfortunate.

DANTON: It would, wouldn't it? If the Austrians were at the gates? And you were delivering the city over to them out of respect for the judicial process?

ROBESPIERRE: Well, I suppose you'd ... you'd have to alter the standard of proof in court. Or widen the definition of conspiracy.

DANTON: You would, would you?

ROBESPIERRE: Would that be an example of a lesser evil averting a greater one? I am not usually taken in by this simple, very comforting, very infantile notion – but I know that a successful conspiracy against the French people could lead to genocide.

DANTON: Perverting justice is a very great evil in itself. It leaves no hope of amendment.

ROBESPIERRE: Look, Danton, I don't know, I'm not a theorist.

DANTON: I know that. You're a practitioner. I know all about the sneaky little slaughters you try to fix up behind my back.

ROBESPIERRE: Why do you condone the death of a thousand, and baulk at two politicians?

DANTON: Because I know them, I suppose, Roland and Brissot. I don't know the thousand. Call it a failure of imagination.

ROBESPIERRE: If you couldn't prove things in court, I suppose you could detain your suspects without trial.

DANTON: Could you indeed? It's you idealists who make the best tyrants.

ROBESPIERRE: It seems a bit late to be having this conversation. I've had to take up violence now, and so much else. We should have discussed it last year.

A FEW DAYS LATER Robespierre was back at the Duplays': his head throbbing from three sleepless nights in a row, a giant hand wringing his intestines. Chalk-white and shaky, he sat with Mme Duplay in the small room filled with his portraits. He didn't much resemble any of them; he didn't think he'd ever look healthy again.

'Everything is as you left it,' she said. 'Dr Souberbielle has been sent for. You are under a great strain, and you can't tolerate any disturbance in your life.' She covered his hand with her own. 'We have been like people bereaved. Eléonore has hardly eaten, and I've not been able to get two words out of her. You must never go away again.'

Charlotte came, but they told her that he had taken a sleeping draught, and that she should please lower her voice. They would let her know, they said, when he was well enough for visitors.

SÈVRES, the last day of November: Gabrielle had lit the lamps. They were alone; the children at her mother's house; the circus left behind in the rue des Cordeliers. 'You're going to Belgium?' she said. This is why he has turned up tonight; to give her this news, and then go.

'You remember Westermann, don't you? General Westermann?'

'Yes. The man who Fabre says is a crook. You brought him home with you on 10 August.'

'I don't know why he says that. Anyway, whatever Westermann has been, he's an important man now, and he's come back from the front himself as a messenger from Dumouriez. That will tell you how urgent it is.'

'Wouldn't a government courier have been as fast? Has he wings on his heels as a result of his promotion?'

'He has come himself to impress on us the gravity of the situation. I think that Dumouriez would have come in person, if he could have been spared.'

'That tells us something. Westermann can be spared.'

'It's like talking to Camille,' he grumbled.

'Is it? Do you know you have collected some of his mannerisms yourself? When I knew you at first you never used to wave your hands around so much. They say that if you keep a pet dog, after a while you grow to look like it. It must be something the same.'

She got up and moved to the window, looking out over the lawns crisp with frost; a small November moon showed to her a lost drifting face. 'August, September, October, November,' she said. 'It seems a lifetime.'

'You like the new house? You are comfortable here?'

'Oh, yes. But I didn't think I'd be alone here so much.'

'You'd prefer to go back to Paris? It's warmer at the apartment. I'll take you tonight.'

She shook her head. 'I'm fine here. I've got my parents.' She looked up at him. 'I will miss you, though, Georges.'

'I'm sorry. It's unavoidable.'

Darkness was gathering in the corners of the room. The fire blazed up; shadows leapt and plunged across his dark scarred face. Carefully he kept his hands still, left fist in right palm, his body hunched forward to the warmth, his elbows on his knees. 'We've known for a long time that Dumouriez had problems. He can't get supplies, and the English have flooded the country with counterfeit money. Dumouriez is quarrelling with the War Office – he doesn't like people safe in Paris querying what he does in the field. And the Convention didn't expect to see him propping up the existing order as he does – they expect the Revolution to be propagated. It is a complicated situation, Gabrielle.' He reached forward to put another log on the fire. 'Beechwood,' he said. 'It burns well.' An owl hooted from the copse. The watchdog grumbled under the window. 'Not like Brount,' he said. 'Brount just watches, he doesn't make a noise.'

'So there is an emergency? Dumouriez wants someone to come and see his problems on the spot?'

'Two of the commission have set out already. Deputy Lacroix and I are to go tomorrow.'

'Who is Lacroix?'

'He's . . . well . . . a lawyer.'

'What's his first name?'

'Jean-François.'

'How old is he?'

'I don't know – forty?'

'Is he married?'

'Haven't a clue.'

'What does he look like?'

Danton thought. 'Nothing much. Look, he'll probably tell me his life-story on the journey. If he does, I'll tell it you when I get back.'

She sat down, hitched her chair around, to protect her cheek from the heat of the blaze. Face half in shadow, she said, 'How long will you be away?'

'It's hard to say. I might even be back in a week. You can be sure we'll not waste any time, with Louis's trial going forward here.'

'Are you really so anxious to be in at the kill, Georges?'

'Is that what you think of me?'

'I don't know what to think,' she said wearily. 'I am sure that, like Belgium and General Dumouriez and everything else, it is much more complicated than I know. But I know it will end with the King's death, unless someone with your influence takes his part. The whole Convention is to try him, you say – and I know you can sway the Convention. I understand your power.'

'But what you don't understand is the consequence of exercising it. Let's drop the subject, shall we? I have only an hour.'

'Is Robespierre better?'

'He is – at least, he spoke in the Convention today.'

'And he's staying with the Duplays now?'

'Yes.' Danton sat back in his chair. 'They're keeping Charlotte away from him. What I hear is, she sent her servant round with some jam, and Mme Duplay wouldn't let the girl in. She sent a message back that she didn't want him poisoned.'

'Poor old Charlotte.' Gabrielle half-smiled. His face showed relief. She was diverted to the trivial, the domestic: to where he preferred her.

'It is only two months now. And perhaps a week.' To the birth of the child, she meant. She pushed herself from her chair, crossed the room; she drew the heavy curtains against the night. 'You will at least be back to see the new year in with me?'

'I'll try my best.'

When he had gone, she put her head back against a cushion and fell into a doze. The clock ticked on towards the small hours, and embers rustled into the grate. Outside the owls' wings beat the cold air, and small animals screamed in the undergrowth. She dreamt she was a child again, at morning, in the sun. Then the sounds of the pursuit entered her dreams, and she became, by turns, the hunter and the prey.

ROBESPIERRE to the Convention, January:

There is no case to plead here. Louis is not a defendant, you are not judges. If Louis can be tried, Louis can be acquitted; he may be innocent. But if Louis can be acquitted, if Louis can be presumed innocent, what becomes of the Revolution? ... You have no verdict to give for or against a man, but a measure of public safety to adopt, an act of Providence to carry out ... Louis must die so that the nation can live.

IV. *Blackmail*

(1793)

THE RUE DES CORDELIERS, 13 January: 'Do you think,' Fabre asked, 'that Mr Pitt will send us some money? For the New Year?'

'Ah,' Camille said, 'Mr Pitt only ever sends his good wishes.'

'The great days of William Augustus Miles are over.'

'I think we'll be at war with England soon.'

'You're not supposed to look like that about it, Camille. You're supposed to burn with patriotic fervour.'

'I can't see how we can win. Suppose the British populace doesn't rise in revolt, and so on? They might prefer native oppression to liberation by Frenchmen. And now, of course' – he thought of recent decisions of the Convention – 'it seems to be our policy to annex territories. Danton approves it, at least in the case of Belgium, but to me it just seems the way Europe has always been run. Imagine trying to annex England. People who bore the Convention would be sent as special commissioner to Newcastle-on-Tyne.'

'You're in no danger of boring them, my dear. All my years of careful training, and you never open your mouth.'

'I spoke in the debate about attaching Savoy. I said that the republic should not behave like a king, grabbing territory. No one took the least notice. Fabre, do you think that Mr Pitt really cares whether we have Louis executed?'

'Personally? Oh no, no one gives a damn for Louis. But they think it is a bad precedent to cut off monarchs' heads.'

'It was the English who set the precedent.'

'They try to forget that. And they will declare war on us, unless we do it first.'

'Do you think Georges-Jacques has miscalculated? He had this idea that he could use Louis's life as a bargaining point, keep him alive as long as England stays neutral.'

'I don't think they care about the man's life, in Whitehall. They care about commerce. Shipping. Cash.'

'Danton will be back tomorrow,' Camille said.

'He must be aggrieved that the Convention has sent for him. Another week and Capet's trial would have been over, he wouldn't have needed to commit himself one way or the other. Besides, such a good time he's been having! A pity the stories had to come to his wife's ears. She should have stayed in Sèvres, away from the gossip.'

'I suppose you have not been passing it on to her.'

'What interest would I have, in adding to their difficulties?'

'Just your normal day to day malice would suffice.'

'I do no damage. This is damage, this.' He picked up a paper from Camille's desk. 'I can't read your writing, but I take it the general tenor is that Brissot should go and hang himself.'

'Ah well. As long as your conscience is clear.'

'Quite clear. You can see that I am developing a paunch. It shows how comfortable I find myself.'

'No you don't. Your palms sweat. Your eyes flit from face to face. You are like a counterfeiter passing his first gold piece.'

Fabre looked at Camille intently. 'What do you mean by that?' Camille shrugged. 'Come now.' Fabre stood over him. 'Tell me what you mean.' There was a pause. 'Ah well,' Fabre said, 'I doubt you meant anything, did you?'

'So,' Lucile said, coming in. 'You have been at your meaningless prattle again, have you?' She held some letters, just arrived.

'Fabre's had a bad fright.'

'It's the old story. Camille has been heaping scorn on me. He thinks I am not fit to be Danton's dog, let alone his political confidant.'

'No, that is not it. Fabre has something to hide.'

'More things than one, I imagine,' Lucile said. 'And no doubt they had better remain hidden. Here is a letter from your father. I didn't open it.'

'I should hope not,' Fabre said.

'And here is one from your cousin Rose-Fleur. I did.'

'Lucile is jealous of my cousin. We were going to be married, at one time.'

'How quaint of her,' Fabre said, 'to be jealous of one woman, and that one so far away.'

'You can guess what my father says.' Camille was reading the letter.

'Yes, I can guess,' Lucile said. 'Don't vote for Louis's death – abstain. You have so often spoken against him, and you have already published your opinion on the case. Thus you have prejudged him, which is excusable in a polemicist but not in a juror. Decline therefore to be part of the process. By declining you will also safeguard yourself.'

'In case of counter-revolution. Yes, exactly. He means that I could not be charged with regicide then.'

'The dear, whimsical old man,' Fabre said. 'Really, your family are quaint altogether.'

'Do you find Fouquier-Tinville quaint?'

'No, I had forgotten him. He becomes a person of consequence. He makes himself useful. No doubt he will soon attain high office.'

'As long as he remains grateful.' There was an edge to Lucile's voice. 'They can't bear their subservience to the scrapegrace, this family of yours.'

'Rose-Fleur can bear me, and her mother has always been on my side. Her father, though . . . '

'History repeats itself,' Fabre said.

'Your father couldn't imagine how we laugh at his scruples here,' Lucile said. 'Tomorrow Danton will come back from Belgium and vote to condemn Louis the following day, without having heard a scrap of the evidence. What would your father say to that?'

'He'd be appalled,' Camille said, seeing it in that light for the first time. 'So would I. In fact, I am. But then, you know what Robespierre says. It isn't a trial at all, in the usual meaning of the word. It's a measure we have to take.'

'For the public safety,' Lucile said. This was an expression that was coming up in the world; for the last few weeks it had been on everyone's lips. 'The public safety. But somehow, whatever measures are taken, one never feels any safer. I wonder why that is?'

THE COUR DU COMMERCE, 14 January: Gabrielle had been sitting quietly, waiting for Georges to finish sifting through the pile of letters that had come while he was away. He took her by surprise, appearing in the doorway, filling it with his bulk. His big face was deathly white.

'When did this arrive?' He held the letter out to her, at arms' length.

Antoine looked up from the game he was playing on the carpet. 'He's worried,' the little boy informed her.

'I don't know,' she said. She looked away from the pulse hammering at his temple. She had seen him for a moment as a stranger might see him, and she was afraid of the violence contained by his massive body.

'Can't you remember?' He held it under her nose. Did he mean her to read it?

'December 11. That's more than a month ago, Georges.'

'When did it arrive?'

'I'm sorry, I can't tell you. Someone has slandered me,' she said faintly. 'What is it, what have I done?'

He crumpled the letter in his fist with a sound of sneering impatience. 'This is nothing to do with you. Oh God, oh God, oh God.'

She looked up warningly, indicating Antoine with a weak little gesture. The child pulled at her skirt, whispering into it: 'Is he cross?'

She put her finger to her lips.

'Who is the president of the Convention?'

She tried to think; the office revolved, it changed every fortnight. 'I don't know. I'm sorry, Georges.'

'Where are my friends? Where are they when I need them? Robespierre would be informed, he only has to snap his fingers for anything he wants.'

'Oh, don't be ridiculous.' They hadn't heard Camille come in. 'I know I should be at the Riding-School,' he said, 'but I couldn't bear the speeches about Louis. We'll go together later. Why were you – ' Antoine launched himself from the floor, trampling his soldiers. He ran to Camille, impending screams stiffening his face. Camille picked him up. 'What's happened, Georges? You were fine an hour ago.'

Gabrielle's lips parted. She looked from one to the other. 'Oh, you were there first. You went to Lucile, before you came to me.'

'Stop this,' Danton said ferociously. The child began a red-faced wail. His father bellowed for Catherine, and the servant came, clasping and unclasping her hands. 'Take the baby.' Catherine made clucking noises, unthreading the child's little fingers from Camille's hair. 'What a homecoming. You go away for a month and your sons have attached themselves to another man.'

Catherine carried the child away. Gabrielle wanted to cover her ears to shut out his panic-stricken screams, but she was afraid to move and make herself conspicuous. Rage seemed to be running from his pores. He took hold of Camille, and pushed him down on the sofa beside her. 'Here.' He tossed the letter on to her lap. 'From Bertrand de Molleville, the ex-minister, who is now ensconced in London. Read it together. You two can suffer for me for a bit.'

She took it, smoothed it out on her knee, fumbling with it, then holding it up for Camille's short-sighted eyes; but he had the gist of it while she was puzzling over the first sentence, and turned his face away, his thin, fine hands flying to his forehead, holding his skull poised as if it were disaster about to break out. 'Very helpful, Camille,' her husband said. Slowly she looked away from Camille's horrified face, and returned her eyes to the letter.

I do not feel, Monsieur, that I should any longer keep you ignorant of the fact that, among a pile of papers which the late M. Montmorin left in my care towards the end of June last year – and which I brought abroad with me – I found a memorandum detailing various sums paid over to you from the British Foreign Office Secret Fund, complete with dates of payment, the circumstances in which you received them, and the names of the persons through whom . . .

'Oh yes,' he said, 'I am precisely what you thought.'

She ran her eye down the page: 'I have a note in your own handwriting ... I hereby give you warning that both documents are attached to a letter I have written to the president of the National Convention ...' 'Georges, what does he want?' she whispered.

'Read,' he said. 'The letter and the two documents are sent to a friend of his here in Paris, to be forwarded to the president of the Convention, if I do not save the King.'

Her eyes skimmed over the threat, and the terms: '. . . if you do not comport yourself, in the matter of the King, as befits a man whom the King has paid so handsomely. If, however, you render the services in this matter of which you are well capable, be assured that they will not go unrecompensed.'

'It is a blackmail letter, Gabrielle,' Camille said flatly. 'Montmorin was Louis's Foreign Minister; we forced him out of office after the King tried to escape, but he was always in Louis's inner circle. He was killed in prison in September. This man de Molleville was Louis's Minister of Marine.'

'What will you do?' She put out a hand to Danton, as if to offer comfort; but there was only dismay in her face.

He moved away from her. 'I should have killed them all,' he said. 'I should have slaughtered them while I had the chance.'

In the next room, Antoine was still crying. 'I have always believed,' Gabrielle said, 'that your heart was not in this Revolution. That you were the King's man.' He turned and laughed in her face. 'Keep faith with him. You've taken his money and lived on it, bought land – please keep faith now. You know it's the right thing to do, and if you don't do it – ' She didn't know how to finish. She couldn't imagine what would happen. Would it mean public disgrace? Or worse? Would they put him on trial? 'Surely you must save him,' she said. 'You have no choice.'

'And do you really believe they would reward me, my dear? You really think that? The child would know better. If I save Louis – and they're right, I can do it – then they'll put their evidence back in safekeeping, and hold it over me, and use me as their puppet.

When I'm no more use to them, when my influence is lost – then they'll bring their documents out. They'll do it out of spite, and to sow confusion.'

'Why don't you ask for the documents back?' Camille said. 'Make it part of the bargain? And the cash too? If you thought you could get away with it, you would, wouldn't you? As long as the money's right?'

Danton turned. 'Say exactly what you mean.'

'If there were some way to work it – to save Louis and to keep your credit with the patriots and to extract more money from the English at the same time – you'd do it.'

Time was when he'd have said mildly, I'd be a fool not to; Camille would have smiled, and thought, he always pretends to be worse than he is. But now he saw, perplexity growing on his face, that Danton did not have a reply, did not know what he was going to do, had lost control of himself. He moved. Gabrielle stood up suddenly; she took the open-handed blow full in the face, and it knocked her off her feet, sprawling back on to the sofa. 'Oh Lord,' Camille said. 'That was valorous.'

Danton covered his face with his hands for a moment, gasping, blinking back tears of humiliation and fury. He had scarcely wept since before the bull gored him, since he was a tiny child who could no more control his tears than his bowels. He took his hands away; his wife was looking up at him, dry-eyed. He crouched down beside her. 'I shall never forgive myself for that.'

She touched her lip, gingerly. 'You could smash crockery,' she said, 'not people. We're not even the right people. We just happen to be here.' She clenched her hand so that she wouldn't put it to her face and let him see how much he'd hurt her.

'I don't deserve you,' he said. 'Forgive me. It wasn't meant for you.'

'I wouldn't think the better of you for knocking Camille around the room.'

He straightened up from beside her. 'Camille, I'll kill you one day,' he said simply. 'No, come here. You're all right, you've got a pregnant woman to protect you. You dropped me in the shit in

September, when the prisoners were killed. All organized, you told Prudhomme and everybody within earshot. It's all organized, no problem – when I was trying to deny any knowledge of it. The filthy business was necessary, but at least I had the grace of soul to pretend it was nothing to do with me. You, you'd have fluttered up to take the credit for the Massacre of the Innocents. So don't look down on me from whatever ledge of higher morality you're perched on today. You knew. You knew it all, from the beginning.'

'Yes,' Camille said, 'but I didn't expect you to be caught out like this.' He backed away, smiling. Gabrielle stared at him.

'Oh Camille,' she said, 'you'd better take this seriously.'

'Bathe your face, Gabrielle,' her husband said. 'Yes, because if those documents are made public, my future won't be worth two sous, and neither will yours.'

'I think it might be bluff,' Camille said. 'How would he have a note in your own handwriting?'

'Such a note does exist.'

'You've been a fool then, haven't you? But look now, it is possible that de Molleville has at one time or another seen these documents – but would Montmorin part with such a thing? For safekeeping, de Molleville implies – but what's so safe about being on a cross-channel boat, and carried around in an *émigré*'s luggage? Why would Montmorin have sent the document to London? It's no use to him there. It only has to be sent back. And he didn't know he was going to be killed, did he?'

'You might be right, it's possible you are, but de Molleville's allegations alone could ruin me. If they're circumstantial. If they're detailed. They've been saying for long enough that I work for Pitt. In fact, at this moment – they will be expecting me in the Convention, now.'

'There's no point in panicking, is there? If it is a bluff, if there are no documents, anything de Molleville says will carry much less weight. All you can do is hope it is. But I wonder – which president of the Convention is he talking about? Because today's president is Vergniaud.'

Danton turned away. 'Christ,' he said.

'Yes, I know. You've neglected either to bribe or to frighten him. How could you have been so remiss?'

'You'd better go now,' Gabrielle said. 'Go now and speak for the King.'

'Give in to them?' Danton said. 'I'd rather be dead. If I step in now, at this stage, they'll say I've been bought, just as surely as if the documents become public. Either way, as soon as I turn my back I'll get a patriot's dagger between my shoulder blades. Ask him,' he yelled. 'He'd put one there himself.'

The absurd question held in her eyes, Gabrielle turned her face to Camille.

'No doubt they'd ask me to help with the arrangements. After all, I wouldn't want to share your fate.'

'Why don't you go back to Robespierre?' Danton said.

'No, I'm staying with you, Georges-Jacques. I want to see what you do.'

'Go on, why don't you run and tell him everything? You'll be all right, he'll look after you. Or are you afraid you've been replaced in his affections? You shouldn't worry. You'll always find somebody to run to. With your attributes.'

Gabrielle stood up. 'Is this the way to keep your friends?' She had never spoken to him like this before. 'You lamented the absence of your friends, but when they come to you, you insult them. I think you are trying to destroy yourself. I think you are conspiring with this man de Molleville to destroy yourself.'

'Wait,' Camille said. 'Listen to me Gabrielle – listen, both of you, before there's a massacre. I'm quite unused to being the cool voice of reason, so don't test my abilities in that line.' He turned to Danton. 'If Vergniaud has the documents you're finished, but would Vergniaud wait so long? Today is the last day when you could intervene in the debate. These are the last hours. He has been president three days now – we must wonder why he has not acted. We must wonder, at least, if he has the papers at all – or if it is some earlier president who has them. What is the date of the letter?'

'December 11.'

'Defermon was president.'

'He's – '

'A worm.'

'A moderate, Gabrielle,' Danton said. 'Surely though – he's no friend of mine – and after all this time, four weeks, he'd have said something, done something . . . ?'

'I don't know, Georges-Jacques. Perhaps you don't know how much you frighten people. Why don't you go to his house, and frighten him some more? If he has the papers, you've everything to gain. If he hasn't, you've nothing to lose.'

'But if Vergniaud has them – '

'Then it will hardly matter if you've terrified Defermon gratuitously. Nothing will matter, then. Don't think of that. And don't wait. Defermon may have a tender conscience. Because he has not spoken out so far doesn't mean he will never speak. He may be waiting till the voting begins.'

Fabre missed the last words. 'You're back, Danton. And whatever has happened here?'

His immediate impression was that the quarrel – the inevitable quarrel – had come about at last. He had already heard that Danton had arrived in town and gone straight to the Desmoulins's apartment. How the whole business had moved around the corner, he had yet to find out, but the air of the room was clogged with violence. He did not see de Molleville's letter, because Gabrielle was sitting on it. 'My dear, your face,' he said.

'I got in the way.'

'It was ever thus,' Fabre said, as if to himself. 'Danton, one would never take you for the guilty party. No, you have the face of someone who has been wronged.'

'Fabre, what are you talking about?' Danton said.

'Guilty?' Camille said. 'Never. His innocence shines forth.'

'I'm glad you think so,' Fabre said.

'There's a letter – ' Gabrielle began.

'Be quiet,' Camille said. 'Before he hits you again. On purpose, this time.'

'What letter?' Fabre said.

'No letter,' Camille said. 'There never was a letter. I hope not, anyway. You know, Georges-Jacques, a good deal depends on whether the courier was intelligent. Most people aren't intelligent, don't you find?'

'Trying to confuse me,' Fabre complained.

Danton bent to kiss his wife. 'I may yet save myself.'

'You think so?' She averted her face. 'Yet you are still destroying yourself.'

He looked at her intently for a second, then straightened up. He turned to Camille and put a hand into his hair, pulling his head back. 'You won't wring any apologies from me,' he said. 'Fabre, do you know a deputy, timid and obscure, they call him Defermon? Can you find him for me? Tell him that Danton will visit him at his own house one hour from now. No excuses. He must be there. It is Danton in person who requires to see him. Be sure to stress that. Go on. Don't stand about.'

'Just that? No other message?'

'Go.'

Fabre turned at the door and shook his head at Camille. He talked to himself, as he hurried along the street: think they can fool me, do they, I'll soon find out what's what.

Danton walked into his study and slammed the door; later, they heard him moving about, in different rooms of the apartment.

'What will he do?' Gabrielle said.

'Well, you know, with other people a complicated problem needs a complicated solution, but with Georges-Jacques solutions are usually rather simple and quick. It's true what I said, people are frightened of him. They remember August, when he dragged Mandat around City Hall. They don't know what he might do next. It's true, you know, Gabrielle. Money from England, from the Court – all that.'

'I know. I'm not that much of a simpleton, even though he's always taken me for one. He had an expensive mistress and a child when we married. He thinks I don't know. That's why we were so poor at first. He bought his practice from his mistress's new lover. Did you know that? Yes, of course you did, I don't know why I'm saying all this.' Gabrielle lifted her arms, began repinning her hair;

an automatic action, but her fingers were clumsy, looked swollen. Her face too looked swollen, quite apart from the damage that Georges had done, and her eyes were shadowed, without life. 'I've annoyed him, you see, all these years, by pretending to keep some form of integrity. So have you – that's why he's angry with us both, that's why he's persecuting us together. Both of us knew everything and wouldn't admit it. Oh, I'm no saint, Camille – I knew where the money came from, and I took it, to make a more comfortable life for us. Once you're pregnant for the first time you don't mind what happens, you just think about your children.'

'So you don't really care – about the King, say?'

'Yes, I do care, but I've had to be very accommodating this past year, very tolerant, very easy. Or he would have divorced me, I think.'

'No. He would never have done that. He's an old-fashioned sort of person.'

'Yes, but – we see this all along – his passions take a greater hold on him than his habits do. It would have depended – if Lucile had been as compliant as she pretends to be. But she would never leave you.' She turned to ring the bell for a servant. 'When he brought out the letter – so angry – I wondered what I had done. I thought it was one of those anonymous letters, and that someone had slandered me.'

'Libelled you,' Camille said automatically.

Marie came from the kitchen, wrapped in her large linen apron, her face drawn. 'Catherine has taken the child upstairs to Mme Gély,' she said, without being asked.

'Marie, bring me a bottle of something from the cellar. I don't know – Camille, what would you like? Anything, Marie.' She sighed. 'Servants grow familiar. I wish, I do wish that I had talked to you before.'

'I think you were afraid to admit that we had a common predicament.'

'Oh, that you are in love with my husband – I've known that for years. Don't look so stunned – be truthful now, if you had to describe your own feelings towards him, what else could you say?

But I don't think I'm in love, not any more. Today has been the day I met someone I've been waiting to meet for a very long time. I've been thinking – I'm not such a feeble creature that I needed to marry that kind of man. But what does it matter now?'

Danton stood in front of them. Some of the sudden exhilaration had worn off. He held his hat in his hand, and his caped greatcoat over his arm. He had shaved; he wore a black coat, and a very plain white muslin cravat.

'Shall I come with you?' Camille said.

'God, no. Wait here.'

He marched out. Again, 'What will he do?' Gabrielle whispered. Conspiracy seemed to have set in between them. She sat drinking deeply, her glass cupped in her palm, her face still and thoughtful; after five minutes had passed, she reached out and took Camille's hand in hers.

He said, 'We must suppose, we must hope it is Defermon who has the letter. We must suppose he has been trembling over it for a month, waiting for Louis's trial to begin. He'll have thought, "If I take this letter seriously, if I read it out in the Convention, the Mountain will fall on me. And Deputy Lacroix is fast friends with Danton since they were in Belgium, and Lacroix has influence with the Plain." Defermon will see that the only people he will please are Brissot and Roland and their cronies. And he will say, Danton comes here boldly, not like a guilty man, and he says it is a forgery, a trick – Defermon will want to believe him. We are supposed to be such thugs, that if he upsets Danton he will fear for his life. You heard the message that Fabre took – "It is Danton in person who requires to see him." Defermon will be waiting for him, thinking, "What shall I do? What shall I do?" He will begin to feel guilty, simply because the letter has been delivered to him. Georges-Jacques will – overbear him.'

Darkness fell. They sat still, their fingers plaited together. She thought of her husband, overbearing people. Every day since '89, his corpulence flung into the breach. She ran her fingertips along the edges of Camille's carefully kept nails. She could feel his pulse racing, like a small animal's.

'Georges is not frightened any more.'

'Yes, but I come from the meeker portion of humanity.'

'Meek? Stop acting, Camille. You're as meek as a serpent.'

He smiled and turned his head away. 'I used to think,' he said, 'that he wasn't a very complicated person. But he is – very complicated, very subtle, in himself. It's only his wants that are simple. Power, money, land.'

'Women,' Gabrielle said.

'Why did you say, just now, that he was destroying himself?'

'I'm not sure now what I meant. But at the time – when he was so angry and sneering and insulting – I saw it very clearly. This view he has of himself – he thinks, people may call me corrupt, but I'm just playing the system, I'm still my own man, nothing touches me. But it doesn't work like that. He's forgotten what he wanted. The means have become the end. He doesn't see it, but he's corrupt all through.' She shivered, swirled her glass with the last half-inch of wine settling red and sticky. 'Oh,' she said, 'life, liberty and the pursuit of happiness.'

Danton came home. Catherine walked in before him, touching a spill to tall wax candles in their branched silver sticks. Pools of sweet yellow light washed through the room. His great shadow stretched itself across the wall. He sank to one knee at the hearth and produced papers from his pocket.

'See?' he said. 'Bluff. You were right. It was almost an anticlimax.'

'After the scene you made here,' Camille said, 'I shall find the Last Judgement an anticlimax.'

'The timing was just right. The letter was with Defermon, as you said. The letter in my handwriting wasn't enclosed. Nor the receipts. There was just this.' He held the papers to the blaze. 'Just a tissue of denunciations from de Molleville. Everything made to sound as sinister as it possibly could be, claims that documents exist – but no actual evidence. I raged about, I said to Defermon, "So, you have letters from *émigrés*, do you?" I pounced on it, I said, "See how they libel me." Defermon said, "You're right, Citizen. Oh dear, oh dear."'

Camille watched the flames eat the pages. He didn't, he thought, allow me to read it; what else has de Molleville been saying? Gabrielle thinks we know everything, but you've got to be good to keep up with Georges-Jacques. 'Who was the courier?'

'The worm did not know. It was no one the concierge recognized.'

'It would not have been so easy with Vergniaud, you know. It might not have been possible at all. And these documents – perhaps they do exist somewhere. Perhaps they are still here in Paris.'

'Well, whatever,' Danton said. 'There's not much I can do about that. But I tell you one thing – when de Molleville signed that pathetic letter of his, he signed Louis's death warrant. I'll not lift a finger for Capet now.'

Gabrielle dropped her head. 'You lost,' her husband said to her. He touched her lightly on the back of the neck. 'Go and rest,' he said. 'You need to lie flat. Camille and I will drink another bottle. Today has wasted my time and effort.'

And tomorrow everyone will behave as if nothing has happened. But Danton moved restlessly about the room. He had not quite recovered his colour, since the shock of opening the letter. Only now self-control seemed to be coming back, seeping to muscles and nerves. He would never be so sure of it again. He was going downhill now. He knew it.

V. *A Martyr, a King, a Child*

(1793)

THE KING'S TRIAL is over. The city gates have been closed. One cannot reign innocently, the Convention has decided. Merely to have been born condemns Louis to die? 'That is the logic of the situation,' Saint-Just says calmly.

Five a.m. At a house in the Place Vendôme, all the lights are burning. They have sent for surgeons, the best the republic can offer; they have sent, too, for the artist David, so that he can see what a martyr looks like, so that he can watch moment by moment as death effaces the features and immortality sets them into a better mould. This is the republic's first martyr, who now hears a babble of voices, some near, half-familiar, some fading and far away; whose senses fade, moment by moment, while his funeral is planned in the next room. He is Michel Lepelletier, once a nobleman, now a deputy. There is nothing to be done for him: not in this world, at any rate.

David takes out his pencils. Lepelletier is an ugly man, that cannot be helped. The features are softening already; an arm lies slack and naked, like the arm of Christ carried to the tomb. The clothes, cut from his body, are stiff and black with blood. David handles the shirt, mentally re-clothes the moribund figure on the bed.

A few hours before, Lepelletier had been dining out, at the Restaurant Feurier in the Jardin de l'Égalité (as we call the Palais-Royal these days). A man approached him – a stranger, but quite friendly – perhaps to congratulate him on his republican firmness in voting for Capet's death. Affable, but weary after the many all-night sittings, the deputy leaned back in his chair; the stranger produced from his coat a butcher's knife, and hacked into the deputy's torso, on the right-hand side below the ribs.

Lepelletier is carried to his brother's house, intestines torn, blood pumping over his attendants, possessed of a wound that you could put your fist into. 'I am cold,' he whispers. 'I am cold.' They heap covers on him. He whispers, 'I am cold.'

Five a.m.: Robespierre is asleep in his room on the rue Saint-Honoré. His door is locked and double-bolted. Brount lies outside, his jaws gaping a little, his great dreaming paws twitching in pursuit of better days.

Five a.m.: Camille Desmoulins slides out of bed wide awake, as he used to do years before at Louis-le-Grand. Danton wants a speech, to try to force the resignation of Roland from the ministry. Lolotte turns, mutters something, stretches out a hand for him. He tucks the covers round her. 'Go back to sleep,' he whispers. Danton will not use the speech. He will hold the pages crumpled in his fist, and make it up as he goes along ... Still, he is not doing this because he has to, but to keep in practice, and to pass the time till dawn.

The cold is like knives against his thin dark skin. He moves quietly, feeling his way across the room, splashing icy water on to his face. If he makes any noise Jeanette will be up to light a fire and to tell him he has a weak chest – which he hasn't – and to ply him with food he can't eat. First of all he writes a letter home ... 'Your son, the regicide'. He reaches for fresh sheets of paper, for the speech. Lolotte's cat dabs a tentative paw at his pen, its eyes suspicious; he runs a hand over its arched back, watching a reluctant dawn creep up over the eastern suburbs. His candle gutters in a strong draught, and he flicks his head around, taut with apprehension; he is alone, with the black outlines of the furniture and the engravings on the walls. As gently as the cat, his cold fingers brush the barrel of the small pistol in the drawer of his desk. Freezing rain hisses into the mud of the streets.

Seven-thirty a.m. Crouching by a stove in a small room, a priest, and Louis the Last. 'There dwells on high an incorruptible judge ... you can hear the National Guard beginning to assemble ... What have I done to my cousin Orléans, that he should persecute me in this way? ... I can endure everything ... these people see daggers and poisons everywhere, they fear I shall destroy myself . . . I am occupied, wait for me a few moments . . . give me your last benediction, and pray that it may please God to support me to the end . . . Cléry, my valet, give him my watch and my clothes . . .'

10.30 a.m. The coat is snatched away from Sanson's assistants, and cut up into snippets. Hot pies and gingerbread are for sale in the Place de la Révolution. People are swarming around the scaffold, soaking rags in the spilled blood.

Lepelletier, the martyr, lies in state.

Louis, the King, is quicklimed.

BY THE END of the first week of February, France is at war with England, Holland and Spain. The National Convention has promised armed support to any people who wish to rise against oppression: *war to the châteaux, peace to the cottages.* Cambon, of the Finance Committee: 'The further we penetrate enemy territory, the more ruinously expensive the war becomes.'

At home there is a food shortage, soaring inflation. In Paris the Commune battles with the Girondist ministers and tries to placate the militants of the Sections; it controls bread prices at three sous, and Minister Roland never ceases to complain about such fecklessness with public money. In the Convention the Mountain is still no more than a vociferous minority.

JACQUES ROUX, sansculotte, at the Bar of the Convention:

There must be bread, for where there is no more bread there is no more law, no more freedom and no more republic.

Riots in Lyon, in Orléans, Versailles, Rambouillet, Étampes, in Vendôme, in Courville, and here, in the city itself.

DUTARD, an employee of the Ministry of the Interior, on the Gironde:

They wish to establish an aristocracy of the rich, of merchants and of men of property . . . If I had the choice I should prefer the old regime; the nobles and the priests had some virtues, and these men have none. What do the Jacobins say? It is necessary to put a check on these greedy and depraved men; under the old regime the nobles and the priests made a barrier that they could not pass. But under the new regime there is no limit to their ambitions; they would starve the people. It is necessary to put some barrier in their way, and the only thing to do is to call out the mob.

CAMILLE DESMOULINS, on the Minister Roland:

The people are to you just the necessary means of insurrection; having served to effect a revolution, they are to return to the dust and be forgotten; they are to allow themselves to be led by those who are wiser than they, and who are willing to take the trouble of governing them. Your whole conduct is marked out on these criminal principles.

ROBESPIERRE on the Gironde:

They think they're the gentlemen, the proper beneficiaries of the Revolution. We're just the riff-raff.

FEBRUARY 10: quite early in the morning, Louise Gély took Antoine to his Uncle Victor's house. The two babies – the Desmoulins's child, and François-Georges, who has just had his first birthday – will be shuttled about by their wet-nurse, who will try, amid the day's predicted events, to see that they do not get too hungry.

Louise sprinted back to the Cour du Commerce, and found Angélique in possession of the ground. Her mother said, 'Mind, young lady, if it's going to be tonight, we don't want you under our feet.'

Angélique said to her, 'Don't sulk, child, it makes you plain.'

Next, Lucile Desmoulins arrived. Nothing would make *her* plain, Louise thought spitefully. Lucile wore a black wool skirt, an elegant waistcoat; her hair was tied up with a tricolour ribbon. 'God above,' she said, throwing herself into a chair, stretching out her legs to admire the toes of her riding-boots. 'If there's one thing I loathe, it's an obstetric drama.'

'I suppose you'd pay somebody to have them for you if you could, my sweet,' Angélique said.

'I certainly would,' Lucile said. 'I really think there ought to be some better way of managing about it.'

The women seemed to find things for Louise to do, shutting her out of the conversation. She heard Gabrielle say she was 'very sweet, very helpful'. Her cheeks burned. They shouldn't discuss her.

Then, when Lucile came to go, she turned to Mme Gély: 'Please, if you need me at all, you know I can be here in half a minute.' Lucile's dark eyes were enormous. 'To me, Gabrielle doesn't seem herself. She says she is afraid. She wishes Georges-Jacques were here.'

'That can't be helped,' Mme Gély said harshly. 'He has his business in Belgium, it seems, which cannot wait.'

'Still – send for me,' Lucile said.

Mme Gély gave her a curt nod. In her eyes, Gabrielle was a good, pious girl who'd been badly wronged; Lucile was little better than a prostitute.

Gabrielle said she'd like to rest. Louise trailed back upstairs, to the cramped dowdiness of her parents' apartment. Mid-afternoon, and dusk already. She sat and thought about Claude Dupin. If Lucile knew how serious he was about her – how very soon she might be a wife – would she dare to treat her as a little ninny?

Her mother had smiled, indulgently; but secretly, she was triumphant. Such a good catch! After your next birthday, she said, then we'll begin to talk about it. Fifteen is too young. Only the aristocracy get married at fifteen.

Claude Dupin himself was only twenty-four, but he was (already, her father said) the secretary-general of the Seine *département*. She found it hard to get excited about that. But he was good-looking, too.

She had taken him to meet Gabrielle a fortnight ago. She had thought him very polished, at his ease; not that Gabrielle would set out to intimidate anyone. She could read approval in Gabrielle's eyes; she squirmed in pleasure to think that tomorrow she would be able to sit with Gabrielle and talk artlessly, casually, about Claude Dupin and say, didn't you think he was this, didn't you think he was that? If Gabrielle were really really in favour, if she liked him as much as she seemed to, then perhaps she'd have a word with her parents, and they'd say, well, you've always been grown-up for your age, perhaps fifteen is old enough? Why wait? Life's too short.

But just as everything was going along politely, quietly and wonderfully – in poured Citizen Danton and his crew. Introductions were made. 'Ah, the infant prodigy,' Citizen Fabre said. 'The famous child administrator, a wonder from his cradle. Now let us see what we see.'

And he had viewed Claude Dupin through his lorgnette.

Citizen Hérault had given Claude Dupin a sort of glassy stare, and seemed unable to comprehend who or what he was. 'Gabrielle darling,' he had said, and kissed their hostess; he seated himself, poured himself a glass of Citizen Danton's best cognac, and proceeded to amuse in his loud drawly voice with anecdotes about Louis Capet, whom of course he'd known intimately. This was bad, but Citizen Camille was much the worst: 'Claude Dupin, I have longed to meet you,' he sighed, 'I have lived for this moment.' He curled up in a corner of the sofa, put his head on Gabrielle's shoulder, and fixed his eyes on Claude Dupin's face: continuing, from time to time, to sigh.

Citizen Danton had subjected Claude Dupin to a sharp interrogation about the *département*'s affairs; she did not blame him, it was the way he worked. Claude Dupin was on his mettle, and his replies were intelligent, assertive, she thought; only, when he said anything particularly to the point, Citizen Camille would close his eyes and shiver, as if it were too exciting for him. 'So young, and so perfectly bureaucratic,' Fabre murmured. Louise did think that if Gabrielle had any regard for her she might induce Citizen Camille to take his head off her shoulder and stop being so satirical. But Gabrielle seemed to be consumed by merriment. She placed her traitorous arm around Citizen Camille, and looked sickeningly affectionate.

As soon as they had come into the room – she could not deny it – Claude Dupin had seemed to shrink. He looked plain, ordinary. Once Citizen Danton's questions had been answered, he had lost interest in him. Thereafter, Claude Dupin experienced difficulty in wedging a word into the conversation. She decided it was time to

go. She stood up. Claude Dupin stood up too. 'Don't go so soon!'
Citizen Fabre cried. 'You'll break Camille's little heart!'

Citizen Danton caught her eye. He made her look up into his
unnerving face. He didn't precisely smile.

She was foolish enough to tell her mother about this upset to her
feelings. 'I don't know if he's ... quite what I want. Do you
understand me?'

'No, I do not,' her mother said. 'Last week on your knees begging
me to order up the wedding breakfast, and this week telling me he's
a mere nothing by the side of that evil bunch of people you meet
downstairs. We should have kept you at home, we should never
have allowed you to mix with them.'

Very quietly, her father reminded her mother that he owed his
living to Citizen Danton.

AND NOW, downstairs (she ran up and down, every couple of
minutes), Dr Souberbielle had been in to see Gabrielle, and the
midwife had arrived. Angélique Charpentier caught her at the door,
shooed her out. 'Look, my dear, you think you want to be here, but
you don't. Will you please believe me?' Mme Charpentier looked, at
this stage, quite collected. 'Everything is going nicely, just according
to time. Off to bed with you, now. In the morning we'll have a
lovely baby for you to play with.'

Upstairs again. She felt a furious resentment. She is my friend. *I*
am her true, her best friend; I cannot help being fifteen, I should be
with her, I am the one she wants beside her. She thought, I wonder
where Citizen Danton is tonight: and with whom? I don't, she
thought, have as many illusions as they suppose I have.

Ten p.m.: her mother put her head around the door. 'Louise,
would you come down? Mme Danton is asking for you.' Her face
said, this is against my better judgement.

Vindication! She tripped over her feet in her haste. 'What's happening?'

'I don't know,' her mother said. 'Are you prepared?'

'Of course I am.'

'I warn you, she's isn't well. The labour has not progressed. She had – I hardly know – some kind of upset, convulsion. Things are not as they should be.'

She ran ahead of her mother. They met the midwife coming out of the room. 'You're not letting this child in?' the woman said. 'Madame, I can't answer . . .'

'I told her last week,' Louise cried, agonized. 'I said I'd be with her. I said, if anything happened, I'd look after the children.'

'Did you? Then you're a little fool, aren't you? Making promises you can't keep.' Her mother lifted her hand, and flicked her smartly on the side of the head.

AT MIDNIGHT, Louise went upstairs again, leaving Gabrielle's apartment at her own request. She stretched out on her bed, half-dressed. The closed, solemn faces of the women appeared behind her eyelids. Lucile had been there, no longer making a joke about anything; she had sat on the floor, still in her riding-boots, Gabrielle's hand drooping into hers.

Louise slept. God forgive me, she thought later; but I did sleep, and all that had happened wiped itself from my mind, and I dreamed cheerfully, inconsequentially, and of nothing I would later care to report. The morning's first traffic woke her. It was 11 February. The building seemed quite silent. She got up, washed in a perfunctory way, pulled herself into her clothes. She opened the door into her parents' bedroom, just a crack; looked in, saw her father snoring, saw that her mother's side of the bed had not been disturbed. She drank half a glass of stale, flat water, quickly unplaited and combed out her hair. She ran downstairs. On the landing, she met Mme Charpentier. 'Madame – ' she said.

Angélique was muffled into her cape, her shoulders drawn up, her eyes on the ground. She pushed past Louise. She didn't seem to see her at all; her face was glazed, streaked, angry. Then at the head of the stairs she stopped. She turned back. She said nothing; but then she seemed to feel that she must speak. 'We lost her,' she said. 'She's gone, my sweetheart. My little girl has gone.' She walked outside, into the rain.

Inside the apartment the fires had not been lit. On a footstool in the corner sat the nurse, Lucile Desmoulins's baby fastened to her breast. She looked up when she saw Louise, and covered the baby's face with her hand, protectively. 'Run away now,' she said to her.

Louise said, 'Tell me what has happened.'

Only then did the woman seem to realize that she had seen Louise before. 'From upstairs?' she said. 'Didn't you know? Five o'clock. That poor lady, she was always good to me. Jesus grant her rest.'

'The baby?' Louise said. She had gone ice-cold. 'Because I said I would take care of it . . .'

'A little boy. You can't be sure, but I don't think we'll have him long. My friend was to take him, who lives by me. Mme Charpentier says that will be all right.'

'Whatever,' Louise said. 'If the arrangements were made. Where is François-Georges?'

'With Mme Desmoulins.'

'I'll go and get him.'

'He's all right for an hour or two, I should leave him –'

O God, Louise thought. I made promises. She saw in a minute that the babies were not moral bonds, but physical beings, with fragile, impatient demands she could not fulfil.

'Mme Danton's husband will be coming home,' the woman said. 'He will say what should be done and who should go where. You don't need to worry your little head.'

'No, you don't understand,' Louise said. 'Madame said I was to look after them. Promises have to be kept.'

IT TOOK TIME for the message to get though. It was five days later, 16 February, when Georges-Jacques turned up at home. His wife was buried, but there had not been time to tidy her away; and besides, they had waited on his wishes, as if they knew not to pre-empt him, as if they could predict the violence of his anger and guilt and grief.

Her dresses hung limp in a closet, like victims of torture. Under the old regime, women had been burned alive, and men broken on the wheel; had they suffered more than she had? He didn't know.

No one would tell him. No one wanted him to have any details. In this death house, drawers and chests exhaled a light flower scent. Cupboards were in order. She had kept an inventory of the china, he found. Two days before her death, she'd dropped a cup. At Sèvres just now they were designing a new demitasse. As you sip your mocha you might admire the dripping head of Capet – scattering golden drops of blood, and held in Sanson's golden hand.

The maid found a handkerchief of hers, under the bed in which she had died. A ring that had been missing turned up in his own writing desk. A tradesman arrived with fabric she had ordered three weeks ago. Each day, some further evidence of a task half-finished, a scheme incomplete. He found a novel, with her place marked.

And this is it.

VI. *A Secret History*

(1793)

THE BABY was still alive, but he didn't want to see it. He made no comment on the arrangements that had been made. Letters of condolence lay heaped on his desk. As he opened them, he thought, each of these writers is a decent hypocrite: each of them knows what I did to her. They write as if they did not. They write to bring themselves to my attention, to make their names stick in my mind.

Robespierre's letter was long and emotional. It would slide from the personal to the political – this being Max – and then – this being Max – it would slide back. I am more than ever your friend, it said, and I will be your friend till death. 'From this moment you and I are one ... ' it said. Even in his present condition, Danton thought it an overstatement of the case. He wondered at its distraught tone.

Camille did not write him a letter. He sat without speaking, his head bowed, and let Danton talk about the past, and shed tears, and rant on at him for one dereliction or another. He did not know why he was in the line of fire, why his whole career and character were suddenly under review, but it seemed to do Danton good to shout at him. Danton grew exhausted by the business. He slept at last. He'd wondered if sleep would ever be possible again. Gabrielle seemed to haunt the red-walled study, haunt the octagonal dining room where his clerks had once toiled; she haunted the alcove in the bedroom where they had lain in their separate beds, the distance widening between them month by month.

He turned up her journal, kept sporadically in a bold hand. He read each page, and the mechanics of his past were laid bare for him. Unwilling that anyone else should see the book, he burned it, putting it on the fire a leaf at a time, watching it curl and char.

Louise sat in a corner of the apartment, her eyes puffy and her features coarsened and blurred. He did not send her away; he hardly seemed to notice her. On 3 March he left for Belgium again.

MARCH WAS near-disaster. In Holland the depleted armies crashed to defeat. In the Vendée insurrection became civil war. In Paris mobs looted shops and smashed Girondin printing presses. Hébert demanded the heads of all the ministers, all the generals.

On 8 March Danton mounted the tribune of the Convention. The patriots never forgot the shock of his sudden appearance, nor his face, harrowed by sleepless nights and the exhaustion of travelling, pallid with strain and suffering. Complex griefs caught sometimes at his voice, as he spoke of treason and humiliation; once he stopped and looked at his audience, self-conscious for a moment, and touched the scar on his cheek. With the armies, he has seen malice, incompetence, negligence. Reinforcements must be massive and immediate. The rich of France must pay for the liberation of Europe. A new tax must be voted today and collected tomorrow. To deal with conspirators against the Republic there must be a new court, a Revolutionary Tribunal: from that, no right of appeal.

From the body of the hall someone called, 'Who killed the prisoners?' The Convention erupted: chants of *septembriseur* rocked the walls. The deputies of the Mountain rose as one to their feet. The president screamed for order; his bell clanged. Danton stood with his face turned to the public galleries. His fists were clenched at his side. As soon as the noise passed its climax, he threw his voice against it: 'If there had been such a tribunal in September, the men who have so often and so savagely been reproached for those events would never have stained their reputations with one drop of blood. But I do not care about reputation or good name. Call me a drinker of blood, if you will. I will drink the blood of humanity's enemies, if it means Europe will be free.'

A voice from the Gironde: 'You talk like a king.'

He threw up his chin. 'You talk like a coward.'

He had spoken for almost four hours. Outside a mob was gathering, chanting his name. The deputies stood in their massed ranks and applauded. Even Roland, even Brissot were on their feet; they wanted to escape. Beside himself, Fabre shouted, 'This was your supreme performance, supreme.' The Mountain came down to him. He was surrounded by the press of his supporters; the applause rang in his ears. Threading through the solid-packed bodies, like a coffin-worm at a wedding feast, came Dr Marat: plucking at his sleeve. He looked down into the bloodshot eyes.

'Now is your moment, Danton.'

'For what?' he said dispassionately.

'For the dictatorship. All power is yours.'

He turned away. At that moment a magnetic ripple of deference swept the deputies aside. Robespierre walked towards him. Every time I come home, Danton thought, I find you a greater man. Robespierre's face was taut with strain; he looked older, the muscles bunched at the sides of his jaw. But when he spoke it was in a low voice, with a hesitant gentleness: 'I wanted to see you, but I didn't want to intrude. I'm not the best person at thinking of things to say, and we've never been so close that nothing needs to be said. That's my fault, I suppose. And I regret it.'

Danton put a hand on his shoulder. 'My good friend, thank you.'

'I wrote – I thought, you know, these letters don't do any good. But I wanted you to know you can count on me.'

'I will.'

'There is no rivalry between us. We have no difference of policy.'

'Look at this,' Danton said. 'Listen to them cheering me. It's only weeks since they were spitting in my face because I couldn't produce the ministry's accounts.'

Fabre elbowed his way up. Already he had been taking soundings. 'The Gironde will split over the Tribunal. Brissot will back you, so will Vergniaud. Roland and his friends are opposed.'

'They have defected from republicanism,' Danton said. 'They spend their energies trying to destroy me.'

Still the deputies surged and jostled around him, hemming him in. Fabre was bowing to left and right, as if he took the credit. Collot, the actor, was shouting, 'Bravo, Danton, bravo!' his bilious face conjested by emotion. Robespierre had retreated. Still the applause went on. Outside, a crowd was shouting for him. He stood still, and passed a hand over his face. Camille had struggled through to him. Danton flung an arm across his shoulders. 'Camille, let's just go home,' he said.

LOUISE KEPT her ears open now. As soon as she heard that he was back in Paris, she went downstairs and set Marie and Catherine to work. The children were at Victor Charpentier's house, and perhaps it was as well if he did not see them yet. She would have supper ready for him, at whatever hour he came home; he must not come to a house empty except for servants. Her mother came down five times to fetch her. 'What do you mean,' she said, 'by entangling yourself with that brute? You have no duty to him!'

'He may be a brute. But I know what Gabrielle would have wanted. She would have wanted everything to be done for his comfort.'

She sat in Gabrielle's chair, as if to baulk her ghost. From here, she thought, Gabrielle had seen governments broken. From here she had seen the throne totter and fall. She had been plain, unaffected in her manners; her habits were those of a quiet housewife. She had lived with these sanguinary men.

Midnight struck. 'He'll not come home now,' Catherine said. 'We want to get to bed, even if you don't. He'll be round the corner, we reckon. He'll not come home tonight.'

At six o'clock the next morning, Citizen Danton let himself in quietly, in search of a change of clothes. She gave him a shock, the pale child, slumped without grace into Gabrielle's chair. He picked her up in his arms and transferred her to the sofa. He threw a rug over her. She didn't wake. He took what he needed and left the house.

Around the corner Lucile was up and dressed and making coffee. Camille was writing, making the outline of the speech Danton would deliver to the Convention later that day. 'An air of quiet industry prevails,' Danton said. 'That's what I like to see.' He put his arms around Lucile's waist and kissed the back of her neck.

'Glad to see you back in your routine,' Camille said.

'Do you know, the little girl was waiting for me. Gély's daughter. She'd gone to sleep in a chair.'

'Really?' Lucile and her husband flicked their dark eyes at each other. They don't really need to speak, these days. They have perfected communication by other means.

MARCH 10: it was bitterly cold, the kind of weather that makes breathing painful. Claude Dupin called, made her his formal proposal. Her father told him that although she was so young they were disposed to allow the marriage to go ahead within the year; things have been difficult round here, he said, and he told Claude Dupin (in confidence), 'We'd like to get her into a different atmosphere. She sees and hears too much for a girl of her age. She's lost her friend, of course, she's had a bad shock. Wedding arrangements will take her mind off it.'

She said to Claude Dupin, 'I'm really really sorry, but I can't marry you. Not yet, anyway. Would you be prepared to wait a year? I made a promise, to my friend who is dead, that I would look after her children. If I were your wife I'd have other duties and I'd have to go and live in another street. I think that, Citizen Danton being what he is, he will very soon find himself a new wife. When they have a stepmother, I shall be happy to leave here, but not until then.'

Claude Dupin looked stunned. He'd thought everything was settled. 'I can't take this in,' he said. 'Gabrielle Danton seemed a sensible woman to me. How could she let you make such a promise?'

'I don't know how it came about,' Louise said. 'But it did.'

Dupin nodded. 'Fine,' he said. 'I can't say that I understand you, or that I like this, but if you say wait, I'll wait. A promise is a promise, however unfortunate. But my dear, do one thing for me – so far as you can, stay away from Georges Danton.'

She braced herself for the row. After Claude Dupin had left, her mother burst into tears; her father sat looking solemn, as if very very sorry for all concerned. Her mother called her a fool; she took her by the shoulders and shook her, and said don't tell me you made a promise, it's not that at all; admit it, spit it out, you must be besotted with one of these people. Who is it, come on – it's that journalist, isn't it? You can say his name, Louise said. It won't call up the devil. She had a sudden, hideously painful vision of Gabrielle laughing, sitting on her sofa and giggling at Claude Dupin, Gabrielle warm, alive, her swollen hand trailing on Camille's shoulder. Scalding tears flooded down her cheeks. You little tart, her mother said; and slapped her hard across the face.

This was the second time in a month. Up here, she thought, is getting just like down there.

'YOU'RE GOING to Belgium again?' she asks Danton.

'This will be the last time, I hope. I am needed in the Convention, these days.'

'And the children, are they to come home?'

'Yes. The servants can take care of them.'

'I won't leave them to servants.'

'You've done too much. You shouldn't be playing nursemaid. You should be out enjoying yourself.'

He wonders, vaguely, what a respectable girl-child of fifteen does for enjoyment.

'They're used to me,' she says. 'I like taking care of them. Can you explain what you'll be doing while you're away?'

'I'm going to see General Dumouriez.'

'Why do you have to keep going to see him?'

'Well, it's complicated. Some of the things he's doing recently don't seem to be very revolutionary. For instance, we had Jacobin Clubs set up all over Belgium, and he's closing them down. The Convention wants to know why. They think he may have to be arrested, if he isn't a patriot.'

'Not a patriot? What is he then? A supporter of the Austrians? Or of the King?'

'There is no King.'

'Yes, there is. He's shut up in prison. The Dauphin is the King now.'

'No, he's not anything – he's just an ordinary little boy.'

'If that's true, why do you keep him shut up?'

'What an argumentative child you are! Do you follow events? Do you read the newspapers?'

'Yes.'

'Then you will know that the French have decided not to have a King.'

'No, Paris has decided. That's quite different. That's why we have a civil war.'

'But child – deputies from all over France voted for the end of the monarchy.'

'They wouldn't allow a referendum, though. They didn't dare.'

Danton doesn't seem pleased. 'Are these your parents' views?'

'My mother's. Mine too. My father doesn't have views. He would like to, but he can't take the risk.'

'You must be very careful, because clearly your parents are royalists, and that is not a safe thing to be nowadays. You must be careful what you say.'

'Are people not allowed to say what they like? I thought it was in the Declaration of the Rights of Man. Free speech.'

'You are allowed to express your opinion – but we are at war, and so your opinion must not be treasonable or seditious. Do you understand what they mean, those words?'

She nods.

'You must remember who I am.'

'You don't let a person forget, Citizen Danton.'

'Come here,' he says. 'Let me try to explain.'

'No.'

'Why won't you?'

'My parents have forbidden me to be alone with you.'

'But you are. What's the matter, do they think I might make you little Jacobin?'

'No, it's not my politics they worry about. It's my virginity.'

He grinned. 'So that's what they think of me?'

'They think you're in the habit of taking what you want.'

'They think I'm not to be trusted alone with a little girl?'

'Yes, they think that.'

'I wish you would go and tell them,' he said, 'that I have never in my life forced my attentions on a woman. Despite some dire provocation from a pretty creature around the corner – tell your mother that, she'll know just what I mean. Tell me, have they singled me out for this? Have they warned you about Camille? Because, I can assure you, if you were alone in an empty house with Camille he would consider it his positive duty to deflower you. His positive patriotic duty.'

'Deflower? What an expression!' she said. 'I thought Camille had been having an affair with his mother-in-law?'

'Where the hell do you get these stories from?' Suddenly she has touched the anger that is never far below the surface. 'To tell you the truth, it disgusts me that your parents think so badly of me. My wife has been dead a month – do they think I'm a monster?'

That is exactly what they do think, she says to herself. 'Have you given up women, then?'

'Probably not forever. For now, yes.'

'Do you think that very moral?'

'I think it shows respect for my wife, who is dead.'

'It would have shown more respect if you had done it while she was alive.'

'We ought not to continue this conversation.'

'Oh, I think we ought. When you come home from Belgium.'

HE LEFT PARIS on 17 March, with Deputy Lacroix at his side. By now they knew each other quite well; he could have told Gabrielle everything she wanted to know.

On 19 March he was in Brussels; but by the time they caught up with Dumouriez, he had lost a battle at Neerwinden. They found him in the thick of a rearguard action: 'Meet me in Louvain,' he said.

'What is the Convention anyway?' he asked angrily, that same night. 'Three hundred fools, led by two hundred scoundrels.'

'You will at least observe the decencies,' Danton suggested.

The general stared at him. For a moment he saw himself spitted on his sword; but without a toga, it didn't look quite right.

'I mean,' Danton said, 'that you should at least write a letter to the Convention, promising a detailed explanation of your conduct, of your closure of the Jacobins Clubs, of your refusal to work with the Convention's representatives. Oh, and of your defeat.'

'God dammit,' Dumouriez said. 'I was promised thirty thousand men. Let the Convention write a letter to me, and explain why they've got lost on the way!'

'Do you know there is a move to have you arrested? They are fire-eaters, on the Committee of General Security. Deputy Lebas has spoken against you – and I hear he's a young fellow for whom Robespierre has a high regard. And David, too.'

'Committees?' the general said. 'Let them try it! In the midst of my armies? What's David going to do, hit me with his paintbrush?'

'It would be wise not to be flippant, General. Think about the Revolutionary Tribunal. I do not think it will make much distinction between failure and treason, and you are the man who has just lost France a battle. You had better be careful what you say to me, because I am here to judge your attitude and report on it to the Convention and the General Defence Committee.'

He was taken aback. 'But Danton – haven't we been good friends? We've worked together – in God's name, I hardly recognize you. What's the matter?'

'I don't know. Perhaps it's the effect of prolonged sexual abstinence.'

The general looked up into Danton's face. It yielded nothing. Again, turning away, he muttered, *'Committees.'*

'Committees are effective, General. So we are beginning to find. If the members work together, and work hard, then it is surprising how much can be achieved. Committees will soon be running the Revolution. The ministers already act under their surveillance. It is not so important to be a minister, these days.'

'Yes – what did I hear – about the ministers being prevented from going to the Convention?'

'A temporary detention only. The mob barricaded them into the Foreign Ministry to prevent them interfering with the debate. The Minister of War, you may be glad to know, showed a bold martial character, and escaped by vaulting over a wall.'

'This is no joke,' the general said. 'This is anarchy.'

'I wanted my measures passed,' Danton said.

Dumouriez allowed himself to fold into a chair. He rested his forehead on a clenched fist. 'Christ,' he said, 'I'm done for. At my age a man should be thinking of retirement. Tell me, Danton, how is it in Paris? How are all my devoted friends? Marat, for instance?'

'The doctor is the same. A little yellower, perhaps, rather more shrunken. He takes special baths now, to soothe his pains.'

'Any baths would be an improvement,' the general muttered. 'Quite ordinary ones.'

'They keep him at home sometimes, the special baths. I'm afraid they don't improve his temper.'

'Camille can still talk to him?'

'Oh yes. We have a line of communication. It is necessary – his influence over the people has no rival. Hébert dreams that one day he may have as much. But, when you come down to it, people aren't fools.'

'And young Citizen Robespierre?'

'Looking older. Working hard.'

'Not married that gawky girl yet?'

'No. He's sleeping with her, though.'

'Is he now?' The general raised his eyebrows. 'It's an advance, I suppose. But when you think of the good time he could have, if he wanted . . . it's a tragedy, Danton, a tragedy. I suppose he is not sitting on any of these committees?'

'No. They keep electing him, and he refuses to serve.'

'It's strange, isn't it? He wasn't meant for politics. I've never known anyone fight shy of power like he does.'

'He has plenty of power. He prefers it unofficial, that's all.'

'He baffles me. He baffles you too, I suppose. Still, leave that alone – tell me, how's the beauteous Manon?'

'Still in love, they say. Women in love are supposed to be soft little creatures, aren't they? You should hear the speeches she writes for her friends in the Convention.'

'Did your baby live?'

'No.'

'I'm sorry.' The general looked up. 'Listen, Danton. There's something I want to tell you. But you will have to reciprocate.'

'I love you too.'

'Now it's you who are flippant. Listen. Pay attention. Roland wrote me a letter. He asked me to turn the armies and march them on Paris. To restore order there. Also, to – as he put it – crush a certain faction. The Jacobins, he meant. Crush Robespierre. And you.'

'I see. You have this letter?'

'Yes. But I won't give it you. I didn't tell you this so that you could hale Roland before your Revolutionary Tribunal. I told you to show what you owe to my forbearance.'

'You were tempted to try it?'

'Well, Citizen – how are your friends in Brittany?'

'I don't know what you're talking about.'

'Come, Danton, you're too intelligent to waste time like this. You have contacts with the *émigré* rebels in Brittany. You're keeping in with them in case they're successful. You have friends on the Girondist benches and in the House of Commons. You have men with the armies and in every ministry, and you've had money from every Court in Europe.' He looked up, propping his chin on his knuckles. 'There hasn't been a pie baked in Europe these last three years that you haven't had a finger in. How old are you Danton?'

'Thirty-three.'

'Lord. Well, I suppose revolution is a young man's business.'

'Is there some point to all this, General?'

'Yes. Go back to Paris, and prepare the city for the entry of my armies. Prepare them for a monarchy, a monarchy which will of course be subject entirely to the constitution. The little Dauphin on the throne, Orléans as regent. Best for France, best for me and best for you.'

'No.'

'What will you do, then?'

'I shall go back and indict Roland – and Brissot too, more to the point. I shall throw them out of the Convention. Robespierre and I will put together our talents and our influence and we will fight our way to a peace settlement. But if Europe won't make peace – then count on it, I'll put the whole nation in arms.'

'You believe that? That you can throw the Girondists out of the Convention?'

'Of course I can do it. It may take months, rather than weeks. But I have the resources for it. The ground is prepared for me.'

'Don't you ever get tired?'

'I'm always tired now. I've been trying to struggle out of this bloody business ever since I got into it.'

'I don't believe you,' Dumouriez said.

'As you please.'

'The Republic is six months old, and it's flying apart. It has no cohesive force – only a monarchy has that. Surely you can see? We need the monarchy to pull the country together – then we can win the war.'

Danton shook his head.

'Winners make money,' Dumouriez said. 'I thought you went where the pickings were richest?'

'I shall maintain the Republic,' Danton said.

'Why?'

'Because it is the only honest thing there is.'

'Honest? With your people in it?'

'It may be that all its parts are corrupted, vicious, but take it altogether, yes, the Republic is an honest endeavour. Yes, it has me, it has Fabre, it has Hébert – but it also has Camille. Camille would have died for it in '89.'

'In '89, Camille had no stake in life. Ask him now – now he's got money and power, now he's famous. Ask him now if he's willing to die.'

'It has Robespierre.'

'Oh yes – Robespierre would die to get away from the carpenter's daughter, I don't doubt.'

'You are determined to be the complete cynic, General. There is nothing I can do about that. But watch us – we are going to make a new constitution. It will be different from anything the world has ever seen before. It will provide for everyone to be educated, and for everyone to have work.'

'You will never put it into practice.'

'No – but even hope is a virtue. And still, it will add to the glory of our names.'

'We have arrived at the core of you, Danton. You are an idealist.'

'I must sleep, General, I have a journey ahead.'

'You will arrive in Paris and go straight to the Convention, to denounce me. Or to one of your Committees.'

'Don't you know me better than that? I'm not a denouncer. Though don't delude yourself – there will be others to do it.'

'But the Convention will expect your report.'

'It can savour its expectations till I'm ready.'

The general stood up suddenly, trim and alert in the flickering light. 'Good-night, Citizen Danton.'

'Good-night, General.'

'Change your mind?'

'Good-night.'

PARIS, 23 MARCH: 'Shh,' Danton said.

'You're here,' Louise said. 'At last.'

'Yes. Shh. What were you doing?'

'Watching from the window.'

'Why?'

'I just had a feeling that you might come home.'

'Have your father and mother seen me?'

'No.'

Marie said, 'Oh, Monsieur.' She put her hand over her mouth. 'No one told us to expect you.'

'What is all this?' Louise said. She was whispering.

'It's a secret. You like secrets, don't you? Are the babies asleep?'

'Of course they're asleep. It's past nine o'clock. You mean the secret is just that you're here?'

'Yes. You've got to help me hide.'

He had the satisfaction of seeing her pretty mouth drop open.

'Are you in trouble?'

'No. But if people know I'm back I'll have to report straight to the Convention. I want to sleep for twenty-four hours – no Riding-School, no committees, no politics at all.'

'It's what you need, I'm sure. But General Dumouriez — aren't they expecting to hear what he said?'

'They'll know soon enough. So you'll help me to hide, will you?'

'I don't see how one can hide such a large man as you.'

'Let's try, shall we?'

'All right. Are you hungry?'

'We seem to be falling into a spurious domesticity,' he said. Abruptly he turned away from her and dropped into a chair, plaiting his fingers over his eyes. 'I just can't think, now, of any way to go on ... of how to carry on my life. The only way I can honour her is by sticking to ideas she didn't share ... to say to myself, we didn't see eye-to-eye, but she valued the truth. By pursuing that truth I move further from anything she believed or would have found acceptable ... ' She saw that he was crying. 'Forgive me for this,' he said.

She moved forward to stand behind his chair, a hand resting on the back of it.

'I suppose you loved her,' she said. 'According to your lights.'

'I loved her,' he said. 'I loved her by anyone's lights. By anyone's measure. Perhaps there was a time I thought I didn't, but I know different now.'

'If you loved her, Citizen Danton, why did you spend your nights in other women's beds?'

He looked up at her for a second. 'Why? Lust. Policy. Self-aggrandizement. I suppose you think I'm blunt, insensible? I suppose you think I can tolerate this sort of inquisition?'

'I don't say it to be cruel. I only say it because you mustn't start regretting something that didn't exist. You were dead to each other — '

'No.'

'Yes. You don't understand what you are. Remember, she talked to me. She felt lonely, she felt under threat; she thought, you know, that you were planning to divorce her.'

He was aghast. 'It hadn't entered my head! Why should I divorce her?'

'Yes, why should you? You had all the convenience of marriage, and none of its obligations.'

'I would never have divorced her. If I'd known she was thinking that . . . I could have reassured her.'

'You couldn't even see that she was afraid?'

'How could I? She never told me.'

'You were never here.'

'Anyway, I have never understood women.'

'Damn you,' she said. 'You make that a point of pride, don't you? Listen, I am familiar with you great men, in all your manifestations, and I'm sure I don't know the words for how you disgust me. I have sometimes sat with your wife while you were saving the country.'

'We have to discharge our public duties.'

'Most of you discharge your public duties by beginning to drink at nine o'clock in the morning and spend your day plotting how you can stab each other in the back and make off with each other's wives.'

'There is an exception to that.' He smiled. 'His name's Robespierre. You wouldn't like him. Of course, it never struck me before how we must appear to you – a set of drunken, middle-aged lechers. Well, Louise – what do you think I should do?'

'If you want to save yourself as a human being, you should get out of politics.'

'As a human being?' he queried gently. 'What are the other possibilities?'

'I think you know what I mean. You haven't lived like a proper human being these last few years. You have to get back to the man you were before – ' She gestured.

'Yes, I know. Before the folly. Before the blasphemy.'

'Don't. Just don't laugh.'

'I'm not laughing. But your judgements are very harsh, aren't they? I'm not sure there is much hope for me. If I wanted to abandon my career, I don't know how I'd begin to do it.'

'We could find a way, if you made up your mind.'

'We could? You think so?'

He is laughing, she thought. 'If I had only heard of you, from the newspapers, I should think you were a devil. I should be afraid to breathe the same air as you. But I know you.'

'I see that you have set yourself a task. You mean to save me from myself, don't you?'

'I was told to. I promised.'

When she thinks about it now she cannot be sure what the terms of the promise were. Gabrielle had bequeathed her children, but had she also bequeathed her husband?

THE NEXT MORNING she instructed the servants strictly. They were to mention to no one that Monsieur was home. She had come down early, before seven. He was already up and dressed, reading his letters. 'So you are going out after all, Citizen Danton?'

He glanced up, and saw that she was disappointed. 'No, I'm staying. But I couldn't sleep . . . too much on my mind.'

'What if people come, and ask if you are back yet?'

'Tell lies.'

'You mean it?'

'Yes. I need time to think.'

'I suppose it would not be any great sin.'

'You are grown very liberal, since last night.'

'Don't keep laughing at me. If anyone comes, I shall not let them in, and if I meet anyone when I go to do the shopping –'

'Send Marie.'

'I'm keeping her in. She might give you away. I shall say, I haven't seen you, and you're not expected.'

'That's the spirit.' He turned back to his letters. He spoke kindly enough, but there was too a hint of weariness and boredom. I have no idea how to talk to him, she thought. I wish I were Lucile Desmoulins.

At nine o'clock, she was back, out of breath. He was sitting with a blank sheet of paper before him, his eyes closed. 'Can't write,' he said, opening them. 'Oh, words go down, but they're hardly soul-searing stuff. Good thing I own a journalist.'

'When are you planning to emerge?'

'Tomorrow, I think. Why?'

'I don't think you can hide any longer. I saw your journalist. He knows you're here.'

'How?'

'Well, he doesn't know, but he thinks you are. I denied it, of course. I'm lucky to be in one piece, I can tell you. He didn't believe a word I said.'

'Then you'd better go and give him your apologies, and tell him – in confidence – that he is right. Appeal to him to protect me from marauding committeemen – tell him I haven't decided yet what I ought to do about Dumouriez. And tell him to drop anything he's doing tonight and come and get drunk with me.'

'I'm not sure I ought to convey that message. It's dissolute.'

'If you think that's what people do for debauchery,' he said, 'you've got a lot to learn.'

NEXT MORNING, Louise was up even earlier. Her mother came blundering out of her bedroom, fastening her wrap. 'At this hour!' she said. She knew very well that Danton's servants sleep, not in the apartment, but on the mezzanine floor. 'You will be alone with him,' she said. 'Anyway, how will you get in?'

Louise showed her the key in the palm of her hand.

She let herself in very quietly, opening and closing doors to the study, where Danton would be if he were up; but she doubted he would be. Camille was standing by the window: shirt, breeches, boots, hair not brushed. There were papers all over Danton's desk, covered in someone else's handwriting. 'Good morning,' she said. 'Are you drunk?'

She noticed what a split second it took for him to flare into aggression. 'Do I look it?'

'No. Where is Citizen Danton?'

'I've done away with him. I've been busy dismembering him for the last three hours. Would you like to help me carry his remnants down to the concierge? Oh really, Louise! He's in bed and asleep, where do you think he is?'

'And is he drunk?'

'Very. What is all this harping on intoxication?'

'He said that was what you were going to do. Get drunk.'

'Oh, I see. Were you shocked?'

'Very. What have you been writing?'

He drifted over to Danton's desk, where he could sit down in the chair and look up full into her face. 'A polemic.'

'I have been reading some of your work.'

'Good, isn't it?'

'I think that it's incredibly cruel and destructive.'

'If nice little girls like you thought well of it I wouldn't be achieving much, would I?'

'I don't think you can have kept your part of the bargain,' she said. 'I don't think you can have been very drunk, if you wrote all that.'

'I can write in any condition.'

'Perhaps that explains some of it.' She turned the pages over. She was conscious of his solemn black eyes fixed on her face. Around his neck there was a silver chain; what depended from it was hidden in the folds of his shirt. Did he perhaps wear a crucifix? Were things perhaps not as bad as they seemed? She wanted to touch him, very badly, feeling under the pious necessity of finding out; she recognized at once a point of crisis, what her confessor would call the very instant of temptation. He felt the direction of her gaze; he took from inside his shirt a chased-silver disc, a locket. Inside – without speaking, he showed her – was a fine curled strand of hair.

'Lucile's?'

He nodded. She took the locket in the palm of her left hand; the fingers of her right hand brushed the skin at the base of his throat. It's done – in a moment it's done, finished with. She would like, at one level of her being, to cut her hand off. 'Don't worry,' he said. 'You'll grow out of me.'

'You are incredibly vain.'

'Yes. There seems no reason why I should learn to be less so. But you, Citizeness, will have to learn to keep your hands to yourself.'

His tone was so scathing that she almost burst into tears. 'Why are you being so nasty to me?'

'Because you opened the conversation by asking me if I were drunk, which is not considered polite even by today's standards, and also because if someone trots out their forces at dawn you assume they have stomach for a fight. Get this very clear in your mind, Louise: if you think that you are in love with me, you had better re-think, and you had better fall out of love at lightning speed. I want no area of doubt here. What Danton is allowed to do to my wife, and what I am allowed to do to his, are two very different things.'

A silence. 'Don't bother to arrange your face,' Camille said. 'You've arranged everything else.'

She began to shake. 'What did he say? What did he tell you?'

'He's infatuated with you.'

'He told you that? What did he say?'

'Why should I indulge you?'

'When did he say it? Last night?'

'This morning.'

'What words did he use?'

'Oh, I don't know what words.'

'Words are your profession, aren't they?' she shouted at him. 'Of course you know what words.'

'He said "I am infatuated with Louise".'

All right; she doesn't believe that; but let's get on.

'He was serious? How did he say it?'

'How?'

'How.'

'In the usual four-in-the-morning manner.'

'And what is that?'

'When you're married, you will have the opportunity to find out.'

'Sometimes,' she said, 'I think you're evil. It's a strong word, I know, but I do think it.'

Camille lowered his eyelashes bashfully. 'One tries, of course. But Louise, you shouldn't be too brutal with me, because you're going to have to live with me, in a manner of speaking. Unless you're going to try and turn him down, but you wouldn't try that, would you?'

'I'll see. But I don't necessarily believe you. About anything.'

'He wants to sleep with you, that's the thing, you see. He can't think of any way of doing it, except by marrying you. An honour-able man, Georges-Jacques. An honourable, peaceable, domestic sort, he is. If I had formed the ambition, of course, it would be rather different.'

Camille suddenly slumped forward, elbows on the desk, hands over his mouth. For a moment she didn't know whether he was laughing or crying, but it soon became apparent which it was. 'You can laugh if you want,' she said bleakly, 'I'm getting used to it.'

'Oh good, good. When I tell Fabre,' he said between sobs and gasps, 'about this conversation – he won't believe me.' He wiped his eyes. 'There's a lot you must get used to, I'm afraid.'

She looked down at him. 'Aren't you cold like that?'

'Yes.' He stood up. 'I suppose I had better get myself together. Georges-Jacques and I are being elected to a committee today.'

'Which committee?'

'You don't really want the details, do you?'

'How can you know, anyway, until the election is held?'

'Oh, you have a great deal to learn.'

'I want him out of politics.'

'Over my dead body,' Camille said.

Dawn looked peevish, a sullen red sun. She felt sullied by the encounter. Danton slept on.

DANTON SPOKE to the Convention, later to the Jacobin Club. 'More than once I was tempted to have Dumouriez arrested. But, I said to myself, if I take this drastic step, and the enemy learns of it – think what it will do for their morale. If they had profited by my decision, I might even be suspected of treachery. Citizens, I put it to you – what would you have done in my place?'

'Well, what would you have done?' he asked Robespierre. April has almost come in; there is a stiff fresh night breeze on the rue Honoré. 'We'll walk home with you. I'll pay my respects to your wife, Duplay.'

'You're very welcome, Citizen Danton.'

Saint-Just spoke. 'It does seem to be one of those situations when it would have been better to do *something*.'

'Sometimes it's better to wait and see, Citizen Saint-Just. Does that ever occur to you?'

'I would have arrested him.'

'But you weren't there, you don't know. You don't know the state of the armies, there is so much to understand.'

'No, of course I don't know. But why did you seek our opinions if you were going to shout them down?'

'He didn't seek yours,' Camille said. 'It is not thought he values it.'

'I shall have to go to the front myself,' Saint-Just said, 'and begin to penetrate these mysteries.'

'Oh, good,' Camille said.

'Will you stop being so childish?' Robespierre asked him. 'Well, Danton, as long as you're satisfied in your own mind, as long as you acted in good faith, what more can one ask?'

'I can think of more,' Saint-Just said under his breath.

In the Duplay yard, Brount ran out grumbling to the end of his chain. Approached, he placed his paws on his master's shoulders. Robespierre had a word with him; along the lines, one supposed, of containing himself in patience, until perfect liberty was practicable. They went into the house. The Robespierre women (as one tended to think of them now) were all on display. Madame looked actively, rather intimidatingly benevolent; it was her aim in life to find a Jacobin who was hungry, then to go into the kitchen and make extravagant efforts, and say, 'I have fed a patriot!' Robespierre, in this respect, was no use to her. He seemed to spurn her best efforts.

They sat in the parlour where Robespierre's portraits were hung. Danton looked around him, Robespierre looked back: smiling, half-smiling or earnest, delicate in profile or tense and combative full-face, studious or amused, with a dog, with another dog, without a dog. The original seemed no more than an item in the display; he was quiet tonight, while they talked of Brissot, Roland, Vergniaud. The interminable topics: young Philippe Lebas moved into a corner and began to whisper with Babette. He was not to be blamed, Danton thought. Robespierre caught Danton's eye, and smiled.

Another love affair, then, in the intervals of blood-letting. One finds time, one finds time.

*

WHEN THE MINISTER of War went to Belgium to investigate the situation there, Dumouriez arrested him, along with four of the Convention's official representatives, and handed them over to the Austrians. Soon afterwards he put out a manifesto, announcing that he would march his armies on Paris to restore stability and the rule of law. His troops mutinied, and fired on him. With young General Égalité – Louis-Philippe, the Duke's son – he crossed the Austrian lines. An hour later they were both prisoners of war.

Robespierre to the Convention: 'I demand that all members of the Orléans family, known as Égalité, be brought before the Revolutionary Tribunal ... And that the Tribunal be made responsible for proceeding against all Dumouriez's other accomplices ... Shall I name such distinguished patriots as Messieurs Vergniaud, Brissot? I rely on the wisdom of the Convention.'

You wouldn't have thought the Convention had much wisdom, considering the scenes that followed. The Gironde had an arsenal of charges against Danton: lying, skulking, misappropriating funds. As he strode to the rostrum the Right screamed their favourite insult: *drinker of blood*. As the president put his head in his hands and all but wept, opponents met head to head, punches were thrown, and Citizen Danton must physically grapple with deputies who were trying to prevent him from speaking in his own defence.

Robespierre looked down from the Mountain; his face was horrified. Danton gained the tribune, leaving a trail of casualties in his wake; he seemed stimulated by the disorder: 'Daylight holds no fears for me!' he bawled across the benches of the Right. Philippe Égalité was aware that the colleagues on either side of him had slid further away, as if he were Marat. And here is Marat, limping towards the tribune as Danton stepped down.

He brushed past Danton; there was a flicker of contact between their eyes. He put his hand to the pistol in his belt, as if he were easing it for use. Turning his body almost sideways, he stretched one arm along the ledge of the tribune and surveyed his audience from behind it. Perhaps, Philippe Égalité thought, I shall never again see him do that.

Marat tilted his head back. He looked around the hall. Then, after a long-drawn, exquisite pause – he laughed.

'This man makes my blood run cold,' Deputy Lebas whispered to Robespierre. 'It's like meeting something in a graveyard.'

'Shh,' said Robespierre. 'Listen.'

Marat reached up, pulled once at the red kerchief wrapped around his neck; this was the signal that the joke was over. He stretched out his arm again, fearfully leisured. When he spoke he sounded calm, dispassionate. His proposal was simply this: that the Convention abolish the deputies' immunity from prosecution, so that they could put each other on trial. The Right and the Left glared at each other, each deputy imagining for his personal enemies a procession to Dr Guillotin's beheading machine. Two deputies of the Mountain, sitting a few feet apart, turned and looked at each other; their eyes met, then darted away in shock. No one looked Philippe in the face. Marat's motion was carried, supported from all sides.

Citizens Danton and Desmoulins left the Convention together, applauded by a crowd that had gathered outside. They walked home. It was a clear, chilly April evening. 'I could wish myself elsewhere,' Danton said.

'What are we going to do about Philippe? We can't just throw him to Marat.'

'We might find some comfortable provincial fortress to put him in for the while. He'll be safer in gaol than he will be at large in Paris.'

They were in their own district by now, the republic of the Cordeliers. The streets were quiet; news of the scenes in the Convention would soon leak out, and news of the Convention's fearful decree. Elsewhere, deputies were limping home to nurse their contusions and sprains. Did everyone go slightly mad this afternoon, perhaps? Citizen Danton did have the air of a man who had been in a fight; but then he often had that air.

They stopped outside the Cour du Commerce. 'Coming up for a glass of blood, Georges-Jacques? Or shall I open the burgundy?'

They went up, decided on the burgundy, sat on till after midnight. Camille scribbled down the salient points of the pamphlet he was planning to write. Salient points were not enough though; each word must be a little knife, and it would take him a few weeks yet to sharpen them.

*

MANON ROLAND was back in her old cramped apartment on the rue de la Harpe. 'Good morning, good morning,' Fabre d'Églantine said.

'We did not invite you here.'

'Ah, no.' Fabre seated himself, crossing his legs. 'Citizen Roland not at home?'

'He is taking a short walk. For the state of his health.'

'How *is* his health?' Fabre inquired.

'Not good, I'm afraid. We hope the summer may not be too hot.'

'Ah,' Fabre said. 'Warm weather, cold weather, they all have their demerits for the invalid, don't they? We feared as much. When one noticed that Citizen Roland's letter of resignation from the Ministry was in your hand, one said to Danton, it must be that Citizen Roland is unwell. Danton said – but never mind.'

'Perhaps you have a message to leave for my husband.'

'No, for I didn't come specifically, you see, to talk to Citizen Roland – but merely for a few minutes of your charming company. And to find Citizen Buzot here with you is an added pleasure. You are often together, aren't you? You must be careful, or you will be suspected of' – he chuckled – 'conspiracy. But then, I think a friendship between a young man and an older woman can be a very beautiful thing. So Citizen Desmoulins always says.'

'Unless you state your business very soon,' Buzot said, 'I may throw you out.'

'Really?' Fabre said. 'I was hardly aware that we had reached that pitch of hostility. Do sit down, Citizen Buzot, there's no need to be so physical.'

'As president of the Jacobin Club,' she said, 'Marat has presented to the Convention a petition for the proscription of certain deputies. One is Citizen Buzot, whom you see here. Another is my husband. They want us in front of your Tribunal. Ninety-six people have signed this. What pitch of hostility is that?'

'No, I must protest,' Fabre said. 'Marat's friends have signed it, though I confess myself amazed to learn that Marat has ninety-six friends. Danton has not signed it. Robespierre has not.'

'Camille Desmoulins has.'

'Oh, we have no control over Camille.'

'Robespierre and Danton will not sign it simply because it is Marat who has put it forward,' she said. 'You are hopelessly divided. You think you can frighten us. But you will not throw us out of the Convention, you have not the numbers or force to do it.'

Fabre looked at them through his lorgnette. 'Do you like my coat?' he asked. 'It's a new English cut.'

'You will never achieve anything and you don't represent anybody. Danton and Robespierre are afraid that Hébert will steal their thunder, Hébert and Marat are afraid of Jacques Roux and the other agitators on the streets. You're terrified of losing your popularity, of not being out in front of the Revolution any more – that's why you have given up any pretence at decent gentlemanly conduct. The Jacobins are ruled by their public gallery, and you play to them. But be warned – this cityful of ragged illiterates that you pander to is not France.'

'Your vehemence amazes me,' Fabre said.

'In the Convention there are decent men from all over the nation, and you Paris deputies won't be able to browbeat them all. This Tribunal, this end to immunity, it doesn't work for you alone. We have our plans for Marat.'

'I see,' Fabre said. 'Of course, you know, in a sense all this was unneccessary. If only you'd been halfway civil to Danton, not made those unfortunate remarks about how you wouldn't like to have sexual intercourse with him. He's a good fellow, you know, always ready to do a deal, and he's not in the least out for blood. It's just that recently, with his personal misfortunes, he's not so easy-going as he was.'

'We don't want a deal,' she said, furious. 'We don't want to do a deal with the people who organized the massacre last September.'

'That's very sad,' Fabre said deliberately. 'Because up till now, you know, it's been a business of compromises, more acceptable or less acceptable, and accommodation, and perhaps making yourself – I don't deny it – a little bit of money on the side. But it's turning awfully serious now.'

'Not before time,' she said.

'Well,' he stood up, 'shall I convey your compliments to anyone?'

'I'd rather you didn't.'

'Do you see much of Citizen Brissot?'

'Citizen Brissot is running his own version of the Revolution,' she said, 'and so is Vergniaud. They have their own supporters and their own friends, and it is monstrously stupid and unfair to lump us together with them.'

'I'm afraid it's unavoidable really. I mean if you see each other, exchange information, vote the same way, however coincidentally – well, to outsiders it does seem that you are a sort of faction. That's how it would seem to a jury.'

'On that basis, you would be judged with Marat,' Buzot said. 'I think you're a little premature, Citizen Fabre. You must have a case before you can have a trial.'

'Don't be too sure,' Fabre muttered.

On the stairs he met Roland himself. He was on his way to draft a petition – his eighth or ninth – for an examination of the accounts of Danton's ministry. He had a dilapidated air, and he smelled of infusions. He looked away from Fabre's eyes; his own were lustreless and aggrieved. 'Your Tribunal was a mistake,' he said without preliminary. 'We are entering a time of terror.'

BRISSOT: reading, writing, scurrying from place to place, gathering his thoughts, scattering his good will; proposing a motion, addressing a committee, jotting down a note. Brissot with his cliques, his factions, his whippers-in and his putters-out; with his secretaries and messengers, his errand-boys, his printers, his claque. Brissot with his generals, his ministers.

Who the devil is Brissot anyway? A pastry-cook's son.

Brissot: poet, businessman, adviser to George Washington.

Who are the Brissotins? A good question. You see, if you accuse people of a crime (for example, and especially, conspiracy) and refuse to sever their trials, then it will at once be seen that they are a group, that they have cohesion. Then if we want to say, you're a Brissotin, you're a Girondist – prove that you're not. Prove that you have a right to be treated separately.

How many are there? Ten eminences: sixty or seventy non-entities. Take, for instance, Rabaut Saint-Étienne:

When the National Convention shall be purged of that kind of man, so that people shall ask what a Brissotin was, I will move that to preserve a perfect specimen of one this man's skin be stuffed, and that the original may be kept entire at the Museum of Natural History; and for this purpose, I will oppose his being guillotined.

Brissot: his contributors and his orators, his minutes and his memoranda, his fixers and his dupes.

Brissot: his ways and his means and his means to an end, his circumstances, his ploys, his *faux pas* and his *bons mots*; his past, his present, his world without end.

I establish it as a fact that the Right wing of the Convention, and principally their leaders, are almost all partisans of royalty and accomplices of Dumouriez; that they are directed by the agents of Pitt, Orléans and Prussia; that they wanted to divide France into twenty or thirty federative republics, that no Republic might exist. I maintain that history does not furnish an example of a conspiracy so clearly proved, by so many weighty probabilities, than the conspiracy of Brissot against the French Republic.

Camille Desmoulins, a pamphlet: 'A Secret History of the Revolution'

VII. *Carnivores*

(*1793*)

AT THE TOP of the Queen's Staircase at the Tuileries, there is a series of communicating chambers, crowded every day with clerks, secretaries, messengers, with army officers and purveyors, officials of the Commune and officers of the courts: with government couriers, booted and spurred, waiting for dispatches from the last room in the suite. Look down: outside there are cannon and files of soldiers. The room at the end was once the private office of Louis the Last. You cannot go in.

That room is now the office of the Committee of Public Safety. The Committee exists to supervise the Council of Ministers and to expedite its decisions. At this stage people call it the Danton Committee, wondering what he is doing in that green sanctum, green wallpaper, his elbows propped on the great oval table covered by a green cloth. He finds the colour negative, disturbing. A crystal chandelier tinkles above his head; the mirrored walls reflect his bull-neck and scarred face. Sometimes he looks out of the windows, over the gardens. In the Place Louis XV, now the Place de la Révolution, the guillotine is at work. From this room, as he negotiates for peace, he imagines he can hear Sanson making a living; hear the creak of the machine's moving parts, the clump of the blade. Army officers, for the moment; at least they should know how to die.

In April there were seven executions; undramatically, the numbers will increase. The Section committees will be very ready to yelp for arrests, very quick with their accusations that such a one is a lukewarm patriot, an aristo sympathizer, black-marketeer or priest. House searches, food-issue, recruiting, passports, denunciations: hard to know where the Section committees end and the good offices of the Commune begin. There was a day when the Palais-

Royal was cordoned off by the police, and all the girls were herded together. Their identity cards were taken from them; for an hour or so, they stood barracking their captors in small flocks, their faces hard and hopeless under their paint; then the cards were handed back, they were told to go where they liked. The little Terror of Pierre Chaumette.

From here he has to watch the Austrians and the Prussians, the English and the Swedes: the Russians and the Turks and the Faubourg Saint-Antoine: Lyon, Marseille, the Vendée and the public gallery: Marat at the Jacobin Club and Hébert at the Cordeliers: the Commune and the Section committees and the Tribunal and the press. Sometimes he sits and thinks of his dead wife. He can not imagine the summer without her. He is very tired. He begins to stay away from the Jacobins and the evening meetings of the Committee. Danton is letting his reputation slide, some people say: he is letting go. Other people say *he wouldn't dare*. Sometimes Robespierre comes to see him, panicked and asthmatical, twitching at the sleeves and collars of his very correct clothes. Robespierre is turning into a caricature of himself, Lucile remarks. When Danton is not at home, with little Louise skirting around him, he is with the Desmoulins, living with them practically, as Camille once lived with him.

His pursuit of Lucile is a formality now, a habit. He begins to see how different she is from the earnest, busy, simple women he requires for his domestic comfort. After a day poring over her Rousseau she will announce a scheme for a bucolic retirement from the capital, and drive into the country with her infant, screaming at being separated from his grandmother; there she will formulate plans for his education. Her hair streaming down her back and a large straw hat on her head, she will do a little dilettante weeding in the herb-beds, by way of getting close to nature; she will read poetry in the afternoon, in a garden swing under an apple tree, and go to bed at nine o'clock.

Two days pass, and the bawling of Robespierre's godchild will be driving her out of her mind; scattering orders about the sending after of fresh eggs and salad, she will charge back to the rue des

Cordeliers, worrying all the way about missing her music lessons and whether her husband has left her. You look a complete wreck, she will say to him crossly; what have you been eating, whoever have you been sleeping with? Then for a week it will be parties and staying up all night; the baby departs to grandmother, nurse scuttling after.

In a different kind of mood, she takes up her station early, lies on the blue *chaise-longue*; she is wrapped so deeply in daydreams that no one dares to interrupt her, no one dares to say a word. One day she stirs from her reverie and says, do you know, Georges-Jacques, I sometimes think I may have fantasized the Revolution completely – it seems too unlikely to be true. And Camille – what if he is something I have simply fabricated, just a phantom I have called up out of the depth of my nature, a ghostly second self who works out my discontents?

He thinks of this, and then of his own creations: two dead children, and a woman killed – he believes – by unkindness; his plans for peace aborted, and now the Tribunal.

The Tribunal sits at the Palais de Justice, in a hall adjoining the prison of the Conciergerie: a gothic hall, marble-flagged. Its president, Montané, is a moderate man, but when necessary he will be replaced. Come next autumn, we will have the spectacle of Vice-President Dumas, a red-faced, red-haired man, who is sometimes assisted to his place in an alcoholic daze. He presides with two loaded pistols on the table before him, and his apartment in the rue de Seine is like a fortress.

The Tribunal has a pool of jurors, proven patriots, chosen by the Convention. Souberbielle, Robespierre's doctor, is one of them; he rushes distractedly between the courtroom, his hospital and his most important private patient. Maurice Duplay is also a juror. He dislikes the work and never talks about it at home. Another, Citizen Renaudin, is a violin-maker by profession and responsible for a sudden flare-up of violence at the Jacobins one evening, one of the causeless, chilling incidents that are always happening these days; standing up to oppose Citizen Desmoulins, he despaires of logic, advances on him and knocks him clear across the room. Pounced on by the ushers, dragged out by brute force, his voice is heard even over the indignant bawling of the public galleries: 'Next time I'll kill you, next time I'll kill you.'

The Public Prosecutor is Antoine Fouquier-Tinville, a quick, dark man, who takes up moral stances: not such a showy patriot as his cousin, but far more hard-working.

The Tribunal often acquits: in these early days, at least. Take Marat, for instance; he is indicted by the Gironde, Citizen Fouquier is perfunctory, the courtroom is packed with Maratists from the streets. The Tribunal throws the case out: a singing, chanting mob carries the accused shoulder-high to the Convention, through the streets and to the Jacobin Club, where they enthrone the grinning little demagogue in the president's chair.

In May, the National Convention moves from the Riding-School to the former theatre of the Tuileries, which is refurbished for it. Entertain no notion of pink, dimpling Cupids, the crimson curve of boxes, powder and perfume, the rustle of silk. Think of this scenery: straight lines and right angles, plaster statues with plaster crowns, of plaster laurel and plaster oak. A square tribune for the speaker; behind it, hung almost horizontal, three immense tricolour flags; beside it, *memento mori*, the bust of Lepelletier. The deputies take their seats in a tiered semi-circle; they are without desks or tables, so that they have nowhere to write. The president has his handbell, his inkstand, his folio book; much they avail him, when three thousand insurrectionists pour from the Faubourgs and mill about on the floor below him. Sunlight slides narrowly through the deep windows; on winter afternoons, faces loom, indistinct, from hostile benches. When the lamps are lit, the effect is ghastly; they deliberate in catacombs, and accusation drip from unseen mouths. In a greater dimness, the public galleries barrack and bay.

In this new hall the factions regroup in their old places. Legendre the butcher bawls out a Brissotin: 'I'll slaughter you!' 'First,' says the deputy, 'have a decree passed to say that I am an ox.' And one day a Brissotin stumbles, mounting the nine awkward steps to the tribune: 'It's like mounting the scaffold,' he complains. Delighted, the Left yell at him: make use of the rehearsal. A weary deputy puts his hand to his head, sees Robespierre watching him, and withdraws it hurriedly: 'No, no,' he says, 'he will suppose I am thinking of something.'

As the year goes on, certain deputies – and others, high in public life – will appear unshaven, without coat or cravat; or they will jettison these marks of the polite man, when the temperature rises. They affect the style of men who begin their mornings with a splash under a backyard pump, and who stop off at their street-corner bar for a nip of spirits on their way to ten hours' manual labour. Citizen Robespierre, however, is a breathing rebuke to these men; he retains his buckled shoes, his striped coat of olive green. Can it be the same coat that he wore in the first year of the Revolution? He is not profligate with coats. While Citizen Danton tears off the starched linen that frets his thick neck, Citizen Saint-Just's cravat grows ever higher, stiffer, more wonderful to behold. He affects a single earring, but he resembles less a corsair than a slightly deranged merchant banker.

The Section committees sit in disused churches. Republican slogans are scrawled in black paint on the walls. From these committees you obtain your card of citizenship, with a note of your address, employment, age and appearance: a copy is forwarded to City Hall.

Women hawkers go from door to door, with big baskets of linen for sale; under the linen are fresh eggs and butter, which are far more desirable. The men in the woodyards are always on strike for more pay, and firewood cost twice what it did in '89. Poultry may be obtained, at midnight and for a price, in an alley at the back of the Café du Foy.

A child passed by the market, carrying a loaf; a woman who had the tricolour cockade in her hat threw him down, seized the bread, tore it into pieces and threw it away, saying that, since she had none, she did not want others to have any. The citizenesses of the market pointed out to her the stupidity of such an act; she screamed abuse at them, telling them that they were all aristocrats, and soon all women over thirty years of age would be guillotined.

*

ROBESPIERRE sat propped up on four pillows. Convalescent now, he looked young again. His curly red-brown hair was unpowdered. There were papers all over the bed. The room smelt faintly of orange peel.

'Dr Souberbielle says, no, no, you must not eat oranges, Citizen. But I can't eat anything else. He says, your addiction to citrus fruits is such that I cannot be responsible for you. Marat sent me a note – Cornélia, my dear, could you get me some more cold water? But very cold, I mean?'

'Of course.' She reached for the jug, bustled out.

'Well done,' Camille said.

'Yes, but I have to keep thinking of increasingly difficult things I want. I always told you that women were nothing but a damned nuisance.'

'Yes, but your experience was only academic then.'

'Bring your chair over here. I can't raise my voice much. I don't know what we're going to do in the new hall, I know it was a theatre but it's no better. The only people we'll be able to hear are Georges-Jacques and Legendre. It was bad enough at Versailles, and then the Riding-School, and now this – I've had a sore throat for four years.'

'Don't talk about it. I have to speak at the Jacobins tonight.'

His pamphlet against Brissot was already in the press, and the club – tonight – would vote to reprint and distribute it. But they wanted to see and hear him. Robespierre understood: one must be seen and heard. 'I can't afford to be ill,' he said. 'What about Brissot, has he been seen around much?'

'No.'

'Vergniaud?'

'No.'

'If they're so quiet they must be plotting something.'

'There's your sister Charlotte arriving downstairs. Why can I hear everything today?'

'Maurice has stopped the men working. He thinks I have a headache. That's good, anyway. Eléonore will have to stay downstairs to see that Charlotte doesn't come up.'

'Poor Charlotte.'

'Yes, but poor Eléonore too, I suppose. While I think about it, you might ask Danton not to be so rude about her. I know she's rather plain, but every girl has a right to conceal that fact from people who haven't seen her. Danton keeps telling people. Ask him not to talk about her.'

'Send another messenger.'

'Tell me,' Robespierre said irritably, 'why doesn't he come to see me? Danton, I mean. Tell him from me that he's got to make this Committee work. They're all patriots, he must mobilize them. The only thing that will save us now is a strong central authority – the ministers are ciphers, the Convention is factious, so it must be the Committee.'

'Hush,' Camille said. 'Think of your throat.'

'The Gironde are trying to make the country ungovernable by stirring up the provinces against us, and the Committee must keep a close watch – tell him the ministers mustn't do anything without the Committee's say-so. He must have a written report every day from every *département* – but what's the matter, is that not a good idea?'

'Max, I know you're frustrated because you want to make a speech – but you're supposed to be taking a complete rest, aren't you? Of course one doesn't mind the Committee having such power, if it's run by Danton. But the Committee is elective, isn't it?'

'If he wants to stay elected, then he will. How is he, by the way? I mean, in himself?'

'Brooding.'

'He will think of marrying again, I suppose.'

Maurice Duplay opened the door. 'Your water,' he whispered. 'Sorry. Eléonore – I mean Cornélia – is downstairs entertaining your sister. You don't want to see her, do you? No, of course you don't. How's your head?'

'I haven't got a headache,' Robespierre said loudly.

'Shh. We have to get him back on his feet,' Duplay hissed at Camille. 'It's a pity he'll miss hearing you tonight. I'll be there.' Camille put his hands over his face. Duplay patted him on the shoulder and tiptoed out. 'Don't make him laugh,' he mouthed from the doorway.

'Oh, this is ludicrous,' Robespierre said, and began to laugh a little anyway.

'What were you saying about Marat? He sent you a note?'

'Yes, he is ill too, he can't leave his house. Did you hear about that girl, Anne Théroigne?'

'What's she done now?'

'She was making a speech in the Tuileries gardens, and a group of women attacked her – rough women from the public gallery. She's attached herself to Brissot and his faction, for some reason only she understands – I can't believe Brissot is delighted. She found the wrong audience – I don't know, but perhaps they thought she was some woman of fashion intruding on their patch. Marat was passing by, it seems.'

'So he joined in?'

'He rescued her. Charged in, told the women to desist – rare chivalry, for the doctor, wasn't it? He believes they might have killed her.'

'I wish they had,' Camille said. 'Excuse me for a moment from the necessity to do invalid-talk, I can't be temperate about this matter. I will never forgive the bitch for what she did on 10 August.'

'Oh well, Louis Suleau – of course, we had known him for all those years, but he ended up on the wrong side, didn't he?' Robespierre dropped his head back against the pillows. 'And then, so did she.'

'That is a callous thing to say.'

'It might happen to us. I mean, if we follow our judgements, our consciences, and if they lead us in certain directions, we may have to suffer for it. Brissot – after all – may be in good faith.'

'But I have just written this pamphlet – Brissot is a conspirator against the Republic – '

'So you have convinced yourself. So you'll convince the Jacobins tonight. Certainly in power his people have been mistaken, stupid, criminally negligent, and we have to erase them from political life.'

'But Max, you wanted them killed in September. You tried to set it up.'

'I thought it was best to be rid of them before they did any more damage. I thought of the lives that might be saved . . .' He moved his legs, and some of the papers slithered to the floor. 'It was a considered judgement. And Danton,' he smiled slightly, 'has been wary of me since then. He thinks I am an unpredictable beast, with the key to my own cage.'

'And yet you say Brissot may be in good faith.'

'Camille, we're judging by results, not intentions. Quite possibly he isn't guilty of what you'll charge him with tonight, but I'll let you do it. I want them out of the Convention – but myself, I'd be happy if it went no further. The damage is done, we can't recall the past by persecuting them. But the people won't see things like that. They can't be expected to.'

'You would save them. If you could.'

'No. There are periods in revolution when to live is a crime, and people must know how to yield their heads if they are demanded. Perhaps mine will be. If that time comes, I won't dispute it.'

Camille had walked away, turning his back, running his hand along the grain of the shelves that Maurice Duplay had built. Above them on the wall was a curious emblem he had carved: a great and splendid eagle with outstretched claws, like an eagle of the Romans.

'Such heroism,' Camille said slowly, 'and in a nightshirt too. Policy is the servant of reason. It is a sort of blasphemy to make human reason contradict itself and advise in the name of policy what it forbids in the name of morality.'

'You say that,' Robespierre said tiredly, 'yet you are corrupted.'

'What, by money?'

'No. There are more ways than that of being corrupted. You can be corrupted by friendship. Your attachments are too . . . too vehement. Your hatreds are too sudden, too strong.'

'You mean Mirabeau, don't you? You'll never let that topic go. I know he used me, and he used me to propagate sentiments in which – it turned out – he didn't believe. But now you – it turns out – are just the same. You don't believe a word of what you "let" me say. I find this hard to accept.'

'In a way,' Robespierre said patiently, 'if we want to rise above being like Suleau, and the girl, we have to avoid the snares of what we personally believe, hope for — and see ourselves just as instruments of a destiny that has been worked out already. You know, there would have been a Revolution, even if we had never been born.'

'I don't think I believe that,' Camille said. 'I think it injures my place in the universe to believe that.' He started picking up the papers from the floor. 'If you really want to annoy Eléonore, I mean Cornélia,' he said, 'you can keep throwing them on the floor and asking for them again, like the baby does. Lolotte gets out of the way when she sees that trick starting.'

'Thank you, I'll try.' A spasm of coughing.

'Has Saint-Just been to see you?'

'No. He has no patience with illness.'

Under Robespierre's eyes there were deep purple stains against the skin. Camille remembered his sister, in the months before her death. He pushed the thought aside; refused to have it. 'It's all right for you, you and Danton. I have to go and stutter for two hours at the Jacobins and probably be knocked down again by maddened violin-makers and trampled by all sorts of tradesmen. Whilst Danton spends his evenings feeling up his new girlfriend and you lie around here in a nice fever, not too high. If you're an instrument of destiny, and anyone would do instead, why don't you take a holiday?'

'Well, still, our individual fate is some concern of ours. If I took a holiday, Brissot and Roland and Vergniaud would start planning to cut off my head.'

'You said you wouldn't mind. You'd sort of take it in your stride.'

'Yes, but there are things I want to do first. And it wouldn't be a very pleasant vacation, thinking about it, would it?'

'Saints don't take holidays,' Camille said. 'And I prefer to think that although we are instruments of destiny, no one else will do, because we are like saints, agents of a divine purpose, and filled with the grace of God.'

Charlotte was on her way out too. She was getting worse than she deserved, he thought. They stood on the rue Honoré and tears spilled out of her eyes and down her pert, feline face. 'He wouldn't treat me like this if he knew how I felt,' she said. 'Those monstrous women are turning him into something that none of us will recognize. They make him smug, they make him think about himself all the time, how wonderful he is. Yes, he is wonderful, but he doesn't need telling. Oh, he has no common sense, he has no sense of proportion.'

He took her back to the rue des Cordeliers. Annette was there. She looked Charlotte over very carefully, and listened to her problems. She always looked, these days, like a person who could give advice but never did.

Everyone was coming that evening to sit in reserved places in the gallery at the Jacobins. 'It will be a triumph,' Lolotte said. As the afternoon wore on, panic began to fight inside him like cats in a sack.

What kind of fear is it? He can take any number of fights with violin-makers: that isn't a problem. What he hates is that creeping sense of the big occasion; the hour approaching, the minutes ticking away; that gathering up of papers and conspicuous walk to the tribune, with a perceptible swell and rustle of animosity detectable as soon as he leaves his place. Claude had said, 'You are the Establishment now'; but that is not quite true. Most of the deputies of the Centre and Right think he should not be a member of the Convention, that his extreme views and his advocacy of violence should exclude him; when he gets up to speak they shout 'Lanterne Attorney' and '*septembriseur*'. Some days this gives him a jaunty feeling, feeds his arrogance; other days it makes him feel sick and cold. How could you know in advance which sort of day it was going to be?

The day the Gironde brought in their indictment against Marat – that had been one of the bad ones. They had packed the benches with their supporters; when you looked up at the Mountain, it was surprising how many people had stayed away. Who will speak up for Marat, mad and poisonous and repellent? He will. And they must have expected it, for the noise was orchestrated; we will put Marat on trial, they yelled, *and you with him*. Much more, in the usual vein: *blood-drinker*. Get down from the tribune, they yell, before we drag you down; four years of revolution, and he is as much under threat as he ever was at the Palais-Royal, when the police closed in.

He had stood his ground for as long as he could, but the president was helpless, indicated by a gesture of his hands that there was nothing to be done. What the deputies felt for Marat was an extremity of loathing and dread, and they had transferred those feelings to him, and he was aware – one must always be aware – that the deputies do not attend sittings unarmed. Danton would have faced them out, he would have dominated them, forced their taunts back down their throats; but he did not have those abilities. He stopped trying to speak, contented himself with one long glance over the howling benches: nodded to the president, pushed back his hair, said to himself, 'Well, Dr Marat, first blood to them.'

When he walked shakily back to the Mountain's benches, Danton was not there, Robespierre was not there; they wanted no involvement in this matter. François Robert, who was afraid of Marat and detested him, looked away. Fabre glanced towards him, raised one eyebrow, bit his lip. Antoine Saint-Just gave him a half-smile. 'That cost you an effort, didn't it?' Camille had said fiercely. He'd wished desperately to be outside, to breathe less hostile air, but if he had walked out at once, the Right would have added that to their list of triumphs: not only did we silence Marat's chief supporter, but we also drove him out of our hall.

After an interval, he was able to pick his way out, into the gardens of the Tuileries. Four years in stale and airless rooms; four years of contention and fright. Georges-Jacques thinks the Revolution is something to make money out of, but now the Revolution is exacting its own price. Most of his colleagues have taken to alcohol, some to opium; some of them have developed a repertoire of strange and sudden illnesses, others have a habit of bursting into unmanly tears in the middle of the day's business. Marat is an insomniac; his cousin Fouquier, the Public Prosecutor, has confided in him that he is harassed every night by dreams of dead people trailing him in the street. He is, by the general standard, coping quite well; but he is not equipped for an upset like today's.

He had become aware, at this point, that two men were following him. Making his decision, he turned to face them. They were two of the soldiers who guarded the National Convention. They approached to within three paces. He put his hand to his heart. He was taken aback by the small flat tone of his own voice. 'Of course, you've come to arrest me. I suppose the Convention has just decreed it.'

'No, Citizen, it's not that. If we'd come to arrest you there'd be more than two of us. It is only that we saw you walking here by yourself and we know these are evil times and we were mindful of the way the good Citizen Lepelletier was struck down and died.'

'Yes, of course. Not that there would be much you could do. Unless you were minded to step heroically in the way?' he said hopefully.

'We might catch somebody,' the soldier said. 'An assassin. We're always on the look-out for these conspirators, you know, just as Citizen Robespierre tells us. Now,' he hesitated, turned to his colleague, trying to remember what he was supposed to say. 'Oh yes – can we offer you an escort, Citizen Deputy, to a place of greater safety?'

'The grave,' Camille said. 'The grave.'

'Only would you,' said the second soldier, 'take your hand away from that pistol that you've got in your coat pocket? It's making me nervous.'

That day – and that second of freakish despair – was not a day he wished to remember. Tonight at the Jacobins he will be – for the most part – among friends. Danton will be there, and so he will sit in his usual place beside him. Danton will be deliberately silent, impassive, knowing that one cannot talk or joke his nervousness away. When the time comes he will make his way slowly towards the tribune, because patriots will step out of their places to embrace him, and from the dark parts of the gallery where the sansculottes gather there will be applause and coarse shouts of encouragement. Then silence; and as he begins, thinking carefully ahead so that he can control any tendency to stutter, so that he can circumvent words and pluck them out and slot in others, he will be thinking, no wonder this business is such a bloody mess, no one ever knows what anyone else is saying. No one knew at Versailles; no one knows now; when we are dead and a few years have passed they will grow tired of trying to hear us, they will say, what does it matter? We have elected our own place in the silences of history, with our weak lungs and our speech impediments and our rooms that were designed for something else.

Cour du Commerce:

Gély: Have pity on us, Monsieur.

Danton: Pity? What do you want pity for? Personally I'd have thought it was a stroke of good luck for you.

Gély: We have only one child.

Mme Gély: He wants to kill her like he killed his first wife.

Gély: Be quiet.

Danton: Oh, let her say it. Let her get it out of her system.

Gély: We don't understand why you want her.

Danton: I have a certain feeling for her.

Mme Gély: You might at least have the grace to say you love her.

Danton: It seems to me that's something you find out about a few years on.

Gély: There are more suitable people.

Danton: That's for me to decide, isn't it?

Gély: She's fifteen.

Danton: I'm thirty-three. Marriages like that are made every day.

Gély: We thought you were older than that.

Danton: She's not marrying me for my looks.

Gély: Why not a widow, someone experienced?

Danton: Experienced in what? You know, if you think I have this gigantic sexual appetite, it's just a myth I put about, I'm quite normal really.

Mme Gély: Please.

DANTON: Perhaps after all you should send this female out of the room.

GÉLY: I meant experienced in bringing up a family.

DANTON: The children are attached to her. As she is, to them. Ask her. Also, I don't want a middle-aged woman, I want more children. She knows how to run a household. My wife taught her.

GÉLY: But you entertain, you receive important visitors. She wouldn't know about all that.

DANTON: Anything I decide on is good enough for them.

MME GÉLY: You are the most arrogant person alive.

DANTON: Well, if you do feel so sorry for my friends, you can always come down and advise her. If you feel qualified. Look, she can have an army of servants if she wants. We can move to a bigger place, that might be a good thing all round, I don't know why I stay here, habit I suppose. I'm a rich man. All she has to do is to say what she wants and she can have it. Her children will inherit from me equally with the children of my first marriage.

GÉLY: She isn't for sale.

DANTON: She can have a bloody private chapel and a priest of her own, if she wants. As long as he's a priest loyal to the constitution.

LOUISE: Monsieur, I'm not marrying you in a civil ceremony. I may as well tell you that now.

DANTON: I beg your pardon, my love?

LOUISE: What I mean is, all right, I'll go through that silly business at City Hall. But there must be a real marriage too, with a real priest who hasn't taken the oath.

DANTON: Why?

LOUISE: It wouldn't be a proper marriage otherwise. We'd be living in a state of sin, and our children would be illegitimate.

DANTON: Little fool – don't you know God's a revolutionary?

LOUISE: A proper priest.

DANTON: Do you know what you're asking?

LOUISE: Or not at all.

DANTON: You'd better think again.

LOUISE: I'm trying to make you do the right thing.

DANTON: I appreciate that, but when you're my wife you'll do as you're told, and you can begin now.

LOUISE: That's the only condition I'm making.

DANTON: Louise, I'm not used to having conditions made to me.

LOUISE: This is a good start.

HAVING FAILED in their offensive against Marat, the Girondist deputies set up a new committee, to investigate those persons who – they say – are prejudicing the authority of the National Convention. This committee arrests Hébert. Pressure from the Sections and the Commune forces his release. May 29, the Central Committee of the Sections goes into 'permanent session' – what a fine, crisis-ridden sound it has, that term! May 31, the tocsin rings at three in the morning. The city gates are closed.

Robespierre: 'I invite the people to demonstrate in the Convention itself and drive out the corrupt deputies . . . I declare that, having received from the people the mission of defending their rights, I regard as my oppressor whoever interrupts me or refuses to let me speak, and I declare I will lead a revolt against the president and all the members who try to silence me. I declare that I will punish traitors myself, and I promise to look upon every conspirator as my personal enemy . . .'

Isnard, a Girondist, president of the Convention: 'If there should be any attack made on the representatives of the nation, then I declare to you in the name of the whole country that Paris would be utterly destroyed – people would be searching along the banks of the Seine to find out whether Paris had ever existed.'

'FOR THE LAST few days people haven't been sleeping at home,' Buzot said. 'It isn't safe. Have you thought of leaving now?'

'No,' Manon said. 'I hadn't thought of that.'

'You have a child.'

She put her head back against a cushion, stretching her smooth white throat for him to notice. 'That' – she closed her eyes – 'can't be allowed to influence my actions.'

'It would, for most women.'

'I'm not most women. You know that.' She opened her eyes. 'Do you think I'm without feeling? That's not it. But there is more at stake here than my feelings. I am not leaving Paris.'

'The Sections are in insurrection.'

'Are you afraid?'

'I am ashamed. That it should come to this. After all we've worked and hoped for.'

The moment of languor was gone; she sat up, her face alight. 'Don't give up! Why should you talk like this? We have the majority in the Convention. What does Robespierre think he can do against our numbers?'

'You should never underestimate what Robespierre can do.'

'To think that I offered him the shelter of my house, at the time of the Champs-de-Mars! I esteemed him. I thought him the citadel of everything that was logical and reasonable and decent.'

'You aren't the only person whose judgement he's led astray,' he said. 'Robespierre has never forgiven his friends the injuries he has done them, nor the kindnesses he has received from them, nor the talents some of them possess that he doesn't. You made the wrong choice, my love, you should have held out your hand to Danton.'

'That blackguard repels me.'

'I did not mean in the literal sense.'

'Shall I tell you what Danton thinks? None of you seems to know. In his eyes you, my husband, Brissot, all of you – you're a collection of mild-mannered, played-out intellectuals. The men for him are cynics with strong stomachs, flatterers, carnivores – men who destroy for the love of destruction. That is why he treats you with contempt.'

'No, Manon, that's not true. He offered to negotiate. He offered a truce. We turned him down.'

'So you say, but in fact you know it is not possible to negotiate with him. He lays down terms, and he expects you to fall in with them. In the end, he always gets his way.'

'Yes, possibly you're right. So there's not much left, is there? And us, Manon – we've had nothing.'

'The thing about nothing,' she said, 'is that Danton can't take it away.'

ARMED DEMONSTRATIONS outside the Convention. Inside, delegates from the Sections with the list of deputies they wanted ejected and proscribed. Still the majority wouldn't crack. Robespierre was as white as the sheet of paper that slipped once from his hand; he clung for support to the tribune, and between each sentence there was a laboured pause. Vergniaud called out, 'Finish then!' Robespierre's head snapped back. 'Yes, I'll finish you.'

Two days later, the Convention was surrounded by an immense crowd, mostly armed, which rapid estimates put at eighty thousand strong; in the front ranks were National Guardsmen, with fixed bayonets and cannon. The people's demand was for the expulsion of twenty-nine deputies. Among them were Buzot, Vergniaud, Pétion, Louvet, Brissot. It seemed the Guardsmen and the sansculottes intended to imprison the deputies till they agreed. Hérault de Séchelles, who was president that day, led a crocodile of deputies from the hall into the open air; this gesture, it was hoped, would defuse the mutual hostility. The gunners stood by their cannon. Their commandant glared down from his horse and harangued the president of the Convention. He was to understand that he, Hérault, was regarded as a patriot; but he was to understand that the people would not be thwarted.

Hérault smiled, an abstracted smile. He and his colleagues were putting the final touch to the republican constitution, the document that would give France freedom for ever: and here – 'One perfectly grasps the situation,' he remarked, scarcely audible. Walking before the long procession, he led the trapped men back into the chamber. A number of good sansculottes were now lounging on the benches, exchanging compliments with those deputies of the Mountain who knew exactly what was going on and who had not troubled to stir.

Deputy Couthon, the saint in the wheelchair, had the floor: 'Citizens, all members of the Convention should now be assured of their liberty. You have marched out to the People. You have found them everywhere good, generous and incapable of threatening the security of their delegates – but indignant against conspirators who wish to enslave them. Now that you recognize that you are free in your deliberations, I move a decree of accusation against the denounced members.'

Robespierre put his head in his hands. Given the unlikely nonsense that the saint had just spouted, perhaps he was laughing? Or perhaps he was feeling ill again? No one dared to ask. Each bout of sickness left him perversely strengthened, it seemed.

MANON ROLAND spent a day in the president's antechamber, waiting, a black shawl over her head. Vergniaud brought her the bad news hour by hour. She had written an address to the Convention which she wished to read out, but each time the door opened a terrifying riot of noise washed over her. Vergniaud said, 'You can see for yourself what the situation is. No one can address the deputies while the present tumult continues. You might, as a woman, receive a little more respect, but frankly – ' He shook his head.

She waited. The next time he came in, he said, 'An hour and a half, maybe, but I can't promise that. Nor can I promise what sort of reception you'll get.'

An hour and a half? She had already been away from home too long. She did not know where her husband was. Still – she had waited all day, she would stay a little longer, go through with it. 'I'm not afraid, Vergniaud. Perhaps I can say things that you can't say. Warn our friends,' she said. 'Tell them to be ready to support me.'

'Most of them are not here, Manon.'

She gaped at him. 'Where then?'

He shrugged. 'Our friends have spirit. But I'm afraid they have no stamina.'

She left, took a cab to Louvet's house. He wasn't there. Another cab – home. The streets were crowded, the carriage moved at a walking pace. She called out to the driver to stop. She climbed down, paid him. She began to walk rapidly, then breathlessly, the dark cloth pulled about her face, like a guilty woman in a novel running to meet her lover.

At the gate of her house, the concierge took her by the arm; Monsieur has locked up and gone, he went to the landlord's apartment, there at the back. She beat on the door. Roland has already left, they said. Where? A house down the street. 'Madame, rest just a little, he is safe, take a glass of wine.'

She sat down before the empty grate; it was June after all, and the night was fine, still, warm. They brought her a glass of wine. 'Not so strong,' she said. 'Cut it with water.' All the same, her head swam.

He was not at the next house; but she found him at the one after that. She found him pacing the floor. She was surprised; she had imagined his long bony frame folded into a chair, coughing, coughing. 'Manon,' he said to her, 'we must go. Look, I have friends, I have plans. We leave this damn city tonight.'

She sat down. They brought her a cup of chocolate with cream floating on top. She said, 'This is a nice thing to have.' The richness soothed her throat, the throat in which words had died.

'You understand?' he said. 'There is no question of false heroics, of sitting the situation out. I am compelled to take steps to save myself in case at some future date it is necessary for me to resume office. I must preserve myself if I am to be of any use to the nation. You understand?'

'I understand. I myself, I must go back to the Convention tonight.'

'But Manon – think of your safety, think of our child's safety – '

She put her cup down. 'How strange,' she said. 'It's not late, and yet it feels as if it is.' Their lives were being rolled away around them. They were like the tenants of an empty house; when the removers have finished, you are left with the bare floors, the forgotten bit of cracked china, the dust you have disturbed. They are like the last diners in a café, when the clocks are chiming with menace and the waiters are clearing their throats; you must conclude your conversation now, you must split the bill, and go out into the cold street. Rising neatly, she crossed the room to him. He stood still. Reaching up, she kissed his cheek, feeling with her lips the bones of the skull beneath.

'Did you betray me?' he said. 'Oh, did you betray me?'

She put her finger softly for a second against his lips, and then her cheek against his, catching for a second the faint mephitic odour of his diseased lungs. 'Never,' she said. 'Take great care now. Avoid spirits and any meat that is not well-cooked. Do not touch milk unless you can get it from somewhere clean. Eat a little poached white fish. Drink an infusion of valerian if you feel agitated. Keep your chest and throat warm, don't go out in the rain. Take a warm drink to help you sleep. Write to me.'

She closed the door softly behind her. She would never see him again.

VIII. *Imperfect Contrition*

(*1793*)

'I THINK we were somewhat – er – infirm of purpose,' Danton said. 'House arrest proved not to be very effective. We must remember that for the future. I know we have the little lady secure, but I would rather have had her husband, and Buzot, and some of the others who are now on their way to cosy provincial bolt-holes.'

'Exile,' Robespierre said. 'Outlawry. I wouldn't call the condition of a fugitive comfortable. Anyway, they're gone.'

'To stir up trouble.'

'The troublemakers in the provinces are mostly making royalist trouble.' Robespierre began to cough. 'Damn.' He dabbed his lips with his handkerchief. 'Most of our Girondist absconders are regicides. Still, I'm sure they'll try their best.'

Danton was discomfited. Talking to Robespierre, one tried to make the right noises; but what is right, these days? Address yourself to the militant, and you find a pacifist giving you a reproachful look. Address yourself to the idealist, and you'll find that you've fallen into the company of a cheerful, breezy, professional politician. Address yourself to means, and you'll be told to think of ends: to ends, and you'll be told to think of means. Make an assumption, and you will find it overturned; offer yesterday's conviction, and today you'll find it shredded. What did Mirabeau complain of? *He believes everything he says.* Presumably there was some layer of Robespierre, some deep stratum, where all the contradictions were resolved.

Brissot was on his way to Chartres, his home town; from there to the south. Pétion and Barbaroux were headed for Caen, in Normandy.

*

'THIS ATTIC you live in . . . ' Danton said to the priest. He was dismayed. In his experience priests always attended to their comfort.

'It's not too bad now the winter's over. Better than prison, anyway.'

'Oh, you've been in prison?' The priest didn't answer. 'I wonder, Father, why you dress like a banker's clerk, or a respectable shopkeeper? Should you not be sansculotte?'

'In the places where I go, I am less conspicuous dressed like this.'

'You minister to the middle classes?'

'Not exclusively.'

'And you find that they cling to the old order? That surprises me.'

'The working people are very much afraid of authority, M. Danton, whoever represents it. And are much occupied, as always, with getting together the necessities of life.'

'And in consequence are spiritually degraded, you mean?'

'Monsieur, you did not come to argue politics with a priest. You know my function. I render to Caesar, otherwise I do not concern myself.'

'But you don't think I'm Caesar, do you? You can't claim to be above politics but pick and choose your Caesar.'

'Monsieur, you came so that I could hear your confession, before your marriage to a daughter of the church. Please don't argue, because in this matter you can't win or lose. The case is unfamiliar to you, I know.'

'May I know your name?'

'I am Father Kéravenen. Once of Saint-Sulpice. Would you care for us to begin?'

'It must be half a lifetime since I did this. It taxes the memory, half a lifetime.'

'But you are a young man still.'

'Ah yes. But the years have been crowded with incident.'

'When you were a child you were taught to examine your conscience each night. Have you left off that practice?'

'A man must sleep.'

The priest smiled sadly. 'Perhaps I can help you. You are a son of the church, you have had no dealings I suppose with one heresy or the other – you have been lax perhaps, but you recognize that the church is the one true church, that it is the route to salvation?'

'If there is salvation, I can't see any other route to it.'

'You do believe in God, Monsieur?'

Danton thought. 'Yes. But . . . I would add a list of qualifications to that.'

'Let the one word stand, would be my advice. It is not for us to add qualifications. Your own worship, your obligations as a Catholic – you have performed them, or neglected them?'

'Refused them.'

'But those in your care – you have provided for their spiritual welfare?'

'My children are baptised.'

'Good.' The priest seemed easily encouraged. He looked up. The keenness of his eyes took Danton by surprise.

'Shall we survey the field of your possible derelictions? Murder?'

'Not as such.'

'You can say this in full confidence?'

'This is a sacrament of the church, is it not? It is not a debate in the National Convention.'

'Point taken,' said the priest. 'And the sins of the flesh?'

'Yes, most of those. The common ones, you know. Adultery.'

'How many times?'

'I don't keep a diary, Father, like some love-sick girl.'

'You are sorry for it?'

'The sin? Yes.'

'Because you see how it offends God?'

'Because my wife is dead.'

'What you express is imperfect contrition – that which arises from our human apprehension of punishment and pain – rather than that perfect contrition which arises from the love of God. Nevertheless, it is all that the church requires.'

'I know the theory, Father.'

'And you have a firm purpose of amendment?'

'I intend to be faithful to my second wife.'

'I might now come to other matters – to envy, perhaps, to anger, pride . . . '

'Ah, the Deadly Sins. Put me down for the whole seven. No, leave out sloth. Put in rather that I have been too diligent. A bit more sloth, and I might not have been so sinful in other directions.'

'And then, calumny – '

'That's the politician's stock-in-trade, Father.'

'Again, Monsieur, when you were a child you were taught of the two sins against the Holy Ghost: Presumption and Despair.'

'My tendency these days is more towards despair.'

'You know I don't speak of mundane matters – I speak of spiritual despair. Despair of salvation.'

'No, I don't despair of it. Who knows? God's mercy is very strange. That's what I say to myself.'

'Monsieur, it is to your credit that you have come here today. You have set your foot upon the path.'

'And what's at the end of it?'

'At the end of the path is the face of the crucified Christ.'

Danton shuddered. 'So you will give me absolution?'

The priest inclined his head.

'I'm not much of a penitent.'

'God is willing to stretch a point.' The priest raised his hand. He inscribed a cross on the air; he murmured the formula. 'It is a beginning, M. Danton,' he said. 'I told you I had been in prison – I was so fortunate as to escape, last September.'

'Where have you been since?'

'Never mind that. Only know that I shall be there when you need me.'

'AT THE JACOBINS last night – '

'Don't tell me, Camille.'

'They said, where is Danton? Missing again!'

'I am occupied with the Committee.'

'Mm. Sometimes. Not often enough.'

'I thought you didn't approve of the Committee.'

'I approve of you.'

'And?'

'And if you go on as you do now you'll not be re-elected.'

'Doesn't this remind you of anything? When you were first married, and you wanted a bit of time to yourself? And Robespierre used to come round and nag you and hector you and lecture you on your public duties? Look, I think you should be the first to know. I'm going to marry Gély's daughter.'

'Imagine!' Camille said.

'We plan to sign the marriage contract in four days' time. Will you glance over it for me? In my allegedly giddy and irresponsible frame of mind, I might have put the words in the wrong order. And, you know, a mistake could be expensive.'

'Why – is there something unusual about the settlement?'

'I'm turning over my property to her. The whole of it. I shall manage it during my lifetime.'

There was a long silence. Danton broke it. 'You never know. I might meet with an accident. At the hands of the state. If I lose my head, there's no reason why I should also lose my land. Now, why are you exhibiting symptoms of rage?'

'Get another lawyer,' Camille shouted at him. 'I refuse to be party to your Decline and Fall.' He slammed out of the room.

Louise came down from the apartment above. She looked up into his face, very solemn; put her child's hand in his. 'Where has Camille gone?'

'Oh, to see Robespierre, I expect. He always goes to Robespierre, when we have a row.'

Perhaps, Louise thought, one day he'll not come back. She didn't voice this; her husband-to-be was, she realized, in many ways a vulnerable man. 'You know each other very well, you and Camille,' she said.

'Intolerably well. So my love, I have a thing to say to you – no, nothing to do with politics at all, just a specific word of warning. If I ever come into a room and find you alone with Camille, I'll kill you.'

'If you ever find me alone with Camille, one of us will be dead.'

'I WISH YOU every happiness, Danton,' Robespierre said. 'Camille says you've gone mad but, good heavens, I suppose you know your own mind. There's just one thing I would say – if you will pardon me – that your attitude to your public duties in the last two months has not been all that the Republic is entitled to expect.'

'What about your increasingly frequent illnesses, Robespierre?'

'I can't help those.'

'I can't help getting married. I must have women.'

'We see you must,' Robespierre murmured, 'but need they occupy so much of your time? Can't you satisfy yourself and then get back to work?'

'*Satisfy* myself! Christ, you have a low opinion of me! I meant I must have a home – I must have a wife, my children around me, my house running smoothly – I thought that you more than anyone would understand that.'

'Really? I should have thought that, as a bachelor, I was the last person who could be expected to understand.'

'That's up to you. I thought you valued family life – that was my impression. Anyway, whatever you understand or don't understand – I resent this implication that everything I do is public property.'

'There's no need to get angry.'

'Sometimes I think I'll just pack and go, go tomorrow, get out of this city, go back where I belong, farm my land –'

'Sentimental,' Robespierre said. 'You can be, Danton, you know. Well, if you must you must, we'd prefer to have you with us but no one's indispensable. Come and see me before you go, won't you? We can have a few drinks or something.'

Robespierre resisted the temptation to look back, to where Danton stood gaping after him. He can be such fun to torment, he thought, with those big, blundering, uncouth emotions of his. No wonder Camille has spent ten years at it.

CAMILLE LAY on Robespierre's bed looking up at the ceiling, his hands behind his head. Robespierre sat at his desk. 'Seems a peculiar business,' he said.

'Yes. There were dozens of women he could have married. She's not that pretty, and she won't bring him any money. He's besotted with her, he's lost his sense of proportion. And her family are royalists and possessed by religious mania.'

'No, I'm sorry, I was harking back to what we said earlier, about the Dumouriez business. Still, go on.'

'Oh, it's just – she's putting all sorts of ideas into his head.'

'I shouldn't have thought a little girl like that could put ideas into Danton's head.'

'At the moment he's susceptible.'

'You mean, royalist ideas?'

'Not quite that, but he's softening up. He said to me that he didn't want Antoinette brought to trial. Of course he rationalizes it, says that she's our last bargaining counter, that her relatives in Europe are more likely to listen to peace terms if she's still alive.'

'Her relatives don't give a damn about her. If she doesn't go on trial the existence of the Tribunal is a farce. She has given our military plans to the Austrians, she's a traitor.'

'Then he says, what's the point of hounding down Brissot's people, now they're out of the Convention – though you did say that yourself.'

'Only strictly in private, Camille. Remember, it was just a personal view, it was not a recommendation to the nation.'

'My public views and my private views are the same. They will go on trial, if I have my way.'

'And if Dr Marat has his.' Robespierre turned a few papers over. 'Danton's peace initiatives don't seem to be conspicuously successful, do they?'

'No. He's wasted four million, I should say, in Russia and Spain. Soon it will be peace at any price. That's one whole aspect of him. People don't know. Peace and quiet.'

'Does he still see this Englishman, Mr Miles?'

'Why?'

'I just wondered.'

'Did you now! I think they have dinner together from time to time.'

Robespierre picked up his little volume of Rousseau. He began to work through it absent-mindedly, just flicking the pages with his thumb. 'Tell me, Camille – be entirely honest with me – do you think Georges-Jacques has behaved quite scrupulously with regard to army contracts?'

'How am I to answer that? You know how he finances himself.'

'Cut-ins, kickbacks – yes, we have to take him with all his faults and failings, don't we, though I can hardly imagine what Saint-Just would say if he heard me voice that sentiment. I suppose he'd say I was conniving at corruption, which is really just another way of being corrupt oneself ... Tell me, do you think we could save Danton from himself? Scoop up some of the small fry?'

'No.' Camille turned onto his side and looked at Robespierre, propping his head on his hand. 'Small fry lead to bigger fry, whatever they are. Danton's too valuable to be put into difficult positions.'

'I should hate to see him lose his value. About this marriage settlement – this worries me. Of course, it means only one thing – that at some point in the future he fears he might find himself on trial.'

'You said almost the same thing yourself. That at some point you might, despite yourself, become an obstacle to the Revolution. That you were prepared.'

'Oh, *mentally* prepared – I mean, a little humility is a good thing for us all, but I wouldn't settle my affairs in anticipation. What we must do – we must do our best to steer Danton away from dangerous involvements.'

'I don't see any prospect of an immediate divorce.'

Robespierre smiled. 'Where are they today?'

'At Sèvres with Gabrielle's parents. All the best of friends, terribly cosy. And they are to get a cottage, where they can be absolutely alone together, and none of us are to know where it is.'

'Why did he mention it then?'

'He didn't. It was Louise who made a point of telling me.' Camille sat up. 'I must go. I have a dinner engagement. Not with Mr Miles.'

'But with?'

'No one you know. I mean to have a very good time. You'll be able to read all about it in Hébert's scandal-sheet. No doubt he's inventing the menu this very minute.'

'Doesn't it bother you?'

'Hébert? No, I like to see him pulled down by the accumulated weight of his pettiness.'

'No, I mean – when you spoke in the Convention last, some fool shouted, "You dine with aristocrats." In itself it means nothing, but –'

'They call everyone an aristo who's intelligent. Anyone with good taste.'

'You know that these people, these *ci-devants*, they're only interested in you for the power you hold.'

'Oh yes. Well, not Arthur Dillon – he likes me. But after all, since '89 people have been interested in me only for the power I hold. Before '89, no one was interested in me at all.'

'All the people who counted were.' An intense moment; Robespierre's eyes, with their fugitive blue-green light, rest on him. 'You were always in *my* heart.'

Camille smiles. Sentimentality; after all, it is the fashion of the era. It occurs to him that it is, anyway, more soothing than being yelled at by Georges-Jacques. Robespierre breaks the moment, gives him a good-tempered dismissive wave. But after Camille has gone, he sits and thinks. Virtue, is the word that springs to his mind – or rather *vertu*, meaning strength, honesty, purity of intent. Does Camille understand these words? Sometimes he seems to comprehend them very well; no one has more *vertu*. The trouble is, he thinks he's an exception to every rule. He's been saying things, today, that he'll wish he hadn't said. That doesn't mean I'm not obliged to take notice of them. If he hadn't told me, I'd never have known about Georges-Jacques's marriage settlement. Danton must be feeling very anxious about something. A man like that doesn't worry over trifles. A man like that doesn't give away that he's worried. A man like that feels under threat only when there's some huge guilt pressing on his mind, or a great accumulation of threats and fears . . .

Guilt, of course: there must be. He abused the good young woman's trust; and she was the mother of his little sons. When she died I imagined him so hurt that he would never recover, and I wrote to console him, I opened my mind and heart, laying aside all reservations, suspicions, doubts – 'you and I are one'. I grant you, the sentiment was overblown. I should have guarded my pen, but I felt so raw . . . No doubt he smiled at it. No doubt he thought (no doubt he said, aloud, to smirking people) what is it with this little man? How dare he claim to be *one* with me? How could *Robespierre* – the bachelor, who has only the most skulking attachments, and those he denies – how could *Robespierre* presume to know what I feel?

And now he says to himself, hands resting on his desk: Danton is a patriot. Nothing more is necessary; it doesn't matter if his manners displease me. Danton is a patriot.

He rises from his desk, eases open a drawer, takes out a notebook. One of those little notebooks he uses: a fresh one. He opens the first page. He seats himself, dips his pen, writes DANTON. He would like to add something: don't read this, it's my private book. Yet, though he doesn't claim to know much about people, he knows this: such a plea would drive them on, sniffing and ferreting, reading in excited gulps. He frowned. So, let them read . . . or he could perhaps carry this book with him, all the time? Not liking himself very much, he began to record what he could remember of his conversation with Camille.

MAXIMILIEN Robespierre:

In our country we want to substitute morality for egotism, probity for the code of personal honour, principles for conventions, public duties for social obligations, the empire of reason for the tyranny of fashion, contempt of vice for contempt of misfortune, love of glory for love of money, good people for good society, merit for intrigue, the greatness of Man for the pettiness of the Great, a magnanimous, powerful and happy people for a frivolous and miserable one: in other words, all the virtues and miracles of the republic for all the ridiculous vices of the monarchy.

*

CAMILLE Desmoulins:

Till our day it has been thought, with the lawgivers of old, that Virtues were the necessary basis of a republic; the eternal glory of the Jacobin Club will be to have founded one on vices.

ALL JUNE, disasters in the Vendée. At different times the rebels have Angers, Saumur, Chinon; are narrowly defeated in the battle for Nantes, where off the coast the British navy waits to support them. The Danton Committee is not winning the war, nor can it promise a peace. If by autumn there is no relief from the news of disaster and defeat, the sansculottes will take the law into their own hands, turning on the government and their elected leaders. That at least is the feeling (Danton present or absent) in the chamber of the Committee of Public Safety, whose proceedings are secret. Beneath the black tricorne hat which is the badge of his office, Citizen Fouquier becomes more haggard each day, peering over the files of papers stacked on his desk, planning diversions for the days ahead: acquiring a lean and hungry look which he shares with the Republic herself.

And if a diversion is needed, why not arrest a general? Arthur Dillon is a friend of eminent deputies, a contender for the post of Commander-in-Chief of the Northern Front; he has proved himself at Valmy and in a half-dozen actions since. In the National Assembly he was a liberal; now he is a republican. Isn't it then logical that he should be thrown into gaol, 1 July, on suspicion of passing military secrets to the enemy?

THEY HAD MADE a conspiracy that Claude's health required walks, long walks, every day. His physician had joined in, on the grounds that no amount of gentle exercise does any harm, and if one of the nastiest members of the Convention wanted to have an affair with his mother-in-law, it did not behove him to stand in his way.

Annette, in fact, found her life less exciting than was generally believed. Each morning she occupied herself with the provincial press; she scanned the papers, took cuttings, made extracts. She would sit beside her son-in-law, they would open his letters, she would scribble on them what was to be done, or sent, or said, whether she could reply, whether he should do it, whether the letter could be consigned straight to the drawing-room fire. Who'd have thought, she'd say, that I'd end up your secretary? It's almost ten years now since we haven't been sleeping together and cruelly deceiving the rest of the family. They tried to remember the exact date – it would be sometime in '84 – when Fréron had bowed himself in to Annette's drawing room with Camille in tow. She wasn't, in those days, diligent about writing things down.

If they could remember it, they thought, they could give a party. Any excuse for a party! Annette said. They fell silent for a moment, thinking of the last ten years. Then they went back to discussing the Commune.

And here's Lucile, walking in unexpected and unannounced: 'Really!' her mother said. 'To walk in like this, when we are having an intimate discussion of Hébert – '

Lucile didn't laugh. She started talking. At first he thought she was saying Dillon was dead, killed in action; a miserable blankness descended on his mind, and he went to sit quietly at the desk by the fireplace, looking at the grain of the wood. It was a minute or two before he took in the message: Dillon's here, he's in prison, what are we going to do?

The morning's *joie de vivre* seemed to drain out of Annette. 'This is a complication,' she said. Immediately she thought, I can't see the end of this. Who's behind it? Is it one of the damned committees? The Committee of General Security, which everybody calls the Police Committee? Is it really directed against Arthur Dillon, or is it directed at Camille?

Lucile said, 'You have to get him out, you know. If he's convicted –' her face showed she knew what conviction meant – 'they'll look at you and say, see how hard he pushed Dillon's career. And you did – you have.'

'Convicted?' Camille was on his feet now. 'There'll be no conviction because there won't be a trial. I'll break my cousin's fucking neck.'

'No, you won't,' Annette said. 'Moderate your language, sit down again, have a nice soothing think.'

No hope of that. Camille was outraged – and it's not the cold simulated outrage of the politician, it's the real thing, the kind of outrage that says, *Do you know who I am?* 'There's your name through the mud again,' Annette murmured to her daughter. Outrage will go to the Convention; but first it will go to Marat's house.

THE COOK let him in. Why does Marat employ a cook? It's not as if he gives dinner-parties. Probably this title, 'cook', conceals some more energetic, revolutionary pastime. 'Don't trip over the newspapers,' the woman said. They lay in great bales, in a dingy, half-lit passage. Having issued her warning, she rejoined her employers, who were sitting in a semi-circle like people preparing for a seance. Why don't they clean the place up, he wondered irritably. But Marat's women are unacquainted with the domestic arts. Simone Evrard was there, and her sister Catherine; Marat's sister Albertine had gone on a trip to Switzerland, they said, to visit the family. Marat has a family? I mean a mother and a father and the usual things? The ordinary arrangement, the cook said. Odd really, I never thought of Marat having a beginning, I thought he was thousands and thousands of years old, like Cagliostro. Can I see him?

'He's not well,' Catherine said. 'He's taking one of his special baths.'

'I really need to see him urgently.'

Doe-eyed Simone: 'Dillon?' She got up. 'Yes, come with me. He was laughing about it.'

Marat was encased in a slipper bath in a hot little room, a towel around his shoulders and a cloth wrapped around his head. There was a heavy, medicinal smell. His face had bloated; beneath its ordinary yellow tinge there was something worse, something blue. There was a board balanced across the bath to act as a desk.

Simone indicated a straw-bottomed chair, giving it a gracious kick.

Marat looked up from the proofs he was correcting. 'Upset, are we? The chair is for sitting on, Camille. Do not stand on it and make a speech.'

Camille sat. He tried to avoid looking at Marat. 'Yes, aesthetic, aren't I?' Marat said. 'A work of art. I ought to be in an exhibition. The number of people who come tramping through, I feel like an exhibit anyway.'

'I'm glad you've found something to make you laugh. In your condition I should not be cheerful.'

'Oh, Dillon. I can spare you five minutes on that topic. Inasmuch as Dillon is an aristocrat by birth, he should be guillotined – '

'He can't help his birth.'

'There are certain defects in you that you can't help, but we can't go on making allowances for ever. Inasmuch as Dillon is your wife's lover, you only demonstrate your perverse temperament if you try to do anything for him. Inasmuch as committees have done this – go for them, and bless you my child.' Marat bounced his clenched fist on his writing-board. 'Do some damage,' he said.

'I am afraid that if Dillon goes before the Tribunal on these ludicrous charges – if he goes before the Tribunal, totally innocent, as he is – he may still be condemned. Is it possible, do you think?'

'Yes. He has enemies, very powerful ones. So what do you expect? The Tribunal is a political instrument.'

'The Tribunal was set up to replace mob law.'

'So Danton claimed. But it will go beyond that. There are some rare fights coming up, you know.' Marat looked up. 'As for you, if you make the welfare of these *ci-devants* your concern, something nasty will happen to you.'

'And you?' Camille said dispassionately. 'Are you worse? Are you going to die?'

Marat tapped the side of the bath. 'No ... like this ... drag on, and on.'

SCENES IN the National Convention. Danton's friend Desmoulins and Danton's friend Lacroix shouted at each other across the benches, as if it were a street-meeting. Danton's friend Desmoulins attacked the Danton Committee. Standing at the tribune, he was bawled out from both sides of the House. From the Mountain, Deputy Billaud-Varennes screamed, 'It is a scandal, he must be stopped, he is disgracing his own name.'

Another walk-out. It was becoming familiar. Fabre followed him. 'Write it down,' he said.

'I will.' Already the letter that Dillon had sent to him from prison was made public, he had read it out to the deputies. I have done nothing, Dillon said, that is not for my country's good. 'A pamphlet,' Camille said. 'What shall I call it?'

'Just call it "A Letter to Arthur Dillon". People like reading other people's letters.' Fabre nodded in the direction of the Convention's hall. 'Settle a few scores, while you're about it. Launch a few campaigns.'

Fabre thought, what am I doing, what am I doing? The last thing he needed was to get dragged into the Dillon business.

'What did Billaud mean, I am disgracing my own name? Am I some sort of institution?'

He knew the answer: yes. He *is* the Revolution. Now, apparently, they thought the Revolution had to be protected from itself.

An elderly, grave deputy approached him, defied his murderous expression, drew him aside, and suggested they have a cup of coffee somewhere. Do you know Dillon well? the man asked him. Yes, very well. And do you know, the man said – look, I don't want to upset you, but you ought to know – about Dillon and your wife? Camille nodded. He was writing a paragraph in his head. You don't deserve this, the deputy said. You deserve better, Camille. It is the old story, I suppose – you are occupied with public affairs, the girl is bored, she is fickle, and you don't have Dillon's looks.

So there is kindness in the world – this strained, patient man, stumbling into a situation he didn't understand, catching the tail-end of the lurid gossip, wanting to put a young man's life right; betrayed himself twenty years ago, who knows? Camille was touched. Thank you, he said politely. As he left the café and headed home to his desk, he felt that singular fluid running in his veins; it was like the old days on the *Révolutions*, the power of words moving through his bloodstream like a drug. For the next couple of weeks he would be slightly out of his mind. When he was not writing, or engaged in a shouting-match, the life seemed to drain out of him;

he felt passive, a husk, a ghost. Strange fantasies possessed him; the language of public debate took a violent, unexpected turn.

'After Legendre,' he wrote, 'the member of the National Convention who has the highest opinion of himself is Saint-Just. One can see by his bearing that he feels his head to be the cornerstone of the Revolution; he carries it as if it were the Holy Sacrament.'

Saint-Just looked down at the passage, which some helpful person had underscored in green ink. There was very little expression in his face; he did not sneer, as people do in novelettes. 'Like the Holy Sacrament,' he says. 'I will make him carry his like Saint Denis.'

'Oh that's quite good,' Camille said, when it was relayed. 'For Antoine, that's quite witty. I wonder if he is going to be clever when he grows up?'

Soon he was rummaging through the bookshelves: 'Lucile, where is Saint-Just's disgusting poem, the epic poem in twenty books? There was a verse beginning "If I were God". Let us see how it continued, I'm sure it will provide the occasion for mockery.'

Then suddenly he stopped, sat down or rather fell into a chair. 'What am I doing? Saint-Just and I are supposed to be on the same side. We are Jacobins, we are republicans . . .'

'I'll find it for you,' Lucile said quietly.

'Perhaps better not.'

For he had begun to see visions: visions of that saint, France's patron, who had walked for several leagues with his severed head in his hand. He first saw Denis in the Place de Grève, picking his way over the cobbles. He was neatly truncated, there was no gore; but the head swinging almost casually from his left wrist was Camille's own. He saw him again going stealthily into the Duplay house, for a private meeting with Robespierre; he saw him waiting outside the entrance to the Jacobin Club – a newly arrived patriot, modest and provincial, wanting an introduction to the great world.

After a day or two it came to him that the only thing to do was to take the initiative. It would be quite easy to kill Saint-Just. He could see him alone, any time, at a convenient place; then a pistol-shot, or (not to advertise the incident) a knife. He could see the pain brimming in Saint-Just's velvet eyes.

And then, he would need a Plot: Saint-Just's conspiracy against the Republic, which he had detected with the instinct of the impeccable and tested patriot. *I am the Revolution.* Who would fail to believe that he had slaughtered Saint-Just in an outburst of patriotic rage? He was not known for containing his temper. To avoid awkward questions it would have to be a small knife, the kind you would hardly know that you were carrying.

Don't be stupid, he said to himself. Saint-Just isn't going to kill you, any more than you're going to kill him. Or even less.

He attended the Committee of War, of which he was secretary, and from its rooms wrote a sensible and chatty letter home, asking his father not to mention Rose-Fleur so much in their correspondence, as Lucile was mad with jealousy.

But still, the fantasy had moved into his brain, it had taken up occupation, he could not evict it. He thought of the hole in Lepelletier's side, the wound made by a butcher's killing-knife, the wound he took the whole night to die of. He would have to be quick; it would have to be one true, telling blow; Saint-Just was a good deal bigger and stronger than he was, and he would have just one chance. At the Jacobins, when he heard the young man's sonorous voice, he would smile to himself. He would dream of his plan in the Convention, when Saint-Just was at the tribune, his left hand making brief chopping motions in the air.

JULY 13: 'A person from Caen,' Danton said. 'Pétion and Barbaroux are believed to have been there these last weeks. It is a Girondist conspiracy. Let me assure you, it was not I who arranged it.'

Camille said, 'I heard someone in the street, shouting *assassination* . . . I was afraid that I . . . in a moment of . . . no, nothing, never mind.'

Danton stared at him for a second. 'Anyway,' he said, 'this finishes the Gironde. Murderers and cowards. They sent a woman.'

THERE WAS A CROWD in the narrow street, a near-silent and stolid mass, its eyes riveted in fascination on two brightly lit windows of Marat's apartment. It was an hour after midnight, strangely light, the heat subtropical. Camille waved away the sansculotte who guarded the bottom of the iron-railed steps. The man did not move – not right away.

'Never seen you close up,' he said. His eyes measured Camille. 'How's Danton taking it?'

'He is shocked.'

'I'll bet. And you'll be telling me next he's sorry.'

Camille was used to the crowd calling out his name. This was a different, more unpleasant, kind of familiarity.

'Some are saying that Danton and Robespierre have put him where he'll be quiet,' the man said. 'Then again, some are saying it's the royalists, some are saying it's Brissot.'

'I know you,' Camille said. 'I've seen you running behind Hébert, haven't I? What are you doing here?'

He knew: squabbling over the legacy already.

'Ah,' the man said, 'Père Duchesne has his interests. The People will need a new Friend. It won't be any of you – '

'Jacques Roux, perhaps?'

'You with that filthy swine Dillon – '

Camille pushed past him. Legendre was already in the house, his tricolour sash knotted untidily about his blustering, bulging person: taking charge. The ground seemed to shiver beneath his feet, as if the women's screams were still rattling the windows; but all was quiet now, except for some stifled sobbing from behind a closed door. You have not eaten much today, Camille said to himself; that is why the walls seem liquid, why the air is disturbed.

The assassin sat in the parlour. Her hands were tied tightly, and behind her chair were two men with pikes. Before her was a small table covered with a scruffy white cloth, and on it were her assassin's possessions: a gold watch, a thimble, a reel of white thread, a few loose coins. A passport, a birth certificate; a handkerchief edged with lace; the cardboard sheath of a kitchen knife. On the dusty rug by her feet was a black hat with three brilliant green ribbons.

He stood against the wall, watching her. She had that kind of thin, translucent skin that reddens and marks easily, catches every nuance of the light. A healthy full-breasted girl, fed on fresh farm butter and the cream of the milk: the kind of girl who smiles at you in church, be-ribboned and flower-scented on the Sundays after Easter. I know you well, he thought; I remember you from when I was a child. The remains of an elaborate coiffure hung about her face: the kind of hair-do a girl from the provinces would have before she went out to commit a murder.

'Yes, make her blush,' Legendre said, 'you can easily make her blush. But blush for her crime, she won't blush for that. I thank Providence that I am alive, because she was at my house earlier today. She denies it, but she was there. They were suspicious, wouldn't let her in. Oh, she denies it, but I was her first choice.'

'Congratulations,' Camille said. He knew that the girl was in pain because of the way they had tied her hands.

'She won't blush,' Legendre said, 'for assassinating our greatest patriot.'

'If that was what she had in mind, she would hardly have wasted her time on you.'

Simone Evrard was outside the door where they had the body. She had collapsed against the wall, wracked, tear-stained, hardly able to keep her feet. 'So much blood, Camille,' she said. 'How will we ever get the blood off the floor and the walls?'

As he opened the door she made a feeble motion to stop him. Dr Deschamps looked swiftly over his shoulder. One of his assistants stepped forward with an outstretched arm to bar Camille's way. 'I have to know for sure . . .' Camille whispered. Deschamps turned his head again. 'I beg your pardon, Citizen Camille. I didn't know it was you. Be warned, it's not pleasant. We are embalming the body, but in this heat . . . with the condition of the corpse after four, five hours,' the doctor wiped his hands on a towel, 'it's as if he were decaying while he was still alive.'

He believes, Camille thought, that I am here from the Convention, on some question of protocol. He looked down. Dr Deschamps put a hand under his elbow. 'It was instantaneous,' he said. 'Or almost so. He had just time to cry out. He can't have felt anything. This is where the knife went.' He indicated. 'Into the right lung, through the artery, piercing the heart. We couldn't close his mouth, so we had to cut out the tongue. All right? You see, he's still quite identifiable. Now, let me get you out of here. I'm burning the strongest aromatics I can find, but it is not a smell for the layman.'

Outside Simone was still propped against the wall. Her breath rasped. 'I told them to give this woman an opiate,' Deschamps said crossly. 'Do you want me to sign anything? No, I see. Look, I assume you have an official escort? I don't know what this nonsense is, everyone knows that Marat is dead. I've already had someone from the Jacobins throwing up over my assistants. You look like the fainting type, so I should get outside as soon as you can. Order something done about the wife, or whoever she is, will you?'

The door clicked shut. Simone slumped into his arms. From the next room came voices raised in curt questioning. 'I was his wife,' Simone moaned. 'He didn't marry me in church, he didn't take me to City Hall, but he swore by all the gods in creation that I was his wife.'

What is it, Camille thought, does she want me to advise her on her rights? 'You will be recognized as his relict,' he said. 'No one these days pays much attention to the formalities. It's all yours now, the printing press and the paper for the next edition. Be careful with it. I should think the state will be paying for the funeral.'

Outside in the street he looked back once, to the windows where the busy shadows of Deschamps and his assistants moved against the light. Rain began to fall, big warm drops. There was thunder somewhere in the distance – over Versailles perhaps. The crowd stood, patient, shoulder to shoulder, waiting for what would happen next.

DAVID TOOK CHARGE of arrangements. The body was to be sealed in a coffin of lead, and enclosed in a larger sarcophagus of purple porphyry, taken from the Collection of Antiquities at the Louvre. But for the funeral procession, it was desired to carry the deceased on a bier, swathed in a tricolour (the cloth drenched in spirits). One bare arm, sewn on from a better class of corpse, bore a laurel wreath; young girls dressed in white and bearing cypress branches surrounded the bier.

After them the Convention, the Clubs, the People. The procession began at five in the afternoon; it ended at midnight, by the light of torches. He was to be buried as he had preferred to live, underground, the cellar-like tomb overhung with blocks of stone and fenced about by iron.

The heart, embalmed separately, was placed in an urn; the patriots of the Cordeliers Club bore it away, to keep it on their premises for ever and ever, till the last day of the world. 'Sacred heart of Marat', the people wailed.

HERE LIES MARAT

THE PEOPLE'S FRIEND

KILLED BY THE PEOPLE'S ENEMIES

13 JULY

1793

THE DEMEANOUR of Robespierre in the funeral procession was remarked upon by one observer. He looked, the witness said, as if he were conducting the corpse to a rubbish-tip.

IX. *East Indians*

(*1793*)

JULY 25: Danton threw his weight back in his chair, threw his head back, laughed uproariously. Louise flinched; she was always worrying about the furniture, and he was always assuring her that there was plenty of money for replacing it. 'The day I parted company with the Committee,' he said, 'I saw something I thought I'd never see – I saw Fabre d'Églantine deprived of speech.' Danton was slightly tipsy; every so often he would lean across the table to squeeze the hand of his new wife. 'So, Fabre, still struck dumb, are you?'

'No, no,' Fabre said uncertainly. 'It's true, I wouldn't wish it on anybody, sitting on a committee with Saint-Just. And it's true, as you say, that Robert Lindet's elected, and he's a solid patriot who we can trust. And Hérault's elected, and he's our friend . . . '

'You're not convinced. Look, Fabre, I am *Danton*, can you get that through your skull? The Committee may need me, but I don't need the Committee. Now, allow me to propose a toast to myself, since no one else has the grace to do it. To me – the newly elected president of the Convention.' He raised his glass to Lucile. 'Now more toasts,' he demanded. 'To my friend General Westermann, may he prosper against the rebels in the Vendée.'

He was lucky, Lucile thought, to get Westermann his command back, after that last defeat; Westermann is lucky to be at large. 'To the Sacred Heart of Marat,' Danton said. Louise gave him a sharp look. 'I'm sorry, my love, I don't mean to blaspheme, I'm just repeating what is said by the poor deluded rabble on the streets. Why did the Gironde go after Marat? He was half-dead anyway. Then again, if the bitch was acting on her own initiative, as she claimed, doesn't it just prove what I've always said, that women have no political sense? She should have gone for Robespierre, or me.'

Oh, don't say that, Louise begged him; at the same time she found it difficult to imagine a kitchen knife slicing through those solid layers of muscle and fat. Danton looked down the table. 'Camille,' he said, 'one drop of ink disposed by you is worth all the blood in Marat's body.'

He refilled glasses. He will drink another bottle, Louise thought, and then perhaps he will fall asleep right away. 'And to Liberty,' he said. 'Raise your glass, General.'

'To Liberty,' said General Dillon, feelingly. 'Long may we, if you know what I mean, be at liberty to enjoy it.'

JULY 26: Robespierre sat with his head bowed, his hands knotted together between his knees; he was the picture of misery. 'Do you see?' he asked. 'I have always resisted such involvement, I have always refused office.'

'Yes,' Camille said. He had a headache, from last night. 'The situation changes.'

'Now, you see – ' Robespierre had developed a minute facial tic, distressing to him; every so often he would break off what he was saying and press his hand against his cheek. 'It's clear that a firm central authority . . . with the enemy advancing on every front . . . You know I have always defended the Committee, always seen the need for it . . . '

'Yes. Stop apologizing. You've won an election, not committed a crime.'

'And there are factions – shall I say Hébert, shall I say Jacques Roux – who wish France to have no strong government. They take advantage of the natural discontents of the man in the street, exploit them, and make all the trouble they can. They put forward measures that can only be called ultra-revolutionary, measures that seem disgusting and threatening to decent people. They bring the Revolution into disrepute. They try to kill it by excess. That is why I call them agents of the enemy.' He put his hand to his face again. 'If only,' he said, 'Danton were not so chronically careless.'

'Clearly he doesn't think the Committee as important as you do.'

'Put it on record,' Robespierre said, 'that I didn't seek the office.

Citizen Gasparin fell ill, it was thrust upon me. I do hope they won't start calling it the Robespierre Committee. I shall be just one among many . . . '

One best friend off the Committee. The other best friend on. Camille is used to being the experimental audience for speeches Robespierre is rehearsing; it has been like this since '89. Ever since that charged, emotional moment at the Duplays' house – 'you were always in my heart' – he has felt that more is expected of him. Robespierre is becoming one of those people in whose company it is impossible to relax for a moment.

Two days later the Committee of Public Safety is given the power to issue warrants for arrest.

JACQUES ROUX, whose following grows, announced that the new author of his news-sheet was 'the ghost of Marat'. Hébert advised the Jacobins that if Marat needed a successor – and the aristocrats another victim – he was ready. 'That talentless little man,' Robespierre said. 'How dare he?'

On 8 August Simone Evrard appeared at the Bar of the Convention, and made an impassioned denunciation of certain persons who were leading the sansculottes to perdition. All her views, she said, were those expressed by the martyr, her husband, in his last hours. It was a fluent, confident tirade; just occasionally she paused to peer more closely at her notes, to puzzle out Citizen Robespierre's tiny, uneven handwriting.

A WEEK LATER there is another addition to the Committee of Public Safety: Lazare Carnot, the military engineer whom Robespierre had first met at the Academy of Arras. 'I don't particularly get on with military men,' Robespierre said. 'They seem to be full of personal ambition, and to have a strange set of priorities. But they are a necessary evil. Carnot always,' he added distantly, 'seemed to know what he was talking about.'

Thus Carnot, later to be known as the Organizer of Victory: Robespierre, the Organizer of Carnot.

When the president of the Revolutionary Tribunal was arrested (suspected of mishandling the trial of Marat's assassin) his replacement was Citizen Hermann, late of the Arras Bar. Hadn't he, all those years ago, been the only one to recognize that Robespierre was talking sense? 'I knew him,' he said to Mme Duplay, 'when I was a young man.'

'What do you think you are now?' she asked him.

The outgoing president was taken away by gendarmes while the Tribunal was actually in session. Fouquier-Tinville liked a drama; his cousin had no monopoly.

WHEN THE MINISTER of the Interior resigned, the two rivals for the post were Hébert and Jules Paré, now a lawyer of note. The latter was appointed. 'We all know why, of course,' said Hébert. 'He was once Danton's managing clerk. We get so big for our boots that we don't actually do any work ourselves, we just let our minions exercise power on our behalf. He has his other clerk, Desforgues, at the Foreign Office. Paré and Danton are as thick as thieves. Just as,' he added, 'Danton was with Dumouriez.'

'Odious runt,' Danton said. 'Isn't it enough for him to have his creatures all over the War Office, and his so-called newspaper distributed to the troops?'

He asserted himself at the Jacobin Club; won some applause. As he quit the rostrum, Robespierre rose to speak. 'No one,' he told the club, 'has the right to voice the least breath of criticism against Danton. Anyone who seeks to discredit him must first prove a match for him in energy, forcefulness and patriotic zeal.'

More applause; some members rose to their feet. Danton was cheered; sprawled on the bench, *sans* cravat and badly shaven, he inclined his head. Robespierre was cheered; patting his cuffs into place – a gesture like some ersatz Sign of the Cross – he bobbed his head to his admirers and gave the club his diffident smile. Then – presumably for simply existing – Citizen Camille was applauded. This is what he likes, isn't it? He was back centre-stage, the sweetheart of the Revolution, the *enfant terrible* whose whims will always be indulged. Presumably somewhere on the benches skulked Renaudin the violin-maker, with his memorable right-hook; but for the moment the only danger was the enthusiasm of the patriots, ambushing him with bear-hugs. For the second time, he found himself crushed against Maurice Duplay's shoulder. He thought of the first time, when he had his precarious escape from Babette.

'What are you looking so worried for?' Danton asked him.

'I'm worried about preserving this accord between you.' He made a small gesture, to show how he was preserving it; it seemed to be the size of a hen's egg, and as fragile.

LATE AUGUST, conscription came in, and General Custine (*ci-devant* Comte de Custine) lost his head; it encouraged the others. On the 26th, Elisabeth Duplay married Deputy Philippe Lebas: a young man who was decidedly not handsome, but who was a good republican, and who had a pleasant, loyal, steadfast nature. 'At last!' Camille said. 'What a relief!' Robespierre was surprised. He approved of the match, true; but she's only *seventeen*, he said.

The queues outside the bakers' shops grew restive. Bread was cheap, but there wasn't much of it, and it was poor stuff. The Montagnard deputy Chabot took issue with Robespierre about the new constitution; he waved documents in his face. 'It fails to abolish beggary from the Republic. It fails to assure bread to those who have none.'

Robespierre was stopped in his tracks. This was the dearest wish of his heart: to ensure bread to those who had none. Every aim apart from this could be picked to pieces, hacked apart, assassinated. Surely this aim was simple, achievable? Yet he could not address the larger problem, because of all the petty problems that got in the way. He said, 'I wish I could do that. I wish the poor would be no longer with us. But we are working within the bounds of possibility.'

'You mean that the Committee, with all the powers we have given it – '

'You have given the Committee some powers and many more problems, you have charged us with questions we can't possibly answer. You have given us – for instance – a conscript army to provision. You expect everything from the Committee, and yet you're jealous of its powers. If I could produce a miracle of loaves and fishes, I suppose you'd say we'd exceeded our mandate.' He raised his voice, for those around to hear. 'If there's no bread, blame the English blockade. Blame the conspirators.'

He walked away. He had never liked Chabot. He tried not to be prejudiced by the fact that Chabot looked, as everyone said, like a turkey: red, mottled, swelling. He had once been a Capuchin friar. It was hard to imagine him obedient to his vows: poverty, chastity. He and Deputy Julien were members of a committee formed to stamp out illegal speculation. Put there, Robespierre supposed, on the principle of setting a thief to . . . Julien was a friend of Danton, unfortunately. He thought of that egg cradled between Camille's narrow palms. They said that Chabot was thinking of marrying. She was a Jewess, sister of two bankers called Frei; at least, they claimed that was their name, and that they were refugees from the Hapsburgs. After the marriage, Chabot would be a rich man.

'You dislike foreigners on principle,' Camille said to him.

'It doesn't seem a bad principle to have, when we are at war with the rest of Europe. What do they want in Paris, all these Englishmen and Austrians and Spaniards? They must have loyalties elsewhere. Just businessmen, people say. What sort of business, I ask myself. Why should they stay here, to be paid in worthless paper and to be at the dictates of the sansculottes? In this city the women who do the laundry fix the price of soap.'

'Well, why do you think?'

'Because they're spies, saboteurs.'

'You don't understand finance, do you?'

'No. I can't understand everything.'

'There is often a lot of money to be made out of deteriorating situations.'

'Cambon is our government's financial expert. He should explain things to me. I will remind him.'

'But you've already formed your conclusions. And I suppose you will agree to imprisoning these people on suspicion.'

'Enemy aliens.'

'Yes, you say that now – but will it stop there? Every internment law perverts justice.'

'You must see – '

'I know,' Camille said. 'National Emergency, extraordinary measures. You can't say I've been soft on our opponents. I've never flinched – and incidentally, why are you delaying the trial of Brissot's people? – but what is the point of combating the tyrants of Europe if we behave like tyrants ourselves? What is the point of any of it?'

'Camille, this isn't tyranny – these powers we are taking, we may never need to use them, or not for more than a few months. It's for our self-preservation, our survival as a nation. You say you have never flinched, but I've flinched – I flinch all the time. Do you think I'm bloodthirsty? I thought you would have trusted me to do the right thing.'

'I do – yes, I think I do. But do you control the Committee, or are you just their public front?'

'How could I control them?' He threw his hands out. 'I'm not a dictator.'

'You affect surprise,' Camille observed. 'If you are not in control, is Saint-Just leading you by the nose? I ask you this to remind you not to let your grasp on events slip. And if I do think it is tyranny, I shall tell you. I have the right.'

You see what the Revolution has boiled down to, a more biting concentrate: menials now ministers, and old friends who understand one's mind. Up to September the Tribunal has condemned no more than thirty-six of the 260 accused brought before it; this ratio will begin to alter. While the issues grow greater, the manpower diminishes; at any one point, the survivors feel they have known each other a long time.

Camille knew that this summer he had made a bad move; he should have left Arthur Dillon to the Republic's judgement. At the same time, he had demonstrated his personal power. But it was isolation he sensed, as mornings grew fresh, as logs were got in for the winter, as the pale gold sun anatomized the paper leaves in the public gardens. With no particular end in view, he made a chance annotation among his papers:

Pytheus said that in the island of Thule, which Virgil called Ultima Thule, six days' journey from Great Britain, there was neither earth, nor sea, but a mixture of the three elements, in which it was not possible to walk, or go in a vessel; he spoke of it as a thing which he had seen.

SEPTEMBER 2 1793: Address of the Sans-Culottes Section (formerly known as Jardin-des-Plantes) to the Convention:

Do you not know there is no basis to property other than the extent of physical needs? . . . A maximum should be fixed to personal fortunes . . . no one should be able to own more land than can be tilled with a stipulated number of ploughs . . . A citizen should not be allowed to own more than one shop or workshop . . . the industrious workman, tradesman or farmer should be able to get for himself not only those things essential for eking out a bare existence, but also those things that may add to his happiness . . .

ANTOINE SAINT-JUST:

Happiness is a new idea in Europe.

ON 2 SEPTEMBER, the news reached Paris that the people of Toulon had handed their town and their navy over to the British. It was an unprecedented act of treason. France lost sixteen frigates and twenty-six out of her sixty-five ships of the line. This time last year, the gutters ran with blood.

'LOOK,' DANTON SAID. 'You use this. You don't just let it wash over you.' The noise from the hall of the Convention was a dull roar, punctuated by the occasional scream. 'You get hold of it.' His fingers made a motion of folding themselves around something: a throat? 'As a September murderer, I have never felt so popular.'

Robespierre began to say something.

'You'll have to speak up,' Danton said.

They were in one of the little rooms, bare and dusty, entered from the warren of dark passages that led from the debating chamber. They were alone, but they did not feel it, because of the tumult and close press of the mob; it was almost possible to smell them. Camille and Fabre effaced themselves against the dank far wall. September 5 1793: the sansculottes are holding among their representatives a demonstration, or riot.

'I said, Danton, why are you leaning against the door?'

'To stop Saint-Just getting in,' Danton said swiftly. Never explain. Robespierre opened his mouth. 'Now be quiet,' Danton said. 'Hébert and Chaumette organized this.'

Robespierre shook his head.

'Oh well,' Danton said, 'there may be a measure of truth in that. Maybe the sansculottes organized themselves, and that is a precedent I dislike. So make sure we stay ahead of events. Wrap up their demands in one package and give them back as a present from the Mountain. Economic controls, price maximums – very well. Arrest of suspects, very well. Then we stop there – no interference with private property. Yes, Fabre, I know what the businessmen will think of the economic controls, but this is an emergency, we have to give way, and why should I justify myself to you?'

'We have to present a moving target to Europe,' Robespierre said quietly.

'What did you say?'

Nothing: Robespierre waved it away, tense and out of patience.

'You have come around to the idea of interning suspects – Camille, the definition must wait. Yes, I know it is the heart of it, but I need a piece of paper for framing legislation. Will you keep quiet? I won't listen to you now.'

'Will you listen to *me*?' Robespierre shouted at him. Danton stopped. He looked at Robespierre warily.

'All right. Go on.'

'Tomorrow the Committee is due for re-election. We want to add to it Collot d'Herbois and Billaud-Varennes. They are giving us a lot of trouble, criticizing us all the time. We can't think of any other way of keeping them quiet. Yes, I know it is a craven policy. We need our spines stiffening, don't we? The Committee wants you back.'

'No.'

'Please, Danton,' Fabre said.

'I'll give you all the support you need. I'll press for extension of your powers. Just tell me what you want from the Convention and I'll fix it. But I won't sit with you. The business wears me down. God blast it, can't you see? I'm not the type for committees. I like to work on my own, I have an instinct and I like to act on it, I hate your bloody agenda and your minutes and your procedures.'

'Your attitude is extremely exasperating,' Robespierre yelled at him.

The noise from outside increased. Danton nodded his head in its direction. 'Let me handle this for you. I'm probably the only one who can make his voice heard out there.'

'I resent you — ' Robespierre said. His words were lost. 'The People,' he shouted, 'are everywhere good, and if they obstruct the Revolution — even, for example, at Toulon — we must blame their leaders.'

'What are you going on about this for?' Danton asked him.

Fabre launched himself from the wall. 'He is trying to enunciate a doctrine,' he shrieked. 'He thinks the time has come for a bloody sermon.'

'If only,' Robespierre yelled, 'there were more *vertu*.'

'More what?'

'*Vertu*. Love of one's country. Self-sacrifice. Civic spirit.'

'One appreciates your sense of humour, of course.' Danton jerked his thumb in the direction of the noise. 'The only *vertu* those bastards understand is the kind I demonstrate every night to my wife.'

Robespierre's face crumpled, like a child's on the verge of tears. He followed Danton out into the dark passage.

'You wish he hadn't said that, don't you?' Fabre inquired. He gently prised Camille from the wall.

MAXIMILIEN Robespierre, private notebooks: 'Danton laughed at the idea of *vertu*, comparing it to what he did every night with his wife.'

WHEN DANTON began to speak, the demonstrators cheered; the deputies stood up and applauded. It was some moments before he could continue. Shock and gratification chased each other across his face; now what have I done right? Once again he exhorted, conceded, unified, endorsed – saved the day. The day following, when he was elected once more to the Committee, Robespierre called at his house. Stiff-featured, he sat on the very edge of his chair and refused refreshment. 'I have come to urge you to see your duty,' he said. 'If the word retains any meaning for you.'

Danton was in a good humour. 'Don't run away, Louise. You've never met Citizen Robespierre face-to-face, have you?'

'I am sick of this taunting,' Robespierre said. He choked the words out, and at the same time his left eyelid began to jump in spasm. He took off his spectacles and pressed his fingers to it.

'You'll have to calm down,' Danton said. 'Think of Camille, living all his life with a stutter. Though I confess Camille's stutter has considerably more charm.'

'The Convention may override you. May order you to join us.'

'I intend to be,' said Danton pleasantly, 'a thorn in the flesh of all committees.'

'There isn't really any more to say, is there? People are screaming for trials and purges and killings. You prefer to walk away.'

'What do you want me to do? Sweat blood for the Republic? I've told you I'll support you.'

'You want to be the idol of the Convention. You want to get up and make big speeches and cover yourself in glory. Well, let me tell you, there's a lot more to it than that.'

'You'll make yourself ill if you go on like this.'

'You blame me for turning to Saint-Just for support. At least he doesn't make his personal pleasures a touchstone for the Revolution.'

'Who said I did that?'

'You will at least, I hope, try to be civil to me in public?'

'I shall be positively affectionate,' Danton promised.

Robespierre left his door in a government conveyance. Two large men climbed in beside him. 'Bodyguards,' Danton said, watching from the window. 'They were forced upon him in the end. He was suspected of a plot to put his dog on the Committee of Public

Safety. Actually, he'd quite like to be assassinated.' He stretched out a hand for Louise. 'It would be the crowning glory of the hard, miserable life he's made for himself.'

ON THE DAY of the demonstration, the sansculotte leader Jacques Roux was arrested. For some time no proceedings were taken against him, but when in the end he was called before the Tribunal he killed himself in his cell. September saw the institution of Terror as a form of government. The new constitution was to be suspended till the end of the war. On 13 September, Danton proposed that all committees be renewed, and that in future their members be appointed by the Committee of Public Safety. There was a moment when he and Robespierre stood together, as if to acknowledge jointly the applause of the Mountain. 'All right?' he said to Robespierre, and Robespierre answered calmly, 'Yes, that's fine.'

The decree was passed. The moment passed. And now, thought Danton, we ought to be able to bow and walk off stage. Weariness like a parasite seemed to burst into flower from his bones.

The following morning he found he could hardly lift his head from the pillow. He could not remember anything about the previous day. His memory had been taken out, and replaced by a leaden, pulsating pain. A few incidents floated across the pain – disconnected, some from years back. He did not know the date. He thought he saw Gabrielle come into the room, look down at him, smooth his pillow. Only later he remembered that Gabrielle was dead.

Several doctors came. They argued with each other as if their lives depended on it. When Angélique arrived, Louise crumpled into a little sniffling heap on a sofa. Angélique sent the children off to their uncle, and made Louise drink warm milk. Then she routed the doctors. Souberbielle remained. 'He should get out of Paris,' he said. 'A man like that needs to breathe his own air. He has spent all his adult life going against the grain. He has abused his strength, wrecked his constitution.'

'He will get better?' Louise said.

'Oh yes. But he must recover himself outside this city. The

Convention must give him leave of absence. Citizeness, may I advise you?'

'Of course.'

'While he is ill, don't discuss his affairs with anyone. Don't trust anyone to have his interests at heart.'

'I don't.'

'Stay out of arguments. It's known, Citizeness, that you like to air your views. By doing so, you increase the stress on him.'

'I only speak as my conscience dictates. Perhaps this illness is providential. He must give up the Revolution.'

'It's not so simple. My dear, you were twelve years old when the Bastille fell.'

'Gabrielle was weak.'

'That was not my view of her. She confined herself to her sphere.'

'I want to rescue him from himself.'

'Strange,' the doctor said. 'Robespierre has the same ambition.'

'You know Robespierre?'

'Pretty well.'

'Is he a good man?'

'He is honest and scrupulous and he tries to save lives.'

'At the cost of certain other lives.'

'That is sometimes unavoidable. He regrets it.'

'Do you think he *likes* my husband?'

The doctor shrugged. 'I hardly know. They're different types of men completely. Does it matter?'

Of course it matters, she muttered to herself, as he took his leave. The doctors were replaced by Angélique's daughters-in-law, strong and decisive women whom she hardly knew. They chivvied her about and sent her upstairs, to sleep in her old room. She crept out and sat on the stairs. She almost expected to see Gabrielle, returning to her sphere. You're not pregnant, are you? her mother asked her. She could see the way her mother's mind was working; if something's really wrong, if he takes a turn for the worse, if he dies, how fast can we extricate her? If I'm not pregnant, she said, it's not for the want of trying. Her mother shuddered. He is a savage, she said.

David of the Police Committee called, with another deputy, and demanded to see Danton on business. Angélique showed them the door. As they departed, with certain ungallant threats, squawking about their authorization, Angélique said something dark in Italian. They don't, she said, plan that he should have an easy time when he recovers.

AT THE DESMOULINS'S apartment, Fabre sat and worked himself into a panic. 'If we are to have fixed prices,' he said, 'then we must have fixed wages. What I want to know is, what's the official daily rate for a spy? How, please, are we going to win any battles when so much of the able-bodied population is employed in spying for the Committee?'

'Are they spying on you?'

'Of course they are.'

'Have you told Robespierre?'

Fabre looked at him wildly. 'Tell him how? Tell him what? My affairs are so complicated that I lie awake at night trying to explain them to myself. I am being harassed. I am being forced into difficulties. Do you think that officious chit will let me see Georges?'

'No. Anyway, why should he listen? If you can't tell Robespierre, why should Georges concern himself?'

'There are reasons.'

'You mean you've already dragged his name into it.'

'No. I mean he is under certain obligations to me.'

'I should have thought it was the other way around, and I should have thought that one of your obligations would have been to keep him out of any consequences of your inept fumbling with the stock market.'

'There's more to it than that, it's – '

'Fabre, don't tell me. I'd rather not know.'

'It won't be any use your saying that to the police.'

Camille put his finger to his lips. Lucile came in. 'I heard,' she said.

'Just Fabre's shock tactics. He loses his head.'

'That is an unfortunate phrase,' Lucile said.

Fabre jumped up. 'You're persecuting me. Your hands aren't so clean. My God,' he said. He drew his finger across his throat. 'When you fall between two stools, Camille, nobody's going to help you up. They're just going to stand and laugh.'

'He waxes metaphorical,' Lucile said.

'The whole thing – ' Fabre made a shape with his hands, and then exploded it – 'the whole thing is splitting apart like rotten fruit.' Suddenly he was beside himself. 'For God's sake, Camille, put in a good word for me with Robespierre.'

'Yes, all right,' Camille said hurriedly. He wanted to placate him, stop him continuing the scene in front of Lucile. 'Do keep your voice down, the servants can hear you. What do you want me to say to Robespierre?'

'If my name should come up,' Fabre said, breathing hard, 'just drop into the conversation that I've – that I've always been a patriot.'

'Sit down and calm yourself,' Lucile suggested.

Fabre looked round, distractedly. He seized his hat. 'Got to go. Beg your pardon, Lucile. See myself out.'

Camille followed him. 'Philippe,' he whispered, 'there are a lot of what Robespierre calls small fry who have to be landed before you need worry. Try to ride this out.'

Fabre's mouth opened a fraction. 'Why did you call me that? Why did you call me by my first name?'

Camille smiled. 'Take care,' he said.

He returned to Lucile. 'What were you whispering?' she asked.

'Consolation.'

'You are not to keep things from me, please. What has he done?'

'In August – you have heard of the East India Company? Good, because we have made quite a lot of money out of it. You remember the share prices fell, then they went up again – it was just a matter of buying and selling at the right time.'

'My father mentioned it. He said he expected you did very well out of it. My father has some respect for your inside information, but he says, in my day, of course, they would simply have been called crooks, but in my day the august and virtuous members of the National Convention didn't exist to set these things up for each other.'

'Yes, I can imagine your father saying that. Does he know how it was managed?'

'Probably. But don't try and explain it to me. Just tell me the consequences.'

'The company was to be liquidated. There was a discussion in the Convention about how it was to be done. Perhaps the liquidation was not carried out in quite the way the Convention intended. I don't know.'

'But you do know, really?'

'Not the details. It does seem that Fabre may have broken the law – which we didn't do in our earlier dealings – or he may be about to break it.'

'But he spoke as if you were threatened, and Danton.'

'Danton might be implicated. Fabre is saying, you understand, that investigation into Danton's affairs might not be a good thing.'

'Surely,' she struggled for some tactful way of putting it, 'wouldn't Danton evade – I mean, he's adept at shifting the blame?'

'Fabre is his friend, you see. When we were at the ministry I tried to warn him that Fabre was exceeding what were more or less agreed limits. He said, "Fabre is my friend and we've been through a lot together. We know a lot about each other too."'

'So Georges will protect him?'

'I don't know. I don't want either of them to tell me anything about it. If they do I will feel bound to tell Robespierre, who will feel bound to tell the Committee.'

'Perhaps you should. Tell Robespierre. If there's any danger you could be dragged into it, it might be better if you were the one to uncover it.'

'But that would be helping the Committee. And I don't feel like helping the Committee.'

'If the Committee is our only chance of firm government, isn't it irresponsible not to help it?'

'I loathe firm government.'

'When will the big trials begin?'

'Soon. Danton won't be able to hold things up now, he's too ill. And Robespierre won't, not on his own.'

'I suppose we still welcome the trials?'

'How not? Royalists, Brissotins . . .'

LAW OF SUSPECTS. Suspects are those who: have in any way aided tyranny (royal tyranny, Brissotin tyranny . . .): who cannot show that they have performed their civic duties: who do not starve, and yet have no visible means of support: who have been refused certificates of citizenship by their Sections: who have been removed from public office by the Convention or its representatives: who belong to an aristocratic family, and have not given proof of constant and extraordinary revolutionary fervour: or who have emigrated.

It will be alleged later (by Citizen Desmoulins) that 200,000 people are detained under this law. The Watch Committee in each Section is to draw up lists of suspects, take away their papers and detain them in a secure place. These places will be called 'National Buildings' – convents, vacated châteaux, empty warehouses. Collot d'Herbois has a better idea. He suggests that suspects be herded into mined houses, which can then be blown up.

Since he became a member, Collot no longer criticizes the Committee of Public Safety. When he enters the Committee's chambers, Citizen Robespierre leaves, if he can, by another door.

DECREE of the National Convention: 'The government of France is revolutionary until the peace . . . Terror is the order of the day.'

ANTOINE SAINT-JUST: 'You must punish anyone who is passive in the affairs of the Revolution and who does nothing for it.'

'SO THEY'VE CHANGED the calendar,' Danton said. 'It's too much for an invalid.'

'Yes,' Camille said. 'The week now has ten days. It is tidier, and very good for the war effort. Our dates now run from the foundation of the Republic, so we are in Month I, Year II. But Fabre has been asked to think up some ridiculous poetic names for the months. He plans that the first should be Vendémiaire. Then today,' Camille frowned, 'yes, today would be 19 Vendémiaire.'

'In my household, it remains 10 October.'

'You had better learn it. We are supposed to put it on official letters.'

'I have no plans,' Danton said, 'for writing official letters.'

He was out of bed, but he spoke and moved slowly; occasionally he let his head fall against the back of his chair, and closed his eyes for a moment.

'Tell me about the battle near Dunkirk,' he said. 'When I left the world, it was being hailed as a great victory for the Republic. Now I hear that General Houchard is under arrest.'

'The Committee and the War Office put their heads together. They decided he could have inflicted more damage on the enemy. They are charging him with treason.'

'And yet it was the Committee who appointed him. There were scenes in the Convention, I suppose.'

'Yes, but Robespierre had the best of it.'

'He has become a very good committeeman.'

'He undertook it, and he does everything well.'

'I must leave him to it. They say I am fit to travel now. Will you come out to Arcis, as soon as you have a few spare days?'

'There are no spare days.'

'I know that dire turn of phrase. You have been seeing too much of Robespierre.'

'Georges, do you know about Deputy Julien?'

'No.'

'Does Louise let you have no news?'

'I don't think that anything that Julien did would seem of the least importance to her. I don't think she knows he exists.'

'The police have raided his apartment. They've impounded his papers.'

He opened his eyes. 'And?'

'Chabot took me aside. He said, "I've burned everything, you know." I imagine that was a message I was meant to pass on to you.'

Danton hunched his body forward. Attention broke into his eyes: like the shattering of glass. 'Fabre?'

'Fabre has been panicking.'

'Fabre has an excitable temperament.'

'So have I, Georges-Jacques, so have I. What am I expected to do? I think Fabre has committed a forgery. When the East India Company was liquidated, I think certain documents were falsified in the company's interests. These documents were decrees of the Convention, and only a deputy would be able to do it. Chabot is involved, perhaps half a dozen other people. They themselves don't know, I think, who did the actual falsification. Julien might blame Chabot, Chabot might blame Julien. They have secrets, one from the other.'

'But Fabre has confessed to you?'

'He's tried. I won't let him. I tell him I mustn't know. What I am telling you is just what I have been able to work out. It will take longer for the police to come to their conclusions. And to collect evidence, that will take longer still.'

Danton closed his eyes. 'The harvest will be in,' he said. 'We have nothing to do but to keep ourselves warm for the winter.'

'There are other things you should know.'

'Get them over with.'

'François Robert is in trouble. Does she tell you nothing?'

'She wouldn't know that was important, either. He isn't involved in this?'

'No – it's the most ridiculous thing – he's been accused of dealing on the black market. Eight barrels of rum. For his shop.'

'For Christ's sake,' Danton said. He hit the arm of his chair. 'You offer them a chance to make history, and they prefer to remain grocers.'

Louise ran in. 'You were not to upset him!'

'I line their pockets. I don't ask them to exert themselves. I raise them to office and I accede to their little whims. All I ask is their vote, an occasional speech – and that if they choose to become petty criminals they leave me out of it.'

'The rum is petty. The East India Company is not. But still,

François Robert is our associate. It reflects on us. Will you send your wife away, please?'

'You were told to keep calm,' she said mutinously.

'You can leave us, Louise. I'll be calm. I promise. I'm quite calm now.'

'What are you trying to keep from me?'

'No one is keeping anything from you,' Camille said. 'It is not worth the trouble.'

'She's a child. She doesn't understand. She doesn't know who these people are.'

'It was our own Section, the Cordeliers, who denounced François. The Convention agreed with you that it was petty. They refused to lift his immunity. Otherwise – the penalties are severe. He and Louise will have to creep away now and try to be forgotten.'

'What a way to end up,' Danton said. His expression was morose. 'I think back to those days after the Bastille fell, the *Mercure Nationale* run from the back of the shop, that little Louise sticking her well-bred nose in the air and flouncing off to bawl out their printer – and you know, he was a good lad, François. I'd say, "Go and do this, this, this, go and tie some bricks to your boots and jump in the Seine," and he'd' – Danton touched an imaginary forelock – ' "right away, Georges-Jacques, and do you need any shopping while I'm out?" Jesus, what a way to end up. When you see him, tell him I'd be obliged if he forgets he knows me.'

'I don't see him,' Camille said.

'Our own Section, Camille. Oh, I should have left the Jacobins to Robespierre, and stayed on my own side of the river. I should have hung on to power in my own district. Who runs it now? Hébert. We old Cordeliers should have stuck together.'

They were silent for a moment. We old Cordeliers . . . It's four years since the Bastille fell, four years and three months. It feels like twenty. Danton sits here, overweight, his brow permanently furrowed, God knows what going on amid his internal organs. Robespierre's asthma is worse, and one can't help noticing that his hairline is receding. Hérault's fresh complexion is not so fresh as it used to be, and the double chin on which Lucile passed a damning judgement promises a jowly, disappointing middle-age. Fabre has developed breathing difficulties; as for Camille, his headaches are worse, and he can hardly keep any flesh on his small bones. He looks up at Danton now: 'Georges-Jacques, do you know a man called Comte? Just tell me yes or no.'

'Yes. I employed him as an agent in Normandy, on government business. Why?'

'Because he has turned up here in Paris and made a certain allegation. That you were in league with Brissot's people, to put the Duke of York on our throne.'

'The Duke of York? Lord,' Danton said bitterly, 'I thought only Robespierre could dream up anything so wholly fantastic as the Duke of York.'

'Robespierre was deeply disturbed.'

Danton looked up slowly. 'He gave it credence?'

'No, of course not. He said it was a conspiracy to discredit a patriot. It is a good thing that we still have Hérault on the Committee, though. He had Comte arrested before he could do any more damage. It was because of this that David called on you, on behalf of the Police Committee. Just a formality.'

'I see. "Morning, Danton – are you a traitor?" "Certainly not, David – do run away back to your easel." "I'll do that – left a daub half-finished. Get well soon!" That sort of formality? And I suppose that for Robespierre, it's fuel to his flames? It feeds his notions of gigantic conspiracies?'

'Yes. We suppose Comte must be a British agent. After all, we reason with ourselves – we stretch our imaginations to suppose that it might be true – and then we reason with ourselves, how would this nonentity Comte, this servant, this menial, know anything of the plans of a man like Danton? That is how we reason, Robespierre and I.'

'I know what you mean, Camille,' Louise said warningly. 'Why don't you ask him straight out if there is anything in it?'

'Because it is absurd.' Camille lost his temper. 'Because I have other loyalties, and if it is true, they will kill him.'

Louise stepped back. Her hand fluttered to her throat. Camille saw her difficulty at once: she wanted and didn't want him dead.

'Louise, take no notice,' Danton said. 'Go now and make sure our packing is done.' Tiredness crept back into his voice. 'You must learn a little better to distinguish – it is a ridiculous story. It is as Robespierre says. It is a slander.'

She hesitated. 'We're still going to Arcis?'

'Of course. I have written to them to expect us.'

She left the room.

'I have to go,' Danton said. 'I must recover my health. Without that, nothing.'

'Yes, of course you must go.' Camille averted his face. 'You are avoiding the big trials, are you not?'

'Come here.' Danton puts out a hand to him. Camille pretends not to see it. 'I'm sick of the city,' Danton says. 'I'm sick of people. Why don't you come with me, get a change of air?' He thinks, I've lost him, I've lost him, lost him to Robespierre and that rarefied climate of perpetual chill.

'I'll write to you,' Camille says. He crosses the room, touches his lips to Danton's cheekbone. It feels like the least that can be done.

IT WAS LATE when they reached Arcis, and growing cold. As soon as his feet touched the ground, he felt the power draining from the sun, the soil losing its summer warmth. He put out an arm for Louise. 'Here,' he said. 'Here is where I was born.'

Pulling her travelling cape about her, she looked up wonderingly at the manor house, at the milky darkness rolling in from the river. 'No, not here,' he said, 'not in this very house. But close by. Come now,' he said to the children. 'You've come to your grandmother. You remember?'

Silly question. Somehow Georges always thinks his children are older than they are, he expects them to have long memories. François-Georges was a year old when his mother died; now, a big tough baby, he clung to his stepmother and lashed his heels about her fragile ribcage. Antoine, limp and exhausted by the excitement, hung around his father's neck like a child fetched up from a shipwreck.

Anne Madeleine's husband held a torch high. And there she was – it was Louise's first sight of these alarming sisters – running and tripping over her feet, like some schoolgirl. 'Georges, Georges, my brother Georges!' She hurled herself at him. His arm encircled her. She pushed her hair out of her eyes, kissed him on both cheeks, broke away and scooped up the nearest of her children and held up the little boy for his inspection. This was Anne Madeleine, who had pulled him out from under the bull's feet.

And here was Marie-Cécile; her convent had dispersed, she was home, she was where she should be: didn't he say he'd look after her? She still had her nun's deportment; she tried to fold her hands away in the sleeves of a habit she no longer wore. And here was Pierrette, tall, smiling, full-faced, a spinster more matronly than most of the mothers of Paris; Anne Madeleine's latest baby dribbled on to her shoulder. They surrounded Louise and squeezed her; they felt, as they did so, the ghost promise of Gabrielle's opulent flesh. 'My little dove!' they said, laughing. 'You are so young!'

They dived away, the sisters, into the kitchen. 'Bleak little thing! So duty-ridden! No breasts at all!'

'Didn't you think he'd bring that Lucile-thing? That black-eyed girl? That he'd detach her from her black-eyed husband?'

'No, that evil pair, they were born for each other.' The sisters fell about, laughing. The visit of the Desmoulins had been one of the high points of their lives; they couldn't wait for them to come back again, creating a similar metropolitan *frisson*.

They began to play out the scene taking place between Georges-Jacques and their mother: 'It's a comfort,' croaked Marie-Cécile, 'to see you again before I die.'

'Die?' Anne Madeleine said. 'You old fraud, you'll not die. You'll outlive me, I swear it.'

'And how Georges-Jacques does swear!' said Pierrette. 'How he does! Do you think he's fallen into bad company?'

In the parlour of the manor house, Mme Recordain's blue eyes were sparkling into the dusk. 'Come in from the night air, daughter. Sit here by me.' Diagnostic fingers studded themselves into her waist. Two months! And not pregnant! The Italian girl, who was dead, did her duty by Georges-Jacques – now we have one of these skimpy Parisiennes on our hands.

As if fearing that this examination might be taking place, the sisters came surging out from somewhere in the depth of the house. They swarmed about their brother, proposing various kinds of food he might eat, patting his head and making family jokes – soft-bodied countrywomen, in their strange, dowdy, practical clothes.

'IT MIGHT BE BETTER if you were the one to uncover it.' Fabre had not heard Lucile say this, but it was his own thought. On the day Danton left Paris he sat alone in his apartment, fighting his desire to shriek and smash and hammer the walls, like a bad child to whom promises have been broken. He took up again the brief, polite non-committal note that Danton had sent around before his departure; he tore it into tiny strips and burned it shred by shred.

After a tiring and disputatious meeting of the Jacobin Club, he intercepted Robespierre and Saint-Just as they walked side by side from the hall. Saint-Just did not attend assiduously at the evening meetings; he thought the sessions pointless, though he did not say so, and to himself he called the members, opinion-mongers. He was not much interested in anyone's opinions. In a few days he would be in Alsace, with the armies. He was looking forward to it.

'Citizens.' Fabre beckoned. 'Word with you?'

The irritation on Saint-Just's face deepened. Robespierre thought of the pretty new calendar, and fetched up a wintery smile.

'Please?' Fabre said. 'Something of extreme importance. Would you grant me a private interview?'

'Is it a lengthy matter?' Robespierre asked politely.

'Now look, Fabre,' Saint-Just said, 'we're busy.' Robespierre had to smile again at young Antoine's tone: *Max is my friend and we're not playing with you.* He half-expected that Fabre would step back a pace and survey Saint-Just through his lorgnette. But that didn't happen; pale, clumsily urgent, Fabre solicited his attention. Saint-Just's rudeness had thrown him off balance. 'I have to see the Committee,' he said. 'This is business for them.'

'Then don't shout about it.'

'Only conspirators whisper.' Seeing his chance, Fabre recovered suddenly into a grand resonance. 'Soon the whole Republic must know my news.'

Saint-Just looked at him with distaste. 'We are not on the stage,' he observed.

Robespierre darted a glance at Saint-Just, rather shocked. 'You're right, Fabre. If your news concerns the Republic, it must be broadcast.' At the same time, he looked around swiftly to see who had heard.

'It is a matter of public safety.'

'Then he must come to the Committee.'

'No,' Saint-Just said. 'Tonight's agenda will keep us working till dawn. There is no single item that is not a matter of extreme urgency. There is nothing that can be postponed, and I, Citizen Fabre, have to be at my desk by nine tomorrow.'

Fabre ignored him, and took Robespierre by the arm. 'I have to reveal a conspiracy.' Robespierre's eyes widened. 'However, it will not mature overnight – if we move with energy tomorrow, there will be time enough. Young Citizen Saint-Just needs his rest. He is not accustomed to watching late, like we elder patriots.'

It was a mistake. Robespierre looked at him icily. 'I happen to be informed, Citizen Fabre, that most of your watching late is done in a gambling house whose existence is unknown to the patriots of the Commune, in the company of Citizen Desmoulins's winning streak and several women of dubious reputation.'

'For the love of God,' Fabre said, 'take me seriously.'

Robespierre considered him. 'Is it a complicated conspiracy?'

'Its ramifications are enormous.'

'Very well. Citizen Saint-Just and myself meet tomorrow with the Committee of General Security.'

'I know.'

'Will that be suitable?'

'The Police Committee will be most suitable. It will expedite matters.'

'I see. We meet at – '

'I know.'

'I see. Good-night.'

Saint-Just shifted from foot to foot. 'Robespierre, you're expected. The Committee will be waiting.'

'They will not, I hope,' Robespierre said. 'They will be getting on with the business, I hope. No one should be waited for. No one is indispensable.' But he followed.

'The man is untrustworthy,' Saint-Just said. 'He is theatrical. He is hysterical. I have no doubt that this conspiracy is a figment of his too-active imagination.'

'He is a friend of Danton's and a proven patriot,' Robespierre corrected snappily. 'He is a great poet.' He brooded as they walked. 'I am inclined to credit what he says. He was very white in the face, and he had not his lorgnette.'

IT SEEMED, it seemed all too credible. Taut, quiet, motionless, his hands palm down on the table, Robespierre took over the interrogation. He had moved from a corner of the table to a place directly opposite Fabre, and the committeemen, moving fast, had clumsily scraped their chairs out of his way; now they sat silent, skipping to the beat of his intuitions. He would ask sharply for Fabre to stop; he would make a note, and then wiping his pen and putting it aside deliberately he would spread out his fingers on the table top and glance up at Fabre to indicate that he should begin again.

Fabre slumped in his chair. 'And when,' he said, 'within a month, Chabot comes to you and says, there is a plot, I hope you will remember who first gave you these names.'

'You,' Robespierre said, 'shall interrogate him.'

Fabre swallowed. 'Citizen,' he said, 'I am very sorry to be the agent of your disillusionment. You must have believed many of these people to be staunch patriots?'

'I?' Robespierre looked up with a small joyless smile. 'I already have the names of these foreigners in my notebooks. Anyone may see them. That they were corrupt and dangerous I was well aware, but now you speak to me of systematic conspiracy, of money from Pitt – do you think I don't see it clearly, and more clearly than any of you do? The economic sabotage, the extremist policies which they advocate at the Jacobins and the Cordeliers, the blasphemous, intolerant attacks on the Christian religion, which disturb the good people and turn them away from the new order – do you think I suppose these things are not related?'

'No,' Fabre said. 'No, I should have realized that you would make the connection for yourself. You intend to order arrests?'

'I think not.' Robespierre looked around the table, expecting no contradiction. 'As we are fully aware of their manoeuvres now, we can afford to let them exhaust themselves in their labours for a week or two.' He glanced around again. 'In that way we will discover all their accomplices. We will purify the Revolution once and for all. Have you heard enough?' One or two people nodded, their faces strained, at a loss. 'I haven't, but we won't take up any more of your time.' He stood up, tapping his papers together with his fingertips. 'Come,' he said to Fabre.

'Come?' Fabre said stupidly.

Robespierre motioned with his head towards the door. Fabre got up and followed him. He felt weak and shaky. Robespierre turned into a small room, barely furnished, rather like the one they had occupied on the day of the late riot.

'Do you often work in here?'

'As occasion demands. I like to have somewhere private. You can sit down, it's not dusty.'

Fabre saw an army of locksmiths, window-cleaners, old women with brooms, scouring the attics and cellars of public buildings to make clean hiding-places for Robespierre. 'Leave the door open,' Robespierre said, 'as a precaution against eavesdroppers.' He tossed his notes on to the table; Fabre thought, that's an acquired gesture, he got that from Camille. 'You seem nervous,' Robespierre commented.

'What – I mean, what more would you like me to tell you?'

'Just whatever you like.' Robespierre was accommodating. 'Minor points we could clear up now. The real names of the brothers Frei.'

'Emmanuel Dobruska. Siegmund Gotleb.'

'I'm not surprised they changed them, are you?'

'Why didn't you ask me in front of the others?'

Robespierre ignored him. 'This man Proli, Hérault's secretary, we see him at the Jacobins. Some people say that he is the natural son of Chancellor Kaunitz of Austria. Is that true?'

'Yes. Well, quite possibly.'

'Hérault is an anomaly. He's an aristocrat by birth, yet he is never attacked by Hébert.' Hérault, Fabre thinks: and his mind drifts back – as it tends to, these days – to the Café du Foy. He'd been giving readings from his latest – *Augusta* was dying the death at the Italiens – and in came this huge, rough-looking boy, shoe-horned into a lawyer's black suit, whom he'd made a sketch of in the street, ten years before. The boy had developed this upper-class drawl, and he'd talked about Hérault – 'his looks are impeccable, he's well-travelled, he's pursued by all the ladies at Court' – and beside Danton had been this fey, wide-eyed egotist who had turned out to be half the city's extramarital interest. The years pass ... *plus ça change, plus c'est la même chose* ... 'Fabre, are you with me?' said Robespierre.

'Oh, very much so.'

Robespierre leaned forward and plaited his fingers together; and Fabre, dragged up from the deeps of '87, '88, began to sweat. He heard what Robespierre was saying, and it was enough to chill the blood. 'As Hérault is never attacked by Hébert, I feel they must have a common allegiance. Hébert's people are not just misguided fanatics – they are in touch with all these foreign elements you denounce. The object of their violent speeches and actions is to produce fear and disgust. They set out to make the Revolution appear ridiculous, and to destroy its credibility.'

'Yes,' Fabre looked away. 'I understand that.'

'Hand in hand with this go the attempts to discredit great patriots. For example, the allegations against Danton.'

'It is clear,' Fabre said.

'One wonders why such conspirators should approach you.'

Fabre shook his head: wonderingly, glumly. 'They have already met with some success, in the very heart of the Mountain. I suppose it encourages them. Chabot, Julien ... all trusted men. Naturally, when these are examined, they will claim I'm implicated.'

'Our orders to you,' Robespierre put his fingertips together, 'are to keep a careful eye on those people you've named – especially those you suspect of economic crimes.'

'Yes,' Fabre said. 'Er – whose orders?'

Robespierre looked up, surprised. 'The Committee's.'

'Of course. I should have known you spoke for all.' Fabre leaned forward. 'Citizen, I beg you not to be taken in by anything Chabot says. He and his friends are very glib and plausible.'

'You think I'm a complete fool, do you, Fabre?'

'I beg your pardon.'

'You may go now.'

'Thank you. Trust me. Over the next month you'll see everything come to fruition.'

Robespierre dismissed him with a wave of his hand, as thoughtlessly peremptory as any anointed despot. Outside the door Fabre took out a silk handkerchief and dabbed his face. It had been the most unpleasant morning of his life – if you excepted the morning in 1777 when he'd been sentenced to hang – and yet in another way it had been easier than he'd expected. Robespierre had swallowed every suggestion, as if they merely confirmed conclusions he had already reached. 'This foreign plot,' he'd kept saying. Clearly he was interested in the politics, and hardly at all in the East India Company. And will it, as he promised, come to fruition? Oh yes: because you can rely on Hébert to rant, on Chabot to cheat and lie and steal, on Chaumette to harass priests and close down churches – and now, every time they speak they'll condemn themselves out of their own mouths; all these separate strands he sees as knotted together in conspiracy, and who knows, perhaps they are, perhaps they are. A pity he suspects Hérault. I could warn him, but what use? Life anyway is so precarious for the *ci-devants*, perhaps his days were already numbered.

And the main thing is this – *he trusts Danton*. I'm Danton's man. And so perhaps I've cleared myself. By telling him what he wants to hear.

Saint-Just smiled when he saw him. I'm in favour, he thought. Then he noticed the expression in his eyes. 'Is Robespierre in there?'

'Yes, yes, I've just come from him.'

Saint-Just shouldered past. He had to flatten himself against the wall. 'Leave the door open as a precaution against eavesdroppers,' he called. Saint-Just slammed it behind him. Fabre began to hum. He was working on a new play called *The Maltese Orange*, and it suddenly came to him that he might turn it into an operetta.

Inside the room Robespierre looked up. 'I thought you were getting ready for your trip to the frontier?'

'Tomorrow.'

'What do you think?'

'Of Fabre's plot? It fits all your preconceived ideas. I wonder if he knows that?'

Robespierre bridled. 'You cast doubt on it?'

'Any pretext,' Saint-Just said, 'will do to rid us of foreigners and speculators and Hébertists. As long as you bear in mind that Fabre himself is unlikely to be free from blame.'

'So you don't trust him.'

Saint-Just laughed; as much as he ever did laugh. 'The man's old in deception. You're aware that he calls himself "d'Églantine" in commemoration of a literary prize from the Academy of Toulouse?' Robespierre nodded. 'In the year when he claims to have taken the prize, no prize was awarded.'

'I see.' Robespierre looked away: a delicate, sly, side-long glance. 'You could not be mistaken?'

Saint-Just flushed. 'Of course not. I've inquired. I've checked the records.'

'No doubt,' Robespierre said meekly, 'he thought he ought to have won the prize. No doubt he thought he had been cheated.'

'The man's founded his whole life on a lie!'

'Perhaps more a self-delusion.' Robespierre smiled distantly. 'After all, despite what I said, he's not a great poet. Just a mediocre one. This is petty, Saint-Just. How much time have you wasted on it?' The satisfaction wiped itself out of Saint-Just's face. 'You know,' Robespierre went on, 'I'd have liked to win one of those literary prizes myself – something distinguished, not local stuff – Toulouse or somewhere.'

'But those prizes were institutions of the old regime.' Saint-Just sounded hurt. 'That's done with, finished. It's from before the Revolution.'

'There was such a time, you know.'

'You are too much wedded to the manners and appearances of the old regime.'

'That,' Robespierre said, 'is a very serious accusation.'

Saint-Just looked as if he would rather back down. Robespierre rose from his chair. He was the shorter by perhaps six inches. 'Do you wish to replace me, with someone more thoroughly revolutionary?'

'I have no such thought, I protest.'

'I feel you wish to replace me.'

'This is a mistake.'

'If you attempt to replace me, I will look for your part in this plot and I will demand your head in the Convention.'

Saint-Just raised his eyebrows. 'You are deluded,' he said. 'I am going to the armies.'

Robespierre's voice reached out to him as he crashed out of the room: 'I've known about Fabre's prize for years. Camille told me. We laughed about it. What does it matter? Am I the only one who knows what matters? Am I the only one with any sense of proportion at all?'

MAXIMILIEN ROBESPIERRE: 'Over the last two years, 100,000 men have been slain as a result of treason and weakness; it is our feeble attitude towards traitors that is our undoing.'

THE PALAIS de Justice: 'You seem unhappy, cousin,' Camille said.

Fouquier-Tinville shrugged. His dark face was morose. 'We've been in court for eighteen hours. Yesterday we started at eight in the morning and finished at eleven at night. It is tiring.'

'Imagine what it's like for the prisoner.'

'I really can't imagine that,' the Public Prosecutor said truthfully. 'Is it a fine night?' he asked. 'I could do with some fresh air.'

He had no feelings, one way or the other, about trying women on capital charges; he was sensitive, however, to the questions it raised in some minds. The guillotine allowed some dignity in death; the ordeal came beforehand. He liked his prisoners in better condition than this one – scruffy, in need of medical attention. He had organized a man to stand by and fetch her glasses of water, but so far water had not been needed, and neither had the smelling-salts. It was after midnight now; a jury retiring at this hour were unlikely to agonize over their verdict.

'Hébert, yesterday,' he said abruptly. 'Terrible mess. What he has to do with it, why I had to call him, God knows. I take a pride in my work. I'm a family man – I don't want to hear that sort of thing. The woman showed dignity in her replies. She got sympathy from the crowd.'

Hébert had alleged yesterday that, in addition to her other crimes, the woman prisoner had sexually abused her nine-year-old son; that she had taken him into bed beside her, and taught him to masturbate. His guardians had caught him at it, Hébert said, and – tut-tut, where did you learn such behaviour? Mama taught me, said the shifty, frightened little boy. Hébert adduced documentary evidence – the child had freely signed a statement about it. The child's writing – the ancient, wavering hand – had given Citizen Fouquier a moment's disquiet. 'One has children oneself,' he murmured. Citizen Robespierre had done more than murmur. 'That fool Hébert!' he said, enraged. 'Has any more unlikely allegation come before a court in our lifetime? Depend on it – he'll save the woman yet.'

I wonder, Fouquier thought, what sort of a lawyer was Citizen Robespierre, when he practised? A bleeding heart, I'll be bound.

He was turning back to his cousin when President Hermann appeared, crossing the hall from the darkness into the pool of candlelight that bathed the lawyers, the prisoner's chair and the empty place where the witnesses stood. The president held up one finger for Fouquier to follow him.

'Have a word with Chauveau-Lagarde,' Fouquier said. 'Poor devil, he defended the Marat girl too. I doubt his career will ever recover.'

Lagarde looked up. 'Camille – what are you doing here? I wouldn't be here if I could be anywhere else.' Still, he was glad to see him. He was tired of trying to talk to his client. She was not forthcoming.

'Where else should I be? Some of us have waited a long time for this day.'

'Yes – well, if it suits you.'

'I should think it suits us all to see treason punished.'

'You're pre-judging. The jury are still out.'

'There's no chance the Republic will lose this case,' Camille said. He smiled. 'They do give you all the best jobs, don't they?'

'No lawyer in Paris has more experience of impossible defences.' Lagarde was twenty-eight years old; he tried to put the best face on things. 'I asked for mercy,' he said. 'What else could I do? She was accused of being what she was. She was charged with having existed. There was no defence to the charges. Even if there had been – they gave me the indictment on Sunday night, and said you're in court tomorrow morning. I asked your cousin for three days. No chance When her husband was tried, those were more leisurely times. And when she goes to her death, she'll go in a cart.'

'The closed carriage was somewhat undemocratic, I feel. This is something the people have a right to see.'

Lagarde looked at him sideways. 'Hard bastards they breed in your part of the country.' Yet one could understand them, he thought, one could find them – it was a sign of the times – quite reassuring: deadpan Fouquier, lawyer's lawyer, and his volatile, highly placed relative who had got him the job. One could find them preferable to some of the Republic's servants – preferable to Hébert, with his obscene mouthings, his maggot whiteness. There had been times during yesterday's session when he had felt physically sick.

'I know who you're thinking of,' Camille said. 'That expression commonly crosses people's faces. I suspect that Hébert has laid his paws on War Office money, and if I find the proof he'll be one of your next big clients.'

Fouquier hurried over. 'The jury are returning,' he said. 'My commiserations in advance, Lagarde.'

The prisoner was helped across the hall to her chair. One moment she was in darkness; the next moment, light struck her lined and shattered face.

'She seems old,' Camille said. 'She seems hardly able to see where she's going. I didn't know her eyesight was so poor.'

'I can hardly be blamed for that,' the Public Prosecutor said. 'Though no doubt,' he added with foresight, 'when I am dead, people will blame me for it. Excuse me, cousin, please.'

The verdict was unanimous. Leaning forward, Hermann asked the prisoner if she had anything to say. The former Queen of France shook her head. Her fingers moved impatiently on the arm of her chair. Hermann pronounced the death sentence.

The court rose. Guards moved forward to take the prisoner out. Fouquier didn't watch her go. His cousin hurried to help him with his pile of papers. 'Easy day tomorrow,' Fouquier said. 'Here, take these. Somehow you'd think that the Public Prosecutor would have a clerk available.'

Hermann nodded civilly to Camille, and Fouquier bade the president good-night. Camille's eyes were on the widow Capet's shuffling withdrawal. 'It hardly seems much, really, to be the summit of our ambitions. Cutting some dreary woman's head off.'

'I swear you are changeable, Camille. I've never known you give the Austrian a good word. Come. I usually preserve my dignity in my official carriage, but I need some air. Unless you are reporting to Robespierre?'

He was always proud of his cousin, when they were together in public. Especially when he saw him with Danton — he noted those private allusions they shared, the jokes, the sidelong glances, and he saw, as often as not, Danton's beefy arm draped around his cousin, or his cousin in some late-night public assembly close his dangerous eyes and lean comfortably against Danton's shoulder. With Robespierre, of course, it was not like that. Robespierre almost never touched anyone. His face was distant, aloof. But Camille could conjure on to it an expression of lively amiability; they shared memories, and possibly too they shared private jokes. People said — though this felt like a heresy — that they had seen Camille make Robespierre laugh.

Now his cousin shook his head. 'Robespierre will be asleep now. Unless the committee is still sitting. It's not as if there was any chance of your losing, is it?'

'God forbid.' Fouquier put his arm into his cousin's, and they stepped out into the frosty early hours. A policeman saluted them. 'The next big one is Brissot – and all of that crew we've managed to lay hold of. I base my prosecution on your writings – your "Secret History", and the other article you wrote about Brissot after you had that row about your gambling case. Good stuff: I'll lift some of your phrases if you don't mind. I hope you'll be in court to take the credit.'

Think now of those post-Bastille days: Brissot in Camille's office, perched on the desk, Théroigne swishing in and planting a big kiss on his dry cheek. He was my friend, Camille thinks; then along came the gambling case, and we were suddenly on opposite sides, he made it personal, and *I can't stand criticism*. He knows this about himself; he either flares up or folds up, he takes some kind of offensive or – or what? 'Antoine,' he says to his cousin, 'I seem to know all forms of attack. But I seem to know no forms of defence at all.'

'Come now,' the Prosecutor said. He did not understand in the least what his cousin was talking about, but that was nothing new. He put out a hand, ruffled his cousin's hair. Camille flicked his head away as if a wasp had touched him. Fouquier took it quietly. He was in a good humour – looking forward to the bottle of wine he had promised himself when it was all over; he tried not to drink during the big cases. He felt, however, that sleep might elude him: or bring his nightmares back. Perhaps his cousin, with whom he really spent too little time, would like to sit up and talk. For two boys from the provinces, he thought, we are doing extremely well these days.

SOON AFTER ELEVEN the next morning Henri Sanson entered her cell for the preparations. He was the son of the man who had executed her husband. She wore a white dress, a light shawl, black stockings and a pair of high-heeled plum-coloured shoes, which during her imprisonment she had carefully preserved. The executioner tied her hands behind her back and cut off the hair which, according to her maid, she had thought it proper to 'dress high' to meet her judge and jury. She did not move, and Sanson did not allow the steel to touch her neck. Within a few seconds the long tresses, once the colour of honey and now streaked coarsely with grey, lay on the floor of the cell. He scooped them up to be burned.

The tumbrel waited in the courtyard. It was an ordinary cart, once used for carrying wood, now with planks across it for seats. At the sight of it, she lost her composure; she gaped in fear, but she did not cry out. She asked the executioner to untie her hands for a moment, and when he did so she squatted in a corner, by a wall, and urinated. Her hands were tied again, and she was put into the cart. Under the shorn hair and the plain white cap, her tired eyes searched for pity in the faces around her. The journey to the place of execution lasted for an hour. She did not speak. As she mounted the steps, paid, indifferent hands kept her balanced. Her body began to shake, her limbs to give way. In her blindness and terror, she stepped on the executioner's foot. 'I beg your pardon, Monsieur,' she whispered. 'I did not mean to do it.' A few minutes after noon her head was off: 'the greatest joy of all the joys experienced by Père Duchesne'.

X. *The Marquis Calls*

(1793)

BOTH THE MONARCHS are dead, the he-tyrant and the she-tyrant. You'd think there'd be a feeling of freedom, a feeling inside; Lucile finds she doesn't have it. She had pressed Camille for details of the Queen's last hours, anxious to know whether she had been worthy of a place in history; but he seemed reluctant to talk about it. In the end he said that, as she very well knew, nothing would induce him to attend an execution. Hypocrite, she said. You ought to go and see the results of your actions. He stared at her. I know how people die, he said. He made her an old regime bow, very fulsome and ironic, picked up his hat and went out. He seldom quarrelled with her, but revenged himself by mysterious absences, of between ten minutes and several days in duration.

He was back within the hour: could they give a supper party? The notice was very generous, Jeanette said tartly. But good food in sufficient quantity can always be procured if you have money and know where to go. Camille disappeared again, and it was Jeanette, out shopping, who found out what there was to celebrate; the Convention had heard that afternoon that the Austrians had been defeated in a long and bloody battle at Wattignies.

So that night they drank to the latest victory, to the newest commanders. They talked of the progress against the Vendée insurgents, of success against the rebels of Lyon and Bordeaux. 'It seems to me the Republic is prospering immensely,' she said to Hérault.

'The news is good, yes.' But he frowned. He was preoccupied; he had asked the Committee to send him to Alsace in the wake of Saint-Just, and he was to leave soon, perhaps tomorrow.

'Why did you do that?' she asked him. 'We'll be dull without you. I'm pleased you could come tonight, I thought you might be at the Committee.'

'I'm not a lot of use to them these days. They tell me as little as possible. I learn more from the newspapers.'

'They don't trust you any more?' She was alarmed. 'What's happened?'

'Ask your husband. He has the ear of the Incorruptible.' A few minutes later he rose, thanked her, explained that there were last-minute preparations. Camille stood up, and kissed Hérault's cheek. 'Come back soon. I shall so much miss our regular exchange of veiled abuse.'

'I doubt it will be soon.' Hérault's voice was strained. 'At least, at the frontier I can do useful work, and I can see the enemy, and know who they are. Paris is becoming a place for scavengers.'

'I apologize,' Camille said. 'I can see I'm a waste of your time. Can I have my kiss back?'

'I swear,' someone said lazily, 'that if you two were to mount the scaffold together you'd quarrel over precedence.'

'Oh, I fancy I'd have the advantage,' Camille said. 'Though I cannot imagine which way it lies. My cousin decides the order of execution.'

There was a choking sound, and somebody put his glass down hard. Fabre stared at them, red-faced. 'It's not funny,' he said. 'It's in the worst taste imaginable, and it's not even funny.'

There was a silence, into which Hérault dropped his goodbyes. After he had gone the conversation resumed with a forced hilarity, which Fabre led. The party broke up early. Later, lying in bed, Lucile asked, 'What happened? Our parties never fail, never.'

'Oh,' Camille said, 'no doubt it is the end of civilization as we know it.' Then he added, tiredly, 'It's probably because Georges is away.' He turned away from her, but she knew that he was lying awake, listening to the sounds of the city by night: black eyes staring into black darkness.

Something's amiss, she thought. At least, since Saint-Just left Paris, Camille was more with Robespierre. Robespierre understood him; he would find out what was wrong and tell her.

Next day she called on Eléonore. If it was true that Eléonore was Robespierre's mistress, it didn't make her any happier, certainly no more gracious. She was not slow to bring the conversation round to Camille.

'He,' she said with disgust, 'can make Max do anything he wants, and nobody else can make him do anything they want at all. He's just always very polite and busy.' She leaned forward, trying to communicate her distress. 'He gets up early and deals with his letters. He goes to the Convention. He goes to the Tuileries and transacts the Committee's business. Then he goes to the Jacobins. At ten o'clock at night the Committee goes into session. He comes home in the small hours.'

'He drives himself very hard. But what do you expect? That's the kind of man he is.'

'He'll never marry me. He says, as soon as the present crisis is over. But it never will be over, will it, Lucile, will it?'

A few weeks ago in the street Lucile and her mother had seen Anne Théroigne. It had taken them both a moment to recognize her. Théroigne was no longer pretty. She was thin; her face had fallen in as if she had lost some teeth. She passed them; something flickered in her eyes, but she didn't speak. Lucile thought her pathetic – a victim of the times. 'No one could think her attractive now,' Annette said. She smiled. Her recent birthdays had passed, as she put it, without incident. Most men still looked at her with interest.

Once again, she was seeing Camille in the afternoons. He often stayed away from the Convention now. Many of the Montagnards were away on mission; many of the right-wing deputies, those who had voted against the King's death, had abandoned their public duties and fled Paris. More than seventy deputies had signed a protest about the expulsion of Brissot, Vergniaud and the rest; they were in prison now, and only Robespierre's good offices kept them out of the hands of the Tribunal. François Robert was in disgrace, and Philippe Égalité awaited trial; Collot d'Herbois was in Lyon, punishing rebels. Danton was enjoying the country air. Saint-Just and Babette's husband, Philippe Lebas, were with the armies; the burden of the Committee's work often kept Robespierre at the Tuileries. Camille and Fabre grew tired of counting the empty places. There was no one they much liked, and no one they much wanted to shout down. And Marat was dead.

Théroigne turned up at the rue des Cordeliers a few days after the supper party. Her clothes hung on her; she looked unwashed and somehow desperate. 'I want to see Camille,' she said. She had developed a way of turning her head away from you as she spoke, as if she were engaged in a private monologue into which you mustn't intrude. Camille heard her voice; he had been sitting doing nothing, staring into space. 'Well my dear,' he said, 'you have deteriorated. If this is all you can do by way of feminine charm, I think I prefer the way you were before.'

'Your manners are still exquisite,' Théroigne said, looking at the wall. 'What's that? That engraving? That woman's going to have her head cut off.'

'That is Maria Stuart, my wife's favourite historical personage.'

'How strange,' she said tonelessly.

'Sit down,' Lucile said. 'Do you want something? A warm drink?' She was overwhelmed by pity; someone ought to feed her, brush her hair, tell Camille not to speak to her like that. 'Would you rather I left you?' she said.

'No, that's all right. You can stay if you want. Or go. I don't mind.'

As she moved slowly into a better light, Lucile saw the scars on her face. Months ago, she knew, she had been beaten in the street by a gang of women. How she has suffered, Lucile thought; God preserve me. Her throat tightened.

'What I want won't take long,' Théroigne said. 'You know, don't you, what I think?'

'I don't know that you do,' Camille said.

'You know where my sympathies lie. Brissot's people go on trial this week. I'm one of them, Brissot's people.' There was no passion in her voice. 'I believe in what they stand for and what they've tried to do. I don't like your politics and I don't like Robespierre's.'

'Is that it? Is that what you came for?'

'I want you to go, right away, to the Section committee and denounce me. I'll come with you. I won't deny anything you say about me. I'll repeat exactly what I just said.'

Lucile: 'Anne, what's the matter with you?'

'She wants to die,' Camille said. He smiled.

'Yes,' she said, in the same listless whisper. 'I do.'

Lucile crossed the room to her. Théroigne pushed her hands away, and Camille gave her a sharp, fierce look. She dropped back, looking from one to the other.

'It's easy,' Camille said. 'You go out on the street and shout "Long live the King." They'll arrest you right away.'

Anne raised a bony hand and touched her eyebrow. A white mark showed where the flesh had been split open. 'I made a speech,' she said. 'This happened. They hit me with a whip. They kicked me in the stomach and trod on me. I thought I was finished then. But it was a wretched way to die.'

'Try the river,' Camille said.

'Denounce me. Let's go to the Section now. You'd be pleased to do it. You want your revenge.'

'Yes,' he said, 'I do want revenge, but why should you have the benefit of a civilized end? I may detest Brissot's people, but they shouldn't have their names linked to scum like you. No, Théroigne, you can die in the street – like Louis Suleau did. You can take your death where you find it, and from whoever hands it out. I hope you wait a long time.'

Her expression didn't change. Humbly, her eyes sliding across the carpet, she said, 'I beg of you.'

'Go away,' Camille said.

She inclined her head. Her face averted, her gait beaten and slow, Théroigne moved towards the door. Lucile cried out for her to come back. 'She means to take her life.' Stupidly, she was pointing after her, as if to make herself clear.

'No, she doesn't,' Camille said.

'Oh, you are wicked,' Lucile whispered. 'If there's a hell, you'll burn in it.' The door closed. She rushed across the room. She wanted to injure him, to hurt him in reparation for the ghost-like creature who had crept out into the rain. His expression distant, he held her wrists, thwarting her. Her whole body shook, and a rush of tears scalded her cheeks. 'I'm sorry,' she said. 'I know you couldn't do what she said, it's absurd, but surely there's some way to help her and make her want to live? Everybody must want to live.'

'That's not true. Every day people are taken up off the streets. They wait for a patrol to come along, and then they shout out for the Dauphin, or for Robespierre to be guillotined. There are a multitude of deaths waiting. She only has to choose one.'

She dragged herself from his grasp, ran into the bedroom and slammed the door. Her chest heaved, her heart rose and throbbed in her throat. With all the desperate passions in our heads and bodies, one day these walls will split, one day this house will fall down. There will be soil and bones and grass, and they will read our diaries to find out what we were.

9 BRUMAIRE, the Palais de Justice. Brissot seemed to have aged. He was more papery and stooped, and the hair at his temples had receded further. De Sillery looked old; where were his gambling passions now? He would not bet on the outcome of this; this was a certainty. Only, sometimes, he wondered how he got made into a Brissotin. He should be sitting beside Philippe; Philippe, the lucky devil, has another week to live.

He leant forward. 'Brissot, do you remember? We were witnesses at Camille's wedding.'

'So we were,' Brissot said. 'But then you know, so was Robespierre.'

Vergniaud, who was always careless about his clothes, was immaculate tonight, as if to show that imprisonment and trial had not broken his spirit. His face was carefully devoid of expression; he would give nothing away, give his tormentors no satisfaction. Where was Buzot tonight, he wondered? Where was Citizen Roland? Where was Pétion? Alive or dead?

The clock struck 10.15. Outside it was pitch black, raining. The jury were back; at once they were surrounded by officers of the court. Citizen Fouquier, his cousin with him, strolled across the marble, into the light; there were twenty-two verdicts to be pronounced, twenty-two death sentences to be read, before he could go home to a late meal and a bottle.

His cousin Camille was very pale; his voice shook, he was on edge. For six days he, Fouquier, had been quoting his cousin's assertions at the jury, his accusations of federalist conspiracy, of monarchist plots. Occasionally, when some now-famous phrase fell on their ears, the accused would turn as one man and look at Camille. It was as if they had rehearsed it; no doubt they had. It had been a strain, Fouquier supposed. He had already ordered the tumbrels; when there were twenty-two accused, you had to be mindful of these details.

There is, Fouquier reflected, something theatrical about the scene, or something for an artist's brush; the black and white of the tiles, the flare of candle flames, the splashes, here and there, of the tricolour. Light touches his cousin's face; he takes a chair. The foreman of the jury rises. A clerk flicks from a file a sheaf of death warrants. Behind the Public Prosecutor, someone whispered, 'Camille, what's the matter?'

Suddenly, from the ranks of the accused, there was a single sharp cry. The accused men leapt to their feet, the guards closed in on them, the officers of the court threw down their papers and scrambled from their places. One of the accused, Charles Valazé, had slid backwards from his bench. There were screams from women in the crowd, a rush to see what had happened; guards struggled to hold the spectators back.

'What a way to end it,' a juryman said.

Vergniaud, his face still impassive, motioned to Dr Lehardi, one of the accused. Lehardi knelt by the fallen body. He held up a long dagger, which was bloody to the hilt. The Public Prosecutor immediately removed it from his hand. 'I shall have something to say about this,' Fouquier complained. 'He might have used it on me.'

Brissot sat slumped forward, his chin on his chest. Now Valazé's blood trailed scarlet over the black and white. A space was cleared. Valazé, looking small and very dead, was picked up by two gendarmes and borne away.

The drama was not over yet. Citizen Desmoulins, attempting to get out of the courtroom, had fallen over in a dead faint.

*

17 BRUMAIRE: execution of Philippe, known as Citizen Égalité. At his last meal he consumed two cutlets, a quantity of oysters, the greater part of a good bottle of Bordeaux. To attend the scaffold he wore a white piqué waistcoat, a green frock-coat and yellow buckskins: very English. 'Well, my good man,' he said to Sanson, 'let's hurry it up, shall we?'

THE EXECUTIONER. His overheads have gone up shockingly since the Terror began. He has seven men to pay out of his own wages, and soon he will be hiring up to a dozen carts a day. Before, he managed with two assistants and one cart. The kind of money he can offer doesn't attract people to the work. He has to pay for his own cord for binding the clients, and for the big wicker baskets to take the corpses away afterwards. At first they'd thought the guillotine would be a sweet, clean business, but when you have twenty, perhaps thirty heads to take off in a day, there are problems of scale. Do the powers-that-be understand just how much blood comes out of even one decapitated person? The blood ruins everything, rots things away, especially his clothes. People down there don't realize, but he sometimes gets splashed right up to his knees.

It's heavy work. If you get someone who's tried to do away with himself beforehand, he can be in a mess, maybe collapsed through poison or loss of blood, and you can strain your back trying to drag him into position under the blade. Recently Citizen Fouquier insisted they guillotine a corpse, which everybody thought was a lot of unnecessary work. Again, take someone who's crippled or deformed; they can't be tied to the plank without a lot of sweat and heaving, and then the crowds (who can't see much anyway) get bored and start hissing and catcalling. Meanwhile a queue builds up, and the people at the end of the queue get awkward and start screaming or passing out. If all the clients were young, male, stoical and fit, he'd have fewer problems, but it's surprising how few of them fall into all those categories. The citizens who live nearby complain that he doesn't put down enough sawdust to soak up the blood, and the smell becomes offensive. The machine itself is quiet, efficient, reliable; but of course he has to pay the man who sharpens the knife.

He's trying to make the operation as efficient as he can, get the speed up. Fouquier shouldn't complain. Take the Brissotins; twenty-one, plus the corpse, in thirty-six minutes flat. He couldn't spare a skilled man to time it, but he'd got a friendly spectator to stand by with his watch: just in case he heard any complaints.

In the old days the executioner was esteemed; he was looked up to. There was a special law to prevent people calling him rude names. He had a regular audience who came to see skilled work, and they appreciated any little troubles he took. People came to executions because they wanted to; but some of these old women, knitting for the war effort, you can see they've been paid to sit there, and they can't wait to get away and drink up the proceeds; and the National Guardsmen, who have to attend, are sickened off after a few days of it.

Once the executioner had a special Mass said for the soul of the condemned; but you couldn't do that now. They're numbers on a list now. You feel that before this death had distinction; for your clients it was a special, individual end. For them you had risen early and prayed and dressed in scarlet, composed a marmoreal face and cut a flower for your coat. But now they come in carts like calves, mouths sagging like calves' and their eyes dull, stunned into passivity by the speed with which they've been herded from their judgement to their deaths; it is not an art any longer, it is more like working in a slaughterhouse.

'I WRITE THESE WORDS to the sound of laughter in the next room . . .'

From the first day they took her to prison, Manon had been writing. She had to record a justification, a credo, an autobiography. After a time her wrist would ache, her fingers stiffen in the cold, and she would want to cry. Whenever she stopped writing and allowed her mind to dwell on the past itself, rather than on means of expressing it, she felt a great void of longing open inside her: '. . . we have had nothing.' She would lie on her prison bed, staring up into the darkness, consciously fitting herself for heroism.

Every day she expected them to come and tell her that her husband had been captured, that he was being held in some provincial town, that he was on his way to Paris to stand trial with her. But what if François-Léonard were taken? Perhaps they would not tell her at all. This is the price of discretion, this is the prize for good conduct; they had been so discreet, and behaved so well, that even her closest friends would not think Buzot any personal concern of hers.

Her room in prison was bare and cold, but clean. Meals were sent in to her; nevertheless, she had decided to starve herself to death. Little by little she cut down her intake, until they took her away to another room that served as the prison hospital. The prospect was held out to her then that she would be allowed to testify at Brissot's trial; for that she must be strong, and so she began to eat again.

Perhaps it had been a trick from the start? She didn't know. While the trial was in progress she had been taken to the Palais de Justice and held in a side room, under guard. But she never saw the accused, never saw the judges or (such as they were) the jury. One of her keepers brought her the news of Valazé's suicide. One death breeds another. What was it Vergniaud had said, of the calm, smooth-skinned girl who had stabbed Marat? 'She has killed us, but she has taught us how to die.'

They had delayed her own trial – perhaps because they hoped to capture Roland and stand them side by side. One could ask for mercy, of course; but her life was not worth the sacrifice of everything she had lived it for. Besides, there was no mercy to be got. From Danton? From Robespierre? Camille Desmoulins had been in some uncharacteristic mood at Brissot's trial. He had said – a score of people had heard it, her keepers told her – 'They were my friends, and my writings have killed them.' But no doubt he had repented of repentance, before Jacobin hands had scooped him up from the floor.

On the day she was moved to the Conciergerie, she realized that she would never see her child or her husband again. The cells were below the hall where the Tribunal sat; this was the last stage, and even if Roland were taken now she would be dead before he reached Paris. She appeared before the Tribunal on 8 November – 18 Brumaire, by the reckoning of that charlatan Fabre d'Églantine. She wore a white dress, her auburn hair down, gathering and accreting to itself the last rays of the afternoon light. Fouquier was efficient. She was bundled into a cart that same evening. The bitter wind whipped colour into her cheeks, and she shivered inside her muslin. It was growing dark, but she saw the machine against the sky, the sinister geometry of the knife's edge.

AN EYEWITNESS:

'Robespierre came forward slowly … He wore spectacles which probably served to conceal the twitchings of his pallid face. His delivery was slow and measured. His phrases were so long that every time he stopped and raised his spectacles one thought that he had nothing more to say, but after looking slowly and searchingly over the audience in every part of the room, he would readjust his glasses and add a few more phrases to his sentences, which were already of inordinate length.'

Nowadays when he came up behind people they would jump, startled and guilty. It was as if the fear he often felt had communicated itself to them. Since he was not naturally heavy-footed, he wondered what he should do to warn them – cough, barge into the furniture? He knew that they thought he was there, listening, before they saw him, and all their self-doubts and mutinous half-thoughts came swarming to the surface of their skins.

At the meetings of the Committee he often sat in silence; he did not want to force his views on them, and yet when he abstained from comment he knew that they suspected him of watching them, of noting things down. And he did; he noted a great many things. Sometimes when he gave his opinion Carnot drily contradicted him; Robert Lindet looked very grave, as if he had reservations. He would snap at Carnot to reduce him to silence. What did the man think, that he had some sort of privilege, because he had known him before? His colleagues would exchange glances. Sometimes he would extract a few papers from Carnot's portfolio, complaints from commanders whose men had dysentery or no shoes, or whose mounts were dying from lack of fodder. He would read them quickly and spread them out on the table like a gambler laying down his hand, his eyes engaging Carnot's; I wonder, he would say, if you think your appointment is working out for the best? Carnot sucked on his lower lip.

When his colleagues spoke, Robespierre sat with his narrow chin propped on thumb and forefinger, his face tilted to the ceiling. There was nothing they could tell him about day-to-day politics, about publicity good and bad, about handling the Convention and obtaining a majority. He remembered his schooldays, toiling in the shade of more flamboyant characters; he remembered Arras, where he was chivvied about by the claims of his family, slapped down by local magistrates, blackballed because of his politics by the local Bar's dining club.

He's not like Danton; he didn't want to go home. Here's home: under the midnight lamps, and out in the rainy street. But sometimes while they're talking he finds himself, for a moment, elsewhere; he thinks of those grey-green meadows and quiet town squares, the lines of poplars bending in an autumn wind.

20 BRUMAIRE. A 'Festival of Reason' is held in the public building formerly known as Notre-Dame. The religious embellishments, as people like to call them, have been stripped from the building, and a cardboard Greek temple has been constructed in the nave. An actress from the Opéra impersonates the Goddess of Reason, and is enthroned while the crowd sing the 'Ça Ira'.

Under pressure from the Hébertists, the Bishop of Paris appears before the Convention, and announces his militant atheism. Deputy Julien, who had once been a Protestant pastor, took the occasion to announce his at the same time.

Declared Deputy Clootz (a radical, a foreigner): 'A religious man is a depraved beast. He resembles those animals that are kept to be shorn and roasted for the benefit of merchants and butchers.'

Robespierre came home from the Convention. His lips were pale, his eyes cold with fury. Someone is going to suffer, Eléonore thought.

'If there is no God,' he said, 'if there is no Supreme Being, what are the people to think who live all their lives in hardship and want? Do these atheists think they can do away with poverty, do they think the Republic can be made into heaven on earth?'

Eléonore turned away from him. She knew better than to hope for a kiss. 'Saint-Just rather thinks it,' she said.

'We cannot guarantee bread to people. We cannot guarantee justice. Are we also to take hope away?'

'It sounds as if you only want a God because he fills the gaps in your policies.'

He stared at her. 'Perhaps,' he said slowly. 'Perhaps you're right. But Antoine, you see, he thinks everything can be achieved by wishing it – each individual makes himself over, becomes a better person, a person with more *vertu*, then as individuals change, society changes, and it takes – what? A generation? The problem is, Eléonore, that you lose sight of this when you're bogged down in the detail, you are worrying all the time about supplying boots for the army, and you're thinking, *every day I fail at something* – and it begins to look like one gigantic failure.'

She put her hand on his arm. 'It's not a failure, my darling. It's the only success there's ever been in the world.'

He shook his head. 'I can't always see it now in such absolute terms, I wish I could; I feel sometimes I'm losing my direction. Danton understands, he knows how to talk about this. He says, you make a few botches, you have a few successes, and that's what politics is about.'

'Cynical,' Eléonore said.

'No, it's a viewpoint – the way he looks at it, you do have your general principles to guide you, but you have to make the best of each situation as it arises. Now Saint-Just, he thinks differently – in his opinion, you have to see in each particular circumstance a chance to make your principles operate. Everything, for him, is an opportunity to state the larger case.'

'And where do you stand?'

'Oh, I'm just –' he threw his hands out – 'floundering. Only here, with this issue, I do know where I am. I will not have this intolerance, I will not have this bigotry, I will not have the lifetime's faith of simple people pulled from under them by dilettantes with no idea of what faith means. They call the priests bigots, but they are the bigots, who want to stop Mass being said.'

You 'won't have it', she thought. That means the Tribunal, if they don't back down. She herself was not inclined to believe in a God; or not in a beneficent one, anyway.

Up in his room he wrote a letter to Danton. He read it over, corrected it minutely, as he corrected everything, scoring it over, refining his meaning, stating his case. He was not satisfied with it; he tore it up – into small pieces, because he was not too angry to be careful – and wrote another. He wanted to ask Danton to come to Paris and help him crush Hébert. He wanted to say that he needed help, but would not be patronized: needed an ally, but would not be dominated.

Even the second draft was not satisfactory. Why didn't he think of asking Camille to write it? Camille could put his case so simply, had put it so simply earlier that day: 'We don't need processions and rosaries and relics, but we do need, when things are very bad, the prospect of consolation – we do need, when things are even worse, the idea that in the long run there is someone who could manage to forgive us.'

He sat with his head bowed. You have to smile; what would Father Bérardier say? Here we are, when all's said and done, two good Catholic boys. Never mind that he hasn't heard Mass in years, that Camille counts a week wasted if he hasn't broken every Commandment in the book. Strange, really, how you find yourself back where you started. Or not, of course: he remembered Camille being slapped around the head by Father Proyart for taking Plutarch's *Lives* to Mass. 'I'd just got to an exciting bit . . . ' he'd said. In those days Plutarch passed for excitement. No wonder Camille cut loose when he got away from the priests. They asked us to be something more than human. And I, I struggled on, *trying* to be what they wanted – though I didn't know I was doing it, though I thought I was living by another creed entirely.

His lighter mood didn't last long. He addressed himself to a third draft. How *does* one write to Danton? He took out his DANTON notebook and read it over. He was no wiser when he finished, but much more depressed.

JEAN-MARIE ROLAND was in hiding in Rouen. On the day – 10 November – when the news of his wife's execution reached him, he left the house where he was hiding and walked some three miles out of town. He carried his sword-stick in his hand. He stopped in a deserted lane, by an apple orchard, and sat down under one of the trees. This was the place; there was no point in walking any further.

The ground was iron-hard, the trunk of the tree was cold to the touch; winter was in the air. He experimented; the first sight of his own blood dismayed him, turned him sick. But this *was* the place.

The body was found some time later, by a passer-by who had at first taken him to be an elderly man asleep. It was impossible to say for how many hours he had been dead or whether, impaled by the slender blade, it had taken him very long to die.

November 11, in pouring rain, Mayor Bailly was executed; by popular request, a guillotine was set up for the occasion on the Champs-de-Mars, where in '91 Lafayette had fired on the people.

'CAMILLE,' Lucile said, 'there's a marquis to see you.' Camille looked up from *The City of God*, and shook his hair out of his eyes. 'Impossible.'

'Well then, a former marquis.'

'Does he look respectable?'

'Yes, very. All right? I'll leave you then.'

Suddenly, and after all these years, she has no appetite for politics. Vergniaud's dying words keep running through her head: 'The Revolution, like Saturn, is devouring its own children.' It is becoming one of the slogans and pat phrases she seems to have lived by. (Does a father's authority count for nothing? I don't know why people complain they can't make money nowadays, I have no trouble. They were my friends and my writings have killed them.) They run through her dreams every night, she finds them rising to her lips in conversation, the common currency of the last five years. (It's all organized, no one who's innocent will be touched. I loathe firm government. There's nothing to worry about, M. Danton will look after us.) She no longer attends the debates of the Convention, sitting in the public gallery eating sweets with Louise Robert. She went once to the Tribunal, to hear Cousin Antoine bullying his victims; once was enough.

'Some confusion over identity,' de Sade said to Camille. 'I should have sent in my credentials as an official of the Section des Piques. My mind was wandering. That's enough to get someone denounced as suspect.' He reached out one of his small, soft hands and took away Camille's book. 'Devotional reading,' he said. 'My dear. This is nothing to do with . . . ?'

'Fainting? Oh no. Just my usual diversion. I'm writing a work on the Church Fathers.'

'Each to his own,' de Sade said. 'We authors must look out for each other, don't you think?'

He was in his early fifties now, a small man, rather plump, with receding greyish-blond hair and pale blue eyes. He had put on weight, but he still moved with elegance. He wore the dark clothes and tensely purposeful expression of the Terrorist politician, and he carried a folio of papers knotted with a flamboyant tricolour ribbon. 'Obscene illustrations?' Camille inquired, indicating it.

'Good God,' de Sade said, shocked. 'You consider yourself my moral superior, don't you, M. Lanterne Attorney?'

'Well, I am most people's moral superior. I know all the theory, and I have all the ethical scruples. It is only in my conduct that there is something wanting. Can I have Saint Augustine back, please?'

De Sade looked round for a table: and laid the saint face down. 'You unnerve me,' he said. Camille looked pleased. 'I thought you might like to tell me about these regrets you are having,' the Marquis said. He took a chair.

Camille thought for a moment. 'No . . . I don't think I would. But you can tell me about yours, if you like.'

'The Bastille,' de Sade said. 'It's all double-edged, isn't it? Take the fall of the Bastille. It made you famous. And I congratulate you.

It shows how the wicked prosper, and how even the semi-wicked have a distinct advantage. Also it was a great step forward for humanity, whoever they may be. For my part, I was moved out before the trouble started, and in such a hurry that I left the manuscript of my new novel behind. I got out of prison on Good Friday – after eleven years, Camille – and my papers were nowhere to be found. It was a great blow to me, I can tell you.'

'What was it, your novel?'

'*120 Days of Sodom.*'

'Well, heavens,' Camille said, 'it's more than four years, haven't you had time to get it together again?'

'Not any old 120 days,' the Marquis said. 'It was a feat of imagination which in these attenuated times it is difficult to reproduce.'

'What did you come for, Citizen? Not to talk about your novels, surely?'

The Marquis sighed. 'Just to air my views. About the times, you know. I loved what happened at Brissot's trial. To think of you recovering your senses, such as they are, in the arms of all those strong men. So what do you think now – do you think it would have been possible not to kill Brissot's people?'

'I didn't, but now I think – yes, we might have managed it.'

'Even after Marat's death?'

'I suppose there is at least a chance that the girl did it by herself. She claimed she did. But no one even listened to her. Brissot's trial went on for days. They were allowed to speak. They called witnesses. It was all reported in the newspapers. It was only pressure from Hébert that stopped it, or we could have been arguing still.'

'Just so,' de Sade said.

'But in future defendants won't have those rights. It is regarded as not expeditious, not republican. I am afraid of the consequences of cutting the trials short. I think that people are being killed who need not be. But the killings go on.'

'And the judgements,' de Sade said. 'The judgements in the courtroom. You see I approve the duel, the vendetta, the crime of passion. But this machinery of Terror operates with no passion at all.'

'Forgive me – I'm not entirely sure what you're talking about.'

'You know, your first writings were so entirely without pity, so completely devoid of the conventional mouthings – I had hopes for you. But now you're beginning to retrace your steps. Repent. Aren't you? You know, I was secretary of my Section committee in September. Not last September: the one past, when we killed the prisoners. There was something pure and revolutionary and absolutely fitting about the way the blood flowed – the speed, the fear. But now we have the jury's verdict, the hair-cutting, the carts. We have the lawyers' arguments before death. Nature should visit death; it should not be something you argue against.'

'I am sure I do not see why you are visiting this rubbish on me.'

'I suppose that to you – at least in your present frame of mind – it is only the legal process that makes it acceptable. More acceptable, if the trial is fair, and less acceptable if the witnesses are bullied and the trial is cut short. But to me it is all unacceptable, you see. The more they argue, the worse it is. I can't go on any longer.' There was a pause. 'Are you writing anything?' the Marquis asked. 'I mean, besides your theological work?' Misunderstood again; his timid pale eyes were like those of an old hare, expecting traps.

Camille hesitated. 'I'm thinking of writing. I must see what support I have. It is difficult. We know there are conspiracies, our whole lives are eaten away by them. We dare not speak freely to our best friends, or trust our wives or parents or children. Does that sound melodramatic? It is like Rome in the reign of the Emperor Tiberius.'

'I don't know,' de Sade said. 'But if you say so, it probably is. I've been to Rome, you know? Waste of time. They've put up all these little chapels round the Colosseum, it ruins the place. Saw the Pope. Vulgarity incarnate. Still, I suppose Tiberius was worse.' He looked up. 'What would you do with my opinions?'

'About the Pope?'

'About the Terror.'

'I think I'd keep them to myself, if I were you.'

'But I haven't, you see. I've said at a meeting of my Section that the Terror must be stopped. I expect they'll arrest me soon. Then we'll see what we see. I tell you, dear Citizen Camille – it's not the deaths I can't stand. It's the judgements, the judgements in the courtroom.'

DANTON ARRIVED BACK on 20 November. He had in his pocket letters from Robespierre, from Fabre, from Camille. Robespierre's had a hysterical tinge, Fabre's sounded tearful and Camille's was merely strange. He resisted the temptation to fold them up small and wear them as phylacteries.

They reinstalled themselves in the apartment. Louise looked up at him accusingly. 'You're thinking of going out.'

'It's not every day,' he said, 'that Citizen Robespierre requests my company at his revels.'

'All this time, you've been thinking about Paris. I believe you've been longing to get back.'

'Look at me.' He took her hands. 'I know I'm a fool. When I'm here I want to be in Arcis. When I'm in Arcis, I want to be here. But I want you to understand that the Revolution isn't a game that I can leave when I choose.' His voice was very serious; he put a hand to her waist, drew her to him. God, how he loved her! 'In Arcis we avoided speaking of this, we spoke of simpler things. But it's not a game, and it isn't something, either, that I engage in just for my own profit, or gratification.' His fingers touched her mouth, very softly, stopping what she was going to say. 'Once it was, yes. But we have to think very carefully now, sweetheart. We have to think carefully about what will happen to the country. And to us.'

'So that is what you have been doing. Thinking carefully.'

'Yes.'

'And you are going to see Robespierre now?'

'Not directly.' He lifted his chin. His mood was once again worldy, jocular; he was pulling away from her. 'I need to be well-informed before I see him. Robespierre, you know, hurls abuse at any fellow who doesn't keep up with events.'

'Does that bother you?'

'Not much,' he said cheerfully. He kissed her. They were more on terms now, on terms of his choosing; though he felt – and it hurt him – that she was frightened of him. 'Aren't you even a little bit glad to be back?'

'Yes, I suppose so. Back in our own street. Georges, I couldn't live with your mother. We'll have to have our own house.'

'Yes, we'll do that.'

'Will you start seeing about it? Because we don't want to be in Paris for much longer, do we?'

He didn't answer. 'I'll not be long,' he said.

In the minute it took him to walk around the corner, he managed to greet half a dozen people, slap a few backs, hurry on before anyone could stop him to talk. By nightfall it would be all over the city: he's back. Just as he was about to go into the Desmoulins's building, he became aware of something new – some obtrusive detail, nagging at the corner of his eye. He stepped back, looked up. Cut into the stone above his head were the words RUE MARAT.

For a moment he had the urge to turn back around the corner, climb the stairs, shout to the servants not to bother unpacking, they'd be returning to Arcis in the morning. He looked up to the lighted windows above his head. If I go up there, he thought, I'll never be free again. If I go up there I commit myself to Max, to joining with him to finish Hébert, and perhaps to governing with him. I commit myself to fishing Fabre out of trouble – though God alone knows how that's to be managed. I put myself once more under the threat of assassination; I recommence the blood-feuds, the denunciations.

His face hardened. You can't stand in the street calling into question the last five years of your life, just because they've changed the street name; you can't let it alter the future. No, he thought – and he saw it clearly, for the first time – it's an illusion, about quitting, about going back to Arcis to farm. I've been lying to Louise: once in, never out.

'THANK GOD,' Lucile said. 'I was thinking of coming to get you.'

Her lips brushed his cheek. He'd been preparing to interrogate her closely about Camille and Robespierre, but instead he said, 'How beautiful you are. I believe I'd forgotten.'

'In five weeks?'

'I'd never really forget.' He put his arms around her. 'That was very sweet of you, to be so eager for my presence. You should have come to Arcis, I would have liked it.'

'Louise wouldn't, or your mother.'

'It would have given them something in common.'

'I see. As bad as that?'

'A disaster. Louise is too young, too citified and quite the wrong shape. And how are you?'

'Oh Lord – mixed up.' She tried to pull away from him, but he held on to her, tightening his arms around her waist. How strong she was, full of fight; he believed she was afraid of nothing.

'Not pregnant again, Lolotte?'

She shook her head. 'Thank God,' she added.

'Do you want me to give you another son?'

She raised her eyebrows. 'You have a nice wife of your own to take care of, I think.'

'I can accommodate more than one woman in my life.'

'I thought you'd given me up.'

'Absolutely not. Point of honour.'

'But you had, before you left.'

I've got my strength back now, he thought. 'It's no good trying to reform, is it? You can't reform of loving somebody.'

'You don't love me. You just want to have me, and talk about it afterwards.'

'Better than not having you and talking about it afterwards, like everybody else.'

'Yes.' She leaned her forehead against his chest. 'I've been very silly, haven't I?'

'Very silly. Your situation's irretrievable. Our wives will never believe any good of you now. Be honest for once, and go to bed with me.'

'Is that what you came for?'

'Not originally, but – '

'I'm glad about that. I have no intention of complying, and besides, a little while ago Camille came in and flung himself down on our bed and is doing some savage brooding.'

He kissed the top of her head. 'Look at me.' It was the same request, he remembered, that he had made to his wife thirty minutes earlier. 'Tell me what's wrong.'

'Everything's wrong.'

'I'll fix it all.'

'Please.'

CAMILLE LAY with his head buried in his arms. 'Lolotte?' he said, without looking up. Danton sat down beside him and stroked his hair. 'Oh, Georges.'

'Aren't you surprised?'

'Nothing surprises me,' Camille said wanly. 'Don't stop doing that, it's the first nice thing that's happened to me in a month.'

'From the beginning then.'

'You got my letter?'

'It didn't make much sense.'

'No. No, probably not. I can quite see that.'

He turned around and sat up. Danton was startled. In five weeks, the spurious maturity of the last five years had fallen away; the person who looked at him out of Camille's eyes was the scared and shabby boy of '88.

'Philippe is dead.'

'The Duke? Yes, I know.'

'Charles-Alexis is dead. Valazé stabbed himself right in front of me.'

'I heard. They brought me the news. But leave this for a minute. Tell me about Chabot and those people.'

'Chabot and two of his friends have been expelled from the Convention. They're under arrest. Deputy Julien's gone, he ran away. Vadier is asking questions.'

'Is he, now?' The head of the Committee of General Security was gaining himself a reputation for a horrible efficiency in the hounding of suspects. 'The Inquisitor', people called him. He was a man of sixty or so, with a long, yellow face, and long, yellow, many-jointed hands. 'What sort of questions?' Danton said.

'About you. About Fabre and your friend Lacroix.'

Fabre's dreary little confession was in Danton's pocket. He has done . . . he does not appear to know, himself, what he has done. Yes, he amended a government document, in his own hand, and the amendment has been printed as part of the text; but then again, some unknown hand made an amendment to the amendment . . . It makes you tired just to think about it. The possible conclusion is that Fabre is a forger – a *common* criminal, as opposed to some more refined type. All the indications are that Robespierre hasn't an inkling what is going on.

He returned his attention to Camille. 'Vadier obviously thinks he is about to uncover something damning about you, Georges. I spend my time avoiding Fabre. The Police Committee have had Chabot in. He denounced a conspiracy, of course. Said he'd gone along with it to track it to its source. No one believed that. Fabre has been delegated to produce a report of the affair.'

'On the East India Company? Fabre has?' This is becoming completely absurd, Danton thought.

'Yes, and on its political ramifications. Robespierre's not interested in crooked stock-market deals, he's interested in who's behind them, and where their instructions come from.'

'But why didn't Chabot denounce Fabre right away – why didn't he say, Fabre was in it with me from the beginning?'

'What had he to gain? Then they'd be in the dock together. So Chabot kept quiet, thinking Fabre might be grateful, and exonerate him in the report. Another deal struck, you see.'

'And Chabot really thinks that Fabre will remain in the clear?'

'They expect you to use your influence to pull him into the clear.'

'What a mess,' Danton said.

'Anyway, it's all worse now. Chabot's denouncing Fabre, and *everybody* – the only saving grace is that by now no one believes anything he says. Vadier questioned me.'

'Questioned *you*? He's getting a bit above himself.'

'Oh, it was all very informal. One good patriot to another. He said, Citizen, no one imagines you've done anything shady, but have you perhaps done something a little bit sharp? The idea was that I'd tell him all about it and feel much better afterwards.'

'What did you say?'

'Oh, hardly anything. I opened my eyes and said, me, sharp? My stutter was very bad that day. I dropped Max's name into the conversation a lot. Vadier is terrified of crossing him. He knew if he put any pressure on me I'd complain.'

'Well done,' Danton said grimly. But he saw the difficulty that he was in; it was not just a matter of what he did about Fabre, it was the rather larger matter of Camille's conscience.

'I'm lying to Robespierre,' Camille said. 'By implication, anyway. I don't like this, you know. It puts me on shaky ground for what I want to do next.'

'And that is?'

'There is worse news, I'm afraid. Hébert has come out with a story about Lacroix lining his pockets in Belgium last year, when you were on mission together. He claims to have evidence. He has also persuaded the Jacobins to petition the Convention to pull Lacroix and Legendre back from mission in Normandy.'

'What does he say Legendre has done?'

'He's your friend, isn't he? I went to Robespierre and said, we must stop the Terror.'

'You said that?'

'He said, I entirely agree. He does, of course, he hates the killing, it's only me who took so long to see . . . So I said, Hébert is too powerful. He's entrenched at the War Ministry and the Commune, he's got his newspaper circulating to the troops – and Hébert will *not* agree to stop the Terror. It touched his pride. He said, if I want to stop it, I will, even if I have to cut off Hébert's head first. All right, I told him, think about it for twenty-four hours and then we'll decide how to move in on him. I came home and drafted a pamphlet against Hébert.'

'You never learn, do you?'

'I'm sorry?'

'You were bewailing the Gironde. Your part in their downfall.'

'But this is *Hébert*,' Camille said uncomprehendingly. 'Look, don't confuse me. Hébert's the obstacle to stopping the Terror. If we kill him, we won't need to kill anyone else. Anyway, Robespierre – in that twenty-four hours he started to temporize. He came over all twitchy and indecisive. When I went back he said, "Hébert is very powerful, but he is right about some things, and he could be very useful if he were under our control."' Two-faced little bastard, Danton thought; what's he up to? '"It might be better," he said, "if we could find a compromise. We don't want any more unnecessary bloodshed." For once I wished for Saint-Just. I really thought he was going to do it, you know, and then – ' He made an exasperated gesture. 'Saint-Just might have been able to push him into some action.'

'Action?' Danton said. 'He won't take action. He's got no idea when it comes to action. Unnecessary bloodshed, oh my. Violence, how deplorable. He wears me out with his rectitude. That bugger couldn't boil an egg.'

'Oh no,' Camille said. 'Don't, don't.'

'So what does he want to do?'

'He won't be pinned down to an opinion. Go and see him. Just take in what he says. Don't argue.'

Danton thought, but that is how they used to talk about me. He pulled Camille into his arms. His body seemed strange and precarious, made of shadows and angles. Camille buried his head in his shoulder, and said, 'You really are a shocking and cynical man.'

For a moment or two they didn't speak. Then Camille pulled away and looked up at him. His hands rested lightly on Danton's shoulders. 'Has it ever occurred to you that Max feels the same basic contempt for you as you do for him?'

'He feels contempt for me?'

'It is something he feels very readily.'

'No, I hadn't thought that.'

'Well, the whole world isn't driven by your appetites, and people who are not feel themselves your superior, naturally. He struggles very hard to make allowances for you. He is not tolerant, but he is charitable. Or perhaps it is the other way around.'

'One becomes tired of analysing his character,' Danton said. 'As if one's life depended on it.'

*

HE HAD INTENDED to go back to Louise for an hour. He stood at the corner of the Cour du Commerce. He had become used to talking to her, recounting everything that happened and what had been said, waiting for her comments. He told her things he would never have told Gabrielle; her very lack of involvement, lack of knowledge made her valuable to him. But just now, there was nothing to say. He felt a great inarticulate weight inside him. He looked at his watch. It was possible, though not likely, that the Incorruptible would be at home at this hour, and while he stretched his legs in crossing the river he could think what to say. He glanced up at his own lighted window, then strode off vengefully into the evening.

The lanterns were being lit, swinging giddily from ropes in the narrow alleys between the houses, or hanging from iron brackets. There were more of them now than there had been before the Revolution: lights against the conspirators, against the counterfeiters, against the dark night of the Duke of Brunswick. In '89 they had been hanging up an aristo, and he had asked, 'Do you think the light will shine brighter afterwards?' And Louis Suleau, expressing his surprise at being still alive: 'Whenever I pass a lamppost, I see it stretch out towards me, covetously.'

Two young boys passed him, with cheerful country faces and running noses; they were selling rabbits to the townsfolk, and they carried the animals slung upside down on poles, bloodstained bundles caught in the fields in traps. Someone will rob them, he thought, and then they will have neither money nor rabbits on a pole; as they passed him the furry corpses looked meagre, little flesh on the swinging bones. Two women quarrelled in the door of a cookshop, fists on hips; the river was a smudged channel of yellow and dirty grey, creeping up at the winter like the onset of a wasting disease. People hurried off the streets, to be shut away from the city and the night.

The carriage was new, and remarkable because it was smart; even in the gloom you could see fresh polish on new paint. He caught a glimpse of a round, pale face, and the coachman drew up beside him with a ponderous creak of harness; above it, the squeak of the owner's voice. 'My dear Danton, is it you?'

He halted unwillingly. The horses breathed wetly into the raw, wet twilight. 'Hébert, is it you?'

Hébert stuck his head out. 'So it is. One recognizes your bulk. My dear Danton, it grows dark, what are you doing, walking the streets in this democratic fashion? It is not safe.'

'Don't I look as if I can take care of myself?'

'Of course, but don't you realize, there are gangs of armed robbers – can't I take you somewhere?'

'Not unless you're prepared to go back the way you came.'

'Of course. No trouble.'

'All right.' He spoke to the coachman. 'You know Robespierre's house?'

He had the satisfaction of hearing a minute quaver in Hébert's voice. 'And when did you arrive back?'

'Two hours ago.'

'And the family? All well?'

'Hébert, you really are a most unpleasant person,' Danton said, settling himself opposite in the well-upholstered seat, 'so it's no use pretending otherwise.'

'Yes, I see.' Hébert gave a sort of nervous giggle. 'Danton, you may have heard about certain speeches I have made.'

'Attacking my friends.'

'Don't put it like that,' Hébert said reproachfully. 'After all, if they've nothing to be ashamed of – I'm just offering them a chance to show what good patriots they are.'

'They have already shown it.'

'But surely, none of us should be afraid to have our conduct held up to scrutiny? The point is, Danton, that I shouldn't like you to imagine that I was criticizing you, yourself.'

'I don't think you would dare.'

'As a matter of fact, I thought that a tactical alliance between us –'

'I could as confidently form a tactical alliance with a sponge.'

'Well, think about it,' Hébert said, without rancour. 'By the way, Camille's in a bad state, isn't he? Fainting like that.'

'I'll tell him of your concern.'

'Chose the most inopportune moment. People are saying – quite understandably I suppose – that he's regretting his part in bringing Brissot down. Soft-hearted, dear Marat used to say. Though it seems fearfully inconsistent with his past conduct. '89. The lynchings. Mm. Here we are. Now then – how shall I put it? Citizen Robespierre's a slippery fish this month. Hard to handle. Take care.'

'Thank you, Hébert, for transporting me.'

Danton swung down from the carriage. Hébert's white face appeared beside him. 'Persuade Camille to take a holiday,' he said.

'He might,' Danton said, 'take the day off if it were your funeral.'

The unctuous smile froze. 'Is that a declaration of war?'

Danton shrugged. 'As you like,' he said. 'Drive on,' he shouted to the coachman. Standing in the street, he wanted to shout obscenities after Père Duchesne, chase him and drive a fist into his face. Hostilities begin here.

'So how's your little sister liking married life?' Danton asked Eléonore.

Eléonore flushed darkly. 'All right I suppose. Philippe Lebas doesn't amount to so much.'

You poor, spiteful, disappointed cow, he thought. 'I can find my own way,' he said.

There was no answer when he knocked. He pushed the door open and walked straight into Robespierre's belligerent stare. He was sitting at his desk with pen, ink, one small notebook.

'Pretending not to be here, then?'

'Danton.' Robespierre got to his feet. He coloured slightly. 'I'm sorry, I thought it was Cornélia.'

'Well, what a way to treat your lady friend! Sit down, relax. What were you writing? A love-letter to somebody else?'

'No, as a matter of fact I – never mind.' Robespierre flicked the little book shut. He sat down at his desk and joined his hands in an attitude of rather nervous prayer. 'I could have done with you a week ago, Danton. Chabot came to see me. I – well, what did you ever think of Chabot?'

Danton noted the past tense. 'I think he is a red-faced buffoon with a cap of liberty on his head and very little of a brain beneath it.'

'This marriage of his, you know ... the Frei brothers are to be arrested tomorrow. It was the marriage that trapped him.'

'The dowry,' Danton said.

'Just so. The so-called brothers are millionaires. And Chabot, he likes all that – he's susceptible. Well, how not? He's kept too many frozen Lents.'

Danton looked closely at Robespierre. He's softening? Possibly.

'It's the girl I feel sorry for, the little Jewess.'

'Yes, but then,' Danton said, 'they say she's not the sister of either of them. They say she was bought out of a brothel in Vienna.'

'They'll say anything, won't they? I do know one thing – Chabot's servant has given birth to his child since he left her. And this is the man who spoke so touchingly to the Jacobins last September about the rights of illegitimate children.'

You can never tell what will upset Robespierre most, Danton thought: treason, peculation or sex. 'Anyway – Chabot came to see you, you were saying.'

'Yes.' Robespierre shook his head, amused by the human condition. 'He had a packet with him which he said contained 100,000 francs.'

'You should have counted it.'

'It was waste-paper, for all I know. He went on in his usual way about plotters, and I said, "Have you any documentary evidence?" He said, "I do, but,"' Robespierre laughed, '"it's all written in invisible ink." Then he said, "This money was given to me to bribe the Committee of Public Safety with, so I thought the best thing to do was to bring it to you. Can I have a safe-conduct? I think I ought to get out of the country."' He looked up at Danton. 'Pitiable, isn't it? We had him picked up at eight o'clock the next morning. He's in the Luxembourg now. We made the mistake of letting him have pen and ink, so now every day he produces yards and yards of self-justificatory maundering which he sends to the Police Committee. Your name crops up a lot, I'm afraid.'

'And not in invisible ink?' Danton asked. 'Talking of which – '
He took Robespierre's letter out of his pocket and dropped it on
the desk between them. 'Well, my old friend – what's all this about
doing away with Hébert?'

'Ah,' Robespierre said. 'Camille and I got together and had a
little panic.'

'I see. So I came all this way because you had a little panic.'

'I spoiled your holiday? I'm sorry. You're quite better, though?'

'Fighting fit. I'm just trying to work out where's the fight.'

'You know,' Robespierre cleared his throat, 'I really think that by
New Year our position may be quite favourable. As long as we get
Toulon back. And here in Paris, rid ourselves of these anti-religious
fanatics. Your friend Fabre is doing a good job on the so-called
businessmen. Tomorrow I intend to obtain four expulsions from
the Jacobins.'

'Of?'

'Proli, this Austrian who has worked for Hérault. And three of
Hébert's friends. To put them outside the club paralyses them. And
it serves as a warning to others.'

'I must point out that recently expulsion from the club has been
the prelude to arrest. And yet Camille says you favour an end to the
Terror?'

'I wouldn't put it – quite so – I mean, I think in a couple of
months we may be able to relax, but there are still a number of
foreign agents that we have to flush out.'

'And that aside, you'd favour a return to the normal judicial
process, and bringing in the new constitution?'

'We're still at war, that's the trouble. Very much at war. You
know what the Convention said – "The government of France is
revolutionary until the peace."'

' "Terror is the order of the day." '

'It was the wrong word, perhaps. You'd think the populace was
going around with its teeth chattering. But it isn't so. The theatres
are open as usual.'

'For the performance of patriotic dramas. They bore me, patriotic
dramas.'

'They are more wholesome than what the theatre used to provide.'

'How would you know? You never go to the theatre.'

Robespierre blinked at him. 'Well, it seems, logically, that it must be so. I can't oversee everything. I haven't time to go to the theatre. But if we return to the point – you must understand that in my private capacity I don't like what has been happening, but I have to admit that politically it has been necessary. Now if Camille were here he would demolish that, but, well, Camille is a theoretician and I have to get on with things in the Committee and reconcile myself ... as best I can. The way I see it ... externally, our situation is much better, but internally we still have an emergency; we still have the Vendée rebels, and a capital full of conspirators. The Revolution is not safe from day to day.'

'Do you know what the hell it is you do want?'

Robespierre looked up at him helplessly. 'No.'

'Can't you think it out?'

'I don't know what's best to do. I seem to be surrounded by people who claim to have all the solutions, but mostly they involve more killings. There are more factions now than before we destroyed Brissot. I am trying to keep them apart, stop them destroying each other.'

'If you wanted to stop the executions, how much support would you have on the Committee?'

'Robert Lindet for sure, probably Couthon and Saint-André: Barère perhaps – I never know what Barère is thinking.' He kept count on his fingers. 'Collot and Billaud-Varennes would be against any policy of moderation.'

'God,' Danton said reflectively, 'Citizen Billaud, the big tough committeeman. He used to come round to my office, '86, '87, and I used to give him work drafting pleadings, so he could keep body and soul together.'

'Yes. No doubt he'll never forgive you.'

'What about Hérault?' Danton said. 'You've forgotten him.'

'No, not forgotten.' Robespierre avoided his eyes. 'I think you know he no longer enjoys our confidence. I trust you'll sever your links with him?'

Let it pass, Danton thought: let it pass. 'Saint-Just?'

Robespierre hesitated. 'He would see it as weakness.'

'Can you not influence him?'

'Perhaps. He has had remarkable successes in Strasbourg. He will tend to think he is working on the right lines. And when people have been with the armies, a few lives in Paris don't seem so important to them. The others – I can probably pull them into line.'

'Then get rid of Collot and Billaud-Varennes.'

'Not possible. They have the backing of all Hébert's people.'

'Then get rid of Hébert.'

'And we're back to a policy of Terror.' Robespierre looked up. 'Danton, you haven't spoken of your own place in this. You must have an opinion.'

Danton laughed. 'You wouldn't be so confident of that, if you knew me better. I shall bide my time. I suggest you do the same.'

'You know you'll be attacked as soon as you appear in public? Hébert has insinuated certain things about your Belgian venture. I'm afraid your illness was regarded as largely mythical. People were saying you had emigrated to Switzerland with your ill-gotten gains.'

'We need a bit of solidarity, then.'

'Yes. I'll speak for you, of course, at every opportunity. Get Camille to write something, do you think? Take his mind off things? I told him to stay away from trials. He's very emotional, isn't he?'

'You say that as if it were a surprise to you. As if you only met him last week.'

'I suppose the degree of it always does come as a surprise to me. Camille's feelings seem uncontainable. Like natural disasters.'

'That can be useful, or it can be a nuisance.'

'That sounds cynical, Danton.'

'Does it? Well, perhaps it is.'

'So perhaps you feel cynical about Camille's affection for you?'

'No, I rather feel grateful. I take what comes my way.'

'It's a trait we have observed in you,' Robespierre said, with interest.

'Was that the royal plural?'

'No, I meant, Camille and I.'

'You discuss me?'

'We discuss everybody. Everything. But you know that. No one is closer than we are.'

'I accept your rebuke. Our friendships with Camille are both of a high order. Oh, that all his friendships had been the same!'

'I don't see how they could have been, really.'

'No, you are pleased to be obtuse.'

Robespierre put his chin on his hand. 'I am. Because I've had to compromise a lot to keep Camille's friendship. It's like everything else in my life. I spend my days crying, "Don't tell me," and, "Sweep that under the carpet before I come into the room."'

'I didn't know you knew that about yourself.'

'Oh yes. I am not a hypocrite myself, but I breed hypocrisy in other people.'

'You must, of course. Robespierre doesn't lie or cheat or steal, doesn't get drunk, doesn't fornicate – overmuch. He's not a hedonist or a main-chancer or a breaker of promises.' Danton grinned. 'But what's the use of all this goodness? People don't try to emulate you. Instead they just pull the wool over your eyes.'

'They?' Robespierre echoed gently. 'Say "we", Danton.' He smiled.

MAXIMILIEN Robespierre, private notebooks:

What is our aim?

    The use of the constitution for the benefit of the people.

    Who are likely to oppose us?

    The rich and corrupt.

    What methods will they employ?

    Slander and hypocrisy.

    What factors will encourage the use of such means?

    The ignorance of ordinary people.

    When will the people be educated?

    When they have enough to eat, and when the rich and the government stop bribing treacherous tongues and pens to deceive them; when their interests are identified with those of the people.

    When will this be?

    Never.

FABRE: So what will you do?

DANTON: I won't see you humiliated. It would reflect on me.

FABRE: But your plans – you must have plans?

DANTON: I do, but there is no call for you to go around the city saying Danton has plans. I want a reconciliation with the Right in the Convention. Robespierre says we must be united, not factious – he's correct. Patriots should not torment each other.

FABRE: You expect them to forgive you for cutting their colleagues' heads off?

DANTON: Camille will launch a press campaign in favour of clemency. In the end I want a negotiated peace, the controls off the economy and a return to constitutional government. It's a big programme and you can't do it in a country that's falling apart, so we have to strengthen the Committee. Keep Robespierre, get rid of Collot and Billaud-Varennes and Saint-Just.

FABRE: You admit now you were mistaken? You should never have let yourself be voted off the Committee last summer.

DANTON: Yes, I should have listened to you. Well, first you admit your mistakes, then you start to retrieve them. All of us made a mistake in treating Hébert as a hack writer with no talents. Before we had recovered from our mistake he had ministers and generals in his pocket – not to mention the rabble. It will take courage to break him, and luck.

FABRE: And then stop the Terror?

DANTON: Yes. Things have gone too far.

FABRE: I agree with that. I want Vadier's hot breath off my neck.

DANTON: That's all it means to you?

FABRE: Come on, man. What does it mean to you? It's not that you're turning soft, are you? You're not mellowing?

DANTON: No? Perhaps I am. Anyway, I work hard to make my own interest coincide with the national interest.

FABRE: Do you want to run the country again, Georges-Jacques?

DANTON: I don't know. I haven't decided what I want.

FABRE: Christ, you'd better decide soon. You're going to take them all on. It's dangerous. You've got to have your wits about you. You can't go into it half-asleep, or you'll ruin us all. I don't know – you don't seem to have much relish for it. You don't seem to be your old self.

DANTON: It's Robespierre, he confuses me. I have the feeling that he's hedging his bets all the time.

FABRE: Well . . . keep Camille sweet.

DANTON: Yes, I was thinking . . . if Camille gets into any trouble, I mean any more trouble, Robespierre will have to stand up and defend him, and that will mean he commits himself.

FABRE: Yes, what a good idea.

DANTON: It doesn't matter what Camille does. Robespierre will always straighten it out for him.

FABRE: We can rely on that.

FABRE D'ÉGLANTINE: When, of course, your whole name incorporates a lie, you continually seek reassurance of your reality, you are constantly seeking sources of self-esteem.

When the East India Company business blew up, I kept well out of it till I raised my price. When the price was right, I committed a crime. But such a small crime! Bear with me. May I ask your indulgence, your good faith for a moment? You see, it wasn't entirely the money.

I wanted them to say: you are a powerful man, Fabre! I wanted to see how high a price they put on my protection. It wasn't my financial acumen that they were buying. Camille has remarked that my head is entirely filled with greasepaint and old prompt-copies, where the brain should be; for my part I am always struck by how closely life resembles a hackneyed theatrical plot. What they wanted was my influence, the status that a close friend of Danton commands. Indirectly, I'm sure, they thought they were buying Danton too. After all, my colleagues in the venture had dealt with him before. I shouldn't like you to think that the East India business happened in isolation. Forgery was just a logical extension of sharp practice, just a further step from currency speculation and crooked army contracts. Except that little step was on to the wrong side of the law: and for people like me in times like this it's a bad thing to be on the wrong side of any law, any law at all. Now the idiot poet is on one side, and on the other side is Danton and the Incorruptible's inseparable companion in boyhood adventures: looking smug.

I'm afraid I see no good coming of it. There was a point – it may have passed you by – when Danton and I abdicated from self-interest. When I say a point, I mean exactly that, a few seconds in which a decision was taken; I don't say that afterwards we behaved differently, or better. When we planned how to win Valmy, we said we would never speak of it, not even to save our own lives.

Now – from that moment when we admitted to each other that there was *something* we wouldn't do – we started to lurch at our destruction like two drunks in the sick early morning. Because each conviction he holds costs the opportunist double-dear; each time he places his trust, he bleeds a little. Valmy turned the tide for the Republic; since then, the French have been able to hold up their heads in Europe.

Now, Danton would never abandon his friends. If that sounds mawkish, I apologize. To put it another way – and this may make more sense to you – every trail I've padded in recent years leads to Danton at the heart of the wood. All the accusations Hébert levels at Lacroix about his Belgian mission are true of Danton. Hébert knows it. Vadier will find me out. He wants Danton too. Why? I suppose he offends his sense of propriety. Vadier is a moralist; so I think, is Fouquier. It is a tendency I deplore. God knows what risks we take, God knows all that Danton has done. God and Camille. God will keep his mouth shut.

When I began denouncing conspiracies, to take the heat off myself, how did I know that Robespierre would seize on everything I said? He was looking for a conspiracy in the heart of patriotism: God help me, I provided one. Assume its existence, and every word and action seems to prove it, so that sometimes one wonders, of course – what if Robespierre's right, and I'm the fool, what if some con-trick I thought was cooked up in a Palais-Royal café is really a gigantic conspiracy woven in Whitehall?

No, no – I won't think about it. A man could go mad.

In a way I wish they'd move in and arrest me. It may sound absurd, but arrest is the only thing that will prevent me from doing things to complicate it even more. My head aches, thinking about it; I get so depressed. It's this waiting that unnerves me, the halt in the chase; keep moving, that's always been my motto, all my life. Perhaps it is a technique of Vadier's, or perhaps they are waiting till they come up with something else, something worse; or waiting till Danton commits himself to my defence?

I am afraid that if things go on as they are I shall never finish *The Maltese Orange*. It's a good play, there are some very creditable verses in it. Perhaps it would be the big success that has always just eluded me.

Danton, these last few days, looks more like a mangy stuffed bear than someone who's planning to set the nation by the ears. He seems much affected by the executions. He spends hours just thinking; you ask him what he's doing and he says, thinking.

And Camille: they'll never pin corruption charges on him, and I don't think they'll try. According to Rabbit, he and Duplessis spend many a cosy afternoon out at that farm of theirs, talking over the details of the fast ones he's pulled: all strictly legal and below board. It's their only point of contact.

But here I am, indulging in abuse again. The truth is that when I see Camille looking so stricken, with his absurdly over-sensitive airs, I want to take hold of him and shake him and say, I am suffering too. Robespierre would tear his hair and vomit if he knew that de Sade had set him off on all this. Unless Danton does something suddenly and soon – but what do I dare expect?

I wouldn't ask him to act before the time's ripe, if he aims at a coup. I wouldn't expect saving my life to be more than an accidental benefit to him. So put that down, on Philippe Fabre's side: I am, basically, a humble man.

I don't feel well, the last two or three weeks. They say we're in for a mild winter. I hope so. I have a terrible cough. I thought of consulting Dr Souberbielle, but I'm not sure I want to hear his verdict. His medical one, I mean; he's a juror of the Tribunal, but with that verdict I wouldn't have a choice.

I've no appetite, and I get pains in my chest. Oh well, it may not matter soon.

*

DANTON TO THE CONVENTION, asking for state pensions for priests who have lost their livings:

If a priest is without means of support, what do you expect him to do? He will die, or join the Vendée rebels, or become your irreconcilable enemy . . . You have to temper political claims with those of reason and sanity . . . There must be no intolerance, no persecution. [*Applause.*]

DANTON: Scuttled Chaumette. I'll ram his Worship of Reason up – down his throat. We ought to have an end to these anti-religious masquerades. Every day in the Convention we have to listen to a dreary procession of clerics wringing out their souls like laundry, and abjuring their faith takes them as long as a High Mass. There is a limit, and I shall put it to them that the limit has been reached.

CAMILLE: While you were away some sansculottes came in with a skull, they said it was the skull of Saint Denis. They said it was a grisly relic of a superstitious age, and they wanted it off their hands. I'd have had it. I wanted to show it to Saint-Just.

DANTON: Imbeciles.

LOUISE: I wouldn't have taken Citizen Robespierre for a religious man.

DANTON: He's not, in your sense. But he doesn't want to see persecution, and he doesn't want atheism elevated into a policy. Oh, but there's one thing he'd like much better than running the Revolution. He'd like to be Pope.

CAMILLE: Vulgarity incarnate! He aims higher.

DANTON: Saint Maximilien?

CAMILLE: He never talks about God any more, he talks about the Supreme Being. I think I know who that is.

DANTON: Maximilien?

CAMILLE: Right.

DANTON: You'll get into trouble for laughing at people. Saint-Just says that people who laugh at the heads of governments are suspect.

CAMILLE: What fate is reserved for those who laugh at Saint-Just? The guillotine is too good for them.

*

VADIER (on Danton):

We'll clean up the rest of them, and leave that great stuffed turbot till the end.

DANTON (on Vadier):

Vadier? I'll eat his brains and use his skull to shit in.

ROBESPIERRE to the Jacobin Club: the low-key delivery, the fading pauses that do not relate to sense, have now become a practised technique, hypnotic in effect:

'Danton, they accuse you of having ... emigrated, gone off to Switzerland, laden with the spoils of your ... corruption. Some people even say that you were at the head of a conspiracy to enthrone Louis XVII, on the understanding that ... you were to be Regent ... Now I ... have observed Danton's political opinions – because we have sometimes disagreed – I have observed them closely and at times ... with hostility. It is true that ... he was slow to suspect ... Dumouriez, that he failed to show himself implacable against ... Brissot and his accomplices. But if we did not always ... see eye-to-eye ... must I conclude that he was betraying his country? To the best of my knowledge he had always served it zealously. If Danton is on trial here I am on trial ... too. Let all those people who have anything to say against Danton come ... forward now. Let them stand up, those who are more ... patriotic ... than we.'

'IF YOU COULD spare me a few minutes,' Fouquier-Tinville said. His demeanour certainly suggested he didn't have much time to waste. 'Family feeling, you know.'

'Oh yes?' Lucile said.

Fouquier thought, what a prize she is; far too good for anyone in our family. 'May I sit?' he said. 'A regrettable incident – '

'What has happened?' she said. And actually, he noticed with amusement, put her lovely hand to her throat.

'No, no – my description was a true one. Nothing has happened to him, in the sense that you fear.'

How would you know, she thought, in what senses I fear? She sat down opposite the Public Prosecutor. 'Well then, cousin?'

'You recollect the name of Barnave, my dear? He was a deputy in the National Assembly. He had been in prison for some time. We guillotined him today. He had secret dealings with Antoinette.'

'Yes,' she said. 'I knew him. Poor Tiger.'

'Were you aware of your husband's affection for this traitor?'

She looked up quickly. 'Please leave your courtroom manner aside. I'm not in the dock.'

Fouquier threw up his hands. 'I didn't mean to frighten you.'

'That is not what you do.'

'Then I'm sorry I offended you. But it is a proven fact that Barnave was a traitor.'

'What can I say? Treason is a betrayal, so there must be some state of trust and acceptance that precedes it. Barnave never pretended to be a republican. Camille respected him – I think it was mutual.'

'Is respect so rare a thing for my cousin to command?'

'Well yes, I think it is really.'

'Despite his abilities?'

'People do not respect writers, do they? They think it is one of those things they can do without. Like money.'

'I don't think political journalists are expected to sacrifice much for their art. Except veracity. Still, this is trivial.'

'I don't think so. We have never had a discussion before.'

'Well, perhaps it is not trivial, but I have not time for it.' The Revolution, he thought, is suddenly full of disputatious women. Here is this white-skinned beauty, who has equipped herself with a whole repertoire of her husband's mannerisms: and one hears tales of that gawk Eléonore Duplay: one hears even of Danton's child-bride. Fools to themselves, he thinks; the way to save your neck is to keep out of it, and as women they have an excuse for doing so. 'However it comes about,' he said, 'it seems that your husband could not let Barnave go to his death without speaking with him. He came to the Conciergerie just as Barnave was about to step into the tumbrel. I was out of earshot, and I took care to remain so. But

I could not help but notice that your husband showed the liveliest distress and regret at the proper punishment of this traitor.'

'Citizen Fouquier, may one not show distress and regret at the death of a man one has known in happier times? Is there a law to forbid it?'

Fouquier looked at her appraisingly. 'I saw them embrace,' he said. 'I could not stop myself from seeing it. Of course, I did not put any construction on it. I shall remind them to tie people's hands, I cannot think how it was omitted. It is really not a matter of what is permitted. It is a matter of how things appear. Many people would not be able to help putting a construction on such a display of friendship towards a traitor.'

'Have you a heart?' she asked in a low voice.

'I do my job, my dear,' he said swiftly. 'Now you tell my little cousin from me that his attitude is very dangerous. Whatever he is misguided enough to feel, he cannot afford these extravagant displays of sentimentality.'

'Why should he hide his pity?'

'Because he is compromising his friends. If those friends wish to change their policies, no doubt they would like to say so for themselves.'

'I think you may hear them say so, before long.' I should not have said that, she thought; but he makes me angry, his long face, his hypocrisy. He only worries that he may be out of a job.

Fouquier smiled bleakly. 'If they speak in concert, I shall be surprised. Any relaxation of Terror will split the Committee. It is only the Committee that is holding things together – the revenue, the armies, the food supplies.'

'The composition of the Committee could be changed.'

'Indeed? Is that Danton's plan.'

'Are you spying for someone?'

Fouquier shook his head. 'I am no one's agent. I am the agent of the law. All the conspiracies pass through my hands. The Committee, you know, draws its present unity from being conspired against. I do not know what would happen if the policy of believing in conspiracies were changed. Also, some of the members are by now quite naturally attached to it as an institution. The war, of course, is the major reason for the Committee's existence. And they say Danton wants peace.'

'So does Robespierre. He's always wanted it.'

'Ah, but can they work together? Robespierre would demand the sacrifice of Lacroix and Fabre. Danton would not agree to work with Saint-Just. So it goes. *Praising* each other is all very well. Let us see how they manage when they get to the stage beyond praise.'

'It is a grim outlook then, cousin,' she said lightly.

'All my outlooks are grim,' Fouquier said. 'Perhaps it's the nature of my work.'

'What would you advise my husband to do? I mean, supposing he were inclined to take your advice?'

They both smiled; seeing, separately, the unlikelihood of this. Fouquier considered for a moment. 'I think I would advise him to do exactly as Robespierre says – nothing less, and certainly nothing more.'

There was a pause. Lucile was disturbed; he had put, for the first time, certain possibilities into her head. Surprising herself, she asked, 'Do you think Robespierre can survive?'

'Do you mean, do I think he is too good to live?' Fouquier stood up. 'I don't make predictions. It's enough to make a person suspect.' He kissed her cheek, in the manner of an uncle with a little girl. 'Concentrate on surviving yourself, my love. I do.'

DANTON [*in the National Convention*]: We must punish traitors, but we must distinguish between error and crime. The will of the people is that Terror should be the order of the day, but it must be directed against the real enemies of the Republic and against them alone. A man whose only fault is lack of revolutionary vigour should not be treated as a criminal.

DEPUTY FAYAU: Danton has, unintentionally I'm sure, employed certain expressions that I find offensive. At a time when the people need to harden their hearts, Danton has asked them to show *mercy*.

MONTAGNARDS: He didn't! He didn't!

PRESIDENT: Order!

DANTON: I did not use that word. I did not suggest showing
leniency to criminals. I ask for vigorous action against them. I
denounce conspirators!

IN THE LUXEMBOURG, the ex-Capuchin Chabot declined to let the
state of the nation weigh on his spirits. He missed his little bride, it
was true – but one must sleep, drink, eat. On 17 November he had
bread, soup, four cutlets, a chicken, a pear and some grapes. On the
18th, bread and soup, boiled beef and six larks. On the 19th he
omitted the larks and instead ordered a partridge. On 7 December,
another partridge: next day, a chicken cooked with truffles.

He wrote verses, and had a miniature painted by Citizen Bénard.

XI. *The Old Cordeliers*

(1793–1794)

ANOTHER DIARY finished: not one of the red books, but one of the little insignificant brown ones. The early works are a feast of embarrassment, Lucile thought; she had taken to ripping the pages out, to burning them, and because of this the books were falling apart.

Nowadays, what she put in the official diaries – as she thought of them – was very different from what went into the brown notebooks. The tone of the official diaries became more and more anodyne, with the occasional thoughtful or striking passage to titillate or mislead. The private diaries were for dark, precise thoughts: unpalatable thoughts, recorded in a minute hand. When one book was finished she sealed it up in a packet, breaking the seal only to place another one beside it, perhaps a year later.

On a chilly, misty day, footfalls muffled in the streets, the great buildings distant and shimmering, she went into Saint-Sulpice, to the High Altar where she had been married three years before. On the wall letters in red paint told her THIS IS A NATIONAL BUILDING: LIBERTY, EQUALITY, FRATERNITY OR DEATH. The Virgin held in her arms a headless child, and her face was battered beyond recognition.

Perhaps if I had not met Camille, she thought, I could have had an ordinary kind of life. No one would have encouraged my fantasies. No one would have taught me to think. When I was eleven, all the possibilities of being ordinary stretched out in front of me. When I was twelve, Camille came to the house. I was committed to him the first time I saw him.

Her life is rewriting itself for her; she believes this.

At the apartment Camille was working in a bad light. He was living on alcohol and sleeping three hours a night. 'You'll ruin your eyes,' she said automatically.

'They're ruined already.' He put his pen down. 'Look, a news-paper.'

'So you are going to do it.'

'I think I must call it more a series of pamphlets, as I shall be the sole author. Desenne is going to print for me. In the first issue – here – I just talk about the British government. I shall point out that, after Robespierre's recent speech in praise of Danton, anyone who criticizes Danton gives a public receipt for the guineas of Mr Pitt.' He stopped to write down the last phrase. 'It will not really be controversial, but it will be another setback to Danton's detractors, and it will prepare the way for an appeal for mercy in the courts and the release of some of the suspects.'

'But Camille, do you dare do that?'

'Of course, if I have Danton and Robespierre to back me. Don't you think?'

She put her hands together. 'If they are in agreement,' she said. She had not told him that Fouquier had called.

'They are,' he said calmly. 'Only Robespierre is cautious, he needs pushing on a bit.'

'What did he say to you about the Barnave affair?'

'There wasn't a "Barnave affair". I went to say goodbye to him. I didn't think he should have been executed. I told him so.' That was what Fouquier escaped hearing, she thought. 'Not that it did him much good for me to absolve him, but it did me good to be forgiven, for whatever part I had in bringing him there.'

'But what did Max say?'

'I think he understood. It wasn't really his business, was it? I met Barnave at my cousin de Viefville's apartment in Versailles. I hardly spoke with him, but he took notice of me, as if he thought he would see me again. That night I decided to go to Mirabeau.' He closed his eyes. 'The print order is 50,000.'

In the afternoon Louise came. She was lonely, though she didn't admit it. She didn't want her mother's company, which was forced on her if she stayed at home. Angélique had taken the children for a few days; in their absence, and especially when her husband was not in the house, she would become once again a shy girl darting up and down the stairs. Danton's answer to her lack of occupation was, 'Go and spend some money.' But there was nothing she wanted for herself, and she hesitated to make any changes in the apartment. She did not trust her taste; besides, she thought that her husband might prefer Gabrielle's arrangements left as they were.

A year, eighteen months before, she would have been taken as Danton's wife to the afternoon salons with their mordant gossip, to sit stiffly among the wives of ministers and Paris deputies, self-possessed women of thirty and thirty-five who had read all the latest books and discussed their husband's love affairs with drawling boredom. But that had not been Gabrielle's way; and there was enough of a battle of wits with the visitors she did receive. Either she was tongue-tied, or far too forthright. The things they talked about seemed so trivial that she was convinced that they must have a double meaning to which she was not privy. She had no choice but to join their game; in consideration of her status they had tossed her a book of rules, but they had left her to read it by flashes of lightning.

So – and she could not have predicted this – the apartment round the corner was the most comforting place to be. These days Citizeness Desmoulins kept to her family and a few close friends; she could not be bothered with the stupidities of society, she said. Louise sat in her drawing room day by day, trying to reconstruct the recent past from hints that came her way. Lucile never asked personal questions; herself, she didn't know any other kind to ask. Sometimes they talked about Gabrielle: softly, naturally, as if she were still alive.

Today Louise said, 'You're very gloomy.'

'I have to finish writing this,' Lucile said. 'Then I'll be with you and we'll try to cheer up.'

Louise played for a while with the baby, a doll-like creature who could not possibly have been Danton's child. He talked a lot now – mostly in a meaningless language, as if he knew he were a politician's child. When he was taken away to sleep, she picked up her guitar and fingered it softly. She scowled. 'I don't think I have any talent,' she said to Lucile.

'You should concentrate when you are playing, and do the easier pieces. But I cannot preach, as I never practise.'

'No, you never do now. You used to go to art exhibitions and concerts in the afternoon, but now you only sit and read and write letters. Who do you write to?'

'Oh, several people. I have a great correspondence with Citizen Fréron, our old family friend.'

Louise was on the alert. 'Very fond of him, aren't you?'

Lucile seemed amused. 'More so when he's away.'

'Would you marry him, if Camille died?'

'He's married already.'

'He'd get a divorce, I expect. Or his wife might die.'

'That would be altogether too much of a coincidence. What is all this about dying?'

'There are hundreds of diseases. You can never tell.'

'I used to think that. When I was first married, and everything frightened me.'

'But you would not stay a widow, would you?'

'Yes, I would.'

'Camille wouldn't want that, surely?'

'I don't know why you think he wouldn't. He is very egotistical.'

'If you died, he'd remarry.'

'Within the week,' Lucile agreed. 'If my father died too. In your scheme of things, with people passing away in pairs, that would be quite likely.'

'There must be other men you would like enough to marry.'

'I can't think of any. Unless Georges.'

That was how she ended conversations, when she thought Louise had probed too far – reminding her with a neat brutality of where they stood. She did not enjoy it; but she knew that other people had less scruple. Louise sat gazing into the ruins of the year, in the shifting grey and blue light, trying out pieces that were too difficult for her. Camille was working. The only sound in the apartment were the dissonant chords and broken notes.

At four o'clock he came in with a stack of papers. He sat on the floor in front of the fire. Lucile gathered up the papers and began to read. After a while she looked up. 'It's very good,' she said shyly. 'I think it's going to be the best thing you've done.'

'Do you want to read it, little Louise?' he asked. 'It says nice things about your husband.'

'I like to take an interest in politics, but he doesn't want me to.'

'Perhaps,' he said, exasperated, 'he wouldn't mind if your interest were an informed one. It's your silly, vulgar prejudices he doesn't want to hear.'

'Camille,' Lolotte said softly, 'she's a child. How do you expect her to know things?'

At five o'clock Robespierre came. He said, 'How are you, Citizeness Danton?' as if she were a grown-up person. He kissed Lucile on the cheek and patted Camille on the head. The baby was brought; he held him up and said, 'How goes it, godson?'

'Don't ask him,' Camille said. 'He makes five-hour speeches, like Necker used to do, and they're just as incomprehensible.'

'Oh I don't know.' Robespierre held the little boy against his shoulder. 'He doesn't look like a banker to me. Is he going to be an ornament of the Paris Bar?'

'A poet,' Camille decided. 'Live in the country. Generally have a very nice time.'

'Probably,' Robespierre said. 'I doubt his boring old godfather will manage to keep him on the straight and narrow.' He handed the child over to his father. He was all business now, sitting in his upright way in a chair by the fire. 'When the proofs are ready, tell Desenne to send them straight round to me. I'd read it in manuscript but I detest wrestling with your handwriting.'

'You must correct the proofs then, or it will all take too long. Don't mess about with my punctuation.'

'Ah, Camille d'Églantine,' Robespierre said mockingly. 'No one is going to be interested in the punctuation, only in the content.'

'It is easy to see why you will never win a literary prize.'

'I thought you were heart and soul in this new paper, I thought you felt passionately?'

'I do feel passionately, and about punctuation too.'

'When will the second issue be out?'

'It will be every five days, I hope – 5 December, 10th, *ci-devant* Christmas, so on – till the job is done.'

Robespierre hesitated for a moment. 'But show me everything, won't you? Because I don't want you attributing to me things I haven't said, and foisting on me opinions I don't hold.'

'Would I do that?'

'You would, and you do. Look at your baby, turning his eyes on you. He knows your true character. What are you going to call it?'

'I thought the "Old Cordelier". It was a phrase Georges-Jacques used. "We old Cordeliers", he said.'

'Yes I like that. You see,' he said, turning to the women, 'it puts the new Cordeliers – Hébert's people – neatly in their place. The new Cordeliers don't represent anything, they don't stand for anything – they just oppose and criticize what other people do, and try to destroy it. But the old Cordeliers – they knew what kind of revolution they wanted, and they took risks to get it. Those early days, they didn't seem so heroic at the time, but they do looking back.'

'Was it in those days they used to call you "The Candle of Arras", Citizen Robespierre?'

'In those days!' Robespierre said. 'The child talks as if it were in the reign of Louis XIV. I suppose your husband told you about that?'

'Oh yes – I don't know anything by myself.'

Camille and his wife exchanged glances: strangle her now, or later?

'It's quite true,' Robespierre said. 'It was because they called Mirabeau "The Torch of Provence". The idea was,' he added remorselessly, 'to bring home to me my own insignificance.'

'Yes. He explained that. Why do you think then that those days were heroic?'

'Why do you think that all heroes are people who make a great stir in the world?'

'I hadn't thought about it. I suppose, because of books.'

'Someone should direct your reading.'

'Oh, she is a married woman,' Camille said. 'She is beyond education.'

'I see you don't like to be reminded of it,' Louise said. 'I am sorry. I didn't mean to give offence.'

Robespierre smiled, shook his head. But he turned away from her: no time for this little girl now. 'Camille, remember what I say. Go carefully. We can't take any power from the Tribunal. If we do, and there are any reverses in the war, it will be like September again. The people will take the law into their own hands, and we've seen that, and it's not pleasant. The government must be strong, it can't be tentative – otherwise, what are the patriots at the front to think? A strong army deserves a strong government behind it. We must aim at unity. Force can overturn a throne, but only prudence can maintain a republic.'

Camille nodded, recognizing the unclothed bones of a speech to come. He felt guilty, about laughing at Max and saying he wanted to be God; he wasn't God, God's not so vulnerable.

Max left. Camille said, 'I feel like an egg in a dog's mouth.' He looked up at Louise. 'I hope you are sufficiently reproved? Otherwise, please go home to your husband, and tell him to beat you.'

'Oh dear,' Louise said. 'I thought it was all in the past.'

'One doesn't really forget. Not that kind of thing.'

Danton came in a few minutes later. 'Ah, the Old Cordelier himself,' Lucile said.

'There you are,' he said to his wife. 'Have I just missed our friend?'

'You know damn well you have,' Camille said. 'You must have skulked in a doorway till you saw him go.'

'We work together better when we're apart.' He collapsed into a chair, stretched his legs, regarded Camille. 'What's so worrying?' he asked him abruptly.

'Oh . . . he keeps telling me to go carefully, as if – as if, I mustn't do anything he wouldn't do himself, but he won't tell me what it is he would do.'

Camille was still sitting on the floor, and now Lucile was kneeling beside him: their flattering, wide-eyed attention fixed on Georges-Jacques, and the baby rolling about between them. Really, Louise thought, hating them, it's as if they're always waiting for somebody to come along with a crayon and a sketching-block. When you think of her with her string of lovers ... It's sickening, how easy they find it to put on their act. Camille was saying, 'Max doesn't like to be cornered with an untried opinion. But there you are – some risks have to be taken. I don't mind if I'm the first to take them. Would that count as a heroic sentiment, Louise?'

She spoke sharply: 'Hero's your vocation, isn't it?'

So everybody laughed, at Camille.

DECEMBER 5: 'To the Old Cordeliers.' Fabre raised his glass. His face was hollow and flushed. 'May the second issue prosper like the first.'

'Thank you.' Camille actually looked modest; at least he lowered his head and dropped his eyes, which is the outward sign of the inward grace. 'I didn't expect it to be so successful. As if people were waiting for it ... I feel quite overwhelmed by the public support.'

Deputy Philippeaux – one of these mystery deputies who are always on mission, whom he hardly knew until last week – leaned forward and patted his hand. 'It's wonderful, that's why! It – well, you know, I've written my own pamphlet, but I feel that if you'd seen the things I've seen, you'd have done it so much better. You can –' the deputy touched his elegant cravat – 'you can move the heart, I can only appeal to the conscience. Slaughter is what I've seen, you know?' Strong language didn't come easily to him. He'd sat with the Plain, not the Mountain, and carefully trimmed his opinions: until now.

'Oh, slaughter,' Fabre said. 'Our boy couldn't stand it. One Brissotin with a small dagger hidden in his defence papers, that's enough for him. He couldn't take an atrocity, I'm afraid. Faints, I fear. Gracefully, mind.'

Amazing, how resilient Fabre is. Camille, too. A small part of him feels like lead; the rest of him is ready for the fray, making the most of his capacity to drive people to a finger-twitching fury, or into a long, swooning, sentimental decline from sense. He feels light, very young. The artist Hubert Robert (whose speciality, unfortunately, is picturesque ruins) is always on his heels these days; the artist Boze is constantly giving him hard looks, and occasionally walks over to him and with unfeeling artist hands pulls his hair about. In his worse moods he thinks – get ready to be immortalized.

The main thing is, the constraints have come off style. What we are saying now is that the Revolution does not proceed in a pitiless, forward direction, its politics and its language becoming ever more gross and simplistic: the Revolution is always flexible, subtle, elegant. Mirabeau said: 'Liberty's a bitch who likes to be fucked on a mattress of corpses.' He knows this is true: but he will find some gentler way of presenting it to his reader.

He could be himself now ... that is to say, as different from Hébert as one could imagine. He need make no concession to street language, he need not rant, he need not present himself as Marat's heir; though still he thought of Simone's plump body slumped in his arms, and of the fashion-plate who killed his friend. Forget Marat, and the black distress he bred; he's going to create a new, Ultima Thule atmosphere, very plain, very bright, every word translucent, smooth. The air of Paris is like dried blood; he will (with Robespierre's permission and approval) make us feel that we breathe ice, silk and wine.

'By the way,' Deputy Philippeaux said, 'did you know that de Sade has been arrested?'

'DEPUTY PHILIPPEAUX, Deputy Philippeaux,' Robespierre said. 'Returning from mission, he attacks the conduct of the war. The commanders in the Vendée,' he flicked open Philippeaux's little publication, 'are the commanders who Hébert has in his pocket, and legitimate objects of suspicion. If we except Westermann, who is Danton's friend. Unfortunately,' he reached for his pen, 'Deputy Philippeaux doesn't stop there.' He bent his head, began to underline certain phrases. 'He levels accusations at the Committee, as the Committee has ultimate responsibility for the war. He seems to say that it would have been over a lot sooner, if it hadn't been kept going to line people's pockets.'

'Philippeaux has been a great deal with Danton and Camille,' the committeeman said. 'I only mention it.'

'It's the kind of thesis that would appeal to Camille,' Robespierre said. 'Do you believe it? Oh, I don't know.'

'You question the good faith of your colleagues on the Committee?'

'Yes, actually,' Robespierre said. 'Yet I'm quite persuaded of the need to keep the Committee functioning. Stories are coming back from Lyon about the doings of our friend Collot. They say that he has taken his orders to punish rebels as meaning he should massacre the populace.'

'Oh, they say.'

Robespierre put his fingertips together. 'Collot is an actor, isn't he, a theatrical producer? Once he would have had to satisfy himself by putting on plays about earthquakes and multiple murders. Now he can enact what he dreams. Four years of Revolution, Citizen – and everywhere the same greed, pettiness and egoism, the same brutal indifference to the suffering of others, and the same diabolic thirst for blood. I simply can't fathom the depth of people.' He rested his forehead on his hand. His colleague stared at him, stunned. 'Meanwhile,' he said, 'what is Danton doing? Can he be encouraging Deputy Philippeaux?'

'He would do it – if he saw some temporary advantage. The Committee must silence Philippeaux.'

'No need.' He stabbed his pen at the printed page. 'You see he attacks Hébert? Hébert will do it for us. Let him make himself useful, for once.'

'But you allow Camille to attack Hébert, here in his second issue. Oh,' the committeeman said. 'Both ends against the middle? You are clever, aren't you?'

DECREE of the National Convention:

The Executive Council, the ministers, generals and all constituted bodies, are placed under the supervision of the Committee of Public Safety.

CAMILLE: I don't see why I should expect any plaudits for the third issue. Anyone could have done it. It's a kind of translation. I was reading Tacitus, on the reign of the Emperor Tiberius. I said to de Sade that it was the same, and I checked it, and it was. Our lives now are what the annalist describes: whole families wiped out by the executioner, men committing suicide to save themselves from being dragged through the streets like common criminals; men denouncing their friends to save their own skins; the corruption of all human feeling, the degradation of pity to a crime. I remember when I first read it, years and years ago; and Robespierre will remember when he first read it, too.

There didn't seem much to add – it was enough to bring the text to the public's attention. Take out the names of these Romans, and substitute instead – in your own mind – the names of Frenchmen and women, the names of people you know, people who live on your street, people whose fate you have seen and whose fate you may soon share.

Of course I have had to rearrange the text a bit – bugger about with it, as Hébert would say. I didn't show it to Robespierre. Yes, I imagine it will be a shock to him. But a salutary one, don't you think? I mean, if he recognizes this state of affairs, he will have to think of his own part in creating it. It seems ridiculous to say that Robespierre is a Tiberius, and of course that isn't what I'm saying; but with a certain sort of man about him – yes indeed, I do mean Saint-Just – I don't know what he might become.

There is a description in Tacitus of the Emperor 'without pity, without anger, resolutely closing himself against the inroad of emotion'.

This seemed familiar.

THE 'VIEUX CORDELIER', No. 3:

As soon as words had become crimes against the state, it was only a small step to transform into offences mere glances, sorrow, compassion, sighs, even silence . . .

It was a crime against the state that Libonius Drusus asked the fortune tellers if he would ever be rich . . . It was a crime against the state that one of Cassius' descendants had a portrait of his ancestor in his house. Mamercus Scaurus committed a crime by writing a tragedy in which certain verses were capable of a double meaning. It was a crime against the state that the mother of the consul Furius Geminus mourned for the death of her son ... It was necessary to rejoice at the death of a friend or relative, if one wished to escape death oneself.

Was a citizen popular? He might start a faction. Suspect.

Did he try instead to retreat from public life? Suspect.

Are you rich? Suspect.

Are you – to all appearances – poor? You must be hiding something. Suspect.

Are you melancholy? The state of the nation must upset you. Suspect.

Are you cheerful? You must be rejoicing at national calamities. Suspect.

Are you a philosopher, an orator or a poet? Suspect.

'YOU DIDN'T show me this,' Robespierre said. His voice was toneless. The breeze whipped the last of the year's dead leaves past his face. He caught one, and held it up between finger and thumb so that its veins were sharply exposed against the afternoon light. It had been a fine day; sunset was liquid and crimson; the last rays touched the river in a manner more sinister than picturesque.

'Like blood,' Camille said. 'Well that is what it would suggest. I didn't keep anything from you. You probably have Tacitus on your bookshelves.'

'You are being disingenuous.'

'You must admit it is very apt. If it were not apt it would not have caught the public imagination. Yes, it is a portrait of the way we live now.'

'And you hold it up to Europe? Could you not restrain yourself? Do you want to make yourself the Emperor's favourite reading? Do you expect a message of congratulation from Mr Pitt? Fireworks in Moscow, and your health drunk in the *émigré* camps across the Rhine?' He spoke with a flat calm, as if the questions were reasonable ones. 'Well, tell me.' He put his hands, palms down, on the stonework of the bridge and turned to look into Camille's face; he waited.

'What are we doing out here?' Camille said. 'It's getting cold.'

'I'd rather talk outside. Inside, you can't keep secrets.'

'You see – you admit it. You're eaten away with the thought of conspiracy. Will you guillotine brick walls and doorposts?'

'I'm not eaten away with anything – except perhaps the desire to do what's best for the country.'

'Then stop the Terror.' Camille shivered a little. 'You have the moral leadership. You're the one who can do it.'

'And have the government fall apart around us? Bring the Committee down?' His voice now was a rapid, urgent whisper. 'I can't do it. I can't take that risk.'

'Let's walk on a little way.' They walked. 'Change the Committee,' Camille said. 'That's all I ask. Collot and Billaud-Varennes are not fit for you to associate yourself with.'

'You know why they're there. They're our sop to the Left.'

'I keep forgetting that we're not the Left.'

'Do you want us to have insurrection on our hands?'

Camille halted again, looked across the river. 'Yes, if necessary. Yes.' He was trying to stop the panic bubbling up inside him, stop the racing of his heart; Robespierre was not used to opposition now, and he was not used to opposing him. 'Let's fight it out once and for all.'

'Is that Danton's wish? More violence?'

'Max, what do you think is being done every day in the Place de la Révolution?'

'I'd rather sacrifice aristocrats than sacrifice each other. I have a loyalty to the Revolution and the men who made it. But you are defaming it in the face of all Europe.'

'Do you think that loyalty is covering up, pretending that reason and justice prevail?' The light had faded into the river, and now a night wind was getting up; it pulled at their clothes with cold insistent hands. 'What did we have the Revolution for? I thought it was so that we could speak out against oppression. I thought it was to free us from tyranny. But this is tyranny. Show me a worse one in the history of the world. People have killed for power and greed and delight in blood, but show me another dictatorship that kills with efficiency and delights in virtue and flourishes its abstractions over open graves. We say that everything we do is to preserve the Revolution, but the Revolution is no more than an animated corpse.'

Robespierre would not look at him; but without doing so, he reached out for his arm. 'Everything you say is true,' he whispered, 'but I don't know how to proceed.' A pause. 'Come, let's go home.'

'You said we couldn't talk inside.'

'There's no need to talk, is there? You've said it all.'

HÉBERT, Le Père Duchesne:

Here, my brave sansculottes, here is a brave man you've forgotten. It is really ungrateful of you, for he declares that without him there would never have been a Revolution. Formerly he was known as My Lord Prosecutor to the Lanterne. You think I am speaking of that famous cut-throat who put the aristocrats to flight – but no, the man we're speaking of claims to be the most pacific of persons. To believe him, he has no more gall than a pigeon; he is so sensitive, that he never hears the word 'guillotine' without shivering to his very bones. It is a great pity that he is no orator, or he would prove to the Committee of Public Safety that it has no idea how to manage things; but if he cannot speak, M. Camille can make up for it by writing, to the great satisfaction of the moderates, aristocrats and royalists.

PROCEEDINGS of the Jacobin Club:

CITIZEN NICOLAS [*intervening*]: Camille, you are very close to the guillotine!
CITIZEN DESMOULINS: Nicolas, you are very close to making a fortune! A year ago you dined on a baked apple, and now you're the government printer.
(Laughter.)

HÉRAULT DE SÉCHELLES came back from Alsace in the middle of December. The job was done. The Austrians were in retreat and the frontier was secure; Saint-Just would be following in a week or two, trailing glory.

He called on Danton, and Danton was not at home. He left him a message, arranging a meeting, and Danton did not come. He went to Robespierre's house, and was turned away by the Duplays.

He stood at a window of the Tuileries, to watch the death-carts on their route, and sometimes he followed them to the end of the journey and mingled with the crowds. He heard of wives who denounced their husbands to the Tribunal, and husbands wives; mothers who offered their sons to National Justice and children who betrayed their parents. He saw women hustled from their lying-in, suckling their babies till the tumbrel arrived. He saw men and women slip and fall face down in the spilt blood of their friends, and the executioners haul them up by their pinioned arms. He saw dripping heads held up for the crowds to bay at. 'Why do you force yourself to watch these things?' someone asked him.

'I am learning how to die.'

29 FRIMAIRE, Toulon fell to the Republican armies. The hero of the hour was a young artillery officer called Buonaparte. 'If things go on as they are with the officers,' Fabre said, 'I give Buonaparte three months before he gets his head cut off.'

Three days later, 2 Nivôse, government forces smashed the remains of the rebel army of the Vendée. Peasants taken under arms were outlaws to be shot out of hand; nothing remained except the bloody manhunt through fields and woods and marshes.

In the green room with the silver mirrors, the disparate and factious members of the Committee of Public Safety were settling their differences. They were winning the war, and keeping the precarious peace on the Paris streets. 'Under this Committee,' said the People, 'the Revolution is on the march.'

IT HAD GROWN DARK. Eléonore thought that the room was empty. When Robespierre turned his head, the movement startled her. His face was white in the shadows. 'Are you not going to the Committee?' she said softly. He turned his head away, so that he was looking at the wall again. 'Shall I light the lamp?' she said. 'Please speak to me. Nothing can be so bad.'

She stood behind his chair and slipped a hand on to his shoulder. She felt him stiffen. 'Don't touch me.'

She removed her hand. 'What have I done wrong?' She waited for an answer. 'You're being childish. You can't sit here in the cold and dark.'

No reply. She walked rapidly from the room, leaving the door ajar. She was back in a moment with a taper, which she touched to the wood and kindling laid ready in the grate. She knelt down by the hearth, tending the infant flames, her dark hair sliding over her shoulder.

'I will not have lights,' he said.

She leaned forward, placing another splinter of wood, fanning the blaze. 'I know you'll let it go right out if I don't watch it,' she said. 'You always do. I have only just got in from my class. Citizen David commended my work today. Would you like to see? I can run downstairs and get my folio.' She looked up at him, still kneeling, her hands spread out on her thighs.

'Get up from there,' he said. 'You are not a servant.'

'No?' Her voice was cool. 'What am I? It would be against your principles to speak to a servant as you speak to me.'

'Five days ago,' he said, 'I proposed to the Convention that we should set up a Committee of Justice to examine the verdicts of the Tribunal and to look into the cases of those imprisoned on suspicion. I thought this was what was needed; apparently not, though. I have just seen the fourth issue of the "Old Cordelier". Here.' He pushed the pamphlet across the desk. 'Read it.'

'I can't, in this light.' She lit the candles, lifting one high to look into his face. 'Your eyes are red. You have been crying. I didn't think you cried when you were criticized in the press. I thought you were beyond that.'

'It's not criticism,' he said. 'It's not criticism that's the problem, it's quite other, it's the claims, it's the claims made on me. I am addressed by name. Look.' He pointed to the place on the page. 'Eléonore, who has been more merciful than I have? Seventy-five of Brissot's supporters are in prison. I have fought the committees and the Convention for these men's lives. But this is not enough for Camille – it's not nearly enough. He wants to force me into some – some kind of bullring. Read it.'

She took the pamphlet, brought a chair up to his desk to get the light. 'Robespierre, you are my old school comrade, and you remember the lesson history and philosophy taught us: that love is stronger and more enduring than fear.' *Love is stronger and more enduring than fear*; she glanced up at him, then down at the printed page. 'You have come very close to this idea in the measure passed at your instance during the session of 30 Frimaire. What has been proposed is a Committee of *Justice*. Yet why should *mercy* be looked upon as a crime under the Republic?'

Eléonore looked up. 'The prose,' Robespierre said. 'It's so clean, no conceits, no show, no wit. He means every word. Formerly, you see, he meant every other word. That was his style.'

'Release from prison the 200,000 citizens you call "suspects". In the Declaration of the Rights of Man there is no provision for imprisonment on suspicion.

'You seem determined to wipe out opposition by using the guillotine – but it is a senseless undertaking. When you destroy one opponent on the scaffold, you make ten more enemies among his family and friends. Look at the sort of people you have put behind bars – women, old men, bile-ridden egotists, the flotsam of the Revolution. Do you really believe they constitute a danger? The only enemies left in your midst are those who are too sick and too cowardly to fight; all the brave and able ones have fled abroad, or died at Lyon or in the Vendée. Those who are left do not merit your attention. Believe me – freedom would be more firmly established, and Europe brought to her knees, if you established a Committee of Mercy.'

'Have you read enough?' he asked her.

'Yes. They're trying to force your hand.' She looked up. 'Danton's behind it, I suppose?'

Robespierre didn't speak, not at first. When he did it was in a whisper, and not to the point. 'When we were children, you know, I said to him, Camille, you're all right now, I am going to look after you. You should have seen us, Eléonore – you would have been quite sorry for us, I think. I don't know what would have become of Camille, if it weren't for me.' He buried his face in his hands. 'Or of me, if it weren't for him.'

'But you're not children now,' she said softly. 'And this affection you speak of no longer exists. He's gone over to Danton.'

He looked up. His face is transparent, she thought; he would like the world transparent too. 'Danton's not my enemy,' he said. 'He's a patriot, and I've staked my reputation on it. But what's he done, these last four weeks? A few speeches. Grand-sounding rhetoric that keeps him in the public eye and means nothing at all. He fancies himself as the elder statesman. He's risked nothing. He has thrown my poor Camille into the furnace while he and his friends stand by warming their hands.'

'Don't be upset, it doesn't help.' She averted her face. She was studying the pamphlet again. 'He implies that the Committee has abused its powers. It seems clear that Danton and his friends see themselves as an alternative government.'

'Yes.' He looked up, half-smiled. 'Danton offered me a job once before. No doubt he'd do it again. They expect me to go along with them, you see.'

'Go along with them? With that gang of swindlers? You'd go along with them as you'd go along with brigands who were holding you to ransom. All they want is to use your name, use your credit as an honest man.'

'Do you know what I wish?' he said. 'I wish Marat were alive. What a pass I've come to, when I wish that! But Camille would have listened to him.'

'This is heresy,' Eléonore said. She bent her head over the page. She read, it seemed to him, with a tortured slowness; she seemed to weigh every word. 'The Jacobins will expel him.'

'I will prevent it.'

'What?'

'I said, I will prevent it.'

She shook the paper at him. 'They'll blame you for this. Do you think you can protect him?'

'Protect him? Oh, Christ — I think at any time, at any time before now, I'd have died for him. But I feel, now — perhaps I have a duty to remain alive?'

'A duty to whom?'

'To the people. In case worse befalls them.'

'I agree. You do have a duty to remain alive. Alive and in power.'

He averted his head. 'How easily the phrases fall from your lips. As if you had grown up with them, Eléonore. Collot is back from Lyon, did you know? He has finished his *work*, as he describes it. His path of righteousness is very clear and straight and broad. It's so easy to be a good Jacobin. Collot hasn't a doubt or scruple in his head – indeed, I doubt if he has much in it at all. Stop the Terror? He thinks we haven't even begun.'

'Saint-Just will be here next week. He won't want to know about your school-days, Max. He won't accept excuses.'

Robespierre lifted his chin, blindly and vicariously proud. 'He'll not be offered excuses. I know Camille. He's stronger than you think, oh, not visibly, not evidently – but I do know him, you see. It's a kind of iron-clad vanity he has – and why not, really? It all comes from 12 July, from those days before the Bastille. He knows exactly what he did, exactly what risk he took. Would I have taken it? Of course not. It would have been meaningless – no one would even have looked at me. Would Danton have taken it? Of course not. He was a respectable fellow, a lawyer, a family man. You see, here we are, Eléonore, four years on – still in awe of what was done in a split second.'

'Stupid,' she said.

'Not really. Everything that's important is decided in a split second, isn't it? He stood up before those thousands of people, and his life turned on a hair. Everything after that, of course, has been an anticlimax.'

Eléonore got up, moved away from him. 'Will you go to see him?'

'Now? No. Danton will be there. They will probably be having a party.'

'Well, why not?' Eléonore said. 'I know the reign of superstition is over, but it is Christmas day.'

'IT IS INCREDIBLE,' Danton said. He tipped his head back and tossed another glass down his throat. He did not look like an elder states-man. 'There are demonstrators outside the Convention calling for a Committee of Mercy. They are standing six deep outside Desenne's bookshop demanding another edition. The cover price was two sous and now they're changing hands for twenty francs. Camille, you're a one-man inflationary disaster.'

'But I wish now I had warned Robespierre. About the content, I mean.'

'Oh, for God's sake.' Danton was vast and brash and hearty, the popular leader of a new political force. 'Somebody go and get Robespierre. Somebody go and drag him out. It's time we got him drunk.' He reached across and dropped his hand on Camille's shoulder. 'It's time this Revolution relaxed a little. The people are sick of the killings, and the reaction to your writings proves it.'

'But we should have got the Committee changed this month. You should be on it now.'

Around them, the buzz of conversation resumed. It was understood to have been one of Danton's heartening pronouncements. 'Let's not push things,' Danton said. 'Next month will do. We're creating the mood for change. We don't want to force the issue, we want people to come to our way of thinking of their own accord.' Camille glanced at Fabre. 'Now why are you not happy?' Danton demanded. 'You have just achieved the greatest success of your career. I order you in the name of the Republic to be happy.'

Annette and Claude arrived soon afterwards. Annette looked wary and withdrawn, but Claude looked as if he were working up to a big speech. 'Ah yes,' he said, addressing the air a foot above his son-in-law's head. 'I have not been lavishly complimentary, have I, in the past? But now I will congratulate you, from my heart. It is an act of great courage.'

'Why do you say that? Do you think they will want to cut off my head?'

A silence, sudden and complete and prolonged. No one spoke and no one moved. For the first time in years Claude found it possible to focus his gaze. 'Oh, Camille,' he said, 'who could want to hurt you?'

'Plenty of people,' Camille said remotely. 'Billaud, because I've always laughed at him. Saint-Just, because he has a rage for leadership and I won't follow. All the members of the Jacobins who've been after my blood since I defended Dillon. Ten days ago they brought up the business of Brissot's trial. What right had I to pass out without informing the club? And Barnave — they wanted to know how I dared to go to the Conciergerie to speak to a traitor.'

'But Robespierre defended you,' Claude said.

'Yes, he was very kind. He told them I was given to emotional outbursts. He said that he had known me since I was ten years old and I had always been the same. He nodded and smiled at me as he came down from the tribune. His eyes were very sharp. He had engraved a valuation on me like a goldsmith's mark.'

'Oh, there was more than that,' Lucile said. 'He praised you very warmly.'

'Of course. The club was touched, flattered. He had allowed them a little insight into his private life — you know, touching evidence of his human nature.'

'What can you mean?' Claude said.

'Well, I revert to my former conviction. Quite clearly he is Jesus Christ. He has even condescended to be adopted by a carpenter. I wonder what he will do at the next meeting, when they demand my expulsion?'

'But nothing can happen to you while Robespierre is in power,' Claude said. 'It's not possible. Come now. It's not possible.'

'You mean I have protection. But it is irksome, to be protected.'

'I won't have this,' Danton said. He put down his glass, leaned forward. He was quite sober, though a few minutes earlier he had seemed not to be. 'You know my policies, you know what I am trying to do. Now that the pamphlets have served their purpose, your job is to keep Robespierre in a good humour, and other than that keep your mouth shut. There is no need to take risks. Within two months, all moderate opposition will have crystallized around me. All I have to do is exist.'

'But that is problematical, in my case,' Camille muttered.

'You think I can't protect my followers?'

'I am sick of being protected,' Camille yelled at him. 'I am tired of pleasing you and placating Robespierre and running between the two of you smoothing things over and ministering to your all-

devouring egos and your monstrous, arrogant self-conceits. I have
had enough of it.'

'In that case,' Danton said, 'your use for the future is very
limited, very limited indeed.'

THE COMMITTEE of Justice which Robespierre had proposed fell
victim next day to Billaud-Varennes's revolutionary thoroughness.
He told the Jacobins quite bluntly, in Robespierre's presence, that it
had been a stupid idea from the start.

That night Robespierre didn't sleep. It was not a defeat he
brooded upon; it was a humiliation. He could not remember a time
when his express wishes had been flouted; or rather, he could
remember it, but dimly, like something from a past incarnation.
The Candle of Arras had illuminated another world.

He sat alone at his window, up at the top of the house; watched
the black angles of the rooftops, and the stars between. He would
have liked to pray; but no words he could formulate seemed likely
to move or even reach the blindly purposive deity that had taken
his life in hand. Three times he got up to see if the door was barred,
the bolt firmly drawn and the key turned in the lock. The darkness
shifted, waned; the street below seemed peopled with shades. *In
the reign of the Emperor Tiberius . . .* The ghosts of souls departed
begged their admittance, with faces of clay; they trailed the covert,
feral odours, the long, slinking shadows of circus beasts.

NEXT DAY CAMILLE went to the Duplay house. He asked after
Eléonore's health, and about her work. 'Lucile was saying she
would come and see you, but she doesn't know when it would suit
you, because of your classes. Why don't you ever come and see us?'

'I will,' she said, without conviction. 'How's the baby?'

'Oh, he's fine. Marvellous.'

'He's like you, Camille. He has a look of you.'

'Oh, how sweet of you, Cornélia, you're the first person in
eighteen months to say so. May I go up?'

'He's not at home.'

'Oh, Cornélia. You know that he is at home.'

'He's busy.'

'Has he been telling you to keep people out, or just to keep me out?'

'Look, he needs time to sort things out in his mind. He didn't sleep last night. I'm worried about him.'

'Is he very angry with me?'

'No, he's not angry, I think he's – shocked. That you should hold him responsible for violence, that you should blame him in public.'

'I told him I reserved the right to tell him when the country became a tyranny. Our consciences are public property, so how else should I tell him?'

'He is alarmed, that you should put yourself in such a bad position.'

'Go and tell him I'm here.'

'He won't see you.'

'Go and tell him, Eléonore.'

She quailed. 'All right.'

She left him standing, with a dragging ache in his throat. She paused when she was half-way up the stairs, to think; then she went on. She knocked. 'Camille's here.'

She heard the scraping of the chair, a creak: no answer.

'Are you there? Camille's downstairs. He insists.'

He pulled the door open. She knew he'd been standing right behind it. Absurd, she thought. He was sweating.

'You mustn't let him come up. I told you that. I told you. Why do you take no notice of me?' He was trying to speak very calmly.

She shrugged. 'Right.'

Robespierre had rested one hand on the doorknob, sliding it over the smooth surface; he swung the door back and to, in an arc of six inches.

'I'll tell him,' she said. She turned her head and looked down the stairs, as if she thought Camille might run up and shoulder her aside. 'It's another matter whether he accepts it.'

'Dear God,' he said. 'What does he think? What does he expect?'

'Personally I don't see the sense in keeping him out. You both know he's put you in a very difficult position. You know you're going to defend him, and I think he knows it too. It's not a matter of whether you'll smooth over your disagreements. Of course you will. You'll risk your own reputation to vindicate him. Every principle you've ever had goes out of the window when you're faced with Camille.'

'That is not true, Eléonore,' he said softly. 'That is not true and you are saying it out of twisted jealousy. It is not true and he must be made to realize it. He must be made to think. Listen,' the agitation crept back into his voice, 'how does he look?'

Tears had sprung into her eyes. 'He looks as usual.'

'Does he seem upset? He's not ill?'

'No, he looks as usual.'

'Dear God,' he said. Wearily, softly, he took his perspiring hand from the doorknob, and wiped it, stiff-fingered, down the sleeve of his other arm. 'I need to wash my hands,' he said.

The door closed softly. Eléonore went downstairs, scrubbing at her face with her fist. 'There,' she said. 'I told you. He doesn't want to see you.'

'I suppose he thinks it's for my own good?' Camille laughed nervously.

'I think you can understand his feelings. You have tried to use his affection for you to trap him into supporting you when you put forward policies he disagrees with.'

'He disagrees with them? Since when?'

'Perhaps since his defeat yesterday. Well, that is for you to work out. He doesn't confide in me, and I know nothing of politics.'

A blank misery had dropped into his eyes. 'Very well,' he said. 'I can exist without his approbation.' He walked ahead of her to the door. 'Goodbye, Cornélia, I don't think I'll be seeing much of you from now on.'

'Why? Where are you going?'

In the open doorway he turned suddenly: pulled her towards him, slipped a hand under her breast and kissed her on the lips. Two of the workmen stood and watched them. 'Poor you,' Camille said. He pushed her gently back against the wall. Watching him go, she put the back of her hand against her lips. For the next few hours she could feel the phantom pressure of his cupped hand beneath her breast, and she kept it in her guilty thoughts that she had never really had a lover.

A LETTER to Camille Desmoulins, 11 Nivôse, Year II:

I am not a fanatic, or an enthusiast, or a man to pay compliments: but if I should survive you I mean to have your statue, and to carve on it: 'Wicked men would have had us accept liberty kneaded together of mud and blood. Camille made us love it, carved in marble and covered in flowers.'

'It isn't true, of course,' he said to Lucile, 'but I shall put it away carefully among my papers.'

'I SEE YOU MAKE a very splendid effort to come and speak to me,' Hérault said. 'You could have turned and gone the other way. I shall begin to think I am a case for your charity, like Barnave. By the way, did you know Saint-Just is back?'

'Oh.'

'Perhaps there is a case for not going so far to antagonize Hébert?'

'My fifth pamphlet is in preparation,' Camille said. 'I shall rid the public of that posturing, mindless obscenity, if it's the last thing I do.'

'It may well be that.' Hérault smiled, but not pleasantly. 'I know you enjoy a privileged position, but Robespierre doesn't like defeat.'

'He favours clemency. Very well, there's been a reverse. We'll find another way.'

'How? I think it will seem more than a reverse to him. He has no power base, you know – except in patriotic opinion. He has very few friends. He has placed some old retainers of his on the Tribunal, but he has no ministers in his pocket, no generals – he's neglected all that. His power is entirely in our minds – and I'm sure he knows it. If he can be defeated once, why not twice, why not continuously?'

'Why are you trying to frighten me?'

'For my amusement,' Hérault said coolly. 'I've never been able to understand you, quite. You play on his feelings for you – yet he always says we should leave our personal feelings aside.'

'Oh, we all say that. It is the only thing to be said. But we never do it.'

'Camille, why did you do what you did?'

'Don't you know?'

'I have really no idea. I suppose you wanted to be running out in front of public opinion again.'

'Do you? Do you think that? People say it is a work of art, that I have never written anything better. Do you think I am proud of my sales?'

'I would be, if they were mine.'

'Yes, the pamphlets are a great success. But what does success matter to me now? I am sick of the sight of all this accumulated injustice and ingratitude and wrong.'

A nice epitaph, Hérault thought, should you need one. 'Tell Danton – for what it's worth – and I realize that it may be a liability – the campaign for clemency has my sympathy and support.'

'Oh, Danton and I are not on good terms.'

Hérault frowned. 'How not on good terms? Camille, what are you trying to do to yourself?'

'Oh . . .' Camille said. He pushed his hair back.

'Have you been rude about his wife again?'

'No, not at all. Good heavens – we always leave our personal feelings aside.'

'So what's your quarrel? Something trivial?'

'Everything I do is trivial,' Camille said, with a sudden savage hostility. 'Don't you see that I am a weak and trivial person? Now Hérault – is there any other message?'

'Only that I think he's carrying the time-biding to excess.'

'You are afraid the policy of clemency will come in too late for you?'

'Every day it is too late for someone.'

'He probably has good reasons. All these obscure coalitions . . .

Fabre thinks I know everything about Georges, but I don't. I don't think I could take knowing everything, do you? Actually, I don't think anyone could.'

'Sometimes you sound exactly like Robespierre.'

'It is long association. It is what I am counting on.'

'I had a letter this morning,' Hérault said, 'from my colleagues on the Committee. I am accused of leaking our secret proceedings to the Austrians.' His mouth twisted. 'The documentary evidence will need a little addition, before it comes to court, but that will be no trouble to Saint-Just. He tried to ruin me in Alsace. I am not a stupid man, but I found it hard to keep a step ahead. Not that there was any point.'

'It is the accident of your birth.'

'Just so. I am on my way now to tender my resignation from the Committee. You might tell Georges. Oh, and wish him a happy new year.'

SAINT-JUST: Who is paying Camille to write this?

ROBESPIERRE: No, no, you don't understand. He's been so shaken by the direction of things –

SAINT-JUST: He's a very good actor, I will say that for him. He seems to have taken most of you in.

ROBESPIERRE: Why must you take everything he does in bad faith?

SAINT-JUST: Will you face it, Robespierre? Either he's in bad faith and he's a counter-revolutionary, or he's gone politically soft and he's a counter-revolutionary.

ROBESPIERRE: Oh that's very neat. You weren't here in '89.

SAINT-JUST: We have a new calendar now. '89 doesn't exist.

ROBESPIERRE: You can't judge Camille, because you know nothing about him.

SAINT-JUST: His actions speak. Anyway, I've known Camille for years. He drifted along in life until he found a niche as a literary prostitute. He's for sale to the highest bidder, and that's why he and Danton have so much in common.

ROBESPIERRE: I don't see how you can call it literary prostitution and so on to ask for clemency.

SAINT-JUST: No? Then can you explain why he's the toast of every aristocrat's dinner table for the last month? Can you explain why people like the Beauharnais woman are sending him letters of thanks and adulation? Can you .explain why civil disorder has resulted?

ROBESPIERRE: It was not civil disorder. Lawful petitioners to the Convention.

SAINT-JUST: With his name in their mouths. He's the hero of the hour.

ROBESPIERRE: Well, that is the second time for him.

SAINT-JUST: People can use such egotism for very sinister ends.

ROBESPIERRE: Like?

SAINT-JUST: Like conspiracy against the Republic.

ROBESPIERRE: Who conspires? Camille conspires with no one.

SAINT-JUST: Danton conspires. With Orléans. With Mirabeau. With Brissot. With Dumouriez, with the court, with England and with all our foreign enemies.

ROBESPIERRE: How dare you?

SAINT-JUST: Do you dare break with him? Bring him before the Tribunal and let him answer these charges.

ROBESPIERRE: Take an example. He associated with Mirabeau. I suppose this is what you mean. Mirabeau fell from grace, but when Danton first knew him he was believed to be a patriot. It was not a crime to have dealings with him, and you can't make it so, retrospectively.

SAINT-JUST: You did not share the general blindness about Riquetti, I understand.

ROBESPIERRE: No.

SAINT-JUST: Surely therefore you warned Danton?

ROBESPIERRE: He took no notice. That's not a crime, either.

SAINT-JUST: No? I do suspect a man who – let us say – fails to *hate* the Revolution's enemies. If it was not a crime, it was something a good deal worse than carelessness. There was money involved. With Danton there always is. Learn that. Accept that hard cash is the height and depth of Danton's patriotism. Where are the Crown Jewels?

ROBESPIERRE: Roland was responsible for them.

SAINT-JUST: Roland is dead. You're refusing to accept what stares you in the face. There is a conspiracy. This clemency business, it is just a device to sow dissension among the patriots and pick up some cheap goodwill. Pierre Philippeaux is part of the plot, with his attacks on the Committee, and Danton is at its head. Wait and see. The next issue of the 'Old Cordelier' will launch the real attack on Hébert, because they have to put him out of the way before they can seize power. It will also attack the Committee. My own belief is that they are planning a military coup. They have Westermann, and Dillon too.

ROBESPIERRE: Dillon's been arrested again. Some business about plotting to rescue the Dauphin. Sounds unlikely to me.

SAINT-JUST: Camille won't be able to get him off this time. Not that the prisons are secure.

ROBESPIERRE: Oh, the prisons! The people are saying that if the supply of meat doesn't improve they are going to break into the prisons and roast the prisoners and eat them.

SAINT-JUST: The people are degraded, in their present state of education.

ROBESPIERRE: What do you expect? I had forgotten to worry about the meat supply.

SAINT-JUST: I think you are getting off the point.

ROBESPIERRE: Danton is a patriot. Bring me the evidence against him.

SAINT-JUST: Robespierre, you are a very obstinate man. What kind of evidence do you want?

ROBESPIERRE: Anyway, how do you know what letters Camille has?

SAINT-JUST: Oh, when I was giving you the list of those with whom Danton conspired, I forgot to include Lafayette.

ROBESPIERRE: Well, that's just about everybody then, isn't it?

SAINT-JUST: Yes, I think that's just about everybody.

IN THE FIRST WEEK of the new year certain papers were brought to Robespierre, which proved beyond doubt Fabre's involvement in the East India Company fraud – an affair that Fabre himself, with the cooperation of the Police Committee, had been investigating for more than two months. For half an hour Robespierre sat over the papers, shaking with humiliation and rage, fighting for control. When he heard Saint-Just's voice, he would have liked to get out of the room; but there was only one exit.

SAINT-JUST: What do you say now? Camille must have known. Something about it.

ROBESPIERRE: He was protecting a friend. Oh, he shouldn't have done that. He should have told me.

SAINT-JUST: Fabre really took you in.

ROBESPIERRE: The conspiracies he spoke of were real.

SAINT-JUST: Oh yes. All the men he names have behaved as he predicted. What do we think of someone so close to the heart of perfidy?

ROBESPIERRE: We know what to think now.

SAINT-JUST: Fabre has been at Danton's side throughout.

ROBESPIERRE: And so?

SAINT-JUST: Don't show yourself more naïve than you have been.

ROBESPIERRE: I will have Fabre out of the Jacobins at the next meeting. I trusted him, and he's made me look a fool.

SAINT-JUST: They have all made you look a fool.

ROBESPIERRE: I must begin to think again. I am too well-disposed towards people.

SAINT-JUST: I have a certain amount of evidence that I can put before you.

ROBESPIERRE: I know what people call evidence these days. Hearsay and denunciation and empty rhetoric.

SAINT-JUST: Are you determined to persist in your error?

ROBESPIERRE: You sound like a priest, Antoine. It's what they say when you're at confession — do you recall? I've been mistaken, I agree, in my course of action. I have been looking at what people do, listening to what they say, but I should have been looking into their hearts. I am going to find out all the conspirators now.

SAINT-JUST: Whoever they are. However great their credit in the Revolution, it must now be examined. The Revolution has got frozen up. They have frozen it up with their talk of moderation. To stand still in Revolution is to slip backwards.

ROBESPIERRE: You are mixing your metaphors.

SAINT-JUST: I am not a writer. I have more than phrases to offer.

ROBESPIERRE: Back to Camille again.

SAINT-JUST: Yes.

ROBESPIERRE: He has been misled.

SAINT-JUST: That is not my view, or the general view of the Committee. We believe him responsible for his actions, and we feel strongly that he should not escape what he deserves because of any personal feelings you might entertain for him.

ROBESPIERRE: What are you accusing me of?

SAINT-JUST: Weakness.

ROBESPIERRE: I did not get where I am through weakness.

SAINT-JUST: Remind us of it.

ROBESPIERRE: His conduct will be investigated, just as if he were anyone else. He is only an individual ... O my God, how I hoped to avoid this.

THE FIFTH ISSUE of the 'Old Cordelier' appeared on 5 January, 16 Nivôse. It attacked Hébert and his faction, compared his writings (unfavourably) to an open sewer, accused him of corruption and of complicity with the enemy. It attacked Barère and Collot, members of the Committee of Public Safety.

PROCEEDINGS of the Jacobin Club (1):

CITIZEN COLLOT [*at the tribune*]: Philippeaux and Camille Desmoulins –

CITIZEN HÉBERT: Justice! I demand a hearing!

PRESIDENT: Order! I put it to the meeting that the fifth issue should be read out.

JACOBIN: We have all read it.

JACOBIN: I should be ashamed to admit that I had read an aristo pamphlet.

JACOBIN: Hébert does not want it read, he does not want the truth given wider currency.

CITIZEN HÉBERT: No, no, by no means should it be read out! Camille is trying to complicate everything. He is trying to divert attention from himself. He is accusing me of stealing public funds, and it is completely false.

CITIZEN DESMOULINS: I have the proofs of it here in my hand.

CITIZEN HÉBERT: Oh God! He wants to assassinate me!

PROCEEDINGS of the Jacobin Club (2):

PRESIDENT: We are calling on Camille Desmoulins to justify his conduct.

JACOBIN: He's not here.

JACOBIN: To Robespierre's relief.

PRESIDENT: I am going to call his name three times, so that he has the opportunity to come forward and justify himself before the Society.

JACOBIN: It is a pity he has not got a cockerel that he could persuade to crow thrice. It would be illuminating to see what Danton would do.

PRESIDENT: Camille Desmoulins –

JACOBIN: He isn't here. He knows better.

JACOBIN: It's no use calling his name and calling his name, if he's not here.

CITIZEN ROBESPIERRE: We will discuss instead –

CITIZEN DESMOULINS: I *am* here, actually.

CITIZEN ROBESPIERRE [*loudly*]: I said we will move instead to a discussion of the crimes of the British government.

JACOBIN: Always a safe topic.

CITIZEN DESMOULINS [*at the tribune*]: I suppose . . . I suppose you are going to say that I have been mistaken. I admit I may have been – about Philippeaux's motives, perhaps. I have made a lot of mistakes in my career. I must ask the Society for guidance because I really . . . I really don't know where I am in these matters any more.

JACOBIN: I knew he would go to pieces.

JACOBIN: Always a safe tactic.

JACOBIN: Look at Robespierre, on his feet already.

CITIZEN ROBESPIERRE: I demand to speak.

CITIZEN DESMOULINS: But Robespierre, let me –

CITIZEN ROBESPIERRE: Be quiet, Camille, I want to speak.

JACOBIN: Sit down, Camille, you will only talk yourself into more trouble.

JACOBIN: That's right – give way, and let Robespierre extricate you. Wonderful, isn't it?

CITIZEN ROBESPIERRE [*at the tribune*]: Citizens, Camille has promised us he will renounce his errors and put aside all the political heresies with which the pages of these pamphlets are filled. He has sold vast numbers of copies and the aristocrats in their false-ness and treachery have been heaping praise upon him, and it has all gone to his head.

JACOBIN: He has dropped this manner of his, you know, the long pauses.

CITIZEN ROBESPIERRE: These writings are dangerous, because they disturb public order and fill our enemies with hope. But we have to distinguish between the author and his work. Camille – oh, Camille is just a spoiled child. His inclinations are good but he has fallen in with bad people and he has been seriously misled. We must repudiate these writings, which even Brissot would not have dared acknowledge, but we must keep Camille amongst us. I demand that – as a gesture – the offending issues of the 'Old Cordelier' be burned before this Society.

CITIZEN DESMOULINS: *Burning is not answering.*

JACOBIN: How true! Rousseau said it!

JACOBIN: That we should live to see the day!

JACOBIN: Robespierre confounded by his god Jean-Jacques! He looks green.

JACOBIN: I should not like to have to live with the consequences of being that clever.

JACOBIN: He may not have to.

CITIZEN ROBESPIERRE: Oh, Camille – how can you defend these writings, which are such a delight to the aristocrats? Camille, if you were anyone else, do you think we should treat you with such indulgence?

CITIZEN DESMOULINS: I don't understand you, Robespierre. Some of the writings which you condemn you read yourself in proof. How can you imply that only aristocrats read my work? The Convention and all this Society have read it. Are they all aristocrats?

CITIZEN DANTON: Citizens, may I suggest you pursue your deliberations calmly? And remember – if you strike at Camille, you strike at the freedom of the press.

CITIZEN ROBESPIERRE: All right. Then we won't burn the pamphlets. Perhaps a man who clings to his mistakes with such tenacity is worse than misled. Perhaps soon we shall see behind his arrogant façade the men at whose dictation he has been writing.

[*Fabre d'Églantine rises to leave.*]

CITIZEN ROBESPIERRE: D'Églantine! Stay there.

JACOBIN: Robespierre has something to say to you.

CITIZEN FABRE D'ÉGLANTINE: I can justify myself –

MEMBERS OF THE SOCIETY: Guillotine him! Guillotine him!

LUCILE DESMOULINS to Stanislas Fréron:

23 Nivôse, Year II

... Come back, come back quickly. There is no time to lose. Bring with you all the old Cordeliers you can find, we need them badly. [Robespierre] has seen that when he doesn't think and act in accordance with the views of certain people, he is not all-powerful. [Danton] is becoming weak, he is losing his nerve. D'Églantine is arrested and in the Luxembourg; they are bringing very serious charges ...

I don't laugh any more: I don't play at being a cat; I never touch my piano; I have no dreams; I am nothing but a machine now.

XII. *Ambivalence*

(*1794*)

THIS IS OUR situation now. Danton has asked the Convention to give Fabre a hearing, and they have refused. So? Danton says. He is unwilling to admit that for the moment he is not the Convention's master, and that Hébert disposes of the power in the Sections. 'So? I'm not like Robespierre, wringing my hands over a single defeat. I've come through this whole thing winning, losing, winning again. There was a time,' he tells Lucile, 'when he had nothing but defeats.'

'No doubt that is why he is prejudiced against them.'

'Never mind his prejudices,' he says. 'That damned Committee is looking over their shoulder at me now. One mistake and they're out and I'm in.'

Fighting talk. And yet, this is not the man she knows. Some people say Danton has not fully recovered his health, but he seems fit enough to her. Others say the evident happiness of the second marriage has softened him; but she knows the value of such romantic hogwash. To her mind, it's the first marriage that is affecting him. Since Gabrielle's death he lacks something: some final ruthlessness. It's hard to put into words, and she hopes, of course, that she's wrong. She believes ruthlessness will be needed.

This too is our situation: Robespierre has had Camille reinstated at the Jacobins. At a price: the price of breaking down at the tribune, almost weeping in the face of the bemused Society. Hébert rants in his newspaper about the 'one misguided man' who is protecting Camille – for his own personal and unfathomable reasons. Privately, he goes around sniggering.

The Cordeliers Club is seeking an injunction to stop Camille using their name for his pamphlets. Not that it matters, since

Desenne refuses to print any further issues, and no other publishers, much as they would like the sales, dare touch it.

'Come and see Robespierre with me,' Danton says to Lucile. 'Come on. Pick your baby up and let's go round there now and have a big emotional scene. A reconciliation. We'll drag Camille along and make him apologize nicely, and you will strike your Republican Family pose, and Maximilien will be duly edified. I shall be conciliatory in all sorts of practical ways and remember not to slap him on the back in the hearty man-to-man fashion he finds so terrifying.'

She shakes her head. 'Camille won't come. He's too busy writing.'

'Writing what?'

'The true history of the Revolution, he says. The secret "Secret History".'

'What does he mean to do with it?'

'Burn it, probably. What else would it be fit for?'

'UNFORTUNATELY, everything I say seems to make things worse.'

'I don't know why you should say that, Danton.' Robespierre had been reading – his Rousseau, unfortunately – and now he removed his spectacles. 'I don't see how your saying anything at this point . . .' The phrase trailed off, in his usual style. For a moment his face seemed naked and desperately harassed; then he replaced his spectacles, and his expression became once more intractable and opaque. 'I have really only one thing to say to you. Cut off your contacts with Fabre, repudiate him. If not, I can have nothing more to do with you. But if you will – then we can begin to talk. Accept in all matters the guidance of the Committee, and I will personally guarantee your safety.'

'Christ,' Danton said. 'My *safety*? Are you threatening me?'

Robespierre looked at him speculatively. 'Vadier,' he suggested. 'Collot. Hébert. Saint-Just.'

'I'd prefer to guarantee my own safety, Robespierre, by my own methods.'

'Your methods are likely to ruin you.' Robespierre closed his book. 'Just make sure they don't ruin Camille.'

Danton was suddenly angry. 'Be careful,' he said, 'that Camille doesn't ruin you.'

'What do you mean?'

'Hébert is going round talking about Camille, giggling, and saying this is no ordinary friendship, I'm sure.'

'Of course it is no ordinary friendship.'

Is he not understanding, or is he refusing to understand? This is one of his weapons, this professional, cultivated obtuseness. 'Hébert is instituting further inquiries into Camille's private life.'

Robespierre flung out a hand, palm towards Danton; so theatrical, the gesture, that Fabre might have coached him.

'They ought to make a statue of you,' Danton said, 'in that position. Come on, you know what I'm talking about. I know you weren't around in the Annette days, but I can tell you, he furnished us with some entertainment, your friend – afternoons languishing semi-respectably in Annette's drawing room, and evenings over at the Île de la Cité, committing unnatural acts among the affidavits. You never met Maître Perrin, did you? There were others, of course.' Danton laughed. 'Take that look off your face – nobody thinks Camille's taste would run to you. He likes men who are very large, very ugly and devoted to women. He just wants what he can't have. Well, that's the way I see it, anyway.'

Robespierre reached out a hand for his pen. Then he seemed to change his mind. He let it lie. 'Have you been drinking, Danton?' he said.

'No. Well, not more than my usual intake for this time of day. Why?'

'I thought you might have been. I was looking for an excuse for you.' Behind the concealing blue-tinted lenses, his eyes flickered to Danton's face and away again. The sudden absence of emotion seemed to have pared away his face to the bone; his features were so thin that they seemed etched on air. 'I think you've strayed from the point,' he said. 'Fabre, I think, was the issue.' Again his hand crept towards the pen; he did not seem able to help himself.

(Robespierre, private notebooks: 'Danton spoke contemptuously of Camille Desmoulins, attributing to him a secret and shameful vice.')

'Well, have you made a decision?' His voice was empty of inflection, like God speaking within a rock.

'What am I to say? What do you expect me to do? I can't *repudiate* him, what a stupid word.'

'It is true that he's been your close associate. It is not easy to disentangle yourself.'

'He's been my *friend*.'

'Oh, your friend.' Robespierre smiled faintly. 'I know how you value your friends – but then I dare say he has not Camille's defects. The safety of the country is at issue, Danton. A patriot should be eager to put the safety of the country above his wife or child or friend. There is no place for individual sentiment now.'

Danton gasped, and tears sprang into his eyes. He rubbed at his face and held up his wet fingers. He tried to speak, but found it difficult.

(Maximilien Robespierre, private notebooks: 'Danton made himself ridiculous, producing theatrical tears ... at Robespierre's house.')

'This is unnecessary,' Robespierre said. 'And useless.'

'You are a cripple,' Danton said at last. His voice was weary, flat. 'It's not Couthon who's a cripple, it's you. Don't you know, Robespierre, don't you know there's something wrong with you? Do you ever ask yourself what God left out, when he made you? I used to make jokes at your expense, I used to say you were impotent, but it's more than balls you're missing. I wonder if you're real, I see you walk and talk, but where's the life in you?'

'I do live,' Robespierre looked down. He touched his fingertips together, like a nervous witness. 'I do live. In my fashion.'

'WHAT HAPPENED, Danton?'

'Nothing happened. We don't see eye-to-eye about Fabre. The interview had,' he put one fist reflectively into the other palm, 'no result.'

FIVE-THIRTY A.M., the rue Condé; there was a hammering at the doors below, and Annette pulled the covers over her head and didn't want to know. The next moment she sat up, shocked into wakefulness. She flung herself out of bed: what's happened, what's happened now?

Someone was shouting in the street. She reached for her wrap. She heard Claude's voice, and the voice of her maid, Elise, raised in alarm. Elise was a lard-faced Breton girl, superstitious, familiar and clumsy, with an imperfect grasp of French; she stuck her head round the door now and said, 'It's people from the Section. They want to know if you've got your lover there, they say, come on, don't tell them lies, they weren't born yesterday.'

'My lover? You mean they're looking for Camille?'

'Well, you said it, Madame,' Elise smirked.

The girl was in her shift. In one hand she had a smoking stump of tallow candle. Annette struck out at her as she pushed past, so that the light spun out of her hand and expired on the floor. The girl's complaint pursued her: 'That was my candle-end, not yours.'

In black darkness, Annette collided with someone. A hand shot out and took her by the wrist. She could smell last night's wine on the man's breath. 'What have we here?' the man said. She tried to pull away and he tightened his grip. 'Here we have milady, with hardly any clothes on.'

'Enough, Jeannot,' another voice said. 'Hurry up, we need some lights.'

Someone opened the shutters. Torchlight from the street clawed across the walls. Elise had produced more candles. Jeannot stood back and leered. He wore the coarse, baggy clothes of the practising sansculotte; a red cap with a knitted tricolour cockade was pulled down to his eyebrows. He looked such an oaf that – in other circumstances – she would have laughed. Now a half-dozen men jostled into the room, staring around them, rubbing their cold hands, cursing. The People, she thought. Max's beloved People.

The man who had called off Jeannot stepped forward. He was a mouse-faced boy in a shabby black coat. He had a wad of papers in his hands.

'Health and Fraternity, Citizeness. We are the representatives of the Section Mutius Scaevola.' He flicked the top sheet of paper at her; 'Section Luxembourg' was crossed out, and the new name inked in beside it. 'I have here,' he pawed through the documents, 'a warrant for the arrest of Claude Duplessis, retired civil servant, resident at this address.'

'This is imbecilic,' Annette said. 'There is a mistake. Arrest on what charges?'

'Conspiracy, Citizeness. We have orders to search the premises, and impound any suspicious papers.'

'How dare you come here, at this hour – '

'When Père Duchesne has one of his great cholers,' one of the men said, 'you don't wait for the sun to come up.'

'Père Duchesne? I see. You mean that Hébert dare not strike at Camille, so he sends you and your rabble to terrorize his family. Give me those papers, let me see your warrant.'

She snatched at them. The clerk stepped back defensively. One of the sansculottes caught her outstretched hand, and with his other hand pulled her wrap aside, half-exposing her breasts. With all her strength she dragged herself away from him. She gathered up her wrap to her throat. She was shaking, but – and she hoped they knew this – much more with fury than with fear. 'Are you Duplessis?' the clerk said, looking over her shoulder.

Claude had managed to get dressed. He seemed dazed, but a faint smell of burning crept out from the room behind him. 'You are inquiring for me?' His voice shook a little.

The clerk waved the warrant. 'Hurry up. We can't keep standing about. These citizens want to get the search over and home for their breakfasts.'

'They deserve their breakfast, expeditiously,' Claude said. 'Why, they have had the trouble of waking up a peaceful household, and terrifying my wife and my servants. Where were you thinking of taking me?'

'Pack a bag,' the clerk said. 'Quick about it.'

Claude gave him a measured nod. He turned.

'Claude!' Annette called after him. 'Claude, remember I love you.'

He glanced over his shoulder and gave her a grim nod. A chorus of ribaldry followed him to his room; but the diversion had been effective, because while they were jeering he slammed his door, and she heard the key turn in the lock, and the grunts of effort as they put their shoulders to the door.

She turned to the clerk. 'What's your name?'

'It is of no importance.'

'I'm sure it's not, but I'll find out. You'll suffer. Begin your search. You'll find nothing to interest you.'

'What sort of people are they?' she heard one of the men ask Elise.

'Godless, Monsieur, and very stuck-up.'

'Is she really, you know, with Camille?'

'Everybody knows it,' Elise said. 'They spend hours locked away. Reading the newspapers, she says.'

'What does the old man do about it?'

'Fuck-all,' Elise said.

The men laughed. 'We might have to get you down to the Section,' one of them said. 'Ask you a few questions. I bet you've got some very pretty answers.' He put out his hand, fingered the cloth of her shift, pinched one of her nipples. She gave a little shriek: mock-horror, mock-pain.

As if, Annette thought, there were not enough of the real thing. She took the clerk by the arm. 'Get these people under control. Do they also have a warrant to molest my domestic staff?'

'She talks like the Capet woman's sister,' Jeannot remarked.

'This is an outrage, and you may be sure that within hours it will be discussed in the Convention.'

Jeannot spat at the fireplace, with a pitiful lack of accuracy. 'Pack of lawyers,' he said. 'Revolution? This? Not till the buggers are all dead.'

'At the present rate,' the clerk said, 'it won't be long.'

Claude was back, with two of the sansculottes on his heels. He had put on his greatcoat and was drawing on his new gloves, very carefully, very smoothly. 'Imagine,' he said, 'they accused me of burning papers. Stranger still, they insisted on interposing themselves between my person and the window. There is a citizen beneath it with a pike. As if a person of my years would leap through a first-floor casement, and deprive myself of the pleasure of their company.' One of the men took his arm. Claude shook him off. 'I'll walk by myself,' he said. 'Now, please allow me to say goodbye to my wife.'

He took her hand in his gloved hand and raised her fingertips to his lips. 'Don't cry,' he said. 'Don't cry, my Annette. Get a message to Camille.'

Across the street a shiny new carriage was drawn up. A pair of eyes peered out; the blind was cautiously lowered.

'How thoroughly displeasing,' said Père Duchesne the furnace-maker. 'We picked the wrong night, or did we pick the wrong rumour? There are many other rumours, as good or better. It would have been worth rising early to drag Camille from his comfortable, incestuous bed and see if he could be provoked to violence. I was hoping that we could arrest him for a breach of the peace. Still, this will give him a fright. I wonder who he'll run to hide behind this time?'

ANNETTE WAS AT the rue Marat an hour later, distraught. 'And they have torn the place apart,' she finished. 'And Elise. Elise may be thoroughly unsatisfactory, but I will not stand by and see my menials pawed by ruffians off the streets. Lucile, give me a glass of brandy, will you? I need it.' As her daughter left the room, she whispered, 'Oh Camille, Camille. Claude ran around burning papers. All your letters to me have gone up in smoke. I think. Either that, or the Section committee has got them.'

'I see,' Camille said. 'Well, I expect they're quite chaste.'

'But I want them.' Tears in her eyes. 'I can't bear not having them.'

He ran a fingertip down her cheek. 'I'll write you some more.'

'I want those, those! How can I ask Claude if he burned them? If he burned them, he must have known where I kept them and what they were. Do you think he'd read them?'

'No. Claude's honourable. He's not like you and me.' He smiled. 'I'll ask him, Annette. As soon as we get him home.'

'You look quite cheerful, husband.' Lucile was back with the brandy.

Annette glanced up at him. So he does, she thought: surely he's indestructible? She drank her brandy in one gulp.

CAMILLE'S SPEECH to the Convention was short, audible and alarming. There were murmurs that the relatives of politicians might be suspect as much as anyone else; but most of his audience looked as if it knew precisely what he was talking about when he described the invasion of the Duplessis household. They were lucky if it hadn't happened to them, he said; soon, perhaps, it would.

Looking around the half-empty benches, the deputies knew he was right. There was applause when he referred to the uncontrolled depredations of a former theatre box-office attendant: a mutter of agreement when he deplored a system that could let such a loathsome object flourish. As he left, Danton was on his feet, calling for an end to the arrests.

At the Tuileries, 'Present my compliments to Citizen Vadier and tell him the Lanterne Attorney is here,' Camille said. Vadier was brought out of a session of the Police Committee by his clerks. 'Close down my paper and you get me in person,' Camille said, smiling kindly and giving Vadier a shove against the wall.

'Lanterne Attorney!' Vadier said. 'I thought you'd repented of all that?'

'Call it nostalgia,' Camille said. 'Call it habit. Call it what you like, but do realize that you won't get rid of me until I have some answers from you.'

Vadier looked morose, and pulled his long Inquisitor's nose. He swore by the limbs of the Supreme Being that he knew nothing of the affair. Yes, he admitted, it could be that the Section officials were out of control; it was possible, yes, that Hébert was acting out of personal malice; no, he had no knowledge of any evidence against Claude Duplessis, retired civil servant. He looked at Camille with frank detestation and considerable alarm. 'Hébert is a fool,' he muttered as he hurried away, 'to give Danton's mob a chance to try their strength.'

Robespierre appeared blinking and preoccupied from the Committee of Public Safety, summoned by an urgent message. He hurried forward and took Camille's hands, dictated a rapid stream of orders to a secretary and signified his intention of seeing Père Duchesne in hell. The onlookers noted his tone, the haste, the handclasp above all. Hastily, they memorized the signs on his face, to puzzle over and interpret later; immediately, with the lift of an eyebrow, a glance held a second too long, the questioning twitch of a nostril sniffing the political wind – immediately, imperceptibly, allegiances began to drift. By midday, the expression on Hébert's face had become less complacent; he was, in fact, on the run, and remained so in his own mind until well after Claude Duplessis's release: until some weeks later, when he himself heard a patrol in the early morning, and found he had no friends.

THE NEW CALENDAR wasn't working. Nivôse wasn't snowy, and spring would be here before Germinal. It would arrive immoderately early, so that flower-girls congregated on street corners and the seamstresses were busy with simple patriotic dresses for the summer of '94.

In the Luxembourg Gardens trees hung out unseasonable flags of green among the cannon foundries. Fabre d'Églantine watched the season change, from his prison room in the National Building that was once the Luxembourg Palace. The raw, bright, blustery days made the pain in his chest worse. Each morning he examined himself in the fine mirror he had sent home for, and noted that his face was thinner and his eyes suspiciously bright, with a brightness that had nothing to do with his prospects.

He heard that Danton's initiatives didn't prosper, that Danton didn't see Robespierre. Danton, see Robespierre, he demanded of his prison wall: bully, beg, deceive, demand. Sometimes he lay awake listening for the sound of the Dantonist mob roistering through the city; silence answered back. Camille is friends with Robespierre again, his gaoler told him; adding that he and his wife didn't believe that Camille was an aristocrat, and that Citizen Robespierre was a true friend of the working man, his continued good health the only guarantee of sugar in the shops and firewood at reasonable prices.

Fabre ran over in his mind all the things he had ever done for Camille; they were not many. He sent out for his complete set of the *Encyclopédie*, and for his small ivory telescope; with them for company he settled down to await either his natural or unnatural death.

17 PLUVIÔSE — it wasn't raining — Robespierre spoke to the Convention, outlining the basis of his future policy, his plans for the Republic of Virtue. As he left the hall a rustle of consternation followed him. He seemed more tired than one could reasonably be, even after his hours at the tribune; his lips were bloodless, his eyes dark and hollow with exhaustion. Some of the survivors from those days mentioned Mirabeau's sudden collapse. But he appeared punctually for the next session of the Committee; his eyes travelled from face to face, to see who was disappointed.

22 Pluviôse, he woke in the night fighting for breath. In the intervals of panic he forced himself to his writing table. But he had forgotten what he wanted to write; a wave of nausea brought him to his hands and knees on the floor. You do not die, he said, as he fought to expel the air trapped in his lungs, you do not, he said with each aspiration, die. You have survived this before.

When the attack passed he ordered himself up from the floor. I will not do it, his body said: you have finished me, killed me, I refuse to serve such a master.

His head dropped. If I stay here, he thought, I shall stretch out and go to sleep on the floor, just where I am, I will then take a chill, everything will be finished.

So, said the body, you should not have treated me as your slave, abusing me with fasting and chastity and broken sleep. What will you do now? Tell your intellect to get you off the floor, tell your mind to keep you on your feet tomorrow.

He took hold of the leg of a chair, then its back. He watched his hand creep along the wood; he was falling asleep. His hand became infinitely distant. He dreamed of his grandfather's household. There are no barrels for this week's brewing, someone said; all the wood has been used for scaffolding. Scaffolding or scaffolds? Anxiously he felt in his pocket for a letter from Benjamin Franklin. The letter told him, 'You are an electrical machine.'

Eléonore found him at first light. She and her father stood guard over the door. Souberbielle arrived at eight o'clock. He spoke very slowly, very distinctly, as if to a deaf person: cannot answer for the consequences, he said, cannot answer for the consequences. He nodded to show that he understood. Souberbielle bent to catch his whisper. 'Shall I make my will?'

'Well, I don't think so,' the doctor said cheerfully. 'Have you much to bequeath, by the way?'

He shook his head; let his eyes close, and smiled slightly.

'There is never anything the matter with them,' Souberbielle said. 'I mean, in the sense that it is this disease, or that disease. In September we thought we'd lost Danton. So many years of hard work and panics can reduce even a strong man like that to a wreck – and Citizen Robespierre is not strong. No, of course he is not dying. Nobody actually dies of the things that are wrong with him, they just have their lives made harder. How long? He needs to rest, that's the thing, to be well out of everything. I'd say a month. If he leaves that room sooner, I'll not be responsible.'

Members of the Committee came. It took him a moment to work out their individual faces, but he knew at once it was the Committee. 'Where is Saint-Just?' he whispered. By now he had got into the habit of whispering. Don't struggle for breath, the doctor had said. The committeemen exchanged glances.

'He has forgotten,' they said. 'You have forgotten,' they told him. 'He went to the frontier. He will be back in ten days.'

'Couthon? Could he not be carried up the stairs?'

'He's ill,' they said. 'Couthon is also ill.'

'Is he dying?'

'No. But his paralysis has become worse.'

'Will he be back tomorrow?'

'No, not tomorrow.'

Then who will rule the country? he asked himself. Saint-Just. 'Danton – ' he said. Don't struggle for breath. If you don't struggle for it it will come, the doctor said. He put his hand to his chest in panic. He could not take that advice. It was not his experience of life.

'Will you let Danton have my place?'

They exchanged glances again. Robert Lindet leaned over him. 'Do you wish it?'

He shook his head vehemently. He hears Danton's drawling voice: 'unnatural acts among the affidavits ... Do you ever ask yourself what God left out?' His eyes searched for the eyes of this solid Norman lawyer, a man without theories, without pretensions, a man unknown to the mob. 'Not to have it,' he said at last. 'Not to rule. No *vertu*.'

Lindet's face was expressionless.

'For a little while I shall not be with you,' Robespierre said. 'Then, again, I will be with you.'

'Those are familiar words,' Collot said. 'He can't remember where he has heard them before. Don't worry, we didn't think it was time for your apotheosis yet.'

Lindet said gently, 'Yes, yes, yes.'

Robespierre looked up at Collot. He is taking advantage of my weakness, he thought. 'Please give me some paper,' he whispered. He wanted to make a note: that as soon as he was well, Collot must be *reduced*.

The members of the Committee spoke very politely to Eléonore. They did not necessarily believe Dr Souberbielle, who said he would be better in a month; she understood that if by any chance he should die, she would be treated as the Widow Robespierre, as Simone Evrard was the Widow Marat.

The days passed. Souberbielle gave him permission to have more visitors, to read, to write – but only his personal letters. He might receive the news of the day, if it were not agitating; but all the news was agitating.

Saint-Just came back. We go on very well, in the Committee, he said. We are going to crush the factions. Does Danton still talk of negotiating a peace? he asked. Yes, Saint-Just said. But no one else does. Good republicans talk of victory.

Saint-Just was now twenty-six years old. He was very handsome, very forceful. He spoke in short sentences. Speak of the future, Robespierre said. He talked then of his Spartan republic. In order to breed a new race of men, he said, children would be taken from their parents when they reached five years old, to be trained as farmers, soldiers or lawmakers. Little girls too? Robespierre asked. Oh no, they do not matter, they will stay at home with their mothers.

Nervously, Robespierre's hands moved across the bedcovers. He thought of his godson, one day old, his fluttering skull steadied by his father's long fingers; his godson, a few weeks ago, gripping his coat collar and making a speech. But he was too weak to argue. People said now that Saint-Just was attached to Henriette Lebas, the sister of Babette's husband Philippe. But he didn't believe this; he didn't believe he was attached to anyone, anyone at all.

He waited till Eléonore was out of the room. He was stronger now, could make his voice heard. He beckoned to Maurice Duplay. 'I want to see Camille.'

'Do you think that's a good thing?'

Duplay sent the message. Oddly enough, Eléonore seemed neither pleased nor displeased.

When Camille came they did not talk about politics, or about recent years at all. Once, Camille mentioned Danton; he turned his head away, with his old gesture of rigid obstinacy. They talked of the past, their common past, with the forced cheerfulness that people assume when there is a dead body in the house.

Left alone, he lay dreaming of the Republic of Virtue. Five days before he became ill, he had defined his terms. He meant a republic of justice, of community, of self-sacrifice. He saw a free people, gentle, bucolic and learned. The darkness of superstition had drained away from the people's lives: brackish water, vanishing into soil. In its place flourished the rational, jocund, worship of the Supreme Being. These people were happy; their hearts were not wracked or their flesh tormented by questions without answers or desires without resolution. Men came with gravity and wit to matters of government; they instructed their children, and harvested plain and plentiful food from their own land. Dogs and cats, the animals in the field: all were respected, for their own natures. Garlanded girls, in soft robes of pale linen, moved sedately among colonnades of white marble. He saw the deep dark glint of olive groves, and the blue enamel sky.

'Look at this,' Robert Lindet said. He unrolled the newspaper and shook out of it a piece of bread. 'Feel,' he said, 'go on, taste it.'

It crumbled easily in his fingers. It had a sour musty smell. 'I thought you might not know,' Lindet said, 'if you were living on your usual diet of oranges. There's plenty of the stuff at the moment, but you can see for yourself the quality. People can't live on this. There is no milk either, and the poorer people use a lot of milk. As for meat, people are lucky to get a scrag-end for soup. The women start queuing outside the butchers' at three in the morning. This week the National Guard has had to break up fights.'

'If this goes on – I don't know.' He passed a hand over his face. 'People starved every year under the old regime. Lindet, where is it, where is all the food? The land still produces.'

'Danton says we have frozen trade up with our regulations. He says – it's true enough – that the peasants are afraid to bring their produce into the cities in case they get on the wrong side of some regulation and end up being lynched for profiteering. We requisition where we can, but they hide the stuff, they prefer to let it rot. Danton's people say that if we took the controls off, supply would begin to move again.'

'And what do you say?'

'The agitators in the Sections support controls. They tell the people it is the only way to do things. It is an impossible situation.'

'So . . .'

'I await your guidance.'

'What does Hébert say?'

'Excuse me. Give me the newspaper.' He shook it out, and crumbs showered on to the floor. 'There.'

'The butchers who treat the sansculottes like dogs and give them nothing to gnaw upon but bones should be guillotined like all the enemies of the ordinary people.'

Robespierre's lip curled. 'Very constructive,' he said.

'Unfortunately, the mass of the people has not gained much in wisdom since '89. This sort of suggestion seems a solution, to them.'

'Is there much unrest?'

'Of a sort. They are not demanding liberty. They don't seem to be interested in their rights now. Camille and the release of suspects were very popular, around Christmas. But now they only think about the food supply.'

'Hébert will exploit this,' Robespierre said.

'There's a good deal of agitation, trouble, in the arms factories. We can't afford strikes. The army is under-supplied as it is.'

Robespierre lifted his head. 'The agitators must be rounded up, in the streets, factories, wherever. I understand that the people have grievances, but we can't let everything go now. People must sacrifice themselves for the nation. It will work out, in the long term.'

'Saint-Just and Vadier on the Police Committee keep a tight hand on things. Unfortunately,' Lindet hesitated, 'without a political decision at the highest level, we can't move against the real trouble-makers.'

'Hébert.'

'He will get up an insurrection if he can. The government will fall. Read the newspaper. There is a movement at the Cordeliers – '

'Don't tell me,' Robespierre said. 'I know it all too well. The bombast to get your courage up, and the meetings in back rooms. It is only Hébert that balances out the influence of Danton. Here I am, helpless, and everything is falling apart. Won't the people be loyal to the Committee, after we have saved them from invasion, and fed them as best we can?'

'I'd hoped to spare you this,' Lindet said. He reached into a pocket and took out a piece of card, which he unfolded. It was an official notice, giving the hours and wage-rates for government workshops. There was a ragged tear at each corner, where it had been ripped from the wall.

Robespierre stretched out his hand for it. The notice bore the reproduced signatures of six members of the Committee of Public Safety. Underneath them, crudely scrawled in red, were the words:

CANNIBALS. THIEVES. MURDERERS.

Robespierre let it fall on to the bed. 'Were the Capets abused like this?' He dropped his head back against the pillows. 'It is my duty to hunt out the men who have misled and betrayed these poor people and put these wicked thoughts into their heads. I swear to you, from now on I shall not let the Revolution out of my own hands.'

After Lindet had gone he sat for a long time, propped up by pillows, watching the afternoon light change and flit across the ceiling. Dusk fell. Eléonore crept in with lights. She put a log on the fire, shuffled together the loose papers that lay about the room. She stacked up books and replaced them on the shelves, refilled his jug of water and drew the curtains. She stood over him and gently touched his face. He smiled at her.

'You are feeling better?'

'Much better.'

Suddenly she sat down at the foot of the bed, as if all the strength had left her; her shoulders slumped, she cradled her head in her hands. 'Oh,' she said, 'we thought at first you'd die. You looked like a corpse, when we found you on the floor. What would happen if you died? None of us could go on.'

'I didn't die,' he said. His tone was pleasant, decisive. 'Also I'm more clear now about what has to be done. I shall be going to the Convention tomorrow.'

The date was 21 Ventôse – 11 March, old style. It was thirty days since his withdrawal from public life. He felt as if all the years past he had been enclosed by a shell, penetrable to just a little light and sound; as if his illness had split it open, and the hand of God had plucked him out, pure and clean.

MARCH 12: 'The mandate of the Committee was renewed by the Convention for a further month,' Robert Lindet said. 'There was no opposition.' He said it very formally, as if he were a speaking gazette.

'Mm,' Danton said.

'There wouldn't be, would there?' Camille leapt up to pace about the room. 'There wouldn't be any opposition. The members of the Convention stand up and sit down to the applause of the galleries. Which the Committee had packed, I imagine.'

Lindet sighed. 'You're right. Nothing is left to chance.' His eyes followed Camille. 'Will you be glad of Hébert's death? I suppose you will.'

'Is it a foregone conclusion?' Danton asked.

'The Cordeliers Club calls for insurrection, for a "day". So does Hébert in his newspaper. No government in five years has stood up to insurrection.'

'But then,' Camille said, 'Robespierre was never the government.'

'Exactly. Either he'll snuff it out before it begins, or smash it by force of arms.'

'Man of action,' Danton said. He laughed.

'You were, once,' Lindet said.

Danton swept an arm out. 'I am the Opposition.'

'Robespierre threatened Collot. If Collot had shown the slightest leaning towards Hébert's tactics, he would be in prison now.'

'What has that to do with me?'

'Saint-Just has been at Robespierre, every day for a week. You have to understand that Robespierre has respect for him – Saint-Just never puts a foot wrong. We think that in the long run they may have some divergence of opinion, but we're not concerned with theory now. Saint-Just's attitude is, if Hébert goes, Danton must go. He talks of – balancing out the factions.'

'They wouldn't dare. I'm not a faction, Lindet, I'm at the Revolution's core.'

'Look, Danton, Saint-Just believes you are a traitor. He is actively seeking proofs of your involvement with the enemy. How many times must I tell you? However ludicrous it seems, this is what he believes. This is what he is saying to the Committee. Collot and Billaud-Varennes back him up.'

'But Robespierre,' Camille said quickly. 'He's the important one.'

'I suppose you must have quarrelled, Danton, last time you met. I'm afraid he has the air of a man who is trying to make his mind up. I don't know what it would take – some small thing. He doesn't speak against you, but he doesn't defend you as he used to. He was very quiet, in today's session. The others think it is because he's not over his illness yet, but it's more than that. He made a note of everything that was said. He watched all the time. If Hébert falls, you must go.'

'Go?'

'You must get out.'

'Is that the best advice you have for me, friend Lindet?'

'I want you to survive. Robespierre's a prophet, he's a dreamer – and I ask you, what record have prophets, as heads of government? When he's gone, who will maintain the republic, if you do not?'

'Dreamer? Prophet? You're very persuasive,' Danton said. 'But if I thought that whey-faced eunuch had any designs on me I'd break his neck.'

Lindet dropped back in his chair. 'Well, I don't know. Camille, can you make him understand?'

'Oh . . . my position is somewhat . . . ambivalent.'

'That's a damn good word for you,' Danton observed.

'Saint-Just spoke against you in the Committee today, Camille. So did Collot, so did Barère. Robespierre let them get through with it, then he said that you were led astray by stronger personalities. Barère said that they were sick of hearing that, and here was some evidence from the Police Committee, from Vadier. Robespierre took the papers and put them under his own on the table, and sat with his elbows on them. Then he changed the subject.'

'Does he often do things like that?'

'Surprisingly often.'

'I shall appeal to the people,' Danton said. 'They must have some idea what sort of government they want.'

'Hébert is appealing to the people,' Lindet said. 'The Committee calls it projected insurrection.'

'He has not my status in the Revolution. Nothing like it.'

'I don't think the people care any more,' Lindet said. 'I don't think they care who sinks or swims, you, Hébert, Robespierre. They're exhausted. They come to the trials as a diversion. It is better than the theatre. The blood is real.'

'One might think you despaired,' Camille said.

'Oh, I don't have any truck with despair. I just keep an eye on the food supplies, as the Committee has told me to do.'

'You have your loyalties to the Committee.'

'Yes. So I won't come again.'

'Lindet, if I come out on top of this, I'll remember your good offices.'

Robert Lindet nodded – made, in fact, a sort of humorous, half-embarrassed bow. He was of another generation; the Revolution had not made him. Dogged and clear-headed, he made it his business to survive from day to day; Monday to Tuesday was all he asked.

SOME VIOLENT RHETORIC in the Sections: a minor demonstration at City Hall. 23 Ventôse, Saint-Just read a report to the Convention, alleging a foreign-inspired plot among certain well-known factional-ists to destroy representative government and starve Paris. 24 Ventôse, in the early hours, Hébert and his associates were taken away from their houses by the police.

ROBESPIERRE: I am at a loss to see what purpose our friends thought this meeting would serve.

DANTON: How is the trial going?

ROBESPIERRE: No problems really. We hope it will be over tomor-row. Oh, perhaps you don't mean Hébert's trial? Fabre and Hérault will be in court in a few days time. The exact date escapes me, but Fouquier will know.

DANTON: You wouldn't be trying to frighten me, by any chance? All this relentless labouring of the point.

ROBESPIERRE: You seem to think I have something against you. All I have asked you to do is to disassociate yourself from Fabre. Unfortunately there are people who say that if Fabre is on trial you should be, too.

DANTON: And what do you say?

ROBESPIERRE: Your activities in Belgium were not perhaps above reproach. However, I chiefly blame Lacroix.

DANTON: Camille –

ROBESPIERRE: Never speak to me again of Camille.

DANTON: Why not?

ROBESPIERRE: The last time we met you spoke abusively of him. With contempt.

DANTON: Suit yourself. The point is, in December you were ready to admit that the Terror should be mitigated, that innocent people –

ROBESPIERRE: I dislike these emotive phrases. By 'innocent' you mean 'persons of whom for one reason or another I approve'. That is not the standard. The standard is what the court finds. In that sense, no innocent person has suffered.

DANTON: My God! I don't believe what I'm hearing. He says no innocent person has suffered.

ROBESPIERRE: I hope you're not going to produce any more of your tears. It is the kind of talent Fabre and the actors have, and not becoming to you.

DANTON: I appeal to you for the last time. You and I are the only people capable of running this country. All right – let's admit it finally – we don't like each other. But you don't really suspect me, any more than I suspect you. There are people around us who would like to see us destroy each other. Let's make life hard for them. Let's make common cause.

ROBESPIERRE: There's nothing I'd like better. I deplore factions. I also deplore violence. However, I would rather destroy the factions by violence than see the Revolution fall into the wrong hands and be perverted.

DANTON: You mean mine?

ROBESPIERRE: You see, you talk so much about innocence. Where are they, all these innocent people? I never seem to meet them.

DANTON: You look at innocence, but you see guilt.

ROBESPIERRE: I suppose if I had your morals and your principles, the world would look a different place. I would never see the need to punish anyone. There would be no criminals. There would be no crimes.

DANTON: Oh God, I cannot stand you and your city for a moment longer. I am taking my wife and my children to Sèvres, and if you want me you know where to find me.

*

SÈVRES, 22 MARCH: 2 Germinal. 'So here you are,' Angélique said. 'And you can enjoy the fine weather.' She kissed her grand-sons, ran her eyes down Louise, and found occasion to put an arm round her waist and squeeze her. Louise kissed her cheek dutifully. 'Why didn't you all come? ' Angélique asked. 'I mean, Camille and family? The old people could have come too, there's plenty of room.'

Louise made a mental note to pass on the description of Annette Duplessis as an old person. 'We wanted some time to ourselves,' she said.

'Oh, did you?' Angélique shrugged; it was a desire that she couldn't comprehend.

'Has my friend Duplessis recovered from his ordeal?' M. Charpentier asked.

'He's all right,' Danton said. 'He seems old, lately. Still, wouldn't you, if you had Camille for a son-in-law?'

'You've not spared me grey hairs yourself, Georges.'

'How the years have flown by!' Angélique said. 'I remember Claude as a handsome man. Stupid, but handsome.' She sighed. 'I wish I could have the last ten years over again – don't you, daughter?'

'No,' Louise said.

'She'd be six,' Danton said. 'But Christ, I wish I could have them! There'd be things to do different.'

'You wouldn't necessarily have hindsight,' his wife said.

'I remember an afternoon,' Charpentier said. 'It would be '86, '87? Duplessis came into the café and I asked him to supper. He said, we're up to our eyes at the Treasury – but we will sort out a date, as soon as the present crisis is over.'

'Well?' Louise said.

Charpentier shook his head, smiled. 'They haven't been yet.'

Two days later the weather broke. It turned grey, damp and chilly. There were draughts, the fires smoked. Visitors from Paris arrived in a steady stream. Hasty introductions were made: Deputy So-and-so, Citizen Such-a-one of the Commune. They shut themselves up with Danton; the conversations were brief, but the household heard voices raised in exasperation. The visitors always said that they had to get back to Paris, that they could by no means stay the night. They had about them the air of grim irresolution, of shifty bravado, that Angélique recognized as the prelude to crisis.

She went to ask the necessary questions. Her son-in-law sat in silence for some time, his broad shoulders slumped and his scarred face morose.

'What they want me to do,' he said finally, 'is to go back and throw my weight about. By that, I mean . . . they have plans to rally the Convention to me, and also, Westermann has sent me a letter. You remember my friend, General Westermann?'

'A military coup.' Her dark ageing face sagged. 'Georges, who suffers? Who suffers this time?'

'That's it. That's the whole point. If I can't remedy this situation without bloodshed, I'll have to leave it to someone else. That's – just how I feel these days. I don't want any more killings at my door, I don't want them on my conscience. I no longer feel sure enough of *anything* to risk a single life for it. Is that so hard to understand?' Angélique shook her head. 'My friends in Paris can't understand it. They think it's some fanciful scruple, some whim of mine, or some kind of laziness, a paralysis of the will. But the truth is, I've travelled that road, and I've reached the end of it.'

'God will forgive you, Georges,' she whispered. 'I know you have no faith, but I pray every day for you and Camille.'

'What do you pray for?' He looked up at her. 'Our political success?'

'No, I – I ask God to judge you mercifully.'

'I see. Well, I'm not ready for judgement yet. You might include Robespierre, when you're petitioning the Almighty. Although I'm sure they speak privately, more often than we know.'

MID-AFTERNOON, another carriage rumbling and squeaking into the muddy courtyard, the rain streaming down. In an upstairs room the children were screaming at the tops of their voices. Angélique was harassed; her son-in-law sat talking to the damp dog at his feet.

Louise rubbed a window-pane to look out. 'Oh, no,' she breathed. She left the room with the contemptuous twitch of her skirts which she had perfected.

Runnels of water poured and slithered from Legendre the butcher's travelling clothes: oceans, fountains and canals. 'Will you look at this weather?' he demanded. 'Six paces and I'm drowned.'

'Don't raise my hopes like that,' said the sodden shape behind him.

Legendre turned, hoarse, pink, spluttering, to compliment his travelling companion: 'You look like a rat,' he said.

Angélique reached up to take Camille's face in her hands, and put her cheek against his drenched black curls. She whispered something meaningless or Italian, breathing in the scent of wet wool. 'I don't know what I'm going to say to him,' he whispered back, in a kind of horror. She slid her arms around his shoulders and saw suddenly, with complete vividness, the sunlight slipping obliquely across the little marble tables, heard the chatter and the chink of cups, smells the aroma of fresh coffee, and the river, and the faint perfume of powdered hair. Clinging to each other, swaying slightly, they stood with their eyes fixed on each other's faces, stabbed and transfixed with dread, while the leaden clouds scudded and the foggy dismal torrent wrapped them like a shroud.

Legendre sat himself down heavily. 'I want you to believe,' he said, 'that Camille and myself don't go jaunting about the countryside together without good reason. Therefore what I've come to say, I'm going to say. I am not an educated man – '

'He never tires of telling us,' Camille said. 'He imagines it is a point not already impressed.'

'This is a business you have to face head on – not wrap it up and pretend it happened to Roman emperors.'

'Get on then,' Danton said. 'You may imagine what their journey has been like.'

'Robespierre is out for your blood.'

Danton stood in front of the fire, hands clasped behind his back. He grinned.

Camille took out a list of names and passed it to him. 'The batch of 4 Germinal,' he said. 'Thirteen executions in all. The Cordeliers leadership, Hérault's friend Proli, a couple of bankers, and of course Père Duchesne. He should have been preceded by his furnaces; they could have turned it into a sort of carnival procession. He was not in one of his great cholers when he died. He was screaming.'

'I dare say you would scream,' Legendre said.

'I am quite sure I should,' Camille said coldly. 'But my head is not going to be cut off.'

'They had supper together,' Legendre said meaningfully.

'You had supper with Robespierre?' Camille nodded. 'Well done,' Danton said. 'Myself, I don't think I could eat in the man's presence. I think I'd throw up.'

'Oh, by the way,' Camille said, 'did you know that Chabot tried to poison himself? At least, we think so.'

'He had a bottle in his cell from Charras and Duchatelle, the chemists,' Legendre said. 'It said "For external application only". So he drank it.'

'But Chabot will drink anything,' Camille said.

'He's survived, then? Botched the job?'

'Look,' Legendre said, 'you can't afford to stand there laughing and sneering. You can't afford the time. Saint-Just is nagging at Robespierre night and day.'

'What does he propose to charge me with?'

'Nothing and everything. Everything from supporting Orléans to trying to save Brissot and the Queen.'

'The usual,' Danton said. 'And you advise?'

'Last week I'd have said, stand and fight. But now I say, save your own skin. Get out while there's time.'

'Camille?'

Camille looked up unhappily. 'We met on good terms. He was very amiable. In fact, he had a bit too much to drink. He only does that when he's – when he's trying to shut out his inner voices, if that doesn't sound too fanciful. I asked him, why won't you talk about Danton? He touched his forehead and said, because he is *sub judice*.' He turned his head away. 'You might think of going abroad.'

'Abroad? Oh no. I went to England in '91, and you stood in the garden at Fontenay and berated me.' He shook his head. 'This is my nation. Here I stay. A man can't carry his country on the soles of his shoes.'

The wind howled and rattled in the chimneys; dogs barked across the countryside from farm to farm. 'After all you said about posterity,' Camille muttered. 'You seem to be speaking to it now.' The rain slackened to a grey penetrating drizzle, soaking the houses and fields.

IN PARIS THE SWAYING lanterns are lit in the streets; lights shine through water, fuzzy, diffuse. Saint-Just sits by an insufficient fire, in a poor light. He is a Spartan after all, and Spartans don't need home comforts. He has begun his report, his list of accusations; if Robespierre saw it now, he would tear it up, but in a few days time it will be the very thing he needs.

Sometimes he stops, half-glances over his shoulder. He feels someone has come into the room behind him; but when he allows himself to look, there is nothing to see. It is my destiny, he feels, forming in the shadows of the room. It is the guardian angel I had, long ago when I was a child. It is Camille Desmoulins, looking over my shoulder, laughing at my grammar. He pauses for a moment. He thinks, there are no living ghosts. He takes hold of himself. Bends his head over his task.

His pen scratches. His strange letter-forms incise the paper. His handwriting is minute. He gets a lot of words to the page.

XIII. *Conditional Absolution*

(1794)

COUR DU COMMERCE: 31 March, 10 Germinal: 'Marat?' The black bundle moved, fractionally. 'Forgive me.' Danton put his hand to his head. 'A stupid thing to say.'

He moved to a chair, unable to drag his eyes from the scrap of humanity that was the Citizeness Albertine. Her garments were funereal layers, an array of wraps and shawls, belonging to no style or fashion that had ever existed or ever could. She spoke with a foreign accent, but it was not the accent of any country to be found on a map.

'In a sense,' she said, 'you are not mistaken.' She raised a skeletal hand, and laid it somewhere among her wrappings, where it might be supposed her heart beat. 'I carry my brother here,' she said. 'We are never separated now.'

For several seconds he found himself unable to speak. 'How can I oblige you?' he said at last.

'We did not come to be obliged.' Dry voice: bone on bone. She paused for a moment, as if listening. 'Strike now,' she said.

'With respect —'

'He is at the Convention now. Robespierre.'

'I am haunted enough.' He got up, blundered across the room. Superstitious dread touched him, at his own words. 'I can't have his death on my hands.'

'It's yours or his. You must go to the Convention now, Danton. You must see the patriot walk and talk. You must judge his mood and you must prepare for a fight.'

'Very well, I'll go. If it will please you. But I think you're wrong, Citizeness, I don't think Robespierre or any of the Committee would dare to move against me.'

'You don't believe they would dare.' Mockery. She approached him, tilted up her yellow wide-lipped face. 'Do you know me?' she asked. 'Tell me, Citizen, when were we ever wrong?'

RUE HONORÉ: 'You're wasting my time,' Robespierre said. 'I told you my intentions before the Convention met. The papers for Hérault and Fabre are with the Public Prosecutor. You may draw up warrants for the arrest of Deputy Philippeaux and Deputy Lacroix. But for no one else.'

Saint-Just's voice shook the little sitting room. His fist hammered a table. 'Leave Danton at large and you will be locked up yourself tomorrow. Your head will be off before the week is out.'

'There is no need for this. Calm yourself. I know Danton. He has always been a cautious man, a man who weighs a situation. He will make no move unless he is forced into it. He must be aware you are collecting evidence against him. He is no doubt preparing to refute it.'

'Yes – to refute it by force of arms, that will be his idea. Look – call in Philippe Lebas. Call in the Police Committee. Call in every patriot in the Jacobin Club, and they will tell you what I am telling you now.' Scarlet flared against his perfect white skin: his dark eyes shone. He is enjoying himself, Robespierre thought in disgust. 'Danton is a traitor to the Republic, he is a killer, he has never in his life known how to compromise. If we don't act today he will leave none of us alive to oppose him.'

'You contradict yourself. First you say, he has never been a republican, he has accommodated every counter-revolutionary from Lafayette to Brissot. Then you say, he has never compromised.'

'You are quibbling. What do you think, that Danton is fit to be at large in the Republic?'

Robespierre looked down, considering. He understood the nature of it, this republic that Saint-Just spoke of. It was not the Republic that was bounded by the Pyrenees and the Rhine, but the republic of the spirit; not the city of flesh and stone, but the stronghold of virtue, the dominion of the just. 'I cannot be sure,' he said. 'I cannot make up my mind.' His own face looked back at him, appraisingly, from the wall. He turned. 'Philippe?'

Philippe Lebas stood in the doorway between the little parlour and the Duplay's larger sitting room. 'There is something which may help make up your mind,' he said.

'Something from Vadier,' Robespierre said sceptically. 'From the Police Committee.'

'No, something from Babette.'

'Babette? Is she here? I don't follow you.'

'Would you come in here, please? It won't take very long.' Robespierre hesitated. 'For God's sake,' Lebas said passionately, 'you wanted to know if Danton was fit to live. Saint-Just, will you come and listen?'

'Very well,' Robespierre said. 'But another time, I should prefer not to conduct these arguments in my own house.'

All the Duplays were present in the salon. He looked around them. The room was live with tension; his skin crawled. 'What is this?' he asked gently. 'I don't understand.'

No one spoke. Babette sat alone at the big table, as if she were facing some sort of commission. He bent to kiss her forehead. 'If I'd known you were here, I'd have cut this stupid argument short. Well?'

Still no one spoke. Seeing nothing else to do, he pulled up a chair and sat down beside her at the table. She gave him her soft little hand. Babette was five or six months pregnant, round and flushed and pretty. She was only a few months older than Danton's little child-bride, and he could not look at her without an uprush of fear.

Maurice was sitting on a stool by the fire, his head lowered: as if he had heard something that had humbled him. But now he cleared his throat, and looked up. 'You've been a son to us,' he said.

'Oh, come now,' Robespierre said. He smiled, squeezed Babette's hand. 'This is beginning to seem like the third act of some dreadful play.'

'It is an ordeal for the girl,' Duplay said.

'It's all right,' Elisabeth said. She dropped her head, blushed; her china-blue eyes were half-hidden by their lids. Saint-Just leaned against the wall, his own eyes half-closed.

Philippe Lebas took up his station behind Babette's chair. He wrapped his fingers tightly round the back of it. Robespierre glanced up at him. 'Citizen, what is this?'

'You were debating the character of Citizen Danton,' Babette said softly. 'I know nothing of politics, it is not a woman's province.'

'If you want to have your say, you can do. In my opinion, women have as much discernment as men.' He gave Saint-Just a venomous glance, begging contradiction. Saint-Just smiled lazily.

'I thought you might like to know what happened to me.'

'When?'

'Let her tell you in her own way,' Duplay said.

Babette slid her hand out of his. She joined her fingers on the polished table top, and her face was dimly reflected in it as she began to speak. 'You remember when I went to Sèvres, last autumn? Mother thought I needed some fresh air, so I went to stay with Citizeness Panis.'

Citizeness Panis: respectable wife of a Paris deputy, Etienne Panis: a good Montagnard, with a record of sterling service on 10 August, the day the monarchs were overthrown.

'I remember,' Robespierre said. 'Not the date – it would be October, November?'

'Yes – well, Citizen Danton was there at that time, with Louise. I thought it would be nice to call on her. She's nearly the same age as me, and I thought she might be lonely, and want someone to talk to. I'd been thinking, you know, about what she has to put up with.'

'What is that?'

'Well, some people say that her husband married her for love, and other people say he married her because she was happy to look after his children and run his household while he was occupied with Citizeness Desmoulins. Though most people say, of course, that the Citizeness likes General Dillon best.'

'Babette, keep to the point,' Lebas said.

'So I went to call on her, and she wasn't at home. And Citizen Danton was. He can be – well, very pleasant, quite charming. I felt a little sorry for him – he was the one who seemed to need someone to talk to, and I thought, perhaps Louise is not very intelligent. He said, stay and keep me company.'

'She didn't realize that they were alone in the house,' Lebas said.

'No, of course – I had no way of knowing. We talked: about this and that. Of course, I had no idea what it was leading up to.'

'And what was it leading up to?' Robespierre sounded faintly impatient.

She looked up at him. 'Don't be angry with me.'

'No, of course – I'm not angry. Did I sound angry? I'm sorry. Now, the thing is – Danton made some remark, in the course of your conversation, which you feel you must report. You are a good girl, and you are doing what you see as your duty. No one will blame you for that. Tell me what he said – and then I can see what weight to give it.'

'No, no,' Mme Duplay said faintly. 'He is so good. He has no idea of half the things that happen in the world.'

He glared at the interruption. 'Now, Babette.' He took her hand again, or did rather less than that: he placed the tips of his fingers against the back of her hand.

'Come on,' her husband said: more roughly than he would have liked. 'Say what happened, Babette.'

'Oh, he put his arm around me. I didn't want to make a fuss – one must grow up, I suppose, and after all – he put his hand inside my dress, but I thought, of course, he's been seen in the most respectable company too – well, I mean the things he has done with Citizeness Desmoulins, I have heard people say that he has quite fallen upon her, in public, and of course that it is of no consequence, because he won't actually go to the extreme. All the same, I did try very hard to pull away from him. But he is a very strong man you know, and the words he used – I couldn't repeat them –'

'I think you must,' Robespierre said. His voice was frozen.

'Oh, he said that he wanted to show me how much better it could be with a man who had experience with women than with some high-minded Robespierrist virgin – then he tried – ' She put her hands, fingers interlaced, before her face. Her voice came almost inaudibly from behind them. 'Of course, I struggled. He said, your sister Eléonore is not so moral. He said, she knows just what we republicans want. I think, then, that I fainted.'

'Is there any need to go on?' Lebas said. He moved: transferred his hands to the back of Robespierre's chair, so that he stood looking down at the nape of his neck.

'Don't stand over me like that,' Robespierre said sharply. But Lebas didn't move. Robespierre looked around the room, wanting a corner, an angle, a place to turn his face and compose it. But from everywhere in the room, the eyes of the Duplay family stared back. 'So: when you came to yourself?' he said. 'Where were you then?'

'I was in the room.' Her mouth quivered. 'My clothes were disordered, my skirt – '

'Yes,' Robespierre said. 'We don't need details.'

'There was no one else in the room. I composed myself and I stood up and looked around. I saw no one so I – I ran out of the front door.'

'Are you – let's be quite clear – are you telling me Danton raped you?'

'I struggled for as long as I could.' She began to cry.

'And what happened then?'

'Then?'

'Presumably you got home. What did Panis's wife say?'

She raised her face. A perfect tear rolled down her cheek. 'She said I must never tell anyone anything about it. Because it would make the most dreadful trouble.'

'So you didn't.'

'Until now. I thought I must – ' She dissolved into tears again. Unexpectedly, Saint-Just straightened up from the wall, leaned over her, patted her shoulder.

'Babette,' Robespierre said. 'Now, dry your tears, listen to me. When this happened, where were Danton's servants? He is not a man to do without them, there must have been somebody in the house?'

'I don't know. I cried out, I screamed – nobody came.'

Mme Duplay spoke. She had been, of course, extraordinarily

forbearing, to keep silent for so long, and now she was hesitant. 'You see, Maximilien – the fact of what happened is bad enough, but there is a further problem –'

'I'm sure he can count on his fingers,' Saint-Just said.

It was a moment before he understood. 'So then, Babette – at that date, you didn't know –'

'No.' She dropped her face again. 'How can I know? Perhaps I had already conceived – I can't be sure. Of course, I hope I had. I hope I'm not carrying his child.'

She had said it out loud: they had all arrived at the idea, but now it was spoken out loud it made them gasp with shock.

Only he, Robespierre, exercised self-control. To resist temptation is important now: temptation to look in like a beggar at the lighted window of emotion. 'Listen, Babette,' he said. 'This is very important. Did anyone suggest to you that you should tell this story to me today?'

'No. How could anyone? Until today, nobody knew.'

'You see, Elisabeth, if this were a courtroom – well, I would ask you a lot of questions.'

'It is not a courtroom,' Duplay said. 'It is your family. I saved your life, three years ago in the street, and since then we have cared for you as if you were a child of our own. And your sister, and your brother Augustin – you were orphans, and you had nobody except each other, and we have done our best to be everything to you.'

'Yes.' Defeated, he sat at the head of the table, facing Elisabeth. Mme Duplay moved, brushing lightly against him, to take her daughter in her arms. Elisabeth began to sob, with a sound that pierced him like steel.

Saint-Just cleared his throat. 'I'm sorry to take you away now, but the Police Committee will be meeting our Committee in an hour. I have drawn up a preliminary report regarding Danton – but it needs supplementation.'

'Duplay,' Robespierre said, 'you understand that this matter cannot come to court. There is no need, really – in the context of other charges, I'm afraid it's trivial. You will not sit as a juror at Danton's trial. I shall tell Fouquier to exempt you. It would not be just.' He shook his head. 'No, it would not be equitable.'

'Before we leave,' Saint-Just asked, 'would you go upstairs and get those notebooks of yours?'

THE TUILERIES, eight p.m.: 'I am going to be very plain with you, Citizen,' the Inquisitor said. Robespierre transferred his attention from Vadier's long sallow face to his hands, to his peculiar fingers obsessively re-sorting papers on the green-draped oval table. 'I shall be plain with you, on behalf of your own colleagues, and my colleagues on the Police Committee.'

'Then please do proceed.' His mouth was tight. His chest hurt. There was blood in his mouth. He knew what they wanted.

'You will agree with me,' Vadier said, 'that Danton is a powerful and resourceful man.'

'Yes.'

'And a traitor.'

'Why are you asking me? The Tribunal will determine what he is.'

'But the trial, in itself, is a dangerous business.'

'Yes.'

'So every precaution must be taken.'

'Yes.'

'And every circumstance that might unfavourably influence the course of the trial must be attended to.'

Vadier took his silence for consent. Slowly, like primitive animals, the Inquisitor's fingers curled up. They formed a fist. It hit the table. 'Then how do you expect us to leave this aristocrat journalist at large? If Danton's course since '89 has been treasonable, how do you exonerate his closest associate? Before the Revolution, his friends were the traitor Brissot and the traitor d'Église. No, don't interrupt me. He has no acquaintance with Mirabeau – yet suddenly, he moves in with him at Versailles. For months – the months when Mirabeau was plotting his treason – he was never out of his company. He is impecunious, unknown – then suddenly he appears nightly at Orléans's supper table. He was Danton's secretary during his treasonable tenure at the Ministry of Justice. He is a rich man, or he lives like one – and his private life does not bear discussion.'

'Yes.' Robespierre said. 'And he led the people, on 12 July. He raised revolt, and then the Bastille fell.'

'How can you exonerate this man?' Vadier bawled at him. 'One person to whom the misguided people may have some – some sentimental attachment?' He made a sound expressive of disgust. 'You think you can leave him at liberty, while his friend Danton is on trial? Because once, five years ago, he was bribed to talk to a mob?'

'No, that is not why,' Saint-Just said smoothly. 'The reason is that he himself has a sentimental attachment. He appears to put his personal feelings before the welfare of the Republic.'

'Camille has made a fool of you for too long,' Billaud said.

Robespierre looked up. 'You slander me, Saint-Just. I put nothing before the welfare of the Republic. I do not have it in me to do so.'

'Let me just say this.' Vadier's yellow fingers uncurled themselves again. 'No one, not even your admirable and patriotic self, may stand out against the people's will. We are all against you. You are on your own. You must bow to the majority, or else here and now, tonight and in this room, your career is finished.'

'Citizen Vadier,' Saint-Just said, 'sign the order for arrest, then pass it around the table.'

Vadier reached out for a pen. But Billaud's hand leapt out, like a snake from a hole; he snatched the document and signed his name with a flourish.

'He wanted to be first,' his friend Collot explained.

'Was Danton so tyrannical an employer?' Robert Lindet asked.

Vadier took back the paper, signed it himself, and pushed it along the table. 'Rühl?'

Rühl, of the Police Committee, shook his head.

'He is senile,' Collot suggested. 'He should be turned out of government.'

'Perhaps he's just deaf.' Billaud's forefinger stabbed at the paper. 'Sign, old man.'

'Because I am old, as you say, you can't browbeat me by threatening to end my career. I do not believe that Danton is a traitor. Therefore I will not sign.'

'Your career may end sooner than you think, then.'

'No matter,' Rühl said.

'Then pass the paper on to me,' Lebas said savagely. 'Stop wasting the Republic's time.'

Carnot took it. He looked at it thoughtfully. 'I sign for the sake of the unity of the committees. No other reason.' He did so, and laid the paper in front of Lebas. 'A few weeks, gentlemen, three months at the outside, and you'll be wishing you had Danton to rally the city for you. If you proceed against him, you pass into a new phase of history, for which I think you are ill-prepared. I tell you, gentlemen – you will be consulting necromancers.'

'Quickly,' Collot said. He snatched the paper from a member of the Police Committee, and scribbled his name. 'There you are, Saint-Just – quickly, quickly.'

Robert Lindet took the warrant. Without glancing at it, he passed it on to his neighbour. Saint-Just's eyes narrowed. 'No,' Lindet said shortly.

'Why not?'

'I am not obliged to give my reasons to you.'

'Then we are bound to put the worst construction on them,' Vadier said.

'I am sorry you feel so bound. You have put me in charge of supply. I am here to feed patriots, not to murder them.'

'There is no need for unanimity,' Saint-Just said. 'It would have been desirable, but let's get on. There are only two signatures wanting, I think, besides those who have refused. Citizen Lacoste, you next – then be so good as to put the paper in front of Citizen Robespierre, and move the ink a little nearer.'

THE COMMITTEES of Public Safety and General Security hereby decree that Danton, Lacroix (of the Eure-et-Loire *département*), Camille Desmoulins and Philippeaux, all members of the National Convention, shall be arrested and taken to the Luxembourg, there to be kept in secret and solitary confinement. And they do command the Mayor of Paris to execute this present decree immediately on receipt thereof.

COUR DU COMMERCE, nine p.m.: 'Just a moment,' Danton said. 'Introductions.'

'Danton –'

'Introductions. My dear, this is Fabricius Pâris, an old friend of mine, and the Clerk of the Court to the Tribunal.'

'Delighted to meet you,' Pâris said hurriedly. 'Your husband got me my job.'

'And that's why you're here. You see, Louise, I inspire loyalty. Now?'

Pâris was agitated. 'You know I go every evening to the Committee. I collect the orders for the following day.' He turned to Louise. 'Orders for the Tribunal; I take them to Fouquier.' She nodded. 'When I arrived the doors were locked. Such a thing had never happened before. I said to myself, it may be useful to a patriot to know what is going on in there. I know the building, you see. I went by a back way, and I found – forgive me – a keyhole – '

'I forgive you,' Danton said. 'And you put your eye to the keyhole, and then your ear, and you saw and heard Saint-Just denouncing me.'

'How do you know?'

'It is logical.'

'Danton, they were sitting in silence, listening to every lie he uttered.'

'What exactly has he in mind? Do you know? Was there a warrant?'

'I didn't see one. He was talking about denouncing you before the Convention, in your presence.'

'Couldn't be better,' Danton said. 'He wants to match his oratory against mine, does he? And his experience? And his name in the Revolution?' He turned to his wife. 'It's perfect. It is exactly as I wanted. The imbecile has chosen to meet me on my own ground. Pâris, it couldn't be better.'

Pâris looked incredulous. 'You wanted it forced to this point?'

'I shall crucify that smug young bastard, and I shall take the greatest pleasure in driving in the nails.'

'You will sit up and write your speech, I suppose,' Louise said.

Danton laughed. 'My wife doesn't know my methods yet. But you do, Pâris? I don't need a speech, my love. I get it all out of my head.'

'Well, at least go and get the report of it written in advance for the newspapers. Complete with "tumultuous applause", and so on.'

'You're learning,' he said. 'Pâris, did Saint-Just mention Camille?'

'I didn't wait, as soon as I caught the drift I got around here. I suppose he's not in danger.'

'I went to the Convention this afternoon. Didn't stay. He and Robespierre were deep in conversation.'

'So I heard. I was told they appeared very friendly. Is it possible then . . . ?' He hesitated. How to ask someone if his best friend has reneged on him?

'In the Convention tomorrow I shall put him up to confront Saint-Just. Imagine it. Our man the picture of starched rectitude, and looking as if he has just devoured a beefsteak; and Camille making a joke or two at our man's expense and then talking about '89. A cheap trick, but the galleries will cheer. This will make Saint-Just lose his temper – not easy, since he cultivates that Greek statue manner of his – but I *guarantee* that Camille can do it. As soon as our man begins to bawl and roar, Camille will fold up and look helpless. That will get Robespierre on his feet, and we will all generate one of these huge emotional scenes. I always win those. I shall go round now – no, I won't, we'll plan this in the morning. I ought to leave Camille alone. Bad news from home. A death in the family.'

'Not the precious father?'

'His mother.'

'I'm sorry,' Pâris said. 'Bad timing. He may not be so keen to play games. Danton – I suppose you wouldn't consider any less risky course of action?'

RUE MARAT, 9.30 p.m.: 'I could have gone home,' Camille said. 'Why didn't he tell me she was ill? He was here. He sat in the chair where you sit now. He didn't say a word.'

'Perhaps he wanted to spare your feelings. Perhaps they thought she'd get better.'

One day at the end of last year, a stranger had come to the door:

a distinguished man of sixty or so, spare, remote, with an impressive head of iron-grey hair. It had taken her a long moment to work out who he was.

'My father has never spared my feelings,' Camille said. 'He has never understood the concept of sparing feelings. In fact, he has never understood the concept of feelings at all.'

It had been a brief visit – a day or two. Jean-Nicolas came because he had seen the 'Old Cordelier'. He wanted to tell his son how much he admired it, how much he felt that he had done the right thing at last; how much, perhaps, he missed him, and wanted him to come home sometimes.

But when he tried to do this, a kind of hideous embarrassment swept over him, like the socially disabling blush of a girl of thirteen. His voice had strangled in his throat, and he had confronted, speechless, the son who usually preferred not to speak anyway.

It had been, Lucile thought, one of the worse half-hours in her life. Fabre had been there, bemoaning his lot as usual; but at the sight of the elder Desmoulins in such straits, he had actually found tears in his eyes. She had seen him dab them away; Camille had seen it, too. Better that *they* had cried, Fabre said later; haven't they a lot to cry for? When Jean-Nicolas gave up the effort at speech, father and son had embraced, in a minimal and chilly fashion. The man has some defect, Fabre had said later: I think there's something wrong with his heart.

There was, of course, another aspect to the visit. Even Fabre wouldn't mention it. It was the *will you survive this?* aspect. They couldn't either, mention it tonight. Camille said, 'When you think of Georges-Jacques and his mother, it's odd. She may be a tedious old witch, but they're always on some sort of terms, they're always connected. And you, and your mother.'

'Practically the same person,' Lucile said, acidly.

'Yes, but think of me – it's hard to believe I'm related to my mother at all, perhaps Jean-Nicolas found me under a bush. I've spent my whole life trying to please him, and I've never succeeded, and I've never given up. Here I am, father, I am ten years old, I can read Aristophanes as my sisters read nursery rhymes. Yes, but why did God give us a child with a speech impediment? Look, Father, I have passed every examination known to man – are you pleased? Yes, but when will you make some money? See, Father, you know that revolution you've been talking about for twenty years? I've just started it. Oh yes, very nice – but not quite what we had in mind for you, and what will the neighbours say?' Camille shook his head. 'When I think, of the years of my life that I've spent, if you add it up, writing letters to that man. I could have learned Aramaic, instead. Done something useful. Put my head together with Marat, and worked on his roulette system.'

'He had one, did he?'

'So he said. It was just that he was so generally deplorable as a person that the gaming houses wouldn't let him in.'

They sat in silence for a minute or two. The topic of Camille's mother was exhausted. He didn't know her, she didn't know him, and it was that lack of knowledge that made the news of her death so miserable: that feeling of having calculated on a second chance, and missed it. 'Gamblers,' she said. 'I keep thinking of Hérault. He's been in prison for a fortnight now. But he knew that they were going to arrest him. Why didn't he run?'

'He is too proud.'

'And Fabre. Is it true that Lacroix will be arrested?'

'They say so. And Philippeaux. You can't defy the Committee and live.'

'But Camille, you have defied them. You've done nothing but attack the Committee for the last five months.'

'Yes, but I have Max. They can't touch me. They'd like to. But they can't, without him.'

She knelt before the fire. Shivered. 'Tomorrow I must send to the farm for more wood.'

COUR DU COMMERCE: 'Deputy Panis is here.' Louise had picked up fear in an instant from the man who stood at the door.

It was a quarter to one, the morning of 12 Germinal. Danton was in his dressing-gown. 'Forgive me, Citizen. The servants are in bed and we were just going ourselves. Come to the fire – it's cold out.'

He knelt before the embers. 'Leave that,' Panis said. 'They are coming to arrest you.'

'What?' he turned. 'You're misinformed. Fabricius Pâris was here before you.'

'I don't know what he told you, but he was not at the meeting of the two committees. Lindet was. He sent me. There is a warrant out. They mean to deny you a hearing before the Convention. You are never to appear there again. You are to go straight to prison, and from there to the Tribunal.'

Danton was silenced for a moment: the shock made his face a blank. 'But Pâris heard Saint-Just say he wanted to fight it out with me, before the Convention.'

'So he did. What do you think? They talked him down. They knew the risk and they were not prepared to let him take it. They are not novices – they know you can start a riot in the public galleries. He was furious, Lindet said. He stormed out of the room, and he – ' Panis looked away.

'Well, he what?'

Panis put a hand before his mouth. 'Threw his hat into the fire.'

'What?' Danton said. The Deputy's eyes met his own. They began to laugh, with a silent, contained, unsuitable mirth.

'His hat. It blazed up merrily, Lindet said. His notes would have followed his hat, but some benighted so-called patriot wrested them from his hand, as he was about to skim them into the flames. Oh, he did not care to be deprived of his moment of glory, I tell you. Not at all.'

'His hat! Oh, that Camille had been there!' Danton said.

'Yes,' the deputy agreed. 'Camille would have been the one to appreciate it most.'

And then Danton remembered himself. No joke, he thought, none at all. 'But you are saying they have signed a warrant? Robespierre too?'

'Yes. Lindet says you should take the chance, your last chance. At least get out of your apartment, because they may come here at any time. And I must go now – I must go round the corner, and tell Camille.'

Danton shook his head. 'Leave it. Let them sleep, let them find out in the morning. Because this will be a cruel business for Camille. He will have to face Robespierre, and he won't know what to say.'

Panis stared at him. 'My God, you don't realize, do you? He'll not be saying anything to Robespierre. He'll be locked up with you.'

Louise saw his body sag. He folded into a chair, and sat with his hand before his eyes.

TWO O'CLOCK. 'I came,' Lindet said, 'hoping to find that you were no longer here. For God's sake, Danton, what are you trying to do? Are you bent on helping them destroy you?'

'I can't believe it,' Danton said. He stared into the dying fire. 'That he would have Camille arrested – and just this afternoon I saw them deep in conversation, he was friendly, smiling – oh, the consummate hypocrite!'

Louise had dressed hurriedly. She sat apart from them, hiding her face in her hands. She had seen his face, seen the will and power drain out of him. Tears seeped between her fingers. But at the back of her mind, an insistent little message hammered out its rhythm: you will be free, you will be free.

'I thought they would let me go before the Convention. Lindet, did no one remind them that the Convention has to agree to our arrest, that it has to lift our immunity?'

'Of course. Robespierre reminded them. Billaud told him that they would get the consent when you were safely under lock and key. They were very frightened men, Danton. They bolted the doors, and still they acted as if they expected you to burst through them at any minute.'

'But Lindet, what did he say? About Camille?'

'I felt sorry for him,' Lindet said abruptly. 'They drove him into the ground. They gave him a straight choice. And the poor devil, he thinks he has to stay alive for the Republic. Much good his life will be to him, after this.'

'Marat was indicted before the Tribunal,' Danton said. 'The Gironde arrested him and put him on trial, and the business blew up in their hands. The Tribunal acquitted. The people carried him through the streets in triumph. He came back stronger than ever.'

'Yes,' Lindet said. But, he thought, in those days, the Tribunal guarded its independence. Marat had a trial; do you think it will be a trial, what you'll get?

But he did not speak. He watched Danton gather himself; saw him take heart. 'They can't gag me, can they?' he said. 'They can arrest me, but they have to let me speak. All right – I'm ready to take them on.' Lindet stood up. Danton slapped him on the shoulder. 'We'll see what those buggers look like by the time I've finished with them.'

RUE MARAT, three a.m.: Camille had begun to talk, in little more than a whisper, but fluently, without hesitation, as if a part of his mind had been set free. Lucile had finished crying; she sat and watched him now, in the drugged, hypnotized state that succeeds extreme emotion. In the next room, their child slept. There was no sound from the street outside; no sound in the room, except this low sibilation: no light, except the light of one candle. We might be cut adrift from the universe, she thought.

'You see, in '89 I thought, some aristocrat will run me through. I shall be a martyr for liberty, it will be very nice, it will be in all the papers. Then I thought, in '92, the Austrians will come and shoot me, well, it will be over quickly, and I will be a national hero.' He put his hand to his throat. 'Danton says he doesn't care what they think of him, the people who come after us. I find I want their good opinion. But I don't think I'm going to get it, do you?'

'I don't know,' Lindet said.

'But after all this, to die on the wrong side of patriotism – to be accused of counter-revolution – I can't bear it. Robert, will you help me to escape?'

Lindet hesitated. 'There's no time now.'

'I know there is no time, but will you?'

'No, I don't think so,' Lindet said gently. 'We would both be sacrificed. I'm very sorry, Camille.'

At the door Lindet put an arm around her. 'Go to your mother and father. By morning this will be no place for you.' Suddenly he turned back. 'Camille, did you mean it? Are you really prepared to run for it? Not go to pieces on me, and do as I say?'

Camille looked up. 'Oh no,' he said. 'No, I don't really want to. I was just testing you.'

'For what?'

'Never mind,' Camille said. 'You passed.' He dropped his head again.

Robert Lindet was fifty years old. His age showed in his dry administrator's face. She wondered how anyone survived to attain it.

'IT MUST BE ALMOST DAWN,' Lucile said. 'No one has come yet.'

And she hopes — hope takes you by the throat like a strangler, it makes your heart leap — is it possible that Robespierre has somehow reversed the decision, that he has found courage, talked them down?

'I wrote to Rabbit,' she said. 'I didn't tell you. I asked him to come back, give us his support.'

'He didn't reply.'

'No.'

'He thinks, when I am dead, he will marry you.'

'That's what Louise said.'

'What does Louise know about it?'

'Nothing. Camille? Why did you call him Rabbit?'

'Are people still trying to work out why I called him Rabbit?'

'Yes.'

'No reason.'

She heard, below, boots on cobblestones; she heard the patrol halt. That might be, she thought, just the regular patrol; it is time for them, after all. How the heart deceives.

'There,' Camille stood up. 'I'm glad Jeanette is away tonight. That's the street door now.'

She stood in the middle of the room. She was aware of a puppet-like stiffness in her limbs. She seemed unable to speak.

'Are you looking for me?' Camille said. She watched him. She remembered 10 August, after Suleau's death: how he had cleaned himself up and gone back into the screaming streets. 'You're supposed to ask me who I am,' he told the officer. 'Are you Camille Desmoulins, you're supposed to say, profession journalist, deputy to the National Convention – just as if there might be two of us, very similar.'

'Look, it's very early,' the man said. 'I know damn well who you are and there aren't two of you. Here's the warrant, if you're interested.'

'Can I say goodbye to my little boy?'

'Only if we come with you.'

'I wanted not to wake him. Can't I have a moment on my own?'

The men moved, took up stations before the doors and windows. 'A man last week,' the officer said, 'went to kiss his daughter and blew his brains out. Man across the river jumped out of a window, fell four floors, broke his neck.'

'Yes, you can't understand why he'd bother,' Camille said. 'When the state would have broken it for him.'

'Don't give us any trouble,' the man said.

'No trouble,' Camille promised.

'Take some books.' She was appalled to hear her voice come out, full of bravado. 'It will be boring.'

'Yes, I'll do that.'

'Hurry up then.' The officer put his hand on Camille's arm.

'No,' she said. She flung herself at Camille. She locked her arms around his neck. They kissed. 'Come on now,' the officer said. 'Citizeness, let him go.' But she clung tighter, shrugging off the hand on her arm. A moment later the officer tore her away bodily, and with her fist she caught him one good blow on the jaw, felt the impact of it run through her own body, but felt nothing as her head hit the floor. As if I were a fly, she thought, or some little bird: I am just brushed away, I am crushed.

She was alone. They had hustled him out of the room, down the stairs, out of the house. She sat up. She was not hurt, not at all. She picked up a cushion from the sofa, and held it against her, rocking herself a little, eyes blank: and the scream she had meant to scream, and the words of love she had meant to speak, locked into her throat and set there like iron. She rocked herself. What now? She must dress herself. She must write letters and deliver them. She must see every deputy, every committeeman. She knows how she must set things moving. She must act. She rocks herself. There is the world and there is the shadow-play world; there is the world of freedom and illusion, and then there is the real world, in which we watch, year by year, the people we love hammer on their chains. Rising from the floor, she feels the fetters bite into her flesh. I'm bound to you, she thinks: *bound to you.*

AROUND THE CORNER in the Cour du Commerce, Danton turned over the warrant, read it with some interest. He was in a hurry. He did not ask if he could say goodbye to his children, and kissed his wife in a cursory way on the top of her head. 'The sooner I go, the sooner I'll be back,' he said. 'See you in a day or two.' He stepped out briskly, under guard, into the street.

EIGHT A.M. at the Tuileries: 'You wanted to see us,' Fouquier-Tinville said.

'Oh yes.' Saint-Just looked up and smiled.

'We thought we were coming to see Robespierre,' Hermann said.

'No, Citizen President: me. Any objection?' He didn't ask them to sit down. 'Earlier this morning we arrested four persons – Danton, Desmoulins, Lacroix, Philippeaux. I have drawn up a report on the case which I shall present to the Convention later today. You, for your part, will begin preparations for the trial – drop everything else, treat it as a matter of urgency.'

'Now just stop there,' Hermann said. 'What sort of a procedure is this? The Convention hasn't yet agreed to these arrests.'

'We may take it as a formality.' Saint-Just raised his eyebrows. 'You're not going to fight me over this, are you, Hermann?'

'Fight you? Let me remind you where we stand. Everybody knows, but cannot prove, that Danton has taken bribes. The other thing everybody knows – and the proof is all around us – is that Danton overthrew Capet, set up the Republic and saved us from invasion. What are you going to charge him with? Lack of fervour?'

'If you doubt,' Saint-Just said, 'that there are matters of substance alleged against Danton, you are welcome to look through these papers.' He pushed them across the desk. 'You will see that some sections are in Robespierre's hand and some in mine. You may ignore the passages by Citizen Robespierre which relate to Camille Desmoulins. They are only excuses. In fact, when you have finished, I will delete them.'

'This is a tissue of lies,' Hermann said, reading. 'It is nonsense, it is a complete fabrication.'

'Well,' Fouquier said, 'it is the usual. Conspired with Mirabeau, with Orléans, with Capet, with Brissot. We've handled it before – it was Camille, in fact, who taught us how. Next week, if we have an expeditious verdict, we may be able to add "conspired with Danton". As soon as a man's dead it becomes a capital crime to have known him.'

'What are we to do,' Hermann asked, 'when Danton begins to play to the public gallery?'

'If you need to gag him, we will provide the means.'

'Oh, dramatic!' Fouquier said. 'And these four accused are all lawyers, I think?'

'Come, Citizen, take heart,' Saint-Just said. 'You have always shown yourself capable. I mean, that you have always been faithful to the Committee.'

'Yes. You're the government,' Fouquier said.

'Camille Desmoulins is related to you, isn't he?'

'Yes. I thought he was related to you, too?'

Saint-Just frowned. 'No, I don't think so. It would be unsettling to think that it might influence you.'

'Look, I do my job,' Fouquier said.

'That's fine then.'

'Yes,' Fouquier said. 'And I'd be grateful if you didn't keep harping on it.'

'Do you like Camille?' Saint-Just asked.

'Why? I thought we agreed it had nothing to do with anything.'

'No, I only wondered. You needn't answer. Now – you recall I said it was a matter of urgency?'

'Oh yes,' Hermann said. 'The Committee will be sweating till these heads are off.'

'The trial must begin either tomorrow or the day after. Preferably tomorrow.'

'What?' Fouquier said. 'Are you mad?'

'It is not a proper question to put to me,' Saint-Just said.

'But man, the evidence, the indictments – '

With one fingernail, Saint-Just tapped the report in front of him.

'The witnesses,' Hermann said.

'Need there be witnesses?' Saint-Just sighed. 'Yes, I suppose you must have some. Then get about it.'

'How can we subpoena their witnesses till we know who they want to call?'

'Oh, I would advise you,' he turned to Hermann, 'not to allow witnesses for the defence.'

'One question,' Hermann said. 'Why don't you send in some assassins to kill them in their cells? God knows, I am no Dantonist, but this is murder.'

'Oh come.' Saint-Just was irritated. 'You complain of lack of time, and then you use it up with frivolous questions. I am not here to make small-talk. You know quite well the importance of doing these things in the public eye. Now, the following people are to be charged with the four I have already named. Hérault, Fabre – all right?'

'The papers are ready,' Fouquier said sourly.

'The swindler Chabot, and his associates Basire and Delaunay, both deputies – '

'To discredit them,' Hermann said.

'Yes,' Fouquier said. 'Mix up the politicians with the cheats and thieves. The public will think, if one is on trial for fraud, all the rest must be.'

'If you'll allow me to continue? With them a batch of foreigners – the brothers Frei, the Spanish banker Guzman, the Danish businessman Diedrichsen. Oh, and the army contractor, the Abbé d'Espanac. Charges are conspiracy, fraud, hoarding, currency speculation, congress with foreign powers – I'll leave it to you,

Fouquier. There's no shortage of evidence against any of these people.'

'Only against Danton.'

'Well, that's your problem now. By the way, Citizens – do you know what these are?'

Fouquier looked down. 'Of course I know. Blank warrants, signed by the Committee. That's a dangerous practice, if I may say so.'

'Yes, it is dangerous, isn't it?' Saint-Just turned the papers around and entered a name on each. 'Do you want to see them now?' He held them up between finger and thumb, flapping them to get the ink dry. 'This one is yours, Hermann – and this one, Citizen Prosecutor, is for you.' He smiled again, folded them, and slipped them into an inside pocket of his coat. 'Just in case anything goes wrong at the trial,' he said.

THE NATIONAL Convention: the session opens in disorder. First on his feet is Legendre. His face is haggard. Perhaps noises in the street woke him early?

'Last night certain members of this Assembly were arrested. Danton was one, I'm not sure about the others. I demand that the members of the Convention who are detained be brought to the Bar of the House, to be accused or absolved by us. I am convinced that Danton's hands are as clean as mine – '

A whisper runs through the chamber. Heads turn away from the speaker. President Tallien looks up as the committees enter. Collot's face seems flaccid, unused: he does not assume a character till the day's performance begins. Saint-Just wears a blue coat with gold buttons, and carries many papers. A rustle of alarm sweeps the benches. Here is the Police Committee: Vadier with his long, discoloured face and hooded eyes, Lebas with his jaw set. And in the small silence they command, like the great tragedian who delays his entrance – Citizen Robespierre, the Incorruptible himself. He hesitates in the aisle between the tiered benches, and one of his colleagues digs him in the small of the back.

When he had mounted the tribune he said nothing; he folded his hands on his notes. The seconds passed. His eyes travelled around the room – resting, it was said, for the space of two heartbeats on those he mistrusted.

He began to speak: quite calmly, evenly. Danton's name was raised, as if some privilege attached to it. But there would be no privilege, from now on; rotten idols would be smashed. He paused. He pushed his spectacles up on to his forehead. His eyes fixed upon Legendre, fixed with their glacial, short-sighted stare. Legendre pressed together his huge slaughterer's hands, his throat-cutting and ox-felling hands, until the knuckles grew white. And in a moment he was on his feet, babbling: you have mistaken my intention, you have mistaken my intention. 'Whoever shows fear, is guilty,' Robespierre said. He descended from the tribune, his thin, pale mouth curved between a smile and a sneer.

Saint-Just read for the next two hours his report on the plots of the Dantonist faction. He had imagined, when he wrote it, that he had the accused man before him; he had not amended it. If Danton were really before him, this reading would be punctuated by the roars of his supporters from the galleries, by his own self-justificatory roaring; but Saint-Just addressed the air, and there was a silence, which deepened and fed on itself. He read without passion, almost without inflection, his eyes on the papers that he held in his left hand. Occasionally he would raise his right arm, then let it fall limply by his side: this was his only gesture, a staid, mechanical one. Once, towards the end, he raised his young face to his audience and spoke directly to them: 'After this,' he promised, 'there will be only patriots left.'

RUE MARAT: 'Well, my love,' Lucile said to her child, 'are you coming with me to see your godfather? No, perhaps not. Take him to my mother,' she said to Jeanette.

'You should bathe your face before you go out. It is swollen.'

'He might expect me to cry. He might predict it. He won't notice what I look like. He doesn't.'

'If it's possible,' Louise Danton said, 'this place is in a worse state than ours.'

They stood in the wreck of Lucile's drawing room. Every book they possessed was piled broken-spined on the carpet; drawers and cupboards gaped open, rifled. The ashes in the hearth had been raked over minutely. She reached up and straightened her engraving of Maria Stuart's end. 'They have taken all his papers,' she said. 'Letters. Everything. Even the manuscript of the Church Fathers.'

'If Robespierre agrees to see us, what shall we say? Whatever shall we say?'

'You need say nothing. I will do it.'

'Who would have thought, that the Convention would hand them over like that, with no protest?'

'I would have thought it. No one – except your husband – can stand up to Robespierre. There are letters here,' she told Jeanette, 'to every member of the Committee of Public Safety. Except Saint-Just, there is no point in writing to him. Here are the letters for the Police Committee; this is for Fouquier, and these are for various deputies, you see that they are all addressed. Make sure they go right now. If I get no replies, and Max won't see me, I'll have to think of some new tactics.'

AT THE LUXEMBOURG, Hérault assumed the role of gracious host. It had been, after all, a palace, and was not designed as a prison. 'Secret and solitary, you'll find it isn't,' Hérault said. 'From time to time they do lock us away, but generally we live in the most delightfully sociable way – in fact I have seen nothing like it since Versailles. The talk is witty, manners are of the best – the ladies have their hair dressed, and change three times a day. There are dinner parties. Anything you want – short of firearms – you can get sent in. Only be careful what you say. At least half the people here are informers.'

In what Hérault described as 'our salon', the inmates inspected the newcomers. A *ci-devant* looked over Lacroix's sturdy frame: 'That fellow would make a fine coachman,' he remarked.

General Dillon had been drinking. He was apologetic about it. 'Who are you?' he said to Philippeaux. 'I don't know you, do I? What did you do?'

'I criticized the Committee.'

'Ah.'

'Oh,' Philippeaux said, realizing. 'You're Lucile's – Oh Christ, I'm sorry, General.'

'That's all right. I don't mind what you think.' The general swayed across the room. He draped his arms around Camille. 'Now that you're all here, I'll stay sober, I swear it. I warned you. Didn't I warn you? My poor Camille.'

'Do you know what?' Hérault said. 'The thieving Arts Commission have laid their paws on all my first editions.'

'He says,' said the general, pointing to Hérault, 'that against the charges they will bring he disdains to defend himself. What sort of attitude is that? He thinks it is suitable, because he is an aristocrat. So am I. And also, my love, I am a soldier. Don't worry, don't worry,' he said to Camille. 'We're going to get out of here.'

RUE HONORÉ: 'So you see,' Babette said, 'there are a great many patriots with him, and he can't be disturbed.'

Lucile laid a letter down on the table. 'In common humanity, Elisabeth, you will see that this is put into his hand.'

'It won't do any good.' She smiled. 'He's made his mind up.'

At the top of the house Robespierre sat alone, waiting for the women to go. As they stepped into the street the sun burst from behind a cloud, and they walked down to the river in heady green spring air.

FROM THE LUXEMBOURG prison, Camille Desmoulins to Lucile Desmoulins:

I have discovered a crack in the wall of my room. I put my ear to it and heard someone groaning. I risked a few words and then I heard the voice of a sick man in pain. He asked my name. I told him, and when he heard it he cried out, 'O, my God,' and fell back on the bed from which he had raised himself. I knew then it was Fabre d'Églantine's voice. 'Yes, I am Fabre,' he said, 'but what are you doing here? Has the counter-revolution come?

*

PRELIMINARY examination at the Luxembourg:

L. Camille Desmoulins, barrister-at-law, journalist, deputy to the National Convention, age thirty-four, resident rue Marat. In the presence of F.-J. Denisot, supplementary judge of the Revolutionary Tribunal: F. Girard, Deputy Registrar of the Revolutionary Tribunal: A. Fouquier-Tinville, and G. Liendon, Deputy Public Prosecutor.

Minutes of the examination:

Q. Had he conspired against the French nation by wishing to restore the monarchy, by destroying national representation and republican government?

A. No.

Q. Had he counsel?

A. No.

We nominate, therefore, Chauveau-Lagarde.

LUCILE AND ANNETTE go to the Luxembourg Gardens. They stand with their face raised to the façade, eyes hopelessly searching. The child in his mother's arms cries; he wants to go home. Somewhere at one of the windows her Camille stands. In the half-lit room behind him is the table where he has sat for most of the day, drafting a defence to charges of which he has not yet been notified. The raw April breeze rips through Lucile's hair, snaking it away from her head like the hair of a woman drowned. Her head turns; eyes still searching. He can see her; she can't see him.

CAMILLE DESMOULINS to Lucile Desmoulins:

Yesterday, when the citizen who brought you my letter came back, 'Well, have you seen her?' I said, just as I used to say to the Abbé Laudréville; and I caught myself looking at him as if something of you lingered about his person or his clothes . . .

THE CELL DOOR CLOSED. 'He said he knew I'd come.' Robespierre leaned back against the wall. He closed his eyes. His hair, unpowdered, glinted red in the torchlight. 'I shouldn't be here. I shouldn't have come. But I wanted . . . I couldn't prevent myself.'

'No deal then,' Fouquier said. His face expressed impatience, some derision; it was impossible to say at whom it was directed.

'No deal. He says Danton gives us three months.' In the dimness, his blue-green eyes sought Fouquier's, inquiringly.

'It is just something they say.'

'I think that, for a minute, he thought I'd come to offer him the chance to escape before the trial.'

'Really?' Fouquier said. 'You're not that sort of person. He should know that.'

'Yes, he should, shouldn't he?' He straightened up from the wall, then put his hand out, let his fingers brush the plaster. 'Goodbye,' he whispered. They walked away in silence. Suddenly Robespierre stopped dead. 'Listen.' From behind a closed door they heard the murmur of voices, and over the top of them a huge, unforced laugh. 'Danton,' Robespierre whispered. His face was awestruck.

'Come,' Fouquier said: but Robespierre stood and listened.

'How can he? How can he laugh?'

'Are you going to stand there all night?' Fouquier demanded. With the Incorruptible he had always been warily correct, but where was the Incorruptible now? Sneaking around the prisons with deals and offers and promises. Fouquier saw an undergrown young man, numb and shaking with misery, his sandy lashes wet. 'Move Danton's mob to the Conciergerie,' Fouquier said, over his shoulder. 'Look,' he said, turning back, 'you'll get over him.'

He took the Candle of Arras by the arm, and hustled him out into the night.

PALAIS DE JUSTICE, 13 Germinal, eight a.m.: 'Let's get right down to business, gentlemen,' Fouquier said to his two deputy prosecutors. 'We have in the dock today a disparate company of forgers, swindlers and con-men, plus half a dozen eminent politicians. If you look out of the window, you will see the crowds; in fact, there is no need, you can hear them. These are the people who, if mishandled, could send this business lurching the wrong way and threaten the security of the capital.'

'It is a pity there is not some way to exclude them,' Citizen Fleuriot said.

'The Republic has no provision for trials in camera,' Fouquier said. 'You know quite well the importance of doing these things in the public eye. However, there is to be nothing in the press. Now – – as for our case, it is non-existent. The report we were handed by Saint-Just is – well, it is a political document.'

'You mean lies,' Liendon suggested.

'Yes, substantially. I have no doubt, personally, that Danton is guilty of enough to get him executed several times over, but that doesn't mean he is guilty of the things we will charge him with. We have had no time to prepare a coherent case against these men. There are no witnesses we can put up without the fear that they will blurt out something extremely inconvenient for the Committee.'

'I find your attitude defeatist,' Fleuriot remarked.

'My dear Fleuriot, we all know that you are here to spy for Citizen Robespierre. But our job is to pull nasty forensic tricks – not to mouth slogans and pat phrases. Now – please consider the opposition.'

'I take it,' Liendon said, 'that by "the opposition" you don't mean those unfortunates selected as defence counsel.'

'I doubt they will dare to speak to their clients. Danton is of course well-known to the people; he is the most forceful orator in Paris, and also a much better lawyer than either of you two. Fabre we need not worry about. His case has received a lot of publicity, all of it unfavourable to him, and as he is very ill he'll not be able to give us any trouble. Hérault is a different matter. If he condescends to argue, he could be very dangerous, as we have almost no case against him.'

'I think you have a certain document, relating to the woman Capet?'

'Yes, but as I have had to arrange for alterations to it I am not very anxious for it to be brought forward. Now, we must not under-estimate Deputy Philippeaux. He is less well-known than the others but I am afraid he is utterly intransigent and appears not to be afraid of anything we can do to him. Deputy Lacroix is of course a cool-headed man, something of a gambler. Our informant reports that so far he treats the whole thing rather as a joke.'

'Who is our informant?'

'In the prison? A man called Laflotte.'

'I am afraid of your cousin Camille,' Fleuriot said.

'Again, our informant has made useful observations. He describes him as hysterical and distraught. It seems he claims that Citizen Robespierre visited him secretly at the Luxembourg, and offered him his life to testify for the prosecution. An absurd story, of course.'

'He must be out of his mind,' Liendon said.

'Yes,' Fouquier said. 'Perhaps he is. Our aim from the first hour of the trial must be to unnerve, browbeat and terrorize him; this is not particularly difficult, but it is essential that he be prevented from putting up any sort of defence, as the people who remember '89 are somewhat attached to him. But now, Fleuriot – what are our assets, would you say?'

'Time, Citizen.'

'Precisely. Time is on our side. Procedure since Brissot's trial is that if after three days the jury declares itself satisfied, the trial can be closed. What does that suggest, Liendon?'

'Take care in selecting the jury.'

'You know, you two are really getting quite good. Shall we get on with it then?' Fouquier took out his list of the regular jurors of the Revolutionary Tribunal. 'Trinchard the joiner, Desboisseaux the cobbler – they sound a staunch plebeian pair.'

'Reliable men,' Fleuriot said.

'And Maurice Duplay – who could be sounder?'

'No. Citizen Robespierre himself has vetoed his presence on the jury.'

Fouquier bit his lip. 'I shall never understand that man. Well then – Ganney the wig-maker, he's always cooperative. I suppose he needs the job – there can't be much call for wigs. And Lumière.' He ticked off another name. 'He may need some encouragement. But we'll provide it.'

Liendon peered over the Public Prosecutor's shoulder.

'How about Tenth-of-August Leroy?'

'Excellent,' Fouquier said. He put a mark by the name of the man who had once been Leroy de Montflobert, Marquis of France. 'And now?'

'We'll have to put in Souberbielle.'

'He's a friend of Danton and Robespierre both.'

'But I think he has the right principles,' Fleuriot said. 'Or can be helped to develop them.'

'To balance him out,' Fouquier said, 'we'll have Renaudin the violin-maker.'

Fleuriot laughed. 'Excellent. I was at the Jacobins myself that night he knocked Camille down. But what was the cause of the quarrel? I never knew.'

'Only God knows,' Fouquier said. 'Renaudin is no doubt demonstrably insane. Can you remember, if you address my cousin in court, not to call him by his Christian name?' He frowned over the list. 'I don't know who else is absolutely solid.'

'Him?' said Liendon, pointing.

'Oh no, no. He is fond of reasoning, and we don't want people who reason. No, I'm afraid we'll have to go ahead with a jury of seven. Oh well, they're hardly in a position to argue. You see, I've been talking as if there were some sort of contest. But we aren't, here, playing any game we can lose. See you in court at eleven o'clock.'

'MY NAME IS DANTON. It is a name tolerably well-known in the Revolution. I am a lawyer by profession, and I was born at Arcis, in the Aube country. In a few days' time, my abode will be oblivion. My place of residence will be History.'

Day One.

'That sounds distinctly pessimistic,' Lacroix says to Philippeaux. 'Who are all these people?'

'Fabre of course you know, this is Chabot – delighted to see you looking so well, Citizen – Diedrichsen, this is Philippeaux – this is Emmanuel Frei, Junius Frei – you are supposed to have conspired with them.'

'Delighted to meet you, Deputy Philippeaux,' one of the Frei brothers says. 'What did you do?'

'I criticized the Committee.'

'Ah.'

Philippeaux is counting heads. 'There are fourteen of us. They're going to try the whole East India fraud. If there were any justice, that would take a court three months. We have three days.'

Camille Desmoulins is on his feet. 'Challenge,' he says, indicating the jury. He is being as brief as possible in the hope that he can avoid stuttering.

'Route it through your counsel,' Hermann says shortly.

'I am defending myself,' Desmoulins snaps back. 'I object to Renaudin.'

'On what grounds?'

'He has threatened my life. I could call several hundred witnesses.'

'That is a frivolous objection.'

THE REPORT of the Police Committee is read out, relating to the East India affair. Two hours. The indictments are read. One hour more. Behind the waist-high barriers at the back of the court, the spectators stand packed to the doors: out of the doors, and along the street. 'They say the line of people stretches as far as the Mint,' Fabre whispers.

Lacroix turns his head in the direction of the forgers. 'How ironic,' he murmurs.

Fabre passes a hand over his face. He is slumped in the armchair which is normally reserved for the chief person accused. Last night when the prisoners were transferred to the Conciergerie he was hardly able to walk, and two guards had assisted him into the closed carriage. Occasionally one of his fits of coughing drowns out the voice of Fabricius Pâris, and the Clerk of the Court seizes the opportunity to pause for breath; his eyes travel again and again to the impassive face of his patron, Danton. Fabre takes out a handkerchief and holds it to his mouth. His skin looks damp and bloodless. Sometimes Danton turns to look into his face; another few minutes, and he will turn to watch Camille. From above the jury, corrosive shafts of sunlight scour the black-and-white marble. Afternoon wears on, and an unmerited halo forms above the head of Tenth-of-August Leroy. In the Palais-Royal, the lilac trees are in bloom.

*

DANTON: 'This must stop. I demand to be heard now. I demand permission to write to the Convention. I demand to have a commission appointed. Camille Desmoulins and myself wish to denounce dictatorial practices in the Committee of Public – '

The roar of applause drowns him. They call his name; they clap their hands, stamp their feet, and sing the 'Marseillaise'. The riot travels backwards into the street, and the tumult becomes so great that the president's bell is inaudible; in frenetic dumb-show, he shakes the bell at the accused, and Lacroix shakes his fist back at the president. Don't panic, don't panic, Fouquier mouths: and when Hermann makes his voice heard, it is to adjourn the session. The prisoners are led below to their cells. 'Bastards,' Danton says succinctly. 'I'll make mincemeat out of them tomorrow.'

'SOLD? I, SOLD? There is not a price high enough for a man like me.'

Day Two.

'Who is this?'

'Oh, not another,' Philippeaux says. 'Who is this man?'

Danton looks over his shoulder. 'That is Citizen Lhuillier. He is the Attorney-General – or used to be. Citizen, what are you doing here?'

Lhuillier takes his place with the accused. He does not speak, and he looks stunned.

'Fouquier, what do you say this man's done?'

Fouquier looks up to glare at the accused, and then back to the list he holds in his hand. He confers with his deputies in a furious whisper. 'But you *said* so – ' Fleuriot insists.

'I said subpoena him, I didn't say arrest him. Do everything your bloody self!'

'He doesn't know what he's done,' Philippeaux says. 'He doesn't know. But he'll soon think of something.'

'Camille,' Hérault says, 'I do believe your cousin's incompetent. He's a disgrace to the criminal Bar.'

'Fouquier,' his cousin asks him, 'how did you get this job in the first place?'

The Public Prosecutor rummages among his papers. 'What the hell,' he mutters. He approaches the judge's table. 'A fuck-up,' he tells Hermann. 'But don't let them know. They'll make us a laughing-stock.'

Hermann sighs. 'We are all under a great deal of pressure. I wish you would employ more seemly language. Leave him there, and on the last day I'll direct the jury that there's insufficient evidence and they must acquit.'

Vice-President Dumas reeks of spirits. The crowd at the back moves, restive and dangerous, bored by the delays. Another prisoner is brought in. 'God in Heaven,' Lacroix says, 'Westermann.'

General Westermann, victor of the Vendée, places his belligerent bulk before the accused. 'Who the hell are all these people?' He jerks his thumb at Chabot and his friends.

'Divers criminal elements,' Hérault tells him. 'You conspired with them.'

'Did I?' Westermann raises his voice. 'What do you think, Fouquier, that I'm just some military blockhead, some oaf? I was a lawyer at Strasbourg before the Revolution, I know how things should be done. I have not been allotted counsel. I have not been put through a preliminary investigation. I have not been charged.'

Hermann looks up. 'That is a formality.'

'We are all here,' Danton says drily, 'by way of a formality.'

There is an outburst of rueful laughter from the accused. The remark is relayed to the back of the court. The public applaud, and a line of sansculotte patriots take off their red caps, wave them, sing the 'Ça Ira', and (confusingly) yell *à la Lanterne*.

'I must call you to order,' Hermann shouts at Danton.

'Call me to order?' Danton explodes to his feet. 'It seems to me that I must recall you to decency. I have a right to speak. We all have a right to a hearing. Damn you, man, I set up this Tribunal. I ought to know how it works.'

'Can you not hear this bell?'

'A man on trial for his life takes no notice of bells.'

From the galleries the singing becomes louder. Fouquier's mouth is moving, but nothing can be heard. Hermann closes his eyes, and all the signatures of the Committee of Public Safety dance before his lids. It is fifteen minutes before order is restored.

THE AFFAIR of the East India Company again. The prosecutors know they have a case here, so they are sticking to the subject. Fabre lifts his chin, which had fallen on to his chest. After a few minutes he lets it return there. 'He should have a doctor,' Philippeaux whispers.

'His physician is otherwise engaged. On the jury.'

'Fabre, you're not going to die on us, are you?'

Fabre makes a sick effort at a smile. Danton can feel the fear which holds Camille rigid between himself and Lacroix. Camille spent the whole of last night writing, because he believes that in the end they are bound to let him speak. So far the judges have put him down ferociously whenever he has opened his mouth.

Cambon, the government's financial expert, takes the stand to give evidence about profits and share certificates, banking procedure and foreign currency regulations. He will be the only witness called in the course of the trial. Danton interrupts him:

'Cambon, listen: do you think I'm a royalist?'

Cambon looks across at him and smiles.

'See, he laughed. Citizen Clerk of the Court, see that it goes down in the record that he laughed.'

HERMANN: Danton, the Convention accuses you of showing undue favour to Dumouriez; of failing to reveal his true nature and intentions; and of aiding and abetting his schemes to destroy freedom, such as that of marching on Paris with an armed force to crush republican government and restore the monarchy.

DANTON: May I answer this now?

HERMANN: No. Citizen Pâris, read out the report of Citizen Saint-Just – I mean, the report that the citizen delivered to the Convention and the Jacobin Club.

TWO HOURS. The accused have now separated into two camps, the six politicians and the general trying to put a distance between themselves and the thieves: but this is difficult. Philippeaux listens attentively, and takes notes. Hérault appears sunk in his own thoughts; one cannot be sure he is listening to the court at all. From time to time the general makes an impatient noise and hisses in Lacroix's ear for some point to be elucidated; Lacroix is seldom able to help him.

For the first part of the reading the crowds are restless. But as the implications of the report become clear, a profound silence takes possession of the court, stealing through the darkening room like an animal coming home to its lair. The chiming of the clocks marks off the first hour of the report, Hermann clears his throat, and behind his table, back to the accused, Fouquier stretches his legs. Suddenly Desmoulins's nerve snaps. He puts a hand to his face, wonders what it is doing there, and anxiously flicks back his hair. He looks quickly at the faces to the left and right of him. He holds one fist in the other palm, his mouth pressed against the knuckles; taking his hands from his face, he holds the bench at each side of himself until the nails grow white with pressure. Dictum of Citizen Robespierre, useful in criminal cases: whoever shows fear is guilty. Danton and Lacroix take his hands and hold them surreptitiously by his sides.

Pâris has finished, voice cracking over the final phrases. He drops the document on the table and its leaves fan out. He is exhausted, and if there had been any more he would have broken down and wept.

'Danton,' Hermann says, 'you may speak now.'

As he rises to his feet, he wonders what Philippeaux has recorded in his notes. Because there is not one allegation he can drag screaming into disrepute; not one charge that he can hold up and knock down again and trample on. If only there were a specific accusation ... that you, Georges-Jacques Danton did on the 10th day of August 1792 traitorously conspire ... But it is a whole career he has to justify: a whole life, a life in the Revolution, to oppose to this tissue of lies and innuendo, this abortion of the truth. Saint-Just must have made a close study of Camille's writings against Brissot; that was where the technique was perfected. And he thinks fleetingly of the neat, malicious job Camille would have done on his career.

After fifteen minutes he finds the pleasure and the power of rolling out his voice into the hall. The long silence is over. The crowd begins to applaud again. Sometimes he has to stop and let the noise defeat him; then he draws breath, comes back stronger. Fabre taught him, he taught him well. He begins to imagine his voice as a physical instrument of attack, a power like battalions; as lava from the mouth of some inexhaustible volcano, burning them, boiling them, burying them alive. *Burying them alive.*

A juryman interrupts: 'Can you enlighten us as to why, at Valmy, our troops did not follow up the Prussian retreat?'

'I regret that I cannot enlighten you. I am a lawyer. Military matters are a closed book to me.'

Fabre's hand unclenches from the arm of his chair.

Sometimes Hermann tries to interrupt him at crucial points; Danton overbears him, contemptuously. At each of the court's defeats, the crowds cheer and whistle and shout derisive comments. The theatres are empty; it is the only show in town. And that is what it is – a show, and he knows it. They are behind him now – but if Robespierre were to walk in, wouldn't they cheer him to the echo? Père Duchesne was their hero, but they laughed and catcalled when his creator begged for mercy in the tumbrel.

After the first hour his voice is as strong as ever. At this stage the physical effort is nothing. Like an athlete's, his lungs do what he has trained them to do. But now he is not clinching an argument or forcing a debating point, he is talking to save his life. This is what he has planned and waited and hoped for, the final confrontation: but as the day wears on he finds himself talking over an inner voice that says, they are allowing this confrontation because the issue is decided already: you are a dead man. A question from Fouquier brings him to a pitch of boiling rage: 'Bring me my accusers,' he shouts. 'Bring me a proof, part proof, the flimsiest shadow of a proof. I challenge my accusers to come before me, to meet me face to face. Produce these men, and I will thrust them back into the obscurity from which they should never have emerged. Come out, you filthy imposters, and I will rip the masks from your faces, and deliver you up to the vengeance of the people.'

And another hour. He wants a glass of water, but he dares not stop to ask for one. Hermann sits hunched over his law books, watching him, his mouth slightly ajar. Danton feels as if all the dust of his province has got into his throat, all the choking yellow country beyond Arcis.

Hermann passes a note to Fouquier. 'IN HALF AN HOUR I SHALL SUSPEND DANTON'S DEFENCE.'

Finally, denying it while he can, he knows his voice is losing its power. And there is still tomorrow's fight; he cannot afford to become hoarse. He takes out a handkerchief and wipes his forehead. Hermann springs.

'The witness is exhausted. We will adjourn until tomorrow.'

Danton swallows, raises his voice for a last effort. 'And then I resume my defence.'

Hermann nods sympathetically.

'And then tomorrow, we have our witnesses.'

'Tomorrow.'

'You have the lists of the people we wish to call.'

'We have your lists.'

The applause of the crowd is solid. He looks back at them. He sees Fabre's lips move, and bends to catch the words. 'Go on speaking, Georges. If you stop now they will never let you speak again. Go on, now – it's our only chance.'

'I can't. My voice must recover.' He sits down, staring straight ahead of him. He wrenches off his cravat. 'The day is over.'

14 GERMINAL, evening, the Tuileries: 'You'll probably agree with me,' Robespierre said, 'that you've not got very far.'

'The riot has to be heard to be believed.' Fouquier paced the room. 'We are afraid the crowd will tear them out of our hands.'

'I think you can put your mind at rest on that score. It has never happened yet. And the people have no particular affection for Danton.'

'With respect, Citizen Robespierre – '

'I know that, because they have no particular affection for anyone, these days. I have the experience, I know how to judge these things. They like the spectacle. That's all.'

'It remains impossible to make progress. During his defence Danton constantly appeals to the crowd.'

'It was a mistake. It was a cross-examination that was needed. Hermann should not have allowed this speech.'

'Make sure he doesn't continue it,' Collot said.

Fouquier inclined his head. He remembered a phrase of Danton's: *the three or four criminals who are ruining Robespierre.* 'Yes, yes, naturally,' he said to them.

'If things go no better tomorrow,' Robespierre said, 'send a note to us. We'll see what we can do to help.'

'Well – what could you do?'

'After Brissot's trial we brought in the three-day rule. But it was too late to be helpful. There is no reason why you shouldn't have new procedures when you need them, Fouquier. We don't want this to take much longer.'

Ruined, corrupted, Fouquier thought, a saviour bled dry: they have broken his heart. 'Yes, Citizen Robespierre,' he said. 'Thank you, Citizen Robespierre.'

'The Desmoulins woman has been making a lot of trouble,' Saint-Just said suddenly.

Fouquier looked up. 'What kind of trouble could little Lucile make?'

'She has money. She knows a lot of people. She's been about town since the arrests. She seems to be desperate.'

'Start at eight tomorrow,' Robespierre said. 'You might foil the crowds.'

CAMILLE DESMOULINS to Lucile Desmoulins:

I have walked for five years along the precipices of the Revolution without falling, and I am still living. I dreamt of a republic which all the world would have adored; I could never have believed that men could be so ferocious and so unjust.

'ON A DAY LIKE THIS, one year ago, I founded the Revolutionary Tribunal. I ask pardon of God and man.'

Day Three.

'We will proceed,' Fouquier says, 'to the examination of Emmanuel Frei.'

'Where are my witnesses?'

Fouquier affects surprise. 'The matter of witnesses is with the Committee, Danton.'

'With the Committee? What business has the Committee with it? This is my legal right. If you have not got my witnesses ready, I demand to resume my defence.'

'But your co-accused must be heard.'

'Must they?' Danton looks at them. Fabre, he thinks, is dying. It is a moot point whether the guillotine will slice his neck through before something ruptures inside his chest and drowns him in his own blood. Philippeaux did not sleep last night. He talked for hours about his three-year-old son: the thought of the child paralyses him. Hérault's expression makes it clear that they should regard him as *hors de combat*; he will have no dealings with this court. Camille is in a state of emotional collapse. He insists that Robespierre came to see him in his cell and offered him his life to testify for the prosecution: his life, his freedom and his political rehabilitation. No one else saw him: but Danton is willing to believe that it could be so.

'Right, Lacroix,' he says. 'Go on, man.'

Lacroix is on his feet instantly. He has the tense and exhilarated air of a participant in a dangerous sport. 'Three days ago I handed in a list of my witnesses. Not one of them has been called. I ask the Public Prosecutor to explain, in the presence of the people, who see my efforts to clear my name, why my lawful request has been refused.'

Calm and cool, Fouquier says to himself. 'It is nothing to do with me,' he says innocently. 'I have no objection to your witnesses being called.'

'Then order that they be called. It is not enough for me to know that you have no objection.'

Suddenly violence is in the air. Cousin Camille is standing beside Lacroix, one hand on his shoulder for support, bracing himself as though standing against the wind. 'I have put Robespierre on my list of witnesses.' His voice shakes. 'Will you call him? Will you call him, Fouquier?'

Without speaking or moving from his place, Fouquier conveys

the impression that he is about to cross the courtroom and knock his cousin to the ground: and this would surprise no one. With a gasp, Camille subsides back into his place. But Hermann is panicking again. Hermann, Fouquier thinks, is a rubbish lawyer. If this is all the Artois Bar has to offer, then he, Fouquier, could have got to the very very top. But then, he supposes, he is at the top.

With a click of impatience, he crosses to the judges.

'The crowds are worse than yesterday,' Hermann says. 'The prisoners are worse than yesterday. We shall get no further.'

Fouquier addresses the accused. 'It is time this wrangling ceased. It is a scandal, both to the Tribunal and the public. I am going to send to the Convention for directions as to how this trial shall proceed, and we shall follow its advice to the letter.'

Danton leans over to Lacroix. 'This may be the turning point. When they hear about this travesty, they may recover their wits and give us a hearing. I have friends in the Convention, many friends.'

'You think so?' Philippeaux says. 'You mean there are people who owe you favours. Another few hours of this, and they won't be obliged to repay you. And how do we know he will tell them the truth? Or what else Saint-Just will find to scare them with?'

ANTOINE FOUQUIER-TINVILLE to the National Convention:

We have had an extremely stormy session from the moment we started. The accused are insisting, in the most violent manner, on having witnesses examined for the defence. They are calling on the public to witness what they term the refusal of their just claims. Despite the firm stand taken by the president and the entire Tribunal, their reiterated demands are holding up the case. Furthermore, they openly declare that until their witnesses are called they will persist in such interruptions. We therefore appeal to you for an authoritative ruling on what our response to their request for witnesses should be, since the law does not allow us any legitimate excuse for refusing it.

THE TUILERIES: Robespierre's nervous fingers tap the table. He is not pleased with the situation. 'Get out,' he tells the informer Laflotte.

As soon as the door closes, Saint-Just says, 'I think it will do.'

Robespierre stares down at Fouquier's letter, but his eyes are not taking it in. When Saint-Just speaks again, the eagerness in his tone makes Robespierre look up sharply. 'I shall go to the Convention and tell them that a dangerous conspiracy has been thwarted.'

'Do you believe that?' Robespierre says.

'What?'

'A dangerous conspiracy. You see, I don't understand about Lucile. Is it something that is being said in the prison? Is it true? Is it something Laflotte thought of as he came upstairs? Or . . . did you put into his mouth what you wanted to hear?'

'Informers always tell you what you want to hear. Look,' Saint-Just says impatiently, 'it will do. We need it, it's just what we need.'

'But is it true?' Robespierre persists.

'We'll know when we put her on trial. Meanwhile, circumstances force us to act on it. I must say, the whole thing sounds plausible to me. She's been seen about the city since the morning of the arrests, as if she had something in hand. She's no fool, is she? And after all, Dillon is her lover.'

'No.'

'No?'

'She has no lovers.'

Saint-Just laughs. 'The woman is notorious.'

'It is ill-founded gossip.'

'But everyone speaks of it.' The same exuberant tone. 'When they were at the Place des Piques, she lived shamelessly as Danton's mistress. And she was involved with Hérault. Everyone knows these things.'

'They think they know them.'

'Oh, you only see what you want to see, Robespierre.'

'She has no lovers.'

'How do you account for Dillon then?'

'He is Camille's close friend.'

'All right then, Dillon is his lover. I'm sure it is all the same to me.'

'My God,' Robespierre says. 'You are over-reaching yourself.'

'The Republic must be served,' Saint-Just says passionately.

'These sordid private involvements have no interest for me. All I want is to give the Tribunal the means to finish them off.'

'Listen to me,' Robespierre says. 'Now that we have begun on this there is no turning back, because if we hesitate they will turn on us, seize the advantage and put us where they are now. Yes – in your elegant phrase, we must finish them off. I will let you do this, but I don't have to love you for it.' He turns on Saint-Just his cold eyes. 'Very well, go to the Convention. You tell them that through the informer Laflotte you have discovered a plot in the prisons. That Lucile Desmoulins, financed by – financed by enemy powers – in concert with General Dillon, has conspired to free the prisoners of the Luxembourg, raise an armed riot outside the Convention and assassinate the Committee. Then ask the Convention to pass a decree to silence the prisoners and bring the trial to a conclusion either today or tomorrow morning.'

'There is a warrant here for Lucile Desmoulins's arrest. It would add conviction to the business if you were to sign it.'

Robespierre picks up his pen and puts his signature to the paper without looking at it. 'It hardly matters,' he says. 'She will not want to live. Saint-Just?' The young man turns to look at him sitting behind the table, his hands clasped in front of him, pallid, compact, self-contained. 'When this business is over, and Camille is dead, I shall not want to hear your epitaph for him. No one is ever to speak of him again, I absolutely forbid it. When he is dead, I shall want to think about him myself, alone.'

THE TESTIMONY of Fabricius Pâris, Clerk to the Revolutionary Tribunal, given at the trial of Antoine Fouquier-Tinville, 1795:

Even Fouquier and his worthy associate Fleuriot, atrocious as they were, seemed thunderstruck by such men, and the deponent thought they would not have the courage to sacrifice them. He did not know the odious means being employed to this end, and that a conspiracy was being fabricated at the Luxembourg, by means of which ... the scruples of the National Convention were overcome and the decree of outlawry was obtained. This fatal decree arrived, brought by Amar and Voulland [of the Police Committee]. The deponent was in the Witnesses' Hall when they arrived: anger and terror were written on their faces, so much did they seem to fear their victims would escape death; they greeted the deponent. Voulland said to him, 'We have them, the scoundrels, they were conspiring at the Luxembourg.' They sent for Fouquier, who was in the courtroom. He appeared at once. Amar said to him, 'Here is something to make life easier for you.' Fouquier replied with a smile, 'He wanted it badly enough.' He re-entered the courtroom with an air of triumph . . .

'THEY ARE GOING to murder my wife.'

Camille's cry of horror rings over all the noise of the courtroom. He tries to get at Fouquier, and Danton and Lacroix hold him back. He struggles, shouts something at Hermann, and collapses into sobs. Vadier and David, of the Police Committee, are whispering to the jury. His eyes averted from the accused, Fouquier begins to read out the decree of the National Convention:

The president shall use every means that the law allows to make his authority and the authority of the Revolutionary Tribunal respected, and to suppress any attempts by the accused to disturb public order or hinder the course of justice. It is decreed that all persons accused of conspiracy who shall resist or insult the national justice shall be outlawed and shall receive judgement without any further formality.

'For God's sake,' Fabre whispers. 'What does it mean?'

'It means,' Lacroix says dispassionately, 'that from now on they dictate absolutely the form of the trial. If we call for our witnesses, ask to be cross-examined, ask to speak at all, they will close the trial immediately. To put it more graphically – the National Convention has assassinated us.'

When he finishes reading, the Public Prosecutor raises his head cautiously to look at Danton. Fabre has folded forwards in his chair. His ribs heave, and fresh blood splashes and flowers on to the towel he now holds before his mouth. From behind him Hérault puts a hand on his shoulder, hauling him back to an approximately upright position. The aristocrat's face is disdainful; he has not chosen his company, but he means to scrape them up to his standards if he can.

'We may need to assist the prisoner,' Fouquier says to an usher. 'Desmoulins also seems at the point of collapse.'

'The session is adjourned,' Hermann says.

'The jury,' Lacroix says. 'There is still hope.'

'No,' Danton says. 'There is no hope now.' He gets to his feet. For the last time that day, his voice echoes through the hall: and even now he seems impossible to kill. 'I shall be Danton till my death. Tomorrow I shall sleep in glory.'

RUE MARAT: She had written again to Robespierre. When she heard the patrol outside, she shredded the letter in her hands. She moved to the window. They were disposing themselves; she heard the clatter of steel. What do they think, she wondered: that I have my army in here?

By the time they arrived at the door she had picked up her bag, already packed with the few things she might need. Her little diaries were destroyed: the true record of her life expunged. The cat rubbed around her ankles, and she bent and drew her finger along its back. 'Quietly,' she said. 'No trouble.'

Jeanette cried out when the men held up the warrant. Lucile shook her head at her. 'You will have to say goodbye to the baby for me, and to my mother and father, and to Adèle. Give my best wishes to Mme Danton, and tell her I wish her greater good fortune than she has so far enjoyed. I don't think there is any point in a search,' she said to the men. 'You have already taken away everything that could possibly interest the Committee, and much that could not.' She picked up her bag. 'Let's go.'

'Madame, Madame.' Jeanette hung on to the officer's arm. 'Let me tell her just one thing, before you take her.'

'Quickly then.'

'There was a young woman here. From Guise. Look.' She ran to the bureau. 'She left this, to show where she was staying. She wanted to see you, but it's too late now.'

Lucile took the card. 'Citizeness du Tailland,' it said, in a bold angular hand. Underneath, in a hasty bracket: 'Rose-Fleur Godard.'

'Madame, she was in a pitiful state. The old man is ill, she had travelled by herself from Guise. She says they have only just heard of the arrests.'

'So she came,' Lucile said softly. 'Rose-Fleur. Too late.'

She put her cape over her arm. It was a warm evening, and there was a closed carriage at the door, but perhaps the prison would be cold. You would think a prison would be cold, wouldn't you? 'Goodbye, Jeanette,' she said. 'Take care. Forget us.'

A LETTER TO Antoine Fouquier-Tinville:

> Réunion-sur-Oise, formerly Guise
> 15 Germinal, Year II

Citizen and Compatriot,

Camille Desmoulins, my son, is a republican in his heart, in his principles and, as it were, by instinct. He was a republican in heart and in choice before 14 July 1789, and has been so in reality and in deed ever since . . .

Citizen, I ask you only one thing: investigate, and cause an examining jury to investigate, the conduct of my son.

Health and fraternity from your compatriot and fellow-citizen, who has the honour to be the father of the first and most unhesitating of republicans –

> Desmoulins

'HEY, LACROIX. If I left my legs to Couthon, and my balls to Robespierre, the Committee would have a new lease of life.'

Day Four.

The interrogation of the brothers Frei proceeds. Ten, eleven o'clock. Hermann keeps the decree of the Convention under his hand. He watches the prisoners, the prisoners watch him. The signs of the night they have passed are written on their faces. And Hermann has seen the text of a letter to hearten him, from the Committee to the commander of the National Guard:

'Do not – we emphasize, do not – arrest either the Public Prosecutor or the President of the Tribunal.'

AS NOON APPROACHES, Fouquier addresses Danton and Lacroix. 'I have a great number of witnesses available to testify against both of you. However, I shall not be calling them. You will be judged solely on documentary evidence.'

'What the hell does that mean?' Lacroix demands. 'What documents? Where are they?'

He receives no answer. Danton stands up.

'Since yesterday, we may no longer expect observance of the proper forms of law. But you promised me that I might resume my defence. That is my right.'

'Your rights, Danton, are in abeyance.' Hermann turns to the jury. 'Have you heard enough?'

'Yes: we have heard enough.'

'Then the trial is closed.'

'Closed? What do you mean, closed? You haven't read our statements. You haven't called a single one of our witnesses. The trial hasn't even begun.'

Camille stands up beside him. Hérault reaches forward to take hold of him, but he sidesteps and evades his grasp. He takes two paces forward towards the judges. He holds up the papers. 'I insist on speaking. Through these whole proceedings you have denied my right to speak. You cannot condemn people without hearing their defence. I demand to read out my statement.'

'You may not read it.'

Camille crumples the papers in his two hands, and throws them with amazing accuracy at the president's head. Ignominiously, Hermann ducks. Fouquier is on his feet: 'The prisoners have insulted the national justice. Under the terms of the decree, they may now be removed from the court. The jury will retire to consider its verdict.'

Behind the barrier, the crowd is already drifting away, to take its place along the death-route and by the scaffold. Last night Fouquier issued an order for three tumbrels: three tumbrels, mid-afternoon.

Two officers hurry forward to help Fabre.

'We must take you below, Citizens, while the jury is out.'

'Take your hands off me, please,' Hérault says, with a dangerous politeness. 'Come Danton: no point in standing here. Come, Camille – I hope you'll not make a fuss.'

Camille is going to make as much fuss as he can. An officer of the court stands before him. The man knows – it is an article of faith with him – that the condemned don't fight back. 'Please come with us,' he says. 'Please come quietly. No one wants to hurt you, but if you don't come quietly you're going to get hurt.'

Danton and Lacroix begin to plead with Camille. He clings desperately to the bench. 'I don't want to hurt you,' the officer says abjectly. A section of the crowd has detached itself and come back to watch. Camille sneers at the officer. The man tries without success to pull him away. Reinforcements arrive. Fouquier's eyes rest unseeingly on his cousin. 'For God's sake, overpower him, carry him out,' Hermann shouts. He slams a book down in irritation. 'Get them all out of here.'

One of the officers puts his hand into Camille's long hair and jerks his head back violently. They hear the snap of bone and his gasp of pain. A moment later they have knocked him to the floor. Lacroix turns his face away in distaste. 'I want Robespierre to know,' Camille says, as they drag him up from the marble floor. 'I want him to remember this.'

'Well,' Hermann says to Fouquier, 'half the Police Committee are in the jury room, so we may as well join them. If there is any more hesitation, show them the documents from the British Foreign Office.'

Just outside the courtroom, Fabre's strength almost gives way. 'Stop,' he gasps. The two officers assisting him put their hands under his elbows and lean him against the wall. He struggles for breath. Three men pass him, dragging Camille's limp body. His eyes are closed and his mouth is bleeding. Fabre sees him; his face crumples, and suddenly he begins to cry. 'You bastards, you bastards,' he says. 'Oh, you bastards, you bastards, you bastards.'

FOUQUIER LOOKS AROUND the members of the jury. Souberbielle avoids his eye. 'I think that's about it,' he says to Hermann. He nods to Vadier. 'Satisfied?'

'I shall be satisfied when their heads are off.'

'The crowds are reported large but passive,' Fouquier says. 'It is as Citizen Robespierre says; in the end, they have no allegiance. It is finished.'

'Are we to have them back in the courtroom, and go through all that again?'

'No, I think not,' Fouquier says. He hands a sheet of paper to one of the court officials. 'Get them into the outer office. This is the death sentence. Read it to them while Sanson's men are cutting their hair.' He takes out his watch. 'It's four o'clock. He'll be ready.'

'I DON'T GIVE a fuck for your sentence. I don't want to hear it. I'm not interested in the verdict. The people will judge Danton, not you.'

Danton continues talking over the official's voice, so that none of the men with him hears their death sentences being read. In the courtyard beyond the prison's outer office, Sanson's assistants are joking and calling to each other.

Lacroix sits on a wooden stool. The executioner rips open the collar of his shirt and rapidly cuts off the hair that grows over the back of his neck. 'One unconscious,' a guard calls out. 'One unconscious.'

Behind the wooden grille that separates the prisoners from the courtyard, the master executioner raises his hand to show that he has understood. Chabot is covered by a blanket. His face is blue. He is slipping into a coma. Only his lips move.

'He ordered himself some arsenic,' the guard says. 'Well, you can't stop the prisoner's requirements getting through.'

'Yes,' Hérault says to Danton. 'I contemplated it. In the end I thought, to commit suicide under these circumstances is an admission of guilt, and if they insist on cutting your corpse's head off, as they do, it is in questionable taste. One should set an example to this riff-raff, don't you think? In any event, it is better to open a vein.' His attention is drawn to the opposite wall, where a savage scuffle is going on. 'My dear Camille, what is the point?' Hérault asks.

'You are giving us a lot of trouble, you are,' one of the guards says. They have finally got Camille tied up very tightly. They have discussed whether to accidentally knock him unconscious, but if they do that Sanson will get testy and call them bloody amateurs. His shirt was torn off his back when they tried to hold him still to cut his hair, and the rags of it hang on his thin shoulders. A dark bruise is spreading visibly under his left cheek bone. Danton crouches by him.

'We must tie your hands, Citizen Danton.'

'Just one second.'

Danton reaches down, and takes from around Camille's neck the locket that holds a twist of Lucile's hair. He puts it into his bound hands, and feels Camille's fingers close over it.

'You can go ahead now.'

Lacroix digs him in the ribs. 'Those Belgian girls – it was worth it, yes?'

'It was worth it. But not for the Belgian girls.'

HÉRAULT is a little pale as he steps into the first tumbrel. Otherwise, there is no change visible on his face. 'I am glad I don't have to travel with the thieves.'

'Only the best quality revolutionaries in this tumbrel,' Danton says. 'Are you going to make it, Fabre, or shall we bury you *en route*?'

Fabre lifts his head with an effort. 'Danton. They took my papers, you know.'

'Yes, that is what they do.'

'I just wanted to finish *The Maltese Orange*, that was all. There were such beautiful verses in it. Now the Committee will get the manuscript, and that bastard Collot will pass it off as his own.' Danton tips back his head and begins to laugh. 'They will put it on at the Italiens,' Fabre says, 'under that blasted plagiarist's name.'

Pont-Neuf, Quai de Louvre. The cart sways and jolts. He plants his feet apart to keep upright and to steady Camille's sagging weight. Camille's tears seep through the cloth of his shirt. He is not crying for himself but for Lucile: perhaps for their composite self, their eternity of letters, their repertoire of gestures and quirks and jokes, all lost now, vanished: and for their child. 'You are not meeting Hérault's standards,' Danton says softly.

He scans the faces of the crowd. Silent, indifferent, they slow the progress of the carts. 'Let us try to die with dignity,' Hérault suggests.

Camille looks up, snaps out of his coma of grief. 'Oh, fuck off,' he says to Hérault, 'stop being such a *ci-devant*.'

Quai de l'École. Danton raises his eyes to the façade of the buildings. 'Gabrielle,' he murmurs. He looks up as if he expects to see someone there: a face withdrawing behind a curtain, a hand raised in farewell.

Rue Honoré. The interminable street. At the end of it they shout curses at the shuttered façade of the Duplay house. Camille, though, tries to speak to the crowds. Henri Sanson glances over his shoulder apprehensively. Danton drops his head, whispers to him, 'Be calm, now. Let that vile rabble alone.'

The sun is setting. It will be quite dark, Danton thinks, by the time we are all dead. At the tail of the cart, muffled in sansculotte garb, the Abbé Kéravenen recites silently the prayers for the dying. As the cart turns into the Place de la Révolution, he raises his hand in conditional absolution.

THERE IS A POINT beyond which – convention and imagination dictate – we cannot go; perhaps it's here, when the carts decant on to the scaffold their freight, now living and breathing flesh, soon to be dead meat. Danton imagines that, as the greatest of the condemned, he will be left until last, with Camille beside him. He thinks less of eternity than of how to keep his friend's body and soul together for the fifteen minutes before the National Razor separates them.

But of course it is not like that. Why should it be as you imagine? They drag Hérault away first: rather, they touch him on the elbow, and conduct him to his end. 'Goodbye, my friends,' Hérault says, just that; then immediately they have got their hands on Camille. It makes sense. Quickly dispose of anyone who might discomfit the crowds.

Camille is now, suddenly, calm. It is too late for Hérault to see how his example has been beneficial; but Camille nods his head towards Henri Sanson. 'As Robespierre would say – you have to smile. This man's father sued me for libel. Wouldn't you think that I have the grievance now?'

He does smile. Danton's stomach turns over: breathing flesh, dead meat. He sees Camille speak to Sanson: he sees the man take the locket from his bound hands. The locket is for Annette. He will not forget to deliver it; the last wishes are sacred, and he is of an honourable trade. For ten seconds Danton looks away. After that he watches everything, each bright efflorescence of life's blood. He watches each death, until he is tutored to his own.

'Hey, Sanson?'

'Citizen Danton?'

'Show my head to the people. It's worth the trouble.'

RUE HONORÉ: One day, a long time ago, his mother sat by a window, making lace. The broad morning light streamed in on both of them. He saw that it was the gaps that were important, the spaces between the threads which made the pattern, and not the threads themselves. 'Show me how to do it,' he said. 'I want to learn.'

'Boys don't do it,' she said. Her face was composed; her work continued. His throat closed at the exclusion.

Now, whenever he looks at a piece of lace – even though his eyes are bad – he seems to see every thread in the work. At the Committee table, the image rises at the back of his mind, and forces him to look far, far back into his childhood. He sees the girl on the window-seat, her body swollen, pregnant with death: he sees the light on her bent head; beneath her fingers the airy pattern, going nowhere, flying away.

The Times, 8 April 1794:

When the late reconciliation took place, between Robespierre and Danton, we remarked that it proceeded rather from the fear which these two famous revolutionists entertained of each other, than from mutual affection; we added, that it should last only until the more dexterous of the two should find an opportunity to destroy his rival. The time, fatal to Danton, is at length arrived ... We do not comprehend why Camille Desmoulins, who was so openly protected by Robespierre, is crushed in the triumph of this dictator.

Note

LUCILE DESMOULINS and General Dillon were tried for conspiracy and executed on 24 Germinal. Maximilien Robespierre was executed without trial on 10 Thermidor, 28 July old style. So was his brother Augustin, so was Antoine Saint-Just, so was Couthon. Philippe Lebas shot himself.

Louise Danton married Claude Dupin, and became a baroness under the Empire.

Anne Théroigne died in 1817, in the prison–asylum of La Salpêtrière.

Charlotte Robespierre, who never married, was given a small pension by Napoleon. Eléonore remained 'the widow Robespierre'. Maximilien's father – as it turned out – had died in Munich in 1777.

Legendre died in 1795. Robert Lindet survived and prospered. Danton's sons returned to his province and farmed their land.

Stanislas Fréron deserted the cause. After Robespierre's fall, he persecuted Jacobins, leading gangs of vandals and gallants through the streets. He died in Haiti, in 1802.

Both Jean-Nicolas Desmoulins and Claude Duplessis died within a few months of Robespierre's fall. Camille's child was brought up by Annette and Adèle Duplessis. He attended the former Collège Louis-le-Grand, and was called to the Paris Bar. He died, also in Haiti, at the same age as his father. Adèle Duplessis died in Vervins, Picardy, in 1854.